The Complete Dr. Thorndyke

Volume IV:

A Silent Witness
Helen Vardon's Confession
The Cat's Eye

The Complete Dr. Thorndyke

Volume IV:

A Silent Witness
Helen Vardon's Confesion
The Cat's Eye

By

R. Austin Freeman

Edited by
David Marcum

ISBN Hardback 978-1-78705-536-0
ISBN Paperback 978-1-78705-537-7
AUK ePub ISBN 978-1-78705-538-4
AUK PDF ISBN 978-1-78705-539-1

These works are in the Public Domain in Great Britain
Portrait of Dr. Thorndyke by H.M. Brock (1908)

Published in the UK by
MX Publishing
335 Princess Park Manor, Royal Drive,
London, N11 3GX
www.mxpublishing.co.uk

David Marcum can be reached at:
thepapersofsherlockholmes@gmail.com

Cover design by Brian Belanger
www.belangerbooks.com and *www.redbubble.com/people/zhahadun*

CONTENTS

Introductions

Adventures

A Silent Witness

(Continued on the next page . . . .)

Helen Vardon's Confession

(Continued on the next page . . . .)

The Cat's Eye

The Complete Dr. Thorndyke

Volume IV:

A Silent Witness
Helen Vardon's Confesion
The Cat's Eye

Dr. John Thorndyke

5A King's Bench Walk
in the late 1890's when
Thorndyke would have moved in

5A King's Bench Walk
Photographed by the Editor
during his
Sherlock Holmes Pilgrimage No. 3
(September 8th, 2016)

Meet Dr. Thorndyke
by R. Austin Freeman

My subject is Dr. John Thorndyke, the hero or central character of most of my detective stories. So I'll give you a short account of his real origin – of the way in which he did in fact come into existence.

To discover the origin of John Thorndyke I have to reach back into the past for at least fifty years, to the time when I was a medical student preparing for my final examination. For reasons which I need not go into I gave rather special attention to the legal aspects of medicine and the medical aspects of law. And as I read my text-books, and especially the illustrative cases, I was profoundly impressed by their dramatic quality. Medical jurisprudence deals with the human body in its relation to all kinds of legal problems. Thus its subject matter includes all sorts of crime against the person and all sorts of violent death and bodily injury: Hanging, drowning, poisons and their effects, problems of suicide and homicide, of personal identity and survivorship, and a host of other problems of the highest dramatic possibilities, though not always quite presentable for the purposes of fiction. And the reported cases which were given in illustration were often crime stories of the most thrilling interest. Cases of disputed identity such as the Tichbourne Case, famous poisoning cases such as the Rugeley Case and that of Madeline Smith, cases of mysterious disappearance or the detection of long-forgotten crimes such as that of Eugene Aram. All these, described and analysed with strict scientific accuracy, formed the matter of Medical Jurisprudence which thrilled me as I read and made an indelible impression.

But it produced no immediate results. I had to pass my examinations and get my diploma, and then look out for the means of earning my living. So all this curious lore was put away for the time being in the pigeon-holes of my mind – which Dr. Freud would call the *Unconscious* – not forgotten, but ready to come to the surface when the need for it should arise. And there it reposed for some twenty years, until failing health compelled me to abandon medical practice and take to literature as a profession.

It was then that my old studies recurred to my mind. A fellow doctor, Conan Doyle, had made a brilliant and well-deserved success by the creation of the immortal Sherlock Holmes. Considering that achievement, I asked myself whether it might not be possible to devise a detective story of a slightly different kind – one based on the science of Medical Jurisprudence, in which, by the sacrifice of a certain amount of dramatic effect, one could keep entirely within the facts of real life, with nothing fictitious excepting the persons and the events. I came to the conclusion that it was, and began to turn the idea over in my mind.

But I think that the influence which finally determined the character of my detective stories, and incidentally the character of John Thorndyke, operated when I was working at the Westminster Ophthalmic Hospital. There I used to take the patients into the dark room, examine their eyes with the ophthalmoscope, estimate the errors of refraction, and construct an experimental pair of spectacles to correct those errors. When a perfect correction had been arrived at, the formula for it was embodied in a prescription which was sent to the optician who made the permanent spectacles.

Now when I was writing those prescriptions it was borne in on me that in many cases, especially the more complex, the formula for the spectacles, and consequently the spectacles themselves, furnished an infallible record of personal identity. If, for instance, such a pair of spectacles should have been found in a railway carriage, and the maker of those spectacles could be found, there would be practically conclusive evidence that a particular person had travelled by that train. About that time I drafted out a story based on a pair of spectacles, which was published some years later under the title of *The Mystery of 31 New Inn*, and the construction of that story determined, as I have said, not only the general character of my future work but of the hero around whom the plots were to be woven. But that story remained for some years in cold storage. My first published detective novel was *The Red Thumb-mark*, and in that book we may consider that John Thorndyke was born. And in passing on to describe him I may as well explain how and why he came to be the kind of person that he is.

I may begin by saying that he was not modelled after any real person. He was deliberately created to play a certain part, and the idea that was in my mind was that he should be such a person as would be likely and suitable to occupy such a position in real life. As he was to be a medico-legal expert, he had to be a doctor and a fully trained lawyer. On the physical side I endowed him with every kind of natural advantage. He is exceptionally tall, strong, and athletic because those qualities are useful in his vocation. For the same reason he has acute eyesight and hearing and considerable general manual skill, as every doctor ought to have. In appearance he is handsome and of an imposing presence, with a symmetrical face of the classical type and a Grecian nose. And here I may remark that his distinguished appearance is not merely a concession to my personal taste but is also a protest against the monsters of ugliness whom some detective writers have evolved.

These are quite opposed to natural truth. In real life a first-class man of any kind usually tends to be a good-looking man.

Mentally, Thorndyke is quite normal. He has no gifts of intuition or other supernormal mental qualities. He is just a highly intellectual man of great and varied knowledge with exceptionally acute reasoning powers and endowed with that invaluable asset, a scientific imagination (by a scientific imagination I mean that special faculty which marks the born investigator, the capacity to perceive the essential nature of a problem before the detailed evidence comes into sight). But he arrives at his conclusions by ordinary reasoning, which the reader can follow when he has been supplied with the facts, though the intricacy of the train of reasoning may at times call for an exposition at the end of the investigation.

Thorndyke has no eccentricities or oddities which might detract from the dignity of an eminent professional man, unless one excepts an unnatural liking for Trichinopoly cheroots. In manner he is quiet, reserved and self-contained, and rather markedly secretive, but of a kindly nature, though not sentimental, and addicted to occasional touches of dry humour. That is how Thorndyke appears to me.

As to his age. When he made his first bow to the reading public from the doorway of Number 4 King's Bench Walk he was between thirty-five and forty. As that was thirty years ago, he should now be over sixty-five. But he isn't. If I have to let him *"grow old along with me"* I need not saddle him with the infirmities of age, and I can (in his case) put the brake on the passing years. Probably he is not more than fifty after all!

Now a few words as to how Thorndyke goes to work. His methods are rather different from those of the detectives of the Sherlock Holmes school. They are more technical and more specialized. He is an investigator of crime but he is not a detective. The technique of Scotland Yard would be neither suitable nor possible to him. He is a medico-legal expert, and his methods are those of medico-legal science. In the investigation of a crime there are two entirely different methods of approach. One consists in the careful and laborious examination of a vast mass of small and commonplace detail: Inquiring into the movements of suspected and other persons, interrogating witnesses and checking their statements particularly as to times and places, tracing missing persons, and so forth – the aim being to accumulate a great body of circumstantial evidence which will ultimately disclose the solution of the problem. It is an admirable method, as the success of our police proves, and it is used with brilliant effect by at least one of our contemporary detective writers. But it is essentially a police method.

The other method consists in the search for some fact of high evidential value which can be demonstrated by physical methods and which constitutes conclusive proof of some important point. This method also is used by the police in suitable cases. Finger-prints are examples of this kind of evidence, and another instance is furnished by the Gutteridge murder. Here the microscopical examination of a cartridge-case proved conclusively that the murder had been committed with a particular revolver, a fact which incriminated the owner of that revolver and led to his conviction.

This is Thorndyke's procedure. It consists in the interrogation of things rather than persons, of the ascertainment of physical facts which can be made visible to eyes other than his own. And the facts which he seeks tend to be those which are apparent only to the trained eye of the medical practitioner.

I feel that I ought to say a few words about Thorndyke's two satellites, Jervis and Polton. As to the former, he is just the traditional narrator proper to this type of story. Some of my readers have complained that Dr. Jervis is rather slow in the uptake. But that is precisely his function. He is the expert misunderstander. His job is to observe and record all the facts, and to fail completely to perceive their significance. Thereby he gives the reader all the necessary information, and he affords Thorndyke the opportunity to expound its bearing on the case.

Polton is in a slightly different category. Although he is not drawn from any real person, he is associated in my mind with two actual individuals. One is a Mr. Pollard, who was the laboratory assistant in the hospital museum when I was a student, and who gave me many a valuable tip in matters of technique, and who, I hope, is still to the good. The other was a watch- and clock-maker of the name of Parsons – familiarly known as Uncle Parsons – who had premises in a basement near the Royal Exchange, and who was a man of boundless ingenuity and technical resource. Both of these I regard as collateral relatives, so to speak, of Nathaniel Polton. But his personality is not like either. His crinkly countenance is strictly his own copyright.

To return to Thorndyke, his rather technical methods have, for the purposes of fiction, advantages and disadvantages. The advantage is that his facts are demonstrably true, and often they are intrinsically interesting. The disadvantage is that they are frequently not matters of common knowledge, so that the reader may fail to recognize them or grasp their significance until they are explained. But this is the case with all classes of fiction. There is no type of character or story that can be made sympathetic and acceptable to every kind of reader. The personal equation affects the reading as well as the writing of a story.

R. Austin Freeman
(1862-1943)

5A King's Bench Walk
in the early 1900's when
Thorndyke was in practice

Dr. Thorndyke: In the Footsteps
of Sherlock Holmes
by David Marcum

When Sherlock Holmes began his practice as a "Consulting Detective", his ideas of scientific criminal investigations caused the London police to look upon him as a mere "theorist". He was perceived as an amateur to be tolerated, often with amusement – until, that is, his assistance was required. Then they were more than willing to come knocking upon his door, asking for whatever help that they could receive. And usually this help took the form of brilliant solutions to bizarre and otherwise insoluble problems.

Holmes espoused methods and ideas that were considered ludicrous in the late 1800's. For instance, his frustration knew no bounds when a crime scene was disturbed. Holmes realized that so much could be determined from the physical evidence – footprints, fibers, and spatters. The police were happy to trod into and disturb the evidence as if they were herds of field beasts, with the equivalent level of intelligence.

However, Holmes's methods, and the science behind catching criminals, eventually won out and became so important that it's hard to now imagine the world without them. Many of the exact same techniques and methods that he advocated are now standard practice. From being an amateur with unusual ideas, Holmes is now recognized around the world as The Great Detective. In 2002, Holmes received a posthumous Honorary Fellowship from the British Royal Society of Chemistry, based on the fact that he was beyond his time in using chemistry and chemical sciences as a means of solving crimes.

And before that, in 1985, Scotland Yard introduced *HOLMES* (*Home Office Large Major Enquiry System*), an elaborate computer system designed to process the masses of information collected and evaluated during a criminal investigation, in order to ensure that no vital clues are overlooked. This system, providing total compatibility and consistency between all the police forces of England, Scotland, Wales, and Northern Ireland, as well as the Royal Military Police, has since been upgraded by the improved *HOLMES 2* – and like the first version, there is absolutely no doubt as to who is being honored and memorialized for his work in dragging criminology out of the dark ages.

Many famous Great Detectives followed in Holmes's footsteps – Nero Wolfe and Ellery Queen, Hercule Poirot and Solar Pons – each with their own methods and techniques, but before they began their careers, and while Holmes was still in practice in Baker Street, another London consultant – Dr. John Thorndyke – opened his doors, using the scientific methods developed and perfected by Holmes and taking them to a whole new level of brilliance.

Meet Dr. Thorndyke

Dr. John Evelyn Thorndyke was born on July 4th, 1870. We don't know about where he was raised, or if he has any family. At no point will we be introduced to a more brilliant brother who sometimes *is* the British Government. He was educated at the medical school of St. Margaret's Hospital in London, and while there, he met fellow student Christopher Jervis. They became friends but, after completing school in 1895, they lost touch with one another. Over the next six years, Thorndyke remained at St. Margaret's, taking on various jobs, hanging "about the chemical and physical laboratories, the museum and *post mortem* room," and learning what he could. He obtained his M.D. and his Doctor of Sciences, and then was called to the bar in 1896.

He'd prepared himself with the hope of obtaining a position as a coroner, but he learned of the unexpected retirement of one of St. Margaret's lecturers in medical jurisprudence. He applied for the position and, rather to his own surprise, it was awarded to him. (He would continue to maintain his association with the hospital, going on to become the Medical Registrar, Pathologist, Curator of the Museum, and then Professor of Medical Jurisprudence, all while maintaining his own private consulting practice.)

It was when Thorndyke was named lecturer that he obtained his chambers at 5A King's Bench Walk, in the Inner Temple, that amazing and historic area between Fleet Street and the River. Founded over eight-hundred years ago by the Knights Templar, it is one of the four Inns of Court, (along with the Middle Temple, Lincoln's Inn, and Gray's Inn.) The buildings along King's Bench Walk, and particularly No.'s 4, 5, and 6, have a great deal of historical significance – and not just because Dr. John Thorndyke practiced at 5A for a number of years.

Thorndyke was quite fortunate to obtain a suite of rooms on multiple floors at this location, which leads to speculation about his influence and resources – a question which has no answer. In any case, it was there that he opened his practice and began to wait for clients and cases. He also made the acquaintance of elderly Nathaniel Polton, that man-of-all-work with the crinkly smile who ran the household, as well as Thorndyke's upstairs laboratory.

Like Sherlock Holmes during those early years in the 1870's when he had rooms in Montague Street next to the British Museum and spent his vast amounts of free time learning his craft, Thorndyke also found a way to make the empty hours more useful. He had the unique idea of imagining increasingly complex crimes – often a murder or series of them, for instance – and then, when he had planned every single aspect of the crime, he would turn around and work out the solution from the other side. While doing this, he made extensive notes of each of these theoretical exercises, and retained them for their later usefulness when encountering real-life crimes.

His first legal case was *Regina v Gummer* in 1897. Sadly, no further information about this affair is ever revealed to us, but we may be certain that Thorndyke used his considerable skills to bring it to a satisfactory conclusion, adding to his reputation as he did so.

In the meantime, Jervis had a more unfortunate story. As his time at school ended, his funds ran out rather unexpectedly, and after paying his various fees, he was left with earning his living as a medical assistant, or sometimes serving as a *locum tenens*, moving from one low-paying and temporary job to another, with no prospects of improvement.

Jervis is unemployed on the morning of March 22nd, 1901 when he encounters Thorndyke a few doors up from 5A King's Bench Walk. The two friends are happy to see one another, and before long, Jervis is involved in an investigation that will change his life in several ways, as recounted in *The Red Thumb Mark*.

But it should not be assumed that every Thorndyke adventure is narrated by Jervis in a typical Watsonian manner. In fact, the very next book, *The Eye of Osiris*, is instead told from the perspective of one of Thorndyke's students, Dr. Paul Berkeley. It is one of several that provide a look at Thorndyke – and Jervis – from a different perspective. But Jervis returns as narrator in the third novel, *The Mystery of 31 New Inn*, and we see Thorndyke through his eyes for a good many of both the novels and short stories.

Here a word might be mentioned about the Chronology of the Thorndyke stories. For some this is an irrelevant factor, but for others – like me – understanding the correct chronological placement of the stories is very important. Like the volumes that make up the Sherlock Holmes Canon, the Thorndyke stories aren't published in chronological order – a case set in 1907 (such as "Percival Bland's Proxy") might be collected before one that occurs in 1908, ("The Missing Mortgagee"), or it might not. For instance, *The Red Thumb Mark* (1907) is set in March and April 1901. (This chronological placement, by the way, is determined by noticing that a specific date is given three times in the book – in the British fashion of day before month – *9.3.01* – or *March 9th, 1901*. The dates for the events of the rest of the book can be carefully worked out from this fixed point.)

The next book, *The Eye of Osiris* (1911) is primarily set in the summer of 1904 (with Chapter 1, something of a prologue, taking place in late 1902.) Then, the next book to follow, *The Mystery of 31 New Inn* (1912), jumps back to the spring of 1902, about a year after the events of *The Red Thumb Mark*, and before *The Eye of Osiris*. And one of the short stories, "The Man With the Nailed Shoes" occurs in September and October 1901, between the first two books. Clearly, there is a great deal of material for the chronologicist in the Thorndyke Chronicles.

As Jervis becomes a part of Thorndyke's world, following their reacquaintance in March 1901, he meets others in Thorndyke's circle, including policemen such as Superintendent Miller and Inspector Badger, lawyers like Robert Anstey, Marchmont, and Brodribb, and other physicians like Dr. Paul Berkeley and Dr. Humphrey Jardine. He also has more opportunity to learn from his friend as he begins his own studies in order to become a similar specialist in the medico-legal practice – although he'll never be another Thorndyke.

Through Jervis's eyes – as well as others along the way – we build up our knowledge of Dr. Thorndyke. In appearance, he is tall and athletic, just under six feet in height, slender, and weighing around one-hundred-and-eighty pounds. He is exceptionally handsome – and has been called the handsomest detective in literature. He has no vices, except – perhaps – that he enjoys a Trichinopoly cigar upon occasion when he is feeling especially triumphant – although there is one time when the criminal's knowledge of this fact leads to a clever attempt at Thorndyke's murder . . . .

There are several instances where Thorndyke displays a marked resemblance to Sherlock Holmes – and not just in his scientific approach to crime. The two men sometimes say similar things – such as when Holmes says *"It is quite a pretty little problem,"* (in "A Scandal in Bohemia") or *". . . there are some pretty little problems among them"* (in "The Musgrave Ritual"). Thorndyke mimics this in *Felo de Se?* (*"There, Jervis,"* said he, *"is quite a pretty little problem for you to excogitate"*) or *"Ah, there is a very pretty little problem for you to consider"* (in *The Eye of Osiris*).

And who can forget the many instances when Holmes refers to *data*:

- *"It is a capital mistake to theorize before one has data. Insensibly one begins to twist facts to suit theories, instead of theories to suit facts."* – "A Scandal in Bohemia"
- *"I had,"* said he, *"come to an entirely erroneous conclusion which shows, my dear Watson, how dangerous it always is to reason from insufficient data."* – "The Speckled Band"
- *"No data yet,"* he answered. *"It is a capital mistake to theorize before you have all the evidence. It biases the judgment."* – A Study in Scarlet
- *"The temptation to form premature theories upon insufficient data is the bane of our profession."* – The Valley of Fear
- *"Still, it is an error to argue in front of your data."* – "Wisteria Lodge"

Thorndyke's version? *". . . believe me, it is a capital error to decide beforehand what data are to be sought for."* – from *The Mystery of 31 New Inn*. There are others.

Then there is Holmes's quote from "The Man With the Twisted Lip":

> *"You have a grand gift of silence, Watson,"* said he. *"It makes you quite invaluable as a companion."*

Here's the Thorndyke equivalent:

> *"It has just been borne in upon me, Jervis,"* said he, *"that you are the most companionable fellow in the world. You have the heaven-sent gift of silence."*

And then there is the time, in "The Anthropologist at Large", that a client – expecting a Holmes-like performance as based on "The Blue Carbuncle" – presents Thorndyke with an object for examination:

> *"I understand,"* said he, *"that by examining a hat it is possible to deduce from it, not only the bodily characteristics of the wearer, but also his mental and moral qualities, his state of health, his pecuniary position, his past history, and even his domestic relations and the peculiarities of his place of abode. Am I right in this supposition?"*
>
> *The ghost of a smile flitted across Thorndyke's face as he laid the hat upon the remains of the newspaper. "We must*

11

not expect too much," he observed. "Hats, as you know, have a way of changing owners . . . ."

Another area of intersection between Holmes and Thorndyke is the assembly of information. Recall Holmes's *"ponderous commonplace books in which he placed his cuttings"* as mentioned in "The Engineer's Thumb". We find, also in "The Anthropologist at Large", that Thorndyke does the same thing:

> *[H]is method of dealing with [the morning newspaper] was characteristic. The paper was laid on the table after breakfast, together with a blue pencil and a pair of office shears. A preliminary glance through the sheets enabled him to mark with the pencil those paragraphs that were to be read, and these were presently cut out and looked through, after which they were either thrown away or set aside to be pasted in an indexed book.*

No doubt and examination of Thorndyke's lodgings at 5A King's Bench Walk would reveal – in addition to a series of indexed commonplace books filled with clippings – a number of other items and aspects that would remind one of 221b Baker Street.

Like many locations where the detective's residence is almost a character in and of itself – Sherlock Holmes's London address at 221 Baker Street, and the New York homes of Ellery Queen on West 87th Street and Nero Wolfe's Brownstone on West 35th Street – Thorndyke's rooms at 5A King's Bench Walk are a living and vibrant place – from the entry way, where a heavy door known as "The Oak" leads visitors into a most comfortable wood-paneled sitting room, located on the (British) first floor, one flight up from the ground floor. On the next floor up, Polton has his laboratory and workshop, containing everything that is needed (or what might be manufactured) in order to solve the case.

On the next floor, underneath the attic, are bedrooms belonging to Thorndyke, Jervis, and Polton. Even after Jervis has married – and now you know that he does get married! – he continues to reside a good deal of the time in King's Bench Walk. As he explains in *When Rogues Fall Out* (1932, with the U.S. title of *Dr. Thorndyke's Discovery*):

> *Here, perhaps, since my records of Thorndyke's practice have contained so little reference to my own personal affairs, I should say a few words concerning my domestic habits. As the circumstances of our practice often made it*

12

desirable for me to stay late at our chambers, I had retained there the bedroom that I had occupied before my marriage; and, as these circumstances could not always be foreseen, I had arranged with my wife the simple rule that the house closed at eleven o'clock. If I was unable to get home by that time, it was to be understood that I was staying at the Temple. It may sound like a rather undomestic arrangement, but it worked quite smoothly, and it was not without its advantages. For the brief absence gave to my homecomings a certain festive quality, and helped to keep alive the romantic element in my married life. It is possible for the most devoted husbands and wives to see too much of one another.

Thorndyke's Other Appearances

Through the years, Thorndyke's reputation continues to grow, as presented through a number of adventures. Surprisingly, in light of the tens of thousands of Post-Canonical Sherlock Holmes that have come to light over the years, as discovered by latter-day Literary Agents taking over Watson's first Literary Agent, Sir Arthur Conan Doyle, stopped literary-agenting, there have been almost no additional Thorndyke cases brought to the public's attention. The few exceptions to this statement are *Goodbye, Dr. Thorndyke* (1972) by Norman Donaldson, and *Dr. Thorndyke's Dilemma* (1974) by John H. Dirckx. Both narratives deal with Thorndyke and Jervis in their latter years, and each is written by an expert in the field of Thorndyke scholarship.

Donaldson also wrote what might be the final scholarly word on the subject, *In Search of Dr. Thorndyke* (1971). In fact, he had intended his pastiche, *Goodbye, Dr. Thorndyke*, to be published as the conclusion to this book, but it ended up appearing separately.

To my knowledge, "The Great Fathomer", as Thorndyke is sometimes known, has rarely appeared in other locations. He is mentioned in the Solar Pons tale "The Adventure of the Proper Comma" by August Derleth, which finds Dr. Parker returning "from Thorndyke & Polton with an analysis of the capsules Mrs. Buxton had carried with her . . . ."

In my own book of authorized Solar Pons stories, *The Papers of Solar Pons* (2017), Thorndyke makes two appearances. "The Adventure of the Additional Heirs" has Pons and Parker visiting King's Bench Walk:

At 5A, we learned that our friend Thorndyke, the medical juris-practitioner, was out on some investigation or other, but Pons handed the papers, sans photograph, into the care of Polton, his crinkly-faced laboratory technician, with a detailed explanation of what he wished to learn. The man nodded and smiled, and without any extraneous chit-chat, shut the door, freeing us to return to Fleet Street. We paused at the edge of the walk to look at the photograph, still in Pons's hand.

Later Thorndyke sends Pons a detailed report that helps toward the solution of the problem. And in "The Affair of the Distasteful Society", set in July 1921, Pons and Parker attend the first meeting of a group gathered to honor Sherlock Holmes, where the following conversation occurs:

"I see that you invited Thorndyke, and that little Belgian over on Farraway Street," said Rath.
"And Sexton Blake as well," replied Sir Amory.
"Sexton Blake is a fictional character, Sir Amory," said Pons with a smile.

In my story, "The Adventure of the Two Sisters", included in *The New Adventures of Solar Pons*, Dr. Parker writes:

Pons was not the only detective who offered his services to the London populace, although he might have been the most well-known. We were friends with several others, including the former Belgian policeman who lived in Farraway Street, and another rather mysterious fellow in nearby Bottle Street. And of course, Pons went way back with Thorndyke, whose chambers were across town. It wasn't unusual for Pons and the others to regularly confer on investigations, or simply to sit down and share a few drinks and professional anecdotes.

Thorndyke doesn't just appear in some of my Solar Pons adventures. He's also been referenced off-stage in a couple of Sherlock Holmes adventures that I've pulled from Watson's Tin Dispatch Box – and it's more than likely that others will follow. In "The "London Wheel", contained in *The MX Book of New Sherlock Holmes Stories* –

Part IV: 2016 Annual (2016), Holmes, looking through some documents, states:

> *"I believe," said Holmes, "that I have enough amateur legal training that I can get a sense of the implications of the clauses in question in both of these documents." He pulled the folded pages from his pocket. "I thought about sending a message to my* protégé *Thorndyke in King's Bench Walk for his opinion, as he could have been here very quickly, should he be at home at all and not out on his own business. However, I don't believe that will be necessary.*

Perhaps it is a point of interest that Thorndyke is referred to Holmes's protégé. Possibly more information will be forthcoming, such as that which is hinted in my story, "The Coombs Contrivance" (in *The Irregular Adventures of Sherlock Holmes!*). Set in 1889, when Thorndyke was nineteen years old, Holmes and Watson are discussing a precocious Baker Street Irregular:

> *[Holmes] pinched the bridge of his nose. "Do you trust Levi's judgment, Watson?"*
> *I considered. "For an eight-year-old, he's remarkably perceptive – as much as any of the other Irregulars who have assisted you. The Wiggins family, or the Peakes, or Thorndyke, before he went away to university."*

So was Thorndyke, perhaps, a gifted Irregular who learned from The Master, and then went on to create his own successful practice, taking what he learned to a next very successful level? Possibly. In my forthcoming story "The Inner Temple Intruder", to be found in a volume of Great Detective cross-overs, such an origin story is posited. As Robert Downey, Jr. succinctly stated when playing Holmes in 2009's *Sherlock Holmes*: "Food for thought!"

Thorndyke is also mentioned in Bob Byrne's Holmes story, "The Adventure of the Parson's Son" (*The MX Book of New Sherlock Holmes Stories – Part III: 1896-1929*), wherein Holmes, examining a piece of evidence, cries:

> *"Ha! I believe we have discredited the coat entirely. Though I wish I could get Thorndyke to examine it. Would that we were back in London."*

And it isn't just Thorndyke who has appeared elsewhere. His lawyer friend Marchmont has assisted Holmes and Watson in a small way a couple of my own "The Coombs Contrivance" and the forthcoming adventure *Sherlock Holmes and The Eye of Heka*.

Although I have encouraged these Thorndyke cameos in my own stories or in Holmes and Pons books that I edit, his appearances elsewhere are much more fleeting. In the 2015 BBC radio series *The Rivals*, Inspector Lestrade, Holmes's most frequent associate at Scotland Yard, is placed into the events of the Thorndyke short story "The Moabite Cipher". And Thorndyke has only had a handful of other media appearances. In 1964, the BBC produced seven episodes (now lost) of *Thorndyke*, starring Peter Copley. The episodes were:

- "The Case of Oscar Brodski'
- "The Old Lag"
- "A Case of Premeditation"
- "The Mysterious Visitor"
- "The Case of Phyllis Annesley" – Adapted from "Phyllis Annesley's Peril"
- "Percival Bland's Brother" – Adapted from "Percival Bland's Proxy"
- "The Puzzle Lock"

From 1971 to 1973, Thames TV aired *The Rivals of Sherlock Holmes*, and two stories were adapted: "A Message from the Deep Sea" starring John Neville (who had also played Holmes in 1965's *A Study in Terror*), and "The Moabite Cipher" starring Barrie Ingram. Except for a 1963 BBC Radio adaption of *Mr. Pottermack's Oversight*, and a few on-air readings by a single performer, there have been no other Thorndyke adaptations – which is a terrible shame, as the stories certainly lend themselves to visual and audible interpretations. Perhaps a new generation will discover Thorndyke, Jervis, and the rest, and they will find popularity once again, as they did more than a century ago.

Copley, Neville, and Ingram as Thorndyke

A Few (Hundred) Words About R. Austin Freeman
Thorndyke's Chronicler

Richard Austin Freeman was born on April 11, 1862 in the Soho district of London. He was the son of a skilled tailor and the youngest of five children. As he grew, it was expected that he would become a tailor as well, but instead he had an interest in natural history and medicine, and so he obtained employment in a pharmacist's shop. While there, he qualified as an apothecary and could have gone on to manage the shop, but instead he began to study medicine at Middlesex Hospital.

Austin Freeman qualified as a physician in 1887, and in that same year he married. Faced with the twin facts of his new marital responsibilities and his very limited resources as a young doctor, he made the unusual decision to join the Colonial Service, spending the next seven years in Africa as an Assistant Colonial Surgeon. This continued until the early 1890's, when he contracted Blackwater Fever, an illness that eventually forced him to leave the service and return permanently to England.

For several years, he served as a *locum tenens* for various physicians, a bleak time in his life as he moved from job to job, his income low, and his health never quite recovered. (These experiences were reflected in the narratives of Doctors Jervis and Berkeley.) However, he supplemented his meager income and exercised his creativity during these years by beginning to write. His early publications included *Travels and Live in Ashanti and Jaman* (1898), recounting some of his African sojourns.

In 1900, Freeman obtained work as an assistant to Dr. John James Pitcairn (1860-1936) at Holloway Prison. Although he wasn't there for very long, the association between the two men was enough to turn Freeman's attention toward writing mysteries. Over the next few years, they co-wrote several under the pseudonym *Clifford Ashdown*, including *The Adventures of Romney Pringle* (1902), *The Further Adventures of Romney Pringle* (1903), *From a Surgeon's Diary* (1904-1905), and *The Queen's Treasure* (written around 1905-1906, and published posthumously in 1975.) The specifics of the two men's writing arrangement are unknown to the present day, although much research was carried out by Freeman scholar Percival Mason ("P.M.") Stone, who was actually able to confirm Pitcairn's involvement and influence. Following this association, which apparently helped to train Freeman to be a better writer and to focus on a recurring character, his luck changed, and he was able, within just a few years, to abandon the practice of medicine, which had never been successful, and become a professional author.

In approximately 1904, Freeman began developing a mystery novella based on a short job that he had held at the Western Ophthalmic Hospital. This effort, "31 New Inn", was published in 1905, and it is the true first Dr. Thorndyke story. In it, we meet narrator Dr. Christopher Jervis, working as a *locum tenens*, moving from practice to practice in the same bleak existence that Freeman had experienced. Jervis becomes involved with a patient that may or may not be in danger. Unsure what to do, he recalls his former classmate, the brilliant Dr. John Thorndyke.

Curiously, this novella, (included in Volume II of this newly reissued collection *The Complete Dr. Thorndyke*), has numerous references to the events of the first Thorndyke novel, *The Red Thumb Mark*, which would not be published until 1907. Much of Freeman's life is obscure and unknown, including his writing processes and milestones, but clearly, with so much already clearly defined in this novella about Thorndyke and Jervis, he had firmly established not only fixed aspects of their histories, but the plot of *The Red Thumb Mark* as well, several years before the book's publication. One wonders why he chose to first publish "31 New Inn", since it occurs chronologically a whole year *after* the events of *The Red Thumb Mark*.

Interestingly – at least to a chronologicist such as myself – the original novella of "31 New Inn" is specifically set in April 1900, as indicated internally. However, when it was later revised to become the third Thorndyke novel, *The Mystery of 31 New Inn*, (1912, and included in Volume I of *The Complete Dr. Thorndyke*), the narrative's date is changed to 1902 – which fits, since the events definitely occur after *The Red Thumb Mark*, which takes place in March and April 1901.

Like Rex Stout's Nero Wolfe, who seemed to have sprung fully formed from his creator's brow, Thorndyke and his world are well-defined and immediately real. Although certain characters are added to the circle through the years, the basic layout – with Thorndyke, Jervis, and Polton (the man-of-all-work crinkly-smiled assistant) are always at 5A, ready to spring into action when Jervis – or one of the other varied narrators who show up throughout the series – arrive with a curious problem.

Freeman had found his voice with the Thorndyke books and short stories, and he was able to make use of his lifelong interest in medicine and natural science – often conducting extensive experiments to work out exactly how the solutions in his stories could be discovered. And in Thorndyke's early days, Freeman was able to turn the literary form inside out with the creation of the "Inverted Mystery Story", wherein the criminal is known from the beginning – the motive is explained, the planning and execution of the crime are observed, and the miscreant is left to believe that all is well and that he'll never be caught. And then, in the second part of the story, Thorndyke enters to inexorably follow the trail that is completely invisible to everyone else, scraping away, layer by layer and point by point, until the truth is inevitably revealed.

As Freeman explained:

> *Some years ago I devised, as an experiment, an inverted detective story in two parts. The first part was a minute and detailed description of a crime, setting forth the antecedents, motives, and all attendant circumstances. The reader had seen the crime committed, knew all about the criminal, and was in possession of all the facts. It would have seemed that there was nothing left to tell. But I calculated that the reader would be so occupied with the crime that he would overlook the evidence. And so it turned out. The second part, which described the investigation of the crime, had to most readers the effect of new matter.*

This format went on to be used by a great many authors through the years. For example several of the Lord Peter Wimsey narratives come close to being this type of story, and television's *Columbo* used this type of story-telling as its basis.

While these volumes are an attempt to reintroduce the modern reader to Thorndyke, and are a celebration of him and his world, it must be discussed at some point that Freeman held views that are unacceptable. Unlike Sir Arthur Conan Doyle, who spent his last decades championing spiritualism but never allowed it to creep into the Sherlock Holmes stories, Freeman sometimes did let his own prejudices make their way into the Thorndyke tales. In his book *Social Decay and Regeneration* (1921), he expressed his rather nationalistic view that England had become an "homogenized, restless, unionized working class". Worse, he inexcusably and detestably supported the eugenics movement, arguing that people with "undesirable" traits should not be allowed to reproduce by means such as "segregation, marriage restriction, and sterilization". He referred to immigrants as "Sub-Man", and argued that society needed to be protected from "degenerates of the destructive type."

Some have attempted to excuse his beliefs as being a product of his times. For instance, it has been written that he had a distrust of Jews because of the competition that his father, a tailor, had faced when Freeman was a boy. Later, he served in the Colonial Service in Africa during some of the worst years in terms of treatment of natives by the British, and as an older man, he existed in the Great Britain between the two wars when great upheavals disrupted much of what he had known and expected.

Sadly, there are occasional racial stereotypes and references in the Thorndyke books. As I explain in the *Editor's Caveat*, some of these stereotypes had to be unfortunately maintained within the story in order to accurately reflect the plot and the characters of those times. However, there are some words or phrases that were used in the original stories – vile racial epithets that have no business being repeated or perpetuated anywhere – that I have cheerfully and happily removed. (There weren't many of them, but any are too many.)

These books are intended to bring Dr. Thorndyke and his adventures to a new generation – and not to be an untouchable and sacred literary artifact, with every nasty stain preserved and archived for the historical record. As I warn in the *Caveat*, if readers find that they want to experience the original versions as they were first written, with those hateful words included, then they would be advised to go and seek out the original books, because you won't find that filth here. These versions celebrate Dr. Thorndyke and Dr. Jervis – who do not use the awful stereotyped language, I'm glad to say! – and as such, I felt no need whatsoever to include and perpetuate the objectionable and offensive material

From Thorndyke's creation until 1914, Freeman wrote four novels and two volumes of short stories. Then, with the commencement of the First World War, he entered military service. In February 1915, at the age of fifty-two, he joined the Royal Army Medical Corps. Due to his health, which had never entirely recovered from his time in Africa, he spent the duration of the war involved with various aspects of the ambulance corps, having been promoted very early to the rank of Captain. He wrote nothing about Thorndyke during this period, but he did publish one book concerning the adventures of a scoundrel, *The Exploits of Danby Croker* (1916).

Following the war, he resumed his previous life, writing approximately one Thorndyke novel per year, as well as three more volumes of Thorndyke short stories and a number of other unrelated items, until his death on September 28th, 1943 – likely related to Parkinson's Disease, which had plagued him in later years.

Upon learning the news, *Chicago Tribune* columnist Vincent Starrett wrote:

> *When all the bright young things have performed their appointed task of flatting the complexes of neurotic semi-literates, and have gone their way to oblivion, the best of the Thorndyke stories will live on – minor classics on the shelf that holds the good books the world.*

Raymond Chandler wrote in his famous essay, which initially appeared in a couple of magazines and then was published in the book of the same name, *The Simple Art of Murder* (1950):

> *This man Austin Freeman is a wonderful performer. He has no equal in his genre, and he is also a much better writer than you might think, if you were superficially inclined, because in spite of the immense leisure of his writing, he accomplishes an even suspense which is quite unexpected . . . There is even a gaslight charm about his Victorian love affairs, and those wonderful walks across London.*

In the introduction to *Great Stories of Detection, Mystery, and Horror* (1928), Dorothy L. Sayers, Chronicler of Lord Peter Wimsey, stated:

> *Thorndyke will cheerfully show you all the facts. You will be none the wiser . . . .*

Discovering Dr. Thorndyke

I first encountered Dr. Thorndyke in a rather backwards way – in passing only – and it took several decades to correct that mistake. In approximately 1980, my dad gave me Otto Penzler's *The Private Lives of Private Eyes, Spies, Crime Fighters, and Other Good Guys* (1977). This wonderful oversized book has biographies of twenty-five well-known heroes, along with lists of the original books featuring each one.

My dad bought it for me because it had a chapter about Sherlock Holmes. There were a few others in there that I recognized or had already read about– Ellery Queen and Perry Mason – and soon I would become fanatical about a few more – Nero Wolfe and Hercule Poirot.

Over the next few years I would also find the chapters on James Bond and Lew Archer indispensable, and later than that I would come to appreciate the entries about Philip Marlowe, Sam Spade, Miss Marple, Philo Vance, and Lord Peter Wimsey. But there were a few that, to this day, I've never bothered to read – such as Modesty Blaise or Mr. Moto – and a few others that I skimmed but otherwise ignored. And one of these was the biography of Dr. Thorndyke.

That fact was easily understandable, as throughout the entire time that I was growing up in eastern Tennessee – and in the years since as well – I've never come across a Thorndyke book for sale here in the wild, either in a new bookstore or in a used one. If I'd found one, I might have bought and read it, liked it, and then sought out others. Instead, I was bound to discover Thorndyke by way of Sherlock Holmes.

I've been collecting traditional Sherlock Holmes pastiches since the same time that I discovered the Sherlockian Canon, when I was ten years old in 1975. Since that time, I've collected, read, and chronologicized literally thousands of them. It never gets old, and I'm constantly looking for more – and that means checking Amazon to see what new releases are on the horizon.

In 2012, someone – and I've never determined who – began releasing a variety of Holmes stories for Kindle under the author name *Dr. John H. Watson.* This wasn't too unusual – there have been a number of pastiches that officially list Watson as the author, rather than putting the editor of Watson's papers first. Of course, after determining that these latest entries weren't going to be available as real books, I bought the e-versions, and then printed them on real paper. (I cannot stand e-books – ephemeral electronic blips that you lease instead of buy. I'll only buy those titles if they aren't going to be released as legitimate books – and in this case, it's a good thing that I did, as each of these Kindle stories that I found and paid for were soon withdrawn.)

As I read these latest "Holmes" stories, I noticed that each had a definite style that captured the writing from the late 1800's or early 1900's. (No matter how modern pasticheurs try to achieve that, they never quite pull it off.) But in one of the first two or three titles that I read, I caught a couple of mistakes. In one story, Holmes and Watson leave 221 Baker Street and are immediately in the area around The Temple and Fleet Street, rather than in Marylebone, where Baker Street is properly located. On another occasion, the story's policeman – who had been identified up to that point as Inspector Lestrade – was inexplicably named *Superintendent Miller* – but only in one instance. And in another place in one of the stories, Holmes's address was stated to be *5A King's Bench Walk.*

It was then that some vague memory triggered in my head, and I realized why these stories had captured the style of the late Victorian and early Edwardian eras: *It was because they had actually been written then*. I recalled – from reading Otto Penzler's book of biographies so long ago - that 5A King's Bench Walk belonged to Dr. Thorndyke, and not Sherlock Holmes. Someone was taking the original Thorndyke stories, which I had never before read, and simply changing names: Dr. Thorndyke, Dr. Jervis, and Superintendent Miller became Sherlock Holmes, Dr. Watson, and Inspector Lestrade, respectively.

Between 2012 and 2014, the anonymous author continued to load new Kindle editions on Amazon of Thorndyke-converted to-Holmes stories, and I continued to buy them. As soon as I had one, I would read it, and then try to figure out the original Thorndyke story from which it was taken. When I'd done so, I'd post a review, identifying what this editor was doing, from where he or she was taking the story, and urging that person, whoever it was, give credit to R. Austin Freeman instead of listing the author as Dr. John H. Watson.

Soon after each of my reviews would appear, the story would be withdrawn. I don't know if it was because the editor had made enough money from the initial sales, or if my reviews alerted him or her that they're game had been uncovered. In any case, I still have the printed copies of each of these converted stories – possibly the only copies that are still in existence.

For the record, over that two year period, this editor produced sixteen converted tales – four of the original Thorndyke novels, and twelve short stories. One of the original short stories, "The Mandarin's Pearl", was converted twice, with slight variations – initially published as "The Dragon Pearl", withdrawn, and later revised and reloaded as "The Oriental Pearl":

- "The Bloodied Thumbprint" – Originally the first Thorndyke novel, *The Red Thumb Mark*;
- "The Eye of Ra" – Originally the second Thorndyke novel, *The Eye of Osiris*;
- "The Cat's Eye Mystery" – Originally the sixth Thorndyke novel, *The Cat's Eye*;
- "The Julius Dalton Mystery" – Originally the ninth Thorndyke novel, *The D'Arblay Mystery*;
- "The Green Jacket Mystery" – Originally "The Green Check Jacket";
- "Mr. Crofton's Disappearance" – Originally "The Mysterious Visitor";

- "The Coded Lock" – Originally "The Puzzle Lock";
- "The Duplicated Letter" – Originally "The Stalking Horse";
- "The Bullion Robbery" – Originally "The Stolen Ingots";
- "The Talking Corpse" – Originally "The Contents of a Mare's Nest";
- "The Blue Diamond Mystery" – Originally "The Fisher of Men";
- "The Dragon Pearl" – Originally "The Mandarin's Pearl". (This story was also reworked and published again as a Holmes story under the title "The Oriental Pearl");
- "The Ingenious Murder" – Originally "The Aluminium Dagger";
- "The Bloodhound Superstition" – Originally "The Singing Bone"; *and*
- "The Magic Box" – Originally "The Magic Casket".

For quite a while, I was happy to have these as Holmes stories, and I even considered converting the rest of the Thorndyke adventures into additions to the extended Holmes Canon as well. (For at that time I cared nothing for Dr. Thorndyke.) It was partly with these converted stories in mind that I was motivated to go ahead and publish *Sherlock Holmes in Montague Street* (2014, 2016), which did the same thing to the Martin Hewitt stories, making them early adventures of Holmes before he met Watson and moved to Baker Street. I had long before decided to my own satisfaction that Martin Hewitt *was* a young Sherlock Holmes, with his identity changed through the preparations of a different literary agent than Sir Arthur Conan Doyle.

The taking of old public-domain stories featuring other detectives as the main protagonists and switching them so that Holmes is the main character has also been done by Alan Lance Andersen for his collection *The Affairs of Sherlock Holmes* (2015, 2016), wherein various non-series Sax Rohmer stories from nearly a hundred years ago were reworked as Holmes tales. Other non-Holmes authors have sometimes done the same thing. Raymond Chandler revised some of his early short stories so that the original characters' names were changed to Philip Marlowe. Ross MacDonald – (Kenneth Millar) also rewrote his old stories as well, making them into Lew Archer cases instead. More recently, the British ITV series *Marple* has taken non-Miss Marple Agatha Christie stories and converted them into episodes featuring that character.

So I had no problems with this type of change – and still don't. In fact, in my foreword to *Sherlock Holmes of Montague Street*, I wrote that I would rather have these converted Thorndyke stories as Holmes adventures, because I would rather read about Holmes than Thorndyke. But gradually my mind began to change, and I became more curious about Thorndyke, as presented in the proper fashion.

In 2013, I was able to go to London, as well as other places in England and Scotland, on the first (of three so far) Holmes Pilgrimages. For the most part, if a location wasn't related to Holmes, I didn't visit it. There were a few exceptions – I did intentionally visit Solar Pons's house at 7B Praed Street, Hercule Poirot's two residences, James Bond's flat in Chelsea – but everything else was pretty much pure Holmes.

One day, during my Holmesian rambles, I was making my way east down Fleet Street, and I visited both of the possible locations of "Pope's Court" (as featured in "The Red-Headed League"), Poppin's Court and Mitre Court. (The latter is also one of the locations where Denis Nayland Smith and Dr. Petrie had quarters in some of the Fu Manchu books.) I decided that Mitre Court was certainly the original of "Pope's Court", and I passed through it to find myself unexpectedly in The Temple.

That's the amazing thing about a Holmes Pilgrimage to London – one travels to a site and finds two more very close by. I had planned to visit The Temple, but hadn't realized that I was so close. And now here I was – and more interesting was the fact that I was walking along King's Bench Walk, which runs downhill from the Miter Court passage. I recalled that Thorndyke had lived at 5A, so I made my way there – but without too much awe on that day, because I hadn't actually read any Thorndyke adventures yet – just some converted Holmes stories.

After I returned home, the thought of that side-trip to Thorndyke's front door stuck in my mind, and I sought out and read the first novel in the series, *The Red Thumb Mark*. I was so impressed that I kept going, and discovered a wonderful series of books and stories – fascinating characters and mysteries, and very evocative descriptions of both the London and the countryside of those times.

When I returned on my second Holmes Pilgrimage in 2015, I took the second Thorndyke book with me, reading it while there – while also reading Holmes stories too, of course! This one, *The Eye of Osiris*, has a great deal of London atmosphere, and I spent part of one late afternoon tracking down locations in this book – or what's now left of them – in the area around Fetter Lane to the north of Thorndyke's home in The Temple. It was truly unforgettable.

And of course I made an intentional stop at King's Bench Walk on that 2015 trip, and again on Holmes Pilgrimage No. 3 in 2016. By that point I was a Thorndyke fan, and I took the trouble to write to the current occupiers of 5A before I traveled to see if I could step inside and perhaps spend a moment in Thorndyke's old quarters. Sadly, they did not respond – either because it was simply beneath them to do so, or possibly because they get too many people like me who want to make a literary pilgrimage to what is a functioning and thriving business location.

While making photographs at Thorndyke's old doorway, I had several chances to go inside when someone else would enter or leave – My ever-present deerstalker and I could have simply been bold enough to slip in and then talk my way onward. It worked at other places on my Holmes Pilgrimages – the laboratory at Barts where Holmes and Watson met, for instance, and the site of the (former?) Diogenes Club at No. 78 Pall Mall, where they acted just oddly enough to make me think that the club is still there. But for some reason, barging into Thorndyke's old chambers without proper permission didn't feel quite right. But if or when I make Holmes Pilgrimage No. 4, I'll definitely make an even greater effort to see the doctor's former rooms.

The Editor and his deerstalker at 5A King's Bench Walk
September 2016

With many thanks . . . .

These last few years have been an amazing ride, and I've been able to play in the Sherlockian sandbox more than I'd ever imagined. (And subsequently, the Solar Pons sandbox, and now Thorndyke, too! Along the way, I've been able to meet some incredible people, both in person and in the modern electronic way, and also I've been able to read several hundred new Holmes adventures, as well as to be able to share them with others.

Still, what is most important is my amazingly wonderful wife (of over thirty years!) Rebecca, and our truly awesome son and my friend, Dan. I love you both, and you are everything to me! I am the luckiest guy in the world.

I have all the gratitude in the world for everyone that I've encountered along the way – It's an undeniable fact that Sherlock Holmes authors are the *best* people! I'd like to thank those who offer support, encouragement, and friendship, sometimes patiently waiting on me to reply as my time is directed in many other directions. Many many thanks to (in alphabetical order): Brian Belanger, Derrick Belanger, Bob Byrne, Roger Johnson, Mark Mower, Denis Smith, Tom Turley, Dan Victor, and Marcia Wilson.

In particular, I'd also like to especially thank Steve Emecz, who is always supportive of every idea that I pitch. It's been my particular good fortune that he crossed my path – it changed my life in a way that would have never happened otherwise, and I'm grateful for every opportunity!

I hope that these books will provide pleasure to those discovering Dr. Thorndyke for the first time, and to others who have known him for a long time. As always, I approach these matters from a Sherlockian perspective, so of course these stories, to me, are a peripheral extension of Holmes's world, and as such they are just more tiny threads woven into the ongoing Great Holmes Tapestry. However, they are wonderful on their own, and however one reads them, I wish great joy upon the journey.

David Marcum
(Revised October 2019)

*Questions, comments, and story submissions
may be addressed to David Marcum at*
thepapersofsherlockholmes@gmail.com

27

5A King's Bench Walk
in the late 1890's when
Thorndyke was in residence

Editor's *Caveat*

These stories have been prepared using modern text-converting software, and as such, occasional deviations in punctuation have occurred. Those who absolutely must have the original version, down to each jot and dash, should understand that this version was created in order to present Dr. Thorndyke's adventures to a modern audience, and not to preserve an absolute pristine model for the historical archives.

Similarly, these stories were written in a time when racial prejudice and stereotypes were much more common than today. While some of these stereotypes must be unfortunately maintained within the story in order to accurately reflect the plot and the characters of those times, there are some words that were used in the original stories – vile racial epithets that have no business being repeated or perpetuated anywhere – that I have cheerfully removed. (There weren't many of them, but *any* are *too many*.)

If readers find that they want to experience the original versions as they were first written, with those hateful and ignorant words included, then they would be advised to seek out the original books. These versions celebrate Dr. Thorndyke and Dr. Jervis – who do *not* use the awful stereotyped language, I'm glad to say! – and as such, I felt no need whatsoever to include objectionable and offensive material simply for the sake of honoring or archiving the historical record.

David Marcum
Editor

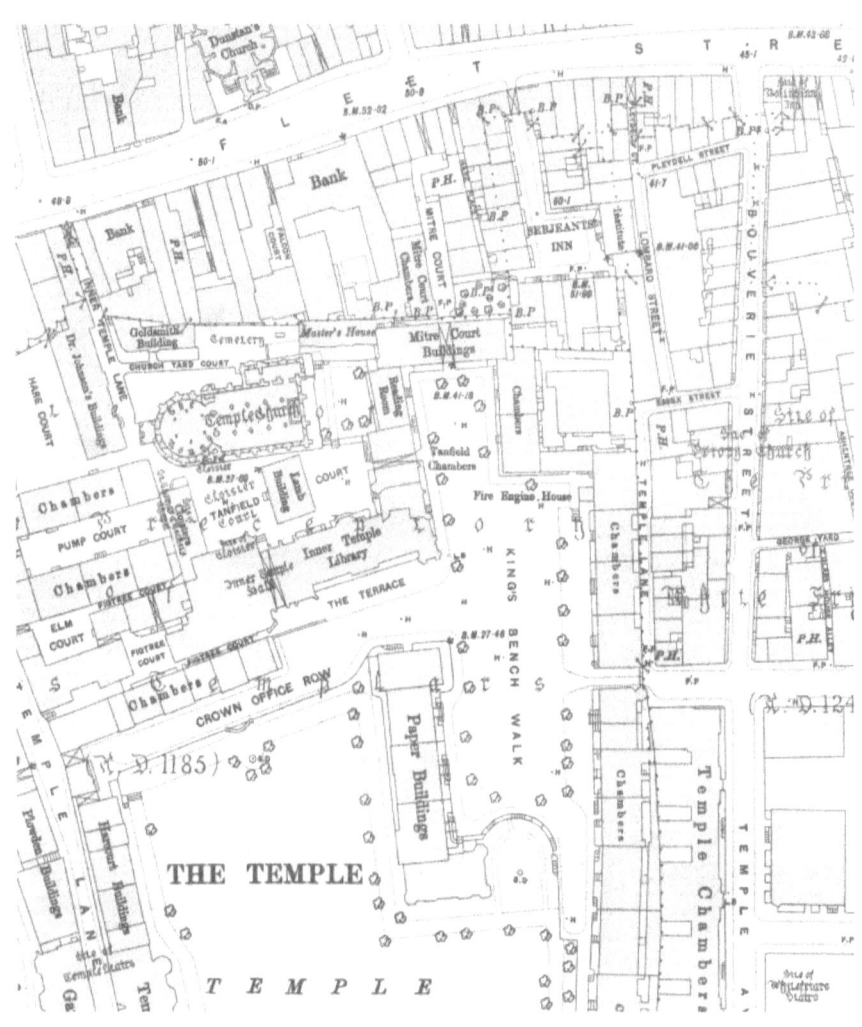

King's Bench Walk and the Temple, London
around 1900

33

1914 Hodder & Stoughton Cover

Chapter I
The Beginning of the Mystery

The history upon which I am now embarking abounds in incidents so amazing that, as I look back on them, a something approaching to skepticism contends with my vivid recollections and makes me feel almost apologetic in laying them before the reader. Some of them indeed are so out of character with the workaday life in which they happened that they will appear almost incredible, but none is more fraught with mystery than the experience that befell me on a certain September night in the last year of my studentship and ushered in the rest of the astounding sequence.

It was past eleven o'clock when I let myself out of my lodgings at Gospel Oak, a dark night, cloudy and warm and rather inclined to rain. But, despite the rather unfavourable aspect of the weather, I turned my steps away from the town, and walking briskly up the Highgate Road, presently turned into Millfield Lane. This was my favourite walk and the pretty winding lane, meandering so pleasantly from Lower Highgate to the heights of Hampstead, was familiar to me under all its aspects.

On sweet summer mornings when the cuckoos called from the depths of Ken Wood, when the path was spangled with golden sunlight, and saucy squirrels played hide-and-seek in the shadows under the elms (though the place was within earshot of Westminster and within sight of the dome of St. Paul's), on winter days when the Heath wore its mantle of white and the ring of gliding steel came up from the skaters on the pond below, on August evenings, when I would come suddenly on sequestered lovers (to our mutual embarrassment) and hurry by with ill-feigned unconsciousness – I knew all its phases and loved them all. Even its name was delightful, carrying the mind back to those more rustic days when the wits foregathered at the Old Flask Tavern and John Constable tramped through this very lane with his colour-box slung over his shoulder.

It was very dark after I had passed the lamp at the entrance to the lane. Very silent and solitary too. Not a soul was stirring at this hour, for the last of the lovers had long since gone home and the place was little frequented even in the daytime. The elms brooded over the road, shrouding it in shadows of palpable black, and their leaves whispered secretly in the soft night breeze. But the darkness, the quiet, and the solitude were restful after the long hours of study and the glare of the printed page, and I strolled on past the ghostly pond and the little thatched cottage, now wrapped in silence and darkness, with a certain wistful regret that I must soon look my last on them. For I had now passed all my examinations but the final "Fellowship", and must soon be starting my professional career in earnest.

Presently a light rain began to fall. Foreseeing that I should have to curtail my walk, I stepped forward more briskly, and, passing between the posts, entered the narrowest and most secluded part of the lane. But now the rain suddenly increased, and a squall of wind drove it athwart the path. I drew up in the shelter of one of the tall oak fences by which the lane is here inclosed and waited for the shower to pass. And as I stood with my back to the fence, pensively filling my pipe, I became for the first time sensible of the utter solitude of the place.

I looked about me and listened. The lane was darker here than elsewhere, a mere trench between the high fences. I could dimly see the posts at the entrance and a group of large elms over-shadowing them. In the other direction, where the lane doubled sharply upon itself, was absolute, inky blackness, save where a faint glimmer from the wet ground showed the corner of the fence and a projecting stump or tree-root jutting out from the corner and looking curiously like a human foot with the toes pointed upward.

The rain fell steadily with a soft, continuous murmur. The leaves of the elm-trees whispered together and answered the falling rain. The Scotch pines above my head stirred in the breeze with a sound like the surge of the distant sea. The voices of Nature, hushed and solemn, oblivious of man like the voices of the wilderness, and over all and through all, a profound, enveloping silence.

I drew up closer to the fence and shivered slightly, for the night was growing chill. It seemed a little lighter now in the narrow, trench-like lane, not that the sky was less murky but because the ground was now flooded with water. The posts stood out less vaguely against the background of wet road, and the odd-looking stump by the corner was almost distinct. And again it struck me as looking curiously like a foot – a booted foot with the toe pointing upwards.

The chime of a church clock sounded across the Heath – a human voice, this, penetrating the desolate silence. Then, after an interval, the solemn boom of Big Ben came up faintly from the sleeping city.

Midnight! And time for me to go home. It was of no use to wait for the rain to cease. This was no passing shower, but a steady drizzle that might last till morning. I re-lit my pipe, turned up my collar, and prepared to plunge into the rain. And as I stepped out, the queer-looking stump caught my eye once more. It was singularly like a foot, and it was odd, too, that I had never noticed it before in my many rambles through the lane.

A sudden, childish curiosity impelled me to see what it really was before I went, and the next moment I was striding sharply up the sodden path. Of course, I expected the illusion to vanish as I approached. But it did not. The resemblance increased as I drew nearer, and I hurried forward with something more than curiosity.

It was a foot! I realized it with a shock while I was some paces away, and, as I reached the corner, I came upon the body of a man lying in the sharp turn of the path, and the limp, sprawling posture, with one leg doubled under, told its tale at a glance.

I laid my finger on his wrist. It was clammy and cold, and not a vestige of a pulse could I detect. I struck a wax match and held it to his face. The eyes were wide-open and filmy, staring straight up into the reeking sky. The dilated pupils were insensitive to the glare of the match, the eyeballs insensitive to the touch of my finger.

Beyond all doubt the man was dead.

But how had he died? Had he simply fallen dead from some natural cause, or had he been murdered? There was no obvious injury, and no sign of blood. All that the momentary glimmer of the match showed was that his clothes were shiny with the wet, a condition that might easily, in the weak light, mask a considerable amount of bleeding.

When the match went out, I stood for some moments looking down on the prostrate figure as it lay with the rain beating down on the upturned face, professional interest contending with natural awe of the tragic presence. The former prompted me to ascertain without delay the cause of death, and, indeed, I was about to make a more thorough search for some injury or wound when something whispered to me that it is not well to be alone at midnight in a solitary place with a dead man – perchance a murdered man. Had there been any sign of life, my duty would have been clear. As it was, I must act for the best with a due regard to my own safety. And, reaching this conclusion, I turned away, with a last glance at the motionless figure and set forth homeward at a rapid pace.

As I turned out of Millfield Lane into Highgate Rise I perceived a policeman on the opposite side of the road standing under a tree, where the light from a lamp fell on his shining tarpaulin cape. I crossed the road, and, as he civilly touched his helmet, I said, "I am afraid there is something wrong up the lane, Constable. I have just seen the body of a man lying on the pathway."

The constable woke up very completely. "Do you mean a dead man, sir?" he asked.

"Yes, he is undoubtedly dead," I replied.

"Whereabouts did you see the body?" enquired the constable.

"In the narrow part of the lane, just by the stables of Mansfield House."

"That's some distance from here," said the constable. "You had better come with me and report at the station. You're sure the man was dead, sir?"

"Yes, I have no doubt about it. I am a medical man," I added, with some pride (I had been a medical man about three months, and the sensation was still a novel one).

"Oh, are you, sir?" said the officer, with a glance at my half-fledged countenance, "then, I suppose you examined the body?"

"Sufficiently to make sure that the man was dead, but I did not stay to ascertain the cause of death."

"No, sir, quite so. We can find that out later."

As we talked, the constable swung along down the hill, without hurry, but at a pace that gave me very ample exercise, and I caught his eye from time to time, travelling over my person with obvious professional interest. When we had nearly reached the bottom of the hill, there appeared suddenly on the wet road ahead, a couple of figures in waterproof capes. "Ha!" said the constable, "this is fortunate. Here is the inspector and the sergeant. That will save us the walk to the station."

He accosted the officers as they approached and briefly related what I had told him. "You are sure the man was dead, sir?" said the inspector, scrutinizing me narrowly. "But, there, we needn't stay here to discuss that. You run down, Sergeant, and get a stretcher and bring it along as quickly as you can. I must trouble you, sir, to come with me and show me where the body is. Lend the gentleman your cape, sergeant. You can get another at the station."

I accepted the stout cape thankfully, for the rain still fell with steady persistency, and set forth with the inspector to retrace my steps. And as we splashed along through the deep gloom of the lane, the officer plied me with judicious questions. "How long did you think the man had been dead?" he asked.

"Not long, I should think. The body was still quite limp."

"You didn't see any marks of violence?"

"No. There were no obvious injuries."

"Which way were you going when you came on the body?"

"The way we are going now, and, of course, I came straight back."

"Did you meet or see anyone in the lane?"

"Not a soul," I answered.

He considered my answers for some time, and then came the question that I had been expecting. "How came you to be in the lane at this time of night?"

"I was taking a walk," I replied, "as I do nearly every night. I usually finish my evening's reading about eleven, and then I have some supper and take a walk before going to bed, and I take my walk most commonly in Millfield Lane. Some of your men must remember having met me."

This explanation seemed to satisfy him for he pursued the subject no farther, and we trudged on for awhile in silence. At length, as we passed through the posts into the narrow part of the lane, the inspector asked, "We're nearly there, aren't we?"

"Yes," I replied, "the body is lying in the bend just ahead."

I peered into the darkness in search of the foot that had first attracted my notice, but was not yet able to distinguish it. Nor, to my surprise, could I make it out as we approached more nearly, and when we reached the corner, I stopped short in utter amazement.

The body had vanished! "What's the matter?" asked the inspector. "I thought this was the place you meant."

"So it is," I answered. "This is the place where the body was lying, here, across the path, with one foot projecting round the corner. Someone must have carried it away."

The inspector looked at me sharply for a moment. "Well, it isn't here now," said he, "and if it has been taken away, it must have been taken along towards Hampstead Lane. We'd better go and see." Without waiting for a reply, he started off along the lane at a smart double and I followed.

We pursued the windings of the lane until we emerged into the road by the lodge gates, without discovering any traces of the missing corpse or meeting any person, and then we turned back and retraced our steps, and as we, once more, approached the crook in the lane where I had seen the body, we heard a quick, measured tramp. "Here comes the sergeant with the stretcher," observed the inspector, "and he might have saved himself the trouble." Once more the officer glanced at me sharply, and this time with unmistakable suspicion. "There's no body here, Robson," he said, as the sergeant came up, accompanied by two constables carrying a stretcher. "It seems to have disappeared."

"Disappeared!" exclaimed the sergeant, bestowing on me a look of extreme disfavor. "That's a rum go, sir. How could it have disappeared?"

"Ah! That's the question!" said the inspector. "And another question is, was it ever here? Are you prepared to make a sworn statement on the subject, sir?"

"Certainly I am," I replied.

"Then," said the inspector, "we will take it that there was a body here. Put down that stretcher. There is a gap in the fence farther along. We will get through there and search the meadow."

The bearers stood the stretcher up against a tree and we all proceeded up the lane to the place where the observant inspector had noticed the opening in the fence. The gravel, though sodden with the wet, took but the faintest impressions of the feet that trod it, and, though the sergeant and the two constables threw the combined light of their lanterns on the ground, we were only able to make out very faintly the occasional traces of our own footsteps.

We scrutinized the break in the fence and the earth around with the utmost minuteness, but could detect no sign of anyone having passed through. The short turf of the meadow, on which I had seen sheep grazing in the daytime, was not calculated to yield traces of anyone passing over it, and no traces of any kind were discoverable. When we had searched the meadow thoroughly and without result, we came back into the lane and followed its devious course to the "kissing-gate" at the Hampstead Lane entrance. And still there was no sign of anything unusual. True, there were obscure foot-prints in the soft gravel by the turnstile, but they told us nothing. We could not even be sure that they had not been made by ourselves on our previous visit. In short, the net result of our investigations was that the body had vanished and left no trace. "It's a very extraordinary affair," said the inspector, in a tone of deep discontent, as we walked back. "The body of a full-grown man isn't the sort of thing you can put in your pocket and stroll off with without being noticed, even at midnight. Are you perfectly sure the man was really dead and not in a faint?"

"I feel no doubt whatever that he was dead," I replied.

"With all respect to you, sir," said the sergeant, "I think you must be mistaken. I think the man must have been in a dead faint, and after you came away, the rain must have revived him so that he was able to get up and walk away."

"I don't think so," said I, though with less conviction, for, after all, it was not absolutely impossible that I should have been mistaken, since I had discovered no mortal injury, and the sergeant's suggestion was an eminently reasonable one.

"What sized man was he?" the inspector asked.

"That I couldn't say," I answered. "It is not easy to judge the height of a man when he is lying down and the light was excessively dim. But I should say he was not a tall man and rather slight in build."

"Could you give us any description of him?"

"He was an elderly man, about sixty, I should think, and he appeared to be a clergyman or a priest, for he wore a Roman collar with a narrow, dark stripe up the front. He was clean shaven, and, I think, wore a clerical suit of black. A tall hat was lying on the ground close by and a walking-stick which looked like a malacca, but I couldn't see it very well, as he had fallen on it and most of it was hidden."

"And you saw all this by the light of one wax match," said the inspector.

"You made pretty good use of your eyes, sir."

"A man isn't much use in my profession if he doesn't," I replied, rather stiffly.

"No, that's true," the inspector agreed. "Well, I must ask you to give us the full particulars at the station, and we shall see if anything fresh turns up. I'm sorry to keep you hanging about in the wet, but it can't be helped."

"Of course it can't," said I, and we trudged on in silence until we reached the station, which looked quite cheerful and homelike despite the grim blue lamp above the doorway. "Well, Doctor," said the inspector, when he had read over my statement and I had affixed my signature, "if anything turns up, you'll hear from us. But I doubt if we shall hear anything more of this. Dead or alive, the man seems to have vanished completely. Perhaps the sergeant's right after all, and your dead man is at this moment comfortably tucked up in bed. Good-night, Doctor, and thank you for all the trouble you have taken."

By the time that I reached my lodgings I was tired out and miserably cold, so cold that I was fain to brew myself a jorum of hot grog in my shaving pot. As a natural result, I fell fast asleep as soon as I got to bed and slept on until the autumn sunshine poured in through the slats of the Venetian blind.

Chapter II
The Finding of the Reliquary

I awoke on the following morning to a dim consciousness of something unusual, and, as my wits returned with the rapidity that is natural to the young and healthy, the surprising events of the previous night reconstituted themselves and once more set a-going the train of speculation. Vividly I saw with my mind's eye the motionless figure lying limp and inert with the pitiless rain beating down on it, the fixed pupils, the insensitive eyeballs, the pulseless wrist, and the sprawling posture. And again I saw the streaming path, void of its dreadful burden, the suspicious inspector, the incredulous sergeant, and the unanswerable questions formulated themselves anew.

Had I, after all, mistaken a living man for a dead body? It was in the highest degree improbable, and yet it was not impossible. Or had the body been spirited away without leaving a trace? That also was highly improbable and yet, not absolutely impossible. The two contending improbabilities cancelled one another. Each was as unlikely as the other.

I turned the problem over again and again as I shaved and took my bath. I pondered upon it over a late and leisurely breakfast. But no conclusion emerged from these reflections. The man, living or dead, had been lying motionless in the lane all the time that I was sheltering, and probably for some time before. In the interval of my absence he had vanished. These were actual facts despite the open incredulity of the police. How he had come there, what had occasioned his death or insensibility, how he had disappeared and whither he had gone, were questions to which no answer seemed possible.

The fatigues of the previous night had left me somewhat indolent. There was no occasion for me to go to the hospital to-day. It was vacation time, the school was closed, the teaching staff were mostly away, and there was little doing in the wards. I decided to take a holiday and spend a quiet day rambling about the Heath, and, having formed this resolution, I filled my pipe, slipped a sketch-book into my pocket, and set forth.

Automatically my feet turned towards Millfield Lane. It was, as I have said, my usual walk, and on this morning, with last night's recollections fresh in my mind, it was natural that I should take my way thither.

44

Very different was the aspect of the lane this morning from that which I had last looked upon. The gloom and desolation of the night had given place to the golden sunshine of a lovely autumn day. The elms, clothed already in the sober livery of the waning year, sighed with pensive reminiscence of the summer that was gone, the ponds repeated the warm blue of the sky, and the lane itself was a vista of flickering sunlight and cool, reposeful shadow.

The narrow continuation beyond the posts was wrapped, as always, in a sombre shade, save where a gleam of yellow light streamed through a chink between the boards of the fence. I made my way straight to the spot where the body had lain and stooped over it, examining each pebble with the closest scrutiny. But not a trace remained. The hard, gravelly soil retained no impress either of the body or even of our footsteps, and as for the stain of blood, if there had ever been any, it would have been immediately removed by the falling rain, for the ground here had a quite appreciable slope and must have been covered last night by a considerable flowing stream.

I went on to the break in the fence – it was on the right-hand side of the path – and was at once discouraged by the aspect of the ground, for even our rough tramplings had left hardly a trace behind. After an aimless walk across the meadow, now occupied by a flock of sheep, I returned to the lane and walked slowly back past the place where I had sheltered from the rain. And then it was that I discovered the first hint of any clue to the mystery. I had retraced my steps some little distance past the spot where I had seen the body, when my eye was attracted by a darkish streak on the upper part of the high fence. It was quite faint and not at all noticeable on the weather-stained oak, but it chanced to catch my eye and I stopped to examine it. The fence which bore it was the opposite one to that in which the break occurred, and, since I had sheltered under it, the side of it which looked towards the lane must have been the lee side and thus less exposed to the rain.

I looked at the stain attentively. It extended from the top of the fence-which was about seven feet high – half-way to the ground, fading away gradually in all directions. The colour was a dull brown, and the appearance very much that of blood which had run down a wet surface. The board which bore the stain was traversed by a vertical crack near one edge, so that I was able to break off a small piece without much difficulty, and on examining that portion of the detached piece which had formed the side of the crack, I found it covered with a brownish-red, shiny substance, which I felt little doubt was dried blood, here protected by the crack and so less altered by contact with water.

Naturally, my next proceeding was to scrutinize very carefully the ground immediately beneath the stain. At the foot of the fence, a few tussocks of grass and clumps of undergrown weeds struggled for life in the deep shade. The latter certainly had, on close examination, the appearance of having been trodden on, though it was not very evident. But while I was considering an undoubted bruise on the stalk of a little dead-nettle, my eye caught the glint of some bright object among the leaves. I picked it out eagerly and held it up to look at it, and a very curious object it was, evidently an article of jewellery of some kind, but quite unlike anything I had ever seen before. It appeared to be a little elongated, gold case, with eight sides and terminating at either end in a blunt octagonal pyramid with a tiny ring at its apex, so that it seemed to have been part of a necklace. Of the eight flat sides, six were ornamented with sunk quatre-foils, four on each side, the other two sides were plain except that each had a row of letters engraved on it – *A.M.D.G.* on one side, and *S.V.D.P.* on the other. There was no hall-mark and, as far as I could see, no means of opening the little case. It seemed to have been suspended by a thin silk cord, a portion of which remained attached to one ring and showed a frayed end where it had broken or chafed through.

I wrapped the little object and the detached fragment of the fence in my handkerchief (for I had broken off the latter with the idea of testing it chemically for blood-pigment), and then resumed my investigations. The appearances suggested that the body had been lifted over the fence, and the question arose, What was on the other side? I listened attentively for a few seconds, and then, hearing no sound of footsteps, I grasped the top of the fence, gave a good spring and hoisting myself up, sat astride and looked about me. The fence skirted the margin of a small lake much overgrown with weeds, amidst which I could see a couple of waterhens making off in alarm at my appearance, and beyond the lake rose the dark mass of Ken Wood. The ground between the fence and the lake was covered with high, reedy grass, which, immediately below my perch, bore very distinct impressions of feet, and an equally distinct set of tracks led away towards the wood – or from the wood to the fence, it was impossible to say which. But in any case, as there were no other tracks, it was certain that the person who made them had climbed over the fence. I dropped down on the grass and, having examined the ground attentively without discovering anything fresh, set off to follow the tracks.

For some distance they continued through high grass in which the impressions were very distinct, then they entered the wood, and here also, in the soft humus, lightly sprinkled with fallen leaves, the footprints were deep and easy to follow. But presently they struck a path, and, as they did not reappear on the farther side, it was evident that the unknown person had proceeded along it. The path was an old one, well made of hard gravel, and, where it passed through the deeper shade of the wood, was covered with velvety moss and grey-green lichen, on which I made out with some difficulty, the imprints of feet. But these were no longer distinct –they did not form a connected track, nor was it possible to distinguish them from the footprints of other persons who might have passed along the path. Even these I soon lost where I had halted irresolutely under a noble beech that rose from a fantastic coil of roots, and was considering how, if at all, I should next proceed, when, there appeared round a curve of the path a man in cord breeches and gaiters, evidently a keeper. He touched his hat civilly and ventured to enquire my business. "I am afraid I have no business here at all," I replied, for I did not think it expedient to tell him what had brought me into the wood. "I suppose I am trespassing."

"Well, sir, it is private property," he rejoined, "and being so near London we have to be rather particular. Perhaps you would like me to show you the way out on to the Heath."

I accepted his offer with many thanks for his courteous method of ejecting a trespasser, and we walked together through the beautiful woodland until the path terminated at a rustic turnstile. "That will be your way, sir," he said, as he let me out, indicating a track that led down to the Vale of Health.

I thanked him once more and then asked, "Is that a private house or does it belong to your estate?" I pointed to a small house or large cottage that stood within a fenced enclosure not far from the edge of the wood.

"That, sir," he replied, "was formerly a keeper's lodge. It is now let for a short term to an artist gentleman who is making some pictures of the Heath, but I expect it will be pulled down before long, as there is some talk of the County Council taking over that piece of land to add to the public grounds. Good-morning, sir," and the keeper, with a parting salute, turned back into the wood.

As I took my way homeward by the Highgate Ponds, I meditated on the relation of my new discoveries to the mystery of the preceding night. It was a strange affair, and sinister withal.

That the tracks led from the lane to the wood and not from the wood to the lane, I felt firmly convinced, and equally so that the body of the unknown priest or clergyman had undoubtedly been spirited away. But whither had it been carried? Presumably to some sequestered spot in the wood. And what better hiding-place could be found? There, buried in the soft leaf-mould, it might lie undisturbed for centuries, covered only the deeper as each succeeding autumn shed its russet burden on the unknown grave.

47

And what, I wondered, was the connection between this mysterious tragedy and the queer little object that I had picked up? Perhaps there was none. Its presence at that particular spot might be nothing but a coincidence. I took it from my handkerchief and examined it afresh. It was a very curious object. As to its use or meaning, I could only form vague surmises. Perhaps it was some kind of locket, enclosing a wisp of hair – the hair perhaps of some dead child or wife or husband or even lover. It was impossible to say. Of course, this question could be settled by taking it to pieces, but I was loth to injure the pretty little bauble. Besides, it was not mine. In fact, I felt that I ought to notify publicly that I had found it, though the circumstances did not make this very advisable. But if it had any connection with the tragedy, what was the nature of that connection? Had it dropped from the dead man or from the murderer – as I assumed the other man to be? Either was equally possible, though the two possibilities had very different values.

Then the question arose as to what course I should pursue. Clearly it would be my duty to inform the police of the mark on the fence and the tracks through the grass. But should I hand over the mysterious trinket to them? It seemed the correct thing to do, and yet there might after all be no connection between it and the crime. In the end I left the matter to be decided by the attitude of the police themselves.

I called at the station on my way home and furnished the inspector with an account of my new discoveries, of which he made a careful note, assuring me that the affair should be looked into. But his manner expressed frank disbelief, and was even a trifle hostile, and his emphatic request that I would abstain from mentioning the matter to anyone left me in no doubt that he regarded both my communications as wild delusions if not as a deliberate hoax. Consequently, though I frequently reproached myself afterwards with the omission, I said nothing about the trinket, and when I left the station I carried it in my pocket.

No communication on the subject of this mysterious affair ever reached me from the police. That they did actually make some perfunctory investigations, I learned later, as will appear in this narrative. But they gave no publicity to the affair and they sought no further information from me. For my own part, I could, naturally, never forget so strange an experience, but time and the multitudinous interests of my opening life tended to push it farther into the background of memory, and there it might have remained for ever had not subsequent events drawn it once more from its obscurity.

Chapter III
"Who is Sylvia?"

The winter session had commenced at the hospital, but at Hampstead the month of October had set in with something like a return to summer. It is true that the trees had lost something of their leafy opulence, and that here and there, amidst the sober green, patches of russet and gold had made their appearance, as if Nature's colour-orchestra were tuning up for the final symphony. But, meanwhile, the sun shone brightly and with a genial heat, and if, day by day, he fell farther from the zenith, there was nothing to show it but the lengthening noonday shadows, the warmer blue of the sky and the more rosy tint of the clouds that sailed across it.

Other and more capable pens than mine have set forth the charm of autumn and the beauties of Hampstead – queen of suburbs of the world's metropolis. Therefore will I refrain, and only note, as relevant to the subject, the fact that on many a day, when the work of the hospital was in full swing, I might have been seen playing truant very agreeably on the inexhaustible Heath or in the lanes and fields adjacent thereto. In truth, I was taking the final stage of my curriculum rather lazily, having worked hard enough in the earlier years, and being still too young by several months to be admitted to the fellowship of the College of Surgeons, promising myself that when the weather broke I would settle down in earnest to the winter's work.

I have mentioned that Millfield Lane was one of my favourite haunts – indeed, from my lodgings, it was the most direct route to the Heath, and I passed along it almost daily, and never, now, without my thoughts turning back to that rainy night when I had found the dead – or unconscious – man lying across the narrow footway. One morning, as I passed the spot, it occurred to me to make a drawing of the place in my sketch-book, that I might have some memorial of that strange adventure. The pictorial possibilities of the lane just here were not great, but by taking my stand at the turn, on the very spot where I had seen the body lying, I was able to arrange a simple composition which was satisfactory enough.

I am no artist. A neat and intelligible drawing is the utmost that I can produce. But even this modest degree of achievement may be very useful, as I had discovered many a time in the wards or laboratories – indeed, I have often been surprised that the instructors of our youth attach such small value to the power of graphic expression, and it came in usefully now, though in a way that was unforeseen and not fully appreciated at the moment. I had dealt adequately with the fence, the posts, the tree-trunks, and other well-defined forms and was beginning a less successful attack on the foliage, when I heard a light, quick step approaching from Hampstead Lane. Intuition – if there is such a thing – fitted the foot-step with a personality, and, for once in a way, was right, as the newcomer reached the sharp bend of the path, I saw a girl of about my own age, simply and serviceably dressed and carrying a pochade box and a small camp-stool. She was not an entire stranger to me. I had met her often in the lane and on the Heath – so often in fact that we had developed that profound unconsciousness of one another's existence that almost amounts to recognition – and had wondered vaguely who she was and what sort of work she did on the panels in that mysterious box.

As I drew back to make way for her, she brushed past, with a single, quick, inquisitive glance at my sketchbook, and went on her way, looking very much alive and full of business. I watched her as she tripped down the lane and passed between the posts out into the sunlight beyond, to vanish behind the trunks of the elms, then I returned to my sketch and my struggles to express foliage with a touch somewhat less suggestive of a birch-broom.

When I had finished my drawing, I sauntered on rather aimlessly, speculating for the hundredth time on the meaning of those discoveries of mine in this very lane. Was it possible that the man whom I had seen was not dead, but merely insensible? I could not believe it. The whole set of circumstances – the aspect of the body, the blood-stain on the fence, the tracks through the high grass, and the mysterious gold trinket – were opposed to any such belief. Yet, on the other hand, one would think that a man could not disappear unnoticed. This was no tramp or nameless vagrant. He was a clergyman or a priest, a man who would be known to a great number of persons and whose disappearance must surely be observed at once and be the occasion of very stringent enquiries. But no enquiries had apparently been made. I had seen no notice in the papers of any missing cleric, and clearly the police had heard nothing or they would have looked me up. The whole affair was enveloped in the profoundest mystery. Dead or alive, the man had vanished utterly, and whether he was dead or alive, the mystery was equally beyond solution.

These reflections brought me, almost unconsciously, to another of my favourite walks, the pretty footpath from the Heath to Temple Fortune. I had crossed the stile and stepped off the path to survey the pleasant scene, when my eye was attracted by a number of streaks of alien colour on the leaves of a burdock. Stooping down, I perceived that

50

they were smears of oil-paint, and inferred that someone had cleaned a palette on the herbage, an inference that was confirmed a moment later by what looked like the handle of a brush projecting from a clump of nettles. When I drew it out, however, it proved to be not a brush, but a very curious knife with a blade shaped like a diminutive and attenuated trowel, evidently a painting-knife and also evidently home-made, at least in part, for the tang had been thrust into a short, stout brush-handle and secured with a whipping of waxed thread. I dropped it into my outside breast pocket and went on my way, wondering if by chance it might have been dropped by my fair acquaintance, and the thought was still in my mind when its object hove in sight. Turning a bend in the path, I came on her quite suddenly, perched on her little camp-stool in the shadow of the hedge, with the open sketching-book on her knees, working away with an industry and concentration that seemed to rebuke my own idleness. Indeed, she was so much engrossed with her occupation that she did not notice me until I stepped off the path and approached with the knife in my hand. "I wonder," said I, holding it out and raising my cap, "if this happens to be your property. I picked it up just now among the nettles near the barn."

She took the knife from me and looked at it inquisitively. "No," she replied, "it isn't mine, but I think I know whose it is. I suspect it belongs to an artist who has been doing a good deal of work about the Heath. You may have seen him."

"I have seen several artists working about here during the summer. What was this one like?"

"Well," she answered with a smile, "he was like an artist. Very much like. Quite the orthodox get up. Wide brimmed hat, rather long hair, and a ragged beard. And he wore sketching-spectacles – half-moon-shaped things, you know – and kid gloves – which were not quite so orthodox."

"Very inconvenient, I should think.

"Not so very. I work in gloves myself in the cold weather or if the midges are very troublesome. You soon get used to the feel of them, and the man I am speaking of wouldn't find them in the way at all because he works almost entirely with painting-knives. That is what made me think that this knife was probably his. He had several, I know, and very skilfully he used them, too."

"You have seen his work, then?"

"Well," she admitted, "I'm afraid I descended once or twice to play the 'snooper'. You see, his method of handling interested me."

"May I ask what a 'snooper' is?" I enquired.

"Don't you know? It's a student's slang name for the kind of person who makes some transparent pretext for coming off the path and passing behind you to get a look at your picture by false pretences."

For an instant there flashed into my mind the suspicion that she was administering a quiet "backhander", and I rejoined hastily, "I hope you are not including me in the genus 'snooper'."

She laughed softly. "It did sound rather like it. But I'll give you the benefit of the doubt in consideration of your finding the knife – which you had better keep in trust for the owner."

"Won't you keep it? You know the probable owner by sight and I don't, and meanwhile you might experiment with it yourself."

"Very well," she replied, dropping it into her brush-tray, "I'll keep it for the present at any rate."

There was a brief pause, and then I ventured to remark, "That looks a very promising sketch of yours. And how well the subject comes."

"I'm glad you like it," she replied, quite simply, viewing her work with her head on one side. "I want it to turn out well, because it's a commission, and commissions for small-oil paintings are rare and precious."

"Do you find small oil pictures very difficult to dispose of?" I asked.

"Not difficult. Impossible, as a rule. But I don't try now. I copy my oil sketches in water-colour, with modifications to suit the market."

Again there was a pause, and, as her brush wandered towards the palette, it occurred to me that I had stayed as long as good manners permitted. Accordingly, I raised my cap, and, having expressed the hope that I had not greatly hindered her, prepared to move away. "Oh, not at all," she answered, "and thank you for the knife, though it isn't mine – or, at any rate, wasn't. Good-morning."

With this and a pleasant smile and a little nod, she dismissed me, and once more I went my idle and meditative way.

It had been quite a pleasant little adventure. There is always something rather interesting in making the acquaintance of a person whom one has known some time by sight but who is otherwise an unknown quantity. The voice, the manner, and the little revelations of character, which confirm or contradict previous impressions, are watched with interest as they develop themselves and fill in, one by one, the blank spaces of the total personality. I had, as I have said, often met this industrious maiden in my walks and had formed the opinion that she looked a rather nice girl – an opinion that was probably influenced by her unusual good looks and graceful carriage. And a rather nice girl she had turned out to be, very dignified and self-possessed, but quite simple and frank – though, to be sure, her gracious reception of me had probably been due to my sketch-book – she had taken me for a kindred spirit. She had a pleasant voice and a faultless accent, with just a hint of the fine lady in her manner, but I liked her none the less for that. And her name was a pretty name, too, if I had guessed it correctly, for, on the inside of the lid of her box, which was partly uncovered by the upright panel, I had read the letters "*Syl*". The panel hid the rest, but the name could hardly be other than Sylvia, and what more charming and appropriate name could be bestowed upon a comely young lady who spent her days amidst the woods and fields of my beloved Hampstead?

Regaling myself with this somewhat small beer, I sauntered on along the grassy lane, between hedgerows that in the summer had been spangled with wild roses and that were now gay with the big, oval berries, sleek and glossy and scarlet, like overgrown beads of red coral, away, across the fields to Golder's Green and thence by Millfield Lane, back to my lodgings at Gospel Oak, and to my landlady, Mrs. Blunt, who had a few plaintive words to say respecting the disastrous effects of unpunctuality – and the resulting prolonged heat – on mutton cutlets and fried potatoes.

It had been an idle morning and apparently void of significant events – but yet, when I look back on it, I see a definite thread of causation running through its simple happenings, and I realize that, all unthinking, I had strung on one more bead to the chaplet of my destiny.

Chapter IV
Septimus Maddock, Deceased

It was getting well on into November when I strolled one afternoon into the hospital museum, not with any specific object, but rather vaguely in search of something to do. During the last few days I had developed a slight revival of industry – which had coincided, oddly enough, with a marked deterioration of the weather – and, pathology being my weakest point, the museum had seemed to call me (though not very loudly, I fear) to browse amongst its multitudinous jars and dry preparations.

There was only one person in the great room, but he was a very important person, being none other than our lecturer on Medical Jurisprudence, Dr. John Thorndyke. He was seated at a small table, whereon was set out collection of jars and a number of large photographs, of which he appeared to be making a catalogue. But intent as he was on his occupation, he looked up as I entered and greeted me with a genial smile. "What do you think of my little collection, Jardine?" he asked, as I approached deferentially. Before replying, I ran a vaguely enquiring eye over the group of objects on the table and was mighty little enlightened thereby. It was certainly a queer collection. There was a flat jar which contained a series of five differently-coloured mice, another with a similar series of three rats, a human foot, a hand, manifestly deformed, a series of four fowls' heads, and a number of photographs of plants. "It looks," I replied, at length, "like what the auctioneers would call a miscellaneous lot."

"Yes," Dr. Thorndyke agreed, "it is a miscellaneous collection in a sense. But there is a connecting idea. It illustrates certain phenomena of inheritance which were discovered and described by Mendel."

"Mendel!" I exclaimed. "Who is he? I never heard of him."

"I daresay not." said Thorndyke, "though he published his results before you were born. But the importance of his discoveries is only now beginning to be appreciated."

"I suppose," said I, "the subject is too large and complex for a short explanation to be possible."

"The subject is a large one, of course," he replied, "but, put in a nutshell, Mendel's great discovery amounts to this, that, whereas certain characters are inherited only partially and fade off gradually in successive generations, certain other characters are inherited completely and pass unchanged from generation to generation. To take a couple of illustrative cases: If a black man marries a European, the offspring are mulattoes – forms intermediate between the black man and the European. If a mulatto marries a European, the offspring are quadroons – another intermediate form, and the next generation gives us the octoroon – intermediate again between the quadroon and the European. And so, from generation to generation, the black character gradually fades away and finally disappears. But there are other characters which are inherited entire or not at all, and such characters appear in pairs which are positive or negative to one another. Sex is a case in point. A male marries a female and the offspring are either male or female, never intermediate. The sex-character of only one parent is inherited, and it is inherited completely. The characters of maleness or femaleness pass down unchanged through the ages with no tendency to diminish or to shade off into one another. That is a case of Mendelian inheritance."

I ran my eyes over the collection and they presently lighted on the rather abnormal-looking foot, hanging, white and shrivelled in the clear spirit. I lifted the jar from the table and then, noticing for the first time, that the foot had a supernumerary toe, I enquired what point the specimen illustrated. "That six-toed foot," Thorndyke replied, "is an example of a deformity that is transmitted unchanged for an indefinite number of generations. This *brachydactylous* hand is another instance. The *brachydactyly* reappears in the offspring either completely or not at all. There are no intermediate conditions." He picked up the jar, and, having wiped the glass with a duster, exhibited the hand which was suspended within, and a strange-looking hand it was, broad and stumpy, like the hand of a mole. "There seem to be only two joints to each finger," I said. "Yes. The fingers are all thumbs, and the thumb is only a demi-thumb. A joint is suppressed in each digit."

"It must make the hand very clumsy and useless," I remarked.

"So one would think. It isn't exactly the type of hand for a Liszt or a Paganini. And yet we mustn't assume too much. I once saw an armless man copying pictures in the Luxembourg, and copying them very well, too. He held his brush with his toes, and he was so handy with his feet that he not only painted really dextrously, but managed to take his hat off to lady with quite a fine flourish. So you see, Jardine, it is not the hand that matters, but rather the brain that actuates it. A very indifferent hand will serve if the motor centres are of the right sort."

He replaced the jar on the table, and then, after a short pause, turning quickly to me, he asked, "What are you doing at present, Jardine?"

"Principally idling, sir," I replied.

"And not a bad thing to do either," he rejoined with a smile, "if you do it thoroughly and don't keep it up too long. How would you like to take charge of a practice for a week or so?"

"I don't know that I should particularly care to, sir," I answered.

"Why not? It would be a useful experience and would bring you useful knowledge – knowledge that you have got to acquire sooner or later. Hospital conditions, you know, are not normal conditions.

"General practice is normal medical practice, and the sooner you get to know the conditions of the great world the better for you. If you stick to the wards too long, you will get to be like the nurses, who seem to think that, '*All the world's a hospital, And men and women only patients.*'"

I reflected for a few moments. It was perfectly true. I was a qualified medical man, and yet of the ordinary routine of private practice I had not the faintest knowledge. To me, all sick people were either in-patients or out-patients. "Had you any particular practice in your mind, sir?" I asked.

"Yes. I met one of our old students just now. He is at his wit's end to find a *locum tenens*. He has to go away to-night or to-morrow morning, but he can't get anyone to look after his work. Won't you go to his relief? It's an easy practice, I believe."

I turned the question over in my mind and finally decided to try the venture. "That's right," said Dr. Thorndyke. "You'll help a professional brother, at any rate, and pick up a little experience. Our friend's name is Batson, and he lives in Jacob Street, Hampstead Road. I'll write it down."

He handed me a slip of paper with the address on it and wished me success, and I started at once from the hospital, already quite elated, as is the way of the youthful, at the prospect of a new experience.

Dr. Batson's establishment in Jacob Street was modest to the verge of dinginess. But Jacob Street, itself, was dingy, and so was the immediate neighbourhood, a district of tall, grimy houses that might easily have seen better days. However, Dr. Batson himself was spruce enough and in excellent spirits at my arrival, as was evident when he bounced into the room with a jovial greeting, bringing in with him a faint aroma of sherry. "Delighted to see you, Doctor!" he exclaimed in his large brisk voice. (That "Doctor" was a diplomatic hit on his part. They don't call newly-qualified men "Doctor" at the hospital.) "I met Thorndyke this morning and told him of my predicament. A busy man is the Great Unraveller, but never too busy to do a kindness to his friends. Can you take over to-night?"

"I could," said I.

"Then do. I want particularly to be off by the eight-thirty from Liverpool Street. Drop in and have some grub about six-thirty, I shall have polished off the day's work by then and you'll just come in for the evening consultations."

"Are there any cases that you will want me to see with you?" I asked.

"Oh, no," Batson replied, rather airily I thought. "They're all plain sailing. There's a typhoid. He's doing well – fourth week – and there's a tonsilitis and a psoas abscess – that's rather tedious, but still, it's improving – and an old woman with a liver. You won't have any difficulty with them. There's only one queer case, a heart."

"Valvular?" I asked.

"No, not valvular, I can tell you that much. I know what it isn't, but I'm hanged if I know what it is. Chappie complains of pain, shortness of breath, faintness, and so on, but I can't find anything to account for it. Heart-sounds all right, pulse quite good, no dropsy, no nothing. Seems like malingering, but I don't see why he should malinger. I think I'll get you to drop in this evening and have a look at him."

"Are you keeping him in bed?" I asked.

"Yes," said Batson, "I am now – not that his general condition seems to demand it. But he has had one or two fainting attacks, and yesterday he must needs fall down flop in his bedroom when there was nobody there, and, by way of making things more comfortable, he drops his medicine bottle and falls on the fragments. He might have killed himself, you know," Batson added in an aggrieved tone. "As it was, a long splinter from the bottom of the bottle stuck into his back and made quite a deep little wound. So I've kept him in bed since, out of harm's way, and there he is, deuced sorry for himself but, as far as I can make out, without a single tangible symptom."

"No facial signs? Nothing unusual in his colour or expression."

Batson laughed and tapped his gold-rimmed spectacles. "Ah! There you are! When you've got minus-five-D and some irregular astigmatism and a pair of glasses that don't correct it, all human beings look pretty much alike – a trifle sketchy, don't you know. I didn't see anything unusual in his face, but you might. Time will show. Now you cut along and fetch your traps, and I'll skip round and polish off the sufferers."

He launched me into the outer greyness of Jacob Street and bounced off in the direction of Cumberland Market, leaving me to pursue my way to my lodgings at Gospel Oak.

As I threaded the teeming streets of Camden Town I meditated on the new experience that was opening to me, and, with youthful egotism, I already saw myself making a brilliant diagnosis of an obscure heart case.

Also I reflected with some surprise on the calm view that Batson took of his defective eyesight. A certain type of painter, as I had observed, finds in semi-blindness a valuable gift which helps him to eliminate trivial detail and to impart a noble breadth of effect to his pictures, but to a doctor no such self-delusion would seem possible. Visual acuteness is the most precious item in his equipment.

I crammed into a large Gladstone bag the bare necessaries for a week's stay, together with a few indispensable instruments, and then mounted the jingling horse-tram of those pre-electric days, which, in due course, deposited me at the end of Jacob Street, Hampstead Road. Dr. Batson had not returned from his round when I arrived, but a few minutes later he burst into the surgery humming an air from *The Mikado*. "Ha! Here you are then! Punctual to the minute!" He hung his hat on a peg, laid his visiting-list on the desk of the dispensing counter, and began to compound medicine with the speed of a prestidigitator, talking volubly all the time. "That's for the old woman with the liver, Mrs. Mudge – Cumberland Market. You'll see her prescription in the day book. S'pose you don't know how to wrap up a bottle of medicine. Better watch me. This is the way." He slapped the bottle down on a square of cut paper, gave a few dextrous twiddles of his fingers and held out for my inspection a little white parcel like the mummy-case of a deceased medicine bottle. "It's quite easy when you've had a little practice," he said, deftly sticking the ends down with sealing-wax, "but you'll make a frightful mucker of it at first." Which prophecy was duly fulfilled that very evening.

"What time had I better see that heart case?" said I.

"Oh, you won't have to see it at all. Man's dead. Message left half-an-hour go. Pity, isn't it? I should have liked to hear what you thought of him. Must have been fatty heart. I'll write out the certificate while I think of it. Maggie! Where's that note that Mrs. Samway left?"

The question was roared out vaguely through the open door to a servant of unknown whereabouts, and resulted in the appearance of a somewhat scraggy housemaid bearing an opened note. "Here we are," said Batson, snatching the note out of its envelope and opening the book of certificate forms.

"Septimus Maddock was the chappie's name, age fifty-one, address 23, Gayton Street, cause of death – that's just what I should like to know – primary cause, secondary causes – I wish these infernal government clerks had got something better to do than fill printed forms with silly conundrums. I shall put '*Morbus Cordis*' – that ought to be enough for them. Mrs. Samway – that's his landlady, you know – will probably call for the certificate during the evening."

"Aren't you going to inspect the body?" I asked.

"Lord, no! Why should I! It isn't necessary, you know. I'm not an undertaker. Wish I was. Dead people good deal more profitable than live ones."

"But surely," I exclaimed, "the death ought to be verified. Why the man may not be dead at all."

"I know," said Batson, scribbling away like a minor poet, "but that isn't my business. Business of the Law. Law wastes your time with a heap of silly questions that don't matter and leaves out the question that does. Asks exact time when I last saw him alive, which doesn't matter a hang, and doesn't ask whether I saw him dead. Bumble was right. Law's an ass."

"But still," I persisted, "leaving the legal requirements out of consideration, oughtn't you for your own sake, and as a public duty, to verify the death? Supposing the man were not really dead?"

"That would be awkward for him," said Batson, "and awkward for me, too, if he came to life before they buried him. But it doesn't really happen in real life. Premature burial only occurs in novels."

His easy-going confidence jarred on me considerably. How could he, or anyone else, know what happened? "I don't see how you arrive at that," I objected. "It could only be proved by wholesale disinterment. And the fact remains that, if you don't verify a reported death, you have no security against premature burial – or even cremation."

Batson started up and stared at me, his wide-open, pale-blue eyes looking ridiculously small through his deep, concave spectacles. "By Jove!" he exclaimed, "I am glad you mentioned that – about cremation, I mean, because that is what will probably happen. I witnessed the chappie's will a couple of days ago, and I remember now that one of the clauses stipulated that his body should be cremated. So I shall have to verify the death for the purpose of the cremation certificate. We'd better pop round and see him at once."

With characteristic impulsiveness he sprang to his feet, snatched his hat from its peg, and started forth, leaving me to follow. "Beastly nuisance, these special regulations," said Batson, as he ambled briskly up the street. "Give a lot of trouble and cause a lot of delay."

"Isn't the ordinary death certificate sufficient in a case of cremation?" I asked.

"For purposes of law it is, though there is some talk of new legislation on the subject, but the Company are a law unto themselves. They have made the most infernally stringent regulations, and, as there is no crematorium near London excepting the one at Woking, you have to abide by their rules. And that reminds me – " here Batson halted and scowled at me ferociously through his spectacles.

"Reminds you?" I repeated.

"That they require a second death certificate, signed by a man with certain special qualifications." He stood awhile frowning and muttering under his breath and then suddenly turned and bounced off in a new direction. "Going to catch the other chappie and take him with us," he explained, as he darted out into the Hampstead Road. "Be off my mind then. A fellow named O'Connor, Assistant Physician to the North London Hospital. He'll do if we can catch him at home. If not, you'll have to manage him."

Batson looked at his watch – holding it within four inches of his nose – and broke into a trot as we entered a quiet square. Halfway up he halted at a door which bore a modest brass plate inscribed "*Dr. O'Connor*" and, seizing the bell-knob, worked it vigorously in and out as if it were the handle of an air-pump. "Doctor in?" he demanded briskly of a startled housemaid, and, without waiting for an answer, he darted into the hall, down the whole length of which he staggered, executing a sort of sword-dance, having caught his toe on an unobserved door-mat.

The doctor was in and he shortly appeared in evening dress with an overcoat on his arm, and apparently in as great a hurry as Batson himself. "Won't it do to-morrow?" he asked, when Batson had explained his difficulties and the service required.

"Might as well come now," said Batson persuasively. "Won't take a minute and then I can go away in peace."

"Very well," said O'Connor, wriggling into his overcoat. "You go along and I'll follow in a few minutes. I've got to look in on a patient on my way up west, and I shall be late for my appointment as it is. Write the address on my card, here."

He held out a card to my principal, and when the latter had scribbled the address on it, he bustled out and vanished up the square. Batson followed at the same headlong speed, and, again overlooking the mat, came out on the pavement like an ill-started sprinter.

Gayton Street, at which we shortly arrived, was a grey and dingy side-street exactly like a score of others in the same locality, and Number 23 differed from the rest of the seedy-looking houses in no respect save that it was perhaps a shade more dingy. The door was opened in answer to Batson's indecorously brisk knock by a woman – or perhaps I should say a lady – who at once admitted us and to whom Batson began, without preface, to explain the situation. "I got your note, Mrs. Samway. Was going to bring my friend, here, round to see the patient. Very unfortunate

60

affair. Very sad. Unexpected, too. Didn't seem particularly bad yesterday. What time did it happen?"

"I can't say exactly," was the reply. "He seemed quite comfortable when I looked in on him the last thing at night, but when I went in about seven this morning he was dead. I should have let you know sooner, but I was expecting you to call."

"Hmm, yes," said Batson, "very unfortunate. By the way, Mr. Maddock desired that his remains should be cremated, I think?"

"Yes, so my husband tells me. He is the executor of the will, you remember, in the absence of any relatives. All Mr. Maddock's relations seem to be in America."

"Have you got the certificate forms?" asked Batson.

"Yes. My husband got all the papers from the undertaker this afternoon."

"Very well, Mrs. Samway, then we'll just take a look at the body – have to certify that I've seen it, you know."

Mrs. Samway ushered us into a sitting-room where she had apparently been working alone, for an unfinished mourning garment of some kind lay on the table. Leaving us here, she went away and presently returned with a sheaf of papers and a lighted candle, when we rose and followed her to a back room on the ground floor. It was a smallish room, sparely furnished, with heavy curtains drawn across the window, and by one wall a bed, on which was a motionless figure covered by a sheet.

Our conductress stood the candlestick on a table by the bed and stepped back to make way for Batson, who drew back the sheet and looked down on the body in his peering, near-sighted fashion. The deceased seemed to be a rather frail-looking man of about fifty, but, beyond the fact that he was clean shaven, I could form very little idea of his appearance, since, in addition to the usual bandage under the chin to close the mouth, a tape had been carried round the head to secure a couple of pads of cotton wool over the eyes to keep the eyelids closed.

As Batson applied his stethoscope to the chest of the dead man, I glanced at our hostess not without interest. Mrs. Samway was an unusual-looking woman, and I thought her decidedly handsome, though not attractive to me personally. She seemed to be about thirty, rather over the medium height and of fine Junoesque proportions, with a small head very gracefully set on the shoulders. Her jet-black hair, formally parted in the middle, was brought down either side of the forehead in wavy, but very smooth, masses and gathered behind in a neat, precisely-plaited coil. The general effect reminded me of the so-called "Clytie", having the same reposefulness though not the gentleness and softness of that lovely head. But the most remarkable feature of this woman was the colour of her eyes, which were of the palest grey or hazel that I have ever seen – so pale in fact that they told as spots of light, like the eyes of some lemurs or those of a cat seen in the dusk, a peculiarity that imparted a curiously intense and penetrating quality to her glance.

I had just noted these particulars when Batson, having finished his examination, held out the stethoscope to me. "May as well listen, as you're here," said he, and, turning to our hostess, he added, "Let us see those papers, Mrs. Samway."

As he stepped over to the table, I took his place on a chair by the bedside and proceeded to make an examination. It was, of course, only a matter of form, for the man was obviously dead, but having insisted so strongly on the necessity of verifying the death I had to make a show of becoming scepticism. Accordingly I tested, both by touch and with the stethoscope, the region of the heart. Needless to say, no heart-sounds were to be distinguished, nor any signs of pulsation – indeed, the very first touch of my hand on the chilly surface of the chest was enough to banish any doubt. No living body could be so entirely destitute of animal heat. I laid down the stethoscope and looked reflectively at the dead man, lying so still and rigid, with his bandaged jaws and blindfolded eyes, and speculated vaguely on his personality when alive and on the hidden disease that had so suddenly cut him off from the land of the living, and insensibly – by habit I suppose – my fingers strayed to his clammy, pulseless wrist. The sleeve of his night-shirt was excessively long, almost covering the fingers, and I had to turn it back to reach the spot where the pulse would normally be felt. In doing this, I moved the dead hand slightly and then became aware of a well-marked *rigor mortis*, or death stiffening in the arm of the corpse, a condition which I ought to have observed sooner.

At this moment, happening to look up, I caught the eye of Mrs. Samway fixed on me with a very remarkable expression. She was leaning over Batson as he filled up the voluminous certificate, but had evidently been watching me, and the expression of her pale, catlike eyes left no doubt in my mind that she strongly resented my proceedings. In some confusion, and accusing myself of some failure in outward decorum, I hastily drew down the dead man's sleeve and rose from the bedside. "You noticed, I suppose," said I, "that there is fairly well-marked *rigor mortis*?"

"I didn't," said Batson, "but if you did it'll do as well. Better mention it to O'Connor when he comes. He ought to be here now."

"Who is O'Connor?" asked Mrs. Samway.

"Oh, he is the doctor who is going to sign the confirmatory certificate."

Again a gleam of unmistakable anger flashed from our hostess' eyes as she demanded, "Then who is this gentleman?"

"This is Dr. Humphrey Jardine," said Batson. "'Pologize for not introducing him before. Dr. Jardine is taking my practice while I'm away. I'm off to-night for about a week."

Mrs. Samway withered me with a baleful glance of her singular eyes, and remarked stiffly, "I don't quite see why you brought him here."

She turned her back on me, and I decided that Mrs. Samway was somewhat of a Tartar – though, to be sure, my presence was a distinct intrusion. I was about to beat a retreat when Batson's apologies were interrupted by a noisy rat-tat at the street door. "Ah, here's O'Connor," said Batson, and, as Mrs. Samway went out to open the door, he added, "Seem to have put our foot in it, though I don't see why she need have been so peppery about it. And O'Connor needn't have banged at the door like that, with death in the house. He'll get into trouble if he doesn't look out."

Our colleague's manner was certainly not ingratiating. He burst into the room with his watch in his hand protesting that he was three minutes late already, and, he added, "if there is one thing that I detest, it's being late at dinner. Got the forms?"

"Yes," replied Batson, "here they are. That's my certificate on the front page. Yours is overleaf."

Dr. O'Connor glanced rapidly down the long table of questions, muttering discontentedly. "'*Made careful external examination?*' Hmm. '*Have you made a* post mortem?' No, of course, I haven't. What an infernal rigmarole! If cremation ever becomes general, there'll be no time for anything but funerals. Who nursed the deceased?"

"I did," said Mrs. Samway. "My husband relieved me occasionally, but nearly all the nursing was done by me. My name is Letitia Samway."

"Was the deceased a relation of yours?"

"No, only a friend. He lived with us for a time in Paris and came to England with us."

"What was his occupation?"

"He was nominally a dealer in works of art. Actually he was a man of independent means."

"Have you any pecuniary interest in his death?"

"He has left us about seventy pounds. My husband is the executor of the will."

"I see. Well, I'd better have a few words with you outside, Batson, before I make my examination. It's all a confounded farce, but we must go through the proper forms, I suppose."

"Yes, by all means," said Batson. "Don't leave any loop-hole for queries or objections." He rose and accompanied O'Connor out into the hall, whence the sound of hurried muttering came faintly through the door.

As soon as we were alone, I endeavoured to make my peace with Mrs. Samway by offering apologies for my intrusion into the house of mourning. "For the time being," I concluded, "I am Dr. Batson's assistant, and, as he seemed to wish me to come with him, I came without considering that my presence might be objected to. I hope you will forgive me."

My humility appeared entirely to appease her, in a moment her stiff and forbidding manner melted into one that was quite gracious and she rewarded me with a smile that made her face really charming. "Of course," she said, "it was silly of me to be so cantankerous and rude, too. But it did look a little callous, you know, when I saw you playing with his poor, dead hand, so you must make allowances." She smiled again, very prettily, and at this moment my two colleagues re-entered the room. "Now, then," said O'Connor, "let us see the body and then we shall have finished."

He strode over to the bed, and, turning back the sheet, made a rapid inspection of the corpse. "Ridiculous farce," he muttered. "Looks all right. Would, in any case though. Parcel of red tape. What's the good of looking at the outside of a body? *Post mortem*'s the only thing that's any use. What's this piece of tape-plaster on the back?"

"Oh," said Batson, "that is a little cut that he made by falling on a broken bottle. I stuck the plaster on because you can't get a bandage to hold satisfactorily on the back. Besides, he didn't want a bandage constricting his chest."

"No, of course not," O'Connor agreed. "Well, it's all regular and straightforward. Give me the form and I'll fill it up and sign it." He seated himself at the table, looked once more at his watch, groaned aloud and began to write furiously. "The Egyptians weren't such bad judges, after all," he remarked as he laid down the pen and rose from his chair.

"Embalming may have been troublesome, but when it was done it was done for good. The deceased was always accessible for reference in case of a dispute, and all this red tape was saved. Good-night, Mrs. Samway." He buttoned up his coat and bustled off, and a minute or so later we followed.

"By jove!" exclaimed Batson, "this business has upset my arrangements finely. I shall have to buck up if I'm going to catch my train. There's all the medicine to be made up and sent out yet, to say nothing of dinner. But dinner will have to wait until the business is all

64

settled up. Don't you hurry, Jardine. I'll just run on and get to work." He broke into an elephantine trot and soon disappeared round a corner, and, when I arrived at the surgery, I found him posting up the day-book with the speed of a parliamentary reporter.

Batson's dexterity with medicine-bottles and wrapping paper filled me with admiration and despair. I made a futile effort to assist, but in the end, he snatched away the crumpled paper in which I was struggling to enswathe a bottle, dropped it into the waste-paper basket, snatched up a clean sheet and – *Slap! Bang!* – in the twinkling of an eye, he had transformed the bottle into a neat, little white parcel as a conjuror changes a cocked hat into a guinea-pig. It was wonderful.

My host was a cheerful soul, but restless. He got up from the table no less than six times to pack some article that he had just thought of, and after dinner, when I accompanied him to his bedroom, I saw him empty his trunk no less than three times to make sure that he had forgotten nothing. He quite worried me. Your over-quick man is apt to wear out other people's nerves more than his own. I began to look anxiously at the clock, and felt a real relief when the maid came to announce that the cab was at the door. "Well, good-bye, Doctor!" he sang out cheerily, shaking my hand through the open window of the cab. "Don't forget to keep the stock-bottles filled up. Saves a world of trouble. And don't take too long on your rounds. Ta! Ta!"

The cab rattled away and I went back into the house, a full-blown general practitioner.

Chapter V
The Lethal Chamber

A young and newly-qualified doctor, emerging for the first time into private practice, is apt to be somewhat surprised and disconcerted by the new conditions. Accustomed to the exclusively professional and scientific atmosphere of the hospital, the sudden appearance of the personal element as the predominant factor rather takes him aback. He finds himself in a new and unexpected position. No longer a mere, impersonal official, a portion of a great machine, he is the paid servant of his patients who are not always above letting him feel the conditions of his service. The hospital patient, drilled into a certain respectful submissiveness by the discipline of the wards, has given place to an employer, usually critical, sometimes truculent, and occasionally addicted to a disagreeable frankness of speech.

The *locum tenens*, moreover, is peculiarly susceptible to these conditions – especially if, as in my case, his appearance is youthful. Patients resent the substitution of a stranger for the familiar medical attendant and are at no great pains to disguise the fact. The "old woman with the liver" (to adopt Batson's pellucid phrase) hinted that I was rather young, adding encouragingly that I should get the better of that in time, while the more morose typhoid bluntly informed me that he hadn't bargained for being attended by a medical student.

Taken as a whole, I found private practice disappointing and soon began to wish myself back in the wards and to sigh for my quiet, solitary rambles on Hampstead Heath. Still, there were rifts in the cloud. Some of the patients appreciated the interest that I took in their cases, evidently contrasting it with the rather casual attitude of my principal, and some were positively friendly. But, in general, my reception was such as to make me slightly apprehensive whenever a new patient appeared.

On the fourth evening after Batson's departure, Mrs. Samway was announced and I prepared myself for the customary snub. But I was mistaken. Nothing could be more gracious than her manner towards me, though the object of her visit occasioned me some embarrassment. "I have called, Dr. Jardine." she said, "to ask you if you could let me have the account for poor Mr. Maddock. My husband is the executor, you know, and, as we shall be going back to Paris quite shortly, he wants to get everything settled up."

I was in rather a quandary. Of the financial side of practice I was absolutely ignorant and I thought it best to say so. "But," I added, "Dr. Batson will be back on Friday evening, if you can wait so long."

"Oh, that will do quite well," she replied, "but don't forget to tell him that we want the account at once."

I promised not to forget, and then remarked that she would, no doubt, be glad to be back in Paris. "No," she answered, "I shall be rather sorry. Of course Camden Town is not a very attractive neighbourhood, but it is close to the heart of London, and then there are some delightful places near and quite accessible. There is Highgate, for instance."

"Yes, but it is getting very much built over, isn't it?"

"Unfortunately it is, but yet there are some very pleasant places left. The old village is still charming. So quaint and old world. And then there is Hampstead. What could be more delightful than the Heath? But perhaps you don't know Hampstead?"

"Oh, yes I do," said I. "My rooms are at Gospel Oak, quite near the Heath, and I think I know every nook and corner of the neighbourhood. I am pining for a stroll on the Heath at this very moment."

"I daresay you are," she said sympathetically. "This is a depressing neighbourhood if you can't get away from it. We found it very dismal, at first, after Paris."

"Do you live in Paris?" I asked.

"Not permanently," she replied. "But we spend a good deal of time there. My husband is a dealer in works of art, so he has to travel about a good deal. That is how we came to know Mr. Maddock."

"He was a dealer too, wasn't he?" I enquired.

"Yes, in a way. But he had means of his own and his dealing was a mere excuse for collecting things that he was not going to keep. He had a passion for buying, and then he used to sell the things in order to buy more. But I am afraid I am detaining you with my chatter?"

"No, not at all," I said eagerly, only too glad to have an intelligent, educated person to talk to. "You are the last caller, and I hope I have finished my day's work."

Accordingly she stayed quite a long time, chatting on a variety of subjects and finally on that of cremation. "I daresay," she said, "it is more sanitary and wholesome than burial, but there is something rather dreadful about it. Perhaps it is because we are not accustomed to the idea."

"Did you go to the funeral?" I asked.

"Yes. Mr. Maddock had no friends in England but my husband and me, so we both went. It was very solemn and awesome. The coffin was laid on the catafalque while a short service was read, and then two metal doors opened and it was passed through out of our sight. We waited some time and presently they brought us a little terra-cotta urn with just a handful or two of white ash in it. That was all that was left of our poor friend Septimus Maddock. Don't you think it is rather dreadful?"

"Death is always rather dreadful," I answered. "But when we look at the ashes of a dead person, we realize the total destruction of the body, whereas the grave keeps its secrets. If we could look down through the earth and see the changes that are taking place, we should probably find the slow decay more shocking than the swift consumption by fire. Fortunately we cannot. But we know that the final result is the same in both."

Mrs. Samway shuddered slightly, and drew her wraps more closely about her. "Yes," she said with a faint sigh, "the same end awaits us all – but it is better not to think about it."

We were both silent for awhile. I sat with my gaze bent rather absently on the case-book before me, turning over her last somewhat gloomy utterance, until, chancing to look up, I found her pale, penetrating eyes fixed on me with the same strange intentness that I had noticed when she had looked at me as I sat by the body of Maddock. As she met my glance, she looked down quickly but without confusion, and with a return to her habitual reposefulness.

Half-unconsciously I returned her scrutiny. She was a remarkable-looking woman. A beautiful woman, too, but of a type that is, in our time and country, rare: An ancient or barbaric type in which womanly beauty and grace are joined to manifest physical strength. I felt that some unusual racial mixture spoke in her inconsistent colouring, her clear, pink skin, her pale eyes and the jet-black hair that rippled down either side of her low forehead in little crimpy waves, as regular and formal as the "archaic curls" of early Greek sculpture.

But predominant over all other qualities was that of strength. Full and plump, soft and almost ultra-feminine, lissom and flexible in every pose and movement, yet, to me, the chief impression that her appearance suggested was strength – sheer, muscular strength. Not the rigid bull-dog strength of a strong man, but the soft and supple strength of a leopard. I looked at her as she sat almost limply in her chair, with her head on one side, her hands resting in her lap and a beautiful, soft, womanly droop of the shoulders, and I felt that she could have started up in an instant, active, strong, formidable, like a roused panther.

I was going on, I think, to make comparisons between her and that other woman who was wont to trip so daintily down Millfield Lane, when she raised her eyes slowly to mine, and suddenly she blushed scarlet. "Am I a very remarkable-looking person, Dr. Jardine?" she asked quietly, as if answering my thoughts.

The rebuke was well merited. For an instant a paltry compliment fluttered on my lips, but I swallowed it down. She wasn't that kind of woman. "I am afraid I have been staring you out of countenance, Mrs. Samway," I said apologetically.

"Hardly that," she replied with a smile, "but you certainly were looking at me very attentively."

"Well," I said, recovering myself, "after all, a cat may look at a king, you know."

She laughed softly – a very pretty, musical laugh – and rose, still blushing warmly. "And," she retorted, "by the same reasoning, you think a king may look at a cat. Very well, Dr. Jardine. Good-night."

She held out her hand, a beautifully-shaped hand, though rather large – but, as I have said, she was not a small woman, and as it clasped mine, though the pressure was quite gentle, it conveyed, like her appearance, an impression of abundant physical strength.

I accompanied her to the door and watched her as she walked up the dingy street with an easy, erect, undulating gait, even as might have walked those women who are portrayed for the wonder of all time on the ivory-toned marble of the Parthenon frieze. I followed with my eyes the dignified, graceful figure until it vanished round the corner, and then went back to the consulting-room dimly wondering why a woman of such manifest beauty and charm should offer little attraction to me.

Batson's practice, among its other drawbacks, suffered from a deadly lack of professional interest. Whether this was its normal condition, or whether his patients had got wind of me and called in other and more experienced practitioners, I know not, but certainly, after the stirring work of the hospital, the cases that I had to deal with seemed very small beer. Hence the prospect of a genuine surgical case came as a grateful surprise and I hailed it with enthusiasm.

It was on the day before Batson's expected return that I received the summons, which was delivered to me in a dirty envelope as I sat by the bedside of the last patient on my list. "Is the messenger waiting?" I asked, tearing open the envelope.

"No, Doctor. He just handed in the note and went off. He seemed to be in a hurry."

I ran my eye over the message, scrawled in a rather illiterate hand on a sheet of common notepaper, and read:

Sir,

Will you please come at once to the Mineral Water Works in Norton Street. One of our men has injured himself rather badly.

Yours truly,

J. Parker

P.S. – He is bleeding a good deal, so please come quick.

The postscript gave a very necessary piece of information. An injury which bled would require certain dressings and surgical appliances over and above those contained in my pocket case, and to obtain these I should have to take Batson's house on the way. Slipping the note into my pocket, I wished my patient a hasty *adieu* and strode off at a swinging pace in the direction of Jacob Street.

The housemaid, Maggie, helped me to find the dressings and pack the bag – for she was a handy, intelligent girl though no beauty, and meanwhile I questioned her as to the whereabouts of Norton Street and the mineral water factory. "Oh, I know the place well enough, sir," said she, "though I didn't know the works were open. Norton Street is only a few minutes' walk from here. It's quite close to Gayton Street – in fact these works are just at the back of the Samway's house. You go up to the corner by the market and take the second on the right and then – "

"Look here, Maggie," I interrupted, "you'd better come and show me the way, as you know the place. There's no time to waste on fumbling for the right turning."

"Very well, sir," she replied, and the bag being now packed with all necessary instruments and dressings, we set forth together. "Is this a large factory?" I asked, as she trotted by my side, to the astonished admiration of Jacob Street, and the neighbourhood in general.

"No, sir," she replied. "It's quite a small place. The last people went bankrupt and the works were empty and to let for a long time. I thought they were still to let, but I suppose somebody has taken them and started the business afresh. It's round here."

She piloted me round a corner into a narrow bystreet, near the end of which she halted at the gate of a yard or mews. Above the entrance was a weather-beaten board bearing the inscription, "International Mineral Water Company" and a half-defaced printed bill offering the premises to let, and at the side was a large bell-pull. A vigorous tug at the latter set a bell jangling within, and, as Maggie tripped away up the street, a small wicket in the gate opened, disclosing the dimly-seen figure of a man standing in the inner darkness. "Are you the doctor?" he inquired.

I answered "Yes," and, being thereupon bidden to enter, stepped through the opening of the wicket, which the man immediately closed, shutting out the last gleam of light from the street lamp outside. "It's rather dark," said the unseen custodian, taking me by the arm.

"It is indeed," I replied, groping with my feet over the rough cobbles. "Hadn't you better get a light of some kind?"

"I will in a minute," was the reply. "You see, all the other men have gone home. We close at six sharp. This is the way. I'll strike a match. The man is down in the bottling-room."

My conductor struck a match by the light of which he guided me through a doorway, along a passage or corridor and down a flight of stone steps. At the bottom of the steps was a flagged passage, out of which opened what looked like a range of cellars. Along the passage I walked warily, followed by the stranger and lighted, very imperfectly, by the matches that he struck, the glimmer of which threw a gigantic and ghostly shadow of myself on the stone floor, but failed utterly to pierce the darkness ahead. I was exactly opposite the yawning doorway of one of the cellars when the match went out, and the man behind me exclaimed, "Wait a moment, Doctor! Don't move until I strike another light."

I halted abruptly, and the next moment I received a violent thrust that sent me staggering through the open doorway into the cellar. Instantly, the massive door slammed and a pair of heavy bolts were shot in succession on the outside.

"What the devil is the meaning of this?" I roared, battering and kicking furiously at the door. Of course there was no answer, and I quickly stopped my demonstrations, for it dawned on me in a moment that the factory was untenanted save by the ruffian who had admitted me, that I had been decoyed here of a set purpose, though what that purpose was I could not imagine.

But it was not long before I received a pretty broad hint as to the immediate intentions of my host. A gentle thumping at the door of my cellar attracted my attention and caused me to lay my ear against the wood. The sound that I heard was quite unmistakable. The crevices of the door were being filled, apparently with pieces of rag, which my friend was ramming home, presumably with a chisel. In fact the door was being "caulked" to make the joints airtight.

The object of this proceeding was clear enough. I was shut up in an air-tight cavity in which I was to be slowly suffocated. That was quite obvious. Why I was to be suffocated, I could form no sort of guess

71

excepting that I had fallen into the hands of a homicidal lunatic. But I was not greatly alarmed. The air in a good-sized cellar will last a considerable time, and I could easily poke out anything that my friend might stuff into the keyhole. Then, when the men arrived in the morning, I could kick on the cellar door, and they would come and let me out. There was nothing to be particularly frightened about.

Were there any men? The injured man was evidently a myth. Supposing the other men were a myth too? I recalled Maggie's remark, that she "had thought the place was to let still." Perhaps it was. That would be rather more serious.

At this point my agitations were broken in upon by sounds from the adjoining cellar, the sound of someone moving about and dragging some heavy body. And it struck me at once as strange that I should hear these sounds so distinctly, seeing the massive door of my own cellar was sealed and the walls were of solid brick, as I ascertained by rapping at them with my knuckles. But I had no time to consider this circumstance, for there suddenly rose a new sound, whereat, I must confess my heart fairly came into my mouth, a loud, penetrating hiss like the shriek of escaping steam. It seemed to come from some part of the cellar in which I was immured, from a spot nearly overhead, and it was immediately echoed by a similar sound in the adjoining cellar and then by a third. Even as the last sound broke forth, the door of the adjoining cellar slammed, the bolts were shot and then faintly mingled with the discordant hissing. I could hear the dull thumping that told me that the cracks of that door, too, were being caulked.

It was a frightful situation. The hissing sound was obviously caused by the escape of gas under high pressure, and that gas must be entering my cellar through some opening. I felt for my match-box, and, groping along the wall towards the point whence the loudest sound – and, indeed, all the sounds – proceeded, I struck a match. The glimmer of the wax vesta made everything clear. Close to the ceiling, about seven feet from the ground, was an opening in the wall about six inches square, and pouring through this in a continuous stream was a cloud of white particles that glistened like snowflakes. As I stood under the opening, some of them settled on my face, and the more than icy coldness of the contact, told the whole, horrible tale in a moment.

This white powder *was* snow – carbonic acid snow. The hissing sound came from three of those great iron bottles, charged under pressure with liquefied carbonic acid, which are used by mineral water manufacturers for aerating the water. The miscreant (or lunatic) who had imprisoned me had turned on the taps, and the liquid was escaping and turning into to snow with the cold produced by its own rapid evaporation and expansion. Of course the snow would quickly absorb heat, and, without again liquefying, evaporate into the gaseous form. In a very short time both cellars would be full of the poisonous gas, and I – well, in a word, I was shut up in a lethal chamber.

It has taken me some time to write this explanation, which, however, flashed through my brain in the twinkling of an eye as the light of the match fell on that sinister cloud of snowflakes. In a moment I had my coat off, and was stuffing it for dear life into the opening. It was but a poor protection against the gas, which would easily enough find its way through the interstices of the fabric, but it would stop the direct stream of snow and give me time to think.

On what incalculable chances do the great issues of our lives depend! If I had been a short man I must have been dead in half-an-hour, for the opening through which the cloud of snow was pouring was well over seven feet above the floor and would have been quite out of my reach. Even as it was, with my six feet of stature and corresponding length of arm, it was impossible to ram my coat into the opening with the necessary force, for I had to stand close to the wall with my arm upraised at a great mechanical disadvantage. Still, as I have said, imperfect as the obstruction was, it served to stop the inrushing cloud of snow. It would take some time for the heavy gas in the adjoining cellar to rise to the level of the opening, and, meanwhile, I could be devising other measures.

I lit another match and looked about me. The cellar was much smaller than I had thought and was absolutely empty. The floor was of concrete, the walls of rough brickwork and the ceiling of plaster, all cracked and falling in. There was plenty of ventilation there, but that was of no interest to me. Carbonic acid gas is so heavy that it behaves almost like a liquid, and it would have filled the cellar and suffocated me even if the top of my prison had been open to the sky. The adjoining cellar was already filling rapidly, and when the gas in it reached the level of the opening, it would percolate through my coat and come pouring down into my cellar. But that, as I have said, would take some time – if the dividing wall was moderately sound. This important qualification, as soon as it occurred to me, set me exploring the wall with the aid of another match, and very unsatisfactory was the result. It was a bad wall, built of inferior brick and worse mortar, and was marked by innumerable holes where wall-hooks and other fastenings had been driven in between the bricks. My brief survey convinced me that, so far from being gas-tight, the wall was as pervious as a sponge, and that whatever I meant to do to preserve my life, I must set about without delay.

But what was I to do? That was the urgent, the vital question. Escape was evidently impossible. There were no means of stopping up the numberless holes and weak places in the wall. The only vulnerable spot was the door. If I could establish some communication with the outer air, I could, for a time at least, disregard the poisonous gas with which I should presently be surrounded.

The first thing to be considered was the keyhole. That must be unstopped at once. Fumbling in my bag – for I had grown of a sudden niggardly with my matches – I found a good-sized probe, which I insinuated into the keyhole, and, in a moment, my hopes in that direction were extinguished. For the end of the probe impinged upon metal. The keyhole was not stopped with rag, but with a plate of metal fixed on the outside. With rapidly-growing alarm, but with a tidiness born of habit, I put the probe back in the bag and began feverishly to review the situation and consider my resources.

And then I had an idea – only a poor, forlorn hope, but still an idea.

There is a certain ingenious type of pocket-knife, devised principally in the interest of the cutlery trade, that innocent persons (usually of the female persuasion) are wont to bestow as presents on their masculine friends. Such a knife I chanced to possess. It had been given to me by an aunt, and sentimental considerations had induced me to give it an amount of room in my trousers' pocket that I continually grudged. However, there it was at this critical moment, with its corkscrew, gimlet, its bewildering array of blades, its hoof-pick, tooth-pick, tweezers, file, screw-driver, and assorted unclassifiable tools, a ponderous lump of pocket-destroying uselessness – and yet, the appointed means of saving my life.

The gimlet was the first tool that I called into requisition. Very gingerly – for these tools are commonly over-tempered and brittle – I bored in the thick plank a hole at about the level of my mouth, and as I worked I turned over my further plans. When the gimlet was through the door, I selected a tool on whose use I had often speculated – a sharp-edged spike, like a diminutive and very stumpy bayonet – which I proceeded to use broach-wise to enlarge the hole. When this tool worked loose, I exchanged it for the screwdriver, with which I managed to broach the hole out to about half an inch in width. And this was as large as I could make it, and it was not large enough. True, one could breathe fairly comfortably through a half-inch hole, but, with the deadly gas circulating around, a freer opening was very desirable.

Then I bethought me that the magic knife contained a saw – a wretched, thick-bladed affair, but still a saw – which would actually cut wood if you gave it time. This implement suggested a simple plan which

74

I forthwith put into execution, working as rapidly as I could without running the risk of breaking the tools. My plan was to make a second hole some two inches diagonally below the first, and from each hole to carry two saw-cuts at right angles to one another. The two pairs of cuts would intersect and take a square piece out of the door, giving me a little window through which I could breathe in comfort.

It was a trifling task, but yet, with the miserable tools I had, it took a considerable time to execute, the more since the saw-blade was wider than the holes, excepting at its point. However, it was accomplished at last, and I had the satisfaction of pushing out the little separated square of wood and feeling that I now had free access to the pure air outside my dungeon.

But it was none too soon. As I rested from my labours, it occurred to me to test the condition of the air inside. Lighting a wax match, I held the little taper so that the flame ascended steadily, and then lowered it slowly. As it descended the flame changed colour somewhat, and about eighteen inches from the floor it went out quite suddenly. There was, then, a layer of the pure gas about eighteen inches deep covering the floor, and, no doubt, rising pretty rapidly.

This was rather startling, and it warned me to have recourse without delay to my breathing hole. For though carbonic acid gas behaves somewhat as a liquid, it is not a liquid: Like other gases, it has the power of diffusing upwards, and the air of the cellar must be already getting unsafe. Accordingly, after carefully wiping the surface of the door with my handkerchief, I applied my mouth, with some distaste, to the opening and took in a deep draught of undoubtedly pure air.

The position in which I had to stand with my mouth to the hole was an irksome one, and I foresaw that it would presently become very fatiguing. Moreover, when the gas reached the level of my head, it would be difficult to prevent some of it from finding its way into my mouth and nostrils, and if it did, I should most assuredly be poisoned. This consideration suggested the necessity of making another hole at a lower level to let out the gas and allow me to rest myself by a change of position. But this new task had to be carried out with my mouth glued to the breathing hole, and very awkward and tiring I found it and very slow was the progress that I made. This second hole was smaller than the first, for time was precious, and I reflected that I could easily enlarge it by fresh saw-cuts, each two of which would take out a triangular piece of wood.

But it was tedious work, and its completion left me with aching arms, indeed, I was beginning to ache all over from the constrained position. Taking a deep breath and shutting my mouth, I stood up and stretched myself. Then I lit a match and looked at my watch. Half-past eight. I had been over two hours in the cellar. And meanwhile the patients were waiting for me at the surgery, and, no doubt, murmuring at the delay. How soon would my absence lead to enquiries? Or were enquiries being made even now?

Looking at the match that I still held in my hand, I noticed that its flame was pallid and bluish, and as I lowered it slowly, it went out when it was a little over two feet from the floor. The gas, then, was still rising, though not so rapidly as I, had feared, but from the altered colour of the flame, it was evident that the air of the cellar, generally, contained enough diffused gas to be actively poisonous.

After a time, the erect position began to grow insupportably fatiguing. I felt that I must sit down for a few minutes' rest, even though prudence whispered that it was highly unsafe. I struggled for awhile, but eventually, conquered by fatigue, sat down on the floor with my mouth applied closely to the lower breathing-hole. I persuaded myself that I would sit only just long enough to recover some of my strength, but minute after minute sped by and still I felt an unaccountable reluctance to rise.

Suddenly I because conscious of a vague feeling of drowsiness, of a desire to lean back against the wall and doze. It was only slight, but its significance was so appalling that I scrambled to my feet in a panic, and, putting my mouth to the upper breathing-hole, took several deep inspirations. But I soon realized that the upright position was impossible. The drowsy feeling continued and there was growing with it a lassitude and weakness of the limbs that threatened to leave me only the choice between sitting or falling. A wave of furious anger swept over me and roused me a little, a burst of hatred of the cowardly wretch who had decoyed me, as I now suspected, to my death. Then this feeling passed and was succeeded by chilly fear, and I sank down once more into a sitting position with my mouth pressed to the lower opening.

The time ran on unreckoned by me. Gradually, by imperceptible degrees, my mental state grew more and yet more sluggish. Anger and fear and ever-dwindling hope flitted by turns across the slowly-fading field of my consciousness. Intervals of quiet indifference – almost of placid comfort – began to intervene, with increasing lassitude and a growing desire for rest. To lie down, that was what I wanted. To lay my head upon the stony floor and sink into sweet oblivion.

At last I must have actually dozed, though, fortunately, without removing my mouth from the breathing-hole, for I had no sense of the passage of time, when I was suddenly aroused by the loud and continuous jangling of a bell.

76

I listened with a sort of dull eagerness and keeping awake with a conscious effort.

The bell pealed wildly and without a pause for what seemed to me quite a long time.

Then it ceased, and again my consciousness began to grow dim. After an interval, I know not how long, there came to me dimly and only half-perceived, the closing of a door, the patter of quick footsteps, and then the voice of a man calling me by name.

I struggled to get on to my feet, but could not move. But I still held the clasp-knife and was able to rap with it feebly on the door. Again I heard the voice – it sounded nearer now, and yet infinitely far away – and again I rapped on the door and shouted through the breathing-hole, a thin, muffled cry, such as one utters in a troubled dream. And then the drowsiness crept over me again and I heard no more.

The next thing of which I was conscious was a sounding thwack on the cheek with something wet that felt like a dead fish. I opened my eyes and looked vaguely into two faces that were close to mine and seemed to be lighted by a lamp or candle. The faces were somehow familiar, but yet I failed clearly to recognize them, and, after staring stupidly for a few moments, I began to doze again. Then the dead fish returned to the assault and I again opened my eyes. Another vigorous flop caused me to open my mouth with an unparliamentary gasp. "Ah! That's better," said a familiar and yet "unplaced" voice. "When a man is able to swear, he is fairly on the road to recovery." Flop!

The renewed attentions of the dead fish (which turned out, later, to be merely a wet towel) evoked further demonstrations on my part of progressing recovery, accompanied by a nervous titter in a female voice. Gradually the clouds rolled away, and to my returning consciousness, the faces revealed themselves as those of Maggie, the housemaid, and Dr. Thorndyke. Even to my muddled wits, the presence of the latter was somewhat of a puzzle, and, in the intervals of anathematizing the deceased fish – which I had not yet identified – I found myself hazily speculating on the problem of how my revered teacher came to be in this place, and what place this was. "Come, now, Jardine," said Dr. Thorndyke, emptying a jug of water on my face, and receiving a volley of spluttered expletives in exchange, "pull yourself together. How did you get in that cellar?"

"Hang' 'f I know," said I, composing myself for another nap. But here the wet towel came once more into requisition, and that with such vigour that, in a fit of exasperation, I sat up and yawned. "I think you'd better fetch a cab," said Thorndyke, as Maggie wrung out the towel afresh, "but leave the gate open when you go out."

"Wasser cab for?" I asked sulkily. "Can't I walk?"

"If you can, it will be better," said Thorndyke. "Let us see if you are able to stand." He hoisted me on to my feet and he and Maggie, taking each an arm, walked me slowly up and down the cobbled yard, which I now began to recognize as appertaining to the Mineral Water Works. At first I staggered very drunkenly, but by degrees the drowsy feeling wore off and I was able to walk with Thorndyke's assistance only. "I think we might venture out now," said he, at length, piloting me towards the gate, and when I had stumbled rather awkwardly through the wicket, we set forth homeward.

On my arrival home, Thorndyke ordered a supply of strong coffee and a light meal, after which – it being obvious that I was good for nothing in a professional sense, he suggested that I should go to bed. "Don't worry about the practice," said he. "I will send for my friend Jervis, and, between us, we will see that everything is looked after. If Maggie will give me a sheet of paper and an envelope I will write a note to him, and then she can take a hansom to my chambers and give the note either to Dr. Jervis or my man Polton. Meanwhile, I will stay here and see that you don't go to sleep prematurely."

He wrote the note, and Maggie, having made such improvements in her outward garb as befitted the status of a rider in hansoms, took charge of it and departed with much satisfaction and dignity. Thorndyke made a few enquiries of me as to the circumstances that had led to my incarceration in the cellar, but finding that I knew no more than Maggie – whom he had already questioned – he changed the subject, nor would he allow me again to refer to it. "No, Jardine," he said. "Better think no more of it for the present. Have a good night's rest and then, if you are all right in the morning, we will go into the matter and see if we can put the puzzle together."

Chapter VI
A Council of War

I awoke somewhat late on the following morning, indeed, I was but half-awake when there came a somewhat masterful and peremptory tap at my bedroom door, followed by the appearance in the room of a rather tall gentleman of some thirty years of age. I should have diagnosed him instantly as a doctor by his self-possessed, proprietary manner of entering, but he left me no time for guessing as to his identity.

"Good-morning, Jardine," he said briskly, jingling the keys and small change in his trousers' pockets, "my name is Jervis. Second violin in the Thorndyke orchestra. I'm in charge here *pro tem*. How are you feeling?"

"Oh, I'm all right. I was just going to get up. You needn't trouble about the practice. I'm quite fit."

"I'm glad to hear it," said Jervis, "but you'd better keep quiet all the same. My orders are explicit, and I know my place too well to disobey. Thorndyke's instructions were that you are not to make any visits or go abroad until after the inquest."

"Inquest?" I exclaimed.

"Yes. He's coming here at four o'clock to hold an inquiry into the circumstances that led to your being locked up in a cellar, and until then I'm to look after the practice and keep an eye on you. What time do you expect the offspring of the flittermouse?"

"Who?" I demanded.

"Batson. He's coming back to-day, isn't he?"

"Yes. About six o'clock to-night."

"Then you'll be able to clear out. So much the better. The neighbourhood doesn't seem very wholesome for you."

"I suppose I can do the surgery work," said I.

"You'd better not. Better follow Thorndyke's instructions literally. But you can tell me about the patients and help me to dispense. And that reminds me that a person named Samway called just now, a rather fine-looking woman – reminded me of a big, sleek tabby cat. She wouldn't say what she wanted. Do you know anything about her?"

"I expect she came about her account. But she'll have to see Batson. I told her so, only a night or two ago."

"Very well," said Jervis, "then I'll be off now, and you take things easy and just think over what happened last night, so as to be ready for Thorndyke."

With this he bustled away, leaving me to rise and breakfast at my leisure.

His advice to me to think over the events of the previous night was rather superfluous. The experience was not one that I was likely to forget. To have escaped from death by the very slenderest chance was in itself a matter to occupy one's thoughts pretty completely, apart from the horrible circumstances, and then there was the mystery in which the whole affair was enveloped, a mystery which utterly baffled any attempt to penetrate it. Turn it over as I would – and it was hardly out of my thoughts for a minute at a time all day – no glimmer of light could I perceive, no faintest clue to any explanation of that hideous and incomprehensible crime.

At four o'clock punctually to the minute, Dr. Thorndyke arrived, and, having quickly looked me over to see that I was none the worse for my adventure, proceeded to business. "Have you finished the visits, Jervis?" he asked.

"Yes, and sent off all the medicine. There's nothing more to do until six."

"Then," said Thorndyke, "we might have a cup of tea in the consulting-room and talk this affair over. I am rather taking possession of you, Jardine," he added, "but I think we ought to see where we are quite clearly, even if we decide finally to hand the case over to the police. Don't you agree with me?"

"Certainly," I agreed, highly flattered by the interest he was taking in my affairs. "Naturally, I should like to get to the bottom of the mystery."

"So should I," said he, "and to that end, I propose that you give us a completely circumstantial account of the whole affair. I have had a talk with your very intelligent little maid, Maggie, and now I want to hear what happened after she left you."

"I don't think I have much to tell that you don't know," said I. "However, I will take up the story where Maggie left off," and I proceeded to describe the events in detail, much as I have related them to the reader.

Thorndyke listened to my story with profound attention, making an occasional memorandum but not uttering a word until I had finished. Then, after a rapid glance through his memoranda, he said, "You spoke of a note that was handed in to you. Have you got that note?"

"I left it on the writing-table, and it is probably there still. Yes, here it is." I brought it over to the little table on which our tea was laid and handed it to him, and as he took it from me with the dainty carefulness of a photographer handling a wet plate. I noted mentally that the habit of delicate manipulation contracted in the laboratory makes itself evident in the most trifling of everyday actions.

"I see," he remarked, turning the envelope over and scrutinizing it minutely, "that this is addressed to '*Dr. H. Jardine*'. It appears, then, that he knows your Christian name. Can you account for that?"

"No, I can't. The only letter I have had here was addressed '*Dr. Jardine*', and I have signed no certificates or other documents."

He made a note of my answer, and, drawing the missive from its envelope, read it through. "The handwriting," he remarked, "looks disguised rather than illiterate, and the diction is inconsistent. The blatantly incorrect adverb at the end does not agree with the rest of the phraseology and the correct punctuation. As to the signature, we may neglect that, unless you are acquainted with anyone in these parts of the name of Parker."

"I am not," said I.

"Very well. Then if you will allow me to keep this note, I will file it for future reference. And now I will ask you a few questions about this adventure of yours, which is really a most astonishing and mysterious affair – even more mysterious, I may add, than it looks at the first glance. But we shall come to that presently. At the moment we are concerned with the crime itself – with a manifest attempt to murder you – and the circumstances that led up to it, and there are certain obvious questions that suggest themselves. The first is: Can you give any explanation of this attempt on your life?"

"No, I can't," I replied. "It is a complete mystery to me. I can only suppose that the fellow was a homicidal lunatic."

"A homicidal lunatic," said Thorndyke, "is the baffled investigator's last resource. But we had better not begin supposing at this stage. Let us keep strictly to facts. You do not know of anything that would explain this attack on you?"

"No."

"Then the next question is: Had you any property of value on your person?"

"No. Five pounds would cover the value of everything I had about me, including the instruments."

"Then that seems to exclude robbery as a motive. The next question is: Does any person stand to benefit considerably by your death? Have you any considerable expectations in the way of bequests, reversions, or succession to landed property or titles?"

"No," I replied with a faint grin. "I shall come in for a thousand or two when my uncle dies, but I believe the London Hospital is the alternative legatee, and I suppose we would hardly suspect the hospital governors of this little affair. Otherwise, the only person who would benefit by my death would be the undertaker who got the contract to plant me."

Thorndyke nodded and made a note of my answer. "That," said he, "disposes of the principal motives for premeditated murder. There remains the question of personal enmity – not a common motive in this country. Have you, as far as you know, an enemy or enemies who might conceivably try to kill you?"

"As far as I know, I have not an enemy in the world, or anyone, even, who would wish to do me a bad turn."

"Then," said Thorndyke, "that seems to dispose of all the ordinary motives for murder, and I may say that I have only put these questions as a matter of routine precaution – *ex abundantia cautelae*, as Jervis says, when he is in a forensic mood – because certain other facts which I have learned seem to exclude any of these motives except, perhaps, robbery from the person."

"You haven't been long picking up those other facts," remarked Jervis. "Why the affair only happened last night."

"I have only made a few simple enquiries," replied Thorndyke. "This morning I called on Mr. Highfield, whose name, as solicitor and agent to the landlords, I copied from the notice on the gate at the works last night. He knows me slightly so I was able to get from him the information that I wanted. It amounts to this.

"About four months ago, a Mr. Gill wrote to him and offered a lump sum for the use of the mineral water works for six months. Highfield accepted the offer and drew up an agreement, as desired, granting Gill immediate possession of the premises and the small stock and plant, of which the residue was to be taken back at a valuation by the landlords at the expiration of the term.

"I noted Gill's address, as it appeared on the agreement, and sent my man, Polton, to make enquiries.

"The address is that of a West Kensington lodging house at which Gill was staying when he signed the agreement. He had been there only three weeks, he left two days after the date of the agreement and the landlady does not know where he went or anything about him."

"Sounds a bit fishy," Jervis remarked. "Did he tell Highfield what he wanted the premises for?"

82

"I understood that something was said about some assay work in connection with certain – or rather uncertain – mineral concessions. But of course that was no affair of Highfield's. His business was to get the rent, and, having got it, his interest in Mr. Gill lapsed. But you see the bearing of these facts. Gill's connection with these works does, as Jervis says, look a little queer, especially after what has happened. But, seeing that he made his arrangements four months ago, at a time when Jardine had no thought of coming into this neighbourhood, it is clear that those arrangements could have no connection with this particular attempt. Gill obviously did not take those works with the intention of murdering Jardine. He took them for some other purpose, quite possibly the purpose that he stated. And we must not assume that Gill was the perpetrator of this outrage at all. Could you identify the man who let you in?"

"No," I replied. "Certainly not. I hardly saw him at all. The place was pitch dark, and whenever he struck a match he was either behind me or in front with his back to me. The only thing I could make out about him was that he had some sort of coarse wash-leather gloves on."

"Ha!" exclaimed Thorndyke. "Then we were right, Jervis."

I looked in surprise from one to the other of my friends, and was on the point of asking Thorndyke what he meant, when he continued. "That closes another track. If you couldn't identify the man, a description of Gill, if we could obtain it, would not help us. We must begin at some other point."

"It seems to me," said Jervis, "that we haven't much to go upon at all."

"We haven't much," agreed Thorndyke, "but still we have something. We find that the motive of this attempt was apparently not robbery, nor the diversion of inheritable property, nor personal enmity. It must have been premeditated, but yet it could not have been planned more than a week in advance, for Jardine has only been in this neighbourhood for that time, and his coming was unexpected. The appearances very strongly suggest that the motive, whatever it was, has been generated recently and probably locally. So we had better make a start from that assumption."

"Is it possible," Jervis suggested, "that this man Gill may be some sort of anarchist crank? Or a sort of thug? It is actually conceivable that he may have taken these premises for the express purpose of having a secure place where he could perpetrate murders and conceal the bodies."

"It is quite conceivable," said Thorndyke, "and when we go and look over the works – which I propose we do presently – we may as well bear the possibility in mind. But it is merely a speculative suggestion. To return to your affairs, Jardine, has your stay here been quite uneventful?"

"Perfectly," I replied.

"No unusual or obscure cases? No injuries?"

"No, nothing out of the common," I replied.

"No deaths?"

"One. But the man died before I took over."

"Nothing unusual about that? Everything quite regular?"

"Oh, perfectly," I answered, and then with a sudden qualm, as I recalled Batson's uncertainty as to the actual cause of death, I added, "At least I hope so."

"You hope so?" queried Thorndyke.

"Yes. Because it's too late to go into the question now. The man was cremated."

At this a singular silence fell. Both my friends seemed to stiffen in their chairs, and both looked at me silently but very attentively. Then Thorndyke asked, "Did you have anything to do with that case?"

"Yes," I replied. "I went with Batson to examine the body."

"And are you perfectly satisfied that everything was as it should be?"

I was on the point of saying "Yes." And then suddenly there arose before my eyes the vision of Mrs. Samway looking at me over Batson's shoulder with that strange, inscrutable expression. And again, I recalled her unexplained anger and then her sudden change of mood. It had impressed me uncomfortably at the time, and it impressed me uncomfortably now. "I don't know that I am, now that I come to think it over," I replied.

"Why not?" asked Thorndyke.

"Well," I said, a little hesitatingly, "to begin with, I don't think the cause of death was quite clear, Batson couldn't find anything definite when he attended the man, and I know that the patient's death came as quite a surprise."

"But surely," exclaimed Thorndyke, "he took some measures to find out the cause of death!"

"He didn't. He assumed that it was a case of fatty heart and certified it as '*Morbus cordis*', and a man named O'Connor confirmed his certificate after examining the body."

"After merely inspecting the exterior?"

"Yes."

My two friends looked at one another significantly, and Thorndyke remarked, with a disapproving shake of the head, "And this is what all the elaborate precautions amount to in practice. A case which might have been one of the crudest and baldest poisoning gets passed with hardly a pretence of scrutiny. And so it will always be. Routine precautions against the unsuspected are no precautions at all. That is the danger of cremation. It restores to the poisoner the security that he enjoyed in the old days when there were no such sciences as toxicology and organic chemistry, when it was impossible for him to be tripped up by an exhumation and an analysis."

"You don't think it likely that this was a case of poisoning, do you?" I asked.

"I know nothing about the case," he replied, "excepting that there was gross neglect in issuing the certificates. What do you think about it yourself? Looking back at the case, is there anything besides the uncertainty that strikes you as unsatisfactory?"

I hesitated, and again the figure of Mrs. Samway rose before me with that strange, baleful look in her eyes. Finally I described the incident to my colleagues. "Mrs. Samway!" exclaimed Jervis. "Is that the handsome Lucrezia Borgia lady with the mongoose eyes who called here this morning? By Jove! Jardine, you are giving me the creeps."

"I understand," said Thorndyke, "that you were making as if to feel the dead man's pulse?"

"Yes."

"There is no doubt, I suppose, that he really was dead?"

"None whatever. He was as cold as a fish, and, besides there was quite distinct *rigor mortis*."

"That seems conclusive enough," said Thorndyke, but he continued to gaze at his open note-book with a profoundly speculative and thoughtful expression.

"It certainly looks," said Jervis, "as if Jardine had either seen something or had been about to see something that he was not wanted to see, and the question is what that something could have been."

"Yes," I agreed, gloomily. "That is what I have just been asking myself. There might have been a wound or injury of some kind, or there might have been the marks of a hypodermic needle on the wrist. I wish I knew what she meant by looking at me in that way."

"Well," said Jervis, "we shall never know now. The grave gives up its secrets now and again, but the crematorium furnace never. Whether he died naturally or was murdered, Mr. Maddock is now a little heap of ashes with no message for anyone this side of the Day of Judgment."

Thorndyke looked up. "That seems to be so," said he, "and really, we have no substantial reasons for thinking that there was anything wrong. So we come back to your own affairs, Jardine, and the question is, What would you prefer to do?"

"In what respect?" I asked.

"In regard to this attempt on your life. You have told us that you have not an enemy in the world. But it appears as if you had, and a very dangerous one, too. Now would you like to put the case into the hands of the police, or would you rather that we kept our own counsel and looked into it ourselves?"

"I should like you to decide that," said I.

"The reason that I ask," said Thorndyke, "is this: The machinery of the police is adjusted to professional crime – burglary, coining, forgery, and so forth – and their methods are mostly based on 'information received'. The professional 'crook' is generally well known to the police, and, when wanted for any particular 'job', can be found without much difficulty and the information necessary for his conviction obtained from the usual sources. But in cases of obscure, non-professional crime the police are at a disadvantage. The criminal is unknown to them. There are no confederates from whom to get information, and consequently they have no starting-point for their enquiries. They can't create clues, and they, very naturally, will not devote time, labour, and money to cases in which they have nothing to go on.

"Now this affair of yours does not look like a professional crime. No motive is evident and you can give no information that would help the police. I doubt if they would do much more than give you some rather disagreeable publicity, and they might even suspect you of some kind of imposture."

"Gad!" I exclaimed. "That's just what they would do. It's what they did last time, and this affair would write me down in their eyes a confirmed mystery-monger."

"Last time?" queried Thorndyke. "What last time is that? Have there been any other attempts?"

"Not on me," I replied. "But I had an adventure one night about six or seven weeks ago that has made the Hampstead police look on me, I think, with some suspicion" – and here I gave my two friends a description of my encounter with the dead (or insensible) cleric in Millfield Lane, and my discoveries on the following morning.

"But my dear Jardine!" Thorndyke exclaimed when I had finished, "what an extraordinary man you are! It seems as if you could hardly show your nose out of doors without becoming involved in some dark and dreadful mystery."

"Well," said I, "I hope I have now exhausted my gifts in that respect. I am not thirsting for more experiences. But what do you think about that Hampstead affair? Do you think I could possibly have been mistaken? Could the man have been merely insensible, after all, as the police suggested?"

Thorndyke shook his head. "I don't think," he replied, "that it is possible to take that view. You see, the man had disappeared. Now he could not have got away unassisted – in fact he could not have walked at all. One would have to assume that some persons appeared directly after you left and carried him away, and that they appeared and retired so quickly as not to be overtaken by you on your return a few minutes later with the police. That is assuming too much. And then there are the traces which you discovered on the following day, which seem to suggest strongly that a body had been carried away to Ken Wood. It is a thousand pities that you encountered that keeper, if you could have followed the tracks while they were fresh you might have been able to ascertain whither it had been carried. But now, to return to your latest experience, what shall we do? Shall we communicate with the police, or shall we make a few investigations on our own account?"

"As far as I am concerned," I replied eagerly, "a private investigation would be greatly preferable. But wouldn't it take up rather a lot of your time?"

"Now, Jardine, you needn't apologize," said Jervis. "Unless I am much mistaken, my respected senior has 'struck soundings', as the nautical phrase has it. He has a theory of your case, and he would like to see it through. Isn't that so, Thorndyke?"

"Well," Thorndyke admitted, "I will confess that the case piques my curiosity somewhat. It is an unusual affair and suggests some curious hypotheses which might be worth testing. So, if you agree, Jardine, that we make at least a few preliminary investigations, I suggest that, as soon as Batson returns, we three go over to the what the newspapers would call 'the scene of the tragedy' and reconstitute the affair on the spot."

"And what about Batson?" I asked. "Shall we tell him anything?"

"I think we must," said Thorndyke, "if only to put him on his guard, for your unknown enemy may be his enemy, too."

At this moment the street door banged loudly, a quick step danced along the hall, and Batson himself burst into the room. "Good Lord!" he exclaimed, halting abruptly at the door and gazing in dismay at our little council. "What's the matter? Anything happened?"

Thorndyke laughed as he shook the hand of his quondam pupil.

"Come, come, Batson," said he. "Don't make me out such a bird of ill-omen."

"I was afraid something awkward might have occurred, police job or inquest or something of that sort."

"You weren't so very far wrong," said Thorndyke. "When you are at liberty I'll tell you about it."

"I'm at liberty now," said Batson, dropping into a chair and glaring at Thorndyke through his spectacles. "No scandal, I hope."

Thorndyke reassured him on this point and gave him a brief account of my adventure and our proposed visit to the works, to which he listened with occasional ejaculations of astonishment and relief. "By Gum!" he exclaimed, "what a mercy you got there in time. If you hadn't there'd have been an inquest and a devil of a fuss. I should never have heard the last of it. Ruined the practice and worried me into a lunatic asylum. Oh, and about those works. I wouldn't go there if I were you."

"Why not?" Thorndyke asked.

"Well, you may have to answer some awkward questions, and we don't want this affair to get about, you know. No use raising a dust. Rumpus of any kind plays the deuce with a medical practice."

Thorndyke smiled at my principal's frank egoism. "Jervis and I went over last night," said he, "and had a hasty look round and we found the place quite deserted. Probably it is so still."

"Then you won't be able to get in. How did you get in last night?"

"I happened to have a piece of stiff wire in my pocket," Thorndyke replied impassively.

"Ha!" said Batson. "Wire, eh? Picklock in fact. I wouldn't, if I were you. Devil of a bobbery if anyone sees you. Hallo! There goes the bell. Patient. Let him wait. 'Tisn't six yet, is it?"

"Two minutes past," replied Thorndyke, rising and looking at his watch. "Perhaps we had better be starting as it's now dark, and the business at the works, if there is any, is probably over for the day."

"Hang the works!" exclaimed Batson. "I wouldn't go nosing about there. What's the good? Jardine's alright and the chappie isn't likely to be on view. You'll only raise a stink for nothing and bring in a crowd of beastly reporters humming about the place. There's that damn bell again. Well, if you won't stay, perhaps you'll look me up some other time Always d'lighted to see you. Jervis too. You're not going, Jardine. I've got to settle up with you and hear your report."

"I'll look in later," said I, "when you've finished the evening's work."

"Right you are," said Batson, opening the door and adroitly edging us out. "Sorry you can't stay. Good-night! Good-night!"

He shepherded us persuasively and compellingly down the hall, with a skill born of long practice with garrulous patients, and, having exchanged us on the doorstep for a stout woman with two children, returned into the house with his prey and was lost to sight.

Chapter VII
An Unseen Enemy

From my late principal's house we walked away quickly down the lamplit street, all – I think, dimly amused at the circumstances of our departure. "Is Batson always like that?" Thorndyke asked.

"Always," I replied. "Hurry and bustle are his normal states."

"Dear, dear," commented Thorndyke, "what a terrible amount of time he must waste. Of course, one can understand now how that cremation muddle came about. Your incurable hustler is always thinking of the things he has got to do next instead of the thing that he is doing at the moment. By the way, Jardine, I am taking it for granted that you would like to inspect these premises. It is not essential. Jervis and I had a preliminary look round last night, and I daresay we picked up most of the facts that are likely to be of importance if we should be going farther into the matter."

"I think it would be as well for me to take a look at the place and show you exactly where and how the affair happened."

"I think so too," said Thorndyke. "It was all pretty evident, but you might be able to show us something that we had overlooked. Here we are. I wonder if Mr. Gill is on the premises – supposing him still to frequent them."

He looked up and down the street, and, taking a key from his pocket, inserted it into the lock. "Why, how on earth did you get the key?" I asked.

Thorndyke looked at me slyly. "We keep a tame mechanic," said he, as he turned the key and opened the wicket.

"Yes, but how did he get the pattern of the lock?" I asked.

Thorndyke laughed softly. "It is only a simple trade lock. The fact is, Jardine, that in our branch of practice we have occasionally to take some rather irregular proceedings. For instance, I usually carry a small set of picklocks – fortunately for you. That is how I got in last night. Then I never go abroad without a little box of moulding wax, a most invaluable material, Jardine, for collecting certain kinds of evidence. Well, with a slip of wood and a bit of wax I was able to furnish my man with the necessary data for filing up a blank key. One doesn't want to be seen using a picklock. Now, can you show us the way?"

He flashed a pocket electric lamp on the ground, and we advanced over the rough cobbles until we reached a door at the side. "This is where

I went in," said I. "It opens into a sort of corridor, and at the end is a door opening on some steps that lead down to the passage below."

Thorndyke tried the handle of the door and pushed, but it was evidently locked or bolted. "I left this door unlocked last night," said he, "so it is clear that someone has been here since. I hardly expected that. I thought our friend would have cleared off for good. But it is possible that Gill had nothing to do with the attempt. The premises may have been used by someone who happened to know that they were unoccupied. It would have been quite easy for such a person to gain admittance, as you see."

While speaking, he had produced from his pocket a little bunch of skeleton keys, with one of which he now quietly unlocked the door. "These builders' locks," said he, "are merely symbolic of security. You are not expected to unfasten them without authority, but you can if you like and happen to have a bit of stiff wire."

We entered the corridor, and, as we proceeded, looked into the rooms that opened out of it. One of them was meagrely furnished as an office, but the thick layer of dust on the desk and stools showed clearly that it had been long disused. The other rooms were empty and desolate, and showed no trace of use or occupation. "The worthy Gill," said Jervis, "seems to have been able, like Diogenes, to get on with a very modest outfit."

"Yes," agreed Thorndyke, "it is a little difficult to guess what his occupation is. The place looks as if it had never been used at all. Shall I go first?"

He halted for a moment, passing the light of his lamp over the massive door at the head of the steps, and then began to descend. It was certainly a horrible and repulsive place, especially to my eyes, with the recollection of my late experience fresh in my mind. The rough brick walls, covered with the crumbling remains of old white-wash, the black masses of cobwebs that drooped like funereal stalactites from the ceiling, the fungi that sprouted in corners, and the snail-tracks that glistened in the lamplight on the stone floor, all contributed to a vault-like sepulchral effect that was most unpleasantly suggestive of what might have been and very nearly had been.

My late prison was easily distinguished by the two holes in the door. We looked in, but that cellar was completely empty save for a few chips of wood and a pinch or two of sawdust, memorials of my sojourn in the lethal chamber at which I could hardly look without a shudder. Then we passed on to the next cellar – the one adjoining my prison – and this was an object of no little curiosity to me. Here, while I was securely bolted into my cell, that unknown villain had, deliberately and in cold blood,

90

made all the arrangements for my murder – arrangements which he little suspected that I should survive to look upon.

Thorndyke, too, was interested. He stood at the open door, looking in as if considering the positions of various objects. As in fact he was. "Someone has been here since last night, Jervis," said he.

"Yes," agreed Jervis.

"That gas bottle has been taken down from the opening. You see, Jardine," he continued, "he had stood that big packing-case up on end and laid the gas bottle along the top, with its nozzle just opposite the hole. Two other bottles were standing upright with their nozzles upwards."

"I understand," said Thorndyke, "that you heard three bottles only turned on?"

"Yes," I answered, "there was the one opposite the hole and two others."

"I ask," Thorndyke said, "because there are, as you see, seven other bottles, lying by the wall. Those are all empty. We tried them when we came here last night."

"I know nothing about those others," said I. "The three bottles that I have mentioned I heard distinctly, and after he had turned on the third, the man went out of the cellar and closed up the door."

"Then," said Thorndyke, "the other seven were presumably used for some other – and let us hope, more legitimate – purpose. I wonder why our friend has been at the trouble of moving the cylinders."

"Perhaps," suggested Jervis, "he thought that the arrangement might be a little too illuminating for the police, if they should happen to pay a visit to the place. He may not be aware that the apparatus had already been inspected *in situ* by us. Or, again, the cylinders may have been moved by someone else. We are assuming that he is a lawful occupant of the premises, but he may be a mere secret intruder like ourselves, who has discovered that the place is more or less unoccupied and has made use of the premises and plant for his own benevolent purposes."

"Yes," agreed Thorndyke, "that is perfectly true. But we can put the matter to the test, at least negatively. If the cylinders have been moved by an innocent stranger they will bear the prints of hands."

"But why shouldn't the man himself leave the prints of his hands on the cylinders?" I asked.

"Because, my dear Jardine, he is too knowing a bird. Jervis and I went carefully over the cylinders last night in the hope of getting a few finger-prints to submit to Scotland Yard, but not a vestige could we find. Our friend had seen to that. We assumed that he had operated in gloves and your description of him confirmed our assumption. Which, in its way, is an interesting fact, for a man who is knowing enough to take these precautions has probably had some previous experience of crime, or, at least, has some acquaintance with the ways of criminals. The suggestion, in fact, is that, although this is not an ordinary professional crime, the perpetrator may be a professional criminal. And the further suggestion is, of course, that of very deliberate premeditation."

While he had been speaking he had produced from his pocket a small, flattened bottle fitted with a metal cap and filled with a yellowish powder. Removing the cap and uncovering a perforated inner cap, like that of an iodoform dredger, he proceeded to shake a cloud of the light powder over the three upper cylinders, jarring them with his foot to make the powder spread. Then he blew sharply on them, one after the other, when the powder disappeared from their surfaces, leaving visible one or two shapeless whitened smears but never a trace of a finger-print or even the shape of a hand.

Thorndyke rose and slipped the bottle back in his pocket. "Apparently," said he, "the cylinders were moved by our unknown friend, with the same careful precautions as on the first occasion. A wary gentleman, this, Jervis. He'll give us a run for our money, at any rate."

"Yes," agreed Jervis, "he doesn't mean to give himself away. He preserves his incognito most punctiliously. I'll say that for him."

"And meanwhile," said Thorndyke, "we had better proceed with our measures for drawing him out of this modest retirement. I want you, Jardine, to look round this cellar and tell us if any of the things that you see in it reminds you of anything that has happened to you, or suggests any thought or reflection."

I looked round, I am afraid rather vacantly. A more unsuggestive collection of objects I have never looked upon. "There are the gas cylinders," I said, feebly, "but I have told you about them. I don't see anything else excepting a few oddments of rubbish."

"Then take a good look at the rubbish," said he. "Remember that it may be necessary at some future time for you to recall exactly what this cellar was like, and what it contained. You may even have to make a sworn statement. So cast your eye round and tell us what you see."

I did so, wondering inwardly what the deuce I was expected to see and what might be the importance of my seeing it. "I see," said I, "a mouldy-looking cellar about fifteen feet by twelve, with very bad brick walls, a plaster ceiling in an advanced stage of decay, and a concrete floor. In the left hand wall is a hole about six inches square opening into the adjoining cellar. The contents are ten gas cylinders, all apparently empty, a key or spanner which seems to have been used to turn the cocks, a large packing-case, which, to judge by its shape, seems to have contained gas cylinders – "

"The word 'large'," interrupted Thorndyke, "is not a particularly exact one."

"Well, then, a packing-case about seven feet long by two-and-a-half-feet wide and deep."

"That's better," said Thorndyke. "Always give your dimensions in quantitative terms if possible. Go on."

"There are a couple of waterproof sheets," said I. "I don't see quite what they can have been used for."

"Never mind their use," said Thorndyke. "Note the fact that they are here."

"I have," said I, "and that seems to complete the list with the exception of the straw in which I suppose the gas cylinders were packed. There is a large quantity of that, but not more than would seem necessary for the purpose. And that seems to complete the inventory, and, I may say, that none of these things conveys any suggestion whatever to my mind."

"Probably not," said Thorndyke, "and it is quite possible that none of these things has any particular significance at all. But as they are the only facts offered us, we must make the best of them. There is one other cellar that we have not yet looked into, I think."

We came out, and, walking along the passage, came to another door which stood slightly ajar. Thorndyke opened it, and, throwing in the light of his lamp, revealed a considerable stack of long iron gas bottles, and one or two packing-cases similar to the one I had already seen. "I presume," said he, "that these are full cylinders, the store from which our friend got his supply, but we may as well make sure."

He ran back into the adjoining cellar, and returned with the spanner, with which he proceeded to turn the cock of one of the topmost cylinders, upon which a loud hiss and a thin, snowy cloud showed that his surmise was correct.

He had just closed the cock and stepped out into the passage to take back the spanner, when I saw him stop suddenly as if listening. And then he sniffed once or twice. "What is it?" asked Jervis, but Thorndyke, without replying, ran quickly along the passage and up the steps, and I heard him trying the door at the top.

"Bring up one of the empty cylinders," he said quietly. "They have bolted us in and apparently set fire to the place."

We did not require much urging to act quickly. Picking up one of the long, ponderous iron cylinders, we ran with it along the passage towards the light of Thorndyke's lamp. As we ascended the steps I became plainly aware of the smell of burning wood and of a crackling sound, faintly audible through the massive door. "There is only one bolt," said Thorndyke, "I noticed it as we came in. I will throw my light on the part of the door where it is fixed, and you two must batter on that spot with the cylinder."

The door was, as I have said, a massive one, but it would have been a massive door indeed that could have withstood the blows of that ponderous iron cylinder, wielded by two strong men whose lives depended on their efforts. At the very first crash of the battering-ram, a tiny chink opened and at each thundering blow, the building shook. Furiously we pounded at the thick, plank-built door, and slowly the chink widened as the screws of the bolt tore out of the woodwork. And as the chink opened, a thin reek of pungent smoke filtered in, and the cold light of Thorndyke's lantern became contrasted with a red glare from without. And then suddenly, the door, under the heavy battering, burst from its fastenings and swung open. A blinding, choking cloud of smoke and sparks rolled in upon us, through which we could see in the corridor outside a pile of straw and crates and broken packing-cases, blazing and cracking furiously. It looked as if we were cut off beyond all hope.

Jervis and I had dropped the now useless cylinder and were gazing in horror at the blazing mass that filled the corridor and cut off our only means of escape, when we were recalled by the voice of Thorndyke, speaking in his usual quiet and precise manner. "We must get the full cylinders up as quickly as possible," said he, and, running down the steps he made straight for the end cellar, whither we followed him. Picking up one of the cylinders, we carried it quickly to the top of the steps. "Lay it down," said Thorndyke, "and fetch another."

Jervis and I ran back to the cellar, and taking up another cylinder, brought it along the passage. As we were ascending the steps, there suddenly arose a loud, penetrating hiss, and as we reached the top, we saw Thorndyke disengaging the spanner from the cock of the cylinder out of which a jet of liquid was issuing, mingled with a dense, snowy cloud.

An instantaneous glance, as we laid down the fresh cylinder, reassured me very considerably. The icy, volatile liquid and the falling cloud of intensely cold carbonic acid snow had produced an immediate effect, as was evident in a blackened, smouldering patch in the midst of the blazing mass. With reviving hope I followed Jervis once more down the steps and along the passage to the end cellar, from which we brought forth a third cylinder.

By this time the passage was so filled with smoke that it was difficult either to see or to breathe, and the bright light that had at first poured in through the open doorway had already pulled down so far that Thorndyke's figure, framed in the opening, loomed dim and shadowy amidst the smoke and against the dusky red background. We found him, when we reached the top of the steps, holding the great gas bottle and directing the stream of snow and liquid on to those parts of the wood and straw from which flames still issued. "It will be all right," he said in his calm, unemotional way. "The fire had not really got an effective start. The straw made a great show, but that is nearly all burnt now, and all this carbonic acid gas will soon smother the burning wood. But we must be careful that it doesn't smother us too. The steps will be the safest place for the present."

He opened the cock of the new cylinder and, having placed it so that it played on the most refractory part of the burning mass, backed to the steps where Jervis and I stood looking through the doorway. The fire was, as he had said, rapidly dying down. The volumes of gas produced by the evaporation of the liquid and the melting snow, cut off the supply of air so that, in place of the flames that had, at first, looked so alarming, only a dense reek of smoke arose. "Now," said Thorndyke, after we had waited on the steps a couple of minutes more, "I think we might make a sortie and put an end to it. If we can get the smouldering stuff off that wooden floor down on to the stone, the danger will be over."

He led the way cautiously into the corridor, and, once more bringing his electric lamp into requisition, began to kick the smouldering cases and crates and the blackened masses of straw down the steps on to the stone floor of the passage, whither we followed them and scattered them with our feet until they were completely safe from any chance of re-ignition. "There," said Jervis, giving a final kick at a small heap of smoking straw, "I should think that ought to do. There's no fear of that stuff lighting up again. And, if I may venture to make the remark, the sooner we are off these premises the happier I shall be. Our friend's methods of entertaining his visitors are a trifle too strenuous for my taste. He might try dynamite next."

"Yes," I agreed, "or he might take pot shots at us with a revolver from some dark corner."

"It is much more likely," said Thorndyke, "that he has cleared off in anticipation of the alarm of fire. Still, it is undeniable that we shall be safer outside. Shall I go first and show you a light?"

He piloted us along the corridor and up the cobbled yard, putting away his lamp as he unlocked the wicket. There was no sign of anyone about the premises nor, when we had passed out of the gate, was there anyone in sight in the street. I looked about, expecting to see some sign of the fire, but there was no smoke visible, and only a slight smell of burning wood. The smoke must have drifted out at the back. "Well," Thorndyke remarked, "it has been quite an exciting little episode. And a highly satisfactory finish, as things turned out, though it might easily have been very much the reverse. But for the fortunate chance of those gas-bottles being available, I don't think we should be alive at this moment."

"No," agreed Jervis. "We should be in much the same condition by this time as Batson's late patient, Mr. Maddock, or at least, well on our way to that disembodied state. However, all's well that ends well. Are you coming our way, Jardine?"

"I will walk a little way with you," said I. "Then I must go back to Batson to settle up and fetch my traps."

I walked with them to Oxford Street and we discussed our late adventure as we went. "It was a pretty strong hint to clear out, wasn't it?" Jervis remarked.

"Yes," replied Thorndyke, "it didn't leave us much option. But the affair can't be left at this. I shall have a watch set on those premises, and I shall make some more particular enquiries about Mr. Gill. By the way, Jardine, I haven't your address. I'd better have it in case I want to communicate with you, and you'd better have my card in case anything turns up which you think I ought to know."

We accordingly exchanged cards, and, as we had now reached the corner of Oxford Street, I wished my friends *adieu* and thoughtfully retraced my steps to Jacob Street.

Chapter VIII
It's an Ill Wind

London is a wonderful place. From the urban greyness of Jacob Street to the borders of Hampstead Heath was, even in those days of the slow horse tram, but a matter of minutes – a good many minutes, perhaps, but still, considerably under an hour. Yet, in that brief and leisurely journey, one exchanged the grim sordidness of a most unlovely street for the solitude and sweet rusticity of open and charming country.

A day or two after my second adventure in the mineral water works, I was leaning on the parapet of the viaduct – the handsome, red brick viaduct with which some builder, unknown to me, had spanned the pond beyond the Upper Heath, apparently with purely decorative motive, and in a spirit of sheer philanthropy. For no road seemed to lead anywhere in particular over it, and there was no reason why any wayfarer should wish to cross the pond rather than walk round it, indeed, in those days it was covered by a turfy expanse seldom trodden by any feet but those of the sheep that grazed in the meadows bordering the pond. I leaned on the parapet, smoking my pipe with deep contentment, and looking down into the placid water. Flags and rushes grew at its borders, water-lilies spread their flat leaves on its surface, and a small party of urchins angled from the margin, with the keen joy of the juvenile sportsman who suspects that his proceedings are unlawful.

I had lounged on the parapet for several minutes, when I became aware of a man, approaching along the indistinct track that crossed the viaduct, and, as he drew near, I recognized him as the keeper whom I had met in Ken Wood on the morning after my discovery of the body in Millfield Lane. I would have let him pass with a smile of recognition, but he had no intention of passing. Touching his hat politely, he halted, and, having wished me good-morning, remarked, "You didn't tell me, sir, what it was you were looking for that morning when I met you in the wood."

"No," I replied, "but apparently, someone else has."

"Well, sir, you see," he said, "the sergeant came up the next day with a plain-clothes man to have a look round, and, as the sergeant is an old acquaintance of mine, he gave me the tip as to what they were after. I am sorry, sir, you didn't tell me what you were looking for."

"Why?" I asked.

"Well," he replied, "we might have found something if we had looked while the tracks were fresh. Unfortunately there was a gale in the night that fetched down a lot of leaves, and blew up those that had already fallen, so that any foot-marks would have got hidden before the sergeant came."

"What did the police officers seem to think about it?" I asked.

"Why, to speak the truth," the keeper replied, "they seemed to think it was all bogey."

"Do you mean to say," I asked, "that they thought I had invented the whole story?"

"Oh, no, sir," he replied, "not that. They believed you had seen a man lying in the lane, but they didn't believe that he was a dead man and they thought your imagination had misled you about the tracks."

"Then, I suppose they didn't find anything?" said I.

"No, they didn't, and I haven't been able to find anything myself, though I've had a good look round."

And then, after a brief pause, "I wonder," he said, "if you would care to come up to the Wood and have a look at the place yourself."

I considered for a moment. I had nothing to do for I was taking a day off, and the man's proposal sounded rather attractive. Finally, I accepted his offer, and we turned back together towards the Wood.

Hampstead – the Hampstead of those days – was singularly rustic and remote. But, within the wood, it was incredible that the town of London actually lay within the sound of a church bell or the flight of a bullet. Along the shady paths, carpeted with moss and silvery lichen, overshadowed by the boughs of noble beeches, or in leafy hollows, with the humus of centuries under our feet, and the whispering silence of the woodland all around, we might have been treading the glades of some primeval forest. Nor was the effect of this strange remoteness less, when presently, emerging from the thicker portion of the wood, we came upon a moss-grown, half-ruinous boat-house on the sedgy margin of a lake, in which was drawn up a rustic-looking, and evidently, little-used punt.

"It's wonderful quiet about here, sir," the keeper remarked, as a water-hen stole out from behind a clump of high rushes and scrambled over the leaves of the water-lilies.

"And presumably," I remarked, "it's quieter still at night."

"You're right, sir," the keeper replied. "If that man had got as far as this, he'd have had mighty little trouble in putting the body where no one was ever likely to look for it."

"I suppose," said I, "that you had a good look at the edges of the lake?"

"Yes," he answered. "I went right round it, and so did the police, for that matter, and we had a good look at the punt, too. But, all the same, it wouldn't surprise me if, one fine day, that body came floating up among the lilies, always supposing, that is," he added, "that there really was a body."

"How far is it," I asked, "from the lake to the place where you met me that morning?"

"It's only a matter of two or three minutes," he answered, "we may as well walk that way and you can see for yourself." Accordingly, we set forth together, and, coming presently upon one of the moss-grown paths, followed it past a large summerhouse until we came in sight of the beech beyond which I had encountered him while I was searching for the tracks. As we went, he plied me with questions as to what I had seen on the night in the lane, and I made no scruple of telling him all that I had told the police, seeing that they, on their side, had made no secret of the matter.

Of course, it was idle, after this long period – for it was now more than seven weeks since I had seen the body – to attempt anything in the nature of a search. It certainly did look as if the man who had stolen into that wood that night had been bound for the solitary lake. The punt, I had noticed, was only secured with a rope, so that the murderer – for such I assumed he must have been – could easily have carried his dreadful burden out into the middle, and there sunk it with weights, and so hidden it for ever. It was a quick, simple and easy method of hiding the traces of his crime, and, if the police had not thought it worthwhile to search the water with drags, there was no reason why the buried secret should not remain buried for all time.

After we had walked for some time about the pleasant, shady wood, less shady now that the yellowing leaves were beginning to fall with the passing of autumn, the keeper conducted me to the exit by which I had left on the previous occasion.

As I was passing out of the wicket, my eye fell once more on the cottage which I had then noticed, and, recalling the remark that my fair acquaintance had let fall concerning the artist to whom the derelict knife was supposed to belong, I said, "You mentioned, I think, that that house was let to an artist."

"It was," he replied, "but it's empty now. The artist has gone away."

"It must be a pleasant little house to live in," I said. "At any rate, in summer."

"Yes," he replied, "a country house within an hour's walk of the Bank of England. Would you like to have a look at it, sir? I've got the keys."

Now I certainly had no intention of offering myself as a tenant, but, yet, to an idle man, there is a certain attractiveness in an empty house of an eligible kind, a certain interest in roaming through the rooms and letting one's fancy furnish them with one's own household goods. I accepted the man's invitation, and, opening the wide gate that admitted to the garden from a byroad, we walked up to the door of the house. "It's quite a nice little place," the keeper remarked. "There isn't much garden, you see, but then, you've got the Heath all around, and there's a small stable and coachhouse if you should be wanting to go into town."

"Did the last tenant keep any kind of carriage?" I asked.

"I don't think so," said the keeper, "but I fancy he used to hire a little cart sometimes when he had things to bring in from town, but I don't know very much about him or his habits."

We walked through the empty rooms together, looking out of the windows and commenting on the pleasant prospects that all of them commanded, and talking about the man who had last lived in the house. "He was a queer sort of fellow," said the keeper. "He and his wife seem to have lived here all alone without any servant, and they seem often to have left the house to itself for a day or two at a time, but he could paint. I have stopped and had a look when he has been at work, and it was wonderful to see how he knocked off those pictures. He didn't seem to use brushes, but he had a lot of knives, like little trowels, and he used to shovel the paint on with them, and he always wore gloves when he was painting – didn't like to get the paint on his hands, I suppose."

"It sounds as if it would be very awkward," I said.

"Just what I should have thought," the keeper agreed. "But he didn't seem to find it so. This seems to be the place that he worked in."

Apparently the keeper was right. The room, which we had now entered, was evidently the late studio, and did not appear to have been cleaned up since the tenant left. The floor was littered with scraps of paper on which a palette-knife had been cleaned, with empty paint-tubes and one or two broken and worn-out brushes, and, in a packing-case, which seemed to have served as a receptacle for rubbish, were one or two canvases that had been torn from their stretchers and thrown away. I picked them out and glanced at them with some interest, remembering what my fair friend had said. For the most part, they were mere experiments or failures, deliberately defaced with strokes or daubs of paint, but one of them was a quite spirited and attractive sketch, rough and unfinished, but skilfully executed and undefaced. I stretched out the crumpled canvas and looked at it with considerable interest, for it represented Millfield Lane, and showed the large elms and the posts and the high fence under which I had sheltered in the rain. In fact, it appeared to have been taken from the exact spot on which the body had been lying, and from which I had made my own drawing – not that there was anything in the latter coincidence, for it was the only sketchable spot in the lane. "It's really quite a nice sketch," I said. "It seems a pity to leave it here among the rubbish."

"It does, sir," the keeper agreed. "If you like it, you had better roll it up and put it in your pocket. You won't be robbing anyone."

As it seemed that I was but rescuing it from a rubbish-heap, I ventured to follow the keeper's advice, and, rolling the canvas up, carefully stowed it in my pocket. And shortly after as I had now seen all that there was to see, which was mighty little, we left the house, and, at the gate, the keeper took leave of me with a touch of his hat.

I made my way slowly back towards my lodgings by way of the Spaniard's Road and Hampstead Lane, turning over in my mind as I went, the speculation suggested by my visit to the wood. Of the existence of the lake I had not been previously aware. Now that I had seen it, I felt very little doubt that it was known to the mysterious murderer – for such I felt convinced he was – who must have been lurking in the lane that night when I was sheltering under the lee of the fence. The route that he had then taken appeared to be the direct route to the lake. That he was carrying the body, I had no doubt whatever, and, seeing that he had carried it so far, it appeared probable that he had some definite hiding-place in view. And what hiding-place could be so suitable as this remote piece of still water? No digging, no troublesome and dangerous preparation would be necessary. There was the punt in readiness to bear him to the deep water in the middle, a silent, easily-handled conveyance. A few stones, or some heavy object from the boat-house, would be all that was needful, and in a moment he would be rid for ever of the dreadful witness of his crime.

Thus reflecting – not without dissatisfaction at the passive part that I had played in this sinister affair – I passed through the turnstile, or "kissing-gate", at the entrance to Millfield Lane. Almost certainly, the murderer or the victim or both, had passed through that very gate on the night of the tragedy. The thought came to me with added solemnity with the recollection of the silent wood and the dark, still water fresh in my mind, and caused me unconsciously to tread more softly and walk more sedately than usual.

The lane was little frequented at any time and now, at mid-day, was almost as deserted as at midnight. Very remote it seemed, too, and very quiet, with a silence that recalled the hush of the wood. And yet the silence was not quite unbroken. From somewhere ahead, from one of the many windings of the tortuous lane, came the sound of hurried footsteps.

I stopped to listen. There were two persons, one treading lightly, the other more heavily, apparently a man and a woman. And both were running – running fast.

There was nothing remarkable in this, perhaps, but yet the sound smote on my ear with a certain note of alarm that made me quicken my pace and listen yet more intently. And suddenly there came another sound, a muffled, whimpering cry like that of a frightened woman. Instantly I gave an answering shout and sprang forward at a swift run.

I had turned one of the numerous corners and was racing down a straight stretch of the lane when a woman darted round the corner ahead, and ran towards me, holding out her hands. I recognised her at a glance, though now she was dishevelled, pale, wild-eyed, breathless and nearly frantic with terror, and rage against her assailant spurred me on to greater speed. But when I would have passed her to give chase to the wretch, she clutched my arm frantically with both hands and detained me. "Let me go and catch the scoundrel!" I exclaimed, but she only clung the tighter.

"No," she panted, "don't leave me! I am terrified! Don't go away!"

I ground my teeth. Even as we stood, I could hear the ruffian's footsteps receding as rapidly as they had advanced. In a few moments he would be beyond pursuit. "Do let me go and stop that villain!" I implored. "You're quite safe now, and you can follow me and keep me in sight."

But she shook her head passionately, and, still clutching my sleeve with one hand, pressed the other to her heart. "No, no, no!" she gasped, with a catch in her voice that was almost a sob, "I can't be alone! I am frightened. Oh! Please don't go away from me!"

What could I do? The poor girl was evidently beside herself with terror, and exhausted by her frantic flight. It would have been cruel to leave her in that state. But all the same, it was infuriating. I had no idea what the man had done to terrify her in this way. But that was of no consequence. The natural impulse of a healthy young man when he learns that a woman has been ill-used is to hammer the offender effectively in the first place, and then to inquire into the affair. That was what I wanted to do, but it was not to be. "Well," I said, by way of compromise, "let us walk back together. Perhaps we may be able to find out which way the man went."

To this she agreed. I drew her arm through mine – for she was still trembling and looked faint and weak – and we began to retrace her steps towards Highgate. Of course the man was nowhere to be seen, and by the time that we had turned the sharp corner where I had found the body of the priest, the man was not only out of sight, but his footsteps were no longer audible.

Still we went on for some distance in the hopes of meeting someone who could tell us which way the miscreant had gone. But we met nobody. Only, some distance past the posts, we came in sight of a sketching box and a camp-stool, lying by the side of the path. "Surely those are your things?" I said.

"Yes," she answered. "I had forgotten all about them. I dropped them when I began to run." I picked up the box and the stool, and debated with myself whether it was worthwhile to go on any farther. From where we stood, nothing was to be seen, for the lane was still enclosed on both sides by a seven foot fence of oak boards. But the chance of overtaking the fugitive was not to be considered, by this time he was probably out of the lane on the Heath or in the surrounding meadows, and meanwhile, my companion, though calmer and less breathless, looked very pale and shaken. "I don't know that it's any use," I said, "to tire you by going any farther. The man is evidently gone."

She seemed relieved at my decision, and it then occurred to me to suggest that she should sit down awhile on the bank under the high fence to recover herself, and to this, too, she assented gladly. "If it wouldn't distress you," I said, "would you mind telling me what had happened?"

She pondered for a few seconds and then answered, "It doesn't sound much in the telling and I expect you will think me very silly to be so much upset."

"I'm sure I shan't," I said, with perfect confidence in the correctness of my statement.

"Well," she said, "what happened was this as nearly as I can remember: I was coming up the path from the ponds and I had to pass a man who was leaning against the fence by the stile. As I came near to him, he looked at me, at first, in quite an ordinary way, and then, he suddenly began to stare in a most singular and disturbing fashion – not at me, so much, as at this little crucifix which I wear hung from my neck. As I passed through the turnstile, he spoke to me. 'Would you mind letting me look at that crucifix?' he asked. It was a most astonishing piece of impertinence, and I was so taken aback that I hardly had the presence of mind to refuse. However, I did, and very decidedly, too. Then he came up to me, and, in a most threatening and alarming manner, said, 'You found that crucifix. You picked it up somewhere near here. It's mine, and I'll ask you to let me have it, if you please.'

"Now this was perfectly untrue. The crucifix was given to me by my father when I was quite a little child, and I have worn it ever since I have been grown up – ever since he died, in fact, six years ago. I told the man this, but he made no pretence of believing me, and was evidently about to renew his demand, when two labourers appeared, coming down the lane. I thought this a good opportunity to escape, and walked away quickly up the lane, it was very silly of me, I ought to have gone the other way."

"Of course you ought," I agreed. "You ought to have got out into a public road at once."

"Yes, I see that now," she said. "It was very foolish of me. However, I walked on pretty quickly, for there was something in the man's face that had frightened me, and I was anxious to get home. I looked back, from time to time, and, when I saw no sign of the man, I began to recover myself, but just as I had got to the most solitary part of the lane, just about where we are now, shut in by these high fences, I heard quick footsteps behind me. I looked back and saw the man coming after me. Then, I suppose, I got in a sudden panic, for I dropped my sketching things and began to run. But as soon as I began to run, the man broke into a run too. I raced for my life, and when I heard the man gaining on me, I suppose I must have called out. Then I heard your shout from the upper part of the lane and ran on faster than ever to gain your protection. That's all, and I suppose you think that I have been making a great fuss about nothing."

"I don't think anything of the kind," I said, "and neither would our absent friend if I could get hold of him. By the way, what sort of person was he? – A tramp?"

"Oh, no, quite a respectable looking person. In fact, he would have passed for a gentleman."

"Can you give any sort of description of him – not that verbal descriptions are of much use except in the case of a hunchback or a Chinaman or some other easily identifiable creature."

"No, they are not," she agreed, "and I don't think that I can tell you much about this man excepting that he was clean-shaved, of medium height, quite well dressed, and wore a round hat and slate-coloured suede gloves."

"I'm afraid we shan't get hold of him from that description," I said. "The only thing that you can do is to avoid solitary places for the present and not to come through this lane again alone."

"Yes," she said. "I suppose I must, but it's very unfortunate. One cannot always take a companion when one goes sketching even if it were desirable, which it is not."

As to the desirability, in the case of a good-looking girl, of wandering about alone in solitary places, I had my own opinions, and very definite opinions they were. But I kept them to myself. And so we sat silent for awhile. She was still pale and agitated, and perhaps her recital of her misadventure had not been wholly beneficial. At the moment that this idea occurred to me, a crackling in my breast-pocket reminded me of the forgotten canvas, and I bethought me that perhaps a change of subject might divert her mind from her very disagreeable experience. Accordingly, I drew the canvas out of my pocket, and, unrolling it, asked her what she thought of the sketch. In a moment she became quite animated. "Why," she exclaimed, "this looks exactly like the work of that artist who was working on the Heath a little while ago."

"It is his," I replied, considerably impressed and rather astonished at her instantaneous recognition, "but I didn't know you were so familiar with his work."

"I'm not very familiar with it," she replied, "but, as I told you, I sometimes managed to steal a glance or two when I passed him. You see, his technique is so peculiar that it's easily recognised, and it interested me very much. I should have liked to stop and watch him and get a lesson."

"It is rather peculiar work," I said, looking at the canvas with new interest. "Very solid and yet very smooth."

"Yes. It is typical knife-work, almost untouched with the brush. That was what interested me. The knife is a dangerous tool for a comparative tyro like myself, but yet one would like to learn how to use it. Did he give you this sketch?"

I smiled guiltily. "The truth is," I admitted, "I stole it."

"How dreadful of you!" she said, "I suppose that you could not be bribed to steal another?"

"I would steal it for nothing if you asked me," I answered, "and meanwhile, you had better take possession of this one. It will be of more use to you than to me."

She shook her head. "No, I won't do that," she said, "though it is most kind of you. You paint, I think, don't you?"

"I'm only the merest amateur," I replied. "I annexed the sketch for the sake of the subject. I have rather an affection for this lane."

"So had I," said she, "until to-day. Now, I hate it. But, might I ask how you managed your theft?"

I told her about the empty cottage and the rejected canvases in the rubbish box. "I'm afraid none of the others would be of any use to you because he had drawn a brushful of paint across each of them."

"Oh, that wouldn't matter," she said. "The brush-strokes would be on dry paint and could easily be scraped off. Besides, it is not the subject but the technique that interests me."

"Then I will get into the cottage somehow and purloin the remaining canvases for you."

"Oh, but I mustn't give you all this trouble," she protested.

"It won't be any trouble," I said. "I shall quite enjoy a deliberate and determined robbery. But where shall I send the spoil?"

She produced her card-case, and, selecting a card, handed it to me, with a smile. "It seems to me," she said, "that I am inciting you to robbery and acting as a receiver of stolen goods, but I suppose there's no harm in it, though I feel that I ought not to give you all this trouble."

I made the usual polite rejoinder as I took from her the little magical slip of pasteboard that, in a moment, transformed her from a stranger to an acquaintance, and gave her a local habitation and a name. Before bestowing it in my pocket-book, I glanced at the neat copper-plate and read the inscription: "*Miss Sylvia Vyne. The Hawthorns. North End*".

The effect of our conversation had answered my expectations. Her agitation had passed off, the colour had come back to her cheeks, and, in fact, she seemed quite recovered. Apparently she thought so herself, for she rose, saying that she now felt well enough to walk home, and held out her hand for the colour-box and stool. "I think," said I, "that if you won't consider me intrusive, I should like to see you safely out on to an inhabited road at least."

"I shall accept your escort gratefully," she replied, "as far as the end of the lane, or farther if it is not taking you too much out of your way."

Needless to say, I would gladly have escorted so agreeable and winsome a protégée from John o' Groats to Land's End and found it not out of my way at all, and when she passed out of the gate into Hampstead Lane, I clung tenaciously to the box and stool and turned towards "The Spaniards" as though no such thing as a dismissal had ever been contemplated. In fact, with the reasonable excuse of carrying the *impedimenta*, I maintained my place by her side in the absence of a definite conge, and so we walked together, talking quite easily, principally about pictures and painting, until, in the pleasant little hamlet, she halted by a garden gate, and, taking her possessions from me, held out a friendly hand. "Good-bye," she said. "I can't thank you enough for all your help and kindness. I hope I have not been very troublesome to you."

I assured her that she had been most amenable, and, when I had once more cautioned her to avoid solitary places, we exchanged a cordial hand-shake and parted, she to enter the pleasant, rustic-looking house, and I to betake myself back to my lodgings, lightening the way with much agreeable and self-congratulatory reflection.

Chapter IX
Thorndyke Takes Up
the Scent

At my lodgings, which I reached at an unconscionably late hour for lunch, I found a little surprise awaiting me, a short note from Dr. Thorndyke asking me if I should be at liberty early on the following afternoon to show him the spot on which I had found the mysterious body. Of course, I answered by return, begging him to come straight on from the hospital to an early lunch, over which we could discuss the facts of the case before setting out. Having dispatched my letter, I called at the offices of the house agent who had the letting of the cottage on the Heath, to see if he had duplicate keys. Fortunately he had, and was willing to entrust them to me on the understanding that they should be returned some time during the next day. I did not, however, go on to the cottage, for it occurred to me that Thorndyke would probably wish to visit the wood, and I could make my visit and purloin the canvases then.

A telegram on the following morning informed me that Thorndyke would be with me at twelve o'clock, and, punctually to the minute, he arrived. "I hope you don't mind me swooping down on you in this fashion," he said, as the servant showed him into the room.

I assured him, very truthfully, that I was delighted to be honoured by a visit from him, and he then proceeded to explain. "You may wonder, Jardine, why I am busying myself about this case, which is really no business of mine, or, at least, appears to be none, but the fact is, that as a teacher and a practitioner of Medical Jurisprudence, I find it advisable to look into any unusual cases. Of course, there is always a considerable probability that I may be consulted concerning any out of the way case, but, apart from that, I have the ordinary specialist's interest in anything remarkable in my own speciality."

"I should think," said I, "that it would be well for me to give you all the facts before we start."

"Exactly, Jardine," he replied, "that is what I want. Tell me all you know about the affair and then we shall be able to test our conclusions on the spot."

He produced a large scale ordnance map, and, folding it under my direction, so that it showed only the region in which we were interested, he stood it up on the table against the water bottle, where we could both see it, and marked on it with a pencil each spot as I described it.

It is not necessary for me to record our conversation. I told him the whole story as I have already told it to the reader, pointing out on the map the exact locality where each event occurred. "It's a most remarkable case, Jardine," was his thoughtful comment when I had finished, "most remarkable, curiously puzzling, and inconsistent too. For you see that on the one hand, it looks like a casual or accidental crime, and yet, on the other, strongly suggests premeditation. No man, one would think, could have planned to commit a murder in what is, after all, a public thoroughfare, and yet, the long distance which the body seems to have been carried, and the apparently selected hiding-place, seem to suggest a previously considered plan."

"You think that there is no doubt that the man was really dead?" I asked.

"Had you any doubt at the time yourself?"

"None at all," I replied. "It was only the disappearance of the body, and, perhaps, the sergeant's suggestion, that made me think it possible that I might have been mistaken."

Thorndyke shook his head. "No, Jardine," said he, "the man was dead. We are safe in assuming that, and on that assumption our investigations must be based. The next question is, how was the body taken away? Did you measure the fence?"

"No, but I should say it is about seven feet high."

"And what kind of fence is it? Are there any footholds?"

"I can show you exactly what the fence is like," I answered. "That sketch, which I have pinned up on the wall, was apparently painted from the exact spot on which the body lay. That fence on the right-hand side is the one under which I sheltered and is exactly like the one over which the body seems to have been lifted."

Thorndyke rose and walked over to the sketch, which I had fixed to the wall with drawing-pins. "Not a bad sketch, this, Jardine," he remarked. "Very smartly put in, apparently mostly with the knife. Where did you get it?"

I had to confess that the canvas was unlawfully come by, and told him how I had obtained it. "You don't know the artist's name?" said Thorndyke, looking closely at the sketch.

"No. In fact, I know nothing about him, excepting that he worked mostly with a small painting-knife, and usually wore kid gloves."

"You don't mean that he worked in gloves?" said Thorndyke.

"So I am told," said I. "I never saw him."

"It's very odd," said Thorndyke. "I have heard of men wearing a glove on the palette-hand to keep off the midges, and many men paint in

108

gloves in exceptionally cold weather. But this sketch seems to have been painted in the summer."

"I suppose," said I, "the midges don't confine their attentions to the palette-hand. And after all, to a man who worked entirely with the knife, a glove wouldn't be really in the way."

"No," Thorndyke agreed, "that is true." He looked closely at the sketch, and even took out his pocket lens to help his vision, which seemed almost unnecessary. It appeared that he was as much interested in the unknown artist's peculiar technique as was my friend, Miss Sylvia Vyne. "By the way," said he, when he had resumed his seat at the table, "you were telling me about some kind of gold trinket that you had picked up at the foot of the fence. Shall we have a look at it?"

I fetched the little gold object from the dispatch box in which I had locked it up, and handed it to him. He turned it over in his fingers, read the letters that were engraved on it, and examined the little piece of silk cord that was attached to one ring. "There is no doubt," said he, "as to the nature of this object, nor of its connection with the dead man. This is evidently a reliquary, and these initials engraved upon it bear out exactly your description of the body. *S.V.D.P.* evidently means *St. Vincent de Paul*, who, as you probably know, was a saint who was distinguished for his works of charity. You have mentioned that the dead man wore a Roman collar, with a narrow, dark stripe up the front. That means that he was the lay-brother of some religious order, probably some philanthropic order, to whom St. Vincent de Paul would be an object of special devotion. The other letters, *A.M.D.G.*, are the initials of the words *Ad Majorem Dei Gloriam* – the motto of the Society of Jesus. But as St. Vincent de Paul was not a Jesuit saint, the motto probably refers to the owner of the reliquary, who may have been a Jesuit or a friend of the Society. It was apparently attached – perhaps to the neck – by this silk cord, which seems to have been frayed nearly through, and probably broke when the body was drawn over the top of the fence."

"I suppose I ought to have shown it to the police," I said.

"I suppose you ought," he replied, "but, as you haven't, I think we had better say nothing about it now."

He handed it back to me, and I dropped it into my pocket, intending to return it presently to the dispatch box. A few minutes later, we sallied forth on our journey of exploration.

It is not necessary to describe this journey in detail since I have already taken the reader over the ground more than once. We went, of course, to the place where I had found the body and walked right through to Hampstead Lane. Then we returned, and reconstituted the circumstances of that eventful night, after which, I conducted Thorndyke to the place where I assumed that the body had been lifted over the fence. "I suppose," I said, "we must go round and pick up the track from the other side."

He looked up and down the lane and smiled. "Would your quondam professor lose your respect for ever, Jardine, if you saw him climb over a fence in a frock coat and a topper?"

"No," I answered, "but it might look a little quaint if anyone else saw you."

"I think we will risk that," he said. "There is no one about, and I should rather like to try a little experiment. Would you mind if I hoisted you over the fence? You are something of an out-size, but then, so am I, too, which balances the conditions."

Of course I had no objection, and, when we had looked up and down the lane and listened to make sure that we had no observers, Thorndyke picked me up, with an ease that rather surprised me, and hoisted me above the level of the fence. "Is it all clear on the other side?" he asked.

"Yes," I answered, "there's no one in sight."

"Then I want you to be quite passive," he said, and with this, he hoisted me up further until I hung with my own weight across the top of the fence. Leaving me hanging thus, he sprang up lightly, and, having got astride at the top, dropped down on the other side, when he once more took hold of me and drew me over. "It wasn't so very difficult," he said. "Of course, it would have been more so to a shorter man, but, on the other hand, it is extremely unlikely that the body was anything like your size and weight."

We now followed the track up to the wood, which we entered by an opening in the fence, through which I assumed that the murderer had probably passed. I conducted Thorndyke by the nearest route to the boat-house, and, when he had thoroughly examined the place and made notes of the points that appeared to interest him, I showed him the way out by the turnstile.

It was here when we came in sight of the cottage that I bethought me of my promise to Miss Vyne, and somewhat sheepishly explained the matter to Thorndyke. "It won't take me a minute to go in and sneak the things," I said apologetically, and was proposing that he should walk on slowly, when he interrupted me.

"I'll come in with you," said he. "There may be something else to filch. Besides, I am rather partial to empty houses. There is something quite interesting, I think, in looking over the traces of recent occupation, and speculating on the personality and habits of the late occupiers. Don't you find it so?"

I said "Yes," truthfully enough, for it was a feeling of this kind that had first led me to look over the cottage. But my interest was nothing to Thorndyke's, for no sooner had I let him in at the front door, than he began to browse about through the empty rooms and passages, for all the world like a cat that has just been taken to a new house. "This was evidently the studio," he remarked, as we entered the room from which I had taken the canvas. "He doesn't seem to have had much of an outfit, as he appears to have worked on his sketching-easel. You can see the indentations made by the toe-points, and there are no marks of the castors of a studio easel. You notice, too, that he sat on a camp-stool to work."

It did not appear to me to matter very much what he had sat on, but I kept this opinion to myself and watched Thorndyke curiously as he picked up the empty paint tubes and scrutinized them one after the other. His inquisitiveness filled me with amused astonishment. He turned out the rubbish box completely, and having looked over every inch of the discarded canvases, he began systematically to examine, one by one, the pieces of paper on which the late resident had wiped his palette-knife.

Having rolled up and pocketed the waste canvases, I expressed myself as ready to depart. "If you're not in a hurry," said Thorndyke, "I should like to look over the rest of the premises."

He spoke as though we were inspecting some museum or exhibition, and, indeed, his interest and attention, as he wandered from room to room, were greater than that of the majority of visitors to a public gallery. He even insisted on visiting the little stable and coachhouse, and when he had explored them both, ascended the ricketty steps to the loft over the latter. "I suppose," said I, "this was the lumber room or store. Judging by the quantity of straw it would seem as if some cases had been unpacked here."

"Probably," agreed Thorndyke. "In fact, you can see where the cases have been dragged along, and also, by that smooth indented line, where some heavy metallic object has been slid along the floor. Perhaps if we look over the straw, we may be able to judge what those cases contained."

It didn't seem to me to matter a brass farthing what they contained, but again I made no remark, and together we moved the great mass of straw, almost handful by handful, from one end of the loft to the other, while Thorndyke, not only examined the straw but even closely scrutinized the floor on which it lay.

As far as I could see, all this minute and apparently purposeless searching was entirely without result, until we were in the act of removing the last armful of straw from the corner, and even then the object that came to light did not appear a very remarkable one under the circumstances, though Thorndyke seemed to find what appeared to me a most unreasonable interest in it. The object was a pair of canvas-pliers, which Thorndyke picked up almost eagerly and examined with profound attention. "What do you make of that, Jardine?" he asked, at length, handing the implement to me.

"It's a pair of canvas-pliers," I replied.

"Obviously," he rejoined, "but what do you suppose they have been used for?"

I opined that they had been used for straining canvases, that being their manifest function. "But," objected Thorndyke, "he would hardly have strained his canvases up here. Besides, you will notice that they have, in fact, been used for something else. You observe that the handles are slightly bent, as if something had been held with great force, and if you look at the jaws, you will see that that something was a metallic object about three quarters of an inch wide with sharp corners. Now, what do you make of that?

I looked at the pliers, inwardly reflecting that I didn't care two-pence what the object was, and finally said that I would give it up. "The problem does not interest you keenly," Thorndyke remarked with a smile, "and yet it ought to, you know. However, we may consider the matter on some future occasion. Meanwhile, I shall follow your pernicious example and purloin the pliers."

His interest in this complete stranger appeared to me very singular, and it seemed for the moment to have displaced that in the mysterious case which was the object of his visit to me. "A strange, vagabond sort of man that artist must have been," he remarked, as we walked home across the Heath, "but I suppose one picks up vagabond habits in travelling about the world."

"Do you gather that he had travelled much, then?" I asked.

"He appears to have visited New York, Brussels, and Florence, which is a selection suggesting other travels."

I was wondering vaguely how Thorndyke had arrived at these facts, and was indeed about to ask him, when he suddenly changed the subject by saying, "I suppose, Jardine, you don't wander about this place alone at night?"

"I do sometimes," I replied.

"Then I shouldn't," he said. "You must remember that a very determined attempt has been made on your life, and it would be unreasonable to suppose that it was made without some purpose. But that purpose is still unaccomplished. You don't know who your enemy is, and, consequently, can take no precautions against him excepting by

112

keeping away from solitary places. It is an uncomfortable thought, but at present, you have to remember that any chance stranger may be an intending murderer. So be on your guard."

I promised to bear his warning in mind, though I must confess his language seemed to me rather exaggerated, and so we walked on, chatting about various matters until we arrived at my lodgings.

Thorndyke was easily persuaded to come in and have tea with me, and while we were waiting for its arrival, he renewed his examination of the sketch upon the wall.

"Aren't you going to have this strained on a stretcher?" he asked.

I replied, "Yes," and that I intended to take it with me the next time I went into town.

"Let me take it for you," said Thorndyke. "I should like to show it to Jervis to illustrate the route that we have marked on the map. Then I can have it left at any place that you like."

I mentioned the name of an artist's-colourman in the Hampstead Road, and, unpinning the canvas, rolled it up and handed it to him.

He took it from me and, rolling it up methodically and carefully, bestowed it in his breast pocket. Then he brought forth the map, and, as we drank our tea and talked over our investigations, he checked our route on it and marked the position of the cottage. Shortly after tea he took his leave, and I then occupied an agreeable half-hour in composing a letter to Miss Vyne to accompany the loot from the deserted house.

Chapter X
The Unheeded Warning

Thorndyke's warning, so emphatically expressed, ought to have been alike unnecessary and effective. As a matter of fact, it was neither. I suppose that to a young man, not naturally timorous, the idea of a constantly lurking danger amidst the prosaic conditions of modern civilization is one that is not readily accepted. At any rate, the fact is that I continued to walk abroad by day and by night with as much unconcern as if nothing unusual had ever befallen me. It was not that the recollection of those horrible hours in the poisoned cellar had in any way faded. That incident I could never forget. But I think, that in the back of my mind, there still lingered the idea of a homicidal lunatic, though that idea had been so scornfully rejected by Thorndyke.

But before I describe the amazing experience by which I once more came within a hair's breadth of sudden and violent death, I must refer to another incident, not because it seemed to be connected with that alarming occurrence, but because it came first in the order of time, and had its own significance later.

It was a couple of days after Thorndyke's visit that I walked down the Hampstead Road with the intention of fetching the sketch from the artist's-colourman's. The shop was within a few hundred yards of Jacob Street, and as I crossed the end of that street, I was just considering whether I ought to look in on Batson, when a lady bowed to me and made as if she would stop. It was Mrs. Samway. Of course, I stopped and shook hands, and while I was making the usual polite enquiries, I felt myself once more impressed with the unusualness of the woman. Even in her dress she was unlike other women, though not in the least eccentric or bizarre.

At present, she was clothed from head to foot in black, but a scarlet bird's wing in the coquettish little velvet toque, and a scarlet bow at her throat, gave an effect of colour that, unusual as it was, harmonized completely and naturally with her jet-black hair and her strange, un-English beauty. "So you haven't started for Paris yet," I remarked.

"No," she replied, "my husband has gone and may, perhaps, come back. At any rate, I am staying in England for the present."

"Then I may possibly have the pleasure of seeing you again," I said, and she graciously replied that she hoped it might be so, as we shook hands and parted. A few minutes later, in the artist's-colourman's shop, I had another chance meeting and a more agreeable one. The proprietor had just produced the sketch, now greatly improved in appearance by being strained on a stretcher, when the glass door opened and a young lady entered the shop. Imagine my surprise when that young lady turned out to be none other than Miss Vyne. "Well," I exclaimed, as we mutually recognized each other, "what an extraordinary coincidence!"

"I don't see that it is very extraordinary," she replied. "Most of the Hampstead people come here because it's the nearest place where you can get proper artist's materials. Is that the sketch you were telling me about?"

"Yes," I answered, "and it's the pick of the loot. But it isn't too late to alter your mind. Say the word and it's yours."

"Well," she replied, with a smile, "I am not going to say the word, but I want to thank you for rescuing those other treasures for me."

She had, as a matter of fact, already thanked me in a very pretty little note, but I was not averse to her mentioning the subject again. We stepped back to the door, and in the brighter light, looked at the sketch together. "It's a pity," she remarked, "that he handled it so carelessly before the paint was hard. Those fingermarks wouldn't matter a bit on a brush-painted surface, but on the smooth knife-surface they are rather a disfigurement."

She placed the sketch in my hand, and I backed nearer to the glass door to get a better light. Happening to glance up, I noticed that a sudden and very curious change had come over her, a look of haughty displeasure and even anger, apparently directed at somebody or something outside the shop.

For a few moments I took no notice, then, half-unconsciously, I looked round just as some person moved away from the door. I looked once more at Miss Vyne. She was quite unmistakably angry. Her cheeks were flushed and there was a resentful light in her eyes that gave her an expression quite new to me.

I suppose she caught my enquiring glance for she exclaimed, "Did you see that woman? I never heard of such impertinence in my life."

"What did she do?" I asked.

"She came right up to the doorway and looked over your shoulder, and then stared at me in the most singular and insolent manner. I could have slapped her face."

"Not through the glass door," I suggested, on which her anger subsided in a ripple of laughter as quickly as it had arisen. "What was this objectionable person like?" I asked. "Was she a charwoman or a slavey?"

"Oh, not at all," replied Miss Vyne. "Quite a ladylike looking person, except for her manners. Rather tastefully dressed, too, a black and vermilion scheme of colour."

The reply startled me a little. "Had she a scarlet bird's wing in her hat?" I asked.

"Yes, and a scarlet bow at her throat. I hope you are not going to say that you know her."

It was a rather delicate situation. I could not actually disavow the acquaintance, but I did not feel inclined to have a black and scarlet fly introduced into the sweet-smelling ointment of my intercourse with the fair Sylvia, so I explained with great care the exact scope of the acquaintance, on which Miss Vyne remarked that "she supposed that doctors could not be held responsible for the people they knew", and proceeded to make her purchases.

I did not take the sketch away with me after all, for it occurred to me that I might as well leave it to be framed, but instead, I carried forth with me the parcel containing Miss Vyne's purchases. I had not far to carry it, for she was returning at once to Hampstead. I was tempted to return, for the sake of enjoying a chat with her, too, but discreetly withstood the temptation, and, having escorted her to a tram, I turned my face south and walked away at a leisurely pace into the jaws of an all-unsuspected danger.

It was some hours, however, before anything remarkable happened.

My immediate objective was Lincoln's Inn Fields, where, at the College of Surgeons, a lecture on Epidermic Appendages was to be delivered by the Hunterian Professor, and there, in the college theatre, I spent a delightful hour while the genial professor took his hearers with him on a personally-conducted tour among structures that ranged from the plumage of the sun-bird to the dermal plates of the crocodile, from the silken locks of beauty to the quills of the porcupine or the mail of the armadillo.

When I came out, the dusk was just closing in. It was a slightly foggy evening. The last glow of the sunse in the western sky lighted up the haze into a rosy back-ground, against which the shadowy buildings were relieved in shapes of cloudy grey. It was a lovely effect, an effect such as London alone can show, and fugitive as a breath on a mirror. As I sauntered westward up the Strand I presently bethought me that, before the light should have faded completely, I would see how the effect looked by the riverside. Walking quickly down Buckingham Street, I came out on to the Embankment and looked into the west. But the light was nearly gone, the shadows of evening were closing in fast, and the fog, creeping up the river, ushered in the night.

I leaned on the parapet and watched the last glimmer die away, watched the darkness deepen on the river and the faint lights on the barges moored on the southern shore at first twinkle pallidly and then fade out as the fog thickened. I lit my pipe and looked down at the dark water swirling past, and gradually fell into a train of half-dreamy meditation.

Not for the first time since the occurrence, my thoughts turned to Mrs. Samway. Why had she stared at Miss Vyne in that singular manner – if indeed it was really Mrs. Samway, and if she really had stared in the manner alleged? It was an odd affair, but, after all, it did not very much matter. And with this, my thoughts rambled off in a new direction.

It was to the cottage on the Heath that they wandered this time, and the picture of Thorndyke's cat-like prowlings and pryings arose before me. That was very queer, too. Was it possible that this learned and astute man habitually went about eagerly probing into the personal habits and trivial actions of chance strangers? The apparently puerile inquisitiveness that he had displayed seemed totally out of character with all that I knew about the man, but then it often happens that the private life of public men develops personal traits that are surprising and disappointing to those who have only known them in connection with their public activities.

I had become so completely immersed in my thoughts as to be almost oblivious of what was happening around. Indeed, there was mighty little happening. The gathering darkness and the thin fog limited my view to a few square yards. Now and again, a muffled hoot from the lower river spoke of life and movement on the water, and at long intervals an occasional wayfarer would pass along the pavement behind me.

My reflections had reached the point recorded above, when a person emerged from the obscurity near to the parapet and approached as if to pass close behind me. I only caught the dusky shape indistinctly with the tail of my eye, so indistinctly that I could not say certainly whether it was that of a man or a woman, for I was still gazing down at the dark water. He or she approached quietly, swerving towards me across the wide pavement, and was in the act of passing quite close to me when the thing happened. Of a sudden, I felt my knees clasped in a powerful grip, and at the same moment I was lifted off my feet and thrust forward over the parapet. Instinctively, I clutched at the stonework, but its flat surface offered nothing for my fingers to grasp. Then my assailant let go, and the next instant I plunged head-first into the icy water.

117

It was fortunate for me that the tide was nearly full, else must I, almost certainly, have broken my neck. As it was, my head struck on the firm mud at the bottom with such force, that for some moments I washalf-stunned. Nevertheless, I must have struck out automatically, for when I began to recover my wits my head was above water, and I was swimming as actively as my clinging garments would let me. But, apparently, in those moments of dazed semi-consciousness, I must have struck out towards the middle of the river, for now I was encompassed by a murky void in which nothing was visible save one or two reddish, luminous patches – presumably, the lamps on the Embankment.

Towards one of these I turned and struck out vigorously. The water was desperately cold, and hampered as I was with my clothing, I felt that I should not be able to keep myself afloat very long, strong swimmer as I was. The dim, red nebula of the unseen lamps moved past slowly, showing me that I was drifting down on the ebb-tide. Before me, I knew, was the long, inhospitable wall of the Embankment. True, there were some steps, if I was not mistaken, by Cleopatra's Needle, but the question was whether I had not drifted past them already. I had given one or two lusty shouts as soon as I had cleared my chest of the mouthful of water that I got in my first plunge, and I was now letting off another yell, when, out of the darkness behind me, came a prolonged hoot.

I looked round quickly in the direction whence the sound had come, and then became aware of the churning of a propeller. Almost at the same moment, a dim, ruddy smudge of light broke through the darkness over the river, and began rapidly to brighten until it took the form of the twin mast-head lights of a tug with a vessel in tow.

For a moment I hesitated. My first impulse was to avoid the danger of being run down, but suddenly I altered my mind. For, as the tug bore down on me, with a roaring of water and a loud clank of machinery, I saw that she was not absolutely end-on, for her green starboard light, which had been for a moment visible, suddenly disappeared. Of what happened during the next few moments, I have but a confused recollection.

A splashing and churning, with the loud wash of water, the throb of the engines and a glare of light which blazed before my eyes for a moment, to vanish in an instant into pitchy darkness, a huge, black object, felt rather than seen to sweep past before me, and then my hand clutched a wooden projection, and I felt myself dragged violently through the water. The projection that I had laid hold of was the lee-board of a sailing barge, as I discovered when the rush of the water banged me against it, and much ado I had to hold on, with the water dragging at me and spouting up over my head. But, with what strength was left to me, I reached out with the other hand and clawed hold of the dwarf bulwark over which the water was lapping, and so, with a last violent effort, contrived to drag myself up on to the deck.

I essayed to stand up, and did, in fact, succeed, but as my sensations suggested those of a leaden statue with india-rubber legs, I sat down hastily on the hatch-cover to avoid going overboard. And there I sat for a minute or two leaning against the lowered mast with my teeth chattering, and seeming to grow more and more chilled and exhausted every moment.

Numb as my mind was by this time, my medical instincts told me that this would not do. Somehow I must get warmth and shelter, for I might as well have been drowned at once as die of exposure and cold. I looked round lethargically. There was no sign of any-one on board. Another barge was towing alongside, and the bows of two others were dimly visible astern. On those rear-most barges there must certainly have been someone steering. But they were inaccessible to me, and I had not the energy to shout, nor could anyone have got across to me if I had.

Suddenly my eye fell on the little chimney that rose by the cabin scuttle. A thin stream of smoke issued from it and blew away astern. Perhaps, then, the crew were below, or, if not, at least there was a fire. I crawled aft, holding on with my hands, and, pushing back the scuttle, backed cautiously down the ladder closing the scuttle after me.

There seemed to be nobody below, and the cabin was in darkness, save for the glow of the fire that burned in the little grate. The air was probably warm, though to me it felt icy, but, at least, there was no wind to play on my wet clothes.

I sat down on the locker as near to the fire as I could, and rested my elbows on the little triangular table. Chilled to the marrow and utterly exhausted, I was sensible of a growing desire to sleep, a desire which I repressed, as I believed, with noble resolution. But apparently my efforts in this respect were not so successful as I had supposed, for the next incident opened with suspicious suddenness.

A vigorous shake, which dislodged one of my elbows, introduced the episode.

I looked up, blinking sulkily, at a bright and most objectionably dazzling light, which further inspection showed to proceed from a hurricane lamp held by a rather dirty hand. "Here, wake up, mister," said a hoarse voice. "This here ain't the Hotel Cecil, you know."

I sat up and stared vaguely at the speaker, or at least, the holder of the lamp, but could not think of anything appropriate to say. Then another voice emerged from nowhere in particular. "'E's been overboard, that's what 'e's been."

"Any fool can see that," said the first man, "but the question is, who is he and what's he a-doin' in my cabin? Who are yer, mister?"

Now, that would seem to be a perfectly simple and straightforward question. But it is not so simple as it seems. To a complete stranger, the bare mention of a name is unilluminating. Further explanations are needed. And at that moment I did not feel equal to explanations. Besides, I was not so very clear on the subject myself. Consequently, I preserved a silence which, perhaps, was wooden rather than golden. "D'ye 'ear?" persisted the first man. "I'm a-arskin' you a question."

"What'a the good of arskin' questions of a man what's been a-rammin' 'is crumpet aginst the bottom of the river?" protested the other man.

"What d'ye mean?" demanded the first mariner.

"Can't you see?" retorted the other, "as 'e's took the ground 'ard? Look at 'is 'ed."

Here the first mariner – Lucifer, or lamp-bearer – wiped his hand over the top of my head and then examined the tip of his forefinger critically as though it were the arming of a deep-sea lead. "You're right, Abel," said he. "That's mud off the bottom, that is. He must have took a regular header. Sooicide perhaps, and altered his mind. Found it a bit damper'n what he expected. Put the kittle on, Abe."

From this moment, the two mariners treated me as if I had been a lay-figure. Silently, they peeled off my wet clothes, and dried my skin with vigorous friction as if it had been a wet deck. They not only asked no further questions, but when I would have spoken they urged me to economize my wind. They inducted me into stiff and hairy garments of uncouth aspect, and finally, Abe set before me on the table a large earthenware mug, the contents of which steamed and diffused through the cabin a strong odour of Dutch gin. "You git outside that, mister," said the luminiferous mariner (who turned out subsequently to be the skipper), "and then you'd best turn in."

The treatment was not strictly orthodox, but I obeyed without demur. Most people would have done the same under the circumstances. But the process of "getting outside" it took time, for the grog was boiling hot and had been brewed with a flexible wrist. By the time that I had emptied the mug I was not only revived, but (so far as my memory serves) rather disposed to be garrulously explanatory and facetious. I even felt a slight inclination to sing. But my friends would stand no nonsense. As soon as the mug was fairly empty, they bundled me, neck and crop, into a sort of elongated cupboard and proceeded to pile on me untold quantities of textile fabrics, including a complete suit of oilskins.

120

Then they commanded me to go to sleep, which I believe I must have done almost instantly.

Chapter XI
A Chapter of Accidents

Awakening in a strange place is always a memorable experience, especially to the young, in whom the capacity for novel sensations has not yet been exhausted by repetition. When I emerged, somewhat gradually, from the unconsciousness of sleep, my first impressions concerned themselves with the unusual appearance of the bedroom wall and its remarkable proximity to my nose. I further noticed that the bedstead had become inexplicably tilted and that the house appeared to be swaying, and as I mused on these phenomena with the vagueness of the half-awake, a loud voice, proceeding apparently from the floor above, roared out the mystic words, "Lee-O!" whereupon there ensued a sound like the shaking of colossal table cloths and the loud clanking of chains, and my bedstead took a sharp tilt to the opposite side. This roused me pretty completely, and turning over in the bunk, I looked out into the barge's cabin.

It was broad daylight and evidently not early, for a square patch of sunlight crept to and fro on the little table, whence presently it slipped down to the floor and slithered about unsteadily, as if Phoebus had overdone his morning dram and could not drive his chariot straight. I watched it lazily for some time and then, becoming conscious of a vacancy within, crept out from under the mountain of bedclothes and made my way to the ladder.

As I put my head through the companion hatch, a man who stood at the wheel regarded me stolidly. "So you've woke up, have yer?" said he.

"Thought you was going right round the clock. Abel! He's woke up. Tell young Ted to stand by with them heggs and that there 'addick."

Here Abel looked round from behind the luff of the mainsail, and having verified the statement, conveyed the order to some invisible person in the fore-peak. Then he came aft with an obvious air of business. The time for explanations had arrived.

Accordingly I proceeded to "pitch them my yarn," as they expressed it, to which they listened with polite attention and manifest disappointment, clearly regarding the story as a fabrication from beginning to end. And no wonder. The whole affair was utterly incredible even to me, to them it must have seemed sheer nonsense. Their own verdict of "sooicide" during very temporary insanity with sudden mental recovery, under the influence of cold water, was so much more rational. Not that they obtruded their views. They listened patiently and said nothing, and nothing that they could have said could have been more expressive.

Meanwhile I looked about me with no little surprise. Some miles away to the south lay a stretch of low land, faint and grey, with a single salient object, apparently a church with two spires. In every other direction was the unbroken sea horizon. "You seem to have made a pretty good passage," I remarked.

"We've had sixteen hours to do it in," replied the skipper, "and spring tides and a nice bit of breeze. If it 'ud only hold – which I'm afraid it won't – we'd be in Folkestone Harbour this time to-morrow, or even sooner. Folkestone be much out of your way?"

I smiled at the artlessness of the question. It was undeniable that the route from Charing Cross to Hampstead by way of Folkestone was slightly indirect. But there was no need to insist on the fact. My hospitable friends had acted for the best and their prudence was justified by the result, for here I was, not a whit the worse for my ducking save that I badly wanted a bath. "Folkestone will suit me quite well," I replied, "if there is enough money left in my pockets to pay my fare home."

"That's all right," said the skipper. "I cleared out your pockets myself. You'll find the things in a mug in the starboard locker. Better overhaul 'em when you go below and see if you've dropped anything. Here comes young Ted with your grub."

As he spoke the apprentice rose through the fore-hatch like a stage apparition – if one can imagine an apparition burdened with a tin tea-pot, two "heggs" and an "'addick" – and came grinning along the weather side-deck, to vanish through the cabin hatchway. I followed gleefully, and, almost before young Ted had finished the somewhat informal table arrangements, fell to on the food with voracious joy. "If you want any more eggs or anythink," said the apprentice, "all you've got to do is just to touch the electric bell and the waiter'll come and take your orders." And having delivered this delicate shaft of irony, he presented me with an excellent back view of a pair of brown dreadnoughts as he retired up the ladder.

As I consumed the rough but excellent breakfast I reflected on the strange events that had placed me in my present odd situation. For the first time, I began fairly to realize that I was in some way involved in a nexus of circumstances that I did not in the least understand. I had an enemy, a vindictive enemy, too, in whose eyes mere human life was a thing of no account. But who could he be? I knew of no one on whom I had ever inflicted the smallest injury. I bore no man any grudge and had never to my knowledge had unfriendly dealings with any human

123

creature. Was this inveterate enemy of mine anyone whom I knew? Or was he some stranger whose path I had crossed without knowing it, and whom I should not recognize even if I saw him?

This last supposition was highly disquieting, especially as it seemed rather probable, for if my enemy was unknown to me, what precautions could I take?

Then, again, there was the question! What was the occasion of this extraordinary vendetta? What had I done to this man that he should pursue me with such deadly purpose? As to Jervis's suggestion, that I had seen something at the Samways' house that I was not wanted to see, there was nothing in it, for, as a matter of fact, I had seen nothing. There was nothing to see. The man Maddock was certainly dead. As to what he died of, that was Batson's affair, but even in that there was no sign of anything suspicious. The man himself had consulted Batson, and had thought so badly of himself that he had made his will in Batson's presence. The patient himself was fully aware of his serious condition. It was only Batson, with his eternal hurry and bustle and his defective eyesight, who had missed observing it. The only circumstance that supported Jervis's view was that the acts of violence seemed to be connected with the locality of Batson's house.

Of course there remained the mystery of the dead priest or lay-brother.

But with that these attempts seemed to have no connection. Nor was there any reason why the murderer should pursue me. I had seen the body, it is true, but nobody believed me and no proceedings were being taken. Nor could I have identified the murderer if I had been confronted with him. Clearly, he had nothing to fear from me.

From the causes of my present predicament I passed to the immediate future. I should have to get back from Folkestone, and I ought to send a telegram to my landlady, Mrs. Blunt, who would probably be in a deuce of a twitter about me. I raised the lid of the locker, and, reaching out the big earthenware mug, emptied its contents on the table. All my portable property seemed to be there, including the little gold reliquary, which I had carelessly carried in my pocket ever since I had shown it to Thorndyke. My available funds were some four or five pounds, amply sufficient to get me home and to discharge my liability to the skipper as well. I swept the things back into the mug, which I returned to the locker, and having cut myself another thick slice of bread, proceeded with the largest breakfast that I have ever eaten.

The skipper's forebodings were justified by the course of events. When I came on deck the breeze had died down to a mere faint breath, hardly sufficient to keep the big red main-sail asleep – as the pretty old nautical phrase has it. The skipper was still at the wheel and Abel was anxiously taking soundings with a hand-lead. "You won't do it, Bill," said the latter, coiling up the lead-line with an air of finality. "This 'ere breeze is a-petering right out."

The skipper said nothing, but stared gloomily at the land which was now right ahead and much nearer than when I had last looked, and from the land his eye travelled to a sand-bank from which rose a tall post at the top of which was an inverted cone. "Ought to a-gone about a bit sooner, Bill," pursued Abel, whereupon the skipper turned on him fiercely.

"What's the good o' saying that now!" he demanded. "If you'd a-told me the wind was going to drop, I a-gone about sooner. What water is there?"

"Five fathom here," replied Abel, "that means one-and-a-quarter on the Woolpack. You'd best shove her nose round now, Bill."

"Oh, all right!" retorted the skipper, "Lee-O! This is going to be an all-night job, this is," and with this gloomy prediction, he spun the wheel round viciously, and once more headed away from the land.

Prophecy appeared to be the skipper's speciality and, like most prophets, he tended to view the future with an unfavourable eye. Gradually the breeze died away into a dead calm, so that we had presently to let go the anchor to avoid drifting on to a great sand-bank which now lay between us and the land. And here we remained not only for the rest of the day and the succeeding night, as the skipper had promised, but throughout the whole of the next day and following night.

I have already remarked on the incalculable chances by which the course of a man's life is determined. Looking back now, I see that the skipper's little miscalculation and his failure to cross the Woolpack Shoal into the inshore channel, was an antecedent determining the most momentous consequences for me. For had the barge been becalmed in the inshore channel, I could, and should, have landed in the boat and returned home forthwith, and if I had, certain events would not have happened and my life might have run a very different course. As it was, miles of sea and the great bank known as the Margate Sand lay between me and the shore, whence I was committed to the wanderings and dallyings of the barge as irrevocably as if we were crossing the Pacific.

We lay, then, in the Queen's Channel, outside Margate Sand, for two whole days and nights, during which time the skipper and Abel slept much and smoked more, and young Ted, having cleaned and dried my clothes, inducted me into the art of bottom-fishing. On the third day, a faint breath of breeze enabled us to crawl round the North Foreland, and the skipper having elected to pass outside the Goodwin, managed to get becalmed again in the neighbourhood of the East Goodwin Lightship. A little breeze at night enabled us to move on a few miles farther, and so we continued to crawl along at intervals, mainly on the tide, until nine o'clock in the morning of the fifth day, when we finally crawled into Folkestone Harbour.

As soon as the barge was brought up to a buoy, young Ted was detailed to put me ashore in the boat. The skipper and Abel had insisted on treating me as a guest, and I had perforce to accept the position. But young Ted had no such pride, and when I ran up the wooden steps by the old fish-market, I left him on the stage below, staring with an incredulous grin at a gold coin in his none-too-delicate palm. I was not sorry to be landed in this unfashionable quarter of the town, for in spite of young Ted's efforts, my turn-out left much to be desired, especially in the matter of shirt-cuffs and collar, and I was, moreover, hatless and somewhat imperfectly shaved. Accordingly, I slunk inconspicuously past the market and the groups of lounging fishermen, and when I saw a well-dressed, lady-like woman preceding me into the little narrow street, known as the Stade, I slackened my pace so as not to overtake her. She sauntered along with a leisurely air as if she were waiting for something or somebody, and this and the fact that she carried a light canvas portmanteau and a rug, suggested to me that she was probably travelling by the cross-channel boat which was due to start presently.

Suddenly my attention was diverted from her by a loud chattering and a series of shouts. A small crowd of men and women ran excitedly past the end of the little street. The clattering rapidly drew nearer, and then a horse, with a light van, swept round the corner and passing under an archway, advanced at a furious gallop. Evidently the horse had bolted and now, mad with terror, dashed forward with trailing reins, zigzagging erratically and making the van sway to and fro, so that it took up the whole of the narrow street. The few wayfarers darted into doorways and sheltered corners, and I was about to secure my own safety in a similar manner, when I noticed that the woman in front of me had apparently become petrified with terror, for she stood stock still, gazing helplessly at the approaching horse. It was no time for ceremony. The infuriated animal and the swaying van were thundering up the street like an insane Juggernaut. With a hasty apology, I seized the woman from behind and half-dragged, half-carried her to the opening of a little yard beside a sail-loft. And even then, I was hardly quick enough, for as the van roared past some projecting object struck me between the shoulders and sent me flying, face downwards, on to a pile of tarred drift-net.

I had had the presence of mind to let go, as I was struck, so that my fair protégée was not involved in my downfall, but in a moment, she was stooping over me, and with many expressions of concern, endeavouring to help me to rise. Beyond a thump in the back, however, I was not hurt in the least, but picked myself up, grinning and turned to reassure her. And then I really did get a shock, for as I turned, the woman gave a shriek and fell back on the steps of the sail-loft, gasping, and staring at me with an expression of the utmost astonishment and terror. I supposed the accident had upset her nerves, but to be sure, my own received, as I have said, a pretty severe shock. For the woman was Mrs. Samway.

We remained for a moment or two gazing at one another in mute astonishment. Then I recollected myself, and advanced to shake hands, but to my discomfiture, she shrank away from me and began to sob and laugh in an unmistakably hysterical fashion. I must confess that I was somewhat surprised at these manifestations in so robust a woman as Mrs. Samway. Unreasonably so, indeed, for all women-kind are more or less prone to hysteria, but whereas the normal woman tends to laugh and cry, the weaker vessels develop inexplicable diseases, with a tendency to social reform and emancipation.

I put on my best bedside manner, at once matter-of-fact and persuasive. "You seem quite upset," I said, "and all about nothing, for the poor beggar of a horse must be half-a-mile away by now."

"Yes," she answered shakily, "it's ridiculous of me, but it was so sudden and so – " Here she laughed noisily, and as the laugh ended in a portentous sniff, I hastened to continue the conversation. "Yes, it was a bit of a facer to see that beast coming up the street as if it was Tottenham Corner. Why on earth didn't you get out of the way?"

"I am sure I don't know." she answered. "I seemed to be paralyzed and idiotic and – " Here the laughter began again.

"Well," I interrupted cheerfully, "you didn't get rolled on those tarred nets, so that's something to be thankful for."

This was a rather unlucky shot, for the semblance of facetiousness started a most alarming train of giggles, interrupted by rather loud sobs, but at this point, a new curative influence made itself manifest. Two smack boys halted outside the opening and surveyed her with frank interest and pleased surprise. Simultaneously, an elderly mariner appeared at the door of the sail-loft, grasping a black bottle and a tea-cup, and rather shyly descending the steps, suggested that "perhaps a drop o' sperits might do the lady good."

Mrs. Samway bounced off the steps, her hitherto pale cheeks aflame with anger. "I am making a fool of myself," she exclaimed. "Let us go away from here."

She walked out into the street, and I, having thanked the old gentleman for his most efficacious remedy, followed. As soon as I caught her up, she turned on me quickly and held out her hand. "Good-bye, Dr. Jardine," she said, "and thank you so very much for risking your life for a – for a wretched giggling woman."

"Oh, you're not going to send me packing like this," I protested, "when we've hardly said good morning. Besides, you're not fit to be left. But you're not to begin laughing again," I added, threateningly, for an ominous twitching of her mouth seemed to herald a relapse, "or I shall go back and get that black bottle."

She shook her head impatiently, but without looking at me. "I would rather you went away, Dr. Jardine," she said in an agitated voice. "I would, really. I wish to be alone. Don't think me ungracious. I am really most grateful to you, but I would rather you left me now."

Of course there was nothing more to be said. She was not really ill or in need of assistance, and probably her instinct was right. Hysteria is not one of those affections which waste their sweetness on the desert air. I shook her hand cordially and, advising her to keep out of the way of stray vans and horses, once more pursued my way towards the town, meditating as I went, on the oddity of the whole affair. It was an astonishing coincidence that I should have run against this woman in this out-of-the-way place. I had left her but a few days since apparently firmly rooted in the Hampstead Road, and now, behold, as I step ashore from the barge, she is almost the first person that I meet. And yet the coincidence, which had evidently hit her as hard as it had me, like most coincidences, tended to disappear on closer inspection. The only really odd feature was my own presence in Folkestone. As to Mrs. Samway, she had probably been sent for by her husband, and was crossing by the boat that was now due to start.

Her anxiety to get rid of me was more puzzling, until I suddenly remembered my bare head, my crumpled collar, and generally raffish and disreputable appearance. The latter was, in fact, at this moment brought to my notice by a man, with whom, in my preoccupation, I collided, who first uttered an impatient exclamation and then, bestowing on me a quick stare of astonishment, muttered a hasty apology and hurried past. The incident emphasized the necessity for some reform, and I mended my pace towards the region of shops in a very ferment of uncomfortable self-consciousness.

With the purchase of a new hat, a collar, a pair of cuffs, a neck-tie, a pair of gloves and a stick, some faint glimmer of self-respect revived in me. I was even conscious of a temptation to linger in Folkestone and spend a few hours by the sea, but a sense of duty, aided by a large, muddy stain on my coat, finally decided me to return to town at once. Accordingly, having sent off a telegram to my landlady and ascertained that a train left for London in about twenty minutes, I betook myself to the station.

There were comparatively few people travelling by this particular train. In fact, when I had established myself with the morning paper in the off-side corner seat of a smoking compartment, I began, with an Englishman's proverbial unsociability, to congratulate myself on the prospect of having the compartment to myself, when my hopes were dashed by the entrance of an elderly clergyman, who not only broke up my solitude, but aggravated the offence by quite unnecessarily seating himself opposite to me. I was almost tempted to move to another corner, for my length of leg gives an added value to space, but it seemed a rude thing to do, and as the train moved off at this moment, I resigned myself to the trifling discomfort.

My clerical friend was a somewhat uncommon-looking man, with a countenance at once strong and secretive, a rectangular, masterful face, with a bull-like dew-lap and a small, and very sharp, Roman nose. On further inspection, I decided that he was either a High-Church parson or a Roman Catholic priest. His proceedings seemed to favour the latter hypothesis, for the train was barely out of the station before he had whisked out of his pocket an ecclesiastical-looking volume, which he opened at a marked place, and instantly began to read. I watched him with inquisitive interest, for his manner of reading was very singular. There was something habitual, almost mechanical, about it, suggesting an allotted and familiar task, and a lack of concentration that suggested a corresponding lack of novelty in the matter. As he read, his lips moved, and now and again I caught a faint whisper, by which I gathered that he was reading rapidly, but the most singular phenomenon was, that when his eyes strayed out of the carriage window, as they did at frequent intervals, his lips went on sputtering with unabated rapidity. Quite suddenly he appeared to come to the end of a sort of literary measured mile, for even as his lips were still moving, he clapped in the book-mark, shut the volume, and returned it to his pocket with a curious air of businesslike finality.

As his eyes were no longer occupied with the book, my observations had to be suspended, and my attention was now turned to my own affairs. Putting my hand in my coat pocket for my pipe and pouch, I became aware of a state of confusion in the said pocket which I had already noticed when making my purchases. The fact is, that I had nearly come away from the barge without my portable property. It was only at the last moment that the skipper, remembering the mug, had

129

fetched it hurriedly from the locker and shot its contents bodily into my coat pocket. The present seemed a good opportunity for distributing the various articles among their proper receptacles. Accordingly I turned out the whole pocketful on the seat by my side, and a remarkably miscellaneous collection they formed, comprising knives, pencils, match-box, keys, the minor implements of my craft, and various other objects, useful and useless, including the little gold reliquary.

My neighbour opposite was, I think, quite interested in my proceedings, though he kept up a dignified pretence of being entirely unaware of my existence. Only for a while, however. Suddenly he sat up, very wide awake, and slewing his head round, stared with undisguised intentness at my little collection. I guessed at once what it was that had attracted his attention. A cleric would not be thrilled by the sight of a clinical thermometer or an ophthalmoscope. It was the reliquary that had caught his eye. That was an article in his own line of business.

With deliberate mischief, I left the little bauble exposed to view as I very slowly and methodically conveyed the other things one by one, each to its established pocket. Last of all, I picked up the reliquary and held it irresolutely as if debating where I should stow it. And at this point His Reverence intervened, unable any longer to contain his curiosity. "Zat is a very remargable liddle opchect, sir," he said in excellent Anglo-German. "Might one bresume to ask vat it's use is?"

I handed the reliquary to him and he took it from me with ill-disguised eagerness. "I understand," said I, "that it is a reliquary. But you probably know more about such things than I do. I haven't opened it so I can't say what is inside."

He nodded gravely. "Zo! I am glad to hear you zay zat. Brobably zere is inside some holy relic vich ought not to be touched egzepting by bious handts." He turned the case over, and, putting on a pair of spectacles – which he had not appeared to require for reading – closely scrutinized the inscriptions, and even the wisp of cord that remained attached to one of the rings. "You zay," he resumed without raising his eyes, "zat you understandt zat zis is a reliquary. Do you not zen know? Ze berson who gafe it to you, did he not tell you vat it gondained?"

"It wasn't given to me at all," I replied. "In fact, it isn't properly mine. I picked it up and am merely keeping it until I find the owner."

He pondered this statement with a degree of profundity that seemed rather out of proportion to its matter, and he continued to gaze at the reliquary, never once raising his eyes to mine. At length, after a considerable pause and a most unnecessary amount of reflection, he asked, "Might one ask, if you shall bardon my guriosity, vere you found zis liddle opchect?"

I hesitated before replying. My first, and natural, impulse was to tell him exactly where and under what circumstances I had found the "opchect". But the way in which my information had been received by the police had made me rather chary of offering confidences, besides which, I had half-promised them not to talk about the affair. And, after all, it was no business of this good gentleman's where I found it. My answer was, therefore, not very explicit. "I picked it up in a lane at Hampstead, near London."

"At Hampstead!" he repeated. "Zo! Zat would be a very good blace to find such sings. I mean," he added, hastily, "zere are many beople in zat blace and some of zem will be of ze old religion."

Now, this last remark was such palpable nonsense that it set me speculating on what he had intended to say, for it was obvious that he had altered his mind in the middle of the sentence and completed it with the first words that came to hand. However, as I could read no sense into it at all, I said that perhaps he was right, which seemed an eminently safe rejoinder to an unintelligible statement.

When he had finished his minute examination of the reliquary, he handed it back to me with such evident reluctance that, if it had been mine, I should have been tempted to ask him to accept it. But it was not mine. I was only a trustee. So I made no remark, but watched him as he, very deliberately, took off his spectacles and returned them to their case, looking meanwhile, at the floor with an air of deep abstraction. He appeared to be thinking hard, and I was quite curious as to what his next remark would be. A considerable interval elapsed before he spoke again, but at last the remark came, in the form of a question, and very disappointing it was. "You are not berhaps very much interested in relics and reliquaries?"

As a matter of fact, I didn't care two straws for either the one or the other, but there was no need to put it as strongly as that. "We are apt," I replied, "to find a lack of interest in subjects of which we are ignorant." That was a fine sentence. It might have come straight out of Sandford and Merton.

"Zat is vat I sink, too," he rejoined. "Ve do not know, ve do not care. But zere is a very eggeilent liddle book vich egsplains all ze gustoms and zeremonies gonnected vid relics of ze zainte. I should like you to read zat book. Vill you bermit me to send you a gobby vich I haf?"

Of course I said I should be delighted. It was an outrageous falsehood, but what else could I say? "Zen," said he, "I shall haf great pleasure in zending it to you if you vill kindly tell me how I shall address it."

I presented him with my card, which he read very attentively before bestowing it in his pocket-book. "I see," he remarked, "zat you are a doctor of medicine. It is a fine brofession, if one does not too much vorget ze spiritual life in garing for zat of ze body."

In this I acquiesced vaguely, and the conversation drifted into detached commonplaces, finally petering out as we approached Paddock Wood, where my reverend acquaintance bought a newspaper and underwent a total eclipse behind it.

As soon as the train started again, I took up my own paper, and the very first glance at it gave me a shock of surprise that sent all other matters clean out of my mind. It was an advertisement in the column headed "*Personal*" that attracted my attention, an advertisement that commenced with the word "*Missing*" in large type, and went on to offer "*Two Hundred Pounds Reward*". Thus –

MISSING – TWO-HUNDRED POUNDS REWARD

Whereas, on the 14th inst., Dr. Humphrey Jardine disappeared from his home and his usual places of resort, the above reward will be paid to any person who shall give information as to his whereabouts, if alive, or the whereabouts of his body if he is dead. He was last seen at 12:20 pm on the above date in the Hampstead Road, and was then walking towards Euston Road. The missing man is about twenty-six years of age, is somewhat over six-feet in height, of medium complexion, has brown hair, grey eyes, straight nose, and a rather thin face, which is clean-shaved. He was wearing a dark tweed suit, and soft felt hat.

Information should be given to Hector Brodribb, Esquire, 65 New Square, Lincoln's Inn, by whom the above reward will be paid.

Here was a pretty state of affairs: It seemed that while I was placidly taking events as they came, smoking the skipper's tobacco and bottom-fishing with young Ted, my escapade had been producing somewhere a most almighty splash. I read the advertisement again, with a self-conscious grin, and out of it there arose one or two rather curious questions. In the first place, who the deuce was Hector Brodribb? And what concern was I of his? And how came he to know that I was walking down Hampstead Road at 12:20 on the 14th inst.?

I felt very little doubt it was actually Thorndyke who was tweaking the strings of the Brodribbian puppet. But even this left the mystery unsolved. For how did Thorndyke know? This was only the fifth day after my disappearance, and it would seem that there had hardly been time for exhaustive enquiries.

Then another highly interesting fact emerged. The only person who had seen me walk away down Hampstead Road was Sylvia Vyne, whence it followed that Thorndyke, or the mysterious Brodribb, had in some way got into touch with her. And reflecting on this, the mechanism of the enquiry came into view. The connecting-link was, of course, the sketch. Thorndyke had, himself, left the canvas with Mr. Robinson, the artist's-colourman, and he must have called to enquire if I had collected it. Then, he would have been told of my meeting with Miss Vyne, and as she was a regular customer, Mr. Robinson would have been able to give him her address. It was all perfectly simple, the only remarkable feature being the extraordinary promptitude with which the inquiry had been carried out. Which went to show how much more clearly Thorndyke had realized the danger that surrounded me than I had myself.

These various reflections gave me full occupation during the remainder of the journey, extending themselves into consideration of how I should act in the immediate future. My first duty was obviously to report myself to Thorndyke without delay – after which, I persuaded myself, it would be highly necessary for me personally to re-assure the fair, and, perhaps, anxious Sylvia. As to how this was to be managed, I was not quite clear, and in spite of the most profound cogitation, I had reached no conclusion when the train rumbled into Charing Cross Station.

Chapter XII
Miss Vyne

As I stepped out on to the platform with a valedictory bow to my reverend fellow-passenger, my irresolution came to an end and my duty became clear. I must, in common decency, report myself at once to Thorndyke, seeing that he had been at so much trouble on my account. His card, which he had given me, I had unfortunately – or perhaps fortunately, as it turned out – left on the mantelpiece at my lodgings, but I remembered that the address was King's Bench Walk and assumed that I should have no difficulty in finding the house. Nor had I, for, as I entered the Temple by the Tudor Street gate – having overshot my mark on the Embankment – I was almost immediately confronted by a fine brick doorway surmounted by a handsome pediment and bearing legibly painted on its jamb, "First pair, Dr. Thorndyke."

I ascended the "first pair" of stairs, which brought me to an open oak door, massive and iron-bound, and a closed inner door, on the brass knocker of which I executed a flourish that would have done credit to a Belgravian footman, whereupon the door opened and a small man of sedate and clerical aspect regarded me with an air of mild enquiry. "Is Dr. Thorndyke at home?" I asked.

"No, sir. He is at the hospital."

"Dr. Jervis?"

"Is watching a case in the Probate Court. Perhaps you would like to leave a message or write a note. A message in writing would be preferable."

"I don't know that it's necessary," said I. "My name is Jardine, and if you tell him that I called that will probably be enough."

The little man gave me a quick, bird-like glance of obviously heightened interest. "If you are Dr. Humphrey Jardine," said he, "I think a few explanatory words would be acceptable. The Doctor has been extremely uneasy about you. A short note and an appointment, either here or at the hospital, would be desirable."

With this he stepped back, holding the door invitingly open, and I entered, wondering who the deuce this prim little cathedral dean might be, with his persuasive manners and his quaintly precise forms of speech. He placed a chair for me at the table, and, having furnished me with writing materials, stood a little way off, unobtrusively examining me as I wrote. I had finished the short letter, closed it up and addressed it, and was rising to go, when, almost automatically, I took out my watch and glanced at it. Of course it had stopped. "Can you tell me the time?" I asked.

My acquaintance drew out his own watch and replied deliberately, "Seventeen minutes and forty seconds past one." He paused for a moment and then added, "I hope, sir, you have not got any water into your watch."

"I'm afraid I have," I replied, rather taken aback by the rapidity of his diagnosis. "But I'll just wind it up to make sure."

"Oh, don't do that, sir!" he exclaimed. "Allow me to examine it before you disturb the movement." He whipped out of his pocket a watchmaker's eyeglass, which miraculously glued itself to his eye, and, having taken a brief glance at the opened watch, produced a minute pocket screw-driver and a sheet of paper, and, in the twinkling of an eye, as it seemed to me, the paper was covered with the dismembered structures which had in their totality formed my timepiece. "It's quite a small matter, sir," was his report, as he rose from his inspection and pocketed his eye-glass. "Just a speck or two of rust. If you will take my watch for the present, I will have your own in going order by the next time you call."

It seemed an odd transaction, but the little man's manner, though quiet, was so decisive that I took his proffered watch, and, affixing it to my chain, thanked him for his kindness and departed, wondering if it was possible that this prim clerical little person could possibly be the "tame mechanic" of whom Thorndyke had spoken.

Travelling in London was comparatively slow in those days – which, perhaps, was none the worse for a near and pleasant suburb like Hampstead. It had turned half-past two when I let myself into my lodgings with a rather rusty key and almost literally, fell into the arms of Mrs. Blunt. I feared, for a moment, that she was going to kiss me. But that was a false alarm. What she actually did was to seize both my hands and burst into tears with such violence as to cover me with confusion and cause the servant maid to rise like a domestic, and highly inquisitive, apparition from the kitchen stairs. I pacified Mrs. Blunt as well as I could and shook hands heartily with the maid, who thereupon retired, much gratified, to the underworld, whence presently issued an odour suggestive of sacrificial rites, not entirely unconnected with fried onions, and accompanied by an agreeable hissing sound. "But wherever have you been all this time?" Mrs. Blunt asked, as she preceded me up the stairs wiping her eyes, "and why didn't you send us a line just to say that you were all right?"

To this question I made a somewhat guarded answer in so far as the cause of my immersion in the river was concerned, but otherwise I gave her a fairly correct account of my adventures. "Well, well," was her comment, "I suppose it was all for the best, but I do think those sailors might have put you on shore somewhere. Dear me, what a time it has been. I couldn't sleep at night for thinking of you, and what Susan and I have eaten between us wouldn't have kept a sparrow alive. And Dr. Thorndyke, too, I'm sure he was very anxious and worried about you, though he is such a quiet, self-contained man that you can't tell what he is thinking of. And Lord, what a lot of questions he do ask, to be sure!"

"By the way, how did he come to know that I was missing?"

"Why I told him, of course. When you didn't come home that night – which Susan and me sat up for you until three in the morning – I thought there must be something wrong, you being so regular in your habits, so next day, the very first thing, I took his card from your mantelpiece and down I went to his office and told him what had happened. He came up here that evening to see if you had come home, and he's been here every day since to enquire."

"Has he really?"

"Yes. In a hansom cab. Every single day. And so has the young lady."

"The young lady!" I exclaimed. "What young lady?"

Mrs. Blunt regarded me with something as nearly approaching a wink as can be imagined in association with an elderly female of sedate aspect. "Now," she protested slyly, "as if you didn't know! What young lady indeed! Why, Miss Vyne, to be sure, and a very sweet young lady she is, and talked to me just as simple and friendly as if she'd been an ordinary young woman."

"How do you know that she isn't an ordinary young woman?" I asked.

Mrs. Blunt was shocked. "Do you suppose, Mr. Jardine, sir," she demanded severely, "that I who have been a head parlour-maid in a county family where my poor husband was coachman, don't know a real gentlewoman when I meet one? You surprise me, sir."

I apologized hastily and suggested that, as so many kind enquiries had been made, the least I could do was to call and return thanks without delay. "Certainly, sir," Mrs. Blunt agreed, "but not until you have had your lunch. It's a small porterhouse steak," she added alluringly, being evidently suspicious of my intentions. The announcement, seconded by an appetizing whiff from below, reminded me that I was prodigiously sharp set, having tasted no food since I had come ashore at Folkestone, and put the grosser physiological needs of the body, for the moment, in the ascendant. But even as I was devouring the steak with voracious gusto, my mind occupied itself with plans for a strategic descent on the abode of the fair Sylvia and with speculations on the reception I should get, and the noise of water running into the bath formed a pleasing accompaniment to the final mouthfuls.

When I had bathed, shaved, and attired myself in carefully selected garments, I set forth, as smart and spruce as the frog that would a-wooing go – saving the opera hat, which would have been inappropriate to the occasion. The distance to Sylvia's house was not great, and a pair of long and rapidly-moving legs consumed it to such purpose that it was still quite reasonable calling time when I opened the gate of The Hawthorns and gave a modest pull at the bell. My summons was answered by a rather foolish-looking maid, by whom I was informed that Miss Vyne was at home, and when I had given her my name – which she seemed disposed to confuse with that of a well-known edible fish – she ushered me down a passage to a room at the back of the house, and, opening the door, announced me – correctly, I was glad to note, whereupon I assumed an ingratiating smile and entered.

Now there is nothing more disconcerting than a total failure of agreement between anticipation and realization. Unconsciously, I had pictured to myself the easy-mannered, genial Sylvia, seated, perhaps, at an easel or table, working on one of her pictures, and had prepared myself for a reception quite simple, friendly and unembarrassing. Confidently and entirely at my ease, I walked in through the doorway, and there the pleasant vision faded, leaving me with the smile frozen on my face, staring in consternation at one of the most appalling old women that it has ever been my misfortune to encounter.

I am, in general, rather afraid of old women. They are, to my mind, a rather alarming class of creature, but the present specimen exceeded my wildest nightmares. It was not merely that she was seated unnaturally in the exact centre of the room and that she sat with unhuman immobility, moving no muscle and uttering no sound as I entered, though that was somewhat embarrassing. It was her strange, forbidding appearance that utterly shattered my self-possession and seemed to disturb the very marrow in my bones.

She was a most remarkable-looking person. An immense Roman nose, a mop of frizzy grey fringe, and a lofty surmounting cap or head-dress of some kind, suggested that monstrous and unreal bird, the helmeted hornbill, and the bird-like character was heightened by her eyes, which were small and glittering and set in the midst of a multitude of radiating wrinkles.

137

To this most alarming person I made a low bow – and dropped my stick, of which the maid had neglected to relieve me and for which I had found no appointed receptacle. As I stooped hastily to pick it up, my hat slipped from my grasp, and, urged by the devil that possess disengaged hats, instantly rolled under a deep ottoman, whence I had to hook it out with the handle of my stick. I rose, perspiring with embarrassment, to confront that immovable figure, and found the glittering eyes fixed on me attentively but without any sign of expression of human emotion. Haltingly I essayed to stammer out an explanation of my visit. "Er – I have – er – called – " Here I paused to collect my ideas and the old lady watched me stonily without offering any remark – indeed no comment was needed on a statement so self-evidently true. After a brief and hideous silence I began again. "I – er – thought it desirable – er – and in fact necessary and – er – proper to call – er and – "

Here my ideas again petered out and a horrid silence ensued, amidst which I heard a still, emotionless voice murmur, "Yes. And you have accordingly called."

"Exactly," I agreed, grasping eagerly at the slenderest straw of suggestion. "I have called to – er – well, the fact is that my – er – very remarkable absence seemed to call for some explanation, especially as certain enquiries – er – "

At this point I stopped suddenly with a horrible doubt as to whether I was not saying more than was discreet, and the misgiving was intensified by that chilly, calm voice, framing the question, "Enquiries made personally?"

Now this was a facer. I seemed to have put my foot in it at the first lead off. Supposing Sylvia had said nothing about her little visits to Mrs. Blunt? It would never do to give her away to this inquisitorial old waxwork. I endeavoured to temporize. "Well," I stammered, "not exactly made personally to me."

"By letter, perhaps?" the voice suggested in the same even, impassive tone.

"Er – no. Not by letter."

There was a short embarrassing pause, and then the old lady, as if summing up the case, said frigidly, "Not exactly personally and not by letter."

I was so utterly confounded by her judicial manner, her immovable, expressionless face and the hypnotic quality of those glittering eyes, that for the moment I could think of nothing to say. "Don't let me interrupt you," said she after some seconds of agonized silence on my part, whereupon I pulled myself together and made a fresh start. "I should, perhaps, have explained that I have been unavoidably absent from home

138

for some time, and, as I was unable to communicate with my friends, I have, I am afraid, caused them some anxiety. It was this that seemed to make it necessary for me to call and give an account of myself."

She pondered awhile on this statement – if a graven image can be said to ponder – and at length enquired, "You spoke of your friends. Are any of them known to me?"

"Well," I replied, "I was referring more particularly to your daughter."

She continued to regard me fixedly, and, after a brief interval, rejoined, "You are referring to my daughter. But I do not recall the existence of any such person. I think you must be mistaken."

It seemed extremely probable, and I hastened to amend the description. "I beg your pardon. I should have said Miss Vyne. But perhaps she is not at home."

"You are evidently mistaken," was the paralyzing reply. "I am Miss Vyne, and I need not add that I am at home."

"But," I demanded despairingly, "is there not another Miss Vyne?"

"There is not," she answered. "But it is possible that you are referring to Miss *Sylvia* Vyne. Is that so?"

I replied sulkily that it was, and being somewhat nettled by this unnecessary and rather offensive hairsplitting, offered no further remark. How the conversation would have proceeded after this, I cannot even surmise. But it did not proceed at all, for the embarrassing silence was brought to an end by a very agreeable interruption. The door opened softly and for one moment Sylvia herself stood framed in the portal, then, with a little cry, she ran towards me with her hands held out impulsively and the prettiest smile of welcome. "So it is really you!" she exclaimed. "That silly little goose of a maid has only just told me you were here. I am glad to see you. When did you graciously please to descend from the clouds?"

"I arrived home this afternoon, and as soon as I had changed and had lunch I came here to report myself."

"How nice of you," said Sylvia. "I suppose you guessed how anxious we should be?"

"I didn't presume to think that you would actually be anxious about me," I replied, with a furtive eye on the waxwork, "though I knew that you had been kind enough to express an interest in my fate."

"What a cold-bloodedly polite way to put it!" laughed Sylvia. "'Express an interest', indeed! We were most dreadfully worried about you."

To a somewhat friendless man like myself this sympathetic warmth was very delightful, and my pleasure was not appreciably damped when a chill, emotionless voice affirmed, "The use of the first person singular would, I think, be preferable."

Sylvia turned on her aunt with mock ferocity. "Well, really!" she exclaimed. "You are a dreadful impostor, Mopsy, dear! Just listen to her, Dr. Jardine. And if you had only seen what a twitter she was in as the time went on and no news came!"

I gasped, and the hair seemed to stir on my scalp. Mopsy! The name was obviously not applied to me. But could it be – was it possible that such a name could be associated with that terrific old lady? It was inconceivable. It was positively profane! It was almost as if one should presume to address the Deity as "Old Chap". I could hardly believe my ears.

I glanced at her nervously and caught her glittering eye, but the grotesque face was as immovable as everlasting granite – though, indeed, by some ventriloquial magic, the word "Rubbish" managed to disengage itself from her person.

"It isn't rubbish," retorted Sylvia. "It's the plain truth. We were both worried to death about you. And no wonder. Dr. Thorndyke was very quiet and matter-of-fact, but there was no disguising his fear that something dreadful had happened to you. And then there was the advertisement in the papers. Did you see that? Oh, it's nothing to grin about. You've given us all a nice fright, and me especially, because, of course, I naturally thought of that ruffian from whom you rescued me in the lane."

"But he never saw me."

"You don't know. He may have done. At any rate, you owe us an explanation, so, when the tea comes in you shall give us the true story of your adventures. I hope you've let Dr. Thorndyke know about your resurrection."

I reassured her on this point, and as the "goose of a maid" now brought in the tea, I proceeded to "pitch my yarn", as the skipper had expressed it, without those reservations that I had considered necessary in the case of Mrs. Blunt.

The old lady, having been unmasked by Sylvia, developed a slight tendency to thaw. She even condescended, in a rigid and effigean fashion, to consume bread and butter, a proceeding that seemed to me weirdly incongruous, as though one should steal into the British Museum in off hours and find the seated statue of Amenhotep the Third in the act of refreshing itself with a sandwich and a glass of beer. But I was less terrified of her now since I had gathered that a core of warm humanity was somewhere concealed within that grim exterior, and even though her little sparkling eyes were fixed on me immovably, I told my story to the end without flinching.

Sylvia listened to my narration with a rapt attention that greatly flattered my vanity and made me feel like a very Othello, and when I had finished, she regarded me for a while silently and with an air of speculation. "It's a queer affair," she said at length, "and there is a smack of mystery and romance about it that is rather refreshing in these commonplace days. But I don't like it. Adventure is all very well, but there seems to have been a deliberate attempt to make away with you, unless you think it may have been a piece of silly horse-play that went farther than it was meant to."

"That is quite possible," I replied untruthfully – for I didn't think anything of the sort, and only made this evasive answer to avoid raising other and more delicate issues.

"I hope that is the explanation," said Sylvia, "though it sounds rather a lame one. You would know if you had an enemy who might wish to get rid of you. I suppose you don't know of any such person?"

It was a rather awkward question, I didn't want to tell an untruth, but, on the other hand, I knew that Thorndyke would not wish to have my affairs discussed while his investigations were in progress, so I "hedged" once more, replying, quite truthfully, that I was not acquainted with anyone who bore me the slightest ill-will.

My adventures done with, the talk drifted into other channels and presently came round to the little crucifix that had been the occasion of Sylvia's disagreeable experience in the lane. In spite of my confusion, I had noticed, on first entering the room, that the old lady was wearing, suspended from her neck, a small enamelled crucifix, and had instantly identified it and wondered not a little that she should be thus disporting herself in borrowed ornaments, but when Sylvia had arrived, behold, the original crucifix was hanging on its chain from her neck. From time to time during my recital my eyes had wandered from one to the other seeking some difference or variation but finding none, and at length my inquisitive glances caught the younger lady's attention. "I can see. Dr. Jardine," said she, "that you are eaten up with curiosity about the crucifix that my Aunt is wearing. Now confess. Aren't you?"

"I am," I admitted. "When I first came in I naturally thought it was yours. Is it a copy?"

"Certainly not," said Miss Vyne, the elder. "They are duplicates."

Sylvia laughed. "You'd better not talk about copies," said she. "My aunt has only acquired her treasure lately, and she is as proud of it as a peacock, aren't you, dear?"

"The sensations of a peacock," replied Miss Vyne, "are unknown to me. I am very gratified at possessing the ornament."

"Gratified indeed!" said Sylvia. "I consider such vanity most unsuitable to a person of your age. But they are very charming, and there is quite a little story attached to them. My father and a cousin of his – "

"By marriage," interposed Miss Vyne.

"You needn't insist on that," said Sylvia, "as if poor old Vitalia were a person to be ashamed of. Well, my father and this cousin were at a Jesuit school in Belgium – at Louvain, in fact – and among the teachers in the school was an Italian Jesuit named Giglioli. Now the respected Giggley – "

" – oli," interposed Miss Vyne in a severe voice.

" – oli," continued Sylvia, "had formerly been a goldsmith, and the Father Superior, with that keen eye to the main chance which you may have noticed among professed religious, furnished him with a little workshop and employed him in making monstrances, thuribles, and church plate in general. It was he who made these two crucifixes, and, with the Father Superior's consent, he gave one to my father and the other to the cousin as parting gifts on their leaving school. As the boys were inseparable friends, the two crucifixes were made absolute duplicates of one another, with the single exception that each had the owner's name engraved on the back. When my poor father died his crucifix became mine, and a short time ago, his cousin – who is now getting an old man – took a fancy that he would like the two crucifixes to be together once more and gave his to my aunt. So here they are, after all these years, under one roof again."

As she finished speaking, she detached the crucifix from her neck and, having given it to me to examine, proceeded to remove its fellow from the neck of the elder lady – who not only submitted quite passively but seemed to be unaware of the transaction – and handed that to me also.

I laid them side by side in my palm and compared them, but could not detect the slightest difference between them. They were complete duplicates. Each was a Latin cross with trefoiled extremities, wrought from a single piece of gold and enriched with champlevé enamel. The body of the cross was filled with a ground of deep, translucent blue, from which the figure stood out in rather low relief, and the space between each of the trefoils was occupied by a single Greek letter – *Iota* and *Chi* at the top and bottom respectively, and at the ends of the horizontal arm *Alpha* and *Omega*. On turning them over, I saw that the back of each bore an engraved inscription carried across the horizontal arm, that on

142

Sylvia's reading: "*A. M. ROBERTUS, D.G.*", while that on the other read: "*A. M. VITALIS, D.G.*"

"They are very charming little things," I said, as I returned them to Sylvia, "and it was a pretty idea of the old Jesuit to make them both alike for the two friends. I suppose he didn't make any more of them for his other pupils?"

"What makes you ask that?" demanded Sylvia.

"I am thinking of that man in the lane. He must have had some reason for claiming the crucifix as his, one would think, and as these are quite unlike any ordinary commercial jewellery, the suggestion is that the worthy Giglioli was tempted to repeat his successes. What do you think?"

"I think," said Miss Vyne, "that the suggestion is inadmissable. Father Giglioli was an artist, and an artist does not repeat himself."

"I am inclined to agree with my aunt," said Sylvia. "An artist does not care to repeat a design, excepting for a definite purpose, as in the case of these duplicates, especially when the thing designed is intended as a gift."

To this I gave a somewhat qualified assent, though I found the argument far from convincing, and, as I had made a very long visitation, especially for a first call, I now rose to depart. "I hope I may be allowed to come and see you again," I ventured to say as Miss Vyne raised a sort of semaphore arm to my extended hand.

"I see no reason why you should not," she replied judicially. "You seem to be a well-disposed young man, though indiscreet. Good-afternoon."

I bowed deferentially and then, to my gratification, was escorted as far as the garden gate by Sylvia, who evidently wished to gather my impressions of her relative, for, as she let me out, she asked with a mischievous smile, "What do you think of my aunt, Dr. Jardine?"

"She is rather a terrifying old lady," I replied.

Sylvia giggled delightedly. "She does look an awful old griffin, doesn't she? But it's all nonsense, you know. She is really a dear old thing, and as soft as butter."

"Well," I said, "she conceals the fact most perfectly."

"She does. She is a most complete impostor. I'll tell you a secret, Dr. Jardine," Sylvia added in a mysterious whisper, as we shook hands over the gate. "She trades on her nose. I've told her so. Her nose is her fortune, and she plays it for all it's worth. Goodbye – or rather, *au revoir*! For you've promised to come and see us again."

With a bright little nod she turned and ran up the garden path, still chuckling softly at her joke, and I wended homewards, very well pleased with the circumstances of my visit, despite the soul-shaking incidents with which it had opened.

Chapter XIII
A Mysterious Stranger

On the following morning I betook myself to the hospital, intending to call later in the day at Dr. Thorndyke's chambers, but that visit turned out to be unnecessary, for, as I ran my eye over the names on the attendance board in the entrance hall, I saw that Thorndyke was in the building, although it was not the day on which he lectured. I found him, as I had expected, in the museum and was greeted with a hearty grip of the hand and a welcome, the warmth of which gratified me exceedingly.

"Well, Jardine," he said, "you've given us all a pretty fine shake up. I have never been more relieved in my life than I was when my man Polton gave me your note. But you seem to have had another fairly close shave. What a fellow you are, to be sure! You seem to be as tenacious of life as the proverbial cat."

"So that little archbishop is your man Polton, is he?"

"Yes, and a most remarkable man, Jardine, and simply invaluable to me, though he ought to be in a very different position. But I think he is quite happy with me – especially now that he has got your watch to experiment on. You will see that watch again some day, when he has rated it to half-a-second. And meanwhile let us go into the curator's room and reconstitute your adventures."

The curator's room was empty at the moment – empty, that is to say, so far as human denizens were concerned. Otherwise it was decidedly full, the usual wilderness of glass jars, sepulchral slate tanks, bones in all stages of preparation, and unfinished specimens, being supplemented by that all-pervading, unforgettable odour peculiar to curator's rooms, compounded of alcohol and mortality, and suggesting a necropolis for deceased dipsomaniacs. Thorndyke seated himself on a well-polished stool by the work-bench, and, motioning me to another, bade me speak on. Which I did in exhaustive detail, giving him a minute history of my experiences from the time of my parting from Sylvia to the present moment, not omitting my encounter with Mrs. Samway and the clerical gentleman in the train.

He listened to my narrative in his usual silent, attentive fashion, making no comments and asking no questions until I had finished, when he cross-examined me on one or two points of detail. "With regard to Mrs. Samway," he asked, "did you gather that she was crossing by the Boulogne boat?"

"I inferred that she was, but she said nothing on the subject."

He nodded and then asked, "Do I understand that you never saw your assailant at all?"

"I never got the slightest glimpse of him – in fact I could not say whether the person who attacked me was a man or a woman excepting that the obvious strength and the method of attack suggest a man."

To this he made no reply, but sat a while absorbed in thought. It was evident that he was deeply interested in the affair, not only on my account but by reason of the curious problems that it offered for solution. Indeed, his next remark was to this effect. "It is a most singular case, Jardine," he said. "So much of it is perfectly clear, and yet so much more is unfathomable mystery. But just now, the speculative interest is overshadowed by the personal. I am rather doubtful as to what we ought to do. It almost looks as if you ought not to be at large."

"I hope, sir, you don't suggest shutting me up," I exclaimed with a grin.

"That was in my mind," he answered. "You are evidently in considerable danger, and you are not as cautious as you ought to be."

"I shall be mighty cautious after this experience," I rejoined, "and you have yourself implied that I have nine lives."

"Even so," he retorted, "you have played away a third of them pretty rapidly. If you are not more careful of the other six, I shall have to put you somewhere out of harm's way. Do, for goodness sake, Jardine, keep away from unpopulated places and see that no stranger gets near enough to have you at a disadvantage."

I promised him to keep a constant watch for suspicious strangers and to avoid all solitary neighbourhoods and ill-lighted thoroughfares, and shortly after this we separated to go our respective ways, he back to the museum and I to the surgical wards

For some time after this, the record of my daily life furnishes nothing but a chronicle of small beer. I had resumed pretty regular attendance at the hospital, setting forth from my lodgings in the morning and returning thither as the late afternoon merged into evening, taking the necessary exercise in the form of the long walk to and from the hospital, and keeping close indoors at night. It began to look as though my adventures were at an end and life were settling down to the old familiar jog-trot.

And yet the beer was not quite so small as it looked. Coming events cast their shadows before them, but often enough those shadows wear a shape ill-defined and vague, and so creep on unnoticed. Thus it was in these days of apparent inaction, though even then there were certain little happenings at which I looked askance. Such an episode occurred within a few days of my return, and gave me considerable food for thought. I had climbed on to the yellow 'bus in the Tottenham Court Road and was seated on the top, smoking my pipe, when, as we passed up the Hampstead Road, I noticed a woman looking into the window of Mr. Robinson, the artist's-colourman. Something familiar or distinctive in the pose of the figure made me glance a second time, and then I think my eyes must have grown more and more round with astonishment as the 'bus gradually drew me out of range. For the woman was undoubtedly Mrs. Samway.

It was really a most surprising affair. This good lady seemed to be ubiquitous, to fly hither and thither and drop from the clouds as if she were the possessor of a magic carpet. Apparently she had not gone to Boulogne after all, or if she had, her stay on the Continent must have been uncommonly short. But if she had not crossed on the boat, what was she doing in Folkestone? It was all very well to say that she had as much right to be in Folkestone as I had. That was true enough, but it was a lame conclusion and no explanation at all.

It was my custom, as I have said, to walk from my lodgings to the hospital, a distance of some five miles, but this was practicable only in fine weather. On wet days I took the tram from the Duke of St. Alban's, and beguiled the slow journey by reading one of my text-books and observing the manners and customs of my fellow-passengers. Such a day was the one that followed the re-appearance of Mrs. Samway. A persistent drizzle put my morning walk out of the question and sent me reluctant but resigned to seek the shelter of the tram, where having settled myself with a volume of Gould's *Surgical Diagnosis*, I began to read to the accompaniment of the monotonous rhythm of the horses' hoofs and the sleepy jingle of their bells. From time to time I looked up from my book to take a glance at the other occupants of the steamy interior, and on each occasion that I did so, I caught the eye of my opposite neighbor roving over my person as if taking an inventory of my apparel. Whenever he caught my eye, he immediately looked away, but the next time I glanced up I was sure to find him once more engaged in a leisurely examination of me.

There was nothing remarkable in this. People who sit opposite in a public vehicle unconsciously regard one another, as I was doing myself, but when I had met my neighbour's eye a dozen times or more, I began to grow annoyed at his persistent inspection, and finally, shutting up my book, proceeded to retaliate in kind.

This seemed to embarrass him considerably. Avoiding my steady gaze, his eyes flitted to and fro, passing restlessly from one part of the vehicle to another, and then it was that my medical eye noted a fact that

147

gave an intrinsic interest to the inspection. The man had what is called a *nystagmus*, that is, a peculiar oscillatory movement of the eyeball. As his eyes passed quickly from object to object, they did not both come to rest instantaneously, but the right eye stopped with a sort of vertical stagger as if the bearings were loose. The condition is not a very common one, and the one-sided variety is decidedly rare. It is usually associated with some defect of vision or habitual strain of the eye-muscles, as in miners' nystagmus, whence my discovery naturally led to a further survey and speculation as to the cause of the condition in the present case.

The man was obviously not a miner. His hands – with a cigarette stain, as I noticed, on the left middle finger – were much too delicate, and he had not in any way the appearance of a labourer. Then the spasm must be due to some defect of eyesight. Yet he was not near-sighted, for, as we passed a church at some distance, I saw him glance out through the doorway at the clock and compare it with his watch, and again, I noticed that he took out his watch with his left hand. Then perhaps he had a blind eye or unequal vision in the two eyes, this seemed the most likely explanation, and I had hardly proposed it to myself when the chance was given to me to verify it. Confused by my persistent examination of him, my unwilling patient suddenly produced a newspaper from his pocket and, clapping a pair of pince-nez on his nose, began to read. Those pince-nez gave me the required information, for I could see that one glass was strongly convex while the other was nearly plane.

The question of my friend's eyesight being disposed of, I began to debate the significance of that stain of the left middle finger. Was he left-handed? It did not follow, though it seemed likely, and then I found myself noting the manner in which he held his paper, until, becoming suddenly conscious of the absurdity of the whole affair, I impatiently picked up my book and reverted to the diagnosis of renal calculus. I was becoming, I reflected disparagingly, as inquisitive as Thorndyke himself, from whom I seemed to have caught some infection that impelled me thus to concern myself with the trifling peculiarities of total strangers.

The trivial incident would probably have faded from my recollection but for another, equally trivial, which occurred a day or two later. I was returning home by way of Tottenham Court Road and had nearly reached the crossing at the north end when I suddenly remembered that I had come to the last of my note-books. The shop at which I obtained them was in Gower Street, hard by, and as the thought of the books occurred to me, I turned abruptly and, running across the road, strode quickly down a by-street that led to the shop.

As I came out into Gower Street, I noticed a small, but rapidly augmenting crowd on the pavement, and, elbowing my way through, found at its centre a man lying on the ground, writhing in the convulsions of an epileptic fit. I proceeded to ward off the well-meant attentions of the usual excited bystanders, who were pulling open his hands and trying to sit him up, and had thrust the corner of a folded newspaper between his teeth to prevent him from biting his tongue when a constable arrived on the scene, upon which, as the officer bore on his sleeve the badge of the St. John's Ambulance Society, I gave him a few directions and began to back out of the crowd.

At this moment, I became aware of a pressure behind me and a suspicious fumbling, strongly suggestive of the presence of a pick-pocket. Instantly, I turned right about and directed a searching look at the people behind me, and especially at a bearded, nondescript person who seemed also to be backing out of the crowd. He gave me a single, quick glance as I followed him through the press and then averted his eyes, and as he did so, I noticed, with something of a start, that his right eye came to rest with a peculiar, rapid up-and-down shake. He had, in fact, a right-sided nystagmus.

The coincidence naturally struck me with some force. A nystagmus is not, as I have said, a very common condition, one-sided nystagmus is actually a rare one, and, of the one-sided instances, only some fifty-per-cent will affect the right eye. The coincidence was therefore quite a notable one, but had it any particular bearing? I had a half-formed inclination to follow the man, but he had not actually picked my pocket or done any other overt act, and one could hardly follow a person merely because he happened to suffer from an uncommon nervous affection.

The man was now walking up the street, briskly, but without manifest hurry, looking straight before him and swinging his stick with something of a flourish. I watched him speculatively, as I walked in the same direction, and then suddenly realized that he was carrying his stick in his left hand, and carrying it, too, with the unmistakable ease born of habit. Then he was left-handed! And here was another coincidence, not a remarkable one in itself, but, when added to the other, so singular and striking that I insensibly quickened my pace.

As my acquaintance reached the corner of the Euston Road, an omnibus stopped to put down a passenger. It was about to move on when he raised his stick, and, following it, stepped on the footboard and mounted to the roof. I was undecided what to do. Should I follow him? And, if so, to what purpose? He would certainly notice me if I did and be on his guard, so that I should probably have my trouble for nothing and possibly look like a fool into the bargain. And while I was thus standing irresolute at the corner, the omnibus rumbled away westward and decided the question for me.

I am not, as the reader may have gathered, a particularly cautious man or much given to suspicion. But recent events had made me a good deal more wary and had taught me to look with less charity on chance fellow creatures, and this left-handed person with the nystagmus occupied my thoughts to no small extent during the next day or two. Was he the man whom I had seen in the tram? Apparently not. The latter had been clean-shaven and dressed neatly in the style of a clerk or ordinary City man, whereas the former wore a full beard and was shabby, almost beyond the verge of respectability. As to their respective statures, I could not judge, as I had seen the one man seated and the other standing, but, superficially, they were not at all alike, and, in all probability they were different persons.

But this conclusion was not at all inevitable. When I reflected on the matter, I saw that the resemblances and differences did not balance. The two men resembled one another in qualities that were inherent and unalterable, but they differed in qualities that were superficial and subject to change. A man cannot assume or cast off a nystagmus, but he can put on a false beard. A left-handed man may endeavour to conceal his peculiarity, but the superior deftness of the habitually used hand will make itself apparent in spite of his efforts, whereas he can make any alterations in his clothing that he pleases. And thus reflecting, the suspicion grew more and more strong that the two men might very well have been one and the same person, and that it would be discreet to keep a bright look-out for a left-handed man with a right-sided nystagmus.

During all this time I had seen nothing of my new friend Miss Sylvia. But I had by no means forgotten her. Without wishing to exaggerate my feelings, I may say that I had taken a strong liking to that very engaging young lady. She was a pleasant, easy-mannered girl, evidently good-tempered, and very frank and simple, a girl – as Mr. Sparkler would have said – "with no by-God nonsense about her". Her tastes ran along very similar lines to my own, and she was clever enough to be a quite interesting companion. Then it was evident that she liked me – which was in itself an attraction, to say nothing of the credit that it reflected on her taste – and, in a perfectly modest way, she had made no secret of the fact. And finally, she was exceptionally good-looking. Now people may say, as they do, that beauty is only skin deep – which is perfectly untrue, by the way – but even so, one is more concerned with the skins of one's fellow creatures than with their livers or vermiform appendices. The contact of persons, as of things, occurs at their respective surfaces.

From which it will be gathered that I was only allowing a decent interval to elapse before repeating my visit to The Hawthorns – indeed, I was beginning to think that a sufficient interval had already passed and to contemplate seriously my second call, when my intentions were forestalled by Sylvia herself. Returning home one Friday evening, I found on my mantelpiece a short letter from her, enclosing a ticket for an exhibition of paintings and sculpture at a gallery in Leicester Square, and mentioning – incidentally – that she proposed to visit the show on the following morning in order to see the works by a good light, which seemed such an eminently rational proceeding in these short winter days, that I determined instantly to follow her example and get the advantage of the morning light myself.

I acted on this decision with such thoroughness that, when I arrived at the gallery, I found the attendant in the act of opening the doors, and, for nearly half-an-hour I was in sole possession of the premises. Then, by twos and threes, other visitors began to straggle in, and among them Sylvia, looking very fresh and dainty and obviously pleased to see me. "I am glad you were able to come," she said, as we shook hands. "I thought you would, somehow. It is so much nicer to have someone to talk over the pictures with, isn't it?"

"Much more interesting," I agreed. "I have been taking a preliminary look around and have already accumulated quite a lot of profound observations to discharge at you as occasion offers. Shall we begin at number one?"

We began at number one and worked our way methodically picture by picture, round the room, considering each work attentively with earnest discussion and a wealth of comment. As the morning wore on, visitors arrived in increasing numbers, until the two large rooms began to be somewhat inconveniently crowded. We had made a complete circuit of the pictures and were about to turn to the sculpture, which occupied the central floor space, when Sylvia touched me on the arm. "Let us sit down for a minute," said she. "I want to speak to you."

I led her to one of the large settees that disputed the floor-space with the busts and statuettes, and, somewhat mystified by her serious tone and by the rather agitated manner, which I now noticed for the first time, seated myself by her side. "What is it?" I asked.

She looked anxiously round the room, and, leaning towards me, said in a low tone, "Have you noticed a man who has been keeping near us and listening to our conversation?"

"No, I haven't," I replied. "If I had I would have given him a hint to keep farther off. But there's nothing in it, you know. In picture galleries it is very usual for people to hang about and try to overhear criticisms. This man may be interested in the exhibits."

"Yes, I know. But I don't think this person was so much interested in the exhibits. He didn't look at the pictures, he looked at us. I caught his eye several times reflected in the picture-glasses, and once or twice I saw him looking most attentively at this crucifix of mine. That was what really disturbed me. I wish, now, that I hadn't unbuttoned my coat."

"So do I. You will have to leave that crucifix at home if it attracts so much undesirable attention. Which is the man? Is he in this room?"

"No, I don't see him now. I expect he has gone into the next room."

"Then let us go there, too, and if you will point him out to me, I will pay him back in his own coin."

We rose and made our way to the door of communication, and, as we passed into the second room, Sylvia grasped my arm nervously. "There he is – don't let him see us looking at him! He is sitting on the settee at the farther end of the room."

It was impossible to make a mistake since the settee held only a single person, a fairly well-dressed, ordinary-looking man, rather swarthy and foreign in appearance, with a small waxed moustache. He was sitting nearly opposite the entrance door and seemed, at the moment to be reading over the catalogue, which he held open on his knee, but, as he looked up almost at the moment when we entered, I turned my back to him and continued my inspection with the aid of the reflection in a picture-glass. "He is probably a journalist," I said. "You see he is scribbling some notes on the blank leaves of his catalogue, probably some of your profound criticisms, which will appear, perhaps to-morrow morning, clothed in super-technical jargon, in a daily paper."

Here I paused suddenly, for I had made a rather curious observation. The reflection in a mirror is, as everybody knows, reversed laterally, so that the right hand of a person appears to be the left, and vice versa. But in the present case, no reversal seemed to have taken place. The figure in the reflection was writing with his right hand. Obviously, then, the real person was writing with his left.

This put a rather different aspect on the affair. Up to the present, I had been disposed to think that Sylvia had been unduly disturbed, for there are plenty of ill-bred bounders to be met in any public place who will stare a good-looking girl out of countenance. But now my suspicions were all awake. It is true that left-handed men are as common as blackberries, but still – "Can you tell me, Miss Vyne," I asked, as we worked our way towards the other end of the room, "if this man is at all like the one who frightened you so in Millfield Lane?"

"No, he is not. I am sure of that. The man in the lane was a good deal taller and thinner."

"Well," said I, "whoever he is, I want to have a good look at him, and the best plan will be to turn our attention to the sculpture. Shall we go and look at that rather remarkable pink bust? That will give our friend a chance of another stare at you, and, if he doesn't take it, I will go and inspect him where he sits."

The bust to which I had referred was executed in a curious, rose-tinted marble, very crystalline and translucent, a material that suited the soft, girlish features of its subject admirably. It stood on an isolated pedestal quite near the settee on which the suspicious stranger was sitting, and I hoped that our presence might lure him from his retreat.

"I don't think," I said, taking up a position with my back to the settee, "that I have ever seen any marble quite like this. Have you?"

"No," replied Sylvia. "It looks like coarse lump sugar stained pink. And how very transparent it is – too transparent for most subjects."

Here she gave a quick, nervous glance at me, and I was aware of a shadow thrown by some person standing behind me. Had our friend risen to the bait already?

I continued the conversation in good audible tones. "Very awkward these isolated pedestals would be for slovenly artists who scamp the back of their work."

With this remark I moved round the pedestal as if to examine the back of the bust, and Sylvia followed. The move brought us opposite the person who had been standing behind me, and, sure enough, it was the gentleman from the settee. I continued to talk – rather blatantly, I fear – commenting on the careful treatment of the hair and the backs of the ears, and meanwhile took an occasional swift glance at the man opposite. He appeared to be gazing in wrapt admiration at the bust, but his glance, too, occasionally wandered, and when it did, the "point of fixation", as the oculists would express it, was Sylvia's crucifix, which was still uncovered.

Presently I ventured to take a good, steady look at him and was for a few moments unobserved. His left eye moved, as I could see, quite smoothly and evenly from point to point, but the right, at each change of position, gave a little, rapid, vertical oscillation. Suddenly he became aware of my, now undisguised, inspection of him, and, immediately, the oscillation became much more marked, as is often the case with these spasmodic movements. Perhaps he was conscious of the fact, at any rate, he turned his head away and then moved off to examine a statuette that stood near the middle of the room.

I looked after him, wondering what I ought to do. That he was the man whom I had seen on the two previous occasions I had not the slightest doubt, although I was still unable to identify his features or anything about him excepting the nystagmus and the left-handed condition. But there could be no question that he was the same man, and this very variability in his appearance only gave a more sinister significance to the affair, pointing clearly, as it did, to careful and efficient disguise. Evidently he had been, and still was, shadowing me, and, what was still worse, he seemed to be taking a most undesirable interest in Sylvia. And yet what could I do? My small knowledge of the law suggested that shadowing was not a criminal act unless some unlawful intent could be proved. As to punching the fellow's head – which was what I felt most inclined to do – that would merely give rise to disagreeable, and perhaps dangerous, publicity.

"My lord is pleased to meditate," Sylvia remarked at length, breaking in upon my brown study.

"I beg your pardon," I exclaimed. "The fact is I was wondering what we had better do next. Do you want to see anything else?"

"I should rather like to see the outside of the building," she answered. "That man has made me quite nervous."

"Then we will go at once, and we won't sign the visitor's book."

I led her to the door, and, as we rapidly descended the carpeted stairs, I considered once more what it were best to do. Had I been alone I would have kept our watcher in view and done a little shadowing on my own account, but Sylvia's presence made me uneasy. It was of the first importance that this sinister stranger should not learn where she lived. The only reasonable course seemed to be to give him the slip if possible. "What did you make of that man?" Sylvia asked when we were outside in the square. "Don't you think he was watching us?"

"Yes, I do. And I may say that I have seen him before."

She turned a terrified face to me and asked, "You don't think he is the wretch who pushed you into the river?"

Now this was exactly what I did think, but it was not worthwhile to say so. Accordingly I temporized. "It is impossible to say. I never saw that man, you know. But I have reason for thinking that this fellow is keeping a watch on me, and it occurs to me that, if he appears still to be following us, I had better put you into a hansom and keep my eye on him until you are out of sight."

"Oh, I'm not going to agree to that," she replied with great decision. "I don't suppose that my presence is much protection to you, but still, you are safer while we are together, and I'm not going to leave you."

This settled the matter. Of course she was quite right. I was much safer while she was with me, and if she refused to go off alone, we must make our escape together. I looked up the square as we turned out of it towards the Charing Cross Road, but could see no sign of our follower, and, as we walked on at a good pace, I hoped that we might get clear away. But I was not going to take any chances. Before turning homewards, I decided to walk sharply some distance in an easterly direction and then see if there was any sign of pursuit, for my previous experiences of this good gentleman led me to suspect that he was by no means without skill and experience in the shadowing art.

We walked down to Charing Cross and turned eastward along the north side of the Strand. I had chosen this thoroughfare as offering a good cover to a pursuer, who could easily keep out of sight among the crowd of wayfarers who thronged the pavement for the first question to be settled was whether we were or were not being shadowed. "Where are we going now?" Sylvia asked.

"We are going up Bedford Street," I answered. "There is a book shop on the right-hand side where we can loiter unobtrusively and keep a look-out. If we see nobody, we will try one of the courts off Maiden Lane where we should be certain to catch anyone who was following. But we will try the bookstall first because, if our friend is in attendance, I have a rather neat plan for getting rid of him."

We accordingly made our way to the bookstall in Bedford Street and began systematically to look through the second-hand volumes, and as we pored over an open book, we were able to keep an effective watch on the end of the street and the Strand beyond. Our vigil was not a long one. We had been at the stall less than a minute when Sylvia whispered to me, "Do you see that man looking in the shop on the farther side of the Strand?"

"Yes," I replied, "I have noticed him. He has only just arrived, and I fancy he is our man. If he is, he will probably go into the doorway so as not to have to keep his back to us."

Almost as I spoke, the man moved into the deep doorway as if to inspect the end of the shop window, and Sylvia exclaimed, "I'm sure that is the man. I can see his profile now."

There could be no doubt of the man's identity, and, at this moment, as if to clinch the matter, he took out a cigarette and lighted it, striking the match with his left hand. "Come along," said I. "We will now try my little plan for getting rid of him. We mustn't seem to hurry."

We sauntered up to the corner of Maiden Lane and there stood for a few moments looking about us. Then we strolled across to the farther side of Chandos Street, and, as soon as we were out of sight of our follower, crossed the road and slipped in at the entrance to the Civil Service Stores. Passing quickly through the provision department, we halted at the glazed doors, from which we could look out through the Bedford Street entrance. "There he is!" exclaimed Sylvia. And there he

155

was, sure enough, walking rather quickly up the east side of Bedford Street. "Now," said I, "let us make a bolt for it. This way."

We darted out through the china, furniture, and ironmongery departments, across the whole width of the building and out of the Agar Street entrance, where we immediately crossed into King William Street, turned down Adelaide Street, shot through the alley by St. Martin's Church, and came out opposite the National Portrait Gallery just as a yellow omnibus was about to start. We sprang into the moving vehicle, and, as it rumbled away into the Charing Cross Road, we kept a sharp watch on the end of King William Street. But there was no sign of our pursuer. We had got rid of him for the present, at any rate. "Don't you think," said Sylvia, "that he will suspect that we went into the Stores?"

"I have no doubt he will, and that is where we have him. He can't come away and leave the building unsearched. Most probably he is, at this very moment, racing madly up and down the stairs and trying to watch the three entrances at the same time."

Sylvia chuckled gleefully. "It has been quite good fun," she said, "but I am glad we have shaken him off. I think I shall stay indoors for a day or two and paint, and I hope you'll stay indoors, too. And that reminds me that I am out of Heyl's white. I must call in at Robinson's and get a pound tube. Do you mind? It won't delay us more than a few minutes."

Now I would much rather have gone straight on to Hampstead, for our unknown attendant certainly knew the whereabouts of my lodgings and might follow us when he failed to find us in the stores. Moreover, I had, of late, given the neighbourhood of the artist's-colourman's shop a rather wide berth, having seen Mrs. Samway from afar once or twice, thereabouts, and having surmised that she tended to haunt that particular part of the Hampstead Road. But the fresh supply of flake white seemed to be a necessity, so I made no objection, and we accordingly alighted opposite the shop and entered. Nevertheless, while Sylvia was making her purchase, I stood near the glass door and kept a watchful eye on the street. When a tram stopped a short distance away, I glanced quickly over its passengers, as well as I could, though without observing anyone who might have been our absent friend. But just as it was about to move on, I saw a woman run out from the pavement and enter, and though I got but an indifferent view of her, I felt an uncomfortable suspicion that the woman was Mrs. Samway.

Looking back, I do not quite understand why I had avoided this woman or why I now looked with distaste on the fact that she was travelling in our direction. She was a pleasant-spoken, intelligent person, and I had no dislike of her, nor any cause for dislike. Perhaps it was the recollection of the offence that she had given Sylvia in this very shop, but a short time since, that made me unwilling to encounter her now in Sylvia's company. At any rate, whatever the cause may have been, throughout the otherwise, pleasant journey, and in spite of an animated and interesting conversation, the thought of Mrs. Samway continually recurred, and this notwithstanding that I kept a constant, unobtrusive look-out for the mysterious spy who might, even now, be hovering in our rear.

We alighted from the tram at the Duke of St. Alban's and made our way to North End by way of the Highgate Ponds. As we crossed the open fields and the Heath, I turned at intervals to see if there was any sign of our being followed, but no suspicious-looking person appeared in sight, though on two separate occasions, I noticed a woman ahead of us, and walking in much the same direction, turn round and look our way. There was no reason, however, to suppose that she was looking at us, and, in any case, she was too far ahead to be recognizable. At last, somewhere in the neighbourhood of the Spaniard's Road, she finally disappeared, possibly into the hollow beyond, and I saw no more of her.

At the gate of The Hawthorns, I delivered up the heavy tube of paint, and thus, as it were, formally brought our little outing to an end, and as we shook hands Sylvia treated me to a parting exhortation. "Now do take care of yourself and keep out of harm's way," she urged. "You are so large, you see," she added with a smile, "and such a very conspicuous object that you ought to take special precautions. And you must come and see us again quite soon. I assure you my aunt is positively pining for another conversation with you. Why shouldn't you drop in to-morrow and have tea with us?"

Now this very idea had already occurred to me, so I hastened to close with the invitation, and then, as she retired up the path with another "Good-bye" and a wave of the hand, I turned away and walked back towards the Heath.

For some minutes I strode on, across furzy hollows or over little hills, traversed by sunken, sandy paths, occupying myself with thoughts of the pleasant, friendly girl whom I had just left and reflections on the strange events of the morning. Presently I mounted a larger hill, on which was perched a little, old-fashioned house. Skirting the wooden fence that enclosed it, I turned the corner and saw before me, at a distance of some forty yards, a rough, rustic seat. On that seat a woman was sitting, and somehow, when I looked at her and noted the graceful droop of the figure, it was without any feeling of surprise – almost that of realized expectation – that I recognized Mrs. Samway.

Chapter XIV
A Lonely Woman

If I had had any intention of avoiding Mrs. Samway, that intention must inevitably have been frustrated, for her recognition was as instantaneous as my own. Almost as I turned the corner, she looked up and saw me, and a few moments later, she rose and advanced in my direction, so that, to an onlooker it would have appeared as if we had met by appointment. There was obviously nothing for it but to look as pleased as I could manage at such short notice, which I did, shaking her hand with hypocritical warmth. "And I suppose. Dr. Jardine," said she, "you are thinking what a very odd coincidence it is that we should happen to meet here?"

"Oh, I don't know that it is so very odd. I live about here and I understood you to say that you often come up to the Heath. At any rate, our last meeting was a good deal more odd."

"Yes, indeed. But the truth is that this is not a coincidence at all. I may as well confess that I came here deliberately with the intention of waylaying you."

This very frank statement took me aback considerably, so much so that I could think of no appropriate remark beyond mumbling something to the effect that it was very flattering of her.

"I have been trying," she continued, "to get a few words with you for some time past, but, although I have lurked in your line of march in the most shameless manner, I have always managed to miss you. I thought, from what you told me, that you passed Robinson's shop on your way to the hospital."

"So I do," I replied mendaciously, for I could hardly tell her that I had lately taken to shooting up bystreets with the express purpose of avoiding that particular stretch of pavement.

"It's rather curious that I never happened to meet you there. However, I didn't, so, to-day, I determined to take the bull by the horns and catch you here."

This last statement, like the former ones, gave me abundant matter for reflection. How the deuce had she managed to catch me here? I supposed that she had seen Sylvia and me in the Hampstead Road and had guessed that we were coming on to this neighbourhood. That was a case of feminine intuition, which, like the bone-setter's skill, is a wonderful thing – when it comes off (and when it doesn't one isn't expected to notice the fact). Then she had gone on ahead – still guessing at our final destination – and kept us in sight while keeping out of view herself. It was not so very easy to understand and not at all comfortable to think of, for there was a disagreeable suggestion that she had somehow ascertained Sylvia's place of abode beforehand. And yet – well, the whole affair was rather mysterious. "You don't ask why it was that I wanted to waylay you," she said, at length, as I made no comment on her last statement.

"There is an old saying," I replied, "that one shouldn't look a gift-horse in the mouth."

"That is very diplomatic," she retorted with a laugh. "But I daresay your knowledge of women makes the question unnecessary."

"My knowledge of women," said I, "might be put into a nutshell and still leave plenty of room for the nut and a good, fat maggot besides."

"Then I must beware of you. The man who professes to know nothing of women is the most deep and dangerous class of person. But there is one item of knowledge that you seem to have acquired. You seem to know that women like to have pretty things said to them."

"If you call that knowledge," said I, "you must apply the same name to the mere blind impulse that leads a spider to spin a nice, symmetrical web."

She laughed softly and looked up at me with an expression of amused reflection. "I am thinking," she said, "what a very fine symmetrical web you would spin if you were a spider."

"Possibly," I replied. "But it looks as if the role of bluebottle were the one that is being marked out for me."

"Oh! Not a bluebottle. Dr. Jardine. It doesn't suit you at all. If you must make a comparison, why not say a Goliath beetle, and have something really dignified – and not so very inappropriate."

"Well, then, a Goliath beetle, if you prefer it – not that he would look very dignified, kicking his heels in the elegant web of the superlatively elegant feminine spider."

"Oh, but that isn't pretty of you at all, Dr. Jardine. In fact it is quite horrid, and unfair, too, because you are trying to get the information without asking a direct question."

"What question am I supposed to ask?"

"You needn't ask any. I will take pity on your masculine pride and tell you why I have been lying in wait for you, although I daresay you have guessed. The truth is, I am simply devoured by curiosity."

"Concerning what?

"Now, how can you ask? Just think! One day I meet you in the Hampstead Road, going about your ordinary business, apparently a fixture, at least for months. A few days later, a hundred miles from London, I feel myself suddenly seized from behind, I turn round and there are you with tragedy and adventure written large all over you."

"I thought the tragedy was rather on your side, and so did the ancient mariner with the black bottle and the tea cup. But – "

"I don't wish to discuss the views of that well-meaning old brute. I want an explanation. I want to know how you came to be in Folkestone and in that extraordinary condition. I am sure something strange must have happened to you."

"Why? Haven't I as much right to be in Folkestone as you have?"

"That is mere evasion. When I see a man who is usually rather carefully and very neatly dressed, walking in the streets of a seaport town without hat or a stick and with a collar that looks as if it had been used to clean out a saucepan, and great stains on his clothes, I am justified in inferring that something unusual has happened to him."

"I didn't think you had noticed my négligé get-up."

"At the time I did not. I was very upset and agitated, I had just had a lot of worry and was compelled to cross to France at a moment's notice, and then there was that horrible horse, and the sudden way that you seized me and then got knocked down, and the – "

"The ancient mariner."

"Yes, the ancient mariner, and the knowledge that I was behaving like an idiot and couldn't help it – though you were so nice and kind to me. So you see, I was hardly conscious of what was happening at the time. But afterwards, when I had recovered my wits a little, I recalled the astonishing figure that you made, and I have been wondering ever since what had happened to you. I assure you. Dr. Jardine, you looked as if you might have swum to Folkestone."

"Did I, by Jove!" I exclaimed with a laugh. "Well, appearances weren't so very deceptive. The fact is that I had swum part of the way."

She looked at me incredulously. "Whatever do you mean?" she asked.

"I mean that you are now looking on a modern and strictly up-to-date edition of Sinbad the Sailor."

"That isn't very explanatory. But I suppose it isn't meant to be. It is just a preliminary stimulant to whet my appetite for marvels, and a most unnecessary one, I can assure you, for I am absolutely agape with curiosity. Do go on. Tell me exactly what had happened to you."

Now the truth is that I had already said rather more than was strictly discreet and would gladly have drawn in my horns. But I had evidently

160

let myself in for some sort of plausible explanation, and a lack of that enviable faculty that enables its possessor to tell a really convincing and workmanlike lie, condemned me to a mere unimaginative adherence to the bald facts, though I did make one slight and amateurish effort at prevarication.

"You want a detailed log of Sinbad's voyages, do you?" said I. "Then you shall have it. We will begin at the beginning. The port of departure was the Embankment somewhere near Cleopatra's Needle. I was leaning over the parapet, staring down at the water like a fool, when some practical joker came along, and, apparently thinking it would be rather funny to give me a fright, suddenly lifted me off my feet. But my jocose friend hadn't allowed for the top-heaviness of a person of my height, and, before you could say 'knife', I had slipped from his hold and taken a most stylish header into the water. Fortunately for me, a barge happened at the moment to be towing past, and, when I had managed to haul myself on board, I fell into the arms of a marine species of Good Samaritan, who, not having a supply of the orthodox oil and wine, proceeded to fill me up with hot gin and water, which is distinctly preferable for internal application. Then the Samaritan aforesaid clothed me in gorgeous marine raiment and stowed me in a cupboard to sleep off the oil and wine, which I did after some sixteen hours, and then awoke to find our good ship on the broad bosom of the ocean. And so – not to weary you with the incidents of the voyage – I came to Folkestone, where I found a beautiful lady endeavouring, very unsuccessfully, to hypnotize a run-away horse, and so to the adventure of the tarred nets and the ancient mariner with the black bottle."

Mrs. Samway smiled a little consciously as I mentioned the last incidents, but the smile quickly faded and left a deeply thoughtful expression on her face. "You take it all very calmly," said she, "but it seems to me to have been a rather terrible experience. You really had a very narrow escape from death."

"Yes, quite near enough. I'm far from wanting any more from the same tap."

"And I don't quite see why you assume that it was a mere clumsy joke that sent you into the river by accident."

"Why, what else could it have been?"

"It looks more like a deliberate attempt to drown you. Perhaps you have some enemy who might want to make away with you."

"I haven't. There isn't a soul in the world who owes me the slightest grudge."

"That seems rather a bold thing to say, but I suppose you know. Still, I should think you ought to bear this strange affair in mind, and be a little careful when you go out at night – to avoid the riverside, for instance. Have you – did you give any information to the police about this accident, as you call it?"

"Good Lord! No! What would have been the use?"

"I thought you might have given them some description of the man who pushed you over."

"But I never saw him. I don't even know for certain that it was a man. It might have been a woman for all that I can tell."

Mrs. Samway looked, up at me with that strangely penetrating expression that I had seen before in those singular, pale eyes of hers. "You don't mean that?" she said. "You don't really think that it could have been a woman?"

"I don't think very much about it, but as I never saw the person who did me the honour of hoisting me overboard, I am clearly not in a position to depose as to the sex of that person. But if it was a woman, she must have been an uncommonly strong one."

Mrs. Samway continued to look at me questioningly. "I thought you seemed to hint at a suspicion that it actually *was* a woman. You would surely be able to tell."

"I suppose I should if there were time to think about the matter, but, you see, before I was fairly aware that anyone had hold of me, I was sticking my head into the mud at the bottom of the river, which is a process that does not tend very much to clarify one's thoughts."

"No, I suppose not," she agreed. "But it is a most mysterious and dreadful affair. I can't think how you can take it so calmly. You don't seem to be in the least concerned by the fact that you have been within a hairsbreadth of being murdered. What do your friends think about it?"

"Well, you see, Mrs. Samway," I replied evasively, "one doesn't talk much about incidents of this kind. It doesn't sound very credible, and one doesn't want to gain a reputation as a sort of modern Munchausen. I shouldn't have told you but that you were already partly in the secret and that you cross-examined me in such a determined fashion."

"But," she exclaimed, "do you mean to tell me that you have said nothing to anyone about this extraordinary adventure of yours?"

"No, I don't say that. Of course, I had to give some sort of explanation to my landlady, for instance, but I didn't tell her all that I have told you, and I would rather, if you don't mind, that you didn't mention the affair to anyone. I should hate to be suspected of romancing."

"You shan't be through anything that I may say," she replied, "though I should hardly think that anyone who knew you would be likely to suspect you of inventing imaginary adventures."

For some minutes after this we walked on without speaking, and, from time to time, I stole a glance at my companion. And, once again, I found myself impressed by something distinctive and unusual in her appearance.

Her unquestionable beauty was not like that of most pretty women, localized and unequal, having features of striking attractiveness set in an indifferent or even defective matrix. It was diffused and all pervading, the product of sheer physical excellence. With most women one feels that the more attractive wares are judiciously pushed to the front of the window while a discreet reticence is maintained respecting the unpresentable residue. Not so with Mrs. Samway. Her small, shapely head, her symmetrical face, her fine supple figure, and her easy movements, all spoke of a splendid physique. She was not merely a pretty woman – she was that infinitely rarer creature, a physically perfect human being, comely with the comeliness of faultless proportion, graceful with the grace of symmetry and strength.

Suddenly she looked up at me with just a hint of shyness and a little heightening of the colour in her cheek. "Are you going to tell me again, Dr. Jardine, that a cat may look at a king? Or was it that a king may look at a cat?"

"Whichever you please," I replied. "We will put them on a footing of equality, excepting that the king might have the better claim if the cat happened to be an exceptionally good-looking cat. But I wasn't really staring at you this time, I was only giving you a sort of friendly look over. You weren't quite yourself, I think, when we met last."

"No, I certainly was not. So you are now making an inspection. May I ask if I am to be informed of the diagnosis, as I think you call it?"

Now, to tell the truth, I had thought her looking rather haggard and worn and decidedly thinner, and when her sprightliness subsided in the intervals of our somewhat flippant talk, it had seemed to me that her face took on an expression that was weary and even sad. But it would hardly do to say as much. "It is quite irregular," I replied. "The diagnosis is for the doctor. The patient is only concerned with the treatment. But I'll make an exception in your case, especially as my report is quite unsensational. I thought you looked as if you had been doing rather too much and not greatly enjoying the occupation. Am I right?"

"Yes. Quite right. I've had a lot of worry and bother lately, and not enough rest and peace."

"I hope all that is at an end now?"

163

"I don't know that it is," she replied, wearily, "or, for that matter, that it will ever be. Fate or destiny, or whatever we may call it, starts us upon a certain road, and along that road we must needs trudge, wherever it may lead."

I was rather startled at the sudden despondency of her tone. Apparently the road that Mrs. Samway trod was not strewn with roses. "Still," I said, "it is a long road that has no turning."

"It is," she agreed, bitterly, "but many have to travel such a road, to find the turning at last barred by the churchyard gate."

"Oh, come!" I protested, "we don't talk of churchyards at your time of life. We think of the jolly wayside inns and the buttercups and daisies and the may-blossom in the hedgerows. Churchyard indeed! We will leave that to the old folk and the village donkey, if you please."

She smiled rather wanly. Her gaiety seemed to have deserted her for good.

"The wayside inns and the wayside flowers," said she, "are your portion – at least, I hope so. They are not for me. And, after all, there are worse things to think of than a nice quiet churchyard, with the village donkey browsing among the graves, as you say."

"I quite agree with you. From the standpoint of the disinterested spectator, not contemplating freehold investments, nothing can be more delightfully rustic and peaceful. It is the personal application that I object to."

Again she smiled, but very pensively, and for a while we walked on in silence. Presently she resumed. "I used to think that the shortness of life was quite a tragedy. That was when I was young. But now – "

"When you were young!" I interrupted. "Why, what are you now? I can tell you, Mrs. Samway, that there is many a girl of twenty who would be only too delighted to exchange personalities with you, and who would stand to make a mighty fine bargain if she could do it. If you talk like this, I shall have to refer you to the great Leonardo's advice to painters."

"What is that?" she asked.

"He recommends the frequent use of a looking-glass." She gave me a quick glance and then blushed so very deeply that I was quite alarmed lest I should have given offence. But her next words reassured me.

"It was nice of you to say that, and most kindly meant. I won't say that I don't care very much how I look, because that would be an ungracious return for your compliment and it wouldn't be quite true. There are times when one is quite glad to feel that one looks presentable – the present moment, for instance."

I acknowledged the compliment, with a bow. "Thank you." I said. "That was more than I deserved. I only wish that your fortune was equal to your looks, but I am afraid it isn't. I have an uncomfortable feeling that you are not very happy."

"I'm afraid I'm not," she replied. "Life is rather a lottery, you know, and the worst of it is that you can only take a single ticket. So, when you find that you've drawn the wrong number and you realize that there is no second chance – well, it isn't very inspiriting, is it?"

I had to admit that it was not, and, after a short pause, she continued, "Women are poor dependent creatures, Dr. Jardine – dependent, I mean, for their happiness on the people who surround them."

"But that is true of us all."

"Not quite. A man – like yourself, for instance – has his work and his ambitions that make him independent of others. But, for a woman, whatever pretences she may make as to larger interests in life – a husband, a home and one or two nice children – form the real goal of her ambition."

"But you are not a lone spinster, Mrs. Samway," I reminded her.

"No, I am not. But I have no children, no proper home, and not a real friend in the world – unless I may think of you as one."

"I hope you always will," I exclaimed impulsively, for there was, to me, something very pathetic in the evident loneliness of this woman. She must, I felt, be friendless indeed if she must needs appeal for friendship to a comparative stranger like myself.

"I am glad to hear you say that," she replied, "for I am making you bear a friend's burden. I hope you will forgive me for pouring out my complaints to you in this way."

"It isn't difficult," said I, "to bear other people's troubles with fortitude. But if sympathy is any good, believe me, Mrs. Samway, when I tell you that I am really deeply grieved to think that you are getting so much less out of life than you ought. I only wish that I could do something more than sympathize."

"I believe you do," she said. "I felt, at Folkestone, how kind you were – as a good man is to a woman in her moments of weakness. That is why, I suppose, I was impelled to talk to you like this. And that is why," she added, after a little pause, "I felt a pang of envy when I saw you pass with your pretty companion."

I started somewhat at this. Where the deuce could she have seen us near enough to tell whether my companion was pretty or not? I turned the matter over rapidly in my mind, and meanwhile, I said, "I don't quite see why you envied me, Mrs. Samway."

"I didn't say that I envied you," she replied, with a faint smile and the suspicion of a blush.

"Or her either," I retorted. "We are only the merest acquaintances."

My conscience smote me somewhat as I made this outrageous statement, but Mrs. Samway took me up instantly. "Then you've only known her quite a short time?"

The rapidity with which she had jumped to this conclusion fairly took my breath away, and I had answered her question before I was aware of it.

"But," I added, "I don't quite see how you arrived at your conclusion."

"I thought," she replied, "that you seemed to like one another very well."

"So we do, I think. But can't acquaintances like one another?"

"Oh, certainly, but if they are a young man and a maiden they are not likely to remain mere acquaintances very long. That was how I argued."

"I see. Very acute of you. By the way, where did you see us? I didn't see you."

"Of course you didn't. Yet you passed quite close to me on the Spaniard's Road, immersed in conversation, and little suspecting that the green eyes of envy were fixed on you."

"Oh, now, Mrs. Samway, I can't have that. They're not green, you know, although what their exact colour is I shouldn't like to say offhand."

"What! Not after that careful inspection?"

"That didn't include the eyes. Perhaps you wouldn't mind if I made another, just to satisfy my curiosity and settle the question for good."

"Oh, do, by all means, if it is such a weighty question."

We both halted and I stared into the clear depths of her singular, pale hazel eyes with an impertinent affectation of profound scrutiny, while she looked up smilingly into mine. Suddenly, to my utter confusion, her eyes filled and she turned away her head. "Oh! Please forgive me!" she exclaimed. "I beg your pardon – I do beg your pardon most earnestly for being such a wretched bundle of emotions. You would forgive me if you knew – what I can't tell you."

"There is no need, dear Mrs. Samway," I said very gently, laying my hand on her arm. "Are we not friends? And may I not give you my warmest sympathy without asking too curiously what brings the tears to your eyes?"

I was, in truth, deeply moved, as a young man is apt to be by a pretty woman's tears. But more than this, something whispered to me

166

that my playful impertinence had suddenly brought home to her the void that was in her life, the lack of intimate affection at which she had seemed to hint. And, instantly, all that was masculine in me had risen up with the immemorial instinct of the male in defence of the female, for, whatever her faults may have been, Mrs. Samway was feminine to the finger-tips.

She pressed my hand for a moment and impatiently brushed the tears from her eyes. "I do hope, Dr. Jardine." she said, looking up at me with a smile, "that your wife will be a good woman. You'll be a dreadful victim if she isn't, with your quick sympathy and your endless patience with feminine silliness. And now I won't plague you any more with my tantrums. I hope I am not bringing you a great deal out of your way. You do live in this direction, don't you?"

"Yes, and I have been assuming that my direction was yours, too. Is that right? Are you going back to Hampstead Road?"

"Not at once. I'm going to make a call at Highgate first."

"Then you'll want to go up Highgate Rise or Swain's Lane, and I will walk up with you if you'll let me."

"I think my nearest way will be up the little path that leads out of Swain's Lane. You know it, I expect?"

"Yes. It is locally known as Love Lane. It leads to the crest of the hill."

"That is right. You shall see me to the top of it and then I'll take myself off and leave you in peace."

We had by this time crossed Parliament Hill Fields and passed the end of the Highgate Ponds. A few paces more brought us out at the top of the Grove and a few more to the entrance of the rather steep and very narrow lane. For some time Mrs. Samway walked by my side in silence, and, by the reflective way in which she looked at the ground before her, seemed to be wrapped in meditation, which I did not disturb. As we entered the lane, however, she looked up at me thoughtfully and said, "I wonder what you think of me, Dr. Jardine."

It was a fine opening for a compliment, but somehow, compliments seemed out of place, after what had passed between us. I accordingly evaded the question with another. "What do you suppose I think of you?"

"I don't know. I hardly know what I think of myself. You would be quite justified in thinking me rather forward, to waylay you in this deliberate fashion."

"Well, I don't. Your curiosity about that Folkestone affair seems most natural and reasonable."

"I'm glad you don't think me forward," she said, "but, as to my curiosity, I am beginning to doubt whether it was that alone that determined me of a sudden to come here and talk to you. I half suspect that I was feeling a little more solitary than usual, and that some instinct told me that you would be kind to me and say nice things and pet me just a little – as you have done."

I was deeply touched by her pathetic little confession, so deeply that I could find nothing to say in return. "You don't think any the worse of me," she continued, "for coming to you and begging a little sympathy and friendship?"

As she spoke, she looked up very wistfully and earnestly in my face, and rested her hand for a moment on my arm. I took it in mine and drew her arm under my own as I replied, "Of course I don't. Only I think it a wonder and a shame that my poor friendship and sympathy should be worth the consideration of a woman like you."

She pressed my arm slightly, and, after a little interval, said in a low voice with just the suspicion of a tremor in it, "You have been very kind to me, Dr. Jardine, more kind than you know. I am very, very grateful to you for taking what was really an intrusion so nicely."

"It was not in the least an intrusion," I protested, "and as to gratitude, a good many men would be very delighted to earn it on the same terms. You don't seem to set much value on your own exceedingly agreeable society."

She smiled very prettily at this, and again we walked on for a while up the slope without speaking. Once she turned her head as if listening for some sound from behind us, but our feet were making so much noise on the loose gravel, and the sound reverberated so much in the narrow space between the wooden fences that I, at least, heard nothing. Presently we turned a slight bend and came in sight of the opening at the top of the hill, guarded by a couple of posts. Within a few yards of the latter she halted, and withdrawing her hand from my arm, turned round and faced me. "We must say 'Good-bye' here," said she. "I wonder if I shall ever see you again."

For a moment I felt a strong impulse to propose some future meeting at a definite date, but fortunately some glimmering of discretion – and perhaps some thought of Sylvia – restrained me. "Why shouldn't you?" I asked.

"I don't know. But mine is rather a vagabond existence, and I suppose you will be travelling about. I hope we shall meet again soon, but if we do not, I shall always think of you as my friend, and you will have a kind thought for me sometimes, won't you?"

"I shall indeed. I shall think of you very often and hope that your life is brighter than it seems to be now."

"Thank you," she said earnestly, "and now 'Good-bye'!"

She held out her hand, and, as I grasped it, she looked in my face with the wistful, yearning expression that I had noticed before, and which so touched me to the heart that, yielding to a sudden impulse, I drew her to me and kissed her. Dim as was the light of the fading winter's day, I could see that she had, in an instant, turned scarlet. But she was not angry, for, as she drew away from me, shyly and almost reluctantly, she gave me one of her prettiest smiles and whispered "Good-bye" again. Then she ran out between the posts, and, turning once again – and still as red as a peony – waved me a last farewell.

I stood in the narrow entrance looking out after her with a strange mixture of emotions – pity, wonder, and admiration, and a little doubt as to my own part in the late transaction. For I had never before kissed a married woman, and cooling judgment did not altogether approve the new departure, for if Mr. Samway was not all that he might be, still he was Mr. Samway and I wasn't. Nevertheless, I stood and watched my late companion with very warm interest until she faded into the dusk, and even then I continued to stand by the posts, gazing out into the waning twilight and cogitating on our rather strange interview.

Suddenly my ear caught a sound from behind me, down the lane – a sound which, while it set my suspicion on the alert, brought a broad grin to my face. It was what I suppose I must call a stealthy footstep, but the stealthiness might have stood for the very type and essence of futility, for, as I have said, the ground sloped pretty steeply and was covered with loose pebbles, whereby every movement of the foot was rendered as audible as a thunderclap. However, absurd as the situation seemed – if the unseen person was really trying to approach by stealth – it was necessary to be on my guard. Moreover, if this should chance to be the person with the nystagmus, the present seemed to be an excellent opportunity for coming to some sort of understanding with him.

Accordingly I wheeled about and began to walk back down the lane. Instantly, the steps – no longer stealthy – began to retire. I quickened my pace, the unknown and invisible eavesdropper quickened his. Then I broke into a run, and so did he, notwithstanding which, I think I should have had him but for an untoward accident. The ground was not only sloping, but, under the loose gravel, was as hard as stone.

Consequently, the foothold was none of the best, as I presently discovered, for, as I raced down one of the steepest slopes, the pebbles suddenly rolled away under my foot and I lost my balance. But I did not fall instantly. Half recovering, I flew forward, clawing the air, stamping, staggering, kicking up the gravel, and making the most infernal hubbub and clatter, before I finally subsided into a sitting posture on the pebbles.

When I rose, the footsteps were no longer audible, though the lower end of the lane was still some distance away.

I resumed my progress at a more sedate pace and kept a sharp look-out for a possible ambush, though the lane was too narrow, even in the darkness that now pervaded it, to furnish much cover to an enemy. Some distance down, I came to an opening in the fence, where one or two boards had become loose, and was half disposed to squeeze through and explore. But I did not, for, on reflection, it occurred to me that if the man was not there it would be useless for me to go, while if he should be hiding behind the fence it would be simply insane of me to put my head through the hole.

When I emerged into the road at the bottom, I looked about vaguely, but, of course there was no sign of the fugitive – nor, indeed, could I have identified him if I had met him. I loitered about undecidedly for a minute or two, and then, realizing the futility of keeping a watch on the entrance of the lane for a man whom I could not recognize, and becoming conscious of a ravenous desire for food I made my way down the Grove in the direction of my lodgings.

Chapter XV
Exit Dr. Jardine

My second visit to The Hawthorns, to which I had looked forward with some eagerness, had, after all, to be postponed indefinitely. I say "had", since, under the circumstances, it appeared to be so unsafe that I could not fairly take the risk that it involved. I had made the engagement thoughtlessly, and, in my preoccupation with Mrs. Samway, had not realized the indiscretion to which I had committed myself until I was brought back sharply to the actual conditions by the incident in Love Lane which I have mentioned. But, after that, I saw that it would be the wildest folly to show myself in the vicinity of Sylvia's house. Evidently the spy, after we had given him the slip so neatly, had made direct for my lodgings and lurked in the neighbourhood, and there it must have been that he had picked me up again as I passed with Mrs. Samway. Of course it was possible that the unseen person in the lane was not really shadowing me at all, but his stealthy approach, his hasty retreat and his mysterious disappearance, left me in very little doubt on the subject.

I was not very nervous about this enigmatical person on my own account. In spite of my alarming experiences, I found it difficult to take him as seriously as I should have done, and still felt a quite unjustifiable confidence in my capability of taking care of myself. But on Sylvia's account I was exceedingly uneasy. The interest that this man had shown in the unlucky little ornament that she wore, associated itself in my mind most disagreeably with her mysterious and terrifying adventure in Millfield Lane, and made me feel that it would be sheer insanity for me to go from my house to hers and so possibly give this unknown villain the clue to her whereabouts.

This conclusion, at which I had arrived overnight, was confirmed on the following morning, for, having taken a brisk walk out in the direction of Harrow, and having kept a very sharp look-out, I was distinctly conscious of the fact that there always appeared to be a man in sight. I never got near him and was not able to recognize him, but at intervals throughout the morning he continually reappeared in the distance, even on the comparatively solitary country roads and the hedge-divided meadows.

It was excessively irritating. Yet what could I do? Even if I could have identified him with the man who had apparently shadowed me before, I really had nothing against him. And cogitating on the matter, with no little annoyance, I determined to take counsel with Thorndyke, and meanwhile to avoid the neighbourhood of The Hawthorns.

After lunch, I wrote a letter to Sylvia, briefly explaining the state of affairs, and, having given it to our maid to deliver, I took the precaution to go out and saunter towards Kentish Town with the object of engaging the spy's attention and preventing him from following my messenger to North End. The rest of the day I spent at home and occupied my time in writing a long letter to Thorndyke in which I gave a pretty detailed account of my recent experiences, which letter was duly posted by Mrs. Blunt herself in time for the evening collection.

I had barely seated myself at the breakfast table on the following morning when a telegram was brought to me. On opening it I found that it was from Thorndyke, advising me that a letter had been dispatched by hand and asking me to stay at home until I had received it, which I did, and within an hour it arrived and was delivered into my own hands by a messenger boy.

It was curt and rather peremptory in tone, desiring me to meet him at one o'clock at Salter's Club in a turning off St. James's Street and concluding with these somewhat remarkable instructions: "*I want you to wear an overcoat and hat of a distinctive and easily recognizable character and to take every means that you can of being seen and, if possible, followed to the club. You had better put a few necessaries in a bag or suit-case and tell your landlady that you may not be home to-night. Follow these instructions to the letter and bring this note with you.*"

At the latter part of these directions I was somewhat disposed to boggle, remembering my worthy teacher's threat to put me somewhere out of harm's way. But Thorndyke was a difficult man to disobey. Suave and persuasive as his manners were, he had a certain final and compelling way with him that silenced objections and produced a sort of frictionless obedience without any sense of compulsion. Hence, notwithstanding a slight tendency to bluster and tell myself that I would see him hanged before I would submit to being mollycoddled like an idiot, I found myself, presently, walking down the Grove in a buff overcoat and a grey felt hat, carrying a green canvas suit-case in which were packed the necessaries for a brief stay away from home, and bearing in my pocket the incriminating letter.

I walked slowly as far as the Junction Road in order to give any pursuer a fair opportunity to take up the chase and to make the necessary observations on my tasteful turn-out. At the Junction I waited for a tram and carefully abstained from staring about in a manner which would have embarrassed any person who might wish unobserved to share the conveyance with me, and from the terminus at Euston Road I proceeded in leisurely fashion on foot, still resisting the temptation to look about and see if I had picked up a companion by the way.

Salter's Club was domiciled in a typical West End house situated in a quiet street of similar houses, graced at one end by a cabstand. I timed my arrival with such accuracy that a neighbouring church-clock struck one as I ascended the steps, and on my entering the hall, I was met by an elderly man in a quiet livery who seemed to expect me, for, when I mentioned Thorndyke's name, he asked, "Dr. Jardine, sir?" and, hardly waiting for my reply, showed me to the cloak-room. "Dr. Thorndyke," said he, "will be with you in a few minutes. When you have washed, I will show you to the dining room where he wished you to wait for him."

I was just a little surprised at even this short delay, for Thorndyke was the soul of punctuality. However, I had not to wait long. I had been sitting less than three minutes at a small table laid for two in the deep bay window, scanning the street through the wire-gauze blinds, when he arrived. "I needn't apologize, I suppose, Jardine," he said, shaking my hand heartily. "You will have guessed why I have kept you waiting."

"You flatter me, sir," I replied with a slight grin. "I haven't your powers of instantaneous deduction."

"You hardly needed them," he retorted. "Of course I was watching your approach and observing the corner by which you entered the street to see who came after you."

"Did anyone come after me?"

"Several persons. I examined them all very carefully with a prism binocular that magnifies twelve times linear, and an assistant is now at the same window – the one over this – following the fortunes of those persons with the same excellent glass."

"Did you spot anyone in particular as looking a likely person?"

"Yes. The second man who came after you seemed to be sauntering in a rather unpurposive fashion and looking a little obtrusively unconcerned. I noticed, too, that he was carrying an umbrella in his left hand. But we needn't concern ourselves. If anyone is shadowing you we are certain to see him. He must expose himself to view from time to time, for he can't afford to lose sight of our doorway for more than a few seconds, and there is practically no cover in this street."

"He might hide in a doorway," I suggested.

"Oh, might he! These are all clubs in this street. He'd very soon have the servants out wanting to know his business. No, he'll have to keep on the move and he'll have to keep mostly in sight of this house. And meanwhile we are going to take our lunch at our leisure and have a little talk to while away the time."

The lunch was on a scale that my youthful appetite approved strongly, though the number of courses and irrelevant, time-consuming kickshaws struck me as rather unusual. And I never saw a man eat so slowly and delay a meal so much as Thorndyke did on that occasion. I believe that it took him fully twenty minutes to consume a fried sole, and even then he created a further delay by drawing my attention to the skeleton on his plate as an illustration of inherited deformity adjusted to special environmental conditions. But all the time, whether eating or talking, I noticed that his eye continually travelled up and down the stretch of street that was visible through the wire blinds. "You haven't told me why you sent for me, sir," I said, after waiting patiently for him to open the subject.

"I dare say you have guessed," he replied, "but we may as well thrash the matter out now. You realize that you are running an enormous and unnecessary risk by going abroad with this man at your heels?"

"Well, I don't suppose he is following me about from sheer affection."

"No. I thought it possible that he might be a plain-clothes policeman, but I have ascertained that he is not. Who he is we don't know, but we have the strongest reasons for suspecting his intentions. There have been three very determined attempts on your life. They were all made with such remarkable caution and foresight that, though they failed, practically no traces have been left. Those attempts imply a strong motive, though to us, an unknown one, and that motive, presumably, still exists. Your enemy may well be getting desperate, and may be prepared to take greater risks to get rid of you, and if he is, the chances are that he will succeed sooner or later. Murder isn't very difficult to a cool-headed man who means business."

"Then what do you propose, sir?"

"I propose that you disappear from your ordinary surroundings and come and stay, for a time, at my chambers in the Temple."

This was no more than I had expected, but my jaw dropped considerably, notwithstanding. "It's awfully good of you, sir," I stammered – and so, to be sure, it was – "but don't you think it would be simpler to turn the tables on this Johnnie and shadow him?"

"An excellent idea, Jardine, and one, I may say, that I am acting on at this moment. But there isn't so much in it as you seem to think. Supposing we identify this man and even run him to earth? What then? We have nothing against him. We know of no crime that has been committed. We may suspect that the man whom you saw at Hampstead had been murdered. But we can't prove it. We can't produce the body or even prove that the man was dead. And we couldn't connect this person with the affair because nobody was known to be connected with it. I should like to know who this man is, but I don't want to put him on his guard, and above all, I can't agree to your going about as a sort of live-bait to enable us to locate him. By the way, that man on the opposite side of the street is the one whom I selected as being probably your attendant. Apparently I was right, as this is the third time he has passed. Do you recognize him?"

I looked attentively at the uncharacteristic figure on the farther side of the street, but could find nothing familiar in his appearance. "No," I replied, "he doesn't look to me like the same man. He is dressed differently – but that's nothing, as he has been dressed differently on each occasion – and that torpedo beard and full moustache are quite unlike, though there's nothing in that either, but the man looks different altogether – distinctly taller, for instance."

Thorndyke chuckled. "Good," said he. "Now look at his feet, as he passes opposite. Did you ever see an instep set at that angle to the sole? And does not your anatomical conscience cry out at a foot of that thickness?"

"Yes, by Jove!" I exclaimed, "there's room for a double row of metatarsals. It is a fake of some kind, I suppose?"

"Cork 'raisers' inside high-heeled boots. Through the glasses I could see that the boots gaped considerably at the instep, as they will when there is a pad inside as well as a foot. But you notice, also, that the man is dressed for height. He has a tall hat, a long coat, and his shoulders are obviously raised by padding. I think there is very little doubt that he is our man."

"It must be a dull job," I remarked, "hanging about by the hour to see a man come out of a house."

"Very," Thorndyke agreed. "I am quite sorry for the worthy person, especially as we are going to play him a rather shabby trick presently."

"What are we going to do?" I asked.

"We are going to let him in for one of the longest waits he has ever had, I am afraid. Perhaps I had better give you the particulars of our *modus operandi*. First, I shall send down to the stand for a hansom, which will draw up opposite the club, and thereupon I have no doubt our friend will hurry down to the cab-stand to be in readiness. At any rate, I shall let him get down to that end of the street before I do anything more. Then I shall take the liberty of putting on your coat and hat and go out to the cab with your suit-case in my hand, I shall stand on the kerb long enough to let our friend get a good view of my back, I shall get into the cab, give the driver the direction through the trap to drive to the hospital, and pay the fare in advance."

"Why in advance?" I asked.

"So that I shall not have to turn round and show my face when I get out at the hospital entrance. I assume that your friend will follow me in another hansom. Also that he will alight at the outer gates, whereas I shall drive into the courtyard right up to the main entrance, so that he will merely see your hat, coat and suit-case disappear into the building. Then, as I say, he will be in for an interminable vigil. I have a lecture to give this afternoon, and, when I have finished, I shall come away in a black overcoat and tall hat (which are at this moment hanging up in the curator's room), leaving your friend to wait for the reappearance of your coat, hat, and suit-case. I only hope he won't wait too long."

"Why?"

"Because he may wear out the patience of my assistant. I have a plain-clothes man keeping a watch from the window above. If your friend sets off in pursuit of your garments, as I anticipate, the plain-clothes man will go straight to the hospital and take up his post in the porter's lodge, which, as you know, commands the whole street outside the gates."

"And what have I got to do?"

"First of all, you will put your tooth brush in your pocket – never mind about your razor – and let me try on your hat, in case we have to pad the lining. Then, when you have seen your friend start off in pursuit and are sure the coast is clear, you will make straight for my chambers and wait there for me."

"And supposing the chappie doesn't start off in pursuit? Supposing he twigs the imposture?"

"Then the plain-clothes man will go out and threaten to arrest him for loitering with intent to commit a felony. That would soon move him on out of the neighbourhood, and the officer might accompany him some distance and try to get his address. Meanwhile, you would be off to King's Bench Walk."

"But wouldn't it be simpler to run the Johnnie in, in any case? Then we should know all about him."

"No, it wouldn't do. The police wouldn't actually make an arrest without an information, and, if they did proceed, they would want me to appear. That wouldn't suit me at all. Until we obtain some fresh evidence, I don't want this man to get any suspicion that the case is being investigated. And now I think the time has come for a move. Let us go to the cloak-room and see if your hat fits me sufficiently well."

It was not a good fit, being just a shade small, but, as it was a soft felt, this was not a vital defect. The overcoat fitted well enough, though a trifle long in the sleeves, and when Thorndyke was fully arrayed in this borrowed plumage, his back view, so far as I could judge, was indistinguishable from my own. "If you will take out your toothbrush and hand me your suit-case," said he, "I will send for a hansom, and then we will watch the progress of events from the dining-room window."

I handed him the green canvas case and we returned to the dining-room and there, when he had ordered the cab, we took up a position at the window, screened from observation by the wire blinds. "Our friend," said Thorndyke, "was walking towards the right hand end of the street when we saw him last. As the cabstand is at the left hand end, we may hope to look upon his face once again."

As he spoke, the air was rent by the shriek of the cab-whistle, and the leading hansom began immediately to bear down on the club. It had hardly come to rest at our door when a figure appeared from the opposite direction, advancing at a brisk walk on our side of the road. I recognized him instantly as the man to whom Thorndyke had directed my attention, and watched him closely, as he approached, to see if I could identify him with the man who had shadowed Sylvia and me at the picture gallery, but, though he passed within a few yards of the window, and I felt no doubt that he was the same man, I could trace no definite resemblance. It is true, that while actually passing the club, he averted his face somewhat, but I had a good view of him within an easy distance, and the face that I then saw was certainly not the face of the man at the gallery. The skilfulness of the make-up – assuming it to be really a disguise – was incredible, and I remarked on it to Thorndyke. "Yes," he agreed, "a really artistic make-up is apt to surprise the uninitiated. And that reminds me that Polton has instructions to make a few trifling alterations in your own appearance."

I stared at him aghast. "You don't mean to say," I exclaimed, "that you contemplate making me up?"

"We won't discuss the question now," he replied a little evasively. "You talk it over with Polton. It is time for me to go now, as our quarry has considerately acted up to our expectations. He little knows what confusion of our plans he would have occasioned by simply staying at the other end of the street."

The spy had, in fact, now halted opposite the cabstand and was apparently making some notes in a pocket-book – facing, meanwhile, in our direction. With a few parting instructions to me, Thorndyke picked up the suit-case and hurried out, and I saw him dart down the steps – with his face turned somewhat to the right – and stand for a few seconds at the edge of the pavement with his back to the cabstand, but in full view, looking at his watch as if considering some appointment. Suddenly he sprang into the cab and, pushing up the trap, gave the driver his instructions and handed up the fare. At the same moment I saw the unknown shadower hail a hansom, and, scrambling to the footboard, give some brief directions to the driver. Then Thorndyke's cabman touched his horse with the whip, and away he went at a smart trot, but hardly had the cab turned the first corner when the second hansom rattled past the club in hot pursuit.

I was about to turn away from the window when a tall, well-dressed man ran down the steps and immediately signalled to the cabstand with his stick. Thinking it probable that this was the plain-clothes policeman, I stopped to watch, and when I had seen him enter the cab and drive off in the same direction as the other two, I decided that the show was over and that it was time for me to take my departure, which I did, after stuffing a couple of envelopes into the lining of Thorndyke's hat, to prevent it from slipping down towards my ears.

That my arrival at number 5A, King's Bench Walk was not quite unexpected I gathered – not only from the fact that the "oak" stood wide open, revealing the inner door, but from the instantaneous way in which this latter opened in response to my knock, and something gleeful and triumphant in Mr. Polton's manner as he invited me to enter, stirred my suspicions and aroused vague forebodings.

He helped me out of my – or rather Thorndyke's – overcoat, and, having taken the hat from me, peered inquiringly into its interior and fished out the two envelopes, which he politely offered to me. Then, having disposed of his employer's property, he returned to confront me, and, wrinkling his countenance into a most singular and highly corrugated smile, he opened his mouth and spoke. "So you have come, sir, The Doctor tells me, to take sanctuary for a time with us from the malice of your enemies."

"I don't know about that," I replied, "but there is a cockeyed transformationist who seems to be dodging about after me, and Dr. Thorndyke thinks I had better give him the go-by for the present."

"And very proper, too, sir. Discretion is the better part of valour, as the proverb says – though I really could never see that it is any part at all. But no doubt our forefathers, who made the proverb, knew best. Did The Doctor mention that he had given me certain instructions about you?"

"He said that I was to talk over some question with you, but I didn't quite follow him. What were his instructions?"

Polton rubbed his hands, and his face became more crinkly than ever. "The Doctor instructed me," he replied, looking at me hungrily and obviously making a mental inventory of my features, "to effect certain slight alterations in your outward personality."

"Oh, did he," said I. "And what does he mean by that? Does he mean that you are to make me up as an old woman or a minstrel?"

"Not at all, sir," replied Polton. "Neither of those characters would be at all suitable. They would occasion remark, which it is our object to avoid, and as to a minstrel, his presence in chambers would undoubtedly be objected to by the benchers."

"But," I expostulated, "why any disguise at all, if I am to be boxed up in these chambers? The chappie isn't likely to come and look through the keyhole."

"He wouldn't see anything if he did," said Polton. "I fitted these locks. But, you see, sir, many strangers come to these chambers, and then, too, you might like to take a little exercise about the inn or the gardens. That would probably be quite safe if you were unrecognizable, but otherwise, I should think, inadmissible. And really, sir," he continued persuasively, "if you do a thing at all you may as well do it thoroughly. The Doctor wishes you to disappear, then disappear completely. Don't do it by halves."

I could not but admit to myself that this was reasonable advice. Nevertheless, I grumbled a little sulkily. "It seems to me that Dr. Thorndyke is making a lot of unnecessary fuss. It is absurd for an able-bodied man to be sneaking into a hiding-place and disguising himself like a runaway thief."

"I can offer no opinion on that, sir," said Polton, "but you're wrong about The Doctor. He is a cautious man but he is not nervous or fussy. You would be wise to act as he thinks best, I am sure."

"Very well," I said, "I won't be obstinate. When do you want to begin on me?"

"I should like," replied Polton, brightening up wonderfully at my sudden submission, "to have you ready for inspection by the time that The Doctor returns. If agreeable to you, sir, I would proceed immediately."

"Then in that case," said I, "we had better adjourn to the green-room forthwith."

"If you please, sir," replied Polton, and with this, having opened the door and cautiously inspected the landing, he conducted me up the stairs to the floor above, the rooms of which appeared to be fitted as workshops and laboratories. In one of the former, which appeared to be Polton's own special den, I saw my watch hanging from a nail, with a rating table pinned above it, and proceeded to claim it. "I suppose, sir," said Polton, reluctantly taking it from its nail and surrendering it to me, "as you are going to reside on the premises and I can keep it under observation, you may as well wear it. The present rate is plus one point three seconds daily. And now I will trouble you to sit down on this stool and take off your collar."

I did as he bade me, and, meanwhile, he turned up his cuffs and stood a little way off, surveying me as a sculptor might survey a bust on which he was at work. Then he fetched a large cardboard box, the contents of which I could not see, and fell to work.

His first proceeding was to oil my hair thoroughly, part it in the middle and brush it smoothly down either side of my forehead. Next he shaved off the outer third of each eyebrow, and, having applied some sort of varnish or adhesive, he proceeded to build up, with a number of short hairs, a continuation of the eyebrows at a higher level. The result seemed to please him amazingly, for he stepped back and viewed me with an exceedingly self-satisfied smirk. "It is really surprising, sir," said he, "how much expression there is in the corner of an eyebrow. You look a completely different gentleman already."

"Then," said I, "there's no need to do any more. We can leave it at this."

"Oh, no we can't, sir," Polton replied hastily, making a frantic dive into the cardboard box. "Begging your pardon, sir, it is necessary to attend to the lower part of the face, in case you should wish to wear a hat, which would cover the hair and throw the eyebrows into shadow."

Here he produced from the box an undeniable false beard of the torpedo type and approached me, holding it out as if it were a poultice. "You are not going to stick that beastly thing on my face!" I exclaimed, gazing at it with profound disfavour.

"Now, sir," protested Polton, "pray be patient. We will just try it on, and The Doctor shall decide if it is necessary."

With this he proceeded to affix the abomination to my jowl with the aid of the same sticky varnish that he had used previously, and, having attached a moustache to my upper lip, worked carefully round the edges of both with a quantity of loose hair, which he stuck on the skin with the adhesive liquid and afterwards trimmed off with scissors. The process was just completed and he had stepped back once more to admire his work when an electric bell rang softly in the adjoining room. "There's The Doctor," he remarked. "I'm glad we are ready for him. Shall we go down and submit our work for his inspection?"

I assented readily, having some hopes that Thorndyke would veto the beard, and we descended together to the sitting-room, where we found that Jervis and his principal had arrived together. As to the former, he greeted my entrance by staggering back several paces with an expression of terror, and then seated himself on the edge of the table and laughed with an air of enjoyment that was almost offensive, particularly to Polton, who stood by my side, rubbing his hands and smiling with devilish satisfaction. "I assume," Thorndyke said, gravely, "that this is our friend Jardine."

"It isn't," said Jervis. "It's the shopwalker from Wallis's. I recognized him instantly."

"Look here," I said, with some heat, "it's all very well for you to make me up like Charley's Aunt and then jeer at me, but what's the use of it? The fifth of November's past."

"My dear Jardine," Thorndyke said, soothingly, "you are confusing your sensations with your appearance. I daresay that make-up is rather uncomfortable, but it is completely successful, and I must congratulate Polton, for the highest aim of a disguise is the utterly common-place, and I assure you that you are now a most ordinary-looking person. Fetch the looking-glass from the office, Polton, and let him see for himself."

I gazed into the mirror which Polton held up to me with profound surprise. There was nothing in the least grotesque or unusual in the face that looked out at me, only it was the face of an utter stranger, and, as Thorndyke had said, a perfectly common-place stranger, at whom no one would look twice in the street. Grudgingly, I acknowledged the fact, but still objected to the beard. "Do you think it is really necessary, sir, in addition to the other disfigurements?"

"Yes, I do," replied Thorndyke. "It is only a temporary expedient, because, in a fortnight, your own beard will have grown enough to serve with a little artificial re-enforcement. And," he continued, as Polton retired with a gratified smile, "I am anxious that your disappearance shall be complete. It is not only a question of your safety – although that is very urgent, and I feel myself responsible for you, as we are not appealing to the police. There are other issues. Assuming, as we do assume, that some crime has been committed, the lapse of time must inevitably cause some of the consequences of that crime to develop. If the man whose body you saw at Hampstead was really murdered, he must presently be missed and enquired for. Then we shall learn who he was and perhaps we may gather what was the motive of the crime. Then, your secret enemy will be left unemployed and may produce some fresh evidence – for he can't wait indefinitely for your reappearance. And finally, certain enquiries which I am making may set us on the right track. And, if they do, you must remember, Jardine, that you are probably the sole witness to certain important items of evidence, so you must be preserved in safety as a matter of public policy, apart from your own prejudices in favour of remaining alive."

"I didn't know that you were actually working at the case," I said. "Have you been following up that man Gill of the mineral water works?"

"I followed him up to the vanishing-point. He has gone and left no trace, and I have been unable to get any description of him."

"Then," said I, "if it is allowable to ask the question, in what direction have you been making enquiries?"

"I have been interesting myself," Thorndyke replied, "in the other case, that of your patient Mr. Maddock, as the attacks on you seemed to be associated with his neighbourhood rather than with that of Hampstead. I have examined his will at Somerset House and am collecting information about the persons who benefited by its provisions. Especially, I am making some enquiries about a legatee who lives in New York, and concerning whom I am rather curious. I can't go into further details just now, but you will see that I am keeping the case in hand, and you must remember that, at any moment, fresh information may reach me from other sources. My practice is a very peculiar one, and there are few really obscure cases that are not, sooner or later, brought to me for an opinion."

"And, meanwhile, I am to eat the bread of idleness here and wait on events."

"You won't be entirely idle," Thorndyke replied. "We shall find you some work to do, and you will extend your knowledge of medico-legal practice. You write shorthand fairly well, don't you?"

"Yes, and I can draw a little, if that is of any use."

"Both accomplishments are of use, and, even if they are not, we should have to exercise them for the sake of appearances. It will certainly become known that you are here, so we had better make no secret of it, but find you such occupation as will account for your presence. And, as you will have to meet strangers now and again, we must find you a name. What do you think of 'William Morgan Howard'?"

"It will do as well as any other," I replied.

"Very well, then William Morgan Howard let it be. And, in case you might forget your alias, as the crooks are constantly doing, we will drop the name of Jardine and call you Howard even when we are alone. It will save us all from an untimely slip."

To this arrangement also I agreed with a sour smile, and so, with some physical discomfort in the neighbourhood of the lower jaw, and a certain relish of the novelty and absurdity of my position, I placed myself, under the name of Howard, on the roster of Thorndyke's establishment.

182

Chapter XVI
Enter Father Humperdinck

On the day following my – and Thorndyke's – masterly retreat from Salter's Club, the plain-clothes officer called to make his report, and even before he spoke, I judged from his rather sheepish expression that he had failed. And so it turned out. He had waited in the porter's lodge, he told us, until midnight keeping a watch on the watcher, who, for his part, lurked in the street, always keeping in sight of the hospital, and whiling away the time by gazing into the shop windows. The spy had evidently failed to recognize Thorndyke, for when the latter left the hospital in company with one of the physicians, he had given only a passing glance at the open carriage in which the two men sat.

After the shops had shut, the persevering shadower had occupied himself with a sort of dismal sentry-go up and down the street, disappearing into the darkness and reappearing at regular intervals. Once or twice, the plain-clothes man went out and followed his quarry in his perambulations, but, not considering it prudent to expose himself too much to view, he remained mostly in the Lodge. It was after one of these sallies that the mischance occurred. Returning to the Lodge, he saw the spy pass the gates and disappear up the dark street, he looked, after the usual interval, for him to reappear. But the interval passed and there was no reappearance. Then the officer hurried out in search of his quarry, but found only an empty street. Even the apparently inexhaustible patience of the spy had given out at last. And so the quest had ended.

I cannot say that Thorndyke impressed me as being deeply disappointed. In fact, I thought that he seemed, if anything, rather relieved at his emissary's failure. This was Jervis's opinion also, and he had no false delicacy about expressing it. "Well," Thorndyke replied, "as the fellow thrust himself right under my nose, I could hardly do less than make some sort of an attempt to find out who he is. But I don't particularly want to know. My investigations are proceeding from quite another direction, and you see, Jervis, how awkward it might have been to have this person on our hands. We could only charge him with loitering with felonious intent, and we couldn't prove the intent after all, for we can't produce any evidence connecting this man with the three attempted murders. He may not be the same man at all. And I certainly don't want to go into the witness box just now, and still less do I want my new clerk, Mr. Howard, put into that position. I don't want to take any action until I have the case quite complete and am in a position to make a decisive move."

"The truth is," said Jervis, addressing me confidentially in a stage whisper, "Thorndyke hates the idea of spoiling a really juicy problem by merely arresting the criminal and pumping his friends. He looks on such a proceeding much as a Master of Foxhounds would look on the act of poisoning a fox."

Thorndyke smiled indulgently at his junior. "There is such a thing," said he, "as failing to poison a fox and only making him too unwell to leave his residence. A premature prosecution is apt to fail, and then the prisoner has seen all the cards of his adversaries. At present I am playing against an unseen adversary, but I am hoping that I, in my turn, am unseen by him, and I am pretty certain that he has no idea what cards I hold."

"Gad!" exclaimed Jervis, "then he is much the same position as I am." And with this the subject dropped.

The first week of my residence in Thorndyke's chambers was quite uneventful, and was mainly occupied in settling down to the new conditions. My letters were sent on by Mrs. Blunt to the hospital whence they were brought by my principal – as I may now call my quondam teacher – with the exception of Sylvia's, which we had agreed were to be sent to the chambers enclosed in an envelope addressed to Thorndyke.

At first, I had feared that the confinement would be unendurable, but the reality proved to be much less wearisome than I had anticipated. A horizontal bar rigged up by Polton in the laboratory gave me the means of abundant exercise of one kind, and in the early mornings, before the gates of the inn were opened, I made it my daily practice to trot round the precincts for an hour at a time, taking the circuit from our chambers through Crown Office Road to Fountain Court and back by way of Pump Court and the Cloisters, to the great benefit of my health and the mild surprise of the porters and laundresses.

Nor was I without occupation in the daytime. Besides an exhaustively detailed account of all the remarkable experiences that had befallen me of late which I wrote out at Thorndyke's request, I had a good deal of clerical work of one kind and another, and was frequently employed, when clients called, in exhibiting my skill as a stenographer, taking down oral statements, or making copies of depositions or other documents which were read over to me by Thorndyke or Jervis.

It was the exercise of these latter activities that introduced me to a certain Mr. Marchmont, and through him to some new and rather startling experiences. Mr. Marchmont was a solicitor, and, as I gathered, an old client of Thorndyke's, for, when he called one evening, about ten days after my arrival, with a bagful of documents, he made sundry references to former cases by which I understood that he and Thorndyke had been pretty frequently associated in their professional affairs. "I have got a lot of papers here," he said, opening the bag, "of which I suppose I ought to have had copies made, but there hasn't been time and I am afraid there won't be, as I have to return them to-morrow. But perhaps, if you run your eye over them, you will see what it is necessary to remember and make a few notes."

"I think," said Thorndyke, "that my friend, Mr. Howard, will be able to help us by taking down the essentials in shorthand. Let me introduce you. Mr. Howard is very kindly assisting me for a time by relieving me of some of the extra clerical work."

Mr. Marchmont bowed, and, as we shook hands, looked at me, as I thought, rather curiously, then he extracted the papers from his bag, and, spreading them out on the table, briefly explained their nature. "There is no need," said he, "to have copies of them all, but I thought you had better see them. Perhaps you will glance through them and see which you think ought to be copied for reference."

Thorndyke ran his eye over the documents, and, having made one or two brief notes of the contents of some, which he then laid aside, collected the remainder and began to read them out to me, while I took down the matter verbatim, interpolating Marchmont's comments and explanations on a separate sheet of paper. The reading and the discussion occupied a considerable time, and, before the business was concluded, the Treasury clock had struck half-past nine. "It's getting late," said Marchmont, folding the papers and putting them back in the bag. "I must be going or you'll wish me at Halifax, if you aren't doing so already." He snapped the fastening of the bag, and, grasping the handle, was about to lift it from the table, when he appeared to recollect something, for he let go the handle and once more faced my principal.

"By the way, Thorndyke," said he, "there is a matter on which I have wanted to consult you for some time past, but couldn't get my client to agree. It is a curious affair, quite in your line, I think: A case of disappearance – not in the legal sense, as creating a presumption of death, but disappearance from ordinary places of resort with a very singular change of habits, so far as I can learn. Possibly a case of commencing insanity. I have been wanting to lay the facts before you, but my client, who is a Jesuit and as suspicious as the devil, insisted on trying to ferret out the evidence for himself and wouldn't hear of a consultation with you. Of course he has failed completely, and now, I think, he is more amenable."

"Are you in possession of the facts, yourself?" asked Thorndyke.

185

"No, I'm hanged if I am," replied Marchmont. "The case is concerned with a certain Mr. Reinhardt, who was a client of my late partner, poor Wyndhurst. I never had anything to do with him, and it unfortunately happens that our old clerk, Bell – you remember Bell – who had charge of Mr. Reinhardt's business, left us soon after poor Wyndhurst's death, so there is nobody in the office who has any personal knowledge of the parties."

"You say it is a case of disappearance?" said Thorndyke.

"Not exactly disappearance, but – well, it is a most singular case. I can make nothing of it, and neither can my worthy and reverend client, so as I say, he is now growing more amenable, and I think I shall be able to persuade him to come round with me and take your opinion on such facts as we have. Shall you be at home to-morrow evening?"

"Yes, I can make an appointment for to-morrow, after dinner, if you prefer that time."

"We won't call it an appointment," said Marchmont. "If I can overcome his obstinacy, I will bring him round and take the chance of your being in. But I think he'll come, as he is on his beam-ends, and if he does, I fancy you will find the little problem exactly to your liking." With this Mr. Marchmont took his departure, leaving Thorndyke and me to discuss the various legal aspects of disappearance and the changes of habit and temperament that usher in an attack of mental alienation. I could see that the solicitor's guarded references to an obscure and intricate case had aroused Thorndyke's curiosity to no small extent, for, though he said little on the subject, it evidently remained in his mind, as I judged by the care with which he planned the disposal of his time of the following day, and the little preparations that he made for the reception of his visitors. Nor was Thorndyke the only expectant member of our little establishment. Jervis also, having caught the scent of an interesting case, made it his business to keep the evening free, and so it happened that when eight o'clock struck on the Temple bell, it found us gathered round the fire, chatting on indifferent subjects, but all three listening for the expected tread on the stairs. "It is to be hoped," said Jervis, "that our reverend friend won't jib at the last moment. I always expect something good from Marchmont. He doesn't get flummoxed by anything simple or common place. I think we have had most of our really thrilling cases through him. And seeing that Jardine has laid in two whole quarto note-blocks and put those delightful extra touches to his already alluring get-up – "

"There is no such person here as Jardine," Thorndyke interrupted.

"I beg his pardon. Mr. Howard, I should have said. But listen! There are two persons coming up the stairs. You had better take your place at the table, Ja-Howard, and look beastly business-like, or the reverend gentleman will want you chucked out, and then you'll lose the entertainment."

I hurried across to the table and had just seated myself and taken up a pen when the brass knocker on our inner door rattled out its announcement. Thorndyke strode across and threw the door open, and as Mr. Marchmont entered with his client I looked at the latter inquisitively. But only for a single instant. Then I looked down and tried to efface myself utterly, for Mr. Marchmont's client was none other than the cleric with whom I had travelled from Folkestone to London.

The solicitor ushered in his client with an air of but half-concealed triumph and proceeded with exaggerated geniality to do the honours of introduction. "Let me make you known to one another, gentlemen," said he. "This is the Very Reverend Father Humperdinck. These gentlemen are Dr. Thorndyke, Dr. Jervis, and Mr. Howard, who will act, on this occasion, as the recording angel to take down in writing the particulars of your very remarkable story."

Father Humperdinck bowed stiffly. He was evidently a little disconcerted at finding so large an assembly, and glanced at me, in particular, with undisguised disfavour, while I, my oiled hair, deformed eyebrows and false beard notwithstanding, perspired with anxiety lest he should recognize me. But however unfavourably the reverend father may have viewed our little conclave, Mr. Marchmont, who had been watching him anxiously, gave him no chance of raising objections, but proceeded to open the matter forthwith.

"I have not brought any digest or *précis* of the case," said he, "because I know you prefer to hear the facts from the actual parties. But I had better give you a brief outline of the matter of our inquiry. The case is concerned with a Mr. Vitalis Reinhardt, who has been closely associated with Father Humperdinck for very many years past, and who has now, without notice or explanation, disappeared from his ordinary places of resort, ceased from communication with his friends, and adopted a mode of life quite alien from and inconsistent with his previous habits. Those are the main facts, stated in general terms."

"And the inquiry to which you referred?" said Thorndyke.

"Concerns itself with three questions," replied Marchmont, and he proceeded to check them off on his fingers. "First, is Vitalis Reinhardt alive or dead? Second, if he is alive, where is he? Third, having regard to the singular change in his habits, is his conduct such as might render it possible to place him under restraint or to prove him unfit to control his own affairs?"

"To certify him as insane, if I may put it bluntly," said Thorndyke. "That question could be decided only on a full knowledge of the nature of the changes in this person's habits, with which, no doubt, you are prepared to furnish us. But what instantly strikes me in your epitome of the proposed inquiry is this: You raise the question whether Mr. Reinhardt is alive or dead, and then you refer to certain changes in his habits, but, since a man must be alive to have any habits at all, the two questions seem to be mutually irreconcilable in relation to the same group of facts."

Father Humperdinck nodded approvingly. "Zat is chust our great diffigulty," said he. "Zome zings make me suspect zat my friend Reinhardt is dead, zome ozzer zings make me feel certain zat he is alife. I do not know vich to zink. I am gombletely buzzled."

"Perhaps," said Thorndyke, "the best plan would be for Father Humperdinck to give us a detailed account of his relations with Mr. Reinhardt and of the latter gentleman's habits as they are known to him, after which we could discuss any questions that suggest themselves and clear up any points that seem to be obscure. What do you say, Marchmont?"

"It will be a long story," Marchmont replied doubtfully.

"So much the better," rejoined Thorndyke. "It will give us the more matter for consideration. I would suggest that Father Humperdinck tells us the story in his own way and that Mr. Howard takes down the statement. Then we shall have the principal data and can pursue any issue that seems to invite further investigation."

To this proposal Marchmont agreed, a little reluctantly, fortifying himself for the ordeal by lighting a cigar, and Father Humperdinck, having cast a somewhat disparaging glance at me, began his account of his missing friend, which I took down verbatim, and which I now reproduce shorn of the speaker's picturesque but rather tiresome peculiarities of pronunciation. "My acquaintance with Vitalis Reinhardt began more than forty years ago, when we were both schoolboys in the Jesuit's house at Louvain. But I did not see much of him then, as I was preparing for the novitiate while he was on the secular side. In spite of his German name, Vitalis was looked upon as an English boy, for his father had married a rich English lady and was settled in England, and Vitalis, being the only child, had very great expectations. When he left school I lost sight of him for some years, and it was only after the war had broken out between Germany and France that we met again. I had then just been ordained and was attached as chaplain to a Bavarian regiment, he had come out from England as a volunteer to attend the sick and wounded, and so we met, soon after the Battle of Saarbrück, in the wards of a temporary hospital. But our career in the field was not a long one. Less than a month after Saarbrück, our little force met a French division and had to retreat, leaving a number of men and guns and all the wounded in the hands of the enemy. Both of us were among the prisoners, and Vitalis was one of the wounded, for, just as the retreat began, a French bullet struck him in the right hip. We were both taken to Paris with the rest of the prisoners, and there, in the hospital for wounded prisoners, I was allowed to visit him.

"His wound was a severe one. The bullet had entered deeply and lodged behind the bone of the hip, so that the repeated efforts of the surgeons to extract it not only failed but caused great pain and made the wound worse. From day to day poor Vitalis grew thinner and more yellow, and we could see plainly that if no change occurred, the end must come quite soon. So the doctors said and so Vitalis himself felt.

"Then it came to me that, if the skill of man failed us, we should ask for help from above. It happened that I possessed a relic of the blessed Saint Vincent de Paul, which was contained in a small gold reliquary, and which I had been permitted by the Father General to keep. I proposed to Vitalis that we should apply the relic and make a special appeal to the saint for help, and also that he should promise to dedicate some part of his great possessions to the service of God.

"He agreed readily, for he had always been a deeply pious man. Accordingly he made the promises as I had suggested, we offered up special prayers to the saint, and, with the permission of the surgeons, I attached the reliquary to the dressings of the wound, praying that it should avail to draw out the bullet."

"And did it?" asked Marchmont in a tone which evidently did not escape the observant Jesuit, for that noble-witted gentleman turned sharply on the lawyer and replied with severe emphasis, "No, sir, it did not. And why? Because there was no need. The very next day after the reliquary was applied, when the dressings were changed, a small shred of filthy cloth came out of the wound. That was the cause of the trouble, not the clean metal bullet. The saint, you see, sir, knew better than the surgeon."

"Evidently," said Marchmont, glancing quickly at me, and the expression that I caught in the eye of that elderly heathen suggested that he had actually contemplated a wink and then thought better of it.

"As soon as the piece of cloth was out of the wound," Father Humperdinck resumed, "all the trouble ceased. The fever abated, the wound healed, and very soon Vitalis was able to get about, none the worse for his mishap.

189

"It was natural that he should be grateful to the saint who had saved his life, for though we look forward to the hereafter, we do not wish to die. Also was it natural that he should feel a devotion to the holy relic which had been the appointed instrument of his recovery. He did, and to gratify him, I obtained the Father General's permission to bestow it on him, which gave him great joy, and thenceforth he always carried the reliquary on his person."

"I hope he kept his promise to the saint," said Marchmont.

"He did, faithfully, and, indeed, handsomely. No sooner was he recovered of his wound than he proposed to me the founding of a new society of brothers of charity to attend the sick and wounded. I consulted with the Father General of my Society – the Society of Jesus – and received his sanction to act as director of the new society or fraternity which was to be affiliated to the Society of Jesus under the title of 'The Poor Brothers of Saint Joseph of Aramithea'."

"Why not Saint Vincent de Paul?" asked Marchmont.

"Because there was already a society named after that saint, and because Saint Joseph was a man of eminent charity. But I shall not weary you with a history of our society. It was founded and blessed by His Holiness, the Pope, it prospered, and it still prospers to the glory of God and to the benefit and relief of the sick, the poor, and the suffering. At first Vitalis paid all the costs, and he has been a generous benefactor ever since."

"This is all extremely interesting," said Marchmont, "but – you will excuse my asking – has it any bearing on your friend's disappearance?"

"Yes, sir, it has," replied Father Humperdinck, "as you shall berceive ven I my narradive gondinue."

Mr. Marchmont bowed, and Father Humperdinck, quite undisturbed by the interruption, "gondinued his narradive."

"Our first house was established in Belgium, near Brussels, and Vitalis came to live with us in community. He did not regularly join the society or take any vows, but he lived with us as one of ourselves and wore the habit of a lay brother when in the house and the dress of one when he went abroad. This he has continued to do ever since. Though bound by no vows, he has lived the life of a professed religious by choice, occupying an ordinary cell for sleeping and taking his meals at the refectory table. But not always. From time to time he has taken little holidays to travel about and mix – with the outer world. Sometimes he would come to England to visit his relatives, and sometimes he would spend a few weeks in one of the great cities of the Continent, looking over the museums and picture-galleries. He was greatly interested in art and liked to frequent the society of painters and sculptors, of whom he

190

knew several, and one, in particular – an English painter named Burton, whose acquaintance he made quite recently – he seemed very much attached to, for he stayed with him at Bruges for more than a month.

"When he came back from Bruges, he told me that he purposed going to England to see his relatives and to make certain arrangements with his lawyers for securing a part of his property to our Society. I had often urged him to do this, but, hitherto, he had retained complete control of his property and only paid the expenses of the Society as they occurred.

"He was most generous, but, of course, this was a bad arrangement, because, in the event of his death, we should have been left without the support that he had promised. It seemed that while he was at Bruges he had discussed this matter with Mr. Burton, who was a Catholic, and that the Englishman also had advised him to make a permanent provision for the Society. It seemed that he had decided to divide his property between our community and a cousin of his who lives in England, a project of which I strongly approved. After staying with us for a month or two, he left for England with the purpose of making this arrangement. That was in the middle of last September, and I have not seen him since."

"Did he complete the arrangements that he had mentioned?" Thorndyke asked.

"No, he did not. He made certain arrangements as to his property, but they were very different ones from those he had proposed. But we shall come to that presently. Let me finish my story.

"A few days after Vitalis left us, our oldest lay brother was taken very seriously ill. I wrote to Vitalis, who was deeply attached to Brother Bartholomew, telling him of this, and, as I did not know where he was staying, I sent the letter to his cousin's house at Hampstead. He replied, on the eighteenth of September, that he should return immediately. He said that he was then booking his luggage and paying his hotel bill, that he had to see his cousin again, but that he would try to come by the night train, or if he missed that, he would sleep at the station hotel and start as early as possible on the following day, the nineteenth. That was the last I ever heard from him. He never came and has never communicated with me since."

"You have made enquiries, of course?" said Thorndyke.

"Yes. When he did not come, I wrote to his lawyer, Mr. Wyndhurst, whom I knew slightly. But Mr. Wyndhurst was dead, and my letter was answered by Mr. Marchmont. From him I learned that Vitalis had called on him on the morning of the nineteenth and made certain arrangements of which he, perhaps, will tell you. Mr. Marchmont ascertained that, on the same day, Vitalis's luggage was taken from the cloak-room in time to catch the boat train. I have made inquiries and find that he arrived at Calais, and I have succeeded in tracing him to Paris, but there I have lost him. Where he is now I am unable to discover.

"And now, before I finish my story, you had better hear what Mr. Marchmont has to tell. He has been very close with me, but you are a lawyer and perhaps know better how to deal with lawyers."

Thorndyke glanced enquiringly at the solicitor, who, in his turn, looked dubiously at the end of his waning cigar. "The fact is," said he, "I am in a rather difficult position. Mr. Reinhardt has employed me as his solicitor, and I don't quite see my way to discussing his private affairs without his authority."

"That is a perfectly correct attitude," said Thorndyke, "and yet I am going to urge you to tell us what passed at your interview with your client. I can't go into particulars at present, but I will ask you to take it from me that there are sound reasons why you should, and I will undertake to hold you immune from any blame for having done so."

Marchmont looked sharply and with evidently awakened interest at Thorndyke. "I think I know what that means," he said, "and I will take you at your word, having learned by experience what your word is worth. But before describing the interview, I had better let you know how Reinhardt had previously disposed of his property.

"About twelve years ago he got Wyndhurst to draft a will for him by which a life interest in the entire property was vested in his cousin, a Miss Augusta Vyne, with reversion to her niece, Sylvia Vyne, the only child of his cousin Robert. This will was duly executed in our office.

"After that our firm had, until quite recently, no special business to transact for Mr. Reinhardt beyond the management of his investments. The whole of his property – which was all personal – was in our hands to invest, and our relations with him were confined to the transfer of sums of money to his bank when we received instructions from him to effect such transfer. He never called at the office, and latterly there has been no one there who knew him excepting Wyndhurst himself and the clerk, Bell.

"The next development occurred last September. On the seventeenth I received a letter from him, written at Miss Vyne's house at Hampstead, saying that he had been discussing his affairs with her and that he should like to call on me and make some slight alterations in the disposal of the property. I replied on the eighteenth, addressing my letter to him at Miss Vyne's house, making an appointment for eleven o'clock on the morning of the nineteenth. He kept the appointment punctually, and we had a short interview, at which he explained the new arrangements which he wished to make.

192

"He began by saying that he had found it somewhat inconvenient, living, as he did, on the Continent, to have his account at an English Bank. He proposed, therefore, to transfer it to a private bank at Paris, conducted by a certain M. Desire, or rather to open an account there, for he did not suggest closing his account at his English bank."

"Do you know anything about this M. Desire?" asked Thorndyke.

"I did not, but I have since ascertained that he is a person of credit – quite a substantial man in fact – and that his business is chiefly that of private banker and agent to the officers of the army.

"Well, Mr. Reinhardt went on to say that he had become rather tired of the monotonous life of a lay brother – which he, after all, was not – and wished for a little freedom and change. Accordingly he intended to travel for a time – which was his reason for employing M. Desire – and did not propose, necessarily, to keep anyone informed of his whereabouts. He was a rich man and he had decided to get some advantage from his wealth, which really did not seem to me at all an unreasonable decision. He added that he had no intention of withdrawing his support from the Society of the Poor Brothers, he merely intended to dissociate himself, personally, from it, and he suggested that any occasions that might arise for pecuniary assistance should be addressed to him under cover of M. Desire.

"Finally, he desired me to transfer one-thousand pounds stock to his new agent seven days from the date of our interview, and gave me an authority in writing to that effect in which he instructed me to accept M. Desire's receipt as a valid discharge."

"And you did so?" asked Thorndyke.

"Certainly I did. And I hold M. Desire's receipt for the amount."

"Did you think it necessary to raise the question of your client's identity, seeing that no one in the office knew him personally?"

"No, I did not. The question did not arise. There could not possibly be any doubt on the subject. He was an old client of the firm, and our correspondence had been carried on under cover of his cousin, Miss Vyne, who had known him all his life. You remember that I wrote to him at Miss Vyne's address, making the appointment for the interview."

"And what happened next?"

"The next development was a letter from Father Humperdinck asking if I could give him Mr. Reinhardt's address. Of course I could not, but I wrote to M. Desire asking him if he could give it to me. Desire replied that he did not, at the moment, know where Mr. Reinhardt was, but would, if desired, take charge of any communications and forward them at the first opportunity. This statement may or may not have been true, but I don't think we shall get any more information out of Desire.

He is Reinhardt's agent and will act on his instructions. If Reinhardt has told him not to give anyone his address, naturally he won't give it. So there the matter ends, so far as I am concerned."

"Did Vitalis make no suggestion as to altering his will?" Father Humperdinck enquired.

"None whatever. Nothing was said about the will. But," Mr. Marchmont added, after a cogitative pause, "we must remember that he has another man of business now. There is no saying what he may have done through M. Desire."

Father Humperdinck nodded gloomily, and Thorndyke addressing the solicitor, asked, "And that is all you have to tell us?"

"Yes. And I'm not sure that it is not a good deal more than I ought to have told you. It is Father Humperdinck's turn now."

The Jesuit acknowledged the invitation to resume his narrative by a stiff bow and then proceeded, "You can now see, sir, that what I said is perfectly correct. The conduct of my friend Vitalis shows a sudden and unaccountable change. It is quite inconsistent with his habits and his way of thinking. And the change is, as I say, so sudden. One day he is coming with the greatest haste to the bedside of his sick friend, Brother Bartholomew, the next he is making arrangements for a life of selfish pleasure, utterly indifferent as to whether that friend is alive or dead. As a matter of fact, the good brother passed away to his reward the day after Vitalis should have arrived, without even a message from his old friend. But now I return to my story.

"When Vitalis failed to appear, and I could get no news of him, I became very anxious, and, as it happened that the business of our Society called me to England, I determined to inquire into the matter. Circumstances compelled me to travel by way of Boulogne and cross to Folkestone. I say 'circumstances', but I should rather say that I was guided that way by the hand of Providence, for, in the train that brought me from Folkestone to London, I had a most astonishing experience. In the carriage, alone with me, there travelled a young man, a very strange young man indeed. He was a very large man – or, I should say, very high – and in appearance rather fierce and wild. His clothes were good, but they were disordered and stained with mud, as if he had been drunk at night and had rolled in the gutter. And this, I think, was the case, for, soon after we had started, he began to turn out his pockets on the seat of the carriage, as if to see whether he had lost anything during his debauch. And then it was that I saw a most astonishing thing. Among the objects that this man took from his pockets and laid on the seat, was the reliquary that I had given so many years ago to Vitalis.

"I could not mistake it. Once it had been mine, and I had been accustomed to see it almost daily since. Moreover the young man had the effrontery to pass it to me that I might examine it, and I found on it the very letters which I, myself, had caused to be engraved on it. When I asked him where he had obtained it, he told me that he had picked it up at Hampstead, and he professed not to know what it was. But his answers were very evasive and I did not believe him."

"Nevertheless," said Mr. Marchmont, "there was nothing improbable in his statement. Mr. Reinhardt had been at Hampstead and might have dropped it."

"Possibly. But he would have taken measures to recover it. He would not have left England until he had found it. He was a rich man, and he would have offered a large reward for this his most prized possession."

"You say," said Thorndyke, "that he habitually carried this reliquary on his person. Can you tell us how he carried or wore it?"

"That," replied Father Humperdinck, "was what I was coming to. The reliquary was a small gold object with a ring at each end. It was meant I suppose, to be worn round the wrist, or perhaps the neck, by means of a cord or chain attached to the two rings, or to be inserted into a chaplet of devotional beads. But this was not the way in which Vitalis carried it. He possessed a small and very beautiful crucifix which he set great store by, because it was given to him by one of the fathers when he left school, and which he used to wear suspended from his neck by a green silk cord. Now, when I gave him the reliquary, he caused a goldsmith to link one of its rings to the ring of the crucifix and he fastened the silk cord to the other ring, and so suspended both the reliquary and the crucifix from his neck."

"Did he wear them outside his clothing so that they were visible?" Thorndyke asked.

"Yes, outside his waistcoat, so that they were not only visible but very conspicuous when his coat was unbuttoned. It was, of course, very unsuitable to the dress of a lay brother, and I spoke to him about it several times. But he was sometimes rather self-willed, as you may judge by his refusal to settle an endowment on the Society, and, naturally, as he was not professed, I had no authority over him. But I shall return presently to the reliquary. Now I continue about this young man.

"When I had heard his explanation, and decided that he was telling me lies, I made a simple pretext to discover his name and place of abode. With the same effrontery, he gave me his card, which I have here, and which, you will see, is stained with mud, owing, no doubt, to those wallowings in the mire of which I have spoken." He drew the card from

195

his pocket-book and handed it to Thorndyke, who read it gravely, and, pushing it across the table to me, said, without moving a muscle of his face, "You had better copy it into your notes, Mr. Howard, so that we may have the record complete."

I accordingly copied out my own name and address with due solemnity and a growing enjoyment of the situation, and then returned the card to Father Humperdinck, who pocketed it carefully and resumed, "Having the name and address of this young man, I telegraphed immediately to a private detective bureau in Paris, asking to have sent to me, if possible, a certain M. Foucault, who makes a speciality of following and watching suspected persons. This Foucault is a man of extraordinary talent. His power of disguising himself is beyond belief and his patience is inexhaustible. Fortunately he was disengaged and came to me without delay, and, when I had given him the name and address of this young man, Jardine, and described him from my recollection of him, he set a watch on the house and found that the man was really living there, as he had said, and that he made a daily journey to the hospital of St. Margaret's, where he seemed to have some business, as he usually stayed there until evening."

"St. Margaret's!" exclaimed Marchmont. "Why that is your hospital, Thorndyke. Do you happen to know this man Jardine?"

"There is, or was, a student of that name, who qualified some little time ago, and who is probably the man Father Humperdinck is referring to. A tall man, quite as tall, I should say, as my friend here, Mr. Howard."

"I should say," said Father Humperdinck, "that the man, Jardine, is taller, decidedly taller. I watched him as I walked behind him up the platform at Charing Cross, and M. Foucault has shown him to me since. But that matters not. Have you seen the man, Jardine, lately at the hospital?"

"Not very lately," Thorndyke replied. "I saw him there nearly a fortnight ago, but that, I think, was the last time."

"Ah!" exclaimed Humperdinck. "Exactly. But I shall continue my story. For some time M. Foucault kept a close watch on this man, but discovered nothing fresh. He went to the hospital daily, he came home, and he stayed indoors the whole evening. But, at last, there came a new discovery.

"One morning M. Foucault saw the man, Jardine, come out of his house, dressed more carefully than usual. From his house, Foucault followed him to a picture gallery in Leicester Square and went in after him, and there he saw him meet a female, evidently by a previous assignation. *And*," Father Humperdinck continued, slapping the table to emphasize the climax of his story, "*From-the-neck-of-that-female-was-hanging-Vitalis-Reinhardt's-Crucifix!*"

Having made this thrilling communication, our reverend client leaned back to watch its effect on his audience. I am afraid he must have been a little disappointed, for Thorndyke was habitually impassive in his exterior, and, as for Jervis and me, we were fully occupied in maintaining a decent and befitting gravity. But Marchmont – the only person present who was not already acquainted with the incident – saved the situation by exclaiming, "Very remarkable! Very remarkable indeed!"

"It is more than remarkable," said Father Humperdinck. "It is highly suspicious. You observe that the reliquary and the crucifix had been linked together. Now they are separated, and since both the rings of the reliquary were unbroken, it follows that the ring of the crucifix must have been cut through and a new one made, by which to suspend it."

"I don't see anything particularly suspicious in that," said Marchmont. "If Jardine found the two articles fixed together, and – having failed to discover the owner – wished to give the crucifix to his friend, it is not unnatural that he should have separated them."

"I do not believe that he found them," Father Humperdinck replied doggedly, "but I shall continue my story and you will see. There is not much more to tell.

"It seems that the man, Jardine, suspected Foucault of watching him, for presently he left the gallery in company with the female, and, after being followed for some distance, he managed to escape. As soon as Foucault found that he had lost him, he went to Jardine's house and waited about the neighbourhood, and an hour or two later he had the good fortune to see him coming from Hampstead towards Highgate, in company with another female. He followed them until they entered a narrow passage or lane that leads up the hill, and when they had gone up this some distance, he followed, but could not get near enough to hear what they were saying.

"And now he had a most strange and terrible experience. For some time past he had felt a suspicion that some person – some accomplice of Jardine's perhaps – was following and watching him, and now he had proof of it. At the top of the lane, Jardine stopped to talk to the female, and Foucault crept on tiptoe towards him, and while he was doing so, he heard someone approaching stealthily up the lane, behind him. Suddenly, Jardine began to return down the lane. As it was not convenient for Foucault to meet him there, he also turned and walked back, and then he heard a sound as if someone were climbing the high wooden fence that enclosed the lane. Then Jardine began to run, and Foucault was compelled also to run but he would have been overtaken if it had not happened that Jardine fell down.

"Now, just as he heard Jardine fall, he came to a broken place in the fence, and it occurred to him to creep through the hole and hide while Jardine passed. He accordingly began to do so, but no sooner had he thrust his head through the hole than some unseen ruffian dealt him a violent blow which rendered him instantly insensible. When he recovered his senses, he found himself lying in a churchyard which adjoins the lane, but Jardine and the other ruffian were, of course, nowhere to be seen.

"And now I come to the last incident that I have to relate. The assault took place on a Saturday, on the Sunday M. Foucault was somewhat indisposed and unable to go out, but early on Monday he resumed his watch on Jardine's house. It was nearly noon when Jardine came out, dressed as if for travelling and carrying a valise. He went first to a house near Piccadilly and from thence to the hospital in a cab. Foucault followed in another cab and saw him go into the hospital and waited for him to come out. But he never came. Foucault waited until midnight, but he did not come out. He had vanished."

"He had probably come out by a back exit and gone home," said Marchmont.

"Not so," replied Humperdinck. "The next day Foucault watched Jardine's house, but he did not come there. Then he made enquiries, but Jardine is not there, and the landlady does not know where he is. Also the porter at the hospital knows nothing and is not at all polite. The man Jardine has disappeared as if he had never been."

"That really is rather queer," said Marchmont. "It is a pity that you did not give me all these particulars at first. However, that can't be helped now. Is this all that you have to tell us?"

"It is all, unless there is anything that you wish to ask me."

"I think," said Thorndyke, "that it would be well for us to have a description of Mr. Reinhardt, and, as we have to trace him, if possible, a photograph would be exceedingly useful."

"I have not a photograph with me," said Father Humperdinck, "but I will obtain one and send it to you. Meanwhile I will tell you what my friend Vitalis is like. He is sixty-two years of age, spare, upright, rather tall – his height is a hundred-and-seventy-three centimetres – "

"Roughly five-feet-nine," interposed Thorndyke.

"His hair is nearly white, he is, of course, clean shaven, he has grey eyes, a straight nose, not very prominent, and remarkably good teeth for his age, which he shows somewhat when he talks. I think he is a little vain about his teeth and he well may be, for there are not many men of

198

sixty-two who have not a single false tooth, nor even one that has been stopped by the dentist. As to his clothing, he wears the ordinary dress of a lay brother, which you are probably familiar with, and he nearly always wears gloves, even indoors."

"Is there any reason for his wearing gloves?" Thorndyke asked.

"Not now. The habit began when he had some affliction of the skin, which made it necessary for him to keep his hands covered with gloves which contained some ointment or dressing, and afterwards for a time to conceal the disagreeable appearance of the skin. The habit having been once formed, he continued it, saying that his hands were more comfortable covered up than when exposed to the air."

"Was he dressed in this fashion when he called at your office, Marchmont?" asked Thorndyke.

"Yes. Even to the gloves. I noticed, with some surprise, that he did not take them off even when he wrote and signed the note of which I told you."

"Was he then wearing the reliquary and crucifix as Father Humperdinck has described, on the front of his waistcoat?"

"He may have been, but I didn't notice them, as I fancy I should have done if they had been there."

"And you have nothing more to tell us, Father Humperdinck, as to your friend's personal appearance?"

"No. I will send you the photograph and write to you if I think of anything that I have forgotten. And now, perhaps you can tell me if you think that you will be able to answer those questions that Mr. Marchmont put to you."

"I cannot, of course, answer them now," replied Thorndyke. "The facts that you have given us will have to be considered and compared, and certain enquiries will have to be made. Are you staying long in England?"

"I shall be here for at least a month, and I may as well leave you my address, although Mr. Marchmont has it."

"In the course of a month," Thorndyke said, as he took the proffered card, "I think I may promise you that we shall have settled definitely whether your friend is alive or dead, and if we find that he is alive, we shall, no doubt, be able to ascertain his whereabouts."

"That is very satisfactory," said Father Humperdinck. "I hope you shall be able to make good your promise."

With this he rose, and, having shaken hands stiffly with Thorndyke, bestowed on Jervis and me a ceremonious bow and moved towards the door. I thought that Marchmont looked a little wistful, as if he would have liked to stay and have a few words with us alone, indeed, he lingered for a moment or two after the door was open, but then, apparently altering his mind, he wished us "Good-night" and followed his client.

Chapter XVII
The Palimpsest

It was getting late when our friends left us, but nevertheless, as soon as they were gone, we all drew our chairs up to the fire with the obvious intention of discussing the situation and began, with one accord, to fill our pipes. Jervis was the first to get his tobacco alight, and, having emitted a voluminous preliminary puff, he proceeded to open the debate.

"That man, Jardine, seems to be a pretty desperate character. Just think of his actually wallowing in the mire – not merely rolling, mind you, but wallowing – and of his repulsive habit of consorting with females, one after the other, too, in rapid succession. It's a shocking instance of depravity."

"Our reverend friend," said Thorndyke, "reaches his conclusions by a rather short route – in some cases, at least. In others, his methods seem a little indirect and roundabout."

"Yes," agreed Jervis, "he's a devil at guessing. But he didn't get much food for the imagination out of the man, Thorndyke. Why were you so extraordinarily secretive? With what he told you and what you knew before, you could surely have suggested a line of inquiry. Why didn't you?"

"Principally because of the man's personality. I could not have answered his questions. I could, only have suggested one or two highly probable solutions of the problem that he offered and partial solutions at that. But I am not much addicted to giving partial solutions – to handing over the raw material of a promising inquiry. Certainly, not to a man like this, who seems incapable of a straight-forward action."

"The reverend father," said Jervis, "does certainly seem to be a rather unnecessarily downy bird. And he doesn't seem to have got much by his excessive artfulness, after all."

"No," agreed Thorndyke, "nothing whatever. Quite the contrary, in fact. Look at his ridiculous conduct in respect of 'the man Jardine'. I don't complain of his having taken the precaution to obtain that malefactor's address, but, when he had got it, if he had not been tortuous, so eager to be cunning – if, in short, he had behaved like an ordinary sensible man, he would have got, at once, all the information that Jardine had to give. He could have called on Jardine, written to him, employed a lawyer, or applied to the police. Either of these simple and obvious plans

201

would have been successful, instead of which, he must needs go to the trouble and expense of engaging this absurd spy."

"Who found a mare's nest and got his head thumped," remarked Jervis.

"Then," continued Thorndyke, "look at his behaviour to Marchmont. Evidently he put the case into Marchmont's hands, but, equally evident, he withheld material facts and secretly tinkered at the case himself. No, Jervis, I give no information to Father Humperdinck until I have this case complete to the last rivet. But, all the same, I am greatly obliged to him, and especially to Marchmont, for bringing him here. He has given us a connected story to collate with our rather loose collection of facts and, what is perhaps more important, he has put our investigation on a business footing. That is a great advantage. If I should want to invoke the aid of the powers that be, I can do so now with a definite *locus standi* as the legal representative of interested parties."

"I can't imagine," said I, "in what direction you are going to push your inquiries. Father Humperdinck has given us, as you say, a connected story, but it is a very unexpected one, to me, at least, and does not fall into line at all with what we know – that is, if you are assuming, as I have been, that the man whom I saw lying in Millfield Lane was Vitalis Reinhardt."

"It is difficult," replied Thorndyke, "to avoid that assumption, though we must be on our guard against coincidences – but the man whom you saw agreed with the description that has been given to us, we know that Reinhardt was in the neighbourhood on that day, and you found the reliquary on the following morning in the immediate vicinity. We seem to be committed to the hypothesis that the man was Reinhardt unless we can prove that he was someone else, or that Reinhardt was in some other place at the time, which at present we cannot."

"Then," said I, "in that case, the bobby must have been right, after all. The man couldn't have been dead, seeing that he called on Marchmont the following day and was afterwards traced to Paris. But I must say that he looked as dead as Queen Anne. It just shows how careful one ought to be in giving opinions."

"Some authority has said," remarked Jervis, "that the only conclusive proof of death is decomposition. I believe it was old Taylor who said so, and I am inclined to think that he wasn't far wrong."

"But," said Thorndyke, "assuming that the man whom you saw was Reinhardt, and that he was not dead – how do you explain the other circumstances? Was he insensible from the effects of injury or drugs? Or was he deliberately shamming insensibility? Was it he who passed over the fence? And if so, did he climb over unassisted or was he helped over?

And what answers do you suggest to the questions that Marchmont propounded? You answer his first question: 'Is Reinhardt alive?' in the affirmative. What about the others?"

"As to where he is," I replied. "I can only say – the Lord knows, probably skulking somewhere on the Continent. As to his state of mind, the facts seem to suggest that, in vulgar parlance, he has gone off his onion. He must be as mad as a hatter to have behaved in the way that he has. For, even assuming that he wanted to get clear of the Poor Brothers of Saint Jeremiah Diddler without explicitly saying so, he adopted a fool's plan. There is no sense in masquerading as a corpse one day and turning up smiling at your lawyer's office the next. If he meant to be dead, he should have stuck to it and remained dead."

"The objection to that," said Jervis, "is that Marchmont would have proceeded to get permission to presume death and administer the will."

"I see. Then I can only suppose that he had got infected by Father Humperdinck and resolved to be artful at all costs and hang the consequences."

"Then," said Thorndyke, "I understand your view to be that Reinhardt is at present hiding somewhere on the Continent and that his mind is more or less affected?"

"Yes. Though as to his being unfit to control his own affairs, I am not so clear. I fancy there was more evidence in that direction when he was forking out the bulk of his income to maintain the poverty of the Poor Brothers. But the truth is, I haven't any opinions on the case at all. I am in a complete fog about the whole affair."

"And no wonder," said Jervis. "One set of facts seems to suggest most strongly that Reinhardt must certainly be dead. Another set of facts seems to prove beyond doubt that he was alive, at least after that affair in Millfield Lane. He may be perpetrating an elephantine practical joke on the Poor Brothers, but that doesn't seem to be particularly probable. The whole case is a tangle of contradictions which one might regard as beyond unravelment if it were not for a single clear and intelligible fact."

"What is that?" I asked.

"That my revered senior has undertaken to furnish a solution in the course of a month, from which I gather that my revered senior has something up his sleeve."

"There is nothing up my sleeve," said Thorndyke, "that might not equally well be up yours. I have made no separate investigations. The actual data which I possess were acquired in the presence of one or both of you, and are now the common property of us all. I am referring, of course, to the original data, not to fresh matter obtained by inference from, or further examination of those data."

Jervis smiled sardonically. "It is the old story," said he. "The magician offers you his hat to inspect. 'You observe, ladies and gentlemen, that there is no deception. You can look inside it and examine the lining, and you can also inspect the top of my head. I now put on my hat. I now take it off again and you notice that there is a guinea pig sitting in it. There was no deception, ladies and gentlemen. You had all the data.'"

Thorndyke laughed and shook his head, "That's all nonsense, Jervis," he said. "It is a false analogy. I have done nothing to divert your attention. The guinea pig has been staring you in the face all the time."

"Very rude of him," murmured Jervis.

"I have even drawn your attention to him once or twice. But, seriously, I don't think that this case is so very obscure, though mind you, it is a mere hypothesis so far as I am concerned, and may break down completely when I come to apply the tests that I have in view. But what I mean is, that the facts known to us suggested a very obvious hypothesis and that the suggestion was offered equally to us all. The verification may fail, but that is another matter."

"Are you going to work at the case immediately?" I asked.

"No," Thorndyke replied. "Jervis and I have to attend at the Maidstone Assizes for the next few days. We are retained on a case which involves some very important issues in relation to life assurance, and that will take up most of our time. So this other affair will have to wait.

"And meanwhile," said Jervis, "you will stay at home like a good boy and mind the shop, and I suppose we shall have to find you something to do, to keep you out of mischief. What do you say to making a longhand transcript of Father Humperdinck's statement?"

"Yes, you had better do that," said Thorndyke, "and attach it to the original shorthand copy. And now we must really turn in or we shall never be ready for our start in the morning."

The transcription of Father Humperdinck's statement gave me abundant occupation for the whole of the following morning. But when that was finished, I was without any definite employment, and, though I was not in the least dull – for I was accustomed to a solitary life – I suppose I was in that state of susceptibility to mischief that is proverbially associated with unemployment. And in these untoward circumstances I was suddenly exposed to a great temptation, and after some feeble efforts at resistance, succumbed ignominiously.

I shall offer no excuses for my conduct nor seek in any way to mitigate the judgment that all discreet persons will pass upon my folly. I make no claims to discretion or to the caution and foresight of a man like

Thorndyke. At this time I was an impulsive and rather heedless young man, and my actions were pretty much those which might have been expected from a person of such temperament.

The voice of the tempter issued in the first place from our letter-box, and assumed the sound of the falling of letters thereinto. I hastened to extract the catch, and sorting out the envelopes, selected one, the superscription of which was in Sylvia's now familiar handwriting. It was actually addressed to Dr. Thorndyke, but a private mark, on which we had agreed, exposed that naively pious fraud and gave me the right to open it, which I did, and seated myself in the armchair to enjoy its perusal at my ease.

It was a delightful letter, bright, gossipy and full of frank and intimate friendliness. As I read it, the trim, graceful figure and pretty face of the writer rose before me and made me wonder a little discontentedly how long it would be before I should look on her and hear her voice again. It was now getting into the third week since I had last seen her, and, as the time passed, I was feeling more and more how great a blank in my life the separation from her had caused. Our friendship had grown up in a quiet and unsensational fashion and I suppose I had not realized all that it meant, but I was realizing it now, and, as I conned over her letter, with its little personal notes and familiar turns of expression, I began to be consumed with a desire to see her, to hear her speak, to tell her that she was not as other women to me, and to claim a like special place in her thoughts.

It was towards the end of the letter that the tempter spoke out in clear and unmistakable language, and these were the words that he used, through the medium of the innocent and unconscious Sylvia: *"You remember those sketches that you stole for me – 'pinched', I think was your own expression. Well, I have cleaned off the daubs of paint with which they had been disfigured and put them in rough frames in my studio. All but one, and I began on that yesterday with a scraper and a rag dipped in chloroform. But I took off, not only the defacing marks but part of the surface as well, and then I got such a surprise! I shan't tell you what the surprise was, because you'll see, when you come out of the house of bondage. I am going to work on it again to-morrow, and perhaps I shall get the transformation finished. How I wish you could come and see it done! It takes away more than half the joy of exploration not to be able to share the discovery with you, in fact, I have a good mind to leave it unfinished so that we can complete the transformation together."*

Now, I need not say that, as to the precious sketches, I cared not a fig what was under the top coat of paint. What I did care for was that this dear maid was missing me as I missed her, was wanting my sympathy with her little interests and pleasures and was telling me, half-unconsciously, perhaps, that my absence had created a blank in her life, as her absence had in mine. And forthwith I began to ask myself whether there was really any good reason why I should not, just for this once, break out of my prison and snatch a few brief hours of sunshine. The spy had been exploded. He was not likely to pick up my tracks after all this time and now that my appearance was so altered, and I did not care much if he did seeing that he had been shown to be perfectly harmless. The only circumstance that tended to restrain me from this folly was the one that mitigated its rashness – the change in my appearance, and even that, now that I was used to it and knew that my aspect was neither grotesque nor ridiculous, had little weight, for Sylvia would be prepared for the change and we could enjoy the joke together.

I was aware, even at the time, that I was not being quite candid with myself, for, if I had been, I should obviously have consulted Thorndyke. Instead of which I answered the letter by return, announcing my intention of coming to tea on the following day, and having sent Polton out to post it, spent the remainder of the afternoon in gleeful anticipation of my little holiday, tempered by some nervousness as to what Thorndyke would have to say on the matter, and as to what "my pretty friend", as Mrs. Samway had very appropriately called her, would think of my having begun my letter with the words, "*My dear Sylvia*".

Nothing happened to interfere with my nefarious plans.

On the following morning, Thorndyke and Jervis went off after an early breakfast, leaving me in possession of the premises and master of my actions. I elected to anticipate the usual luncheon time by half-an-hour, and, when this meal was disposed of, I crept to my room and thoroughly cleansed my hair of the grease which Polton still persisted in applying to it, for, since my hat would conceal it while I was out of doors, the added disfigurement was unnecessary. I was even tempted to tamper slightly with my eyebrows, but this impulse I nobly resisted, and, having dried my hair and combed it in its normal fashion, I descended on tip-toe to the sitting-room and wrote a short, explanatory note to Polton, which I left conspicuously on the table. Then I switched the door-bell on to the laboratory, and, letting myself out like a retreating burglar, closed the door silently and sneaked away down the dark staircase.

Once fairly outside, I went off like a lamplighter, and, shooting out through the Tudor Street gate, made my way eastward to Broad Street Station, where I was fortunate enough to catch a train that was just on the point of starting. At Hampstead Heath Station I got out, and, snuffing the air joyfully, set forth at my best pace up the slope that leads to the summit, and in little over twenty minutes found myself at the gate of The Hawthorns.

There was no need to knock or ring. My approach had been observed from the window, and, as I strode up the garden path, the door opened and Sylvia ran out to meet me. "It was nice of you to come!" she exclaimed, as I took her hand and held it in mine. "I don't believe you ought to have ventured out, but I am most delighted all the same. Don't make a noise, Mopsy is having a little doze in the drawing room. Come into the morning room and let me have a good look at you."

I followed her meekly into the front room, where, in the large bay window, she inspected me critically, her cheeks dimpling with a mischievous smile. "There's something radically wrong about your eyebrows," she said, "but, really, you are not in the least the fright that you made out. As to the beard and moustache, I am not sure that I don't rather like them."

"I hope you don't," I replied, "because, off they come at the first opportunity – unless, of course, you forbid it."

"Does my opinion of your appearance matter so much then?"

"It matters entirely. I don't care what I look like to anyone else."

"Oh! What a fib!" exclaimed Sylvia. "Don't I remember how very neatly turned out you always were when you used to pass me in the lane before we knew one another?"

"Exactly," I retorted. "We didn't know one another then. That makes all the difference in the world – to me, at any rate."

"Does it?" she said, colouring a little and looking at me thoughtfully. "It's very – very flattering of you to say so, Dr. Jardine."

"I hope you don't mean that as a snub," I said, rather uneasy at the form of her reply and thinking of my letter.

"A snub!" she exclaimed. "No, I certainly don't. What did I say?"

"You called me Dr. Jardine. I addressed you in my letter as '*Sylvia – My dear Sylvia*'."

"And what ought I to have said?" she asked, blushing warmly and casting down her eyes.

"Well, Sylvia, if you liked me as well as I like you, I don't see why you shouldn't call me Humphrey. We are quite old friends now."

"So we are," she agreed, "and perhaps it would be less formal. So Humphrey it shall be in future, since that is your royal command. But tell me, how did you prevail on Dr. Thorndyke to let you come here? Is there any change in the situation?"

"There's a change in my situation, and a mighty agreeable change, too. I'm here."

"Now don't be silly. How did you persuade Dr. Thorndyke to let you come?"

"Ha – that, my dear Sylvia, is a rather embarrassing question. Shall we change the subject?"

"No, we won't." She looked at me suspiciously for a moment and then exclaimed in low, tragical tones, "Humphrey! You don't mean to tell me that you came away without his knowledge!"

"I'm afraid that is what it amounts to. I saw a loop-hole and I popped through it, and here I am, as I remarked before."

"But how dreadful of you! Perfectly shocking! And whatever will he say to you when you go back?"

"That is a question that I am not proposing to present vividly to my consciousness until I arrive on the door-step. I've broken out of choke and I'm going to have a good time – to go on having a good time, I should say."

"Then you consider that you are having a good time now?"

"I don't consider. I am sure of it. Am I not, at this very moment looking at you? And what more could a man desire?"

She tried to look severe, though the attempt was not strikingly successful, and retorted in an admonishing tone, "You needn't try to wheedle me with compliments. You are a very wicked person and most indiscreet. But it seems to me that some sort of change has come over you since you retired from the world. Don't you think I'm right?"

"You're perfectly right. I've improved. That's what it is. Matured and mellowed, you know, like a bottle of claret that has been left in a cellar and forgotten. Say you think I've improved, Sylvia."

"I won't," she replied, and then, changing her mind, she added, "Yes, I will. I'll say that you are more insinuating than ever, if that will do. And now, as, you are clearly quite incorrigible, I won't scold you any more, especially as you 'broke out of chokee' to come and see me. You shall tell me all about your adventures."

"I didn't come here to talk about myself, Sylvia. I came to tell you something – well, about myself, perhaps, but – er – not my adventures you know or – or that sort of thing – but, I have been thinking a good deal, since I have been alone so much – about you, I mean, Sylvia – and – er – Oh! The deuce!"

The latter exclamation was evoked by the warning voice of the gong, evidently announcing tea, and the subsequent appearance of the housemaid, who was certainly not such a goose as she was supposed to be, for she tapped discreetly at the door and waited three full seconds before entering, and even then she appeared demurely unconscious of my

208

existence. "If you please, Miss Sylvia, Miss Vyne has woke up and I've taken in the tea."

Such was the paltry interruption that arrested the flow of my eloquence and scattered my flowers of rhetoric to the winds. I murmured inwardly, "Blow the tea!" for the opportunity was gone, but I comforted myself with the reflection that it didn't matter very much, since Sylvia and I seemed to have arrived at a pretty clear understanding, which understanding was further clarified by a momentary contact of our hands as we followed the maid to the drawing-room. Miss Vyne was on this occasion, as on the last, seated in the exact centre of the room, and with the same monumental effect, so that my thoughts were borne irresistibly to the ethnographical section of the British Museum, and especially to that part of it wherein the deities of Polynesia look out from their cases in perennial surprise at the degenerate European visitors. If she had been asleep previously, she was wide enough awake now, but the glittering eyes were not directed at me. From the moment of our entering the room they focussed themselves on Sylvia's face and there remained riveted, whereby the heightening of that young lady's complexion, which our interview had produced, became markedly accentuated. It was to no purpose that I placed myself before the rigid figure and offered my hand. A paw was lifted automatically to mine, but the eyes remained fixed on Sylvia. "What did you say this gentleman's name was!" the waxwork asked frigidly.

"This is Dr. Jardine," was the reply.

"Oh, indeed. And who was the gentleman who called some three weeks ago?"

"Why, that was Dr. Jardine. You know it was."

"So I thought, but my memory is not very reliable. And this is a Dr. Jardine, too? Very interesting. A medical family, apparently. But not much alike."

I was beginning to explain my identity and the cause of my altered appearance, when Sylvia approached with a cup of tea and a carefully dissected muffin, which latter she thrust under the nose of the elder lady, who regarded it attentively and with a slight squint, owing to its nearness. "It's of no use, you know," said Sylvia, "for you to pretend that you don't know him, because I've told you all about the transformation – that is, all I know myself. Don't you think it's rather a clever make-up?"

"If," said Miss Vyne, "by 'make-up' you mean a disguise, I think it is highly successful. The beard is a most admirable imitation."

"Oh, the beard is his own – at least, I think it is."

I confirmed this statement, ignoring Polton's slight additions. "Indeed," said Miss Vyne. "Then the wig – it is a wig, I suppose?"

"No, of course it isn't," Sylvia replied.

"Then," said Miss Vyne, majestically, "perhaps you will explain to me what the disguise consists of."

"Well," said Sylvia, "there are the eyebrows. You can see that they have been completely altered in shape."

"If I had committed the former shape of the eyebrows to memory, as you appear to have done," said Miss Vyne. "I should, no doubt, observe the change. But I did not. It seems to me that the disguise which you told me about with such a flourish of trumpets just amounts to this, that Dr. Jardine has allowed his beard to grow. I find the reality quite disappointing."

"Do you?" said Sylvia. "But, at any rate, you didn't recognize him, so your disappointment doesn't count for much."

The old lady, being thus hoist with her own petard, relapsed into majestic silence, and Sylvia then renewed her demand for an account of my adventures. "We want to hear all about that objectionable person who has been shadowing you, and how you finally got rid of him. Your letters were rather sketchy and wanting in detail, so you have got to make up the deficiency now."

Thus commanded, I plunged into an exhaustive account of those events which I have already chronicled at length and which I need not refer to again, nor need I record the cross-examination to which I was subjected, since it elicited nothing that is not set forth in the preceding pages. When I had finished my recital, however, Miss Vyne, who had listened to it in silence, hitherto, put a question which I had some doubts about answering. "Have you or Dr. Thorndyke been able to discover who this inquisitive person is and what is his object in following you about?"

I hesitated. As to my own experiences, I had no secrets from these friends of mine, excepting those that related to the subjects of Thorndyke's investigations, But I must not come here and babble about what took place in the sacred precincts of my principal's chambers. "I think I may tell you," said I, "that Dr. Thorndyke has discovered the identity of this man and that he is not the person whom we suspected him to be. But I mustn't say any more, as the information came through professional channels and consequently is not mine to give."

"Of course you mustn't," said Sylvia, "though I don't mind admitting that you have put me on tenterhooks of curiosity. But I daresay you will be able to tell us everything later."

I agreed that I probably should, and the talk then turned into fresh channels.

The short winter day was running out apace. The daylight had long since gone, and I began, with infinite reluctance, to think of returning to my cage. Indeed, when I looked at my watch, I was horrified to see how the time had fled. "My word!" I exclaimed. "I must be off, or Thorndyke will be putting the sleuth-hounds of the law on my track. And I don't know what you will think of me for having stayed such an unconscionable time."

"It isn't a ceremonial visit," said Sylvia, as I rose and made my *adieux* to her aunt. "We should have liked you to stay much longer."

Here she paused suddenly, and, clasping her hands, gazed at me with an expression of dismay. "Good Heavens! Humphrey!" she exclaimed.

"Eh?" said Miss Vyne.

"I was addressing Dr. Jardine," Sylvia explained, in some confusion.

"I didn't suppose you were addressing me," was the withering reply.

"Do you know," said Sylvia, "that I haven't shown you those sketches, after all. You must see them. They were the special object of your visit."

This was perfectly untrue, and she knew it, but I did not think it worthwhile to contest the statement in Miss Vyne's presence. Accordingly I expressed the utmost eagerness to see the trumpery sketches, and the more so since I had understood that they were on view in the studio, which turned out to be the case. "It won't take a minute for you to see them," said Sylvia. "I'll just run up and light the gas, and you are not to come in until I tell you."

She preceded me up the stairs to the little room on the first floor in which she worked, and, when I had waited a few moments on the landing she summoned me to enter. "These are the sketches," said she, "that I have finished. You see, they are quite presentable now. I cleaned off the rough daubs of paint with a scraper and finished up with a soft rag dipped in chloroform."

I ran my eye over the framed sketches, which, now that the canvases were strained on stretchers and the disfiguring brush-strokes removed, were, as she had said, quite presentable, though too rough and unfinished to be attractive. "I daresay they are very interesting," said I, "but they are only bare beginnings. I shouldn't have thought them worth framing."

"Not as pictures," she agreed, "but as examples of a very curious technique, I find them most instructive. However, you haven't seen the real gem of the collection. This is it, on the easel. Sit down, on the chair and say when you are ready. I'm going to give you a surprise."

I seated myself on the chair opposite the easel, on which was a canvas with its back towards me. "Now," said Sylvia. "Are you ready? One, two, three!"

She picked up the canvas, and, turning it round quickly, presented its face to me. I don't know what I had expected – if I had expected anything, but certainly I was not in the least prepared for what I saw. The sketch had originally represented, very roughly, a dark mass of trees which occupied nearly the whole of the canvas, but of this the middle had been cleaned away, exposing an under painting. And this it was that filled me with such amazement that, after a first startled exclamation, I could do nothing but stare open-mouthed at the canvas, for, from the opening in the dark mass of foliage there looked out at me, distinct and unmistakable, the face of Mrs. Samway.

It was no illusion or chance resemblance. Rough as the painting was, the likeness was excellent. All the well-known features which made her so different from other women were there, though expressed by a mere dextrous turn of the knife, the jet-black, formally-parted hair, the clear, bright complexion, the pale, inscrutable eyes, all were there, even to the steady, penetrating expression that looked out at me from the canvas as if in silent recognition. As I sat staring at the picture with a surprise that almost amounted to awe, Sylvia looked at me a little blankly. "Well!" she exclaimed, at length, "I meant to give you a surprise, but – what is it, Humphrey? Do you know her?"

"Yes," I replied, "and so do you. Don't you remember a woman who looked in at you through the glass door of Robinson's shop."

"Do you mean that black-and-scarlet creature? I didn't recognize her. I had no idea she was so handsome, for this is really a very beautiful face, though there is something about it that I don't understand. Something – well eerie, rather uncanny and almost sinister. Don't you think so?"

"I have always thought her a rather weird woman, but this is the weirdest appearance she has made. How on earth came her face on that canvas?"

"It is an odd coincidence. And yet I don't know that it is. She may have been some relative of that rather eccentric artist, or even his wife. I don't know why it shouldn't be so."

Neither did I. But the coincidence remained a very striking one – to me, at least, much more so than Sylvia realized, though what its significance might be – if it had any – I could not guess. Nor was there any opportunity to discuss it at the moment, for it was high time for me to be gone. "You will send me a telegram when you get back, to say that you have arrived home safely, won't you," said Sylvia, as we descended the stairs with our arms linked together. "Of course nothing is going to happen to you, but I can't help feeling a little nervous. And you'll go down to the station by the High Street, and keep to the main roads. That is a promise, isn't it?"

I made the promise readily having decided previously to take every possible precaution, and, when I had wished Sylvia "Good-bye" at some length, I proceeded to execute it, making my way down the well-populated High Street and keeping a bright look-out both there and at the station. Once more I was fortunate in the matter of trains, and, having taken a hansom from Broad Street to the Temple, was set down in King's Bench Walk soon after half-past six.

As I approached our building, I looked up with some anxiety at the sitting-room windows, and when I saw them brightly lighted, a suspicion that Thorndyke had returned earlier than usual filled me with foreboding, I had had my dance and now I was going to pay the piper, and I did not much enjoy the prospect. In fact, as I ascended the stairs and took my latch-key from my pocket, I was as nervous as a school-boy who has been playing truant However, there was no escape unless I sneaked up to my bed-room, so, inserting the key into the lock, I turned it as boldly as I could, and entered.

Chapter XVIII
A Visitor from the States

As I pushed open the inner door and entered the room, I conceived the momentary hope of a reprieve from the wrath to come, for I found my two friends in what was evidently a business consultation with a stranger, and was on the point of backing out when Thorndyke stopped me. "Don't run away, Howard," said he. "There are no secrets being disclosed – at least, I think not. We have finished with your affairs, Mr. O'Donnell, haven't we?"

"Yes, Doctor," was the answer, "you've run me dry with the exception – of your own little business."

"Then, come in and sit down, Howard, and let me present you to Mr. O'Donnell, who is a famous American detective and has been telling us all sorts of wonderful things."

Mr. O'Donnell paused in the act of returning a quantity of papers to a large attaché case and offered his hand. "The doctor," he remarked, "is blowing his trumpet at the wrong end. I haven't come here to give information but to get advice. But I guess I needn't tell you that."

"I hope that isn't quite true," said Thorndyke. "You spoke just now of my little business – haven't you anything to tell *me*?"

"I have, but I fancy it isn't what you wanted to hear. However, we'll just have a look at your letter to Curtis and take your questions one by one. By the way, what made you write to Curtis?"

"I saw, when I inspected Maddock's will at Somerset House, that he had left a small legacy to Curtis. Naturally, I inferred that Curtis knew him and could give me some account of him."

"It struck you as a bit queer, I reckon, that he should be leaving a legacy to the head of an American detective agency."

"The circumstance suggested possibilities," Thorndyke admitted.

O'Donnell laughed. "I can guess what possibilities suggested themselves to you, if you knew Maddock. Your letter and the lawyer's, announcing the legacy, came within a mail or two of one another. Curtis showed them both to me and we grinned. We took it for granted that the worthy testator was foxing. But we were wrong. And so are you, if that is what you thought."

"You assumed that the will was not a genuine one?"

"Yes, we thought it was a fake, put up with the aid of some shyster to bluff us into giving up Mr. Maddock as deceased. So, as I had to come

214

across about these other affairs, Curtis suggested that I should look into the matter. And a considerable surprise I got when I did, for the will is perfectly regular and so is everything else. That legacy was a sort of posthumous joke, I guess."

"Then do I understand that Mr. Curtis was not really a friend of Maddock's?"

O'Donnell chuckled. "Not exactly a friend, Doctor," said he. "He felt the warmest interest in Maddock's welfare, but they weren't what you might call bosom friends. The position was this: Curtis was the chief of our detective agency, Maddock was a gentleman whom he had been looking for and not finding for a matter of ten years. At last he found him, and then he lost him again, and this legacy, I take it, was a sort of playful hint to show which hole he'd gone down."

"Was Maddock in hiding all that time?" asked Thorndyke.

"In hiding!" repeated O'Donnell. "Bless your innocent heart, Doctor, he had a nice convenient studio in one of the best blocks in New York a couple of doors from our agency, and he used to send us cards for his private views. No, sir, our dear departed friend wasn't the kind that lurks out of sight in cellars or garrets. It was Maddock, sure enough, that Curtis wanted, only he didn't know it. But I guess I'm fogging you. I'd best answer the questions that you put to Curtis.

"First, do we know anything about Maddock? Yes, we do. But we didn't know that his name was Maddock until a few months ago. Isaac Vandamme was the name we knew him by, and it seems that he had one or two other names that he used on occasion. We now know that the gay Isaac was a particularly versatile kind of crook, and a mighty uncommon kind, too, the Lord be praised, for, if there were many more like him we should have to raise our prices some. He wasn't the kind of fool that make a million dollar coup and then goes on the razzle and drops it all. That sort of man is easy enough to deal with. When he's loaded up with dollars everybody knows it, and he's sure to be back in a week or two with empty pockets, ready for another scoop. Isaac wasn't that sort. When he made a little pile, he invested his winnings like a sensible man and didn't live beyond his means, and the only mystery to me is that, when he died, he didn't leave more pickings. I see from his will – which I've had a look at – that the whole estate couldn't have been above five-thousand dollars. He had a lot more than that at one time."

"He may have disposed of the bulk of his property by gift just before his death," Jervis suggested.

"That's possible," agreed O'Donnell. "He'd escape the death dues that way. However, to return to his engaging little ways. His leading line was penmanship – forgery – and he did it to an absolute finish. He was

215

the most expert penman that I have ever known. But where he had us all was that he didn't only know *how* to write another man's name, he knew *when* to write it. I reckon that the great bulk of his forgeries were never spotted at all, and, of the remainder very few got beyond the bare suspicion that they were forgeries. In the case of the few that were actually spotted as forgeries, his tracks were covered up so cleverly that no one could guess who the forger was."

"And how did you come to suspect him eventually?" Thorndyke asked.

"Ah!" said O'Donnell. "There you are. Every crook – even the cleverest – has a strain of the fool in him. Isaac's folly took the form of suspicion. He suspected us of suspecting him. We didn't, but he thought we did, and then he started to dodge and make some false clues for us. That drew our attention to him. We looked into his record, traced his little wanderings and then we began to find things out. A nice collection there was, too, by the time we had worked a month or two at his biography, forgeries, false notes, and, at least two murders that had been a complete mystery to us all. We made ready to drop on Isaac, but, at that psychological moment, he disappeared. It looked, as if he had left the States, and, as we have no great affection for extradition cases, we let the matter rest, more or less, expecting that he would turn up again, sooner or later. And then came this lawyer's letter and yours, announcing his decease. Of course Curtis and I thought he was at the old game, that it was a bit of that sort of extra caution that won't let well alone. So, as I was coming over, I thought I'd just look into the affair as I told you, and, to my astonishment, I found everything perfectly regular, the will properly proved, the death certificate made out correctly, and a second certificate signed by two doctors."

"Did you go into the question of identity?" asked Thorndyke.

"Oh, yes. I called on one of the doctors, a man named Batson, and ascertained that it was all correct. Batson's eyesight seemed to be none of the best, but he made it quite clear to me that his late patient was certainly our friend Isaac, or Maddock. So that's the end of the case. And if you want to go into it any further you've got to deal with a little pile of bone ash, for our friend is not only dead, he's cremated. That's enough for us. We don't follow our clients to the next world. We are not so thorough as you seem to be."

"You are flattering me unduly," said Thorndyke. "I'm not so thorough as that, but our clients, when they betake themselves to the happy hunting-ground, usually leave a few of their friends behind to continue their activities. Do you happen to know what Maddock's original occupation was? Had he any profession?"

"He was originally an engraver, and a very skilful engraver, too, I understand. That was what made him so handy in working the flash-note racket. Then he went on the stage for a time, and didn't do badly at that, but I fancy he was more clever at making-up and mimicry than at acting in the dramatic sense. For the last ten years or so he was practising as a painter – chiefly of landscape, though he could do a figure subject or a portrait at a pinch. I don't fancy he sold much, or made any great efforts to sell his work. He liked painting and the art covered his real industries, for he used to tour about in search of subjects and so open up fresh ground for the little operations that actually produced his income."

"Was his work of any considerable merit?" Thorndyke asked.

"Well, in a way, yes. It was rather in the American taste, though Maddock was really an Englishman. Our taste, as you know, runs to technical smartness and novelty of handling, and Maddock's work was very peculiar and remarkably smart and slick in handling. He used the knife more than the brush, and he used it uncommonly cleverly. In fact, he was unusually skilful in many ways, and that's the really surprising thing about him, when one considers his extraordinary-looking paws."

"What was there peculiar about his hands?" asked Thorndyke. "Were they noticeably clumsy in appearance?"

"Clumsy!" exclaimed O'Donnell. "They were more than that. They were positively deformed. A monkey's hands would be delicate compared with Maddock's, They were short and thick like the paws of an animal. There's some jaw-twisting name for the deformity that he suffered from – *bronchodaotilious*, or something like that."

"*Brachydactylous*." suggested Thorndyke.

"That's the word, and I daresay you know the sort of paw I mean. It didn't look a very likely hand for a first-class penman and engraver of flash notes, but you can't always judge by appearances. And now as to your other questions: You ask what Maddock was like in appearance. I can only give you the description which I gave to Batson and which he recognized at once."

"Had he noticed the peculiarity of the hands?" enquired Thorndyke.

"Yes. I asked him about it and he remembered having observed it when he was attending Maddock. Well, then, our friend was about five-feet-nine in height, fairly broad and decidedly strong, of a medium complexion with grey eyes and darkish brown hair. That's all I can tell you about him."

"You haven't got his finger-prints, I suppose?"

"No. He was never in prison, so we had no chance of getting them."

"Was he married?"

"He had been, but some years ago his wife divorced him, or he divorced her. Latterly he has lived as a bachelor."

"There is nothing else that you can think of as throwing light on his personality or explaining his actions?"

"Nothing at all, Doctor. I've told you all I know about him, and I only hope the information may be more useful than it looks to me."

"Thank you," said Thorndyke, "your information is not only useful, I expect to find it quite valuable. Reasoning, you know, Mr. O'Donnell," he continued, "is somewhat like building an arch. On a supporting mould, the builder lays a number of shaped stones, or *voussoirs*, but until all the *voussoirs* are there, it is a mere collection of stones, incapable of bearing its own weight. Then you drop the last *voussoir* – the *keystone* – into its place, and the arch is complete, and now you may take away the supports, for it will not only bear its own weight, but carry a heavy superstructure."

"That's so, doctor," said O'Donnell. "But, if I may ask, is this all gratuitous wisdom or has any particular bearing?"

"It has this bearing," replied Thorndyke. "I have myself been, for some time past, engaged, metaphorically, in the building of an arch. When you came here to-night, it was but a collection of shaped and adjusted stones, supported from without. With your kind aid, I have just dropped the keystone into its place. That is what I mean."

The American thoughtfully arranged the papers in his case, casting an occasional speculative glance at Thorndyke. "I'd like to know," he said presently, "what it was that I told you. It doesn't seem to me that I have produced any startling novelties. However, I know it's no use trying to squeeze you, so I'll get back to my hotel and have a chew at what you've told me."

He shook hands with us all round, and, when Thorndyke had let him out, we heard him bustling downstairs and away up King's Bench Walk towards Mitre Court.

For a minute or more after his departure none of us spoke. Thorndyke was apparently ruminating on his newly-acquired information, and Jervis and I on the statement that had so naturally aroused the detective's curiosity.

At length Jervis opened the inevitable debate. "I begin to see a glimmer of daylight through the case of Septimus Maddock, deceased," said he, "but it is only a glimmer. Whereas, from what you said to O'Donnell, I gather that you have the case quite complete."

"Hardly that, Jervis," was the reply. "I spoke metaphorically, and metaphors are sometimes misleading. Perhaps I overstated the case, so we will drop metaphor and state the position literally in terms of good, plain, schoolboy logic. It is this: We had certain facts presented to us in connection with Maddock's death. For instance, we observed that the cause of death was obscure, that the body was utterly destroyed by cremation, and that Jardine, who was an unofficial witness to some of the formalities, was subsequently pursued by some unknown person with the unmistakable purpose of murdering him. Those were some of the observed facts, and the explanation of those facts was the problem submitted to us – that is to say, we had to connect those facts and supply others by deduction and research, so that they should form a coherent and intelligible sequence, of which the motive for murdering Jardine should form a part.

"Having observed and examined our facts, we next propose a hypothesis which shall explain them. In this case it would naturally take the form of a hypothetical reconstruction of the circumstances of Maddock's death. That hypothesis must, of course, be in complete agreement with all the facts known to us, including the attempts to murder Jardine. Then, having invented a hypothesis which fits our facts completely, the next stage is to verify it. If the circumstances of Maddock's death were such as we have assumed, certain antecedent events must have occurred and certain conditions must have existed. We make the necessary inquiries and investigations, and we find that those events had actually occurred and those conditions had actually existed. Then it is probable that our hypothesis is correct, particularly if our researches have brought to light nothing that disagrees with it.

"With our new facts we can probably amplify our hypothesis, reconstruct it in greater detail, and then we have to test and verify it afresh in its amplified and detailed form. And if such new tests still yield an affirmative result, the confirmation of the hypothesis becomes overwhelmingly strong. It is, however, still only hypothesis. But perhaps we light on some final test which is capable of yielding a definite answer, yes or no. If we apply that test – the 'Crucial Experiment' of the logicians – and obtain an affirmative result, our inquiry is at an end. It has passed out of the region of hypothesis into that of demonstrative proof."

"And are we to understand," asked Jervis, "that you have brought Maddock's case to the stage of complete demonstration?"

"No," answered Thorndyke. "I am still in the stage of hypothesis, and when O'Donnell came here to-night there were two points which I had been unable to verify. But with his aid I have been able to verify them both, and I now have a complete hypothesis of the case which has been tested exhaustively and has answered to every test. All that remains to be done is to apply the touchstone of the final experiment."

"I suppose," said Jervis, "you have obtained a good many new facts in the course of your investigations?"

"Not a great many," replied Thorndyke, "and what new data I have obtained, I have, for the most part, communicated to you and Jardine. I assure you, Jervis, that if you would only concentrate your attention on the case, you have ample material for a most convincing and complete elucidation of it."

Jervis looked at me with a wry smile. "Now Jardine-Howard." said he, "why don't you brush up your wits and tell us exactly what happened to the late Mr. Maddock and why some person unknown is so keen on your vile body. You have all the facts, you know."

"So you tell me," I retorted, "but this case of yours reminds me of those elaborate picture puzzles that used to weary my juvenile brain. You had a hatful of irregular-shaped pieces which, if you fitted them together, made a picture. Only the beggars wouldn't fit together."

"A very apt comparison," said Thorndyke. "You put the pieces together, and, if they made no intelligible part of a picture, you knew you were wrong, no matter how well they seemed to fit. On the other hand, if they seemed to make parts of a picture you had to verify the result by finding pieces of the exact shape and size of the empty spaces. That is what I have been doing in this case, trying the data together and watching to see if they made the expected picture. As I have told you, O'Donnell's visit found me with the picture entire save for two empty spaces of a particular shape and size, and from him I obtained two pieces that dropped neatly into those spaces and made the picture complete. All I have to do now is to see if the picture is a true representation or only a consistent work of imagination."

"I take it that you have worked the case out in pretty full detail," said Jervis.

"Yes. If the final verification is successful I shall be able to tell you exactly what happened in Maddock's house, what was the cause of death – and I may say that it was not that given in the certificates – who the person is who has been pursuing Jardine and what is his motive, together with a number of other very curious items of information. And the mention of that person reminds me that our friend has been disporting himself in public, contrary to advice and to what I thought was a definite understanding."

"But surely," I said, "it doesn't matter now. We have given that spy chappie the slip, and, even if he hasn't given up the chase as hopeless, we know that he is quite harmless."

"Harmless!" exclaimed Thorndyke. "Why, my dear fellow, he was your guardian angel. Didn't you realize that from Father Humperdinck's statement? He shadowed you so closely that no attack on you was possible – in fact, he actually caught a rap on the head that was apparently meant for you. You were infinitely safer with him at your heels than alone."

"But we've given the other fellow the slip, too," I urged.

"We mustn't take that for granted," said Thorndyke. "The French detective, you remember, came on the scene quite recently, whereas the other man has been with us from the beginning. He probably saw Jervis and me enter the mineral water works on the night of the fire, for he was certainly there, and he may even have followed us home to ascertain who we were. There are several ways in which he could have connected you with us and traced you here, so I must urge you most strongly not to venture out of the precincts of the Temple for the next few days. In fact, it would be much wiser to keep indoors altogether. It will be only a matter of days unless I get a quite unexpected set back, for I hope to have the case finally completed in less than a week, and when I do, I shall take such action as will give your friend some occupation other than shadowing you."

"Very well," I said. "I will promise not to attempt again to escape from custody. But, all the same, my little jaunt to-day has not been entirely without result. I have picked up a new fact, and a rather curious one, I think. What should you say if I suggested that Mrs. Samway was the wife of that eccentric artist who used to paint on the Heath? The man, I mean, who always worked in gloves?"

"I have assumed that she was in some such relation to him," replied Thorndyke, "but I should like to hear the evidence."

"Mrs. Samway," Jervis said in a reflective tone. "Isn't that the handsome uncanny-looking lady with the mongoose eyes, who reminded me of Lucrezia Borgia?"

"That is the lady. Well, I met with a portrait of her to-day which was evidently the work of the man with the gloves," and here I gave them a description of the portrait and an account of the odd way in which it had been disinterred from the landscape that had been painted over it, to which they both listened with close attention.

"It's a queer incident," said Thorndyke, "and quite dramatic. If one were inclined to be superstitious, one might imagine some invisible agency uncovering the tracks that have been so carefully hidden and working unseen in the interests of justice. But haven't you rather jumped to your conclusion? The existence of the portrait establishes a connection, but not necessarily that of husband and wife."

"I only suggested the relationship, but it seemed a likely one as the portrait had been painted over and thrown into the rubbish box."

Jervis laughed sardonically, and even Thorndyke's impassive face relaxed into a smile. "Our young friend," said the former, "doesn't take as favourable a view of the married state as one might expect from a gay Lothario who breaks out of his cage to go a-philandering. But we'll overlook that, in consideration of the very interesting information that he has brought back with him. Not that it conveys very much to me. It is obviously a new piece to fit into our puzzle, but I'm hanged if I see, at the moment, any suitable space to drop it into."

"I think," said Thorndyke, "that if you consider the picture as a whole, you will soon find a vacant space. And while you are considering it, I will just send off a letter, and then we had better adjourn this discussion. We have to catch the early train to Maidstone to-morrow, and that, I hope, will be the last time. Our case ought to be disposed of by the afternoon."

He seated himself at the writing-table and wrote his letter, while Jervis stared into the fire with a cogitative frown. When the letter was sealed and addressed, Thorndyke laid it on the table while he went to the lobby to put on his hat and coat, and, glancing at it almost unconsciously, I noted that the envelope was of foolscap size and was addressed to the Home Office, Whitehall. The name of the addressee escaped me, for, suddenly realizing the impropriety of thus inspecting another man's letter, I looked away hastily, but even then when Thorndyke had taken it away to the post, I found myself speculating vaguely on the nature of the communication and wondering if it had any relation to the mysterious and intricate case of Septimus Maddock.

Chapter XIX
Tenebrae

The resigned composure with which I accepted Thorndyke's sentence of confinement within doors was not entirely attributable to discretion or native virtue. My resolution to follow scrupulously my principal's very pointed advice was somewhat like the ascetic resolutions formed by the gourmet as he rises replete from the banquet table, for, just as the latter is in a peculiarly favourable condition for the unmoved contemplation of a – temporary – abstinence from food, so I, having enjoyed my little dissipation, could now contemplate with fortitude a brief period of retirement. Moreover, the weather was in my favour, being – as Polton reported, when he returned, blue-nosed and powdered with snow, with a fresh supply of tobacco for me – bitterly cold, with a threatening of smoky fog from the east.

Under these circumstances it was no great hardship to sit in a roomy armchair with my slippered feet on the kerb and read and meditate as I basked in the warmth of a glowing fire – though, to be sure, my reading was perfunctory enough, for the treatise of *The Surface Markings of the Human Body*, admirable as it was, competed on very unfavourable terms with other claimants to my attention. In truth, I had plenty to think about even if I went no farther for matter than to the events of the previous day. There was my visit to Sylvia, for instance. I had not said much to her, but what I had said had pledged me to a life-long companionship, which was a solemn thing to reflect upon even though I looked forward to the fulfilment of that pledge with nothing but hopeful pleasure. The dice were thrown. Of course they would turn up sixes, every one, but still – the dice were thrown.

From my own strictly personal affairs my thoughts rambled by an easy transition to the singular episode of the buried portrait, and thence to the subject of that strange palimpsest. Viewed by the light of Mr. O'Donnell's revelations, Mrs. Samway's position was not all that could have been desired. She and her husband had unquestionably been closely associated with Maddock, but Maddock was, it seemed, a habitual criminal. Could this fact have been known to the Samways? Or was it that the cunning forger and swindler had sheltered himself behind their respectability. It was impossible for me to say.

Then there was the strange and perplexing case of the man Maddock, himself. I could make nothing of that – had not, indeed, been aware that there had been a "case", until Thorndyke's investigations had put me in possession of the fact. And even now I could see nothing on which to base any suspicion, apart from the attempts on my life, which we were assuming to be in some way connected with events that had occurred in Maddock's house. The cause of death was apparently not *"Morbus Cordis"*, which might easily enough be, seeing that the diagnosis of heart disease was a mere guess on Batson's part. But if not *Morbus Cordis*, what was it? Thorndyke apparently knew, and seemed to hint that it was something other than ordinary disease. Could there have been foul play? And, if so, were the Samways involved in it in any way? It seemed incredible, for had not Maddock himself suspected that he was in a dangerous state of health. There was certainly one possibility which I considered with a good deal of distaste – namely, that Maddock had been in a hypochondriacal state and that the Samways had taken advantage of his gloomy views as to his health to administer poison. The thing was actually possible, but I did not entertain it, for, even if one assumed that poison had been administered, at any rate, the cremation of the body was not designed to hide the traces of the crime. The Samways had nothing to do with that, the cremation had been adopted in preference to burial by Maddock's own wish.

So my thoughts flitted from topic to topic, with occasional interludes of Surface Markings, through the lazy forenoon until Polton came to lay my solitary luncheon. And after this little break in the comfortable monotony, another spell of meditative idleness set in. Polton was busy upstairs in the laboratory with some photographic copying operations and I was disposed to wander up and look on, but my small friend politely but very firmly vetoed any such proceeding. On some other occasion he would be delighted to show me the working of the great copying camera, but, just now, he had a big job in hand, and, as he was working against time, he would prefer to be alone. He even suggested that I might attend to any stray callers and make my own tea on the gas-ring so as to avoid interrupting his work, and when I had agreed to relieve him to this extent, he thanked me profusely and retired and I saw no more of him.

For some time after his departure, I stood at the window looking out across the wide space at Paper Buildings and the end of Crown Office Bow. It was a wretched afternoon. The yellow, turbid sky brooded close down upon the houseroofs and grew darker and more brown moment by moment, as if the invisible sun had given the day up in despair and gone home early.

A comfortless powdering of snow filtered down at intervals and melted on the pavements, along which depressed wayfarers hurried with their coat collars turned up and their hands thrust deep into their pockets. I watched them commiseratingly, reflecting on the superior advantages of being within doors and forbidden to go out, and then, having flung another scoopful of coal on the fire, I betook myself once more to the armchair, the Surface Markings and idle meditation.

It was some time past four when my reflective browsings had begun to proceed in the direction of the teakettle, that I heard a light footstep on the landing as of someone wearing goloshes. Then a letter dropped softly into the box, and, as I instantly pushed back my chair to rise, the footsteps retreated. I crossed the room quickly and opened the door, but the messenger had already disappeared down the dark staircase, and had gone so silently on his rubber soles that, though I listened attentively, I could hear no sound from below.

Having closed the door, I extracted the letter from the box and took it over to the window to examine it, when I was not a little surprised to find that it was addressed to *W. M. Howard, Esq.* This was the first communication that I had received in my borrowed name, and my surprise at its arrival was not unreasonable, for, of the few persons who knew me by that name, none – with the exception, perhaps, of Mr. Marchmont – was in the least likely to write to me.

But, if the address on the envelope had surprised me, the letter itself surprised me a good deal more, for though the writer was quite unknown to me, even by name, he seemed to be in possession of certain information concerning me which I had supposed to be the exclusive property of Thorndyke, Jervis, Polton and myself. It bore the address, 29 Fig-tree Court, Inner Temple, and ran thus:

Dear Sir,

I am taking the liberty of writing to you to ask for your assistance as I happen to know that my friends, Drs. Thorndyke and Jervis, are away at Maidstone and not available at the moment, and I understand that you have some acquaintance with medical technicalities.

The circumstances are these. At half-past five today I shall be meeting a solicitor to advise as to action in respect of a case in which I am retained, and the decision as to our action will be vitally affected by a certain issue on which I am not competent to form an opinion for lack of medical knowledge. If Dr. Thorndyke had been within reach I should have taken his opinion, as he is not, it occurred to me to ask

225

if you would fill his place on this occasion, it being, of course, understood that the usual fee of five guineas will be paid by the solicitor.

If you should be unable to come to the consultation, do not trouble to reply, as I am now going out and shall not be returning until five-thirty, the time of the appointment. I am,

Yours faithfully,

Arthur Cortland

The contents of this letter, as I have said, surprised me more than a little. How, in the name of all that was wonderful, had this stranger, whose very name was unknown to me, come to be aware that I had any knowledge of medicine? Not from Thorndyke, I felt perfectly sure, nor from Jervis, who, notwithstanding a certain flippant facetiousness of manner, was really an extremely cautious and judicious man. Could it be that my principal was overseen in his trusted laboratory assistant? Was it conceivable that the suave and discreet Polton had moments of leakiness, when, in unofficial talk outside, he let drop the secrets of which his employer's unbounded confidence had made him the repository? I could not believe it. Not only did Polton appear to be the very soul of discretion, there was Thorndyke himself, he was not the man to give his confidence to anyone until after the most exhaustive proof of the safety of so giving it. Nor was he a man who was likely to be deceived, for nothing escaped his observation, and nothing that he observed was passed over without careful consideration.

My lethargy having been shaken off, I addressed myself to the task of preparing tea, and, as I listened to the homely crescendo of the kettle's song, I turned the matter over in all its bearings. By some means this Mr. Courtland had become aware that I was either a doctor or a medical student. But by what means? Was it possible that he had merely inferred from the circumstance of my being associated with Thorndyke that I was of the same profession? That was just barely conceivable, but, if he had, then, as Jervis had said of Father Humperdinck, he must be "a devil at guessing".

As I made the tea and subsequently consumed it, I continued to ruminate on the contents of that singular letter. No answer to it was required. Then what was Mr. Courtland going to do if I did not turn up? He admitted that the issue, which seemed to be an important one, was beyond him, and yet he had to give an answer to the solicitor. And he

226

was prepared to pay five guineas for the advice of a man of whom he – presumably – knew nothing. That was odd. In fact, the whole tone of the letter, with its inconsistent mixture of urgency and casual trusting to chance, seemed irreconcilable with the care and method that one expects from a professional man.

And there was another point. The time of the consultation was half-past five. Now within an hour of that time Thorndyke would be back – or even sooner if he came by the earlier train as he had done on the previous day – as Mr. Courtland must have known, since he knew whither my principal had gone, and he must have often attended Assizes himself. Could he not have waited an hour? And again, had this business been sprung upon him so suddenly that he had had no time to get Thorndyke's opinion? And, yet again, why had be written at all, instead of dropping in at our chambers with the solicitor, as was so commonly done by Thorndyke's clients?

All of which were curious and puzzling questions which I put to myself, one by one, and had to dismiss unanswered. And then I came to the practical question, to which I had to find an answer, and which was: Could I, under the existing circumstances, accede to Mr. Courtland's request? To go outside the precincts of the Inn was, I recognized, absolutely forbidden, but I had given no actual promise to remain in our chambers, nor had I been positively forbidden to leave them. Thorndyke had advised me to remain indoors, and his advice had been given so pointedly and with so evident a desire that it should be followed that I had not hitherto even thought of leaving our premises. But this was an unforeseen contingency, and the question was: Did it alter my position in regard to Thorndyke's advice?

I think I have never been so undecided in my life. On the one hand, I was strongly tempted to keep the appointment. The prospect of triumphantly handing to Thorndyke a five-guinea fee which I had earned as his deputy appealed to me with almost irresistible force. On the other hand, my knowledge of Thorndyke did not support this appeal. I knew him to be a man to whom a principle was much more important than any chance benefit gained by its abandonment, and my inner consciousness told me that he would be better pleased by a strict adherence to our understanding than by the increment of five guineas.

So my thoughts oscillated, to and fro, now impelling me to risk it and earn the fee, and now urging me to keep to the letter of my instructions, and, meanwhile, the time ran on and the hour of the consultation approached. What decision I should have reached, in the end, it is impossible to say. As matters turned out, I never reached any decision at all, for, just as the Treasury clock struck a quarter past five, I hear a light, quick step on our landing and immediately after a soft but hurried knock at the door.

I strode quickly across the room and threw the door open. And then I started back with an exclamation of astonishment. For the visitor – who stood full in the light of the landing-lamp – was a woman, and the woman was Mrs. Samway.

As I stood gazing at her in amazement, she slipped past me into the room and softly shut the door. And then I saw very plainly that there was something amiss, for she was as pale as death, and had a dreadful, frightened, hunted look which haunts me even now as I write. She was somewhat dishevelled, too, and, though it was a bitter evening, her plump, shapely hands were ungloved and cold as ice, as I noted when I took them in mine. "Are you alone?" she asked, peering uneasily at the door of the little office.

"Yes. Quite alone," I replied.

She gazed at me with those strange, penetrating eyes of hers and said in a half-whisper, "How strange you look with that beard. I should hardly have known you if I had not expected – "

She stopped short, and, casting a strange, scared glance over her shoulder at the dark windows, whispered, "Can they see in? Can anyone see us from outside?"

"I shouldn't think so," I replied, but, nevertheless, I stepped over to the windows and drew the curtains. "That looks more comfortable, at any rate," said I. "And now tell me how in the name of wonder you knew I was here."

She grasped both my wrists and looked earnestly-almost fiercely-into my eyes. "Ask me no questions!" she exclaimed. "Ask me nothing! But listen. I have come here for a purpose. Has a letter been left here for you?"

"Yes," I replied.

"Asking you to go to a place in Fig-tree Court?"

"Good God!" I exclaimed. "How on earth – "

She shook my wrists impatiently in her strong grasp. "Answer me!" she exclaimed. "Answer me!"

"Yes," I replied. "I was to go there at half-past five."

Again her strong grasp tightened on my wrists. "Humphrey," she said, in a low, earnest voice, "you are *not to go*. Do you hear me? You are *not to go!*" And then, as I seemed to hesitate, she continued more urgently, "I ask you – I *beg* you to promise me that you won't."

I gazed at her in sheer amazement, but some instinct, some faint glimmer of understanding, restrained me from asking for any explanation. "Very well," I said. "I won't go if you say I'm not to."

228

"That is a promise?"

"Yes, it's a promise. Besides, it's nearly half-past already, so if I don't go now, the appointment falls through."

"And you won't go outside these rooms to-night. Promise me that, too."

"If I don't go to this lawyer, I shan't go out at all."

"And to-morrow, too. Give me your word that you won't let any sort of pretext draw you out of these rooms to-morrow, or the next day, or, in fact, until Dr. Thorndyke says you may."

For a few moments I was literally struck dumb with astonishment at her last words, and could do nothing but gaze at her in astounded silence. At length, recovering myself a little, I exclaimed, "My dear Mrs. Samway – " but she interrupted me.

"Don't call me by that horrible name! Give me my own name, Letitia, or," she added, a little shyly and in a soft, coaxing tone, "call me Lettie. Won't you, Humphrey, just for this once? You needn't mind. You wouldn't if you knew. I should like, when I think of my friend – the only friend that I care for – to remember that he called me by my own name when he said good-bye. You'll think me silly and sentimental, but you needn't mind indulging me just once. It's the last time."

"The last time!" I repeated. "What do you mean by that, Lettie, and by speaking of our saying good-bye? Are you going away?"

"Yes, I am going away. I don't suppose you will ever see me again. I am going out of your life."

"Not out of my life, Lettie. We are always friends, even if we never see one another."

"Are we?" she said, looking up at me earnestly. "Perhaps it is so, but still, this is good-bye. I ought to say it and go, but Oh God!" she exclaimed with sudden passion, "I don't want to go – away from you, Humphrey, out into the cold and the dark!"

She buried her face against my shoulder, and I could feel that she was sobbing though she uttered no sound.

It was a dreadful situation. Instinctively certain though I was that her grief had a real and tragic basis, I could offer no word of comfort. For what was there to say? She was going, clearly, to a life of wretchedness without hope of any relief or change and without a single friend to cheer her loneliness. That much I could guess, vaguely and dimly. But it was enough. And it wrung my heart to witness her passion of grief and to be able to offer no more than a pressure of the hand.

After a few seconds she raised her head and looked in my face, with the tears still clinging to her lashes. "Humphrey," she said, laying her hands on my shoulders, "I have a few last words to say to you, and then I

229

must go. Listen to me, dearest friend, and remember what I say. When I am gone, people will tell you things and you will come to know others. People will say that I am a wicked woman, which is true enough, God knows. But if they say that I have done or connived at wickedness against you, try to believe that it was not as it seemed, and to forgive me for what I have done amiss. And say to yourself, 'This wicked woman would have willingly given her heart's blood for me.' Say that, Humphrey. It is true. I would gladly give my life to make you safe and happy. And try to think kindly of me in the evil report that will reach you sooner or later. Will you try, Humphrey?"

"My dear Lettie," I said, "we are friends, now and always. Nothing that I hear shall alter that."

"I believe you," she said, "and I thank you from my heart. And now I must go – I must go, and it's good-bye – good-bye, Humphrey, for the very last time."

She passed her arms around my neck and pressed her wet cheek to mine, then she kissed me, and, turning away abruptly, walked across to the door and opened it. On the landing, in the light of the lamp, she turned once more, and I saw that the hot blush that had risen to her cheek as she kissed me, had faded already into a deathly pallor, and that the dreadful, frightened, hunted look had come back into her face. She stood for a moment with her finger raised warningly and whispered, "Good-bye, dear, good-bye! Shut the door now and shut it quietly," and then she passed into the opening of the dark staircase.

I closed the door softly and turned away towards the window, and, as I did so, I heard her stumble slightly on the stair a short way down and utter a little startled cry. I was nearly going out to her, and did, in fact, stand a moment or two listening, but, as I heard nothing more, I moved over to the window, and, drawing back the curtain, looked down on our doorstep to see her go out. My mind was in a whirl of confused emotions. Profound pity for this lonely, unhappy, warm-hearted woman contended with amazement at the revelation of her manifest connection with the mystery that surrounded me, and I stood bewildered by the tumult of incoherent thought, grasping the curtain and looking down on the great square stone that I might, at least, catch a farewell glance at this poor soul who was passing so unwillingly out of my life.

The seconds passed. A man came out of our entry and, turning to the left, walked at a rapid pace towards the Tudor Street gate. Still she did not appear. Perhaps she had heard him on the stairs and was waiting to pass out unnoticed. But yet it was strange.

Nearly a minute had elapsed since she started to descend the stairs. Could I have missed her? It seemed impossible, since I had come to the window almost immediately. A vague uneasiness began to take possession of me. I recalled her white face and frightened eyes, and as I stared down at the door-step with growing anxiety, I found myself listening – listening nervously for I knew not what.

Suddenly I caught a sound – faint and vague, but certainly a sound. And it seemed to come from the staircase. In a moment I had the door open and was stealing on tip-toe out on the landing. The house was profoundly silent. No murmur even penetrated from the distant streets. I crept across the landing, breathing softly and listening. And then, from the stillness below, but near at hand came a faint, whispering sigh or moan. Instantly I sprang forward, all of a tremble and darted down the stairs.

At the first turn I saw, projecting round the angle, a hand – a woman's hand, plump and shapely and white as marble. With a gasp of terror I flew round the turn of the staircase and –

God in Heaven! She was there! Huddled limply in the angle, her head resting against the baluster and one hand spread out on her bosom, she lay so still that she might have been dead but for the shallow rise and fail of her breast and the wide-staring eyes that turned to me with such dreadful appeal, I stooped over her and spoke her name, and it seemed to me that a pitiful little smile trembled for a moment on the bloodless lips, but she made no answer beyond a faint, broken sigh, and it was only when she moved her hand slightly that the overwhelming horror of the reality burst upon me. Then when I saw the crimson stain upon her fingers and upon the bosom of her dress, the meaning of that horrible pallor, the sharpening features and strange, pinched expression flashed upon me with a shock that seemed to arrest the very blood at my heart. Yet, stunned as I was, I realized instantly that human skill could avail her nothing, that I could do nought for her but raise her from the sharp edge of the stair and rest her head on my arm. And so I held her, whispering endearments brokenly, and looking as well as I might through the blinding tears into those inscrutable eyes, that gazed up at me, no longer with that stare of horror but with a vague and childlike wonder. And, even as I looked, the change came in an instant. The wide eye-lids relaxed and drooped, the eyes grew filmy and sightless, the hand slipped from her breast and dropped with a thud on the stair, and the supple body in my arms shrank of a sudden with the horrible limpness of death.

Up to this point my recollection is clear, even vivid, but of what followed I have only a dim and confused impression. The awfulness – the unbelievable horror of this frightful thing that had happened left me so dazed and numb that I recall but vaguely the passage of time of what went on around me in this terrible dream from which there was to be no

231

waking. Dimly I recollect kneeling by her side on the silent staircase – but how long I know not – holding her poor body in my arms and gazing incredulously at the marble-white face – now with its drowsy lids and parted lips, grown suddenly girlish and fragile – while the hot tears dropped down on her dress, choking with grief and horror and a fury of hate for the foul wretch who had done this appalling thing, and who was now far away out of reach. I see – dimly still – the livid marks of accursed fingers lingering yet on the whiteness around the mouth to tell me why no cry from her had reached me, and the dreadful, red-edged cut in the bodice mutely demanding vengeance from God and man.

And then of a sudden the silence is shattered by rushing feet and the clamour of voices. Someone – it is Jervis – leads me forcibly away to our room and places me in a chair by the table. Presently I see her lying on our sofa, drowsy-eyed, peaceful, like a marble figure on a tomb. And I see Thorndyke, with a strange, coppery flush and something grim and terrible in the set calm of his face, showing the letter, which I had left on the table, to a tall stranger, who hurries from the room. Anon come two constables with heads uncovered carrying a stretcher. I see her laid on the sordid bier and reverently covered. The dread procession moves out through the doorway, the door is shut after it, and so, in dreadful fulfilment of her words, she passed out of my life.

Chapter XX
The Hue and Cry

The silence of the room remained unbroken for a quite considerable time after the two bearers had passed out with their dreadful burden. My two friends sat apart and, with a tact of which I was gratefully sensible, left me quietly undisturbed by banal words of consolation, to sustain the first shock of grief and horror and get my emotion under control. Still dazed and half-incredulous, I sat with my elbows on the table and my teeth clenched hard, looking dreamily across the room, half-unconsciously observing my two friends as they silently examined the fatal letter. I saw Thorndyke rise softly and take a small bottle from a cabinet, and watched him incuriously as he sprinkled on the paper some of the dark-coloured powder that it contained. Then I saw him blow the powder from the surface of the paper into the fire and scan the letter closely through a lens. And still no word was spoken. Only once, when Jervis, in crossing the room, let his hand rest for a moment on my shoulder, did any communication pass between us, and that silent touch told me unobtrusively – if it were needful to tell me – how well he understood my grief for the woman who had walked open-eyed into the valley of the shadow, had offered her heart's blood that I might pass unscathed.

In about a quarter-of-an-hour the tall stranger returned, bringing with him an atmosphere of bustling activity that at once dispelled the gloomy silence. His busy presence and brisk, matter-of-fact speech, though distressing to me at the moment, served as a distraction and brought me out of my painful reverie to the grim realities of this appalling catastrophe. "You were quite right, sir," said he. "The chambers were an empty set. Mr. Courtland left them about six weeks ago, so they tell me at the office. I've looked them over carefully, and I think it is pretty clear what this man meant to do."

"Did you go in?" asked Thorndyke.

"Yes. Mr. Polton went with me and picked the lock, so I was able to go right through the rooms. And it is evident that this villain was not acting on the spur of the moment. He'd made a very neat plan, and I should say that it was pretty near to coming off. He had selected his chambers with remarkable judgment, and uncommonly well suited they were to his purpose. In the first place, they were the top set – nothing above them, no chance strangers passing up or down, and they were the

233

only set on that landing. Then some previous tenant had made a little trap or grille in the outer door, a little hole about six inches square with a sliding cover on the inside. That was the attraction, I fancy. The landing lamp was alight – he must have lighted it himself, as the landing was out of use – and I fancy he meant to watch through the grille for your friend to come and shoot him as he knocked at the door."

"That would be taking more risk than he usually did," said Thorndyke.

"You mean that the report of the shot would have been heard. Perhaps it might. But these modern, small-bore, repeating pistols make very little noise, though they are uncommonly deadly, especially if you open the nose of the bullets."

"But," objected Thorndyke, "if he had been heard, there he would have been, boxed up in the chambers with no means of escape."

Our acquaintance shook his head. "No," said he, "that's just what he wouldn't have been, and there is where he had planned the affair so neatly. These chambers are a double set. They have a second entrance that opens on the staircase of the next house. You see the idea. When he's fired his shot and made sure that it was all right – or all wrong, if you prefer it – he would just have slipped through to the other entrance, let himself out, shut the door quietly and walked down the stairs. Then, if the shot had been heard, there was he, coming out of the next house to join the crowd and see what was the matter. It was a clever scheme, and, as I say, it might very well have come off if this poor young lady hadn't given it away. So that's all about the chambers, and now" – here he cast a glance in my direction – "I must ask for a few particulars." He produced a large, black-covered notebook and, opening it on the table, looked at me inquiringly.

"This," said Thorndyke, "is Mr. Superintendent Miller of the Criminal Investigation Department. He has charge of this case, so you must tell him exactly what happened. And try, Jardine, to be as clear and circumstantial as possible."

The Superintendent looked up sharply. "I had an impression," said he, "that this gentleman's name was Howard."

"He has used the name of Howard since he has been staying here, for reasons which no longer exist but which I will explain to you later. His name is Humphrey Jardine, and he is a bachelor of medicine."

Mr. Miller entered these particulars in his book and then said, "I suppose it is not necessary to ask if you were actually present when this poor lady was murdered?"

"No, I was not."

"And I presume you did not see the murderer?"

234

"I saw a man, whom I believe to have been the murderer, come out of our entry and walk quickly towards the Tudor Street Gate. But I can give you no description of him. I saw him from the window and by the light of the entry lamp."

The Superintendent wrote down my answer and reflected for a few moments. "Perhaps," said he, "you had better just give us an account of what happened and we can ask you any questions afterwards. It's very painful for you, I know, but it has to be, as you will understand."

It was more than painful, it was harrowing to reconstitute that hideous tragedy, step by step, with the knowledge that the poor murdered corpse was still warm. But it had to be, and I did it, haltingly, indeed, and with many a pause to command my voice, but in the end, I gave the superintendent a full description of the actual occurrences, though I withheld any reference to those words that my poor dead friend had spoken for my ear alone. When I had read through and signed my statement, Mr. Miller studied his note-book with an air of dissatisfaction and then turned to Thorndyke. "This is all quite clear, Doctor," said he, "and just about what you inferred from that letter. But it doesn't help us much. The question is: Who is this man? I've an inkling that you know, Doctor."

"I have a very strong suspicion as to who he is," replied Thorndyke.

"That will do for me," said Miller. "Your strong suspicion is equal to another man's certainty. Do you know his name, sir?"

"He has recently passed under the name of Samway," replied Thorndyke. "What his real name is, I think I shall be able to tell you later. Meanwhile, I can give you such particulars as are necessary for making an arrest."

The Superintendent looked narrowly at Thorndyke as the latter pressed the button of the electric bell. "Apparently, Doctor," said he, "you have been making some investigations concerning this man, and, as it was not in connection with this crime, it must have been in connection with something else."

"Yes," replied Thorndyke, "you are quite right, Miller, and it will be a matter of the deepest regret to me to my dying day that circumstances have hindered those investigations as they have. The delay has cost this poor woman her life. A few more days and my case would almost certainly have been complete, and then this terrible disaster would have been impossible."

As Thorndyke finished speaking, the door opened quietly and Polton entered with a small, neatly-made parcel in his hand. "Ah!" said Thorndyke, "you guessed what I wanted, and guessed right, as you always do, Polton. How many are there in that parcel?"

"Three-dozen, sir," replied Polton.

"That ought to be enough for the moment. Hand them to the Superintendent, Polton. If you want any more, Miller, we can let you have a further supply, and I am having a half-tone block made which will be ready to-morrow morning."

"Are these portraits of the man you suspect?" asked Miller.

"No, I haven't his portrait, unfortunately, but on each card is a photograph of three of his finger-prints, which are all I have been able to collect, and on the back is a description which will enable you easily to identify him. You can post them off to the various sea-ports and telegraph the description in advance, and I would recommend you especially to keep a watch on Dover and Folkestone, as I know that he has been in the habit of using that route."

"Speaking of finger-prints," said Miller, "have you tried that letter for them?"

"Yes," replied Thorndyke, "I powdered it very carefully, but there is not a single trace of a fingerprint. He must have realised the risk he was taking and worn gloves when he wrote it."

The Superintendent pocketed the parcel with a thoughtful air, and, after a few moments' cogitation, turned once more to Thorndyke. "You've supplied me with the means of arresting the man, Doctor," said he, "but that's all. Supposing I find him and detain him in custody? What then? I don't know that he murdered this poor woman. Do you? Dr. Jardine can't identify him, and apparently no one else saw him. I have no doubt that you have substantial grounds for suspecting him, but I should like to know what they are."

Thorndyke reflected for a moment or two before replying. "You are quite right. Miller," he said, at length, "you ought to have enough information to establish a *prima facie* case. But I think, that on this occasion, I can say no more than that, if you produce the man, you can rely upon me to furnish enough evidence to secure a conviction. Will that do?"

"It will do from you, sir," replied Miller, rising and buttoning his overcoat. "I will get this description circulated at once. Oh – there was one more matter. The name of the deceased lady was Samway – the same as that of the suspected murderer. What was the relationship?"

"She passed as – and presumably was – his wife."

"Ah!" said Miller. "I see. That was how she knew. Well, well. She was a brave woman, to take the risk that she did, and she deserved something very different from what she got. But we are taught that there is a place where people who suffer injustice and misfortune in this world get it made up to them. I hope it's true, for her sake – and for his," he added abruptly with a sudden change of tone.

"Naturally you do," said Thorndyke, "but, meanwhile, our business is with this world. Spread your net close and wide, Miller. I shall never forgive you if you let this villain slip. It is our sacred duty to purge the world of his presence. You do your part, Miller, and be confident that I will do mine."

"You can depend on me to do my best, sir," said Miller, "though I am working rather in the dark. I suppose you couldn't give me any sort of hint as to what you've got up your sleeve. You've no doubt, for instance, that it was really the man Samway who committed this murder?"

Thorndyke, according to his usual habit, considered the Superintendent's question for awhile before answering. At length he replied, "I don't know why I shouldn't take you into my confidence to some extent, Miller, knowing you as I do. But you will remember that this is a confidence. The fact is that I am proposing to proceed against this man on an entirely different charge. But I am not quite ready to lay an information, and I want you to secure his person on the charge of murdering his wife while I complete the other case."

"Is that another case of murder?" asked Miller.

"Yes. The facts are briefly these. A certain Septimus Maddock, who was living with the Samways, died some time ago under what seem to me very suspicious circumstances. He was nursed by Samway and his wife and by no one else. The cause of death given on the certificate was, in my opinion, not the true one, and I am proceeding to verify my theory as to what was the real cause of death."

"I see," said Miller. "You are applying for an exhumation of the body?"

"Well, hardly an exhumation. The man Maddock was cremated."

"Cremated!" exclaimed Miller. "Then we're done. There isn't any body to exhume."

"No," agreed Thorndyke, "there is no body, but there are the ashes."

"But, surely," said Miller, "you can't get any information out of a few handfuls of bone ash?"

"That remains to be proved," replied Thorndyke. "I have applied for an authority to make an exhaustive examination of those ashes, and, if my opinion as to the cause of death is correct, I shall be able to demonstrate its correctness, and that will involve a charge of murder against this man Samway. It will also support a charge against him of attempts to murder Dr. Jardine, and furnish strong evidence connecting him with the horrible crime that has just been committed. So you see,

Miller, that the important thing is to get possession of him before he has time to escape from this country, and hold him in custody, if necessary, while the evidence against him is being examined and completed. And I must impress on you that no time ought to be lost in getting the description circulated."

"No, that's true," said Miller. "I'll go and telegraph it off at once, and I'll send one or two of our best men to watch the likely seaports."

He shook hands with us all round, and, when we had all most fervently wished him success he took his departure.

As soon as he was gone, Jervis turned to his senior, and, looking at him with a sort of puzzled curiosity, exclaimed, "You are a most astounding person, Thorndyke! You really are! I thought I had begun to see daylight in that Maddock case, and now I find that I was all abroad. And I can't, for the life of me, conceive what in the world you expect to discover by examining a few pounds of calcined phosphates. Suppose Maddock was poisoned – what evidence will be obtainable from the ashes? Of the poisons which could possibly have been used under the known circumstances, not one would leave a trace after cremation. But, of course, you've thought of all that."

"Certainly, I have," replied Thorndyke, "and I agree with you that the ashes of a body that has been cremated are highly unpromising material for a primary investigation. But, does it not occur to you that, in a case where certain circumstantial evidence is available, excellent corroborative data might be obtained by the examination of the ashes?"

"No," replied Jervis, "I can't say that it does."

"It is not too late to consider the question," said Thorndyke. "I shall probably not get the authority for a day or two, so you will have time to turn the problem over in the interval. It is quite worth your while, I assure you, apart from this particular case, as a mere exercise in constructive theory. You can acquire experience from imaginary cases as well as from real ones, as I have often pointed out. In fact, much of my own experience has been gained in this way. I think I have mentioned to you that, in my early days, when I had more leisure than practice, it was my custom to construct imaginary crimes of an elaborately skilful type, and then – having, of course, all the facts – to consider the appropriate procedure for their detection. It was a most valuable exercise, for I was thus able to furnish myself with an abundance of problems of a kind that, in actual practice, are met with only at long intervals of years. And since then a quite considerable number of my imaginary cases have presented themselves, in a more or less modified form, for solution in the course of practice, and have come to me with the familiarity of problems that have already been considered and solved. That is what you should do, Jervis.

Try the synthetic method and then consider what analytical procedure would be appropriate to your result."

"I have," Jervis replied, gloomily. "I have worked at this confounded case until I feel like a rat that has been trying to gnaw through a plate-glass window. Still, I'll have another try. By the way, where are you going to make this examination?"

"I think I shall do it here. I had thought of handing the ashes over to one of the more eminent analysts, but it will be only a small operation, well within the capacity of our own laboratory. I think of asking Professor Woodfield to come here and carry out the actual analysis. Polton will give him any help that he may want and, of course, we shall be here to give any further assistance if he should need it."

"Why not have made the analysis yourself?" asked Jervis. "Is there anything specially difficult or intricate about it?"

"Not at all," replied Thorndyke. "But, as the case will have to go into Court on a capital charge – that is, assuming that my hypothesis turns out to be correct – I thought it best to have the analysis made by a man whose name as an authority on chemistry will carry special weight. Neither the judge nor the jury are likely to have much special knowledge of chemistry, but they will be able to appreciate the fact that Woodfield is a man with a world-wide reputation, and they will respect his opinion accordingly."

"Yes," agreed Jervis, "I think you are quite right. A well-known name goes a long way with a jury. I hope your experiment will turn out as you expect, and I hope, too, that some of Miller's men will manage to lay that murderous devil by the heels. But I'm afraid they'll have their work cut out. He is a clever scoundrel, one must admit that. How do you suppose he contrived to track Jardine here?"

"I think," replied Thorndyke, "that he must have seen us on one of the two occasions when we went to the mineral water works and followed us here. Then, when Jardine disappeared from his lodgings, he would naturally look for him here – this being, in fact, the only place known to him in connection with Jardine, excepting Batson's house, on which he also probably kept a watch."

"But how would he have discovered that Jardine actually was here?"

"There are a number of ways in which he might have ascertained the fact. A good many persons knew that we had a new resident. We could not conceal his presence here. Many of our visitors have seen him, and the porter and hangers-on of the inn will have noticed him taking his exercise in the morning. Samway, himself, even, may have seen him, and he would easily have penetrated the disguise if he saw him out of doors, for there is no disguising a man's stature. He might have made enquiries of one of the porters or lamp-lighters, or he might have employed someone else to make enquiries. The fact that someone was staying here and that his name was Howard could not have been very difficult to discover, while, as for ourselves, we are as well known in the inn as the griffin at Temple Bar. From the circumstance that he knew of our attendance at the Maidstone Assizes, it seems likely that he had subsidized some solicitor's clerk who would know our movements."

"And I suppose," said I, "as he is gone now, I may as well go back to my lodgings."

"Not at all," replied Thorndyke. "In the first place, we don't know that he is gone, and we do know that he is now absolutely desperate and reckless. And you must not forget, Jardine, that whether we charge him with murder in the case of Maddock, with the murder of poor Mrs. Samway, or the attempted murder of yourself, in either case you are the chief witness for the prosecution. You are the appointed instrument of retribution in this man's case, and you must take the utmost care of yourself until your mission is accomplished. He knows the value of your evidence better than you do, and it is still worth his while to get rid of you if he can. But you, I am sure, are at least as anxious as we are to see him hanged."

"I'd sooner twist his neck with my own hands," said I.

"I daresay you would," said Thorndyke, "and it is perfectly natural that you should. But it is not desirable. This is a case for a few fathoms of good, stout, hempen rope, and the common hangman. The private vengeance of a decent man would be an undeserved honour for a wretch like this. So you must stay here quietly for a few days more and give us a little help when we need it."

Thorndyke's decision was not altogether unwelcome. Shaken as I was by the shock of this horrible tragedy, I was in no state to return to the solitude of my lodgings. The quiet and tactful sympathy of my two friends – or I should rather say three, for Polton was as kind and gentle as a woman – was infinitely comforting and their sober cheerfulness and the interest of their talk prevented me from brooding morbidly over the catastrophe of which I had been the involuntary cause. And, dreadful as the associations of the place were, I could not but feel that those of my older resorts would be equally painful. For me, at present, the Heath would be haunted by the figure of poor Letitia, walking at my side, telling me her pitiful tale and so pathetically craving my sympathy and friendship. And the Highgate Road could not but wring my heart with the recollection of that evening when we had walked together up the narrow lane – all unconscious of a black-hearted murderer stealing after us and foiled only by that futile spy – when, as we said good-bye I had kissed her and she had run off blushing like a girl.

Moreover, if Thorndyke's chambers were fraught with terrible and gloomy associations, they were also pervaded by an atmosphere of resolute, relentless preparation which was itself a relief to me, for, as the first shock of horrified grief passed, it left me possessed by a fury of hatred for the murderer and consumed by an inextinguishable craving for vengeance. Nor by the time of suspense so long as we had anticipated, as the very next morning a letter arrived from the Home Office containing the necessary authority to make the proposed examination and informing Thorndyke that on the following day the police would take possession of the ashes, which would be delivered to him by an officer who would remain to witness the examination and to resume possession of the remains when it was concluded.

I saw very little more of Thorndyke that day, but gathered that he was busy making the final arrangements for the important work of the morrow and clearing off various tasks so as to leave himself in from engagements. Nor did I enjoy much of Jervis's society, for he, too, was anxious to have the day free for the "Crucial Experiment," which was – we hoped – to solve the mystery of Septimus Maddock's death and explain the villain Samway's strange vindictiveness towards me.

Left to myself, and by no means enamoured of my own society, I wandered up to the laboratory to see what Polton was doing and to distract my gloomy thoughts by a little gossip with him on the various technical processes of which he possessed so much curious information. I found him arrayed in a white apron, with his sleeves turned up, busily occupied with what I took to be a slab of dough, which he had spread on a pastry board and was levelling with a hard-wood rolling-pin. He greeted me as I entered with his queer, crinkly smile, but made no remark, and I stood awhile in silence, watching him cut the paste in halves, sprinkle it with flour, fold it up and once more roll it out into a sheet with the wooden pin. "Is this going to be a meat pie, Polton?" I asked, at length.

His smile broadened at my question – for which I suspect he had been waiting. "I don't think you'd care much for the flavour of it, if it was, sir," he answered. "But it does look like dough, doesn't it. It's moulding-wax, a special formula of The Doctor's own."

"I thought that white powder was flour."

"So it is, sir, the best wheaten flour. It's lighter than a mineral powder and more tenacious. You have to use some powder to reduce the stickiness of the wax, especially in a soft paste like this, which has a lot of lard in it."

"What are you going to use it for?" I asked.

"Ah!" exclaimed Polton, pausing to give the paste a vicious whack with the rolling-pin, "there you are, sir. That's just what I've been asking myself all the time I've been rolling it out. The Doctor, sir – God bless him – is the most exasperating gentleman in the world. He fairly drives me mad with curiosity, at times. He will give me a piece of work to do – something to make, perhaps – with full particulars – all the facts, you understand, perfectly clear and exact, with working drawings if necessary. But he never says what the thing is for. So I make a hypothesis for myself – whole bundles of hypotheses, I make. And they always turn out wrong. I assure you, sir," he concluded with solemn emphasis, "that I spend the best part of my life asking myself conundrums and giving myself the wrong answers."

"I should have thought," said I, "that you would have got used to his ways by now."

"You can't get used to him," rejoined Polton. "It's impossible. He doesn't think like any other man. Ordinary men's brains are turned out pretty much alike from a single mould, like a batch of pottery. But The Doctor's brain was a special order. If there was any mould at all, that mould was broken up when the job was finished."

"What you mean is," said I, "that he has a great deal more intelligence than is given to the rank and file of humanity."

"No, I don't," retorted Polton. "It isn't a question of quantity at all. It's a different kind of intelligence. Ordinary men have to reason from visible facts. He doesn't. He reasons from facts which his imagination tells him exists, but which nobody else can see. He's like a portrait painter who can do you a likeness of your face by looking at the back of your head. I suppose it's what he calls constructive imagination, such as Darwin and Harvey and Pasteur and other great discoverers had, which enabled them to see beyond the facts that were known to the common herd of humanity."

I was somewhat doubtful as to the soundness of Polton's views on the transcendental intellect, though respectfully admiring of the thoughtfulness of this curious little handicraftsman. Accordingly I returned to the more concrete subject of wax. "Haven't you any idea what this stuff is going to be used for?"

"Not the slightest," he replied. "The Doctor's instructions were to make six pounds of it, to make it soft enough to take a squeeze of a stiff feather if warmed gently, and firm enough to keep its shape in a half-inch layer with a plaster backing, and to be sure to have it ready by to-morrow morning. That's all. I know there's an important analysis on to-morrow and I suppose this wax has got something to do with it. But, as to what moulding wax can have to do with a chemical analysis, that's a question that I can't make head or tail of."

Neither could I, though I had more data than Polton appeared to possess. Nor could Jervis, to whom I propounded the riddle when he came in to tea. We went up to the laboratory together and inspected, not only the wax, but the exterior of three large parcels addressed to Professor Woodfield, care of Dr. Thorndyke, and bearing the labels of a firm of wholesale chemists. But neither of us could suggest any solution of the mystery, and the only result of our visit to the laboratory was that Polton was somewhat scandalized by the conduct of his junior employer, who consoled himself for his failure by executing with the wax, a life-sized and highly grotesque portrait of Father Humperdinck.

Chapter XXI
The Final Problem

At exactly half-past-eleven in the following forenoon, Professor Woodfield arrived, bearing a massive cowhide bag which he deposited on a chair as a preliminary to taking off his hat and wiping his forehead. He was a big burly, heavy-browed man, sparing of speech and rather gruff in manner. "Stuff arrived yet?" he asked when he had brought his forehead to a satisfactory polish.

"I think it came yesterday morning," replied Thorndyke.

"The deuce it did!" exclaimed Woodfield.

"Yes. Drapers – Three parcels from Townley and – "

"Oh, you're talking of the chemicals. I meant the other stuff."

"No, the officer hasn't arrived yet, but I expect he will be here in a few minutes. Superintendent Miller is a scrupulously punctual man."

The professor strode over to the window and glared out in the directionof Crown Office Row. "That man of yours got everything ready?" he asked.

"Yes," answered Thorndyke, "and I have looked over the laboratory myself. Everything is ready. You can begin the instant the ashes are delivered to us."

Woodfield expressed his satisfaction – or whatever he intended to express – by a grunt, without removing his eyes from the approach to our chambers. "Cab coming," he announced a few moments later. "Man inside with a parcel. That the officer?"

Jervis looked out over the professor's shoulder. "Yes," said he, "that's Miller, and, confound it! Here's Marchmont with old Humperdinck. Shall we bolt up to the laboratory and send down word that we're all out of town?"

"I don't see why we should," said Thorndyke. "Woodfield won't be inconsolable if we have to leave him to work by himself for a while."

The professor confirmed this statement by another grunt, and, shortly afterwards, the clamour of the little brass knocker announced the arrival of the first contingent, which, when I opened the door, was seen to consist of the solicitor and his very reverend client. "My dear Thorndyke!" exclaimed Marchmont, shaking our principal's hand, "what a shocking affair this is – this murder, I mean. I read about it in the paper. A dreadful affair!"

"Yes, indeed," Thorndyke assented, "a most callous and horrible crime."

"Terrible! Terrible!" said Marchmont. "So unpleasant for you, too, and so inconvenient. Actually on your own stairs, I understand. But I hope they'll be able to catch the villain. Have you any idea who he is?"

"I have a very strong suspicion," Thorndyke replied.

"Ah!" exclaimed Marchmont, "I thought so. The rascal brought his pigs to the wrong market. What? Like doing a burglary at Scotland Yard. He couldn't have known who lived here. Hallo! Why here's Mr. Miller. Howdy-do, Superintendent!"

The officer, for whom I had left the door ajar, entered in his usual brisk fashion, and, having bestowed a comprehensive salutation on the assembled company, deposited on the table an apparently weighty parcel, securely wrapped and decorated with a label bearing the inscription "*This Side Up*".

"There, sir," said he, "there's your box of mystery, and I don't mind telling you that I'm on tenterhooks of curiosity to see what you are going to make of it."

"Professor Woodfield is the presiding magician," said Thorndyke, "so we will hand it over to him. I suppose the casket is sealed?"

"Yes, it was sealed in my presence, and I've got to be present when the seals are broken."

"We'll break the seals up in the laboratory," said Woodfield, "but we may as well undo the parcel here."

He produced a solid-looking pocket knife, fitted with a practicable corkscrew, and, having cut the string, stripped off the wrappings of the parcel. "God bless my soul!" exclaimed Marchmont, as the last wrapping was removed. "Why, it's a cremation urn! What in the name of Fortune are you going to do?"

Miller tapped the lid of the urn with a dramatic gesture. "Dr. Thorndyke," said he, "is going, I hope, to extract from the ashes in this casket an instrument of vengeance on the murderer of Mrs. Samway."

"Ach!" exclaimed Father Humperdinck, "do not speak of vengeance in ze bresence of zese boor remains of a fellow greature. Chustice if you laig, but not vengeance. '*Vengeance is mine, saiz ze Lordt!*'"

"M'yes," agreed Miller, "that's perfectly true, sir, and we quite understand your point of view. Still, we've got our job to do, you know."

"But," said Marchmont, "I don't understand. What is the connection? These appear to be the remains of Septimus Maddock, whoever he may have been, and he seems to have died last November. What has he to do with the murder of this poor woman, Samway?"

245

"The connection is this," replied Thorndyke, "the man who murdered Mrs. Samway murdered the man whose ashes are in this urn. That is my proposition, and I hope, with the skilful aid of my friend Professor Woodfield, to prove it."

"Well," said Marchmont, "it is a remarkable proposition and the proof will be still more remarkable. I certainly thought that a body that had been cremated was beyond the reach of any possible inquiry."

"I am afraid that is so, as a rule," Thorndyke admitted. "But I hope to find an exception in this case. Shall we go upstairs and commence the examination?"

Woodfield having agreed with gruff emphasis, Miller picked up the casket and we all proceeded to the laboratory, where Polton, like a presiding analytical demon, was discovered amidst his beloved apparatus. The casket was placed on a table, the seals broken, and the cover removed by Woodfield, whereupon we all, with one accord, craned forward to peer in at what looked like a mass of fragments of snowy madrepore coral. "Ach!" exclaimed Father Humperdinck, "bot it is a solemn zought zat zese boor ashes vas vunce a living man chust like ourselves."

"Yes," said Marchmont, "it is, and I suppose we shall all be pretty much alike by the time we reach this stage. Cremation is a leveller, with a vengeance. Still, I will say this much: These remains are perfectly unobjectionable in every way. In fact they are almost agreeable in appearance, whereas, an ordinary disinterment after this lapse of time would have been a most horrid business."

"Yes, indeed," agreed Thorndyke. "I have had to make a good many examinations of exhumed bodies, and, as you say, they were very different from this. If I were not a practitioner of legal medicine – in which exhumation often furnishes crucial evidence – I should say that this cleanly and decent method of disposing of the dead was incomparably superior to any other. Unfortunately it has serious medico-legal drawbacks. I think, Woodfield, that we will turn the ashes out on that sheet of paper on the bench, and then, with your permission, I will pick out the recognizable fragments and examine them while you are working on the small, powdery portions."

He took up the urn – which was an oblong, terracotta vessel some fourteen inches in length – and very carefully inverted it over the large sheet of clean white paper. Then, from the dazzling, snowy heap, he picked out daintily the larger fragments – handling them with the utmost tenderness – for, of course, they were excessively fragile – and finally transferring them, one by one, to another sheet of paper at the other end of the bench.

The appearance of the remains was not quite as I had expected. Among the powdery debris was a quite considerable number of larger fragments, most of which were easily recognizable by the anatomical eye, while some of the larger long bones almost gave the impression of having been broken to enable them to be placed in the urn, and suggested that a partial reconstitution, for the purpose of determining the stature or other peculiarities of the skeleton was by no means as impossible as I had supposed. But, large and small alike, the pieces were strangely light and attenuated, like the ghosts of bones or artificial counterfeits in porous, spongy coral.

When Thorndyke had picked out such of the fragments as he wished to examine, Professor Woodfield glanced casually over the collection, but suddenly he paused and, stooping over a large piece of the right innominate bone, narrowly inspected a somewhat shiny yellow stain on its inner surface. "Looks as if you were right, Thorndyke," he said in his laconic way, "qualitatively, at any rate. We shall see what the quantitative test says."

I pored over that dull yellow stain – as did Jervis also – but could make no guess at its nature or conceive any explanation of its presence. What interested me more was a small depression or cavity in the bone at the centre of the stain. That it was not the result of cremation was obvious from the fact that it was surrounded by a small area of sclerosed or hardened bone, which was quite plainly distinguishable on the spongy background, and which clearly pointed to some inflammatory change that had occurred during life. But of its cause, as of that of the stain itself, I could think of no intelligible explanation. "Have you enough of the small fragments to go on with for the present, Woodfield?" Thorndyke asked.

"Plenty," replied Woodfield.

"Then," said Thorndyke, "I will get on with my side of the inquiry. I shall want the whole-plate camera first, Polton."

While his assistant was preparing the camera, he laid several of the fragments on a baize-covered board and secured them in position by threads attached to wooden-headed pins like diminutive bradawls. When the fragments were fixed immovably, he placed the board in a vertical position on a stand in a good light, by which time Polton was ready to make the exposure.

Meanwhile, Professor Woodfield was proceeding – under the horrified supervision of Father Humperdinck – with his part of the investigation. He was a matter-of-fact man, a chemist to the backbone, and to him it was evident that the late Septimus Maddock was simply so many pounds of animal phosphates. Quite composedly he shovelled up a scoopful of the ashes, which he emptied into the pan of a spring-balance, and, having weighed out a pound and a quarter, shot the contents of the pan into a large mortar and forthwith began to grind the fragments to a fine powder, humming a cheerful stave to the ring of the pestle. But his next proceeding scandalized the worthy Jesuit still more deeply. Having weighed out certain quantities of charcoal, sodium carbonate and borax, he pulverized each in a second mortar, mixed the whole together and shot the mixture into the first mortar, which contained the ash, stirring the entire contents up into a repulsive-looking grey powder. "But, my dear sir!" exclaimed Father Humperdinck. "You are destroying ze remains!"

Woodfield looked at him from under his beetling brows, but went on stirring. "Matter is indestructible," he replied stolidly, and with this he tipped the contents of the mortar on to a sheet of paper and transferred them to a large fireclay crucible. "Now, Polton," said he, "is the furnace ready?"

Polton disengaged himself for a moment from the camera, and took up a position by the side of the big fireclay drum with his hand on the gas cock. Then Woodfield, having dropped three or four large iron nails into the crucible, carried the latter over to the furnace and lowered it into the central cavity. The cock was turned on by Polton and a match applied, whereupon a great purplish flame shot up with a roar from the mouth of the furnace, and even when this had been confined by the dropping on of the massive cover, the ironcased cylinder continued to emit a muffled, sullen growl.

While the crucible was heating, I transferred my attention to Thorndyke. The photographic operations were now concluded and the moulding wax had just been produced from a warmed incubator. Polton's curiosity – and mine – was about to be satisfied.

Thorndyke began by laying a thick slab of the warm and pliable wax on the middle of a smooth plate of varnished plaster, at each corner of which was a small, hemispherical pit, and dusting powdered French chalk sparingly over the level surface of the wax. Then he took the large fragment of bone, which bore the mysterious yellow stain, and laid it on the wax with the stained side uppermost, pressing it very gently until it gradually sank into the soft, pasty mass. Next, he took a somewhat smaller slab of wax and, having dusted its surface with French chalk, laid it on the fragment of bone, pressing it on gently but firmly, especially in the neighbourhood of the stain. Having squeezed some irregular-shaped lumps of wax on the back of the top slab, he fastened a strip of india-rubber round the edge of the plaster plate, so that it formed an upright rim, and turned to Polton. "Now mix a bowl of plaster – and mix it extra stiff, so that it will set quickly and hard."

With a soft brush he painted a thin coat of oil on the exposed portion of the plaster plate, up to the edges of the wax, and including the little circular hollows. By the time he had done this, Polton reappeared from the workshop with a basin of liquid plaster, which he was beating up with a spoon as if preparing a custard or batter pudding. As soon as the plaster began to thicken, he poured it on the wax and the oiled slab until it formed a level mass, nearly flush with the top of the india-rubber rim. In a surprisingly short time, the smooth, creamy liquid solidified into a substance having the appearance of icing-sugar, and when Polton had stripped away the india-rubber rim, exposing the edge of the new plaster slab, this part of the process was finished. "We will put this mould aside for the plaster to harden while we make the other mould," said Thorndyke.

"Aren't you going to make moulds of all the fragments?" asked Jervis.

"No," Thorndyke answered, "the photographs of the rest will be sufficient, and I don't think we shall want even those. In fact, what I am doing now is merely by way of extra precaution. We are obliged to destroy the fragments in order to make the analysis, so I am just putting their appearance on record. You never know what an ingenious defending counsel may spring on you."

As Polton produced a second plate of varnished plaster and Thorndyke began to prepare the wax for the next mould, I turned my attention once more to Professor Woodfield. He had now deserted the mortar – in which he had been preparing a further supply of "the stuff" – and taken up a position by the furnace, with a long pair of crucible-tongs in his hand. On the bench, hard by, was an iron plate, and on this an oblong block of iron in which were six conical hollows.

Presently Woodfield glanced at his watch, turned off the gas-cock, removed the cover of the furnace with his tongs, and, reaching down into the glowing interior, lifted out the nearly white-hot crucible. Instantly Marchmont, Humperdinck, and Jervis gathered round to watch, and even Thorndyke left his mould to come and see the result of the first trial.

Having stood the crucible on the iron plate while he picked out the large nails, one by one, Woodfield lifted it and steadily poured its molten contents into the first hollow in the iron block, which they soon filled, and overflowing ran along the iron plate in glowing streams that soon grew dull from contact with the cold surface. I noticed that, as the crucible was slowly tilted, Thorndyke kept his eyes fixed on its interior, as also did Jervis and Woodfield, and, watching closely, I saw just as the vessel was nearly empty, what looked somewhat like a red-hot oil-globule floating in the last of the glowing liquid. This passed out as the crucible was tilted further, and disappeared into the iron mould, when Woodfield, having exchanged a quick, significant glance with Thorndyke, proceeded forthwith, in his matter-of-fact way to fill up the still red-hot vessel with another pound-and-a-quarter of the late Septimus Maddock. "I suppose," said Marchmont, "it is premature to ask you what is the final object of these very interesting operations?"

"It's no use asking me," replied Woodfield, "because I don't know. I am searching for traces of a particular substance, but what may be the significance of its presence, I haven't the slightest idea. You'd better ask Dr. Thorndyke – and he won't tell you."

"No, I know," said Marchmont. "Thorndyke will never tell you anything until he can tell you everything. By the way, will the remains be completely destroyed or will it be possible to recover them?"

"They are not destroyed at all," replied Woodfield. "They are all in the slag that came out of the crucible. We shall simply put the slag in the urn. There is a little charcoal, soda and borax added, but nothing is taken away."

I could see that to the unchemical mind of Father Humperdinck, this was far from satisfactory, and I observed him poring, with obvious disapproval, over the dark-coloured, glassy masses of slag on the iron plate. "*Ashes to Ashes*" was an intelligible formula, but "*Ashes to Slag*" was quite another matter, for which no provision had been made in any known ritual.

After a rather hurried luncheon, the wax moulds were carefully opened and the fragments of bone picked out, when it was seen that each fragment had left a perfect impression on the wax surface into which it had been pressed. These hollow impressions were now filled with liquid plaster, and, when the latter had thickened sufficiently, the two halves of each mould were quickly fitted together and kept in close contact by a weight.

During the interval which was necessary to allow of the plaster setting quite firmly, I had leisure to note that Professor Woodfield had filled two more of the cavities in the iron mould. Now that the furnace was thoroughly hot, he was able to work rather more quickly, and he had economized time by leaving a crucible to heat while we were at lunch. He was preparing to take the fourth charge from the furnace when I observed Polton removing the weight from one of the moulds and hurriedly transferred my patronage to his part of the entertainment. The mould on which he was operating was the one bearing the impressions of the stained fragment of the innominate bone, and when he separated the two halves and exposed the newly-made cast inside one might have thought that the actual bone had been left in, so perfectly did the snowy plaster cast reproduce the dazzlingly-white calcined bone. But, naturally, the stain did not appear in the cast, a defect which Thorndyke proceeded at once to remedy by making a tracing of the exact position and extent of the coloured patch and transferring it to the cast. Then, and not till then, Thorndyke regretfully handed the original fragment to Professor Woodfield, who impassively dropped it into the mortar and pounded it into a mere characterless powder.

After the opening of the second mould and the removal of the casts, the interest of the investigation lapsed for a time. Woodfield's operations were, doubtless, the most important part of the procedure, but they were not thrilling to look on at. In fact they became by unvarying repetition, decidedly tedious, and when the last charge – containing the uttermost crumb of ash – had been placed in the furnace and there was nothing to do but stare at the great fireclay drum, Marchmont and Humperdinck began to yawn in the most portentous manner. I rather wondered that they did not go, for the investigation was no business of theirs, and there was little entertainment in gazing at the outside of the furnace or watching Polton and the Superintendent gather up the masses of slag from the plate and drop them into the casket. But I supposed that they, like myself, were consoling themselves for the tedium of the chemist's manipulations by the prospect of satisfying their curiosity as to the final result of the experiment.

When at length the last charge was ready, Woodfield withdrew the white-hot crucible from the furnace and stood it on the iron plate. But this time he did not pour out the contents. Instead, he tilted the iron mould, and, picking out the conical masses of slag that it contained, one by one, lowered them with his tongs into the hot crucible. Then, having thrown in a little fresh flux, he returned the crucible to the furnace.

"Why didn't he pour out the melted stuff this time?" Marchmont asked.

"Because," Thorndyke replied, "I want, for certain reasons, to have the total result of the analysis in a single mass. Each of those little cones of slag contains the result from a sixth part of the ash, the crucible now contains the matter extracted from the whole of the ashes. For my purposes this is more suitable, as you will see in a few minutes – for we shall not have to leave the crucible in the furnace so long this time."

"I'm glad of that," said Marchmont. "Though this has been a most interesting, and I may say, fascinating experience. I am delighted to have had an opportunity of witnessing these most instructive and – er – aw – "

The rest of the sentence was rendered somewhat obscure by a colossal yawn, but very soon the interest of the proceedings was revived by Woodfield, who approached the furnace with a determined air and removed its cover with somewhat of a flourish. "Now we shall see, Thorndyke," said he, turning off the gas and reaching down into the glowing cavity with his tongs. He lifted out the crucible and, standing it on the iron plate, took out the nails, tapping each on the side of the pot as he withdrew it. "Do you want me to pour it out, or shall I break the pot?" asked Woodfield.

"That rests with you," replied Thorndyke.

"Better break the pot, then," said Woodfield.

This entailed a further spell of expectant waiting, and we all stood round, gazing impatiently at the crucible as it slowly faded from bright red to dull red and from this to its natural dull drab. It was quite a long time before Woodfield considered it cool enough to be broken. Indeed, I half-suspected him of prolonging our suspense with deliberate malice. At length he took up a peculiarly-shaped hammer which Polton had handed to him, and, laying the crucible on its side, struck it sharply near the bottom with the pointed beak, then he turned the pot over and struck a similar blow on the opposite side, upon which the bottom of the crucible broke off cleanly, exposing the mass of dark, glassy slag, and, embedded in it, a bright button of metal. "What metal is that?" Jervis demanded eagerly.

The professor struck the button smartly with the hammer, whereupon it detached itself from the slag and rolled on to the plate. "Lead," said he. "I don't vouch for its purity, but it is undoubtedly lead."

Jervis turned to Thorndyke with a puzzled look. "You can't be suggesting," said he, "that this was a case of acute lead poisoning. The circumstances didn't admit of it, and besides, the quantity of lead is impossibly large."

"I should suppose," interposed Miller, "that the doctor was suggesting a most particularly acute form of lead poisoning, only that it is impossible to imagine that a cremation certificate would be granted in a case where a man had been killed by a pistol shot."

"I am not so sure of that," said Thorndyke, "though it is not likely that a cremation certificate would be applied or under those circumstances. But I am certainly *not* suggesting lead poisoning."

"What do you say is the weight of this button, Thorndyke?" the professor asked.

"That," replied Thorndyke, "depends on its relation to the total content of lead in the ashes. What percentage do you suppose has been lost in the process of reduction?"

"Not more than ten-percent. I hope. You may take this button as representing ninety-percent of the total lead, perhaps a little more."

Thorndyke made a rapid calculation on a scrap of paper. "I suggest," said he, "that the total lead in the ashes was three-hundred-and-eighty-six grains. Deducting a tenth, say thirty-eight-and-a-half grains, we have three-hundred-and-forty-seven-and-a-half grains, which should be the weight of this button."

Woodfield picked up the button and striding over to the glass case which contained the chemical balance, slid up the front, and, placing the button in one pan, put the weight corresponding to Thorndyke's estimate, in the other. On turning the handle that released the balance, it was seen that the button was appreciably heavier than Thorndyke had stated, and Woodfield adjusted the weights with a small pair of forceps until the index stood in the middle of the graduated arc. "The weight is three-hundred-and-forty-nine-and-a-half grains," said Woodfield. "That means that my assay was rather better than I thought. You were quite right, Thorndyke, as you generally are. I wonder what the object was that weighed three-hundred-and-eighty-six grains. Are you going to tell us?"

Thorndyke felt in his waistcoat pocket. "It was an object," said he, "very similar to this."

As he spoke, he produced a rather large, dark-coloured bullet, which he handed to Woodfield, who immediately placed it in the pan of the balance and tested its weight. "Just a fraction short of three hundred-and-eighty-seven grains," said he.

The Superintendent peered curiously into the balance-case, and, taking the bullet out of the pan, turned it over in his fingers. "That's not a modern bullet," said he. "They don't make 'em that size now, and they don't generally make 'em of pure lead."

"No," Thorndyke agreed. "They don't. This is an old French bullet, a *chassepot* of about 1870."

"A *chassepot*!" exclaimed Humperdinck, with suddenly-awakened interest.

"Yes," said Thorndyke, "and this button," – he picked it up from the floor of the balance-case as he spoke – "was once a *chassepot* bullet, too. This, Father Humperdinck," he added, holding out the little mass of metal towards the Jesuit, "was the bullet which struck your friend, Vitalis Reinhardt, near Saarbrück more than thirty years ago."

The priest was thunderstruck. For some seconds, he gazed from Thorndyke's face to the button of lead, with his mouth agape and an expression of utter stupefaction. "But," he exclaimed, at length, "it is impossible! How can it be, in the ashes of a stranger!"

"I take it," said Marchmont, "that Dr. Thorndyke is suggesting that this was the body of Vitalis Reinhardt."

"Undoubtedly I am," said Thorndyke.

"It sounds a rather bold supposition," Marchmont observed, a little dubiously. "Isn't it basing a somewhat startling conclusion upon rather slender data? The presence of the lead is a striking fact, but still, taken alone – "

"But it isn't taken alone," Thorndyke interrupted. "It is the final link in a long chain of evidence. You will hear that evidence later, but, as it happens, I can prove the identity of these remains from facts elicited by the examination that we have just made. Let me put the argument briefly.

"First, I will draw your attention to these plaster casts, which you have seen me make from the original bones, Take, to begin with, these small fragments. Dr. Jervis will tell you what bones they are."

He handed the small casts to Jervis, who looked them over – not for the first time – and passed them to me. "I say that they represent two complete fingers and the first, or proximal, joint of a right thumb. What do you say, Jardine?"

"That is what I had already made them out to be," I replied.

"Very well," said Thorndyke. "That gives us an important initial fact. These remains contained two complete fingers and the first joint of a thumb. But these remains profess to be those of a man named Septimus Maddock. Now this man is known to have had deformed hands, of the kind described as *brachydactylous*. In such hands all the fingers are incomplete – they have only two joints instead of the normal three – and the first, or proximal joint of the thumb is absent. Obviously, then, these remains cannot be those of Septimus Maddock, as alleged.

"But, if not Maddock's remains, whose are they? From certain facts known to me, I had assumed them to be those of Vitalis Reinhardt. Let us see what support that assumption has received. Reinhardt is known to have been wounded in the right hip by a *chassepot* bullet, and the bullet was never extracted. Now I find, among these remains, a considerable portion of the right hip-bone. In that bone is a mark which plainly shows that it has been perforated and the perforation repaired, and there is a cavity in which a foreign body of about the size of a *chassepot* bullet has been partly embedded. The chemical composition of that foreign body is plainly indicated by a stain which surrounds the cavity, which stain is evidently due to oxide of lead. Clearly the foreign body was composed of lead, which will have melted in the cremation furnace and run away, but left a small portion, in the cavity, which small portion, becoming oxidized, the oxide will have liquified and become soaked up by the absorbent bone-ash, thus producing the stain.

"Finally, we find by assay that this foreign body actually was composed of lead and that its weight was – within a negligible amount of error – three hundred and eighty-six grains, which is the weight of a *chassepot* bullet.

"I say that the evidence, from the ashes alone, is conclusive. But this is only corroborative of conclusions that I had already formed on a quite considerable body of evidence. Are you satisfied, Marchmont? I mean, of course, only in respect of a *prima facie* case."

"Perfectly satisfied," replied Marchmont. "And now I understand why you insisted on my being present at this investigation and bringing Father Humperdinck, which, I must admit, has been puzzling me the whole day. By the way, I rather infer, from what you said, that there has been foul play. Is that so?"

"I think," replied Thorndyke, "there can hardly be a doubt that Reinhardt was murdered by Septimus Maddock."

Father Humperdinck's face suddenly turned purple. "And zis man Maddock," he exclaimed fiercely, "zis murderer of my poor friendt Vitalis, vere is he?"

"He is being sought by the police at this moment," replied Thorndyke.

"He must be caught!" Father Humperdinck shouted in a furious voice, "and ven he is caught he must be bunished as he deserves. I shall not vun moment rest until he is hanged as high as Haman." Here I caught a quick glance from Marchmont's eyes and seemed to hear a faint murmur which framed the words "Vengeance is mine."

"But," the Jesuit continued, after a momentary pause, in the same loud, angry tone, "Zis villain has a double grime gommitted, he has murdered a goot, a chenerous, a bious man, and he has robbed ze boor, ze suffering, and ze unfortunate."

"How has he done that?" asked Marchmont.

"By murdering ze benefactor of our zoziety," was the answer.

"Yes, to be sure," agreed the solicitor. "I hadn't thought of that. Of course, the original will in favour of Miss Vyne probably stands without modification."

At this point Superintendent Miller interposed. "You were saying, sir, that the man Maddock is now being sought by the police. Do you mean under that name?"

"No," answered Thorndyke. "I mean under the name of Samway. Septimus Maddock, alias Isaac Van Damme, is written off as deceased. But Samway, alias Maddock, alias Burton of Bruges, alias Gill, is his re-incarnation, and, as such, I commend him to your attention, and I hope,

Miller, you will be able to produce him shortly, in the flesh. The evidence, as you see, is now ready, and all that is lacking is the prisoner."

"He shan't be lacking long, sir, if any efforts of mine can bring him to light. I see a case here that will pay for all the work that we can put into it. And now, with your permission, Doctor, I will take possession of this urn and get off, to see that everything necessary is being done."

The Superintendent, as so often happens with departing guests, infected our other two visitors with a sudden desire to be gone. Father Humperdinck, especially, seemed unwilling to lose sight of the police officer – who was correspondingly anxious to escape – and, having wished us a very hasty *adieu*, hurried down the stairs in his wake, followed, at a greater interval, by his legal adviser.

Chapter XXII
Thorndyke Reviews the Case

When Professor Woodfield, having deliberately packed his bag and – to my great relief and Jervis's – declined Thorndyke's invitation to stay and take tea with us, presently took his departure, we descended to the sitting-room, whither Polton followed us almost immediately with a tea-tray, having, apparently, boiled the kettle in the adjacent workshop while the final act of the analysis was in progress. He placed the tray on a small table by Thorndyke's chair, and, evidently, anticipating the inevitable discussion on the results of the analysis, made up the fire on a liberal scale and retired with unconcealed reluctance.

As soon as we were alone, Jervis opened the subject by voicing his and my joint desire for "more light".

"This has been a great surprise to me, Thorndyke," said he.

"A complete surprise?" Thorndyke asked.

"No, I can't say that. The solution of the problem was one that I had proposed to myself, but I had rejected it as impossible, and it looks impossible still, though I now know it to be the true solution."

"I quite appreciate your difficulty," said Thorndyke, "and I see that if you did not happen to light on the answer to it, the difficulty was insuperable. That was the really brilliant feature in Maddock's plan. But for a single fact which was almost certain to be overlooked, the real explanation of the circumstances would appear utterly incredible. Even if suspicion had been aroused later and the true explanation suggested, there seemed to be one fact with which it was absolutely irreconcilable."

"Yes," agreed Jervis, "that is what I have felt."

"The truth is," said Thorndyke, "that this crime was planned with the most diabolical cleverness and subtlety. We realize that when we consider by what an infinitely narrow margin it failed. Indeed, we can hardly say that it did fail. As far as we can see, it succeeded completely, and if the criminal could only have accepted its success, there seems to be no reason why any discovery should ever have taken place. Looking back on the case, we see that our experience has been the same as O'Donnell's – we had no clue whatever excepting the one that was furnished by the criminal himself in his unnecessary efforts to obtain even greater security. Suppose Maddock, having carried out his plan successfully, had been content to leave it at that, who would have known, or even suspected, that a crime had been committed? Not a soul, I believe. But instead of that he must needs do what the criminal almost invariably does, he must tinker at the crime when all is going well and surround himself by a number of needless safeguards by which, in the end, attention is attracted to his doings. He knows, or believes he knows, that Jardine has in his possession certain knowledge of a highly dangerous character. He does not ask himself whether Jardine is aware that he possesses such knowledge, but, appraising that knowledge at what he, himself, knows to be its value, he decides to get rid of Jardine as the one element of danger. And that was where he failed. If he had left Jardine alone, the whole affair would have passed off as perfectly normal and its details would soon have been lost sight of and forgotten. Even as it was, he missed complete success only by a hair's breadth. But for the most trivial coincidence, Jardine's body might be lying undiscovered in that cellar at this very moment."

"That's a comfortable thought for you, Jardine," my younger colleague remarked.

"Very," I agreed, with a slight shudder at the recollecting of that horrible death-trap. "But what was the coincidence? I never understood how you came to be in that most unlikely place at that very opportune moment."

"It was the merest chance," replied Thorndyke. "I happened to have called in at the hospital that evening, and, having an hour to spare, it occurred to me to look in at Batson's and see if you were getting on quite happily in your new command. As I had induced you to take charge, I felt some sort of responsibility in the matter."

"It was exceedingly kind of you, sir," said I.

"Not in the least," said Thorndyke. "It was just the ordinary solicitude of the teacher for a promising pupil. Well, when I arrived at the house, I found that excellent girl, Maggie, standing on the doorstep, looking anxiously up and down the street. It seemed that, on reflection, she was still convinced that the works were untenanted, and the oddity of the whole set of circumstances had made her somewhat uneasy. I waited a few minutes and disposed of one or two patients, and then, as you did not return, after what seemed an unaccountably long absence, I very easily induced her to show me where the place was, and when we arrived there, the deserted aspect of the building and the notice board over the gate seemed rather to justify her anxiety.

"I rang the bell loudly, as I daresay you know, but I did not wait very long. When I failed to get any response, I too, became suspicious, and proceeded without delay to pick the lock of the wicket – and it is most fortunate that the wicket was unprovided with a bolt, which would have delayed me very considerably. You know the rest. When I shouted your name you must have tried to answer, for I caught a kind of muffled groan and the sound of tapping, which guided me and Maggie to your prison. But it was a near thing, for, when I opened the cellar door, you fell out quite unconscious and accompanied by a gush of carbon dioxide that was absolutely stifling."

"Yes," said I, "it was touch and go. A few minutes more and it would have been all up with me. I realised that as soon as I recovered consciousness. But I couldn't, for the life of me understand why anybody should want to murder me, and I am not so very clear on the subject now. I really knew nothing about Maddock."

"You knew more than anyone else knew, and he thought you knew more than you did. But perhaps it would be instructive to review the case in detail."

"It would be very instructive to me," said Jervis, "for I don't, even now, see how you managed to bridge over those gaps that stopped me in my attempts to make a hypothesis that covered all the circumstances."

"Very well," said Thorndyke, "then we will begin at the beginning, and the beginning, for me, was the finding of Jardine, as I have described it. Here was a pretty plain case of attempted murder, evidently premeditated and apparently committed by some person who had access to these works – evidently, also, conceived and planned with considerable knowledge, skill, and foresight, though with how much foresight I did not realize until I had heard Jardine's story. When I had Jardine's account of the affair, I saw that the crime had been planned with quite remarkable ingenuity and judgment. In fact, the circumstances had been so carefully considered, and contingencies so well provided for that, but for a single tactical error the plan would have succeeded. That error was in making the pretended emergency a surgical injury. If the letter to Jardine had stated that a man was in a fit, instead of suffering from a wound, our friend would have had no need to call at the surgery for appliances but would have gone straight to the works. And there, in all probability, his body would still be lying, for no one would have known whither he had gone, and even if his body had been accidentally discovered, all traces of the means by which he had been killed would probably have been removed. There would have been nothing to show that he had not strayed into the deserted factory and turned on the gas himself. Indeed, it is pretty certain that matters would have been so arranged as to convey that impression to the persons who made the discovery."

"There was the letter," said I. "That would have given things away to some extent."

"But you would have had it in your pocket, from which he would, of course, have removed it. We may be sure that he had not overlooked the letter. It was the need for surgical appliances that he had overlooked, but, in spite of this error, the plan was ingenious, subtle, and clearly not the work of an ignorant man.

"And here I would point out to you that this latter fact was one of great importance in searching for the solution of the mystery. We knew something of our man. He was subtle, resourceful, and absolutely ruthless. Noting this, I was prepared, in pursuing the case, to find his other actions characterized by subtlety, resourcefulness, and ruthlessness. His further actions were not going to be those of a dullard or an ignoramus.

"But this was not all the information that I had concerning the personality of this unknown villain. Jervis and I looked over the cellars that same night within an hour-and-a-half of the rescue and before anything had been moved. We were then in a position to infer that the unknown was probably a somewhat tall man and above the average of strength, as shown by the weight, position, and arrangement of the iron bottles. Moreover, since there was no faintest trace of a finger-print on any of them, it followed that some precaution against them – such as gloves – had been adopted, which again suggested either a professional criminal or a person well acquainted with criminal methods.

"So much for the man. As to the rest of the information that I obtained by looking into the cellar, it seemed, at the time meagre enough, and yet, when considered by the light of Jardine's statement, it turned out to be of vital importance. You remember what it was, Jardine? That cellar contained certain objects. They seemed very unilluminating and commonplace, but, according to my invariable custom, I considered them attentively and made a written list of them. Do you remember what they were?"

"Yes, quite well. There were ten empty cylinders, a spanner, a packing-case – "

"What were the dimensions of the case?" Thorndyke interrupted.

"Seven-feet-long by two-and-a-half wide and deep. Then there were a couple of waterproof sheets and a quantity of straw. That is the lot, I think, and I'll be hanged if I can see what any of them – excepting the three cylinders that were used for my benefit – have to do with the case. Can you, Jervis?"

"I'm afraid I can't," he replied. "They are all such very ordinary objects."

"Ordinary or not," said Thorndyke, "there they were, and I made a note of them on the principle – which I am continually impressing on my students – that you can never judge in advance what the evidential value of any fact will be, and on the further principle that, in estimating evidence, there is no such thing as a commonplace fact or object.

"Until I had heard Jardine's account of the affair there was not much to be gained by thinking about the possibilities that it presented. There was, however one point to be settled, and I dealt with it at once. My slight inspection of the works had shown that no business was being carried on in them, and the question was whether they were completely untenanted or whether there was some person who had regular access to them. My enquiries resulted, as you know, in the unearthing of the mysterious Mr. Gill, but what his relation to the affair might be I was not, at the moment, in a position to judge.

"Then came our talk with Jardine, from which emerged the fact that the ordinary motives of murder apparently did not exist in this case, and that the crime appeared to have its origin in circumstances that had arisen locally and recently. And, on our proceeding to search for such conditions as might conceivably generate an adequate motive, we lighted on a case of cremation.

"Now, it is my habit, whenever I have to deal with death which has been followed by cremation, to approach the case with the utmost caution and scrutinize the circumstances most narrowly. For, admirable as is this method of disposing of the dead regarded from a hygienic standpoint, it has the fatal defect of lending itself most perfectly to the more subtle forms of murder, and especially to the administration of poison. By cremation all traces of the alkaloids, the toxins, and the other organic poisons are utterly destroyed, while of the metals, the three whose compounds are most commonly employed for criminal purposes – arsenic, antimony, and mercury – are volatilized by heat and would be more or less completely dissipated during the incineration of the body. It is true that the most elaborate precautions in the form of examination and certification are prescribed – and usually taken, I presume – before cremation is performed, but, as every medical jurist knows, precautions taken before the event are useless, for, to be effective, they would have to cover every possible cause of death, which would be impracticable. Hence, as suspicion, in case of poisoning, commonly does not arise until some time after death, I always give the closest consideration to the antecedent circumstances in cases where cremation has been performed.

"But in this case of Jardine's it was at once obvious that the circumstances called for the minutest inquiry and that no inquiry had been made. On the face of it the case was a suspicious one, and the curious incident that Jardine described made it look more suspicious still and, moreover, suggested a possible motive for the attempt on his life.

Apparently he had seen, or was believed to have seen, something that he was not desired to see, something that it was not intended that anyone should see.

"Now what might that something have been? Apparently it was connected with the hand or with the part of the arm adjacent to the hand. I considered the possibilities, and at once they fell into two categories. That something might have been a wound, an injury, a hypodermic needle-mark – something, that is to say, related to the cause of death, or it might have been a mutilation, a deformity, a finger-ring, a tattoo-mark – something, that is to say, related to the identity of the deceased. And it followed that the cremation might have been made use of to conceal either the cause of death or the identity of the body. But all this was purely speculative. The case looked suspicious, but there was not a particle of positive evidence that anything abnormal had occurred.

"At this point Jardine exploded on us his second mystery, that of the dead cleric at Hampstead. This gave us, at once, an adequate motive for getting rid of him, for it had every appearance of a case of murder with successful concealment of the body, and Jardine was the only witness who could testify to its having occurred. On hearing of this I was for a moment disposed to dismiss the cremation case, to consider that the suspicious elements in it had been magnified by our imaginations in our endeavours to find an explanation of the assault on Jardine. Moreover, since we now had a sufficient motive for that assault the cremation case appeared to be outside the scope of the inquiry.

"But there was a difficulty. It was now six weeks since Jardine had encountered the body in the lane, and during that time he had been entirely unmolested. The assault had occurred on his moving into a new neighbourhood, to which he had come unexpectedly unannounced. Moreover, the assault had been committed by some person who either had access to the factory or was, at least, well acquainted with it and who, therefore, seemed to be connected with the new neighbourhood, and it was committed within a few days of the cremation incident. Furthermore, the assault was manifestly premeditated and prepared, but yet the circumstances – namely, Jardine's recent and unexpected appearance in the neighbourhood – were such as to make it certain that the crime could have been planned only a day or two before its execution. Which again seemed to connect it with the cremation case rather than with the Hampstead case.

"There were two more points. We have seen that Jardine's would-be murderer was a subtle, ingenious, resourceful, and cautious villain. But a crime adjusted to the conditions of cremation is exactly such a crime as we should expect of such a man, whereas the Hampstead crime –

assuming it to be a crime – appeared to have been a somewhat clumsy affair, though the successful concealment of the body pointed to a person of some capacity. So that the former crime was more congruous with the known personality of the would-be murderer than the latter.

"The second point was made on further investigation. The day after our consultation I looked round the neighbourhood with the aid of a large-scale map, when I discovered that the yard of the factory in Norton Street backed on the garden of the Samways' house in Gayton Street. This, again, suggested a connection between the cremation case and the assault on Jardine, and the suggestion was so strong that once more the cremation incident assumed the uppermost place in my mind.

"I considered that case at length. Assuming a crime to have been committed, what was the probable nature of that crime? Now, cremation, as I have said, tends to destroy two kinds of evidence – namely, that relating to the cause of death and that relating to the identity of the body, whence it follows that the two crimes which it may be used to conceal are murder and substitution.

"To which of these crimes did the evidence point in the present instance? Well we had the undoubted fact that cremation had been performed pursuant to the expressed wishes of Septimus Maddock, the man who was alleged to have been cremated. But if it was a case of murder, the crime must have been hurriedly planned a few days before the man's death – that is, after the execution of the will, for we could assume that Maddock would not have connived at his own murder, whereas, if it was a case of substitution, Maddock, himself, was probably the actual agent. Considering the circumstances – the inexplicable, symptomless illness and the unexpected death – the latter crime was obviously more probable than the former. The illness, in that case, would be a sham illness deliberately planned to prepare the way for the introduction of the substituted body.

"Moreover, the attendant circumstances were more in favour of substitution than of murder. Of the three doctors who saw the body, only one had seen the living man, and that one, Batson, was more than half-blind and wholly inattentive and neglectful. For the purpose of substitution, no more perfectly suitable practitioner could have been selected. The identity of the body was taken for granted – naturally enough, I admit – and no verification was even thought of. Then, as to Jardine's experience. The hand or wrist is not at all a likely region on which to find either a fatal injury or the trace of a hypodermic injection, whereas it is a most important region for purposes of identification. The hand is highly characteristic in itself even when normal, and there is no part of the body that is so subject to mutilation or in which mutilations and deformities are so striking, so conspicuous, and so characteristic. Lost fingers, stiff fingers, webbed fingers, supernumary fingers, contracted palm, deformed nails, *brachydactyly*, and numerous other abnormal conditions are not only easily recognized, but – since the hand is usually unclothed and visible – their existence will be known to a large number of persons.

"The evidence, in short, was strongly in favour of substitution as against murder.

"If, however, the body which was cremated was not that of Maddock, then it was the body of some other person, that is to say that the theory of substitution left us with a dead body that was unaccounted for. And since a dead body implies the death for some person, the theory of substitution left us with a death unaccounted for and obviously concealed, that is to say, it raised a strong presumption of the murder of some unknown person. And here it seemed that our data came to an end, that we had no material whatever for forming any hypothesis as to the identity of the person whose dead body we were assuming to have been substituted for that of Septimus Maddock.

"But while I was thus turning over the possibilities of this cremation case, the other – the Hampstead case – continued to lurk in the background of my mind. It was much less hypothetical. There was positive evidence of some weight that a crime had been committed. And the circumstances offered a fully adequate motive for getting rid of Jardine. Thus it was natural that I should raise the question. Was it possible that the two cases could be in any way connected?

"At the first glance, the suggestion looked absolutely wild. But still I considered it at length, and then it looked somewhat less wild. The two cases had this in common, that if a crime had been committed, Jardine was the sole witness. Moreover, the supposition that the two cases were connected and incriminated the same parties greatly intensified the motive for making away with Jardine. But there was another and much stronger point in favour of this view. If we adopted the theory of substitution, it was impossible, on looking at the two cases, to avoid being struck by the very curious converseness of their conditions. In the Hampstead case we were dealing with a body which had suddenly vanished, no one could say whither, in the Maddock case we were dealing with a body which had suddenly appeared, no one could say whence.

"When I reflected on this very striking appearance of relation it was inevitable that I should ask myself the question. Is it conceivable that these two bodies could have been one and the same? That the body which was cremated could have been the body which Jardine saw in the lane?

"Again, at the first glance, the question looked absurd. The first body was seen by Jardine more than six weeks before the alleged death of Maddock, and the body which he saw at the Samways' house was that of a man newly dead, with *rigor mortis* just beginning. It was, indeed barely conceivable that the Hampstead body was not actually dead and that the man might have lingered on alive for six weeks. But this suggestion failed to fit the known facts in two respects, In the first place, the body which Jardine saw in the lane was, from his description, pretty unmistakably a dead body, and, in the second, the sham illness of Maddock and the elaborate, leisurely preparations suggest a complete control of the time factor, which would be absent if those preparations were adjusted to a dying man who might expire at any moment.

"Rejecting this suggestion, then, the further question arose. Is it possible that the body that was seen in the lane could, after an interval of six weeks, have been produced in Gayton Street, perfectly fresh and in a state of incipient *rigor mortis*? And when the question was thus fairly stated, the answer was obviously in the affirmative. For, is it, not a matter of common knowledge that the bodies of sheep are habitually brought from New Zealand to London, traversing the whole width of the Tropics in the voyage, and are delivered, after an interval of more than six weeks, perfectly fresh and in a state of incipient *rigor mortis*? The physical possibility was beyond question.

"But if physically possible, was such preservation practicable? Well, how are the bodies of the sheep preserved? By exposing them continuously to intense cold. And how is that intense cold produced? Roughly speaking, by the volatilization of a liquified gas – ammonia, in the case of the sheep. But behold! The very man whom we are suspecting of being the agent in this crime is a man who has command of large quantities of a liquefied gas, and who has hired a mineral water factory for no apparent reason and put the premises to no apparent use."

At this point Jervis brought his fist down with a bang on the arm of his chair. "Idiot!" he exclaimed. "Ass, fool, dolt, imbecile that I am! With those cylinders staring me in the face, too! Of course, it was that interval of six weeks that brought me up short. And yet I had actually heard Jardine describe the cloud of carbon dioxide snow that fell on his face! Don't you consider me an absolute donkey, Thorndyke?"

"Certainly not," replied Thorndyke. "You happened to miss a link and, of course, the chain would not hold. It occurs to us all now and again. But, do you see, Jardine, how *'the stone which the builders rejected has become the head of the corner'*? Don't you understand how,

265

when I reached this point, there rose before me the picture of that cellar with the commonplace objects that it contained? The case, seven feet by two-and-a-half – so convenient for preserving a body in a bulky packing, the two waterproof sheets – so well adapted to holding a mass of carbon dioxide snow in contact with the body, the mass of straw – one of the most perfect non-conductors – so admirably fitted for its use as a protective packing for the frozen body, and lastly, those ten empty cylinders, of which seven had been used for some purpose unknown to us? Let this case be a lesson to you, Jardine, not only in legal medicine but in clinical medicine, too, to take the facts as you find them – relevant or irrelevant, striking or commonplace – note them carefully and trust them to find their own places in the inductive scheme."

"It has been a most instructive lesson to me," said I, "especially your analysis of the reasoning by which you identified the criminal."

"Hmm," said Thorndyke. "I didn't know I'd got as far as that."

"But if the body was preserved in a frozen state, there could not be much doubt as to who had preserved it."

"Possibly not," Thorndyke agreed. "But I had not proved that it had been so preserved, but only that it was possible for it to have been, and that the supposition of its having been so preserved was in agreement with the known circumstances of the case. But I must impress on you that up to this point I was dealing in pure hypothesis. My hypothesis was perfectly sound, perfectly consistent in all its parts, and perfectly congruous with all the known facts, but it did not follow therefore that it was true. It was entirely unverified, for hitherto I had not one single item of positive evidence to support it.

"Nevertheless, the striking agreement between the hypothesis and the known facts encouraged me greatly, and, as it was evident that I had now exhausted the material yielded by the cremation incident, I decided to take up the clue at the other end, to investigate the details of the Hampstead affair. To this end I called on Jardine, who very kindly went over the case with me afresh. And here it was that I first came within hail of positive evidence. On his wall was pinned an oil sketch, and on that sketch was a distinct print of a right thumb. It was beautifully clear, for the paint having been dry on the surface but soft underneath, had taken the impression as sharply as a surface of warm wax

"Now, you will remember that I took possession of the letter which summoned Jardine to the mineral water works and I may now say that I tested it most carefully for finger-prints. But paper is a poor material on which to develop invisible prints owing to its absorbent nature and I had very indifferent success. Still, I did not fail entirely. By the combined use of lycopodium powder and photography I obtained impressions of parts

266

of two finger-tips and a portion of the end of a right thumb. They were wretched prints but yet available for corroboration, since one could see part of the pattern on each and could make out that the ridge-pattern of the thumb was of the kind known as a 'twinned loop'.

"Bearing this fact in mind, you will understand that I was quite interested to find that the print on the sketch – also that of a right thumb – had a twinned loop pattern. I noted the fact as a coincidence, but, of course, attached no importance to it until Jardine told me that the artist who painted the sketch habitually worked in gloves, and even then I merely made a mental note that I would ascertain who and what the artist was.

"I need not go over our examination of the scene of the crime. I need only say that I was deeply interested in following the track along which the body had been carried because I was on the look-out for something, and that something was a house or other building in which the body might have been temporarily deposited.

"My hypothesis seemed to demand such a building. For, since the body was quite fresh and *rigor mortis* was only beginning when Jardine saw it at Gayton Street, it must have been frozen very shortly after death. Now, it obviously could not have been carried from Hampstead to Gayton Street on a man's back, the alternative is either a vehicle waiting at an appointed place – and necessarily not far away – or a house or other building to which the body could be taken. But the vehicle would, under the circumstances be almost impracticable. It would hardly be possible to make an appointment with any exactness as to time, and the presence of a waiting or loitering vehicle would, at such an hour – it was about midnight, you will remember – be almost certain to arouse suspicion and inquiry.

"On the other hand, a house to which the body could be conveyed would meet the conditions perfectly. When once the body was deposited there, the danger of pursuit would be practically at an end, and it would be quite possible to have a supply of the liquid gas ready for use on its arrival. This is assuming long premeditation and very deliberate preparation, an assumption supported by Gill's peculiar tenancy of the factory.

"I, therefore, kept a sharp look-out for a likely house or building, and, as Jardine and I came out of Ken Wood by the turnstile, behold! A house which answered the requirements to perfection. It was a solitary house, there was no other house near, and it lay right on the track along which the body had apparently been carried. Instantly, I decided to investigate the recent history of that house and its tenants, but Jardine saved me the trouble. From him I learned that, at the time of the assumed murder, it had been inhabited by the artist whom he had mentioned, but that it had now been empty for a week or two.

"Here were news indeed! This artist, who habitually wore gloves and whose right thumb-print was a twinned loop, had been living in this house at the time of the assumed murder, but had been living elsewhere at the time of the cremation! It was a striking group of facts, and I eagerly availed myself of the opportunity of looking over the house.

"At first, the examination was quite barren and disappointing. The man's habits, as shown by the few discarded articles of use or other traces, were of no interest to me – and still less to Jardine, and of traces of his personality there were none. I searched all the rejected canvases and every available scrap of paper in the hope of collecting some fresh finger-prints, but without the smallest result. In fact, the examination looked like being an utter failure up to the very last, when we entered the stable-loft, but here I came upon one or two really significant traces of occupation.

"The first of these was a smooth, indented line on the floor, as if some heavy, metallic object had been dragged along it, with other, rougher lines, apparently made by a heavy wooden case. Then there was a quantity of straw, not new straw such as you might expect to find in a stable-loft, but straw that had evidently been used for packing. And, finally, there was a pair of canvas pliers which appeared to have been strained by a violent effort to rotate from right to left some hard, metallic body, three-quarters-of-an-inch wide, with sharp corners and apparently square in section – some body, in fact, that in shape, in size, and apparently in material, was identical with the square of the cock on one of the liquid gas bottles, which appeared to have been connected with a screw thread and had clearly required great force to turn it with this inadequate appliance.

"The evidence collected from the loft, suggesting that a large case had been moved in and out and that a gas cylinder had been opened, you will say was of the flimsiest. And so it was. But the effects of evidence are cumulative. To estimate the value of these observations made in the loft, you must add them to the facts just obtained concerning the artist himself, the position of his house, and the date on which he vacated it, and these coincidences and agreements must be added to – or, more strictly, multiplied into – the body of coincidences and agreements which I have already described.

"But the evidence collected at the house was the least important part of the day's 'catch'. On returning to Jardine's rooms I ventured to borrow the sketch and took it home with me, and when I compared the thumb-print on it with the photograph of the thumb-print on the letter –

employing the excellent method of comparison that is in use at Scotland Yard – there could be no possible doubt (disregarding for the moment, the chances of forgery) that they were the prints of one and the same thumb.

"Here, then, at last I had stepped out of the region of mere hypothesis. Here was an item of positive evidence, and one, moreover, of high probative value. It proved, beyond any reasonable doubt, the existence of some connection between the house on the Heath and the factory in Norton Street, and it established a strong presumption that the artist and the man at the factory were the same person, the weak point in this being the absence of proof that the thumb-print on the painting was made by the artist.

"And here, Jardine, I would draw your attention to the interesting way in which, when a long train of hypothetical reasoning has at length elicited an actual, demonstrable truth, that truth instantly reacts on the hypothesis, lifting it as a whole on to an entirely different plane of probability. I may compare the effect to that of a crystal, dropped into a super-saturated solution of a salt, such as sodium sulphate. So long as it is at rest, the solution remains a clear liquid, but drop into it the minutest crystal of its own salt, and, in a few moments the entire liquid has solidified into a mass of crystals.

"So it was in the present case. In the instant when it became an established fact that the house at Hampstead and the factory in Norton Street had been occupied by the same person, the entire sequence of events which I had hypothetically constructed sprang from the plane of mere conceivability to that of actual probability. It was now more likely than unlikely that the unknown cleric had been murdered, that his body had been conveyed to the artist's house, that it had there been frozen, transferred to the factory, preserved there for some weeks, passed over the wall to the Samways' house, and finally cremated under the name of Septimus Maddock.

"All that now remained to be done was the verification and identification of the body. As to the first, I examined the will at Somerset House and found it, as the American detectives suspected, a mere notification to the New York authorities that Septimus Maddock was dead. I wrote to the detective agency and in due course came O'Donnell with the answers to my questions, from which we learned for certain that the artist was Septimus Maddock and that the assumed peculiarity of the hands consisted of *brachydactyly*. And then came the good Father Humperdinck to enable us to give a name to the body and to furnish us with that unlocked for means of identification. Henceforward, all was plain sailing with only one possible source of failure, the possibility that the bullet might have been subsequently extracted. But this was highly improbable. We knew that the wound had healed completely, and it was pretty certain that the bullet was lying quietly encysted or embedded in the bone. Still, I will confess that I have never in my life been more relieved than I was when my eyes lighted on that dent in the ilium with the stain of lead oxide round it."

"So I can imagine," said Jervis. "It was a triumph, and you deserved it. I have never known even my revered senior to work out the theory of a crime more neatly or with less positive matter to work from. And I suppose you have a pretty clear and connected idea of the actual sequence of events."

"I think so," replied Thorndyke, "although much of it is necessarily conjectural. I take it that Maddock, while hiding in Bruges under the name of Burton, made the acquaintance of Reinhardt, and saw in the rich, friendless, eccentric bachelor a suitable subject for a crime which he had probably already considered in general terms. I should think that they were probably somewhat alike in appearance and that the idea of personation was first suggested by the circumstance that they both wore gloves habitually. Maddock will have learned of Reinhardt's intended visit to England and immediately begun his preparations. His scheme – and a most ingenious one it was, I must confess – was clearly to cause Reinhardt to disappear in one locality and produce his body after a considerable interval in another at some distance, and the house on the Heath was apparently taken with this object and to be near Reinhardt's haunts. I take it that on the night of the murder, Reinhardt had an appointment to visit him at that house, but that, having learned at Miss Vyne's of the sudden illness of Brother Bartholomew, he suddenly altered his plans and refused to go. Then Maddock – who had probably waited for him on the road – seeing his scheme on the point of being wrecked, walked with him as he was going home and took the risk of killing him in Millfield Lane. The risk was not great, considering the time of night and the solitary character of the place, and the distance from the house was not too great for a strong man, as Maddock seems to have been, to carry the body.

"Death was almost certainly produced by a stab in the back, and Maddock was probably just about to carry the body away when destiny, in the form of Jardine, appeared. Then Maddock must have lurked, probably behind the fence which had the large hole in it, until Jardine went away, when he must instantly have picked up the body, carried it down the lane, pushed it over the fence – detaching the reliquary as he did so – carried it away to the house, stripped it and proceeded at once to freeze it, having provided a bottle of the gas in readiness.

"The next morning he will have gone to Marchmont's office, probably dressed in Reinhardt's clothes, from thence to Charing Cross, and, with Reinhardt's luggage, gone straight on to Paris, leaving the body packed in an abundance of the carbonic acid snow. At Paris he will have made his arrangements and then disappeared, returning in disguise to England to carry out the rest of the plan. And a wonderfully clever plan it was, and most ingeniously and resolutely executed. If it had succeeded – and it was within a hair's breath of succeeding – the hunted criminal, Maddock, would have been beyond the reach of Justice for ever, and the fictitious Reinhardt might have lived out his life in luxury and absolute security."

As Thorndyke concluded, he rose from his chair, and, stepping over to a cabinet, drew from some inner recess a cigar of melanotic complexion and repulsive aspect.

Jervis looked at it and chuckled. "Thorndyke's one dissipation," said he. "At the close of every successful case he proceeds, as a sort of thanksgiving ceremony, to funk us out of these chambers with the smoke of a Trichinopoly cheroot. But listen! Don't light it yet, Thorndyke. Here comes some harmless and inoffensive stranger."

Thorndyke paused with the cigar in his fingers. A quick step ascended the stairs and then came a sharp, official rat-tat from the little brass knocker. Thorndyke laid the cigar on the mantelpiece and strode over to the door. I saw him take in a telegram, open it, glance at the paper and dismiss the messenger. Then, closing the door, he came back to the fireside with the "flimsy" in his hand. "There, Jardine," said he, laying it on my knee, "there is your order of release."

I picked up the paper and read aloud its curt message. "'*Maddock arrested Folkestone. Now in custody Bow Street. Miller.*'"

"That means to say," said Thorndyke, "that the halter is already around his neck. I think I may light my Trichinopoly now."

And he did so.

There is little more to tell. This has been a history of coincidences and one more coincidence brings it to a close. The very day on which my formal engagement to Sylvia was made public chanced to be the day on which the execution of Septimus Maddock was described in the papers. On that day, too, the portrait of poor Letitia, painted by that skilful and murderous hand, was placed in the handsome ebony frame that I had caused to be made for it. As I write these closing words, it hangs before me, flanked on either side by the little jar of violets that are renewed religiously from day to day by my wife or me. The pale, inscrutable eyes look out on me, her friend whom she loved so faithfully and who so little merited her love, but as I look into them, the picture fades and shows me

271

the same face glorified, waxen, pallid, drowsy-eyed, peaceful, and sweet – the dead face of the woman who gave her heart's blood as the price of my ransom, and who was fated then to pass – out of my life indeed, but out of my heart's shrine and my most loving remembrance, never.

The End

1922 Hodder & Stoughton Cover

Prologue

To every woman there comes a day (and that all too soon) when she receives the first hint that Time, the harvester, has not passed her by unnoticed. The waning of actual youth may have passed with but the faintest regret, if any, regret for the lost bud being merged in the triumph at the glory of the opening blossom. But the waning of womanhood is another matter. Old age has no compensations to offer for those delights that it steals away. At least, that is what I understand from those who know, for I must still speak on the subject from hearsay, having received from Father Time but the very faintest and most delicate hint on the subject.

I was sitting at my dressing table brushing out my hair, which is of a docile habit, though a thought bulky, when amidst the black tress – blacker than it used to be when I was a girl – I noticed a single white hair. It was the first that I had seen, and I looked at it dubiously, picking it out from its fellows to see if it were all white, and noticing how like it was to a thread of glass. Should I pluck it out and pretend that it was never there? Or should I, more thriftily – for a hair is a hair after all, and enough of them will make a wig – should I dye it and hush up its treason?

I smiled at the foolish thought. What a to-do about a single white hair! I have seen girls in their twenties with snow-white hair and looking as sweet as lavender. As to this one, I would think of it as a souvenir from the troubled past rather than a harbinger of approaching age, and with this I swept my brush over it and buried it even as I had buried those sorrows and those dreadful experiences which might have left me white-headed years before.

But that glassy thread, buried once more amid the black, left a legacy of suggestion. Those hideous days were long past now. I could look back on them unmoved – nay, with a certain serene interest. Suppose I should write the history of them? Why not? To write is not necessarily to publish. And if, perchance, no eye but mine shall see these lines until the little taper of my life has burned down into its socket, then what matters it to me whether praise or blame, sympathy or condemnation, be my portion. Posterity has no gifts to offer that I need court its suffrages.

Book 1 – Tragedy

Chapter I
The Crack of Doom

There is no difficulty whatever in deciding upon the exact moment at which to open this history. Into some lives the fateful and significant creep by degrees, unnoticed till by the development of their consequences the mind is aroused and memory is set, like a sleuth-hound, to retrace the course of events and track the present to its origin in the past. Not so has it been with mine. Serene, eventless, its quiet years had slipped away unnumbered, from childhood to youth, from youth to womanhood, when, at the appointed moment, the voice of Destiny rang out, trumpet-tongued, and Behold! In the twinkling of an eye, all was changed.

"Happy," it has been said, "is the nation which has no history!" And surely the same may be said with equal truth of individuals. So, at any rate, experience teaches me, for the very moment wherein I may be said to have begun to have a history saw a life-long peace shattered into a chaos of misery and disaster.

How well I remember the day – yea, and the very moment – when the blow fell, like a thunderbolt crashing down out of a cloudless sky. I had been sitting in my little room upstairs, reading very studiously and pausing now and again to think over what I had read. The book was Lecky's *History of England in the Eighteenth Century*, and the period on which I was engaged was that of Queen Anne. And here, coming presently upon a footnote containing a short quotation from *The Spectator*, it occurred to me that I should like to look over the original letter. Accordingly, laying aside my book, I began to descend the stairs – very softly, because I knew that my father had a visitor – possibly a client – with him in his study. And when I came to the turn of the stair and saw that the study door was ajar, I stepped more lightly still, though I stole down quickly lest I should overhear what was being said.

The library, or book-room as we called it, was next to the study, and to reach it I had to pass the half-opened door, which I did swiftly on tip-toe, without hearing more than the vague murmur of conversation from within. *The Spectator* stood on a shelf close to the door, a goodly row clothed in rusty calf to which the worn gilt tooling imparted a certain sumptuousness that had always seemed very pleasant to my eye. My hand was on the third volume when I heard my father say, "So that's how the matter stands."

I plucked the volume from the shelf, and, tucking it under my arm, stole out of the book-room, intending to dart up the stairs before there should be time for anything more to be said, but I had hardly crossed the threshold, and was, in fact, exactly opposite the study door, when a voice said very distinctly, though not at all loudly, "Do you realise, Vardon, that this renders you liable to seven years' penal servitude?"

At those terrible words I stopped as though I had been, in a moment, turned into stone, stopped with my lips parted, my very breathing arrested, clutching at the book under my arm, with no sign of life or movement save the tumultuous thumping of my heart. There was what seemed an interminable pause, and then my father replied, "Hardly, I think, Otway. Technically, perhaps, it amounts to a misdemeanour – "

"Technically!" repeated Mr. Otway.

"Yes, technically. The absence of any intent to defraud modifies the position considerably. Still, for the purpose of argument, we may admit that it amounts to a misdemeanour."

"And," said Mr. Otway, "the maximum punishment of that misdemeanour is seven years' penal servitude. As to your plea of absence of fraudulent intent, you, as a lawyer of experience, must know well that judges are not apt to be very sympathetic with trustees who misappropriate property placed in their custody."

"Misappropriate!" my father exclaimed.

"Yes, Mr. Otway, I say misappropriate. What other word could you apply? Here is a sum of money which has been placed in your custody. I come here with the intention to receive that money from you on behalf of the trustees, and you tell me that you haven't got it. You are not only unable to produce it, but you are unable to give any date on which you could produce it. And meanwhile it seems that you have applied it to your own uses."

"I haven't spent it," my father objected. "The money is locked up for the present, but it isn't lost."

"What is the use of saying that?" demanded Mr. Otway. "You haven't got the money, and you can't give any satisfactory account of it. The plain English of it is that you have used this trust money for your own private purposes, and that when the trustors ask to have it restored to them, you are unable to produce it."

To this my father made no immediate reply, and in the silence that ensued I could hear my heart throbbing and the blood humming in the veins of my neck. At length my father asked, "Well, Otway, what are you going to do?"

"Do!" repeated Mr. Otway. "What can I do? As a trustee, it is my duty to get this money from you. I have to protect the interests of those whom I represent. And if you have misapplied these funds – well, you must see for yourself that I have no choice."

"You mean that you'll prosecute?"

"What else can I do? I can't introduce personal considerations into the business of a trust, and even if I should decline to move in the matter, the trustors themselves would undoubtedly take action."

Here there followed a silence which seemed to me of endless duration, then Mr. Otway said, in a somewhat different tone, "There is just one way for you out of this mess, Vardon."

"Indeed!" said my father.

"Yes. I am going to make you a proposal, and I may as well put it quite bluntly. It is this. I am prepared to take over your liabilities, for the time being, on condition that I marry your daughter. If you agree, then on the day on which the marriage takes place, I pay into your bank the sum of five-thousand pounds, you giving me an undertaking to repay the loan if and when you can."

"Have you any reason to suppose that my daughter wishes to marry you?" my father asked.

"Not the slightest," replied Mr. Otway, "but I think it probable that, if the case were put to her – "

"It is not going to be," my father interrupted. "I would rather go to gaol than connive at the sacrifice of my daughter's happiness."

"You might have thought of her happiness a little sooner, Vardon," Mr. Otway remarked. "We are not quite of an age, but she might easily find it more agreeable to be the wife of an elderly man than the daughter of a convict. At any rate, it would be only fair to give her the choice."

"It would be entirely unfair," my father retorted. "In effect, it would be asking her to make the sacrifice, and she might be fool enough to consent. And please bear in mind, Otway, that I am not a convict yet, and possibly may never be one. There are certain conceivable alternatives, you know."

"Oh," said Mr. Otway, "if you have resources that you have not mentioned, that is quite another matter. I understood that you had none. And as to sacrifice, there is no need to harp on that string so persistently. Your daughter might be happy enough as my wife."

"What infernal nonsense you are talking!" my father exclaimed, impatiently. "Do you suppose that Helen is a fool?"

"No, I certainly do not," Mr. Otway replied.

"Very well, then, what do you mean by her being happy as your wife? Here am I, standing over a mine – "

"Of your own laying," interrupted Mr. Otway.

"Quite so, of my own laying. And here you come with a lighted match and say to my daughter, in effect, 'My dear young lady, I am your devoted lover. Be my wife – consent this very instant or I fire this mine and blow you and your father to smithereens.' And then, you think, she would settle down with you and live happy ever after. By the Lord, Otway, you must be a devilish poor judge of character."

"I am quite willing to take the risk," said Mr. Otway.

"So you may be," my father retorted angrily, "but I'm not. I would rather see the poor girl in her grave than know that she was chained for life to a cold-blooded, blackmailing scoundrel – "

"Softly, Vardon!" Mr. Otway interrupted. "There is no need for that sort of language. And perhaps we had better shut the door."

Here, as I drew back hastily into the book-room, quick footsteps crossed the study floor and I heard the door close. The interruption brought me back to some sense of my position, though, to be sure, what I had overheard concerned me as much as it concerned anyone. Quickly slipping the book back on the shelf, I ran on tip-toe past the study door and up the stairs, and even then I was none too soon, for, as I halted on the threshold of my room, the study door opened again and the two men strode across the hail.

"You are taking a ridiculously wrong-headed view of the whole affair," I heard Mr. Otway declare.

"Possibly," my father replied, stiffly. "And if I do, I am prepared to take the consequences."

"Only the consequences won't fall on you alone," said Mr. Otway.

"Good afternoon," was the dry and final response. Then the hall door slammed, and I heard my father walk slowly back to the study.

Chapter II
Atra Cura

As the study door closed, I sank into my easy chair with a sudden feeling of faintness and bodily exhaustion. The momentary shock of horror and amazement had passed, giving place to a numb and chilly dread that made me feel sick and weak. Scraps of the astounding conversation that I had heard came back to me, incoherently and yet with hideous distinctness, like the whisperings of some malignant spirit. Disjointed words and phrases repeated themselves again and again, almost meaninglessly, but still with a vague undertone of menace.

And then, by degrees, as I sat gazing at the blurred pages of the book that still lay open on the reading-stand, my thoughts grew less chaotic, the words of that dreadful dialogue arranged themselves anew, and I began with more distinctness to gather their meaning.

Seven years penal servitude!

That was the dreadful refrain of this song of doom that was being chanted in my ear by the Spirit of Misfortune. And ruin – black, hideous ruin – for my father and me was the burden of that refrain, no mere loss, no paltry plunge into endurable poverty, but a descent into the bottomless pit of social degradation, from which there could be no hope of resurrection.

Nor was this the worst. For, gradually, as my thoughts began to arrang themselves into a coherent sequence, I realised that it was not the implied poverty and social disgrace that gave to that sentence it dreadful import. Poverty might be overcome, and disgrace could be endured, but when I thought of my father dragged away from me to be cast into gaol, when, in my mind's eye, I saw him clothed in the horrible livery of shame, wearing out his life within the prison walls and behind the fast-bolted prison doors, the thought and the imagined sight were unendurable. It was death – for him at least, for he was not a strong man. And for me?

Here, of a sudden, there came back to me the rather enigmatical speech of my father's, which I had heard without at the moment fully comprehending, but which I now recalled with a shock of alarm.

"Please bear in mind, Otway, that I am not a convict yet, and possibly may never be one. There are certain conceivable alternatives, you know."

The cryptic utterance had evidently puzzled Mr. Otway, who had clearly misunderstood it as referring to some unknown resources. To me, no such misunderstanding was possible. More than once my father had discussed with me the ethics of suicide, on which subject he held somewhat unorthodox opinions, and I now recalled with terrible distinction the very definite statement that he had made on the occasion of our last talks. "For my part," he had said, "if I should ever find myself in such a position that the continuance of life was less desirable than its termination, I should not hesitate to take the appropriate measures for exchanging the less desirable state for the more desirable."

In the face of such a statement, made, as I felt sure, in all sincerity and with sober judgment, how could I entertain any doubt as to the interpretation of that reference to "certain conceivable alternatives"? To a man of culture and some position and none too robust in health, what would be the aspect of life with its immediate future occupied by a criminal prosecution ending in an inevitable conviction and a term of penal servitude? Could the continuance of such a life be conceived as desirable? Assuredly not.

And then imagination began to torture me by filling in with hideous ingenuity the dreadful details. Now it was a pistol shot, heard in the night, and a group of terrified servants huddled together in the corridor. But no, that was not like my poor father. Such crude and bloody methods appertain rather to the terror-stricken fugitive than to one who is executing a considered and orderly retreat. Then I saw myself, in the grey of the morning, tapping at his bedroom door, tapping – tapping – and at last opening the door, or perhaps bursting it open. I saw the dim room – Oh! How horribly plain and vivid it was! With the cold light of the dawn glimmering through the blind, the curtained bed, the half-seen figure, still and silent in the shadow. Horrible! Horrible!

And then, in instant, the scene changed. I saw a man in our hall – a man in uniform, a railway porter or inspector. I heard him tell, in a hushed, embarrassed voice, of a strange and dreadful accident down on the line . . . And yet again this awful phantasmagoria shifted the scene and showed me a new picture, a search party, prowling with lantern around a chalk pit, and *anon* a group of four men, treading softly and carrying something on a hurdle.

"Dear God!" I gasped, with my hands pressed to my forehead, "must I be – this awful thing! Is there no other way?"

And with that there fell on me a great calm. A chilly calm, bringing no comfort, and yet, in a manner, a relief. For, perhaps, after all, there *was* another way. It was true that my father had rejected Mr. Otway's proposal, and such was my habit of implicit obedience that, with his definite rejection of it, the alternative had, for me, ceased to exist.

But now, with the horror of this dreadful menace upon me, I recalled the words that had been spoken, and asked myself if that avenue of escape were really closed. As to my father, I had no doubt, he would never consent, and even to raise the question might only be to precipitate the catastrophe. But with regard to Mr. Otway, the manner in which my father had met and rejected his proposal seemed to close the subject finally. He had called him a blackmailing scoundrel and used other injurious expressions, which might make it difficult or, at least, uncomfortable to reopen the question. Still that was a small matter. When one is walking to the gallows, one does not boggle at an uncomfortable shoe.

As to my own inclinations, they were beside the mark. My father's life and good name must be saved if it were possible, and it seemed that it might be possible – at a price. Whether it were possible or not depended on Mr. Otway.

I recalled what I knew of this man who had thus in a moment become the arbiter of my father's fate and mine. My acquaintance with him was but slight, though I had met him pretty frequently and had sometimes wondered what his profession was, if he had any. I had assumed, from his evident acquaintance with legal matters, that he was a lawyer. But he was not in ordinary practice, and his business, whatever it was, seemed to involve a good deal of travelling. That was all I knew about him. As to his appearance, he was a huge, unwieldy man, some years older, I should think, than my father, pleasant spoken and genial in a somewhat heavy fashion, but quite uninteresting. Hitherto I had neither liked nor disliked him. Now, it need hardly be said, I regarded him with decided aversion, for if he were not, as my father had said, "a blackmailing scoundrel", he had, at any rate, taken the meanest, the most ungenerous advantage of my father's difficulties, to say nothing of the callous, cynical indifference that he had shown in regard to me and my wishes and interests.

It may seem a little odd that I found myself attaching no blame to my father. Yet so it was. To me he appeared as merely the victim of circumstances. No doubt he had done something indiscreet – perhaps incorrect But discretion and correctness are not qualities that appeal to a woman, whereas generosity – and my father was generous almost to a fault – makes the most powerful appeal to feminine sympathies. As to his honesty and good faith, I never doubted them for an instant. Besides, he had plainly said that no fraudulent intent could be ascribed to him. What he had done I had not the least idea. Nor did I particularly care. It was not the act, but it consequences with which I was concerned.

My meditations were interrupted at length by an apologetic tap at the door, followed by the appearance of our housemaid.

"If you please, Miss Helen, shall I take Mr. Vardon's tea to the study, or is he going to have it with you?"

The question brought me back from the region of tragedy and disaster in which my thoughts had been straying, to the homely commonplaces of everyday life.

"I'll just run down and ask him, Jessie," I answered, "and you needn't wait. I'll come and tell you what he says."

I ran quickly down the stairs, but at the study door I paused with a sudden revival of those terrors that had so lately assailed me. Suppose he should open the subject and have something dreadful to tell me? Or suppose that, even now, already – At the half-formed thought, I raised a trembling hand, and, tapping lightly at the door, opened it and entered. He was sitting at the table with a small pile of sealed and stamped letters before him, and, as I stood, steadying my hand on the door knob, he looked up with his customary smile of friendly welcome.

"Hail! O Dame of the azure hosen," said he, swinging round on his revolving chair, "and how fares it with our liege lady, Queen Anne?"

"She is quite well, thank you," I replied.

"The Lord be praised!" he rejoined. "I seemed to have heard some rumour of her untimely decease. A mere canard, it would seem, a fiction of these confounded newspaper men. Or perchance I have been misled by the jocose and boisterous Lecky."

The whimsical playfulness of speech, habitual as it was to him, impressed me – perhaps for that very reason – with a vague uneasiness. It was not what I had expected after that terrible conversation. The anti-climax to my own tragic thoughts was too sudden, the descent to the ordinary too uncomfortably steep. I perched myself on his knee, as I often did, despite my rather excessive size, and passed my hand over his thin, grey hair.

"Do you know," I said, clinging desperately to the common-place, "that you are going bald? I can see the skin of your head quite plainly."

"And why not?" he demanded. "Did you think my hair grew out of my cranium? But you won't see it long. I've heard of an infallible hair-restorer."

"Indeed!"

"Yes, indeed! Guaranteed to grow a crop of ringlets on a bladder of lard. We'll get a bottle and try it on the carpet broom, and if the result is satisfactory – well, we'll just put Esau in his place in the second row."

"You are a very frivolous old person, Mr. Pater," said I. "Do you know that?"

"I hope so," he replied. "And again I say, why not? When a man is too old to play the fool, it is time to carry him to the bone-yard. Am I going to have any tea?"

"Of course you are. Will you have it here alone or shall we have tea together?"

"What a question!" he exclaimed. "Am I in my dotage? Should I drink tea in musty solitude when I might bask in the smiles of a lovely maiden? Avaunt! No, I'll tell you what we'll do, Jimmy. I'll just telephone down to the office and see if there is any silly nonsense there that may distract me from serious pursuits, and, if there isn't, we'll have tea in the workroom and then we'll polish off that coal-scuttle."

"Finish it! But there's quite a lot to do."

"Then we'll do the lot."

"But why this hurry? There's no particular reason for getting it finished to-night, is there?

"I don't know that there is, but we've had the thing hanging about long enough. Better get it finished and start on something else. Now you trot off and see about tea while I ring up Jackson."

As he turned to the telephone, I hurried away to give instructions to the maid and to set the workshop in order so that we might start without delay on our evening's task, concerning which a few words of explanation would seem to be called for.

My father was by nature designed to be a craftsman. He was never so happy as when he was making something or in some way working with his hands, and remarkably skilful hands they were, with an inborn capacity for the dexterous manipulation of every kind of material, tool, or appliance. And to his natural skill he had added a vast amount of knowledge of methods and processes. He was an excellent woodworker, an admirable mechanic, and a quite passable potter. Our house abounded in the products of his industry: Stools, cupboards, clocks, fenders, earthen-ware jars. Even our bicycles had been built, or, at least, "assembled", by him, and a bronze knocker on our door had been finished by him from castings made in our workshop. If his powers of design had been equal to his manual skill, he would have been a first-class art craftsman. Unfortunately they were not. Left to himself, his tendency was to aim at a neat trade finish, at smooth surfaces and mechanical precision. But he knew his limitations, and had been at great pains to have me instructed in the arts of design, and, as I apparently had some natural aptitude in that direction, I was able to help him by making sketches and working drawings and by criticising the work as it progressed. But my duties did not stop at that. In our happy, united life, I was his apprentice, his journeyman, his assistant – or foreman, as he pleased to call me – and his constant companion, in the house, in the workshop, and in our walks abroad.

As our maid, Jessie, laid the tea-tray on a vacant corner of the work-bench, I examined our latest joint-production, a bronze coal-scuttle, the design of which was based on a Roman helmet that I had seen in the British Museum. There was a good deal more than an ordinary evening's work to be done before it could be finished. A portion of the embossed ornament on the foot required touching up, the foot itself had to be brazed to the body and the handle had to be riveted to the lugs, to say nothing of the "pickling", scouring, and oxidizing. It was a colossal evening's work.

But it was not the magnitude of the task that troubled me, for I shared my father's love of manual work. What had instantly impressed me with a vague discomfort was the urgency of my father's desire to get this piece of work finished and done with. That was not like him at all. Not only had he the genuine craftsman's inexhaustible patience, but he had a habit of keeping an apparently finished work on hand, that he might tinker at it lovingly, smooth and polish it, and bring it to a state of even greater completeness and finish.

Why, then, this strange urgency and impatience? And, as I asked myself the question, all my fears came crowding back on me. Again there came that dreadful sinking at the heart, that strangling terror of the storm-cloud that hung over us, unseen but ready to burst and overwhelm us in ruin at any moment.

But I had little time for these gloomy and disquieting thoughts. The tinkling of the telephone bell in the study told me that my father had finished his talk with his managing clerk, and a few moments later he strode into the workshop and began taking off his coat.

"Where's your apron, Jimmy?" he asked (the pet name "Jimmy" had been evolved out of an ancient fiction that my name was Jemima).

"There's no hurry, Pater, dear," said I. "Let a person have her tea in peace. And do sit down like a Christian man."

He obediently perched himself on a stool as I handed him his tea, but in less than a minute he was on his feet again, prowling, cup in hand, around the end of the bench where the work lay.

"Wonder if I'd better anneal it a bit," he mused, picking up the bronze foot and examining the unfinished space. "Mustn't make it too soft. Think I will, though. We can hammer it up a little on the stake after it's brazed on. That will harden it enough."

He laid the foot down, but only that he might apply a match to the great gas blowpipe, and I watched him with a sinking heart as he stood with his teacup in one hand, while with the other he held the foot, gripped in a pair of tongs, in the roaring purple flame. What did it mean, this strange, restless haste to finish what was, after all, but a work of pleasure? Did it portend some change that he saw more clearly than I? Was he, impelled by the craftsman's instinct, turning in this fashion a page of the book of life? Or was it – Oh! dreadful thought! – was it that he was deliberately writing "*Finis*" before closing the volume?

But whatever was in his secret mind, he chatted cheerfully as he worked, and submitted to be fed with scraps of bread-and-butter and to have cups of tea administered at intervals. Yet still I noted that the chasing hammer flew at unwonted speed, and the depth of the punch-marks on the work that rested on the sand-bag told of an unusual weight in the blows.

"What a pity it is," he remarked, "that social prejudices prevent a middle-class man from earning a livelihood with his hands. Now, here I am, a third-rate solicitor perforce, whereas, if I followed my bent, I should be a first-rate coppersmith. Shouldn't I?"

"Quite first-rate," I replied.

"Or even a silversmith," he continued, "if I could have my mate, Jim, to do the art with a capital *A* while I did the work with a capital *W*. Hmm?"

He looked up at me with a twinkle, and I took the opportunity to pop a piece of bread-and-butter into his mouth, which occasioned a pause in the conversation.

I had entertained faint – very faint – hopes that he might say something to me about his difficulties. Not that I was inquisitive on the subject, but, in view of a resolution that was slowly forming in my mind, I should have liked to have some idea what his position really was. It seemed pretty plain, however, that he did not intend to take me into his confidence, notwithstanding which I decided in a tentative way to give him an opening.

"Wasn't that Mr. Otway who was with you this afternoon?" I asked.

"Yes," he replied. "How did you know?"

"I heard his voice in the hall as you let him out," I answered, with something of a gulp at the implied untruth.

The chasing hammer was arrested for a moment in mid-air, and, as my father's eye fixed itself reflectively on the punch that he held, I could see that he was trying to remember what Mr. Otway had said in the hall.

"Yes," he replied, after a brief pause, "it was Mr. Otway. I should hardly have thought you would have known his voice. Queer fellow,

Otway. No brains to speak of, but yet an excellent man of business in his way."

"What does he do – by way of profession, I mean?"

"The Lord knows. He was originally a solicitor, but he hasn't practised for years. Now he is what is called a financier, which is a little vague, but apparently profitable. And I think he does something in the way of precious stones."

"Do you mean that he deals in them?"

"Yes, occasionally, at least, so I have heard. I know that he is something of a connoisseur in stones, and that he had a collection, which he sold some time ago. I have also heard – and I believe it is a fact – that his name was originally Levy, and that he is one of the Chosen. But why he changed his name I have no notion, unless it was an undesirable one to present to the financial world."

I was half-disposed to pursue my enquiries further, but as he finished speaking, he once more began to ply the hammer with such furious energy that I became quite uneasy.

"You mustn't exert yourself so much, Pater," I remarked. "Remember what Dr. Sharpe said."

"Bah!" he replied. "Sharpe is an old woman. My heart is sound enough. At any rate, it will last as long as the rest of me. An old fellow like me cannot expect to go in for sprinting or high jumping, but there's no need for him to live in splints and cotton wool."

"Nor to endanger his health by perfectly unnecessary exertion. Why on earth are you in such a fever to get this thing finished?"

"I'm not in a fever, my dear," he answered, "I'm only tired of seeing this thing lying about unfinished. You see, as it stands, it is only so many pounds of old bronze, whereas a couple of hours' work turns it into a valuable piece of furniture, fit to take a dignified place in the catalogue when we are sold up. Just consider how finely it would read: '*Handsome bronze scuttle, in form of Roman helmet, the work of the late owner and his charming and talented daughter, capable of serving either as a convenient receptacle for coal or as a becoming head-dress for a person with a suitable cranium.*' Don't you think that would sound rather alluring?"

"Very," I replied, "but as we are not going to be sold up – "

The rest of my sentence was drowned in the din of the beaten metal as my father returned to his hammering, and I only watched in mute discomfort until this part of the work was done and the great brazing jet was once more set a-roaring.

The work progressed apace, for my father was not only skilful and neat, but could be very quick on occasion, and as I watched the completion of stage after stage, I was conscious of a growing uneasiness, a vague fear of seeing the work actually finished, as if this mere toy – for it was little more – held some deep and tragic symbolism. I felt like one looking on at the slow wasting of one of those waxen effigies which the sorceresses of old prepared with magical rites for the destruction of some victim, whose life should slowly wane and flicker away with the wasting of the wax.

And meanwhile, above the roar of the blowpipe flame, my father's voice sounded, now in a cheerful stave of song, and now in lively jest or playful badinage. But yet he did not deceive me. Behind all this show of high spirits was a sombre background that was never quite hidden. For the eye of love is very keen and can see plainly, despite quip or joke or jovial carol, when *"Black Care rides behind the horseman"*.

What a miserable affair it was, this pitiful acting of two poor, leaden-hearted mortals, each hiding from each the desperate resolve with smiles and jests that were more bitter than tears! For I, too, had now my secret, and must needs preserve it with such a show of gaiety as I could muster by sheer effort of will. The resolution of which I have spoken was growing – growing, even as the toy that we were making was growing towards completion, and as I seemed to see, as if symbolized by it, the sands of destiny trickling out before my eyes. So I, too, had my part to play in this harrowing comedy.

Works which have consumed much time in the doing have a way of coming to an end with disconcerting suddenness. When I mixed the acid for the "pickle" in the great earthenware pan, it seemed that a great deal still remained to be done, in spite of my father's feverish energy and swift dexterity. And then, but a few minutes later, as it appeared to me, behold the finished piece standing on the bench its embossed ornament telling boldly against the sulphur-browned background, and my father stretching himself and wiping the blackened oil from his hands, and it was borne in on me that, with the final touch, his interest in the thing had fallen dead.

"*Nunc dimittis!*" he murmured. "It's finished at last. '*Now lettest Thou Thy servant depart in peace.*' And that reminds me, Jim – don't the shops keep open late to-night?"

"Some of them do," I replied.

"Good," said he. "Tell Jessie to bring up the supper while I'm washing. I've got to make a business call to-night, and I want to get some things, so we won't make it a ceremonious meal. Not that I want to put you on short allowance, for I expect you are hungry after your Titanic labours. You mustn't take any notice of me."

As he hurried away, I rang the bell, and, when I had given the necessary instructions, I went up to my bedroom to remove the traces of the evening's work and make myself presentable.

At the supper table, my father preserved the same quiet gaiety of manner – his usual manner, in fact, for he was always cheerful and companionable – though, on this occasion, the speed with which he disposed of his food gave little opportunity for conversation. After a very hurried meal, he rose and, pushing back his chair, glanced at his watch.

"You mustn't mind my running away," said he. "Time, tide, and the shopkeeper wait for no man."

He moved away toward the door, but before he reached it he paused and then came back and stood beside my chair.

"You need'nt sit up for me," he said. "I may possibly be rather late. So I'd better say 'good-night' now.'" He took my head in his hands, and, looking earnestly into my eyes, murmured, "Dear little Jim, best and most loyal of apprentices." Then he kissed me very tenderly and passed his hands over my hair.

"Good-night, sweetheart," said he. "Don't sit up reading, but go to bed early like a sensible girlie – if you will pardon my thopping into Weggish poetry without notice."

He turned away and walked quickly to the door, where he stood for a moment to wave his hand. I heard him go to the study, and sat stiffly in my chair listening. In a few moments he came out and stepped quietly across the hail, there was a brief pause, and then the outer door closed.

He was gone.

At the sound of the closing door, I sprang to my feet with all my terrors revived. Whither had he gone? It was unusual for him to leave his home at night. What was it that had taken him abroad on this night of all others? And what was it that he wanted to buy? And wanted so urgently that he could not wait until the morrow? And why had he wished me "good-night" with such tender earnestness? A foolish question, this, for he was a loving father, and never sought to veil his affection. But to-night I was unstrung, haunted by nameless fears that gave a dreadful significance to every passing incident. And as the chill of mortal terror crept round my heart, the resolution that had been growing – growing – came to its final completion.

It had to be. Horrible, loathsome as, even then, I felt it to be, it was the only alternative to that other nameless and unthinkable. The sacrifice must be made by us both for both our sakes – if it were not too late already.

Too late? Even as the dreadful thought smote like a hammer on my heart, I ran from the room and sped up the stairs on the wings of terror.

With trembling fingers I took my hat and cloak from the wardrobe and hurried down stairs, putting them on as I went. At the dining-room door I called out a hasty message to the maid, and then, snatching up my gloves from the hall table, I opened the door and ran out into darkness.

Chapter III
The Covenant

As I sped swiftly along the quiet roads on the outskirts of the town, the confusion and sense of helplessness began to subside under the influence of action and a definite purpose, by degrees my thoughts clarified, and I found myself shaping out, with surprising deliberation and judgment, the course that I intended to pursue. Mr. Otway's house was about a mile distant from ours, somewhat farther out of town, though on a frequented road, a short distance and quickly covered by my flying feet. Yet, short as it was, and traversed with a phantom of terror in close pursuit, it gave me time to collect my faculties, so that, when I opened the gate and walked up the little drive, I had already to a large extent recovered my self-possession, though I was still trembling with the fear of what might be happening else where at this very moment.

The door was opened by a small frail-looking woman of about fifty, who did not look quite like an ordinary servant, and whose appearance instantly impressed me disagreeably. She stood with her face slightly averted, looking at me out of the corners of her eyes, and holding the door open as she asked, with a slight Scotch accent, "Who would you be wanting?"

"I wish to see Mr. Otway, if he is at home?" I replied.

"If ye'll come in and give me your name, I'll tell him," said she, and with this she showed me into a small room that opened out of the hall, where, when I had told her my name, she left me. In less than a minute Mr. Otway entered, and having carefully closed the door, shook hands gravely and offered me a chair.

"This is quite an unexpected pleasure, Miss Vardon," said he. "Oddly enough, I was just thinking about you. I called on your father only this afternoon."

"I know," said I. "It was about that that I came to see you."

"Your father, then," said Mr. Otway, "has mentioned to you the subject of our not entirely pleasant interview?"

"No, he has not," I replied. "Nothing has passed between us on the subject, and he is not aware that I have come here. The fact is, I overheard a part of your conversation and made it my business to hear as much of the rest as I could."

292

"Ha! Indeed!" He gave me a quick glance, half-enquiring, half-suspicious, and added, "Perhaps, Miss Vardon, you had better tell me what you heard."

"There is no need for me to repeat it in detail," said I, "but, from what I heard, I gathered that my father had rendered himself liable to a prosecution. Is that correct?"

"Yes," said Mr. Otway, "that is unfortunately – most unfortunately – the case."

"And that the proceedings will be taken by you, and that you have the power to stay them if you choose?"

"I wouldn't put it that way, Miss Vardon. That hardly states the position fairly. Do you know nothing of the circumstances at all? Has your father not told you any thing about this unfortunate affair?"

"He has not spoken a word to me on the subject, and he has no idea that I know anything about it."

"Hmm," Mr. Otway grunted, reflectively. "Yes. Well, Miss Vardon, if you wish to talk the matter over with me, perhaps I had better just let you know how the land lies, although, really, your father is the proper person to tell you."

"I think you had better tell me, if you don't mind," said I.

"Very well, Miss Vardon," he agreed. "Then the position is this: A sum of money – five-thousand pounds, to be exact – was handed to your father by the trustees of a certain estate, to be invested by him on behalf of the trust, and the manner of its disposal – into which we need not enter – was quite clearly specified. But your father, instead of disposing of the money as directed, chose to make over the whole of it as a loan to a friend of his who was in temporary difficulties – a manufacturer, as I understand, who had suffered an unexpected loss and was on the verge of bankruptcy. There was no proper security, nor even, as I understand, any satisfactory arrangement as to the payment of interest. The whole affair was most improper, a gross violation of trust. In effect, your father converted this money and made use of it for his own purposes."

"Is the money lost?" I enquired.

Mr. Otway shrugged his shoulders. "Who can say? It may be recoverable some day, or it may not. But that is very little to the point. The position is that it is now demanded of your father and that he can't produce it."

"And so you are going to prosecute him?"

"Oh, please don't put it that way, Miss Vardon. I am a quite involuntary agent. My position is that I am instructed to get this money from your father and dispose of it in a particular way. But I can't get it, and when I report that fact, I shall, of course, be urged – in fact, compelled – to take criminal proceedings. I shall have no choice. It isn't my money, you know."

"But why criminal proceedings?" I asked. "It seems to me that a civil action to recover the money would be the natural course."

Again Mr. Otway shrugged his shoulders. "I don't see that it makes much difference," said he. "The money has been made away with. Even if the trustees took no criminal action, there is the Public Prosecutor and there is the Incorporated Law Society. A prosecution is inevitable."

"And supposing my father is convicted?"

"It is hardly necessary to suppose," said Mr. Otway. "He will be. There is no defence. As to the sentence, I don't imagine that the maximum punishment of seven years penal servitude is likely to be inflicted. Still, your father is a solicitor, and the law is, quite properly, very severe in the case of solicitors who misappropriate their clients' property. He is almost certain to get a term of imprisonment."

To this I made no reply. There was nothing to say. It was only too clear that every avenue of escape was closed – save one, and realizing more fully every moment where that one led, I could not bring myself to make the fateful move. So, for a while, we sat in a hideous silence through which the ticking of a clock penetrated noisily and seemed to keep pace with the thumping of my heart.

As I sat, bracing myself for the effort that had to be made, my eyes travelled, half-unconsciously, over the person of my companion. His appearance was not prepossessing. Huge, unwieldy, and shapeless, although by no means grossly fat, his great size carried no dignity, nor did his very marked and prominent features impart to his face anything of distinction or nobility. He was of a distinctly oriental type, with black and rather curly hair, oiled and combed over a slightly bald head, a large aquiline nose, a wide mouth, rather full and fleshy, and very dark eyes, under which were baggy folds of skin creased by innumerable tiny wrinkles. As I looked at him with growing distaste, I found myself comparing him to a gigantic spider. Suddenly it was borne in on me – perhaps by the measured ticking of the clock – that time was passing, time which might be infinitely precious. To delay further were mere cowardice. Nevertheless, when I spoke, it was in a voice so husky that I had to stop and begin again.

"You spoke, Mr. Otway – I heard you mention to my father that – that on certain conditions, you would – would be prepared to abandon your intention of prosecuting – Or, at least – "

I could get no farther. Fear and shame and loathing of this thing that I was going to do, overpowered me utterly. It was only by the most strenuous effort that I choked down the sob that was rising in my throat. But I had said enough, for Mr. Otway now came to my assistance.

"I told your father that I was prepared to take over his liabilities, for the time being, at least, on condition that you became my wife. He refused, as perhaps you know refused very definitely, I may say."

"And rather rudely, I am afraid."

"He was not at any great pains to wrap his refusal up delicately. But we may let that pass. Is it in respect of this proposal of mine that you have done me the very great honour of calling on me, Miss Vardon?"

I felt myself turn scarlet, but nevertheless I answered, resolutely,

"Yes. I came to ask if my father's very blunt refusal had closed the matter finally, or whether you were prepared to – to re-open it."

"We won't talk about re-opening it. It was never closed, by me. The proposal that I made to your father I now make to you, and if you should see your way to accepting it, I believe you would never have occasion to regret your decision."

He spoke in a dry, commercial tone, as if he were trying to sell me something at a rather high price – as, in fact, he was. And meanwhile I found myself wondering dimly why on earth he wanted to marry me.

"May I ask," he continued, after a pause, "if you are disposed to entertain my proposal?

"I would do anything to save my father," I replied.

"That," said he, "is what I thought, judging from my previous knowledge of you, and it was the knowledge of your devotion to your father that encouraged me to make the proposal. For it seemed to me that a young lady of your attractions who could so completely devote herself to an elderly father might find it possible to devote herself to an elderly husband."

His reasoning did not impress me as very sound, seeing that it took no account of the respective personalities of the father and the proposed husband. But I made no reply, and, after a further pause, he asked, "Am I to understand that you – that you regard my proposal favourably?"

"I can't say that," I replied. "But I came here to-night prepared to accept your conditions, and I am ready to accept them now. But, of course, you understand that I do so under compulsion and not of my own free choice."

"I quite realise that," said he, "but I take it that you will carry out fairly any covenant into which you may enter."

"Certainly I shall," was my reply.

"Then may I take it that you are willing to marry me, on the conditions that I named?"

"Yes, Mr. Otway. I consent to marry you on those conditions and on certain others that I will propose."

"Let us hear the other conditions," said he.

"The first is that you give me a promise in writing that, in consideration of my consent to marry you, you will do what is necessary to get my father out of his present difficulties."

"That is quite fair, though it is rather unnecessary. I shouldn't want a convict for a father-in-law, you know. But, anyhow, I'll agree, as soon as the marriage is over, to pay into your father's bank a cheque for five-thousand pounds, or, if he prefers it, to give him a full discharge for that amount. And I will give you an undertaking in writing to that effect before you leave here to-night. Will that do?"

"It will do quite well," I answered. "But I wish you also to add to that undertaking a *proviso* to the effect that, if at any time before the marriage takes place, any circumstances shall arise by which your pecuniary help shall become unnecessary, then this agreement between you and me shall not take effect, and you shall have no claim of any kind on me."

Mr. Otway looked at me in some surprise, and, indeed, I was somewhat surprised myself at the completeness with which my judgment and self-possession had revived as soon as it came to making terms, though I had considered the matter very carefully on my way to Mr. Otway's house.

"You are a true lawyer's daughter, Miss Vardon," said he, with a somewhat wry smile. "You are not going to give yourself away *gratis*. No play, no pay, hmm? However, you are quite right. You agree to marry me for a certain consideration. If you don't receive the consideration, you don't marry me. Very well. That is a perfectly business-like proposition, and I agree to it. You think that perhaps your father may be able to meet his liabilities, after all?"

"I do not think anything of the kind. The *proviso* was introduced by me in view of a very different contingency. I was making this sacrifice to save my father's life. If I failed in that, the sacrifice would be useless." But I did not think it necessary to mention this to Mr. Otway. I therefore replied that, as I knew very little about my father's affairs, I thought it wise to provide even against the improbable."

"Quite so, Miss Vardon, quite so," he agreed. "One should always make provision for the unexpected. Well, I have said that I accept your first two conditions. What is the next one?"

"I want you to write my father a letter which shall relieve him of all present anxieties, and I want you to give me that letter so that it may be delivered to-night."

At this Mr. Otway's countenance fell somewhat. He pursed up his lips disapprovingly, and, after some moments of reflection, said gravely, "That, you know, Miss Vardon, really anticipates the fulfilment of the contract on my side. Such a letter would commit me to a withdrawal of my demand for immediate payment of this money."

"But," said I, "you have my promise, which I am willing to give you in writing, if you wish me to."

"Well," he replied, dubiously, "that would seem to meet the difficult – not that I am suspecting you of trying to evade fufilment. But, you see, your father has refused his consent and will probably continue to refuse, so that one would rather not raise the question. By the way, I suppose you are over twenty-one?"

"I was twenty-three last birthday."

"Then, of course, his consent is not necessary. Still, one doesn't want a fuss, and if you delivered this letter to him, he would be in possession of the facts, and then there would be trouble."

"I was not proposing to deliver it to him. I should drop it in the letter-box and let him think that you had sent or left it. He would know nothing of my visit to you or of the arrangement we have come to."

"I see. That alters the position somewhat. But is it really necessary? I can understand your wish to relieve his anxiety, but still, it need be only a day or two. Do you really think it is essential?"

"I do, Mr. Otway. I think it absolutely essential. If I had not, I should not have come here to-night. My father is in a desperate position, and one never knows what a desperate man may do."

Mr. Otway gave me a quick glance, and I could see that he was considerably startled. The possibility at which I had hinted would have consequences for him as well as for me, and I saw that he fully realized this. But he did not answer hastily. Perhaps he saw more in my suggestion than I did myself. At any rate, he pondered for some seconds before he finally replied,

"Perhaps you are right, Miss Vardon. I'm sure I shall be very glad to put an end to his suspense. Yes, I'll write the letter and give it to you. Are there any more conditions?"

"No, that is all. So if you will write the letter and the agreement and draft out what you want me to say, we shall have done. And please make as much haste as you can. It is rather late, and I am anxious to get home before my father if possible."

My anxiety apparently communicated itself to Mr. Otway, for he immediately swung his chair round to his desk, and, taking one or two sheets of paper from the rack, began to write rapidly. In two or three minutes he turned, and, handing me what he had written, together with a blank sheet of paper and a pen and ink-bottle, took a fresh sheet himself, and, without a word, began once more to write. The draft which he had handed me was simply and concisely worded as follows:

I, Helen Vardon, of Stonebury, Maidstone, in the county of Kent, spinster, hereby promise to marry Lewis Otway, of the Beeches, Maidstone, in the county of Kent, attorney-at-law, within fourteen days from this present date, in consideration of his assuming the present liabilities of my father, William Henry Vardon, in respect of the estate of James Collis-Hardy, Deceased, this promise to be subject to the conditions set forth in a letter written to me by the said Lewis Otway and dated the 2nd of April, 1908.

(Signed) Helen Vardon
Maidstone, Kent.
21st April, 1908

I read the draft through carefully, noting that it was not only quite simple and lucid, but that it embodied the terms of our agreement with scrupulous fairness and took over my father's liabilities without any limit as to time, then I dipped the pen in the ink and made a fair copy on the blank sheet which I signed, and laid on the corner of the desk.

By the time I had finished my copy, Mr. Otway had completed the first of the documents, which he now handed to me, and as I read it, he took up the paper that I had written, and, having glanced through it, placed it in a drawer and began once more to write. The paper that he had given to me was in the form of a letter, and read thus,

Dear Miss Vardon,

At your request I put on record the terms of the arrangement which has been made between us to-day, and which are:

1. That in consideration of my taking over your father's liabilities in respect of the Collis-Hardy Estate, you agree to marry me within fourteen days of this present date.

2. That on the completion of the marriage ceremony, or at such time thereafter as you may decide upon, I shall pay into your father's bank the sum of five-

298

thousand pounds, or, if he prefers it, give him a full discharge of all liabilities in respect of the Collis-Hardy Estate aforesaid.

3. Provided that if at any time prior to the said marriage, your father shall discharge the said liabilities, or any circumstances shall arise by which the said payment or discharge by me shall become unnecessary, then the agreement between you and me which is herein recorded shall become void, and neither of us, the contracting parties, shall have any claim upon the other.

I am, dear Miss Vardon,
Your obedient servant,

Lewis Otway

Maidstone, Kent.
2 April, 1908

Mr. Otway glanced up from his desk as I folded the paper and bestowed it in my purse, and asked, "Will that do? I think it covers the terms of our arrangement."

"Thank you," I answered, "it will do quite well."

He made no rejoinder, but went on with the letter that he was writing, and meanwhile I sat and watched him, with a strong distaste of his appearance, dimly wondering at this strange interview and at my own curious self-possession and mental alertness. But behind these hazy reflections was a background of haunting terror that had never quite faded even when I was putting the utmost strain upon my wits, terror lest all this bargaining should be useless after all, lest I should arrive home to find that my help had come too late.

These disquieting thoughts were presently interrupted by Mr. Otway, who, laying down his pen and swinging round in his revolving chair, took up the letter that he had just written.

"This is what I have said to your father, Miss Vardon. I think it will make his mind quite easy for the present, which is all we want.

Dear Vardon,

299

Since my talk with you this afternoon, I have been thinking over matters and considering whether it is not possible to give you more time. On looking into the affairs of the trust more closely, I think it can be done. In fact, I am sure it can, with some careful management on my part. So you may take it from me that the demand, which I felt compelled to make, is withdrawn for the time being. When you are in a position to surrender the money, you had better notify me, and in the meantime you have my assurance that no further demand will be made without reasonable notice.

I hope this will relieve your natural anxiety, concerning which I have been a little uncomfortable since I left you.

The Beeches.
2 April, 1908.
Yours sincerely,

Lewis Otway

He handed me the letter when he had finished reading, and I glanced through it quickly before returning it to him.

"I think that ought to relieve him of all anxiety," said he.

"Yes," I answered. "It will do admirably. And if you will kindly seal it and let me have it, I will go at once and drop it in the letter-box. It is most important that it should be in his hands as soon as possible."

"Quite so," he agreed, "and I won't detain you further excepting to point out that, by giving you this letter, I am putting myself entirely in your hands. You will observe that this amounts to a surrender of my claim on your father for the time being. He will, of course, keep the letter, and could produce it in answer to any sudden demand for the restitution of the money. So I am really carrying out my part of the agreement in advance."

"Yes, I see that," I replied, "and I thank you most sincerely, but," I added, rising and holding out my hand for the letter, "you have my solemn promise to carry out my part. If you were better acquainted with me, you would consider that enough."

"But I do, Miss Vardon," he rejoined, hastily, "I do. If I did not trust you implicitly, I should not have written this letter. However, I mustn't delay you. I will make all the necessary arrangements and let you know when everything is ready. Will next Thursday be too soon?"

At the mention of an actual date, and one so near, too, something like a complete realisation of what I was doing flashed into my mind and set my heart thumping painfully. But it had to be, so why haggle for terms? Nor, indeed, since it must be, was there any use in trying to put off the evil day. The urgent need of the moment was to get this letter into my father's hands, if it were not already too late.

"I must leave the arrangement of the affair to you, Mr. Otway," I murmured, shakily. "Do as you think best. And now I must really go."

He shook my hand in a drily courteous fashion and let me out, accompanying me down the drive to the outer gate, which he opened for me with a ceremonious bow. I wished him a hurried "Good-night" and, as soon as I was outside the gate, ran off in the direction of home, holding the precious letter in the little pocket of my cloak.

Chapter IV
The Eleventh Hour

As I drew near the neighbourhood of our house, my fears grew so that I was compelled by sheer breathlessness and the trembling of my limbs to slacken my pace. I was sick with terror. In my mind, pictures, vague and nebulous but unspeakably dreadful, rose like the visions of a nightmare. I clutched the precious order of release in my pocket and set my teeth, trying not to think of what I might find at my journey's end.

At last I came in sight of the house. It was all dark save two of the upper windows – those of the servants' bedrooms. The servants, then, were going to bed as usual, for ours was an early household. This seemed reassuring, but only to a slight degree, for even if – I opened the gate softly – I do not know why, but some how I instinctively avoided noise of any kind – and running up the garden path, let myself in quietly with my latch-key. With one quick and fearful glance around the darkened hall, I stole up to the hat-stand. Apparently my father had not yet come home, for his stick was not in the stand, and one of his hats was missing. I looked at the tall clock and noted that it was not yet half-past ten, I peered out through the open doorway, down the dark road, and listened awhile for the sound of footsteps. Then, slipping the letter into the letter-box – which I could see contained no other missives – I lit one of the candles from the hall table and, having peeped into the study, the book-room, and the workshop, stole silently up the stairs.

First, I went to my father's bedroom and, by the glimmer of gas that the maid had left burning, and the light of my candle, inspected it narrowly. I looked over the trifles on the mantelpiece and on the dressing table, and even opened the little medicine-cupboard to run my eye over the collection of bottles and boxes, pausing from time to time that I might listen for footsteps, strange or familiar, as Fate might decree. But pry as I would, there was nothing unusual, nothing on which the most eager suspicion might fasten. All the details of that room were familiar to me, for it had been my daily task since my girlhood to look them over and see that my father's orderly arrangements were not disturbed by the servants, and everything was in its place, and nothing new or strange or sinister had made its appearance.

When I had finished my inspection, I stole softly along the corridor to my own bedroom, which was at the head of the stairs and, turning up the gas, but leaving the door ajar, began slowly to undress, listening intently the while for any sounds that might confirm or dispel my fears. The house was very quiet and still, so quiet that the tinkle of the water, as I poured it out from the ewer, struck with disturbing harshness on my ear, and even the ticking of the little clock and my own slippered footfalls seemed an impertinent intrusion into that expectant silence.

It was a few minutes past eleven when the sound of a latch-key and the gentle closing of the hall door sent the blood tingling to my very finger-tips. No footsteps had been audible on the garden path, but this, in itself, was characteristic, for my father and I were alike in that we both disliked noise and habitually moved about softly, avoiding the slamming of doors or the production in any way of jarring sounds.

I crept on tip-toe to the door and listened. A stick was carefully put down in the hall-stand, and then I thought – but was not quite sure – that I heard my father unlock the letter-box. A few seconds later I caught a faint creak, which I recognised as proceeding from the study door, and, after a short interval, the creak was repeated and the door closed. Then the hall gas was turned out and soft footfalls began to ascend the stairs.

"Is that you, Pater, dear?" I asked.

"Is it I, indeed, O! Wicked and disobedient child and likewise minx!" was the welcome answer. "Didn't I tell you to go to bed?"

"Yes, you did, and I am going. But I thought I would like to see you safely home from your roysterings."

"*Mures rathi!*" he exclaimed, as he came into the light from my open door. "It is poor old Queen Anne who has been keeping you out of your little nest. I know you."

Here he gave a gentle tug at one of the tails into which I had plaited my hair, and, having kissed me on the tip of my nose, continued, "And you look as tired as the proverbial dog – which is the only kind of dog that ever does get tired. Now go to bed and sleep like a young dormouse. Good-night, Jimmy, dear."

With the aid of the convenient tail, he drew my face to his and kissed me again, then he went off along the corridor singing very softly, but just audibly to me, "*Her father he makes cabbage nets And in the streets does cry 'em, Her mother she sells laces long –* "

Here a rapid diminuendo indicated the closing of the door, and the silence that had been so agreeably broken once again settled down upon the house. Still, I stood at the open door, looking out into the darkness. Had my father seen the letter? He had seemed very cheerful. But then, he would have seemed very cheerful if he had been walking to the scaffold or the stake. That was his nature. Yet his gaiety had appeared to me more genuine than that which he had exhibited earlier in the evening. However, there was no need to speculate – the question could easily be set at rest. Taking the match-box from my candlestick, I stole silently down the stairs, steadying myself by the hand-rail, and groped my way across the hall until I reached the door. Then I struck a match, and by its light, peered through the wire grating into the letter-box.

It was empty. The letter had been taken out.

I blew out the match, and, having dropped it into the salver on the table, crept back up the stairs to my room. Closing the door silently, I made my final preparations, turned out the light and crept into bed, feeling in the sudden ecstasy of relief that I could now shake off all care and bury the anxieties and alarms of this dreadful day in slumber.

My father was saved! No haunting fear of imminent tragedy, no dread of impending ruin and disgrace remained to murder sleep or mingle it with frightful visions. My father was saved. At the eleventh hour I had made my bid for his life and liberty, and the eleventh hour had not been too late.

But it was long – very long – before sleep came to shut out for a time the realities of life. The blessed feeling of escape from this appalling peril, the sense of restored security, was presently followed by the chill of reaction. For the end was not yet. I had bid for my father's life and had bought it in, but the price remained to be paid. And only now, when I could consider it undisturbed by terror for my father's safety, did I begin to realise fully how bitter a price it was. Not that I would have gone back on my bargain, for I had made it with my eyes open, and would have made it over again if the need had been. But it was a terrible price. I had sold my birth-right – my precious woman's birth-right to choose my own mate – for a mess of pottage. It was a price that I should have to pay, and go on paying as long as life lasted.

Hour after hour did I lie, gazing wide-eyed into the darkness, letting my thoughts flit hither and thither, now into the quiet, untroubled past, now into the dim and desolate future, whence they would come hurrying back affrighted. But always, whithersoever they wandered, behind them rose, now vague and remote, now horribly distinct, that unwieldy figure with the impassive oriental face, even, as to the eyes of the fisherman in the Arabian tale, the smoke from the magic jar shaped itself into the menacing form of the gigantic Jinn.

I tried to consider dispassionately the character of Mr. Otway. It was very difficult, for had he not come into our life like some malignant spirit, to dispel with a word and in the twinkling of an eye, all the peace and happiness of our quiet home? To snap off short my serene companionship with my father? To turn into dust and ashes all the vaguely-sweet dreams of maidenhood? To shut out the warm and hazy sunshine from my future and fill the firmament with unrelieved, leaden greyness? Still, I tried to consider him fairly. Callously, cynically, he had driven his Juggernaut car over my father and me, his eyes fixed upon his own desires and seeing nothing else. He was an absolute egoist. That was undeniable. For some reason, he wished to marry me, and to achieve that wish he had been willing to put us both on the rack, and, with passionless composure, to turn the screw until we yielded. It was not a pleasant thing to think of.

On the other hand, he seemed, in his way, to be a just man. By no hair's breadth had he sought to modify the terms that he had first proposed – indeed, in his letter to me he had treated the loan to my father as an almost unconditional gift, and the other details of our agreement he had expressed in writing fully and fairly, with no attempt at evasion. Nor was he niggardly. Five-thousand pounds is a large sum to pay for the privilege of marrying an unwilling bride. Under other circumstances, I might have appreciated the implied compliment. Now, I could only admit that, according to his lights, he seemed not ungenerous.

But when I considered him as the companion with whom I must share the remainder of my life – or, at least, that part of it which mattered – the thought was almost unendurable. To live, day after day and year after year, under the same roof with this huge, dull, uncomely man, to sit at table with him, to walk abroad by his side, to spend interminable evenings alone with him – it was appalling. I could hardly bear to think of it. And yet the horrible reality would be upon me in the course of a few swiftly-passing days.

Nor was it a question of mere companionship – but from this aspect I hurriedly averted my thoughts in sheer cowardice. I dared not let myself think even for a moment of what marriage actually meant. Under normal conditions, it may be permitted to the modesty of an unwedded girl to cast an occasional glance, half-shy and not wholly unpleasurable, at the more intimate relations of married life, but to me, if the thought would rise unbidden, it could call up nought but the quick flush of shame and loathing whereat I would bury my face in the pillow with a moan of shuddering disgust.

It was a relief to turn from the distressful present and the unthinkable future to the past, or even to the future that might have been. For, like most other girls, I had had my day-dreams. The companionship with my father had been happy and full of interest, but it had never seemed final. I had looked on it as no more than the prologue to the real life, which lay, for the moment, hidden behind the near horizon of my maidenhood. And as to that reality, though it offered but a vague picture, yet it had a certain definiteness. To many modern girls, ambition seems to connect itself with the academy and the laboratory, with the platform

305

and the forum. They appear to hanker after fame, or even mere notoriety, and would contend with men – who have nothing better to do – for the high places in politics, in science, or in literature. I had read the impassioned demands of some of these women for political and economic equality with men, and had looked at them with a certain dim surprise to see them so eager to gather this Dead Sea fruit and turn their backs upon the Tree of Life, with its golden burden of love and blessed motherhood.

Ambition of that kind had no message for me. So far my mind was perfectly clear. As to the terms in which I conceived the realities, the blossom and fructification of a woman's life, I am less clear. A home of my own like the pleasant, peaceful home that my father had made, a man of my own, in whom I could feel pride and by whom I could be linked to the greater world outside, and a sweet brood of little people in whom my youth could be renewed and for whom I could even cherish wider ambitions – this was probably what my rambling thoughts would have pictured if they could have been gathered up and brought to a definite focus. But they never had been. The necessary refracting medium had been absent. For what the burning-glass is to the sunbeam, the actual love of some particular man is to the opening mind of a young girl, bringing the scattered rays of thought to a single bright spot in which the wished-for future becomes sharp and distinct. And this influence, in its completeness, had never come into my life. The undoubted liking that I had for the society of men was due, chiefly, to their larger interests and wider knowledge. Of experiences sentimental or romantic there had been none.

And yet the little god had not entirely forgotten me. Indeed, his winged shaft had missed me so narrowly that I could hardly yet be certain that I had passed quite unscathed. That little episode – tame enough in all conscience – had occurred two years ago, when a Mr. Davenant had come from Oxford with a small party of fellow undergraduates, to spend a more or less studious vacation in our neighbourhood. I had met him, in all, three times on the footing of a casual acquaintance, and we had talked "high philosophy" with the eager interest of the very young. That was all. He had been a bird of passage, alighting for a moment on the very outskirts of my life, only to soar away into the unknown and vanish for ever.

It seemed an insignificant affair. A score of other men had come and gone in the same way. But there was a difference – to me. Those other men, too, had talked "high philosophy", but I had forgotten utterly what it was that they had said. Not so had it been in the case of Mr. Davenant. Again and again had I found myself thinking over his talks with me –

not, I suspect, for the sake of the matter – which, to speak the truth, was neither weighty nor brilliantly original – but rather because I had enjoyed talking to him. And sometimes I had been surprised to notice how clearly I remembered those talks, even to the very words that he had used and the tones of his pleasant, manly voice.

Two years had passed since then – a long time in a girl's life, but still Mr. Davenant – his name, by the way, was Jasper, a pleasant-sounding name I had thought it – remained the one figure that had separated itself from the nebulous mass of humanity that had peopled my short existence. And to-night – on this night of misery and despair, when all that was worth living for seemed to be passing away, as I lay staring up into the darkness, the memory of him came back to me again. Once more I heard his voice – how strangely familiar it sounded! – framing those quaintly-abstruse sentences. I recalled the look in his eyes – clear, hazel eyes, they were, that sparkled with vivacity and the fresh interest of youth – and his smile, as he uttered some mild joke – a queer, humorous smile that drew his mouth just a little to one side and seemed to give an added piquancy to the jest by its own trifling oddity. I remembered it all – clearly, vividly, with the freshness of yesterday – the words of wisdom, the humorous turn of speech, the earnest, almost eager tone, the easy manner, friendly yet deferential – all came back to me as it had done a hundred times before, though it was two years ago.

He had been but a stranger – a mere passing stranger who had come and gone – who had sailed across the rim of my horizon and vanished. But even in that swift passage some virtue had exhaled from him by which it had been given to me to look beyond the present into a world hitherto in visible to me. He was my one little romance, a very little one, but all that I had, and, to me, he stood for all those things that might have been and now could never be. And so it happened that, on this night, when I seemed to be bidding farewell to my youth and all its dimly-cherished hopes, the memory of him lingered in my thoughts and was with me still when, at last, sleep – the sleep of utter weariness and exhaustion – closed my eyelids and shut out for a time the realities of that life on which I would have been well content never to look again.

Chapter V
On the Brink

Of the four days that followed, I do not, even now, like to think. The dreadful change that was coming into my life loomed up every moment more distinct, more threatening, more terrible. The hideous realities of what was about to happen to me refused to be ignored. They thrust themselves upon me and filled my thoughts every instant of the day and haunted my dreams at night. There were times when I turned a wistful eye upon that solution of the hopeless difficulties of life at which my father had hinted, but alas! Even that was no solution as matters stood. Death which would have released me from this bondage into which I had sold myself would have left my father unemancipated, and to attain it by my own act would have been a grossly dishonest evasion of the covenant into which I had entered with Mr. Otway. Expediency and honour both demanded that I should carry out the terms of my agreement.

But it was a terrible burden that I bore during those four days, and bore, of necessity, with a cheerful face and as little change as might be from my usual manner. That was the most difficult part of all. To keep up the appearance of quiet gaiety, which was the tone of our house – to smile, to jest, to discuss projected work and to talk over the history which I was supposed still to be reading, and all the time to feel the day of doom creeping upon me, nearer and nearer with every beat of my aching heart. That was the hardest part. But it had to be done and done with thoroughness, for my father's watchful and sympathetic eye would have detected at once the smallest flutter of a signal of distress. And it was imperative that he should be kept in the dark.

And that, perhaps, was the bitterest drop in this bitter potion. For the first time in my life, I had a secret from my father. I was systematically deceiving him. And the secret that I withheld from him and shared with a mere stranger – with an enemy, in fact – was one that concerned him profoundly. And yet that, too, had to be. It was of the essence of the transaction. For, if he had suspected, for one instant, what I proposed to do, he would certainly have interfered, and I knew him well enough to feel sure that his interference would not have taken the form of mere persuasion. He was a quiet man, suave and gentle in manner, even-tempered, patient, forebearing – up to a certain point, but when that point was passed, a change occurred which was apt to surprise those who knew him but slightly. Like a heavy body, he was difficult to move and difficult to stop when moved. If he had suspected Mr. Otway of putting unfair pressure on me – which he would certainly have done – then I would not have answered for the consequences to Mr. Otway.

But strive as I would to keep my secret, the intolerable strain of those days of misery must have made itself visible in some change in my appearance. Once or twice I caught my father looking at me narrowly with something of anxiety in his expression, and hastened to put on a little extra spurt of gaiety and to divert his attention from myself. Still, he was not entirely deceived by my assumed cheerfulness, though he made no remark until the very last evening, when, I suppose, my efforts to conceal the grief and wretchedness that were gnawing at my heart were less successful than usual. Then it was that he took me quite seriously to task.

"I wonder what is the matter with my little girl," he said, looking at me reflectively as we sat at the supper table. "She has been getting a little pale of late, and looks tired and worn. Is it too much Queen Anne and not enough sleep, think you?"

"I am feeling quite well," I replied.

"That is an evasion, my dear, and a tarradiddle to boot, I suspect. You are looking quite well. What is it, Jimmy?"

"I don't think it is anything, Pater, dear," I answered, not without a qualm of conscience at the direct untruth. "I haven't been sleeping so very well lately, but that is not due to my sitting up reading. Perhaps it's the weather."

"Hmm!" he grunted, "perhaps it is – and perhaps it isn't. Are you sure there is nothing troubling you? No – what shall we say? Well, to put it bluntly, no young man, for instance, competing with the good Queen Anne for your attention?"

I laughed a little, bitterly. If only there had been! But, alas! I was only too well secured against any troubles of that sort. So I was able to reply with a moderately clear conscience.

"No, of course there isn't. You know that perfectly well. How could there be when you keep me so securely in my little hutch?"

"That's true, Jimmy," he answered. "I certainly haven't noticed any buck rabbit sniffing around. But perhaps it is the hutch itself that is the trouble. It is a dull life for a girl, to be shut up with an old fellow like me. Coal-scuttles and such-like are all very well for an ancient fossil who has sucked all the juice out of life and must needs content himself with a modest nibble at the rind that's left. But it's not the sort of thing for a girl. Your orange is still unsucked, Jimmy, dear, and we mustn't leave it to get over-ripe."

"I've always been very happy with you, dear old Pater," I said, and a lump rose in my throat as I spoke. How happy I had been! And oh, how thankfully would I have gone on with that serene, peaceful life and never asked for anything different, if only it might have been so!

"I know you have, my dear," he rejoined, "always contented and cheerful and kind to your old father. But still – well, we mustn't get too groovy. We must have a little change now and again. I have been rather preoccupied these last few days, but I shall be more free now. What do you say to a few lays in London? It's quite a long time since we've been to town. Shall we take a week off and dissipate a little? Just spread a thin wash of carmine – quite a thin and delicate one – over the metropolis, and incidentally see for ourselves if the population of the great world doesn't still contain a few presentable human beings? What do you say?"

I don't know what I said, or how I controlled the almost irresistible impulse to fling myself on his neck and sob my secret into his ear. It was terrible to listen to him making these plans for one of those blissful little holidays that we had enjoyed together from time to time, and to know that the morrow would see my own life spoiled irrevocably and his home made desolate. Some vague answer I murmured, and then managed to lead the conversation into a less distressing channel. But once or twice during the evening he reverted to the subject, and when, at a rather early hour, I wished him "Good-night", he said, as he held my hands and looked me over-critically,

"Yes, the blossom is undoubtedly a little faded. We must see to it, Jimmy. Think over my proposal and consider whether there is any particular kind of jaunt that you would like – whether, for instance, you would rather go to the sea than to London."

"Very well, Pater, dear," I replied, "I'll think about it," and with this only too easily fulfilled promise I turned away and went upstairs.

It was my last night at home, the last night of my girlhood and of freedom. Virtually and to all intents, I had said farewell to my father for ever, for though, hereafter, we should meet, I should be his daughter, in the old sense – no more. I should be the chattel of another man, and that man no friend of his.

For long after I went to my room I sat thinking these thoughts and gazing with scared, bewildered eyes into the dark future on whose threshold I already stood. What that future held for me, beyond the certainty of misery and degradation, who could tell? I dared not try to pierce that dread obscurity. From what might lie beyond that threshold my thoughts shrank back, appalled. The whole thing seemed like some hideous dream from which I should presently awaken, trembling, but with a sigh of relief. And yet it was not. Unbelievable as was this awful thing that had descended upon me in a moment, it was yet but too real for any hope of awakening.

And what of my father? For him, too, the old pleasant life was at an end. The quiet gaiety, the serene happiness of his home was gone for ever. Henceforth he would be a lonely man, mourning the loss of his companion and cherishing a bitter resentment against the man who had stolen her away. But what would he feel about this shipwreck of my life – for so he would certainly regard it? What portion of the wretchedness and degradation into which I had sold myself would have to be borne by him? It was a question which I had hardly asked myself before, but now, when I thought of his devotion to me, of his sympathy with me and his self-forgetfulness, a sudden misgiving crept into my mind. Was it worthwhile, after all? If my father and I were both to be made wretched for life, what good had I done by this sacrifice?

I thought of him as he had been this evening and for the last day or two. All his light-heartedness had come back. He was quite himself again. Since I had delivered Mr. Otway's letter, all signs of care had vanished. That letter had apparently put him entirely at his ease – naturally enough, since it had put an end to his immediate difficulties, and since he knew nothing of the price at which it had been purchased. And though I knew better, yet his ease and confidence were not without their effect on me. Under the clear sky and in the sunshine, it was hard to believe that the thunderbolt was still ready to fall. And so it was that, more than once on that night, I found myself asking if it were possible that I had done the wrong thing? Had I been too precipitate?

But it was of no use to think of that now. The bargain had been made, and payment accepted in advance. Nor if it had been possible for me to go back on a promise voluntarily given – which it obviously was not – could Mr. Otway have been held to his. The original situation would have been created afresh.

Before undressing, I sat down at my little bureau and wrote a letter to my father in case there should be no time on the morrow. For the arrangements – which Mr. Otway had communicated to me in a letter addressed in a feminine handwriting – were necessarily of a somewhat clandestine character. Mr. Otway had obtained a special license and had given notice to the clergyman of a small church on the outskirts of the town, and on the by-road leading to the church I was to meet him on Thursday morning as near as possible to eleven o'clock. There was not likely to be any difficulty in carrying out my part of the arrangement, but nevertheless, it was as well to leave nothing to be done on the morrow.

The letter that I wrote to my father was quite short. There was no need for a long one, since the facts to be communicated were of the simplest and I should probably see him in the course of the day. What I wrote was as follows:

My dearest Father,

I am writing to tell you that I am about to do a thing of which I fear you will disapprove. I am going to marry Mr. Otway, and by the time you get this, the marriage will have taken place.

You will understand why I have done this when I tell you that I accidentally became aware of your difficulties and of the claim which he had on you and you will understand, too, why I have kept my intention secret from you. It was the only way out for us, and you are not to think that I have done it for you only. I was equally concerned, and have acted in my own interests as well as yours.

Please, dearest, try to forgive me for taking this step without your sanction. You would never have consented, and yet it had to be.

Your loving daughter,

Helen

I sealed the letter and, having addressed it, placed it in my bureau in readiness for the morning. Then I made various little arrangements of my possessions, tidying up my bureau and wardrobe, tearing up letters that had been answered and packing a small trunk with necessary articles of dress, to be sent for on the morrow, and all this I did with a curious stony calm and the sense of setting my affairs in order as if preparing to bid farewell to life. And this calm – a calm like that which persons of character often exhibit in the face of unavoidable death, or on the eve of a dangerous operation, continued even after I went to bed, so that, in contrast to the perturbed nights that I had passed since my interview with Mr. Otway, I presently fell into a sound sleep and slept late into the morning.

Chapter VI
A Meeting and a Parting

It turned out to be easier than I had expected to keep my appointment with Mr. Otway, for my father had business that took him abroad early, and, when I came down to breakfast, he had already left the house, which was a profound relief to me, since it saved me the added misery of a last farewell and the necessity of further deception.

It was half-past ten when, after placing my letter in the salver on the hall table, I set forth from the house. The most direct way to the church was across the town, but the fear of meeting my father or any of my acquaintances led me to the roads that led out from the environs towards the country, and thus skirt the circumference of the town. I walked at a good pace, unconsciously threading my way through the rather complicated maze of by-roads, and still pervaded by the curious, half-dreamy calm that had possessed me on the preceding evening.

As I approached the vicinity of the little church – which was a kind of mission-chapel, in charge of a supernumerary curate – I glanced at my watch and saw that it was five-minutes-to-eleven, and almost at the same moment, on turning a corner, I came in sight of a figure the very first glance at which so completely shattered my self-possession that I felt ready to sink down upon the pavement. There was no mistaking it, though the back was towards me, a huge, ponderous figure that walked away from me with the peculiar gait of the heavy and unathletic man, a silent, deliberate gait that recalls the action of the hind legs of an elephant.

I followed him breathlessly up the rather sordid-looking street, noting that, from time to time, a thin cloud of blue smoke floated over his shoulder. At length, at the corner of an intersecting road, he turned and saw me, upon which he flung away a cigar, and, retracing his steps towards me, saluted me with a flourish of his hat and held out his hand.

"This is good of you, Miss Vardon," he said, "to be so punctual. I hardly hoped that you would be able to be here so – er – so punctually."

I took his hand limply, but made no reply. The shock of the sudden encounter was slowly passing off and giving place to a sort of benumbed indifference mingled with vague curiosity. I felt as if I had been drugged or were walking abroad in a hypnotic trance, half-conscious and waiting with dull expectancy to see what would happen next. I walked at Mr. Otway's side up the mean little street with a feeling somewhat like that

313

with which one would walk in a dream beside some historical or mythical personage, accepting the incongruous situation from mere mental inertia.

Mr. Otway, too, seemed subdued by the strangeness of the position, or perhaps he was embarrassed by my silence. At any rate, although he occasionally cleared his throat as if about to make a remark, he did not actually speak again until we turned a corner, when there appeared, embedded in a row of mean houses, a small brick building which, in general shape and design, resembled a large dog-kennel.

"That," said he, "is the church, Miss Vardon – or perhaps I should say, *Helen*. It is a little difficult to – ah – get used to these – these intimacies, I may say, at so short a notice. No doubt you find it so?"

"Yes," I answered.

"I am sure you do. Naturally. My own name, you may remember, is Lewis. My Christian name, I mean," he added.

"I remember," said I.

"Quite so. I had no doubt you would. Ahem." He cleared his throat once or twice in an embarrassed manner, and then, as we crossed over towards the church, he continued, "I think we shall find the doors open. The law, I believe, requires it. And we shall find my housekeeper, Mrs. Gregg, inside. She will be one of the witnesses, you know. The other will be the sexton."

The outer door was on the latch, as he had said, and, when he had admitted me, he closed and relatched it. From the dark vestibule, I stepped into the bare, comfortless building, from the white-washed wall of which a great, emblazoned text grinned at me, as if in derision, with the words, "*I was glad when they said unto me, 'Let us go into the House of the Lord'*."

Near the door, on one of the deal benches, the little, frail-looking woman whom I had seen at Mr. Otway's house was seated, conversing with a very bald and rather seedy elderly man, but, as we entered, the man hurried away towards the vestry and the woman rose and came forward a few paces to meet us.

"This is Miss Vardon, Mrs. Gregg," said Mr. Otway, introducing me in a heavy, embarrassed manner.

Mrs. Gregg stared at me with undisguised curiosity and something of hostility in her expression, as she replied, "Ah've seen her before."

"Yes," said Mr. Otway, "I believe you have. Yes. To be sure. Of course. And I – er – hope – in fact, I may say that I – ah – "

What he was going to say I have no idea, and I suspect that he was not very clear himself, but at this moment the man – who was apparently

314

the sexton – emerged from the vestry in company with a young clergyman, vested already in his surplice and carrying a book in his hand.

Apparently everything had been explained and arranged beforehand by Mr. Otway, for, as we advanced up the nave, the curate took his place before the communion table and opened his book. I noticed that he gave me one quick and intense look, full of surprise and curiosity, and thereafter seemed, as far as possible, to avoid even glancing in my direction.

The ceremony began abruptly and without preamble. With dim surprise, I became aware that the clergyman was speaking, or rather reading aloud, in a rapid and indistinct undertone. I listened with but slight attention, and failed, for the most part, to distinguish the words which, I think, was what the curate intended, his half-apologetic mumble being, I believe, designed to mitigate the effect of those coarsely-phrased impertinences with which the service is besprinkled, and which have survived so inappropriately into this age of decent and reticent speech. I tried to fix my thoughts on the ceremony in which I was taking part, but found them constantly wandering away to my father, busying themselves with his present whereabouts and occupation. Was he still at his office? Or had he perchance called in at our house, as he sometimes did, and already seen my letter?

I was brought back to the happenings of the moment by a question addressed to me by name in more distinct tones, and followed by the murmured instruction, "Say I will." I obeyed the gently-spoken command, and then, with my right hand enveloped in a large and flabby grasp, I heard Mr. Otway repeat after the curate the solemn form of words that should mean so much and that was, as now spoken, so empty a mockery, of which the phrase "to have and to hold from this day forward" seemed to separate itself as the only part truly applicable.

Still passive, and conscious only of a certain, dull discomfort and surprise at the incongruity of the whole affair, I permitted our hands to be separated and re-joined, and obediently repeated the form of words as the curate dictated.

"I, Helen Vardon, take thee, Lewis Otway, to my wedded husband, to have and to hold from this day forward, for richer for poorer, in sickness and in health, to love, cherish, and to obey, till death us do part, according to God's holy ordinance, and thereto I give thee my troth."

It was amazing. These burning words, so charged with love, with utter devotion and self-abandonment I was actually addressing to a mere stranger, to a man who, even now, was but a name attached to an unfamiliar, ungracious personality, upon whose corpse, if he had fallen

315

dead at my feet in the very moment of my speaking, I could have looked with no emotion but relief.

It was an astounding situation. The wonder, the incredibility of it filled my mind to the exclusion of all else until, as Mr. Otway began once more to speak at the curate's dictation, and I became aware that a ring had been slipped on my finger, I realised dimly that the ceremony was complete and that the irrevocable change had occurred.

But even then my thoughts quickly flitted away from this significant scene to others that seemed more deeply to concern me. As I knelt at Mr. Otway's side and the monotonous mumble recommenced, I began once more to wonder where my father was and what he was doing. Had he come in and seen my letter, or had the maid noticed it and taken it to the office? And would he be angry or only grieved? Would he think that I had acted rightly? Or would he condemn my action as ill-considered or even unnecessary? And lastly, was it just barely possible that I had done the wrong thing? Had I sacrificed myself – and him – without sufficient cause?

Thus my thoughts wandered to-and-fro to the mumbled accompaniment of the interminable prayers and exhortations that rolled past me in an unheeded stream. At last the ceremony came to an end. Rising from our knees, we trooped after the curate to the vestry, where, as I signed the familiar name in the register, the first clear realization of my changed condition came upon me. But even then the vivid flash of perception was but transient. Hardly had I shaken hands with the clergyman and passed out into the street, when my thoughts sped away once more to my home – my real home – and my father.

For some time after leaving the church, Mr. Otway and I walked in silence. He hemmed once or twice and seemed on the point of speaking, but either he could find nothing appropriate to say or he found some difficulty in opening the subject of his thoughts. And meanwhile I pursued my own reflections. At length, however, after one or two preliminary hems, he managed to make a beginning.

"I am afraid, Helen, you may think that I have put rather unfair pressure on you to marry me."

I roused myself to consider what he had said, and replied, after a slight pause,

"Whatever I may think, I am not complaining. I don't forget that I accepted your proposal of my own free will, and I intend to try to carry out honestly my part of the bargain."

"I am glad to hear you say that, Helen," he said eagerly. "I was afraid you might feel resentful – might think I had driven a rather hard bargain."

"Perhaps I do," I replied. "But that doesn't affect the terms of the bargain. My feelings towards you were no part of the agreement."

"No, that's true," he agreed hastily, but he was visibly crestfallen, and walked by my side for some time without speaking. My thoughts began to wander again, and then, suddenly, there occurred to me a question that I had already asked myself over and over again without finding any answer. Now, moved by a fresh impulse of curiosity, I put it into words.

"Would you mind telling me, Mr. Otway, why you wished to marry me?"

He looked at me in some surprise and a little confusion.

"Why, my dear Helen," he replied hesitatingly, "there is nothing remarkable about it, is there? I wished to marry you for the same reason that any other man would: Because you are a handsome girl – a beautiful girl, I may say – and clever and bright, and, as far as I could judge from your manner to your father, a good, affectionate girl. I have admired you ever since I first met you, a year-and-a-half ago."

I suppose I looked surprised – I certainly felt so, seeing that he had made no effort to cultivate our acquaintance – for he continued, "Yes, Helen, I admired you, but as I had nothing to offer in the way of personal attractions, and I did not suppose that my means would be a sufficient set-off for my – ah – personal disadvantages, I kept my admiration to myself. In fact, I suppose, if it had not been for this lucky chance – lucky for me, I mean – a little unfortunate perhaps for you – though not so unfortunate as it might – er – at least I venture to hope that things may turn out – "

He paused awkwardly, as if expecting me to help him. But I made no comment. My momentary curiosity was satisfied. I had heard his explanation, and a very insufficient one it seemed to be. So the sentence remained unfinished, and, in the silence that ensued, my thoughts went back once more to my father.

When would he get my letter? And what would be his feelings when he realized that his daughter – his companion and playmate, his beloved apprentice – was lost to him for ever? And what would be his attitude to Mr. Otway? Deeply resentful, beyond a doubt. His scornful rejection of the proposal had shown that clearly enough. Yes, he would be angry – furiously angry, for quiet and gentle as his manners were, he was a passionate man. He could even be violent, as I knew from one or two experiences. And our doctor, Dr. Sharpe, knew it, too, and had warned him to be careful, had cautioned him not only to avoid over-exertion, but excessive excitement of any kind. The doctor's words came back to me now with a qualm of uneasiness. I had not thought of that before. His distress, his grief, his anger against the man who had exacted this price from me – all that I had thought of and fretted over. But the actual physical shock that my letter would inflict on him, utterly unprepared as he was – that I had somehow overlooked. And yet it was palpable enough. He would come home expecting to find me waiting for him as usual, and then, without an instant's warning, in the very twinkling of an eye, he would learn that I had been spirited away out of his life for ever. It would be a terrible blow.

The more I thought of it the more uneasy I became. Supposing he should become seriously ill on receiving my letter. It was quite possible, it was even very probable. And if he should have got my letter already! If he should be, at this very moment, lying, prostrated by the shock, with none but the servants to tend him! As I thought of this dreadful possibility, my anxiety grew, moment by moment, and I was beginning to consider how soon I could contrive to escape to him, to satisfy myself that all was well, when the voice of Mr. Otway broke in on my thoughts. I did not at first gather clearly what he was saying until, by an effort, I detached my attention from the agitating subject of my reflections.

"Of course," he was saying as I endeavoured to catch up the thread of his remarks, "it answered my purpose as a solitary bachelor, but it won't do now. We shall have to get quite a different class of house. And we shall want some other servants. I shall keep Mrs. Gregg, if you don't object, as she has been with me so long and knows my ways, but we shall want a couple of maids in addition, I suppose."

"Is Mrs. Gregg your only servant?" I asked, rather absently.

"Yes," he replied, "that is to say, the only resident servant. She has a girl to help her in the mornings with the housework and to mind the place when she goes out shopping. That is how she was able to attend at the church this morning."

As he was speaking, we turned into the quiet, countrified road in which he lived, and a few more steps brought us to the house. Mrs. Gregg, who had apparently hurried on in advance by a different route, was standing at the open door talking to a girl of about sixteen, and, as we ascended the steps, she addressed Mr. Otway.

"I've got to see to some things in the town. D'ye want Lizzie to stay or will ye open the door yourself if anyone comes?"

"Oh, she needn't stay, Mrs. Gregg," was the reply. "I shan't be going out. But don't be any longer than you can help."

On this Mrs. Gregg dismissed the girl, and followed her out, shutting the door after her. Mr. Otway hung his hat on a peg in the hall, and placing his umbrella in the stand, remarked apologetically, "Mrs. Gregg's manner is not all that might be desired in a servant, but she is a capable woman and absolutely trustworthy. She comes from the North, you know, where manners run a little more blunt than with us. Shall I show you your room?"

Without waiting for a reply, he preceded me up the stairs to the first floor, where he ushered me into a bedroom and stood by the door with an embarrassed and rather deprecating air, casting a glance of obvious disparagement over its somewhat meagre appointments.

"It's a poor place to bring you to, Helen," he remarked, "but that can be mended. It was good enough for a bachelor. You'll find the wardrobe and chest of drawers empty when you send for your things. Mine are in the dressing-room – that little room to the right. And now I'll leave you in possession for the present."

With this he went out, closing the door behind him, and I heard his soft, heavy tread descending the stairs.

For some time after he had gone I stood looking about me in absolute dismay. The room was mean almost to sordidness – surprisingly mean for the habitation of an admittedly wealthy man. But it was not that which filled me with consternation. Delicately as I had been brought up, the mere surroundings of life were of no great consideration to me. What appalled me utterly was the fact now brought home to me with overwhelming force, that I was no more my own, that I had surrendered myself to the possession of another person, a strange man, towards whom I felt a growing repugnance. This was not *my* room, it was *our* room. No longer had I any rights of privacy or of personal reticence. I was his, "to have and to hold from this day forward," with no power of escape or protest against the most repulsive familiarities. I had voluntarily surrendered, not only my liberty, but even the appearance of security from the most outrageous intrusions.

Of course I had known all this before. But in the hurry and rush, the alarms and agitations of the events that had forced me to my hasty decision, perception had been partly obscured. I had known what I was doing, but had only dimly realized. It had needed the sight of that mean room, with its significant contents and the presence of that man who stood at my side as joint occupier, to light up the vague perception into realization of the most horrid vividness.

Presently I began, with the dull curiosity of a prisoner introduced to a new cell, to explore the room, opening the empty wardrobe and pulling out the ill-fitting drawers of the plain pine chest. Then I peeped into the dressing-room – a bare little closet, furnished with a wash-stand, a dressing table, and a chest of drawers – and even stepped in to glance over the half-blind down into the garden and street beyond. I was about to turn away when I noticed a man approaching the house at a rapid pace, and in an instant my heart leaped with mingled joy and alarm.

It was my father.

I watched him nervously as he strode towards the house, and my fears rose with each step that he took. Every movement was expressive of excitement and anger – the swift stride, the forward-thrust chin, the very set of the shoulders, the way in which he grasped his stick by the middle, as if aiming a blow, was full of menace. As he drew nearer I shrank behind the curtain, but still watched him, watched him with growing alarm, for now I could see that his eyes were wild under the frowning brows, his mouth was set, and his face was of a strange, blotchy, purple colour. He looked as if he had been drinking, but I knew he had not.

As he reached the gate, he wrenched it open violently, and, entering, slammed it behind him, a thing I had never before known him to do. He strode up the path, without a glance upwards, and disappeared from my sight, and a moment later there came a wild jangling of the bell, followed by a thundering knock at the door.

I hesitated, undecided what I should do. Should I go down and meet him with appeasing words, or should I wait until the first explosion of his wrath had subsided? I crept out of the bedroom to the landing and stood with my hand on the baluster rail, listening. I heard Mr. Otway walk along the hall, softly and rather slowly. I heard him open the door, and then my father's voice rose, loud and fierce.

"Where is my daughter, Otway? Is she here?

"Yes," Mr. Otway replied, "she is upstairs. We have just returned from the church."

"Do you mean to say," my father demanded, "that the marriage has actually taken place?"

"Yes," Mr. Otway answered. "We were married half-an-hour ago."

"What!" roared my father. "After my letter! Did you tell her about that letter? You didn't, you damned scoundrel! You've tricked her! You've swindled her!

"As to your letter, Mr. Vardon," I heard Mr. Otway reply, "I haven't seen it myself, yet. The morning's correspondence is still – "

Here a door closed, and his voice became inaudible. They had gone into one of the rooms. I staggered back into the bedroom and sank on to a chair, trembling from head to foot. In the name of God, what did my father mean? Tricked! Swindled! Could it be true? Was it actually possible that I had been lured into the arms of this ungainly lout by a false pretence? It was incredible. And yet – As the first shock of this amazing statement began to pass off, a storm of anger and indignation arose in my breast, and I was on the point of rising to go down and confront Mr. Otway, when the house shook to a heavy concussion. I sprang from the chair, and flying on the wings of terror down the stairs, opened the first door that I came to.

Years have rolled by since that unforgettable moment, but even now, as I write, the tableau that met my eyes as I opened the door rises before me vivid and distinct as the dreadful reality. I saw it even then but for a single instant, as I darted into the room, but it has remained with me and will remain till my dying day.

My father lay motionless on the floor near the fire-place, his face an awful, livid grey, his eyes staring fixedly at the ceiling, and from a small wound on the right side of his forehead a few drops of dark blood trickled down his temple. Beside him, and stooping over him, stood Mr. Otway, with ashen face and dropped jaw, the very picture of horror and mortal fear, and in Mr. Otway's right hand was grasped my father's stick, a stout Malacca, with a heavily-loaded silver knob.

I flew past him and sank on my knees by my father's side, and in that moment I knew that my father was dead. I had never seen a dead person before. But it was unmistakable. I spoke to him, I called to him in an agonised whisper, I patted his head and touched his face. But all the while I knew that he was dead, that he was gone from me forever. Even as I looked at him, the livid grey of his face faded to a dead white, the staring eyes relaxed and seemed to sink into their sockets, and the mouth slowly fell open. It was death. I knew it. Dazed, stricken, almost bereft of consciousness and the power of thought, I knew it, with the dull certainty of despair.

As I had entered the room, Mr. Otway had started up with a look of terror, and when I sank at my father's side, I had heard him move away softly towards the writing-table. He was now back and once more stooping over my father's body. I felt that he was there, although my eyes were fixed on that pallid face that gave back no answering glance. Presently he spoke, in a hushed, awe-stricken whisper.

"This is terrible, Helen! Can't we do anything?"

I looked up at him with a sudden flush of loathing and detestation, and as I looked, I noticed that he no longer held the stick. I rose slowly to my feet and faced him.

"No," I answered. "He is dead. He is dead. Mr. Otway, you have killed my father."

As I faced him, he shrank away from me, staring at me as if I had been some horrid apparition. His face, blanched to a horrible white and shiny with sweat, was dreadful to look upon, the face of abject, mortal terror.

"Helen!" he gasped. "Helen! For God's sake don't look at me like that! It was not I who killed him. I swear to God it was not. He fainted. I was trying to take the stick from him – I had to, or he would have killed me – and his head struck the mantelpiece. Then he fainted and fell. I am telling you the truth, Helen. I am, before God!"

To this I made no reply. Whether I believed him or not, I cannot say. Stunned as I was by this frightful thing that had befallen, I could only look at him with utter loathing as the cause of it all.

"Helen!" he continued, imploringly, "say you believe me! I swear I never touched him. And don't look at me like that! Helen! Why do you look at me in that awful way?"

He clasped his hands, and, casting a fearful glance at my poor father's corpse, moaned, "My God! my God! but this is horrible! Horrible! Do you think he is really dead? Don't you think – can't we do anything? If a doctor were here – if we only had someone to send – Shall I go and fetch a doctor, Helen?"

"Yes," I answered, "you had better."

"I will," he said. "But you do believe me, don't you? I swear – "

"You had better go at once, Mr. Otway," I interrupted.

He gave me one pitiful glance of appeal, and then, with a despairing moan, turned and left the room. I heard him hurry along the hall and a moment later the outer door closed.

Once more I sank on my knees beside my father, and, taking the passive hand in mine, looked into the pallid face, dimly surprised to find something new and unfamiliar creeping into it. I did not weep. The blow was too crushing, too overwhelming to call forth common emotion. Nor did I think coherently, but knelt, looking dumbly into the face that was my father's, and yet was not, wrapped in a sort of dreadful trance, conscious only of bitter pain and a sense of unutterable loss.

After a time – I do not know how long – I became aware of sounds of movement in the house, and presently soft foot steps approached the room. The door, which Mr. Otway had left ajar, opened with a faint creak, and the voice of Mrs. Gregg ejaculated, "Sakes! What's this?"

She stole on tip-toe into the room until she stood beside me, looking down with a scared expression as my father's corpse.

"Why!" she exclaimed, "the man's dead! Who is he?

"He is my father, Mrs. Gregg," I replied.

She stood for some time in silence, apparently considering the import of my answer. Then she walked round and looked down curiously at the wound on the forehead.

"Where is Mr. Otway?" she asked.

"He has gone to fetch a doctor," I answered.

322

"A doctor!" she repeated. "And what might be the good of a doctor when the man is dead? D'ye know how it happened?"

Before I had time to reply to her question, there came the sound of a latch-key inserted into the hall door. She turned quickly and made as if she would leave the room, but, as she reached the threshold, Mr. Otway entered, followed by the doctor, and she fell back to let them pass. I rose to my feet, and the doctor – a hard-faced, middle-aged man whom I knew by sight – knelt down in my place. He lifted the limp hand and laid his finger on the wrist, he raised the eyelid and touched the glazing eyeball. Then drawing out his stethoscope, he listened for some time at the chest over the region of the heart. And meanwhile we all stood watching him in a profound silence through which the ticking of the clock broke noisily, as it had done on that fateful night when I had sat in this very room unconsciously preparing the elements of this tragedy.

At length the doctor rose and, folding his stethoscope, deliberately slipped it into his pocket and turned to Mr. Otway.

"I am sorry to say that it is as you feared," said he. "He is quite dead. From what you have told me, I should say it was a case of heart failure from over-excitement. Have there been any previous attacks?"

"No," I answered. "But I think Dr. Sharpe considered that his heart was weak."

"Ah! He did, did he? Well, I had better call on Dr. Sharpe and hear what he knows about the case." He walked round, and, stooping down, examined the wound attentively. Then, without looking at Mr. Otway, he asked, "You say he struck his head against the corner of the mantelpiece? This corner, I suppose?"

He touched the right hand corner of the marble shelf, and, as Mr. Otway assented, I saw him place his shoulder against it as if to measure its height.

"Was that when he was in the act of falling?" he asked, with his eyes fixed on the wound.

"Yes," replied Mr. Otway. "At least, I think so – I should say yes, certainly – that is, to the best of my belief. Of course, Dr. Bury, you will understand that I am a little confused in my recollection. The – ah – the circumstances were very agitating and – ah – confusing. Is the point of any importance?"

"Well, you see," the doctor replied a little drily, "when a man dies suddenly and only one person is present – as I understand was the case in this instance – every point is of importance."

"Yes, of course. It would be, naturally."

Mr. Otway spoke these words in a low, husky voice, and, as I looked at him, I saw that he had turned as pale as death and that his face

323

had again broken out into a greasy sweat. Nor was I the only observer. Mrs. Gregg, who had been standing in the corner by the door, quietly attentive to all that passed, was now watching her employer narrowly and with a very curious expression. There was a brief interval of silence, and then Mr. Otway having cleared his throat once or twice, asked, in the same husky, unsteady voice, "I suppose, when you have talked the matter over with Dr. Sharpe, you will be able to certify the death in the usual way?"

"In the usual way?" Dr. Bury repeated. "Yes, in the way that is usual in cases of sudden death. Of course, I shan't be able to give an ordinary certificate. I shall write to the coroner, giving him the facts, and he will decide whether an inquest is necessary or whether he can issue a certificate on my statement."

"I see," said Mr. Otway. "You will report the facts – and, I suppose, you will state what your own views on the case are?"

"I shall make any comments that seem to be called for – but, of course, the facts are what the coroner wants."

"And would you consider that, in a case like this, an inquiry is necessary?

"I don't know that I should," was the reply, "but it doesn't rest with me. Would you like me to help you to move him? You can't leave him lying here, and you can hardly have him carried to his own house by daylight."

"No," Mr. Otway agreed, "we could not. If you will kindly help me to carry him to the drawing-room, we can lay him on the sofa."

The two men raised my poor father, and, while I supported his head, they carried him to the drawing-room and laid him on the sofa, when Dr. Bury, having taken an embroidered cover from a table and spread it over him, drew down the blinds.

"Perhaps," said he, "you had better leave him here until we know what the coroner intends to do. In case he should decide – "

Here he glanced a little uncomfortably at me, and I realised that he would rather speak of the grim details unembarrassed by my presence. Accordingly, I stole from the room and returned to the one from which we had just come. The door was open as we had left it, and, as I came opposite to it, treading softly, as was my habit, I saw Mrs. Gregg standing by the roll-top table with my father's stick in her hand, apparently testing the weight of the heavy lead loading that the silver knob concealed. She started as she suddenly became aware of my presence, but, quickly recovering her self-possession, asked, "Will this be your father's stick?"

I answered that it was, whereupon she remarked, as she stood it in the corner behind the writing-table, whence, I suppose, she had taken it.

"I thought 'twas a stranger to me. A fine stick it is, too, and a trusty companion 'twould be on a dark night and a lonely road."

To this I made no reply, and when she had glanced at the clock and peered curiously into my father's hat, which stood on the table, she turned abruptly and left the room.

Chapter VII
The Terms of Release

When Mrs. Gregg had gone, I shut the door, and, sinking on to the chair by the writing-table, tried to collect my thoughts. But though I was vaguely conscious that this dreadful disaster vitally affected my position, and must in some way affect my actions, overwhelming grief and a sense of irreparable loss rendered coherent thought impossible. My father was dead. That was all I could think of. My one perfect friend, who had absorbed all my affection and given me all of his, had gone out of my life. Henceforward I was alone in the world.

Presently I heard Dr. Bury leave the house, and then the door opened, and Mr. Otway came into the room, looking like a man who had risen prematurely after a severe illness. He dropped limply on a chair, and sat, with his hands on his knees, looking at me with a pitiable expression of misery and consternation.

"This is a terrible affair, Helen," he said in a broken voice. "Terrible! Terrible!"

I made no reply, but looked at him, half-curiously and resentfully. In the extremity of my grief, I had no pity to spare for him who was the cause of this dreadful calamity.

"Won't you speak to me, Helen?" he said, imploringly. "Won't you try to give me some comfort? Think of the awful position I am in."

At his miserable egotism, my grief blazed up into sudden wrath.

"*You!*" I exclaimed, scornfully. "And what of *me*? You have robbed me of my father – of all that matters to me in life – and now you ask *me* to comfort *you*!"

He stretched out his hands to me with a gesture of entreaty.

"Don't say that, Helen!" he implored. "Don't say I robbed you of him. It was an accident that no one could foresee. And after all, you know, Helen," he added, persuasively, "if you have lost a father, you have gained a devoted husband."

At these words I gazed at him in utter amazement, and quite suddenly the confusion of my thoughts began to clear up. I began to realise that some action was called for, though what that action was I could not clearly see at the moment. But what I did see quite clearly was that the thing he was suggesting was utterly unthinkable.

"Do you suppose, Mr. Otway," I demanded, "that I could possibly live with you as your wife after what has happened?"

"But you are my wife, Helen," he protested.

"I agreed to marry you, Mr. Otway, in order to save my father. My father has not been saved."

"That was, no doubt, your motive, Helen," he answered. "I don't deny that. But, actually, you agreed to be my wife on certain specific conditions, which I carried out – or, at least, was prepared – "

He hesitated with sudden embarrassment, and the embarrassment, with the statement, in the midst of which he had broken off, gave me my cue.

"Mr. Otway," I said, "you had a letter from my father. What was in that letter?"

At this question his self-possession broke down completely.

"I have had no letter," he stammered, "at least, that is to say, I haven't seen – he spoke of a letter, but – but the fact is, in my excitement this morning I forgot to look at my correspondence. If there was a letter, it must be in the box still."

"Let us go and see if it is there," said I. My confusion of mind was fast clearing up, and as my wits returned, I found myself shaping a definite course of action. I rose and accompanied him to the hall door and stood by while he unlocked the letter-box. As he opened the trap, I perceived that the box contained a single letter, and even in that agitating moment, the significance of the fact struck me. It was strange, indeed, that the morning's delivery should bring to a man of business no more than a single letter.

He picked the missive out, and, having glanced at it, handed it to me. I looked at it, and, perceiving that it was in my father's handwriting, tore open the envelope and drew out the letter, which I read aloud. It ran thus, –

Stonebury, Maidstone.

25th April, 1908.

Dear Otway,

You will, no doubt, be glad to learn that our little difficulty is at an end. The unexpected has happened. My friend has been able to raise the wherewith to repay the loan that I made to him, and has sent a cheque for the full amount. I have paid it into my bank, but, as a measure of security, in view of the magnitude of the sum, I am waiting until the cheque is cleared before sending you mine.

327

However, you may expect to receive payment in full in the course of three clear days from this date.

With many thanks for your forbearance,

I am, yours very truly,

W. H. Vardon

As I finished reading, I looked Mr. Otway sternly in the face.

"You realize," I said, "that this letter makes our agreement void?"

He did not reply immediately, but stood with his eyes averted from me and his fingers working nervously.

"Do you realize that?" I demanded.

"Well, in a way, yes," he replied, hesitatingly. "If it had reached me sooner – that is to say, if I had seen it – "

"If you had seen it!" I interrupted, angrily. "What has that to do with the question? The letter was delivered to you, as the post-mark shows, before you left the house. It came by the first post. If you chose to leave it unopened, that is your affair. When you met me this morning, the agreement was already at an end."

He glanced nervously along the hall towards the kitchen stairs.

"We needn't stand here," he said. "Let us go into the study and talk this affair over quietly."

He led the way back to the room we had left, and, having shut the door, turned to me deprecatingly.

"It's an unfortunate business, Helen," he said. "Very unfortunate. Of course, I ought to have looked over the morning's post, but, in my natural excitement, I overlooked it, and now I don't see that there is anything for us to do but make the best of it."

I looked at him in amazement. "But," I exclaimed, "you don't seem to realize that our agreement was at an end before the marriage took place."

"No, I don't," he replied. "You see, this letter is only a notification – a conditional promise to pay. It doesn't discharge the debt."

At this my patience gave out completely. "Let us have no evasions or quibbles, Mr. Otway," I said. "Our agreement was at an end before the marriage took place, and I have no doubt that you knew it. You obtained my consent by fraud."

"I don't admit that," said he. "But even if it were so, what would you propose?"

"I propose to have the marriage annulled," I replied.

He shook his head. "That is impossible, Helen," he said. "The marriage is not voidable. An action for nullity can be sustained only on certain conditions, none of which exist in our case."

"But," I exclaimed, "my consent was obtained on a fraudulent pretence! Surely that is a sufficient ground for claiming to have the marriage annulled!"

"I deny the fraud," he replied, doggedly. "But in any case it is not material. The marriage was perfectly regular, you are of full adult age, you gave your consent without compulsion, and there are none of those impediments which the law recognises. I assure you, Helen, that our marriage is not voidable – that it cannot be annulled by ordinary process."

Little as I trusted to his truth or honour, I suspected that what he was now saying was true. But yet the position was unthinkable.

"Do you mean to tell me," I demanded, "that the law would uphold a marriage between a woman and the murderer of her father?"

He winced as if I had struck him a blow, and his face grew sensibly paler.

"For the love of God, Helen," he entreated, "don't talk like that! You don't believe it. I can see you don't. You know I did not kill your father."

"I know nothing," I replied, "but this – that when I came into the room my father was lying dead with a wound on his forehead and that you were standing over him with a formidable weapon in your hand."

I thought he would have fainted. He sank into a chair with a gasp that was almost a sob, and the sweat streamed down his pallid face. He was a pitiable spectacle, but yet I felt no pity for him. I was bent only on escaping from the net in which he had caught me.

"I swear I never touched him, Helen," he protested, breathlessly. "I swear it. But you know I did not. You are only saying this to torture me. You don't believe it. I know you don't."

"It is of little importance what I believe, Mr. Otway." I replied, coldly. "The decision will not rest with me. You will be judged by others on the facts which I have stated."

He made no immediate reply. He seemed absolutely paralysed by terror, and sat, breathing quickly and staring at me, as if he expected me to kill him then and there. At length he spoke in a husky, indistinct voice.

"Helen. What is it you want of me?"

"I want this marriage set aside," I answered.

"But," he protested, "I have told you that is impossible. It cannot be annulled in the ordinary sense. Be reasonable, Helen. Let us talk the matter over and see if we can't come to terms."

"What do you mean?" I asked.

"Well," he said, persuasively, "I should like to meet your wishes if I can. I am not unreasonable. I can see that, as things are, you would not wish to live with me as my wife. We can't get the marriage annulled, but we can arrange a separation – a temporary separation, say, without prejudice to any future arrangements – by mutual consent. What do you say to that?"

"If the marriage cannot be set aside, I suppose a separation would be the next best thing. Do I understand that you are willing to agree to a separation?"

"Yes," he replied, "on certain conditions I am willing to agree to a separation – a temporary separation, you know."

"What are your conditions?" I asked.

He cleared his throat once or twice, as if in doubt how best to put the matter. Then, avoiding my eye, he began, hesitatingly, but with an obsequiously persuasive manner.

"The exact circumstances of your father's most lamentable death, Helen, are known to you and to me and to no one else. As I have told you, and I am convinced that you believe, the heart attack which killed him came as we were struggling for possession of his stick. It was due to the excitement and the violent exertion. Perhaps the blow on the head from the corner of the mantelpiece may have had something to do with it, for the fainting attack came on almost directly afterwards. He relaxed his hold on the stick and fell, leaving it in my hands. There was no violence on my part. I never struck him or did anything that could in any way make me responsible for his death. That is the truth, Helen, and I am convinced that you believe it, in spite of what you have said."

"I have only your word that it is the truth," said I.

"Exactly," he agreed. "But you believe me. You know what your father's state of health was, and you know that he was liable, on occasions, to be – er – somewhat violent. So you believe me. But others, who have not the knowledge that you have – ah – might – ah – might not believe me."

"I haven't said that I do," I interposed. "However, we will let that pass. Go on, please."

He paused to wipe his face with his handkerchief, and then proceeded,

"You said just now that when you entered the room you saw me standing over your father with a weapon in my hand."

"So I did."

"I know you did, Helen. You saw me holding your father's loaded stick. It is quite true. But – it would – ah – greatly simplify matters if –

well, if that circumstance were not communicated to – ah – to anyone else."

"You mean to say," said I, "that you want me to suppress the fact that I saw you standing over my father's dead body holding a loaded stick?"

"I wouldn't use the word 'suppress', Helen," he replied, passing his handkerchief once more over his haggard face. "I only ask you to refrain – in the interests of justice and – ah – of common humanity – from mentioning a circumstance that – ah – mentioned, might mislead the hearers, and might, conceivably, lead them to quite erroneous conclusions. It is a reasonable thing to ask. No doubt you blame me, you look upon me as the cause of this dreadful trouble – which, in a certain sense, I admit I am. But you would not be vindictive, Helen, or unjust. You would not wish to see me placed in the dock – perhaps even convicted – think of that, Helen! Convicted and sentenced when I am absolutely innocent! My God! It would be an awful thing! You wouldn't wish to have such a frightful miscarriage of justice as that on your conscience, I am sure."

"It wouldn't be on *my* conscience," I replied, coldly. "The verdict would not be mine, and besides, I have only your word that you are innocent. You have made the statement to me, and you could make it to others, who would take it for what it is worth."

He clasped his hands passionately and leaned forward towards me with an imploring gesture.

"Helen!" he exclaimed. "Don't be so hard, so cold! Have you no pity for me? Think of my awful position – an innocent man, but yet with appearances so horribly against me. And the whole issue is in your hands. You were not present when – when it happened. You have only to say so and to refrain from making any unnecessary additions to that statement, and no miscarriage of justice can occur. I am not asking you to say anything that is not true, I am only asking you to keep irrelevant and misleading matter out of the inquiry. Do this, Helen, and I promise to execute a deed surrendering all claims on you – at least for a time."

I made no immediate answer. Mr. Otway was perfectly right on one point. I did not believe that he had killed my father. I think I only half-believed it, even at the awful moment of the discovery, for the alarming appearance that my father had presented as he strode up the garden path, with his wild eyes and his strange, blotchy colour, had made me fear a catastrophe, and when the catastrophe had almost immediately followed, it was natural that my mind should refer it to a cause already considered rather than to one totally unexpected. Moreover, Mr. Otway's account of the tragedy was intrinsically probable, it fitted the facts that were known to me, whereas the supposition that he had killed my father was wildly improbable.

It is not to be supposed, however, that, in my present agitated state, I reasoned the matter out consciously in this methodical fashion. But unconsciously, and perhaps vaguely, my mind had worked along these lines to a conclusion, and that conclusion was that Mr. Otway's account of what had happened was substantially correct. Nevertheless, I was not prepared to admit this at the moment – indeed, my whole desire was to be rid of the man's irksome presence – to be alone with my grief.

"I can't give you an answer now, Mr. Otway," I said. "I am not in a condition to discuss anything. I want to go home and be quiet."

He acquiesced with surprising readiness, no doubt encouraged by my tacit abandonment of the accusation.

"Of course you do," he agreed. "It has been a fearful shock for you. Go home and keep yourself quiet. I shall hear from Dr. Bury, in the course of the day, what the coroner intends to do, and I will call and let you know. And I will bring a draft of the deed for you to look at. The sooner we arrive at a settlement, the better. And, Helen, let me beg you not to say anything to anyone about – anything that might complicate matters. You understand what I mean."

I nodded wearily and moved towards the door. I was still wearing my outdoor clothes, so I had no preparations to make. Mr. Otway opened the door for me and I passed out into the hall, but before leaving the house, I turned back into the darkened drawing-room, and, raising the cover from my father's face, kissed his already cold cheek.

"Good-bye, dearest! Good-bye!" I whispered, passionately, and then, feeling the tears rushing to my eyes, I kissed him again, and, replacing the cover, hurried from the room. Mr. Otway was standing at the hall door to let me out, and timidly offered his hand, but I walked quickly past him, and, running down the steps, made my way out through the gate that had admitted me to my ruin and my father to his death.

Chapter VIII
"Whom God Hath Joined – "

Our states of mind in certain unforeseen circumstances are sometimes surprising, even, to ourselves. As I walked away from Mr. Otway's house, I think I was dimly surprised at my own self-possession. The worst had happened. The calamity which I had feared, and which I had made such sacrifices to avert, had befallen, and yet I was comparatively calm. My heart ached, it is true, with a grief such as I had never known before, with a sense of irreparable loss and a feeling of utter loneliness and desolation – but yet, under it all was a certain indefinable peace

Looking back with more natural knowledge and experience, this state of mind is not difficult to understand. My father's sudden death was a crushing calamity but, in the very moment of its happening, the incubus of my relation to Mr. Otway was lifted. For, though I was not at the time conscious of the fact, I now see clearly that, even as I passed out of the house of the man whom the law regarded as my husband, my mind was made up that I had done with Mr. Otway.

Moreover, my new trouble was in other ways more easy to bear than the misery of the last few days. My marriage had seemed, in a manner, to put an end to my life. It had offered nothing but an unending vista of wretchedness, an unending submission to a state of things that was intolerable even to think of. But this new catastrophe was sudden and final. The blow had fallen, once for all, shattering, indeed, my present, but calling upon me instantly to make provision for the future. And in action, the necessity of which forced itself upon me even before I reached home, I found, if not relief from my sorrow, at least some temporary distraction.

As I let myself in with my latch-key, our housemaid met me in the hall to announce that lunch had been waiting for some time, and to ask me if I knew at what time my father would come in.

"My father is dead, Jessie," I replied. "He died suddenly at Mr. Otway's house about an hour ago. I can't tell you any more just now."

I walked past her and ascended the stairs to my room, leaving her standing in the hall as if petrified, but, before I reached the landing, I heard her rush away towards the kitchen, making the house resound with her hysterical shrieks and lamentations. It was very dreadful and distressing, but yet it had a steadying effect on me, reminding me of my isolated position and of the need for firmness and self-control. In a few minutes I came down, and disregarding Jessie's sobs and tears, sat out the simple formalities of lunch as a matter of discipline and example, and even compelled myself to take a certain amount of food.

As I sat at my silent and solitary meal, my thoughts were busy with the many things that had to be done. Not willingly, indeed, for I longed to be quiet and nurse my grief – to forget everything but my sorrow and my great bereavement. But that was impossible. I was practically alone in the world, for I had no near relatives, and all that had to be done must be done, or at least directed, by me. There was my father's funeral to be arranged, the business to be transferred or wound up, the property to be realised – and there was Mr. Otway.

Naturally enough, my thoughts constantly came back to him. As to his moral claim on me, it was null and void. Whether he had, as I suspected, seen my father's letter and deliberately left it unopened, or whether he had simply neglected to look for it, made no difference. It had been delivered to him, and thereupon our agreement had ceased to exist. But if he had no moral claim, he had, apparently, a legal hold on me which would have to be considered. If he could be induced to surrender that, the position would be greatly simplified. And he was ready to surrender it on a certain condition.

To Mr. Otway's proposal my thoughts came back again and again. The condition that he had made was not an unreasonable one, or, at least, it did not appear so to me. My father had died when they were alone together. They had admittedly been quarrelling, my father bore the mark of a heavy blow, and Mr. Otway had been found standing over the body with a loaded stick in his hand. The appearances suggested that he had killed my father. And yet I was convinced that he had not. Profoundly loathing him as the cause of all my misfortunes, I still felt that he was, in this respect, an innocent man, and common justice demanded that he should not be made to suffer for a crime that he had not committed.

Now what was my position in the affair? Practically I held the scales of justice. The one absolutely damning fact was in my sole possession, and I alone, in all probability, would appreciate the misleading appearances which that fact created. That was my dilemma. I could make known the fact itself to those who should judge him, but could I make them understand how little it was worth? It seemed very doubtful. I had trembled for my father's safety and had seen him come in at the gate, already in a dangerous condition. They had not. They might easily fail to weigh his state of health against that one, apparently, sinister fact of the loaded stick. In short, it came to this, that if I mentioned what I had seen, Mr. Otway ran a serious risk of being punished for a crime which he had not committed, whereas if I refrained from mentioning it, justice would take its proper course.

That, I think, is, in effect, how I argued. Neither the logician nor the jurist will commend me. But women have their own ways of looking at things, and one of those ways is somewhat to confuse conviction with knowledge. A thing firmly believed is apt to present itself as a thing known. I had come to the conclusion that Mr. Otway was innocent of my father's death, and having done so, had unconsciously treated his innocence as a fact that was within my knowledge.

After lunch, I telephoned to the office, asking Mr. Jackson, my father's managing clerk, to come and see me, and while I was waiting for him, I took down from the study shelves a treatise of *The Law of Husband and Wife*, and turned over those of its unsavoury pages which dealt with suits for nullity. Apparently Mr. Otway was right. So far as I could make out, the circumstances of our marriage afforded no grounds for such a suit. I was married irrevocably. My complete freedom was gone beyond recall, I should have to be content with such incomplete freedom as is conferred by a deed of separation.

I had just returned the book to the shelf when Mr. Jackson arrived and entered the room looking very flurried and uncomfortable.

"What a dreadful thing this is, Miss Vardon!" he exclaimed. "Shocking! Shocking! So unexpected! I need not say how much we all sympathize with you."

"It is very kind of you," I said, offering him a chair.

"Not at all," he rejoined. "It is a terrible misfortune for all of us. Would it distress you very much to tell me how it happened?"

"It was for that purpose that I sent for you, Mr. Jackson, to tell you exactly what has happened and to ask your advice," and here I gave him a brief account of the events of the morning.

At the mention of my marriage he looked profoundly surprised, but also, I thought, distinctly relieved, but he did not make any comment until I had finished the whole tragic story, when he remarked, "I am very glad to hear that you are married, Miss Vardon – or rather, I should say, Mrs. Otway – to a man of such very substantial means, if I am rightly informed."

"Why are you glad?" I asked.

"Because," he replied, "it disposes of rather a difficulty. Your father was a man of great abilities and an excellent lawyer, but he was somewhat inattentive to the financial side of his profession. I am afraid you would have been left rather badly provided for."

"I am sorry to hear that," said I, "because I am not proposing to live with Mr. Otway. I have asked him to agree to a separation."

Mr. Jackson raised his eyebrows. "May I ask why?" he enquired.

"I don't want to go into details just now," I answered, "but I may say that the marriage was an affair of accommodation. I supposed my father to be in a position of embarrassment, and I made the arrangement with Mr. Otway without his knowledge. It turns out that I was mistaken. He was not embarrassed. When the marriage took place, I was under a misapprehension and I was misled by Mr. Otway. Accordingly, I have asked to have a separation deed drawn up."

"Does he agree to the separation?"

"He has not yet, but I think he will, so I shall have to consider my resources, after all."

"But," Mr. Jackson objected, "he will have to make you an allowance."

"That," I said, "is impossible. If I repudiate the marriage, I could not, of course, allow him to support me."

"Why not?" demanded Mr. Jackson. "He is legally bound to. You are his wife. While the marriage stands, you can't marry anybody else. Besides, he is not likely to raise any objection. He is a lawyer, you know."

"I am not thinking of him, I am thinking of myself. I wish to be under no obligations to Mr. Otway, and I shall not accept any assistance from him."

"I am sorry to hear you say that," Mr. Jackson said, gloomily, "because I am afraid you will be rather badly off. The business is a very personal one, and is worth practically nothing to sell. If I were a qualified solicitor, I might be able to carry it on. But I'm not, and I doubt if anyone would care to buy the good-will at any price. Still, I'll see what can be done. As to your father's will, I happen to know that you are the residuary legatee – practically the sole legatee – but what that amounts to, I shouldn't like to say. Mighty little, I fear. However, it's of no use to worry you with these matters now. If you will authorize me to look into your father's affairs, I will let you know exactly how things stand, and if I could be of service to you in any way, I hope you'll let me know. There's the funeral, for instance – "

He paused suddenly, and ran an uncomfortable eye along the rows of law books on the shelves.

"You are very kind, Mr. Jackson," I said, "and your help will be invaluable. As my father's friend, I should like you to take charge of the funeral arrangements, if you would be so good."

The rest of our conversation was concerned with the various things which had to be done during the next day or two, and it left with a feeling of the warmest gratitude to this quiet and rather dry man of business, whose sympathy took such a practical and acceptable form.

It was past six o'clock when the red-eyed Jessie came to the study to announce that Mr. Otway was waiting in the drawing-room, and there I found him wandering restlessly round by the walls and making a show of examining the pictures. He was still very pale and looked haggard and weary, but yet he held out his hand to me with a certain confidence.

"I think, Helen," said he, "that you will be a little relieved at my news. I have seen Dr. Bury, and he tells me that the coroner will be satisfied with his evidence and Dr. Sharpe's."

"Do you mean that there is to be no inquest?" I demanded, with sudden suspicion.

"No, no," he replied. "Of course, there will be an inquest. But the coroner thinks that the circumstances do not call for a *post mortem*. I thought you would be glad to know that. The – er – body will remain where it is until the jury have viewed it, and then it can be brought here for the – ah – the funeral."

I nodded but made no comment on this statement, and he continued after a brief pause. "I suppose, Helen, you would like me to act for you in regard to the funeral arrangements."

"Thank you, Mr. Otway," I replied, "but Mr. Jackson has very kindly undertaken that for me."

He looked somewhat crestfallen at this, and said, deprecatingly, "I am sorry you did not leave the arrangements to me. It would have looked better." Which it undeniably would – from his point of view.

As I made no rejoinder, there followed a slightly uncomfortable pause, during which he was evidently bracing himself up for what was the real object of his visit. At length he began nervously, "Have you been able to give any more consideration to my proposal, Helen?"

"Yes," I answered, "I have thought about it a good deal. Perhaps we had better go into the study, which is more out of the way of the servants than this."

We crossed the hall, and, when we had entered the study and closed the door, I resumed. "I may as well say, Mr. Otway, that I am prepared to accept your statement. On reflection, I believe that your account of what happened is true."

"Thank God for that!" he ejaculated. "I felt sure you believed me, Helen, but it is an unspeakable relief to hear you say so. And I am sure you will agree with me that the – the apparently incriminating circumstance need not be mentioned."

"I might even agree to that," I replied, "but there must be a clear understanding. I am not going to say anything that is not strictly true."

"Oh, certainly not!" he agreed. "All that I ask is that you refrain from volunteering a perfectly unnecessary and misleading statement. Will you promise to do that?"

"I am not sure that I have any right to make such a promise, Mr. Otway, but still, on the conditions that you mentioned, I am prepared to do so."

His relief was really pathetic. Its intensity made me understand what torments of terror he had been suffering. He flung out his hands as if he would have embraced me, but drew back, as I said, coldly,

"You are prepared on your side, Mr. Otway, to carry out your part? You agree to execute a deed of separation, as I asked?

"If you insist," he replied. "It's a hard bargain, but if you hold me to it, I have no choice. Would not a short, informal separation do?"

"No, Mr. Otway," I replied firmly, "it would not. I am acting somewhat against my conscience in agreeing to suppress this fact, and I want full compensation for doing so. I must have a legally valid deed of separation."

"Very well, Helen," said he, "if it must be, it must. I hope that, later, you will take a kinder view of our relations, but meanwhile I will do exactly as you wish. I have drafted out a deed, in a simple form, with as little legal verbiage as possible. If its terms satisfy you, I will copy it out and sign it."

He handed me a sheet of paper on which the deed was drafted, and I read it through carefully. Like the other documents that he had drawn up, it was lucid, simple, and concise, and set forth quite fairly the conditions to which he had agreed, with one exception. It determined automatically at the end of three months.

"I can't agree to that," I said. "There must be no specified time. It is to be just a separation."

"But," he exclaimed, "you don't propose that the separation should last forever, do you?"

That was precisely what I did propose, but I thought it politic not to express myself too definitely.

"It is impossible," I replied, "to say what may happen in the future, but if you make the separation determinable by mutual consent, that will provide for all eventualities."

He agreed, with a somewhat wry smile, that this was so, and then asked how soon I should like to have the deed executed.

"As it must be signed before I give my evidence," I replied, "it had better be done now. If you will make two copies, I will go and fetch the maids to witness the signatures."

"Dear me, Helen!" he exclaimed. "What an extra ordinarily business-like young lady you are! But I suppose you are right, only I would suggest that you do not acquaint the witnesses with the nature of the document. We don't want to take the world into our confidence, especially just now."

This was reasonable enough, though it would obviously be impossible to keep the world in the dark as to our position, particularly after what I had said to Mr. Jackson. However, I agreed to maintain a discreet reticence, and when he had made the two copies – which I carefully read through – I went out and called Jessie and the cook.

"I want you," said I, "to witness my signature and Mr. Otway's to a couple of documents. You have just to see us sign our names and then sign your own underneath."

The two women came into the study with an air of mystery and awe, gazing furtively from me to Mr. Otway. The two documents lay on the table, each with a sheet of blotting paper spread over it, exposing only the blank spaces which were to receive the signatures, on each of which a red wafer seal had been stuck. Mr. Otway signed first, and then, indicating to the cook the place where she was to write her name, placed the pen in her hand.

"That's right," said he, when she had painfully and with protruded tongue, executed the signature of "*Ivy Stokes*". "Now you will do the same with the other paper as soon as Mrs. Otway has signed."

The cook gazed curiously at me as I signed the second document, and then, in the same strained and laborious fashion, traced the scrawling characters over the name that I had lightly pencilled in for her guidance. Having watched with feverish interest while I marked the next space, she drew back and made way for Jessie, who, by watching her colleague, had learned what was required of her.

When the formalities were completed and the two maids dismissed – to discuss these strange proceedings, doubtless, in the kitchen – Mr. Otway handed me the copy bearing his signature and, taking the other, rose to depart.

"Before I go, Helen," he said, "there is one matter to settle. In the document I thought it best to say nothing about an allowance – "

"You were quite right," I interrupted. "Of course, I should not ask for, or accept, any allowance under the circumstances."

"You won't need one at present," said he. "We know there are five-thousand pounds lying to your father's credit at his bank – "

"That money was not his," I said, "and it is not mine. As soon as the will is proved, it will be paid to you on behalf of your clients."

"But that is quite unnecessary, Helen," said he. "The use, for an unspecified time, of that sum of money was the consideration in respect of which you agreed to marry me. As the marriage has taken place, it is only fair and reasonable that you should receive the consideration. In effect, that five-thousand is yours by the terms of our agreement."

I was on the point of replying that our agreement was null and void, and that I had no intention of carrying out its conditions, but prudence whispered that I had better keep my intentions to myself, at least as to my ultimate conduct. Besides which, Mr. Otway's statement was not entirely correct, as I proceeded to point out.

"The use of this money," I said, "was to relieve my father, who was assumed to be insolvent. But it appears that he was not insolvent, and it is my intention that all his debts shall be paid, in so far as there are funds to meet them. It is certainly what he would have wished."

"But," Mr. Otway protested, "supposing the payment of these debts should consume all the available assets? How are you going to live?"

"I suppose I shall do as other women do when they have no independent means. I shall work for my living. But it is premature to discuss that until I have had Mr. Jackson's report. I don't suppose I shall be absolutely penniless."

He shook his head gloomily. "You are Quixotic, Helen, and wrong-headed, too. There is no reason why you should work for your living. As a married woman, you are entitled to maintenance, and I am willing, and even anxious, to maintain you. But I won't press the matter now. If you want money, you know that you can have it, not as a favour but as a right, And now there is just one other matter that I want to speak about. In the deed of separation I said nothing about our relations other than was actually necessary. I made no stipulation as to your keeping me informed of your whereabouts, but I ask you now, if you should be leaving Maidstone, to let me have your address and to allow me to keep up communication with you. It is a reasonable request, Helen, and I am sure you will not hesitate to accede to it."

I did hesitate, however, for some time. In truth, I was not at all willing to agree to this proposal. My wish was to sponge Mr. Otway, once and for all, out of my life and to make a fresh start. Still, the request was a reasonable one, and could, I suspected, have been enforced as a demand, and, in the end, though very reluctantly, I yielded.

"Thank you, Helen," said he, holding out his hand. "Then I won't worry you any more just now. It is understood that I am not to lose sight of you, and that if you should want help, pecuniary or other, you will let me know. And I may rely on you to say no more at the inquest than is actually necessary?"

340

I gave him the required assurance on this point and, having somewhat frigidly shaken his hand, accompanied him to the hall door and let him out.

As I stood in the open doorway, watching him walk away up the street in his heavy, elephantine fashion, a man entered at the gate, and, approaching with a deferential and rather uncomfortable air, took off his hat and offered me a small, blue envelope, which bore the superscription "*Mrs. Lewis Otway*". I took it from him and, closing the door, went back to the study, where I opened the envelope and extracted the little slip of blue paper that it enclosed, which turned out, as I had expected, to be the subpoena to the Inquest. I glanced through the peremptory phrases of the summons and, laying the slip of paper on the table, went up to my own room to be quiet and think upon all that lay before me.

But thought – orderly, useful thought – was impossible. Everything around me spoke of the life that had been so tragically broken off, rather than of the future that loomed so vague and empty before me. The open book on the reading-stand, the hastily scribbled notes upon the writing-block, the unanswered letters and a little pile of rough drawings on the table – all seemed to call to me to take up afresh the thread that had been dropped, seemed to interpose the unfinished past before the uncommenced future. Restlessly I wandered down to the workshop – where the coal scuttle still stood on the bench, a mute but eloquent memorial of that tragic final evening – only to gather a fresh sense of loss and desolation. And so, for the rest of the day, I haunted the house like some unquiet spirit, watched with pity, not unmixed with fear, by the awe-stricken servants, tearless and outwardly calm, but inwardly torn by grief and a sense of bereavement that seemed to intensify moment by moment.

And yet, when, in the silence of the night, the tears came at last, and my sorrow, no longer mute, voiced itself in sobs and moans of pain – still, under the feeling of utter bereavement and desolation, was a half-felt sense of peace, of respite, and reprieve.

Chapter IX
Testimony and Counsel

Those who are apt to refer in contemptuous terms to the artificiality of the plots of the novelist must have failed to observe the orderly way in which events arrange themselves in real life, how the circumstances of the vital and essential happenings of our lives may, if attentively considered, be separated out in a coherent group of causes and effects as closely knit and inevitably connected as the parts of the story-teller's plot.

The reflection is suggested to me by the distressing experiences of the inquest on my father's death. Clearly enough, indeed, did I realise at the time that this would never have been but for those fateful words so calamitously overheard by me, and for my ill-considered, though well-meant, efforts to avert the apparently impending catastrophe. But I realised not at all – as, indeed, how should I? – that this day of sorrow, of shame and humiliation, was not only the harvest of the irrevocable past, but the seed-time of an even more momentous future.

As I approached the school-house in which the inquest was to be held, I observed Mr. Otway pacing slowly up and down the little court-yard. He was pale and haggard, and though he preserved his usual ponderously reposeful manner, it was not difficult to see that he was in a state of intense, nervous excitement and suppressed anxiety.

He was evidently waiting for me, and turned to meet me as I entered the gate.

"I thought we had better go in together, Helen," he said, as we exchanged a formal greeting. "They know that we are married, and, of course, they don't know that our – ah – our arrangements are in – ah – in suspense. And it would perhaps be as well if no reference were made to – ah – to those – ahem – temporary modifications which – ah – in short, to our provisional agreement."

He looked at me deprecatingly and I nodded. There would be quite enough painful detail to be dragged into the light of day without this sordid addition. Besides, any reference to the deed of separation would start enquiries which neither of us desired, as was plainly evident to Mr. Otway, for he continued in a husky undertone, as we approached the schoolroom door, "And you will fulfil your part of our covenant faithfully, Helen, I am sure."

"Most undoubtedly I shall," I replied. "But you will remember that our covenant does not include false evidence. I shall say as little as is possible, but if I am asked a direct question I must answer it, and answer it truthfully."

"Of course you must," he agreed, "but it is often possible to ward off an inconvenient question which may lead to others still more inconvenient."

"You make take it," I said, "that I shall carry out my part of our bargain in the spirit as well as in the letter."

With this assurance he appeared to be satisfied, and we now moved slowly towards the door of the school-house. While we had been talking, a party of men – the coroner and his jury – had filed past us and entered, and when we followed a minute later, we found them already in their places and the proceedings about to begin. We seated ourselves on the two chairs placed for us, which were next to those of the two medical witnesses, and as I glanced round the Court, I observed Mr. Jackson sitting near the coroner, and by his side a gentleman whose face I seemed to recognise, but to whom I could not give a name. Some dim recollection connected the quiet, strong, intellectual face with my father and the happy past, but not until near the close of the inquiry was I able to bring my memory to a clear focus.

The attitude of the coroner and jury alike – they were all local men and most of them known to me – made my difficult task as easy as was possible. They were all anxious to spare me to the utmost and to make the best of what the coroner described as "a grievous and terrible calamity." Moreover, they restrained in the most delicate manner their evident curiosity as to the relations of Mr. Otway and myself. But, of course, the facts had to be given, and very distressing and humiliating it was to me to have to confess to what must have looked like a mere sordid intrigue with the uncouth creature at my side.

As the only person present when the death occurred, Mr. Otway was necessarily the first witness, and a very nervous, hesitating witness he was, and very fortunate was it for him that he had so sympathetic a court. As he stammered out his evidence I noted, again and again, the searching, grey eye of the strange gentleman fixed upon him, not indeed with any obvious distrust, but with the most concentrated attention.

"Do we understand," asked the coroner, "that Mr. Vardon was angry and excited when he arrived at your house?

"Yes – furiously angry."

"Do you know why he was angry and excited?"

Yes, the witness did know. And as he proceeded to relate, in husky, uncertain tones, the circumstances of the secret marriage, more than one of the jurymen glanced from him to me with hardly-concealed astonishment, and I felt my face burning and my eyes filling with humiliation.

"Was there any reason for this secrecy?" the coroner asked.

"Yes. The deceased had already refused his consent to the marriage."

"But that is hardly a reason for secrecy in the case of an adult. Could he have prevented the marriage from taking place?"

"No. But it seemed better to – ah – to avoid discussion and unpleasantness."

The coroner looked dissatisfied. He considered a few moments, and then asked, "Do you know why the deceased objected to the marriage?

"I think he considered that the – ah – the inequality of age was undesirable," Mr. Otway replied.

Still the coroner looked dissatisfied, and as he paused to reflect, and the jurymen looked at him expectantly, Mr. Otway furtively wiped his forehead with his handkerchief. Evidently, he was profoundly disturbed, as well he might be, for if this line of inquiry were pursued much farther, it must inevitably lay bare the real nature of the transaction.

At length the coroner turned to the jury. "Well, gentlemen," said he, "I suppose the question is not very material. It is clear that the deceased was extremely excited and angry. The ultimate cause of his anger is, perhaps, not very relevant to the subject of our inquiry."

To this the foreman of the jury readily agreed, and I could almost see the sigh of relief with which Mr. Otway hailed the passing of this perilous incident – a relief in which I participated to no small extent.

The narrative was now resumed, and as it proceeded, Mr. Otway's voice became more and more husky and his speech more hesitating. He had a difficult course to steer, and his nerves were at their utmost tension. He had to tell a consistent story without telling the whole truth, and he had to bear in mind that my evidence was yet to be given. It was a position that might have shattered the nerve of a much bolder man than Mr. Otway.

"You tell us that the deceased was violent and threatening in his manner. Do you mean that he was physically violent?

"Yes – at least he threatened to use physical violence."

"He did not actually assault you?"

"Not actually. The blow that he aimed – at least that he was about to aim – ah – did not – er – did not take effect."

The coroner's brows puckered into a puzzled frown. "This is not quite clear," said he. "Did he or did he not aim a blow at you?"

344

"He did – at least, that is to say, he appeared – " Here Mr. Otway mopped his streaming forehead. "Well, I think he actually raised his – ah – his – ah – his clenched fist."

"Did you have to restrain him?"

"No," replied Mr. Otway, with rather unnecessary emphasis. "No, I did not. I stepped back, and – ah – the incident – ah – passed. In fact, it was at this moment that the fatal attack occurred."

"Tell us exactly what happened then."

"He suddenly turned very pale," said Mr. Otway, speaking now with more fluency as he got back to the narration of the actual events, "and seemed to stand unsteadily. Then he staggered backwards and fell, striking his head on the corner of the mantelpiece."

"Did he appear to have fainted before he struck his head?"

"I should say, yes, but – ah – I would not – ah – I was very agitated and alarmed – and – ah – "

"Naturally. But you would say that the fainting attack preceded the blow on the head?"

"There was no blow," Mr. Otway exclaimed quickly, and then, perceiving his mistake, he added, hastily, "That is to say, you are referring to his striking the corner of the mantelpiece?"

"That is what you were telling us about."

"Yes. I should say that he struck – or rather that he fainted and staggered and that he struck his head in falling."

Once more the coroner paused and seemed to reflect, and in the intense silence and stillness that enveloped the court my eye travelled from the huge, ungainly figure of the witness to the face of the tall stranger by Mr. Jackson's side. And a very striking face it was – a handsome, symmetrical face, but strangely – almost unhumanly – reposeful and impassive. Yet, though it was as immobile as a mask of stone, it conveyed an impression of intense attention – almost of watchfulness, and the clear, grey eyes never moved from the face of the witness. To me there was something a little uncanny and disturbing in that immovable mask and that steady, unrelaxing gaze. I found myself hoping that those searching grey eyes would not be fixed on me in that relentless observation when my turn came to give my evidence. And even as this thought flitted through my mind, I remembered who this stranger was. He was a Dr. Thorndyke, an old, though not very intimate, friend of my father's, a famous criminal lawyer and a great authority on medical jurisprudence. I had met him only once, when he had dined, many years ago, at our house, but I had often heard my father speak of him in terms of the highest admiration.

When the coroner resumed his interrogation, it seemed that the crisis was past, so far as Mr. Otway was concerned, for his first question was, "What did you do when the deceased fell down?

"For a moment or two," was the reply, "I was too bewildered to do anything. Then his daughter – my wife – came into the room, and, as he appeared to be dying or dead, I went off to fetch a doctor."

This virtually concluded his evidence, and the next name called was my own, which, in its new form – Helen Otway – I heard with a start of surprise and something like disgust. As I rose to approach the table, I caught an instantaneous glance – a terrified, imploring glance – from Mr. Otway, and as my eye lighted immediately afterwards on Dr. Thorndyke's face, I felt that this momentary look, too, had been noted by that inexorably attentive grey eye. But I was relieved to observe that he did not look at me, but, as I gave my evidence, fixed a steady, introspective gaze upon a spot upon the opposite wall.

My task turned out to be easier than I had hoped, though perhaps it might have been less easy if I had had more time to reflect on the significance of the questions. The coroner began by expressing the sympathy of the court with my bereavement and apologizing for imposing on me the painful duty of attending the inquiry. Then he asked, "You have heard the evidence of Mr. Otway with reference to your marriage and your father's attitude in regard to it. Do you confirm what he has said?

"I do," I replied.

"You were not present at the interview of Mr. Otway with the deceased?"

"No, I was not. When I entered the room my father was lying on the floor and appeared to be already dead."

"Had you seen your father since the solemnization of the marriage?"

"I saw him from the window as he entered Mr. Otway's garden."

"Did you notice anything unusual in his appearance?"

"Yes, his appearance alarmed me very much. He seemed excessively excited, and his face was deeply flushed and of a strange, purplish colour."

"Had you any special reason to be alarmed?"

"Yes. I knew that his doctor had warned him to avoid all excitement and exertion on account of the weak state of his heart."

"You did not hear what passed between your father and Mr. Otway?"

"I heard my father ask where I was, and I heard Mr. Otway tell him that the marriage had taken place."

"Did you hear anything more?"

"My father then called Mr. Otway a scoundrel, and was still speaking loudly and angrily when the study door closed and I heard no more."

"What made you go to the study?"

"I heard and felt the shock when my father fell."

"Would you mind telling us again in what condition you found your father?"

"He appeared to be dead. His face was at first a livid grey, but it faded to marble whiteness as I looked at him. There was a small wound on the right side of his forehead and a drop of blood had run down on to his cheek and on his temple."

The coroner glanced at the jurymen. "I think, gentlemen," he said, "that is all we need ask Mrs. Otway?"

And when the foreman had acquiesced, and he had thanked me for "the very clear and lucid manner" in which I had given my evidence, I was permitted to resume my seat.

"I can never thank you enough, Helen," whispered Mr. Otway, as I sat down. "You managed admirably – admirably."

To this I made no reply, for now that the ordeal was over I began to be assailed by certain doubts as to whether I had been quite candid. I had told all that was really material to the inquiry, but – However, at this point Dr. Sharpe approached the table and picked up the Testament.

His evidence practically settled the verdict. He testified that my father had suffered for some years from a dilated heart and arterial degeneration. "I warned him frequently to avoid excitement and undue exertion, for he was inclined to be careless and take liberties with himself."

"You considered his state of health precarious?"

"I thought he might fall down dead at any moment."

"You have heard the evidence of the two previous witnesses. Does that evidence contain any suggestion to you as to the cause of death?"

"It suggests to me that the deceased hurried to Mr. Otway's house in a towering rage, and that, during the interview, he worked himself up into a fury. I should say that the combined exertion and excitement brought on a fatal attack of syncope."

"You think that death was caused by heart failure?"

"I have no doubt of it."

Dr. Bury's evidence was much to the same effect, though less positive.

"The deceased had apparently been dead about half-an-hour when I arrived. The cause of death was not obvious, but the appearances were consistent with the account given by Mr. Otway. There was a small, contused wound at the junction of the forehead and right temple, apparently caused by the violent impact of some hard and blunt body. Judging by the small amount of bleeding, the wound had been sustained immediately before death. A single drop of blood had trickled down on to the cheek, and one or two drops on to the temple."

"You have heard Mr. Otway's account of the way in which that wound was occasioned. Do you consider that the appearances are in agreement with that account?"

"There is no disagreement. The appearance of the wound was consistent with its production in the manner described."

"Would you say that it was probably so produced?"

"That," replied Dr. Bury, "is a question for the jury. It might have been. I can't go beyond the appearances."

"No, of course you can't. And is that all that you have to tell us?"

"That is all," was the reply, and this virtually brought the inquiry to an end. After a brief summing-up by the coroner, the jury held an equally brief consultation and then unanimously returned a verdict of "Death from natural causes."

On the announcement of the verdict everyone rose, including myself and Mr. Otway, and the latter, turning to me, said in a low voice, "I think I won't wait. I want to get home and be quiet, but I shall call on you to-morrow, if I may, to make – ah – any – ah – arrangements that – ah – in fact, to speak to you about the – ah – the funeral."

"Very well," I said, reluctantly – for, deeply as I loathed him, I could not exclude him even from that sacred ceremony without creating an open scandal. "You had better come early in the forenoon." and with this I dismissed him with a stiff bow, and made my way to where Mr. Jackson and Dr. Thorndyke were standing. As I held out my hand to the latter and recalled to him our meeting years ago, Mr. Jackson said, "Dr. Thorndyke happened to be in Maidstone to-day and to call at our office, so I prevailed on him to come here and watch the proceedings on our behalf in case any complications should arise. But everything has gone off quite smoothly."

"Very smoothly indeed," Dr. Thorndyke agreed, with, as it seemed to me, a certain degree of emphasis.

"Both the coroner and the jury were most considerate," pursued Mr. Jackson.

"Most considerate," assented Dr. Thorndyke, and again I seemed to detect a note of emphasis, as also, I think, did Mr. Jackson, for he glanced quickly at our companion, though he made no remark.

"I wonder," said I, "if you two gentlemen would care to come and take a cup of tea with me?"

Mr. Jackson had an engagement at the office, and as Dr. Thorndyke appeared to hesitate, I added quickly, "I should be very glad if you could, though I don't wish to take up your time if you are busy."

"My time is my own for the next three hours," said Dr. Thorndyke, "and if I should really not be an inopportune visitor, I should like very much to have tea with you."

"Let us go, then," said I. "Mr. Jackson will accompany us as far as Gabriel's Hill, won't you?" And as my old friend assented with a prim, little bow, we set forth.

"I have offered no condolences, Mrs. Otway," said Dr. Thorndyke. "I knew your father, I saw you and him together, and I realize what this loss must mean to you. There is nothing to say except that you have my most real sympathy."

"Thank you," I said, and for a time we walked on in silence. And as we walked I found myself recalling, with a strong, speculative interest, that curious, subtle emphasis which Dr. Thorndyke had conveyed into his agreement with Mr. Jackson. At length, when we had dropped the latter near the Town Hall, I summoned up courage to raise the question.

"I have an impression, Dr. Thorndyke, which may be quite a mistaken one, that you were not completely satisfied with the way in which the inquest was conducted. Am I mistaken?"

"Well," he replied, slowly, "the coroner's methods were not what one would call rigorous."

"I suppose they were not. But in what respect are you disposed to find fault with them?"

"Principally," he replied, "in his failure to elicit a really conclusive verdict. The verdict of the jury was based upon Dr. Sharpe's opinion as to the cause of death. That opinion was probably correct, but it was based upon reasoning which was not sound. His position was this: If certain circumstances – excitement or exertion – should arise, there would be a great probability of their causing sudden death. But those circumstances had actually arisen and sudden death had actually followed. Therefore the death was due to the factors of the said circumstances. But this conclusion is fallacious. It does not prove a fact, it merely indicates a probability."

"But are not all verdicts statements of probability?"

"Too often they are. But it is a coroner's business to bring the conclusions of his court, as far as possible, into the region of ascertained fact. The immediate cause of death can usually be demonstrated by scientific methods, and the inquiry can then be built up on a foundation of certainty. Opinion should never be accepted where knowledge is obtainable."

"Do you think, then, that the verdict was not a proper one?"

"I am not criticizing the verdict," he replied, "but the methods by which it was arrived at. I think that the cause of death should have been established beyond all doubt before any contributory circumstances were inquired into."

"But otherwise, apart from that one point?"

"I thought the examination of the witnesses rather easy going. No doubt it elicited all the relevant facts. But that is impossible to decide on. One cannot judge of the relevancy of a fact until one has got the fact. I think, for instance, that most counsel would have pressed your husband a good deal more closely. The coroner appeared to decide that the matter was not relevant without being quite clear as to what matter he was dealing with."

This, I must confess, had been my own impression, but I had been so relieved at the manner in which the difficult passages had been allowed to pass that I had been little disposed to criticise the considerate and sympathetic coroner. Nor did it seem quite safe to pursue the present discussion much farther, for it was tending in a rather dangerous direction. My own reservations began to weigh on me somewhat – and Dr. Thorndyke was not quite the same type of listener as the coroner. Nevertheless, the conversation pleased me, though I could not but be struck by the oddity of this detached discussion of a matter which was of such vital moment to me. But that very oddity was itself an element of gratification, for a woman is naturally flattered when an intellectual man appears to credit her with the power of impartial judgment of her own conduct and affairs – that faculty not being one by which our sex is peculiarly distinguished.

But at this point, our discussion was brought naturally to an end by our arrival at my house – as I must now call it, and here a quick glance of surprised recognition on my companion's part gave me a new note of warning and prepared me for the inevitable question.

"You are living at your father's house, I see."

"I am, for the present. Mr. Otway remains in his own house."

"Yes. I suppose it will be more convenient to settle everything up here before joining your husband."

I was on the point of temporising by a vague assent, but my lips refused to frame the implied falsehood. It may have been my natural dislike of secrecy and concealment, it may be that my womanly pride resented the very idea of association with that unwieldy human spider. At any rate, an irresistible impulse drove me to say, "I am not going to join my husband at all, Dr. Thorndyke. I am not going to live with Mr. Otway."

I did not look at Dr. Thorndyke as I made this statement, and he made no comment beyond a matter-of-fact "Indeed." But I had the feeling that, in the silence that followed, he was fitting this new fact into its place in some ordered scheme, that he was docketting it as an appendix to Mr. Otway's evidence.

Nothing more was said until we had entered the house and I had given instructions for tea to be brought to the study. But in that interval I was aware of a growing impulse to have done with this miserable secrecy – this sordid fencing and dodging, which must come, in the end, to downright lying – and tell this strong, wise man the whole wretched story. Besides, I wanted counsel and guidance, and who was so fit to give them as he?

Accordingly, when the tray had been laid on the study table, I re-opened the subject.

"I did not mention this matter in my evidence," I said. "It had no bearing on the inquiry."

"I am not clear," he replied, "that you were entitled to make any reservations. A witness's duty is to state the whole truth. The question of relevancy is for the court to consider."

"But unfortunately there were other reservations that had to be made. Dr. Thorndyke, I want to tell you the whole story – in confidence – and to ask your advice."

"I counsel you to make no confidences," he said, gravely, "unless you really wish to consult me in my professional capacity."

"That is what I wish to do," I said.

"Very well," said he. "That places us in the secure relation of lawyer and client, and I need not say that your father's daughter is very welcome to any help or advice that I can give."

With this encouragement, I poured forth the story that I have told in these pages and in almost as much detail. But still I held back one fact. I said nothing of my having found Mr. Otway grasping my father's loaded stick. That single reservation had to be. Not only was I bound by a solemn promise, my silence on that point was the price of my release. The letter of the covenant, indeed, had reference only to my evidence at the inquest, but its spirit sealed my lips even in this my most intimate confidence.

And so, once again, a secret guarded from a friendly eye remained, like a seed dropped in a summer's drought, to germinate and bring forth its fruit in its season.

Chapter X
The Turning of the Page

Dr. Thorndyke listened to my recital of the history of the tragedy, not only with patience, but with close attention and apparently keen interest, interrupting me only at rare intervals to ask a question or elucidate some point that was not quite clear. When I had come to an end I was disposed to be apologetic, for I had told the story in the fullest detail, with only the single reservation that I have noted.

"I am afraid," I said, "that I have been rather victimizing you and trespassing on your very great patience."

"By no means," he replied. "Men and men's actions and motives are my merchandise. If I could listen to a story like yours without the deepest interest I should not be in my present profession. But, now that I have heard it, I think I can guess the subject on which you wish to consult me. You would like to annul your marriage with Mr. Otway."

"Yes, if it is possible."

"It is very natural that you should wish to recover your freedom. I sympathize with you entirely, and I wish I could give you some encouragement. But I fear that you have no remedy."

"It seems rather hard," I said, "that I should be bound for life to this man whom I detest and who has done me such grievous injuries."

"It is very hard," he agreed, "and, humanly speaking, there ought to be some remedy. But the law provides none, nor is it really possible for the law to make provision for every imaginable contingency. Yours is a very exceptional case."

"Yes, I see that, but it seems unreasonable to compel two people to maintain a relationship which is not only unsuitable but quite unreal."

"It does," he admitted. "But the law takes a very unsentimental view of these matters. It regards marriage as an institution concerned with the establishment of families and the orderly devolution of property, and its interference is, in the main, limited to circumstances connected with that assumed function. Of the human aspects of marriage it takes little account. In a purely legal sense – which is what we are considering – your position is this: You were competent to contract a marriage and you did contract one, of your own free will, without any compulsion or misrepresentation that the law would recognise. The circumstances that appeared to exist before the marriage still appear to exist. No new facts have come to light which would affect the competence of either party. It is a case in which one of the parties has disregarded the old legal maxim, *Caveat emptor* – Buyer beware! You bought, at a high price, something which turns out to be of no value. You agreed to marry Mr. Otway for a consideration – the release of your father from his embarrassments – which seemed to be valuable enough to justify the great sacrifice that you contemplated. But it turned out that your father needed no release, and the consideration thereupon ceased to have any value. As far as the law is concerned, you have simply made a very bad bargain."

"Does the law attach no importance to fraud?" I demanded.

"But has there been fraud?" he objected. "No representations, true or false, were made to you by Mr. Otway. You acted on knowledge which you assumed that you possessed. You laid down the conditions, he accepted them. You demanded a certain consideration, he furnished the consideration demanded. Even with regard to the letter from your father, we may – and do – suspect that he knew that it was in the box, and probably guessed at its contents. But we have no proof. Moreover, if he did know that it was there – even if he had opened it and read it, he was under no obligation to communicate its contents to you. Your agreement made no such provision. It laid down specific conditions, and with these Mr. Otway had fully complied. On the plea of fraud, I am afraid you would have no case."

"Apparently not," I agreed. "You are most horribly convincing, Dr. Thorndyke."

"I am putting the case as a lawyer, and very much against my own feeling as a man. But my present office is rather like that of a Devil's Advocate in a theological council. I think that this marriage ought to be annulled, but I am sure that, in point of law, it is not voidable.

"But there is yet another aspect of the case, and you must forgive me if I put it rather bluntly. There are not many women to whom I should have spoken in as downright a fashion as I have to you, and I shall continue to pay you this rather unpleasant compliment. Mrs. Otway, even if, legally speaking, you had a case, you could not take it into court."

"Why not?" I asked, more than a little startled.

"Because of the incidents of the inquest. You have spoken of certain reservations in your evidence. But in the case of Mr. Otway there was more than reservation. There was deliberate mis-statement, and that, too, in respect of a question that was highly material to the inquiry. He was asked the reason of your father's resentment of this marriage, and he stated it to be the disparity of age. But that was not the reason, and he knew it was not. Your father would have raised no obstacle if you had really wished to marry Mr. Otway. He resented the marriage because it had been brought about by means which he regarded as – morally speaking – fraudulent. Mr. Otway's evidence was false evidence, and it was deliberately given with the intention of misleading the jury."

"But it was a small point and of no importance. Besides, Mr. Otway's evidence is no concern of mine."

"Pardon me," Dr. Thorndyke objected, gravely, "the point was of very great importance. It would have started a train of entirely new issues. And Mr. Otway's evidence is very much your concern. You heard it given, you were asked if you confirmed it, and you did confirm it. There upon, Mr. Otway's evidence became your evidence.

"Now, if you were to embark on a suit for the annulment of your marriage, the plea of fraud, on which you would base your claim, would have to be supported by evidence which would conflict with that given by you at the inquest. Your position would be a very uncomfortable one, and it would be made more so by the fact that your evidence was in agreement with Mr. Otway's. When two witnesses agree in a departure from the actual facts known to them, a suspicion of collusion is apt to be raised, and collusion again suggests purpose and motive. I am afraid, Mrs. Otway, that the Devil's Advocate is making out a diabolically complete case. But that, you know, is his business. The conclusion is that a malignant fate has woven around you a mesh of circumstances from which there is no escape, and that the less you struggle the less irksome will be your bonds."

To this conclusion, unsatisfactory as it was, I assented with a readiness born not only of conviction but of a certain amount of alarm. I had heard my father speak with admiration of Dr. Thorndyke's amazing power of analysing evidence and extracting its essentials, and I now began to wonder how much of the actual truth he had extracted from the evidence at the inquest, elucidated by my narrative. His warning as to a possible suspicion of collusion with "a purpose and a motive" in the background set me speculating as to whether he, himself, entertained such a suspicion, and his next question was by no means reassuring on this point.

"You spoke," said he, "of having decided not to live with Mr. Otway, and of having communicated your intention to him. Do I understand that he assents to a separation?"

"Yes. He sees that the position would be quite impossible."

"Is your arrangement with him merely a verbal one, or has it been placed on a regular footing by a document of some kind?"

"Mr. Otway has executed a deed of separation, which I think is quite regular. But I had better let you see it."

With some trepidation, I produced the deed and nervously watched him as he read it through, which he did with an inscrutable expression, and – as it seemed to me – a horrible appearance of seeing through it to the rather questionable circumstances that had brought it into existence.

"Yes," he said, as he handed it back to me, "it is quite regular. You may congratulate yourself on finding Mr. Otway so compliant. It is more than one would have expected of him."

"He could hardly have done otherwise," I answered hastily. "We couldn't possibly have lived together after what had happened. Still, I am glad he took the reasonable view. It leaves me free to make my own arrangements for my future."

"And what arrangements do you propose – if your legal adviser is not too inquisitive."

"Not at all. I was going to ask you to advise me. I don't think there will be enough to support me, and, of course, I can't accept any help from Mr. Otway. I shall have to earn my living in some way."

"You could compel Mr. Otway to support you, but I appreciate your unwillingness to accept an allowance and thereby recognise the relationship. Have you any means of livelihood in your mind?"

I hesitated a little shyly. For I had, but my plan might sound rather an odd one, at least to a stranger.

"I thought," said I, at length, "of trying to get a living by doing what I have been accustomed to do as a hobby – by making simple jewellery and small, ornamental metal objects. I am afraid you will look on it as rather a wild scheme."

"No," he answered. "It is an unconventional scheme, but not in any way a wild one. I think we often appreciate insufficiently the wisdom of the artist's choice of his profession. In choosing a means of livelihood, we are choosing the way in which we shall spend the greater part of our lives. We have something to sell – the bulk of our waking lives – and we are apt to think too much of its selling price – its value to the purchaser – and not enough of its value to ourselves. A man, such as a navvy, a miner, a bank-clerk, or a factory hand, barters the means of subsistence so many hours a day spent in doing something that he does not want to do. He sells the best part of his life. But the artist or craftsman makes a much better bargain, for he contrives to obtain a subsistence by doing what he enjoys doing and what he would elect to do for his own satisfaction. He sells only the by-products of his life, the whole of that life he retains for his own use, to be spent as he would, in any case, wish to spend it. But there is an inevitable *proviso*: His acceptable occupation must really yield a subsistence. His wares must be of value to the purchaser, and he must be able to find a market. Do you think you could satisfy those conditions?"

"I think I could make the things pretty well, but, as to selling them, that is a different matter. I have to find that out. May I show you some of my work?"

"I should like very much to see some of it," he replied.

"I will fetch a few pieces. And meanwhile, that clock on the mantelpiece is partly my work. My father made the clock, itself, but I made the dial, the hands and the case."

Dr. Thorndyke rose, and, stepping over to the mantelpiece, looked at the work with keen interest. It was a little bracket-clock with a bronze dial, a silver circle for the figures, silver-gilt hands, and a simple wooden case decorated with gesso. Leaving my visitor to inspect it, I went away and collected a few samples of my work in metal, a bronze candlestick, an enamelled silver belt-buckle, a gold pendant set with opals, and one or two silver spoons, all of which Dr. Thorndyke examined with that friendly interest – unmistakeable to the artist or craftsman – that evinces some knowledge of and liking for the thing examined.

"Well," he said, as he laid down the last of the spoons, "these things answer the first question. They are quite workmanlike, and they are attractive and tastefully designed. The next question is the economic one. Could you sell them? And if so, would they realize a price that would furnish a reasonable livelihood? You would have to compete with commercial products made in large numbers by cheap processes. Your hammered, embossed, and chased work would compete with work stamped from steel dies or with comparatively rough castings. Of course, your work is infinitely better value, but this is a commercial age, and buyers are bad judges. And then you would have to sell to dealers who would demand not less than fifty-per-cent profit, which, I am afraid, would leave you a pitiable small return for your labour and skill."

"Yes," I agreed. "That is all quite true. But still, I think I will try. The work would be interesting and pleasant, and, as you implied just now, an artist cannot expect to be paid as much for doing what he likes doing as another man receives for doing what he dislikes. Pleasant work is, to some extent at least, its own reward, and if my work doesn't yield enough to live on, I shall have to try something else. But I don't suppose I shall be absolutely without means when my father's estate has been wound up."

"Do you think of continuing to live here?" Dr. Thorndyke asked.

"No. As soon as everything is settled, I propose to go to London. It will be much easier – or, at least, less difficult – to dispose of my work there."

"Undoubtedly. And have you any definite arrangements in your mind – where and how you are going to live, for instance?

"None whatever, at present."

"I ask because I happen to know of a place where you could put up, at least temporarily, where you would be comfortably lodged, well fed and cared for, and where you could pursue your labours under good working conditions and at small expense. There is only one drawback, but you may consider that a fatal one: It is in the immediate neighbourhood of Ratcliff Highway – or, as it has been renamed, St. George's Street."

"Is that a very dreadful place?"

"It is far from being an aristocratic locality. But let me describe the establishment. It is conducted by a Miss Polton, who is the sister of my laboratory assistant – a most expert and talented mechanician. Miss Polton was at one time a nurse, but when her brother entered my employment, he was able to help her to set up in Wellclose Square, Ratcliff, a boarding-house for mercantile marine officers. At the same time, she, being like her brother, a highly-capable, ingenious person, got herself a hand-loom and took up weaving as a hobby. But since then times have changed. Sailing ships have to a great extent disappeared, and Miss Polton's clients with them, while the hobby of making excellent cloth has turned out quite a profitable one. So Miss Polton plies her shuttle industriously, and, in the place of the merchant seamen, has collected a little family of women who also work at handicrafts for their living. I believe they form quite a happy little community and, of course, they are able to assist one another in disposing of their wares. So that is the position. I know that Miss Polton has room for another boarder, for it is quite a large house – Wellclose Square was once the abode of well-to-do shipowners and retired sea-captains – and I am sure she would welcome another novice to her community. The drawback, as I have said, is the neighbourhood, which is – to put it bluntly – just a trifle squalid."

"I don't see that the neighbourhood matters," said I, "and in every other respect it sounds like the very thing I want."

"I think you would be quite well-advised to give it a trial. You would be among friends and fellow-workers and, if you found that the neighbourhood was too much for you, you would be in London and could seek a new residence at your leisure. I will write the address on one of my cards, and if on reflection you decide to give Ratcliff a trial, you can write to Miss Polton and me at the same time."

He wrote the address, and, handing me the card, stood up and glanced at his watch.

"How long will it take me to walk to the station?" he asked.

"Less than twenty minutes."

"I have half-an-hour, so I can walk easily. Good-bye, Mrs. Otway. I wish I could have given you a better account of your position. But I can only advise you to make the best of a bad bargain and keep your own counsel."

"You have been most kind, Dr. Thorndyke," I said, earnestly, "in giving me so much time and patient attention. I don't know how I can thank you."

"I will tell you," said he. "By keeping a good heart and letting me know how your affairs progress."

He shook my hand heartily, and, when I had let him out, strode down the garden path, the very personification of manly dignity, alertness, and vigour. At the gate he turned to raise his hat, with a smile of friendly farewell, and I closed the door and turned back into the house, feeling, for the first time since my father's death, that I was not alone in the world, but that, if the need should arise, the strength of this strong, commanding man was at my call.

The short remainder of my life at Maidstone I shall pass over briefly. It comes back to me in scenes like those of a play, separate but related. I see the interior of the parish church – noble, spacious, cathedral-like. I hear the voice of the clergyman reciting reverently those flowers of ancient poetry rendered into perfect English speech that usher the departed into the realms of silence with so gracious a dignity, I see the flower-strewn coffin sink into the grave wherein sleeps my unremembered mother, while the russet-sailed barges glide past the churchyard on the placid river below towards the mills at Tovil. And so farewell for ever to the best of fathers and the kindest, most lovable of friends.

These closing weeks, in which I wound up my old life and made ready for the new, were full of bustle and unrest. I had written to Miss Polton and Dr. Thorndyke, and from the former had received a kindly letter assuring me of the warmest welcome, and now I was busily collecting my tools and workshop appliances and packing them into travelling boxes to be dispatched with my heavier luggage. There was the furniture to be stored or set aside for sale, the servants to be placed in new situations, and various business to be transacted with Mr. Jackson – who, indeed, relieved me of all that lay within his powers.

Then there was Mr. Otway, from whom I received an abject letter and with whom I must needs have a rather distressing interview. He was really horrified at my proposed mode of life (I suspect he had never done a stroke of manual work in his life), and even more so at my proposed place of residence, and was, I believe, sincerely distressed at my firm refusal to permit him to make me an allowance. Indeed, the devotion

358

which he professed for me, little as I wanted it, seemed to be as real as was possible in the case of a man so self-centred and so callously egoistic. But the very sight of him hardened my heart and lighted up afresh my indignation at the havoc that he had wrought in my life. What I had agreed to do, I did, but I made no hair's breadth of concession. I gave him my future address, and agreed to his addressing letters there, but I refused resolutely to receive any visits from him, or even to enter into any correspondence other than that which circumstances might render necessary.

And now the last day has come, the day of final parting. I see myself wandering through the empty house, stripped of all but the barest necessaries and filled with new and strange echoes, the van drawn up at the gate to take away the last of the furniture, and the tearful Jessie carrying my two little portmanteaux down the path to the porter's barrow. I see her return, wiping her eyes and gazing at me in dumb appeal, and, with a sudden impulse of tenderness, I kiss her and stroke her hair, whereupon she bursts into tears and throws herself sobbing on to my breast.

It was hard to close the old life, which had been so sweet and peaceful, so full and satisfying, to bid farewell to the beautiful old town which was the only place I had known and which I had loved so well. As I took my way through the streets, attaché-case in hand, all my old friends seemed to look on me reproachfully and call on me to stay. The quaint plaster-fronted house in Week Street, the venerable medieval pile at the corner of Gabriel's Hill, the grinning masks on the corbels of the old house-fronts of Middle Row – all the old familiar landmarks had suddenly grown dear and precious, and each exacted its twinge of regret as I looked my last on it. On the bridge, I halted to survey the upper river, with the church and the Old Palace, both embowered in trees and brooding over the quiet water. Often as I had looked upon that view, it had never seemed to me so pleasant and desirable as now. And with this last impression – to be recalled how often in the troubled future! – I turned away and headed resolutely for the station.

BOOK II – ROMANCE

Chapter XI
A Harbour of Refuge

It was the cabman who first made it clear to me that my town address was somewhat out of the common. He had stowed my two portmanteaux on the roof (it was a four-wheeled cab) and, descending to hold the door open for me to enter, shut it after me with a bang and waited while I stated my destination.

"I beg your pardon, Miss," he said, incredulously. "Did you say Wellclose Square?"

"Yes. Number Sixty-nine."

Again he regarded me with wrinkled brows. "That won't be Wellclose Square down by the Docks?" he suggested.

"I don't know if it's near the Docks," I replied, "but it isn't far from Ratcliff Highway."

"That's the place, sure enough," said he. "Number Sixty-nine, Well, I'm jiggered." With this he turned and slowly climbed to the box, looking in at me through the front window as he mounted, and even when he had taken his seat and gathered up the reins, he took yet another confirmatory glance over his shoulder before starting. These mysterious proceedings occasioned me some surprise, not entirely unmixed with anxiety. Dr. Thorndyke had admitted that the neighbourhood was squalid, and the question arose: How squalid was it? The first part of the journey, through Eastcheap and Great Tower Street, was rather reassuring, and as we crossed Tower Hill and the grey pile of ancient buildings loomed up above the trees, I was quite pleasantly impressed. But then came a change for the worse. Long streets of characterless houses, all of a dingy, grey colour – the colour of all-pervading dirt – and growing greyer and dingier as we proceeded, populated by men and women, and especially children, of the same cobwebby tint, with something foreign and unfamiliar in their aspect and manners – a deficiency of artificial head covering with a remarkable profusion of the natural, and a tendency to sit about on doorsteps – these, with a general outbreak on the shop signs of Wowskys, Minskys, Stems, and Popoffs, were the features of the neighbourhood that chiefly attracted my attention as the cab rattled eastward. But there was not much time for extended observation, for I had barely noted these appearances when we turned into a short side-street and emerged into a square, the dingyness of which was somewhat relieved by a group of faded trees in the central enclosure.

Round the square the cab trundled slowly until it drew up opposite a tall house of the Georgian type, with white window frames and a green door. As the cab stopped, the green door opened, and a small elderly lady came forth, while three younger women lurked in the background. Escaping from the cab, I advanced to meet the elderly lady, who received me with a singularly pleasant smile and a few quietly-spoken words of welcome, a proceeding that was observed with furtive interest by the cabman as he transferred my portmanteaux from the cab-roof to the pavement and thence to the hall. Nor did his curious observation of me cease until it was brought to an end by actual invisibility, for, as the cab moved out of the square, I saw his face still turned towards me over the roof, with the same I expression of puzzled surprise.

"You would like to see your room, I expect," said the elderly lady whom I had correctly assumed to be Miss Polton. "Then we will have tea and talk over your arrangements." She moved towards the stairs (up which I had just seen one of the young women hopping with surprising agility, with one of my portmanteaux in either hand), and conducted me to a room on the second floor, where the portmanteaux had been duly deposited, though the bearer had vanished.

"It's rather bare," said Miss Polton, "but you can have some pictures and ornaments if you like. My young ladies usually prefer to have their own things and arrange them in their own way. Your workroom is downstairs. I consulted my brother about it, and he said he thought you would like a room with a stone floor if you were going to do hammered work and use a furnace. So, as I had one with quite a good light, I have kept it for you – that is, of course, if you like it."

"I expect I shall," I replied. "A wooden floor is dreadfully noisy when one is hammering on a stake, and not very safe when there are red-hot crucibles about."

"Yes," she agreed, "and you can have a mat for your feet when you are sitting at the bench. And now I will leave you and go and see about the tea."

Left to myself, I looked around at my new home. The room, though spacious, was undeniably bare, but yet it gave me an impression of comfort. For its bareness was due merely to the absence of superfluities. The empty walls, distempered a pale cream colour, were severe to baldness, but how much better than the usual boarding house walls, covered with staring flowered paper and disfigured with horrible prints or illuminated texts. They, like the empty book-shelves, were ready to

362

receive the personal touches and to become friendly and sympathetic. Of actual necessaries, there were more than in many an over-furnished room: A small wardrobe, a good-sized firm table, a chest of drawers with a looking-glass on it, a small writing chair, a comfortable folding arm-chair, a washing-stand and a sponge bath, besides the book-shelves aforesaid, and a daintily-furnished bed, gave me a foundation of material comfort and convenience on which it would be easy to build and make additions. As I concluded my survey and refreshed myself with a wash, I decided that, whatever the surroundings of the house might be like, its interior seemed to have the makings of a home.

Nor was I less favourably impressed when I went downstairs. The dining-room, in which I found the ladies assembled, was pervaded by an air of spotless cleanliness with a severity approaching bareness. The absence of superfluous furniture and useless ornaments and bric-a-brac struck me, indeed, as rather odd in a household composed – so far as I knew – entirely of women.

"I must introduce you to the family," said Miss Polton, with a pleasant wrinkly smile, "at least those who are at home. There are three more who will come in to dinner. This is Miss Blake, and these ladies are Miss Barnard and Miss Finch."

I shook hands with my new comrades – the last being the little lady who had skipped up the stairs so actively with my luggage – and then we sat down to the table, at the head of which Miss Polton presided, and made the tea in a delightful Delft teapot from a brass kettle on which I cast an expert and somewhat disapproving eye, for it was of a blatantly commercial type and quite unworthy of the teapot. At first, conversation was spasmodic and punctuated by considerable pauses. Miss Polton was evidently a silent, self-contained woman, though genial in a quiet, restful way. Miss Finch, too, who sat by me, was quiet and a little shy, speaking rarely but silently plying me with food. Miss Blake, on the other hand, had a restless manner, and, though she spoke little at first, was undisguisedly interested in me, for whenever I looked at her I caught her wide-open, blue eyes fixed on me with an intensity that was almost embarrassing. She was a rather remarkable-looking girl, with a wealth of red-gold hair, a white-and-pink complexion, and a profile which, with its sharp, projecting chin and *retroussé* nose, might have been taken direct from one of Miss Burne-Jones's allegories – indeed, my first glance at her made me think of the "Briar Rose" and the "Golden Stairs". And now, as I caught her intense gaze again and again, I had the feeling that she was wanting to say something to me, and the more so since I thought I detected a certain expectancy in the expression of her neighbour, Miss Barnard. Nor was I mistaken, for, after one of the periodic pauses in the conversation, she leaned over the table towards me and said in low, portentous tones, "Mrs. Otway, I want to ask you a question, if you won't think me too inquisitive." Here she paused – and Miss Barnard also paused in the conveyance to her mouth of a large piece of bread and marmalade.

Miss Polton explained that "Miss Blake was somewhat of a mystic."

"Like her famous namesake," said I.

"And ancestor," Miss Blake added, eagerly.

"Really!" I exclaimed, clutching at this straw. "You are actually a descendant of William Blake? And I dare say you are a great admirer of his works?"

"I should think she is!" exclaimed Miss Barnard. "You should just see her fashion plates."

Recalling Blake's usual rendering of the human figure and its unadaptability to the conditions of our climate, I secretly resolved to take an early opportunity of examining those fashion plates. Meanwhile, I remarked, "I was thinking of his poems rather than the drawings."

"Yes," said Miss Blake, "though the drawings are very spiritual, too. But to return to my question. You see, I had been looking at your face. It is a face, you know, in which the workings of the subconscious appear, as it were. It's an extraordinary psychic face, do you know?"

"Is it?" said I, noting that Miss Barnard had broken out into a slow smile, which she was trying to obliterate with the lump of bread and marmalade.

"Oh, very. Intensely so."

"I don't suppose your question would be too inquisitive," I said, guardedly.

"It isn't really," said she. "You know, I have been I have been looking at your face, watching it with deep interest, and I have been hoping that, at last, I had met with a kindred spirit. I do hope – I feel convinced – that I have. I've been wondering if you are, as I am, a dweller in the larger world beyond that inhabited by the conscious self, beyond the mere material universe. Is it not so, Mrs. Otway?"

Now this was a "facer". As my dear father would have expressed it in his playful fashion, it "knocked me side-ways". I cast a bewildered glance round the table, and was aware of a very extensive outbreak of tact, Miss Polton was blandly indulgent, her face transformed into a network of amiable wrinkles, Miss Finch was engaged in an intense scrutiny of the bowl of a jam spoon, while Miss Barnard's feats, with the bread and marmalade, were becoming positively dangerous.

"I am not sure I understand your question, Miss Blake," I managed to respond at length.

"Perhaps I did not put my question very clearly – it is difficult to be very definite when one is speaking of the psychic life, but I was wondering if you had ever had experiences that had made you aware of that larger world beyond the world of mere matter and sense-perception, if you had sometimes felt the thoughts of other minds stealing into your own without the aid of speech or bodily presence and even, perhaps, held converse with those dear to you who, while they have passed out of this little, material world, still share with you the greater world in which soul speaks to soul unhampered by the limitations – "

The humorous wrinkles had suddenly faded from Miss Polton's face, leaving it grave and quiet, and now, in a quiet, grave voice, she interposed, "I think, Lilith, dear, that Mrs. Otway's griefs are too new and too real – "

"I know!" Miss Blake exclaimed, impulsively. "I am an egotistical wretch. It was horrid of me to be so wrapped up in my own interests. I am so sorry, so very, very sorry. Please forgive me, dear Mrs. Otway! Let us talk of something else."

"I don't think we must talk of anything much longer," said Miss Polton. "We have finished tea and we ought to get on with our work. Besides, Mrs. Otway will want to unpack her things and set her room in order."

On this there was a general up-rising. Miss Finch immediately fell to work gathering up the debris and returning the cups and saucers to the tray, while Miss Blake renewed her apologies and expressions of sympathy. Then Miss Polton took possession of me and, having shown me my workshop – a smallish, well-lighted room, with a paved floor and a large window looking on an unexpectedly pleasant garden – took me upstairs to a box-room in which my personal luggage had been deposited.

"Supper is at eight o'clock," said she. "We have made it rather late so that everyone may have a good, long day's work and all the wanderers may have come home. It is the social event of the day. And now I will leave you to your unpacking."

She tripped away up a narrow flight of stairs that opened from the landing, towards what I took to be the attics, from whence presently came a rhythmical "click-clack" that I associated with the loom of which Dr. Thorndyke had spoken. Meanwhile, I fell to work on my trunks, with a view to transferring their contents to my room, but I had hardly got them open when Miss Finch appeared at the open door.

"Can I help you?" she asked. "If I carry some of the things down you won't have so many journeys."

"But aren't you busy?" I asked in return.

"Do I look like it? No, I'm lazy this afternoon, but I should like to help you, if you will let me."

Of course I was only too glad, and forthwith loaded her with an armful of books, following her with a second consignment. For some time we continued our journeys up and down the stairs with very little said on either side, and gradually my room began to lose its emptiness and severity, and to take on the friendly aspect of an inhabited apartment.

"It doesn't look so bad," said Miss Finch, surveying it critically. "Looks as if someone lived in it. Do you like the wash-stand?"

"I've been admiring it. It's so simple and so tasteful and unusual."

"Yes, and yet it is only stained deal, with a few touches of gesso. Phillibar made it – Phyllis Barton, you know. You'll meet her at supper.

"Is she a carpenter?"

"No, she makes frames for mirrors and pictures, wooden frames decorated with gesso, or compo, or else carved. But she's very thorough. Does it all herself. Makes up the frames from the plank, makes the compo and the moulds and does the gilding. And she is quite a good wood-worker and carves beautifully."

"And does she make a pretty good living?" I asked, bearing Dr. Thorndyke's observations in mind.

"She does quite well now, though she had a hard struggle at first. But now she works direct for the artists and gets as much as she can do. You will often see her frames in the exhibitions. The floor-cloth is rather nice, too, isn't it, though it is only stencilled sacking. You'd be surprised to see how durable it is. The more it is worn, the better it looks – if it is properly done. This is stencilled with a stain. Lilith did it."

"Lilith? Is that Miss Blake?"

"Yes. Her name is really Winifred, but we call her Lilith because she looks as if she had come out of a stained-glass window. You might think that she was a little – well, a little barmy. But she's awfully clever."

"She does fashion-plates, doesn't she?

"Yes, poor Lilith! She hates them, but she does them rippingly all the same. She would rather paint pictures or mural decorations or design tapestries, but you've got to do what you can sell, you know, if you want to make a living, and Lilith has a little brother whom she keeps at school – an awfully nice little kiddie. She's a really good sort, you know, though frightfully spooky – planchette, crystal ball, and all that sort of tosh, and she thinks she has found a fellow-spook, so you will have to look out."

As Miss Finch paused to take another survey, her eye and mine fell upon the wash-stand, or rather on what it supported.

"I think," I remarked, "that I shall have to treat myself to some new crockery. That jug and basin are hardly worthy of Miss Barton's masterpiece."

"No, they're horrid, aren't they? Regular Whitechapel china-shop stuff. But I believe I've got some – I'll just run up and see."

She tripped away up the stairs and presently returned, bearing a basin and pitcher of simple, reddish-buff earthen ware glazed internally with a fine green glaze.

"They are frightfully crude and coarse," she said apologetically (and with cheeks several shades redder than the ware), "but they aren't vulgar. Would you like to have them until you can get something better?"

"I shall have them a long time, then," said I. "They are charming – delightful – and they suit the wash-stand perfectly. What a house this is for pottery! I noticed the teapot and the beautiful cups and plates, all so interesting and uncommon. And now you produce these wonderful things like some benevolent enchantress. How do you do it? Do you keep a crystal ball, too?"

Miss Finch laughed and blushed very prettily. "We all do our little bit towards making the home presentable and saving expense. Miss Polton distempered these walls, and Joan Allen painted the woodwork – you'll like Joan, I think, she paints portraits when she can get them, and fills in her time by doing magazine covers and book-wrappers. We shall expect a diploma work from you, too. You're a goldsmith, aren't you?"

It was my turn to laugh and blush as this magnificent title was applied to me. "Not exactly a goldsmith," I protested. "Say, rather, a very elementary jeweller and metal-worker, or perhaps a coppersmith. And, as we have finished with this room for the present, I had better begin to get my workshop in going order."

"And you'll let me help you with that, too, won't you?" said Miss Finch, with a wheedling air, and as I gladly accepted her help, she linked her arm in mine and we descended together to the scene of my future labours.

My experience of various workers has led me to observe that manual skill is a much more generalized quality than is commonly realized. The old saw of the "Jack of all trades and master of none" is entirely misleading, for manual skill acquired in the practice of one art is largely transferable to others. The acquirement of a particular kind of skill results in the establishment of a generally increased manual faculty, so that a person who has completely learned one handicraft is already more than half-way towards the attainment of skill in any other. This fact was impressed upon me as I watched little Miss Finch and noted her extraordinary handiness with probably unfamiliar appliances and her instant comprehension of the uses of things that she had probably never seen before. My two benches – the jeweller's and the general bench – had fortunately been made in a portable form, and now had to be joined up with their screw-bolts. But my little assistant took this in at a glance, and, before I had half-finished unpacking the tool cases, she had the bench-tops up-ended, had sorted out the legs, struts and the appropriate bolts, and was hard at work with the spanner. Yet, as she worked, she kept an alert and interested eye on the tools and appliances that came forth from the cases.

"What a jolly little muffle!" she exclaimed, as I deposited the small enamel furnace on the floor, pending the erection of its stand, "but won't it eat up the gas. You'll have to have your own meter – watch it, too, to see that your earnings don't all go to the gas company. And what a little duck of an anvil! But what on earth are those things?" pointing to a bundle of body-tools and snarling irons.

I explained the use of these mysterious appliances and of sundry others and so, with a good deal of gossip, partly personal and partly technical, we worked on until the sound of the first supper-bell sent us to our rooms to make ourselves presentable, by which time the fitting out of the workshop was so far advanced as to make it possible for me to begin work on the morrow.

The great social function of supper introduced me to the rest of my comrades, Phyllis Barton, who turned out, to my surprise, to be a tiny, frail-looking middle-aged woman of meek aspect – I had pictured her as a large, muscular, boisterous young woman. Joan Allen, who really corresponded somewhat to this description, and whom I detected more than once in the act of inspecting me with one eye closed, and a tall, rather shy girl, by name Edith Palgrave, a scrivener and calligrapher, who, I learned from Miss Finch, wrote, by choice, Church service books and illuminated addresses, but, by necessity, gained her principal livelihood by writing shop-tickets.

It was a pleasant genial gathering, homely, informal, and yet quite regardful of the indispensable social amenities. What the social class of my companions might have been I could hardly guess. They were all educated women, of good intelligence and pleasant manners, all keenly interested in one another's doings, but each fully occupied with her own activities. The agreeable impression was conveyed that, in this little human hive, the companionship arising from the community of domestic life tended in no way to hinder a self-contained person like myself from living her own life and pursuing her own interests and satisfactions.

And so, when, somewhat early, I retired to my room to spend an hour with my books before going to bed, my thoughts turned gratefully to Dr. Thorndyke, and I congratulated myself not a little on having found this quiet anchorage in which to rest after the stormy passages of my troubled life.

Chapter XII
The Hidden Hand

I had been settled in my new home about a month when I received a letter from Mr. Jackson. It was principally devoted to a report on business matters concerned with the disposal of my father's practice and the sale of the surplus furniture and effects, but it contained one passage that gave me considerable food for thought. The passage in question had been added as a postscript, and ran thus, *"You have probably heard that Mr. Otway has left Maidstone. I fancy things had become rather uncomfortable for him. From what transpired at the inquest, an impression got abroad that he was, to a great extent responsible for your father's death, and there was consequently a rather strong feeling against him. I don't know where he has gone, but rumour has it that he has migrated to London."*

This was, in more than one respect, somewhat disquieting news. I turned it over again and again as I sat at my bench and tried to estimate its significance. The inquest had "gone off quite smoothly", as Mr. Jackson had expressed it, but it was clear that some, at least, of the persons present had read a meaning into the evidence which the coroner and his jury seemed to have missed. Dr. Thorndyke was one of these, but, as no rumour could be traceable to him, there were evidently others. What did this portend? To Mr. Jackson it meant no more than a local prejudice. To me, conscious of a secret covenant which I had not dared to confide even to Dr. Thorndyke, it conveyed an uneasy feeling that suspicion was abroad, that it might become cumulative, and that, even yet, that covenant might be dragged into the light of day which it would bear so ill.

Ever since my talk with Dr. Thorndyke, my conscience had been somewhat ill at ease. I felt that, as a witness giving testimony on oath, I had been at least uncandid, if not positively untruthful, and the word "collusion" had acquired an unpleasantly personal quality.

And then, what of Mr. Otway? Had he slipped away out of my life to hide himself where suspicion would not reach him? Or had he really migrated to London, and would his sinister shadow presently fall upon my new life as it had done upon the old? My hopes pictured him driven by his fears – for he was a timorous man – far afield, perhaps beyond the seas, but a presentiment whispered that I had not heard or seen the last of him.

It was a few days later, in fact, that I returned from a walk to find a letter from Mr. Otway, requesting me to see him. I met him the following day at the Tower Wharf. He was more agitated even than usual, and rose to greet me with a audible explanation of relief. "Miss Vardon – that is – Mrs. – ah – Helen. I have received a letter."

"Your correspondence is of no interest to me." I told him coldly.

"But the contents of this one are so extraordinary that I ventured to write to you about it. I hoped you would – er – respond to my appeal. It is strange," he added, "considering what our relations are and what your feelings are towards me, that I seem to look to you, and to you alone, for support and counsel in this – er – this unexpected trouble."

"I don't suppose," said I, "that any counsel of mine will be of much value to a man of your experience. But perhaps you had better tell me what the trouble is. Shall we sit down here? You spoke of having received a letter."

"Yes," he replied, as we sat down on a seat near the bridge. "It is an anonymous letter, and its purport is – ah – very singular, and is – ah – to the effect that – er – in fact – "

"Is there any objection to your repeating the actual wording of the letter?" I asked.

"Well, no. Certainly not. Perhaps it would be better. You are really remarkably business-like and clear-headed. I suppose it is your upbringing and being so much with your father. No, there is no objection. In fact – " Here he produced from his pocket, with evident reluctance, a leather wallet, from which he extracted a folded paper. "In fact, you may as well see the letter for yourself."

I took the paper from him, and opening it found it to be a quite short letter, typewritten upon ordinary typist's paper, without any address or other heading, and undated save for Mr. Otway's written and signed endorsement. There was no signature, but in place of one was written in typed characters, "*A Well Wisher*" and this is what it said:

Mr. Lewis Otway,

The undersigned is writing to put you on your guard because Somebody knows something about how Mr. Vardon came by his death, and that somebody is not friend, so you had better keep a sharp look out for your enemy and see what they mean to do. I can't tell you any more at present.

A Well Wisher

I read it through twice, noting, the second time, the peculiar construction, the faulty grammar and punctuation, and especially the confusion in the pronouns which is so characteristic of the writing of an uneducated person. Of course, these peculiarities might have been assumed as a disguise, but they established a probability that the writer was a person of indifferent education, to which class, indeed, the bulk of anonymous letter-writers belong. I handed the document back to Mr. Otway and asked, "Does this letter convey anything to you?"

"Nothing," he replied. "Absolutely nothing. It speaks of somebody knowing something. But that is impossible. There was no one in the house but you and I and – er – your father. Besides, there is nothing to know – excepting what you know."

"Have you any idea or suspicion as to who the writer of this letter may be?"

"None whatever. I have not the faintest clue. You see, there is nobody in the world who has any – er – any special knowledge of the – ah – the exact circumstances but yourself." He paused for a few moments, and then, in a lower tone, asked hesitatingly, "I suppose, Helen, you cannot – er – guess or – ah – surmise who might have – "

I looked up quickly and caught a furtive glance which was instantly averted, and in a moment it was borne in on me that he suspected me of either being the writer or concerned in writing of this letter.

"Mr. Otway," said I, speaking slowly and quietly, the better to command my temper, "if you have any idea that I know anything of this wretched production, dismiss it. If you have any idea that there lurks in my mind any suspicion that your account of my father's death was untrue, dismiss that, too. If I had known, or even had the smallest grounds for suspecting, that my father met with foul play, you would not have had to wait till now to hear from me, nor would my communication have reached you in this form or through these channels."

As I said this, looking at him, I do not doubt, sternly and forbiddingly enough, he turned horribly pale and seemed to shrink visibly. He was completely cowed – so much so that, cordially as I detested him, I felt really sorry for him.

"You mistake me, Helen. You misjudge me," he protested, huskily, "you do, indeed. I had no intention – I never, for one moment, suspected – but why do I say this? Of course, you must know I did not. I merely thought it possible that you might be able to guess – you might know of some person – "

"I do not, Mr. Otway," said I. "No one connected with me has any knowledge that is not public knowledge. Nor do I believe that anyone else has. I should say that this person – apparently a person of the lower

372

class – is just a common blackmailer, who was present at, or has read the report of, the inquest, and is trying to make you believe that some suspicion attaches to you." I could not but admire the adroitness with which Mr. Otway made me a participator in his own difficulties and secured me as an ally against his unseen enemy. And the blackmailer is a rather formidable enemy to a man who is concealing an incriminating fact. We were partners in an unlawful act. That, I had already recognised, and the different significance of that act in our respective cases did not so very much affect our position in the present circumstances.

"Probably you are right, Helen. But you notice that there is no threat – no, direct threat, at least – and that there is no suggestion of any attempt to obtain money from me."

"Perhaps that will come later," said I.

Again he drew a long breath and cast a furtive glance at me. "Perhaps it will," he agreed. "This may be the preliminary move, the laying of ground-bait, so to speak. It's a harassing business, Helen. What do you think I had better do? You see, I rely on you for counsel, although I am so much older. But you have your father's gift of clear judgment and perfect coolness in emergencies."

It was rather a tactless observation, for it recalled vividly my dear father's coolness in that last, fatal emergency, his composure and unruffled cheerfulness when the menace of ruin and disgrace – set up by Mr. Otway – had seemed poised over his head, ready to fall at any moment, and the recollection did not tend to increase my present sympathy.

"For my part," I said, coldly, "I should do nothing at present. I should ignore this letter and wait for the writer to show his hand more clearly. If he should make any threats or demands for hush-money, I should at once put the matter in the hands of the police."

I could see that this advice – particularly the latter part of it – did not greatly commend itself to Mr. Otway. Nor did it to me. But circumstances offered no choice. Any risk is better than that of life-long subjection to a blackmailer.

"It would be very unsafe," said Mr. Otway, "to have – any dealings with the police. They are pretty severe on blackmailers, but they are naturally ready to listen to anyone who professes to have information to give them. And a blackmailer may be very dangerous if he is brought to bay. We couldn't afford to have any enquiries made that might seem to establish what they would call collusion to suppress evidence. We know that the facts that we withheld were not material. Other people would not."

I had nothing further to say, but to repeat that I should ignore the letter, and for a time we sat silent, looking out on the river. Mr. Otway drew a deep breath and reflected gloomily. Perhaps my suggestion was not a very comforting one, for an uncomfortable aspect of the case was that he was right.

"Well," said Mr. Otway, at length, "so be it. We will wait and see what happens. And now let us put this miserable affair away and talk about your future. I have seen some of your work, and I am sure that you could get good prices for it if it were placed in the proper quarter. But the ordinary shops would be of no use to you. The common retailer does not know or care anything about individual work. He just buys from the wholesaler or the manufacturer, and sells to the public. He would probably not look at your work, or if he were willing to buy it, he would pay no more than he pays to the manufacturer who rattles off his goods by the thousand, with the aid of cheap labour and machinery.

"But there are people who know the difference between artists' works and manufactured goods, and are willing to pay for the better things. And there are dealers who supply them. Mr. Campbell is one. I have known him for many years, and I can assure you that he is an excellent judge of works of art and very anxious to get the best for his customers, who are mostly good judges, too. He is well known in artistic circles and, as he is able to dispose of things of real value, he can afford to pay the artist a fair price. I strongly advise you to give him a trial. Of course, I would infinitely rather that you accepted an allowance from me, but if you really – "

"It is very good of you, Mr. Otway, but I assure you that it is out of the question."

"Very well, then. If you are quite resolved, I can only advise you to make the most profitable use of your talents. Go to Mr. Campbell, and I am sure that you will be treated fairly."

I thanked him for his advice and promised to act on it, and very shortly after this I brought the interview to an end.

As I took my way slowly back to Wellclose Square, I reflected on the new developments that my meeting with Mr. Otway had disclosed. That some mischief was brewing there could hardly be a doubt. The disguise of the "Well Wisher" was too thin to create any illusion. As to the somebody who knew something, he was an obvious myth, for, as Mr. Otway had said, the circumstances did not admit of anyone knowing even what was known to me. My own explanation was that some person who had been present at the inquest had observed Mr. Otway's excessive nervousness and had marked him as a likely subject for blackmailing operations. It was a chance shot and nothing more.

374

But Mr. Otway's evident alarm was not difficult to account for. He was a naturally timorous man, he had been subjected to a great and prolonged strain, and he had an incriminating secret. His position was, in fact, one of appreciable danger, as he fully realized. If the details of my father's death had been fully disclosed at the inquest, Mr. Otway's statement and explanation would probably have been accepted without demur. But the suppression of certain material facts put a different complexion on the matter. If the inquiry were now revived, he would have to explain, not only the original circumstances, but his motives for suppressing them. He had very good reason for alarm.

And yet his abject terror produced an uncomfortable impression on me. I could not disguise from myself that the whole tragedy of my father's death was due to an error of judgment on my part. The secret marriage was the outcome of a mistake. Woman-like, I had acted on a strong conviction, and that conviction had been wrong. What if I had once again acted on an erroneous belief? I had assumed that Mr. Otway's account of my dear father's death was correct. There had seemed to be excellent reasons for the assumption. But what if I had been wrong, after all? If I had actually misled a Court of Justice to shield the murderer of my dearly loved father? It was undeniably possible. I had formed my opinion on mere probabilities, backed by a statement that, however plausible, was manifestly worthless as evidence. And that opinion might have been utterly wrong. It was a dreadful thought. So dreadful that, though I tried to put it away and remind myself that I did not entertain and never had entertained it, it haunted me during the whole of my walk home, even to the exclusion of the menace to myself that lurked in this blackmailer's letter.

Chapter XIII
A Crystal-Gazer
and Other Matters

The cheerful atmosphere of the old house in Wellclose Square soon dissipated my gloomy thoughts. It was nearing supper-time when I arrived, and an agreeable clink of china proceeded from the dining-room, accompanied by a faint aroma suggestive of curry. On my landing I found Lilith and Miss Finch engaged in earnest discussion, and both greeted me as if I had returned after a long absence.

"We have been wondering," said the former, "what had become of our Sibyl." (She had bestowed this title on me, presumably, by reason of my peculiarly "psychic" cast of countenance). "As for the poor Titmouse," (this was Miss Finch's pet name), "she has been wandering about like a cat that has lost its kitten."

"Or like a kitten that has lost its cat," I suggested, bestowing an affectionate pinch on my little comrade's ear. "Well, I haven't been far afield, but I have done quite an important stroke of business."

"You don't mean to say you've sold something!" the Titmouse exclaimed, incredulously.

"Not actually sold. But I have discovered a market. I have tidings of a benevolent person – of the Scottish persuasion, I believe – who traffics in works of art and other productions of the human hand."

"A Scotchman!" exclaimed Miss Finch. "When are you going to call on the Laird?

"It is hardly worth while to call on him until I have a fair collection of work to show him," said I.

"I don't agree with you, Sibyl," said Lilith. "The first thing to do is to catch your dealer. To do that, you must find out what he wants. He is sure to have his own personal fancies, and he knows what he can sell most easily. Take him all that you have ready. He will be able to see from that what you can do, and he will tell you what kind of work he will take from you. And don't lose any time. I should go to-morrow if I were you."

"Does an artist have to work to order, then, like salaried journeymen?" I asked.

"Practically, yes," replied Lilith. "And why not? He makes things that he wants people to buy. Surely it is only reasonable that he should consider the needs and the wishes of the buyers. And all good craftsmen do. Chippendale's chairs were not only good to look at, they were comfortable to sit on and serviceable in use. The only difference between an artist craftsman and a commercial producer is that the artist always does his best, for his own satisfaction apart from the question of payment, whereas the commercial producer thinks of the profit only, and turns out the worst stuff that the buyer will put up with."

"But surely an artist may choose what he will make," said I.

"Of course he may," replied Lilith, "if he is willing to keep the thing when he has made it. Not if he is going to ask someone to pay him money for it."

I was inwardly somewhat taken aback by this exhibition of hard-headed reasonableness on the part of the mystical Lilith, so much so that, when she had gone to her room, I remarked on it to Miss Finch.

"Yes," she agreed, "Lilith is an extraordinary girl. In fact, there seem to be two Liliths, one is as cranky as a March hare, and the other is perfectly sane and really very shrewd. I sometimes wonder whether she really believes in all that crystal-gazing tosh and telepathic bunkum. But she practices what she has just been preaching. She does her fashion-plates according to orders – but ever so much better than she need – and does other work to please herself and is content to keep it. You should look in at her studio and see her at work, then you'd understand."

"And you think I had better take her advice?"

"I do. First catch your dealer, and if he wants to keep you turning out the same things over and over again, try to catch another dealer who wants something different. The great thing is to get a market. It's frightfully disheartening to keep on doing good work and having it all left on your hands."

Impressed by this wise counsel, I betook myself after supper to my workshop and reviewed my stock. A month's work had produced no great accumulation, for I was still a slow worker, though the continuous practice was improving that. On the other hand, I had brought with me a certain number of unfinished pieces as well as some of my finished work, so that I had enough to give Mr. Campbell the means of judging my capabilities. When I had looked over the collection and withdrawn one or two pieces that were not up to my present standard, I packed the approved specimens in a hand-bag which I took up with me in readiness for the morrow. I was just opening the door of my room when Lilith came running up the stairs.

"You see," I said, holding up the hand-bag. "I am acting on your advice. I have packed up a selection from my stock to take to the dealer to-morrow morning."

"I am glad of that," said she. "The business side of art is tedious and disagreeable, but you have got to sell if you are to live by your work. Would you mind giving me a private view of your masterpieces?"

"I shall be proud to show them to you," I replied, conducting her into my room and placing the arm-chair by the table, "Let us put out the whole collection."

I emptied the bag of its contents, which I set out on the table to the best advantage, and she examined the pieces one by one.

"They are charming," she exclaimed, enthusiastically. "I can't judge the work, though it looks most expert to my inexpert eye, but the design is delightful. They are all so individual and full of character, and so simple and restrained. You have a fine colour-sense, too. I think your use of enamel quite masterly, and I like your employment of bronze in place of the precious metals. It is fortunate that your dealer is a Scotchman, for the Jews, from Solomon downwards, have always had a leaning towards gold."

"Yes," said I, "bronze is my favourite material, even for personal ornaments. And it is capable of great variety in the patina, especially if one uses the Japanese methods of surface treatment. I wish it took the enamel better."

"You seem to have overcome the difficulties pretty completely," said Lilith. "This pendant, for instance, is beautiful, and so is the belt-clasp. Do you know, Sibyl, I think we might collaborate. Some of my designs might very well include metal ornaments – clasps, buckles, and buttons forming part of the decorative scheme. We must talk it over. And now, my dear Sibyl, I want to say something to you – something quite serious – and I want you to listen without prejudice."

I looked at her, and was instantly aware of a change that had come over her. The shrewd, business-like, capable Lilith had suddenly become transformed into the mystic – wide-eyed, dreamy, yet intense.

"I have avoided talking to you about the things that are to me the great things of life," she said in low, earnest, tones. "I have wished to, but I have been fearful of intruding on your strongly individual, self-contained personality. But I have felt that you have great gifts – great psychic gifts. You are a woman of power. The common herd live their little lives locked up in the prison of the visible and the conscious. If they would convey their thoughts to other minds, they must use the unwieldy means of speech and visible signs. What they know of their fellow-immortals reaches them crudely through the organs of sense, and through those primitive and inadequate media they must needs communicate with others, bound by the limitations of time and space and mere material contact – at least, so long as they are prisoned within a material body.

But there are others for whom no such limitations exist, specially gifted souls who can see without mere material eyes, who can hear without ears, who can speak their thoughts across the gulfs of time and space, who can look into the remote past, and even into the future, who can make their will-power operate at limitless distances and without the aid of gross bodily action. And you are one of these, Sibyl. I am convinced that you are endowed with these powers. But they are latent, unsuspected, because you have never tried to exercise them – because you have never sought to bring the subconscious within the domain of the conscious, or rather to make a contact between the two."

To this strange and rather wild harangue (which the matter-of-fact Titmouse would have called "barmy") I listened with grave attention, though with little enough conviction – for I could not but recall my ignorance and my mistaken judgment in the greatest crisis of my life – noting how like a prophetess the picturesque Lilith looked, with her golden aureole of auburn hair and her great, blue eyes and parted lips. But I made no reply – there was, indeed, nothing to say – and after a short pause she continued,

"Don't think I am saying this with any impertinent intention of trying to force my own views on you. I have a definite practical purpose. You are going to-morrow to make your first essay in a vitally important branch of an artist's calling. On your success depends the possibility of your following art as a profession – that is, if you have not enough to live without work."

"I have not," said I.

"Then artistic success is not sufficient. You must achieve industrial success, you must get a livelihood out of your work. As far as the creation of beautiful things is concerned you are quite competent and will become more so with more practice. Now you have to learn how to dispose of those works profitably, how to make people buy them."

"But surely that will be decided by the suitability of the things themselves."

"Partly, no doubt. But you mustn't leave it at that. You must learn to exercise the power of silent willing combined with suggestion."

"I don't think I quite understand," said I.

"We must talk about this more fully some other time," said Lilith, "and go into the theory and the results of experiments. For the present you must try to take my word for the fact that silent willing and suggestion are real powers. I don't ask you to believe it without proof – I will give you the proof later – but I do beg you, dear Sibyl, to give the method a trial. If it fails in your hands you will be none the worse, but it won't fail if you make up your mind to succeed."

"What do you want me to do, Lilith?" I asked, not a little bit bewildered by her mysterious and rather vague expressions.

"I will tell you what I do myself," she replied. "When I take a batch of drawings to a publisher, I stand outside the office for five minutes and silently will that he shall accept them. Sometimes I write on a piece of paper a command to the publisher to accept my work, and while I am waiting for the interview I keep my eyes fixed on the writing and mentally endorse the command. The writing, you see, helps me to concentrate my will-power. Then, at the interview, I use the method of suggestion. Whatever the editor or publisher may say, whatever objections he may make to my work, I continue steadily to impress on him that he is going to accept it that, in fact, he *has* accepted it. If he refuses it, I ignore the refusal and go on talking as if he had accepted it – not rudely, of course, one must do these things tactfully – and all the time that he is talking, I continue silently to concentrate my will-power on him."

"And what is the result?" I asked.

"The result, my dear Sibyl, is that I sell all the drawings that I offer for sale."

This sounded convincing enough, and would have been more so if I had not happened to know that Lilith's drawings were of the very best of their kind, and that she submitted them to the most rigorous criticism before letting anyone see them. Still, the fact that she sold her work was undeniable, and it was impossible to say how many excellent drawings had failed to gain acceptance. Certainly every capable artist is not a successful one.

"And what is it exactly that you want me to do?" I asked.

"I want you," she replied, "to do just what I do myself. I want you to stand outside the shop for five minutes and silently will that this dealer shall buy your work. It would probably help you if you were to write down the command and keep your eyes fixed on the writing while you are willing, but if the dealer himself should happen to be visible, it would be well to fix your eyes on him so as to direct the will-force with more precision. And when you go into the shop, keep on willing with the greatest concentration that you can command, and when you are talking to the dealer, talk as if he had bought your work, keep on impressing on him that he has bought it, and don't take any notice of contrary statements on his part. If he seems to think that he has refused it, you must correct his mistake and guide his thoughts into the proper channels."

I suppose I must have looked somewhat dismayed at this rather startling programme, for Lilith continued, eagerly, "Now, don't raise

380

objections, Sibyl, dear. It will be quite easy if you will only make up your mind. You have abundant will-power, and I am certain that you have the gift of projecting your mental states into the minds of others. And I am so anxious that you should succeed and that your great gifts should not be wasted. Say you will try, Sibyl, if only to please your friend."

What could I do? Utterly as my mind refused to accept the connection between the alleged cause and effect, I could not say that no such connection existed. I was completely unconvinced, but my unconviction might conceivably be less rational than Lilith's whole-hearted belief. For she declared herself able to support her belief with proof, whereas I had to admit that my scepticism was largely a matter of temperament. And she was so eager, and it was so sweet of her to be so full of anxiety on my behalf, that it would have seemed ungracious to make difficulties. The end of it was that I agreed to carry out her plan of conquest, on which she further inducted me into the arts of silent willing and suggestion and even supervised me while I wrote out, at her dictation, a peremptory command to the dealer, which I promised to use, as directed, for the reinforcement of my will-power at the appropriate time.

On the following morning, after a careful study of my father's atlas of London, which I had brought with me from Maidstone, I set forth, hand-bag in hand and encouraged by the good wishes of my comrades and of Lilith in particular. Entering the Underground Railway at Mark Lane, I came to the surface at Charing Cross Station and bore away northwards across Leicester Square. During the journey, I had turned over in my mind the plan of attack to which I stood committed – with increasing distaste, I must admit, as the time for its execution drew nearer. And as my dislike grew, so also did my scepticism. I found myself recalling the fact that Lilith, successful as she claimed to be, was yet a fashion-plate artist very much against her own wishes, and reflecting that, if her silent willing were as efficacious as she believed it to be, she might surely compel the purchase of the kind of work that she enjoyed doing, instead of being herself compelled to follow a distasteful occupation. However, it was useless to think about it now. I had promised to give the method a trial and must carry out my promise.

These reflections brought me to the bottom of Wardour Street, and my attention was now fully occupied by the search for Mr. Campbell's shop. Mr. Otway had omitted to give me the number of the house, but I remembered his saying that it was on the west side near the Oxford Street end, so I walked slowly up the east side and scanned the shop-fronts across the road. Near the top of the street my eye lighted on a smallish shop, above the window of which was inscribed in faded gold lettering *"Donald Campbell"*, and I immediately crossed the road, becoming aware as I did so of a sudden access of nervousness. For this was a new experience to me. Hitherto all my transactions with shopkeepers had been in the character of a purchaser, and my transformation into a vendor was accompanied by a diffidence and shyness that I had not expected or foreseen. Indeed, in the course of that short journey across the road, my bashfulness increased so much that I had nearly forgotten my promise to Lilith and was on the point of entering the shop when it flashed into my mind.

But even when I recalled Lilith's instructions, they were not easy to carry out. I swerved from the shop door to the side of the window and stood there trying to concentrate my will-power. But it would not be concentrated. In the window was displayed a fascinating array of base metal spoons which instantly riveted my attention, particularly a set of the late seventeenth century, wrought in a fine-coloured latten, and exhibiting in a most charming manner the combined effect of delicate workmanship, with the patina of age and the softening of outlines from use and wear.

Unconsciously, I had begun to compare them with my own cruder productions before I realized that my will-power had escaped control. Then I jerked myself back from the spoons to my present task, and, hastily drawing the paper from my pocket, fixed my eyes on the written command and struggled to concentrate my thoughts on it and to suppress a growing consciousness of the absurdity of the whole proceeding. Presently I raised my eyes from the paper, and as they sought to dodge the spoons, they encountered another object equally disturbing. "It was only a face at the window," as the ridiculous song has it, but it instantly engrossed my attention and transported me in spirit, not to any Highland glen, but straight away to the banks of the Jordan – a fattish face, framed with glossy, black hair that broke out at the temples into rows of little crisp curls like a barrister's wig, a face with small, grey eyes, full under the lids, and surmounted by strong, black eyebrows, with full, red lips and a rather sketchy nose of the general form of a William pear with the stalk uppermost. It was clearly not Mr. Campbell's face, but it appertained to the establishment and, recalling Lilith's instructions to direct my will power with more precision by fixing my eyes on the dealer, I directed a stony stare at the face and willed silently. But here I was countered again, for the owner of the face was also apparently possessed of psychic gifts, and fixed on me a gaze of such intensity that I was covered with confusion. On this I straightway forgot all about will-power, and, hastily pocketing the paper, walked nervously and guiltily into the shop.

The proprietor of the face confronted me impassively across the counter, and such was my trepidation that, although he obviously was not Mr. Campbell, I could think of nothing better than to ask him if he was, whereupon he completed my discomfiture by replying in the affirmative.

"I am Mrs. Otway," said I, at which he suddenly grew keenly attentive, and I continued, "I understand that Mr. Otway – Mr. Lewis Otway – has written to you about me. I had a letter from him to that effect."

"Yes," said Mr. Campbell, "he has, and, if I remember rightly, he suggested that I might be able to dispose of some of your work. I think he said you did some *repoussé* or something of the kind."

Apparently Mr. Campbell was preparing to treat me as an amateur, and my work as the product of a hobby. This would not do at all. Before saying anything further, I opened my bag and handed out the pieces one by one, setting them on the counter before him.

"Oh!" said he. "Yes, ha – hum, this isn't exactly what I expected." He picked up a teaspoon, turned it over between his fingers, closely examined the joining of the shank and bowl and the little bust that formed the knob, and then held it at arm's length with his head on one side. There was something in the action and the facial expression that accompanied it which encouraged me even before he spoke.

"Nithe thpoon that," was his comment as he laid it down. (I observed that he tended to develop a lisp when preoccupied or off his guard.) "Well made, well designed, quite original, too. Spoons are my fancy – you saw that set in the window. If I could afford it, I would specialize in them more than I do. Not but what I'm fond of all goldsmith's work if it's good – or any other art work, for that matter, but I do love a good spoon."

This was pleasant hearing, for I had a weakness for spoons myself. They are useful objects, they admit of infinite variety in design, and their small size adapted them peculiarly to my rather limited resources.

"But there is one thing that you must bear in mind," continued Mr. Campbell. "Single spoons are not very saleable unless they are antique or collectors' pieces. Modern spoons are bought for use as well as ornament, and buyers like them in sets, not all alike, of course, but with a general design running through the set. Twelve spoons, all different, but all brothers, that's what they want."

"Like the apostle sets," said I.

"Yes," he replied, "but we don't want any more apostles. Too many on the market already. The apostles are done. They're a back number.

Everybody does them because they can't think of anything else connected with the number twelve. But there is an opening for something original. If you can do me a set with a good striking design, I think I know where I can place them at a liberal price."

I made a note of this proposal, and Mr. Campbell proceeded with his examination of my samples, accompanying the process with shrewd comments and useful hints. "Now, I'm rather doubtful about this," said he, picking up a bronze paper-weight on which was a little figure with an open book, "it's pretty and might take the fancy of a bookish man, but I question whether you'll get paid for the work that you've put into it. People don't always realize the value of a bronze casting. You must have done this by the *cire perdue* process."

"I did."

"Well, I should save that for more important pieces. Simple modelling and sand-casting is good enough for paper-weights. And you are too lavish with your silver. Just feel this candlestick. You could have done it with half the silver and got paid just as much. The extra cost of the unnecessary silver will have to come off the workmanship – at least, that is the tendency, although it is nominally sold by weight."

As Mr. Campbell was speaking, a woman came out of an inner room and advanced to the counter. I glanced at her casually and then looked again more attentively, for I had instantly the feeling of having seen her before, though I could not recollect where. She was of the dark and sallow type, about my own age, and of a sombre and rather forbidding aspect, and the glance that she cast on my samples, though impassive, was faintly disparaging.

"This is Mrs. Otway, me dear," said Mr. Campbell. "You remember the letter I showed you about her. And these pretty things are her work."

Mrs. Campbell – as I assumed her to be – raised her eyes and bestowed on me a quietly insolent stare, but made no remark. Then she cast another disparaging glance at my wares and said coldly, "They are all right of their kind, but you don't want to fill the place up with modern stuff."

Disagreeable as the remark was, its matter impressed me less than its manner. For again I was sensible of a certain vague familiarity in the voice, the intonation and the accent. She gave me, however, no opportunity for studying either, for, with the curt observation that "she supposed he knew his own business," she retired to the inner room without taking any further notice of me.

"Well," said Mr. Campbell, "there's some truth in what my wife says. I can't afford to lock up my capital in things that I can't sell. But I like your work. It is good work, and you'll improve. I am willing to buy this lot of pieces – at a price. But it will have to be a low price, because I don't know how they will go. If you take my advice, you'll leave them with me and let me try the market with them. When I have sold one or two I shall know what I can do with them, and then I can offer you a fair price based on what they fetch. How will that thoot you?"

It seemed, on the whole, the most satisfactory arrangement, though I should have liked to have some definite idea as to the value of my work. I mentioned this, pointing out that I wanted to know if it would be worth my while to continue this kind of occupation.

"Well," said Mr. Campbell, "you leave the things with me, and I will look them over carefully and weigh the silver. Then I will make you the best offer I can for the lot, and you can either accept it or refuse it, or wait and see what the things fetch. Give me your address and I will write you out a receipt for what you leave. Will that do?"

I replied that it would do admirably, whereupon he supplied me with a slip of paper and pen and ink, and retired to the desk with my collection to write out the receipt. I had taken off my glove and was beginning to write when somebody entered the shop with a quick, light step, suggesting a young and active man. Just behind me the footsteps shopped short, and a pleasant, masculine voice addressed the dealer.

"All right, Mr. Campbell, don't let me disturb you. I'm in no hurry."

"I'm afraid, sir, your things are not quite ready, but if you don't mind waiting a moment I'll make sure."

"I suspected," the voice rejoined, "that I might be a little over-punctual. However, you finish what you are doing, while I browse 'round the museum."

At the first sound of the voice my pen stopped short, and it seemed as if my heart stopped, too – though it soon began to make up for lost time. I was disconcerted and vaguely annoyed that a small surprise should set up such a disproportionate disturbance. Perhaps, too, I was a little startled to find a voice so long unheard elicit such instant and undoubting recognition. But I recovered immediately and resumed my writing, though, to be sure, the pen-point no longer traced the firm and steady lines of the first-written words. Meanwhile, Mr. Campbell had completed his receipt and we now exchanged our documents, I checking his list of my sample works, and he scanning my address with apparent surprise.

"Wellclose Square," he read out. "There is a Wellclose Square somewhere down Wapping way. It won't be that one?"

"Yes. But I think it is actually in Ratcliff. When shall I hear from you?"

"I will write and post the letter this evening."

"Thank you, Mr. Campbell. Good morning."

As we exchanged bows, I turned and met the newcomer approaching the counter. He glanced at me, at first without recognition, then he looked again.

"Why, surely it is Miss Vardon!" he exclaimed.

"Wrong, Mr. Davenant," said I. "It is Mrs. Otway. But that is a mere quibble. I am the person whom you knew as Miss Vardon."

"Well, well," said he, "what a piece of luck to meet you – and here of all places!"

"Is this a peculiarly unlikely place, then?" I asked.

"Well, I suppose it isn't, really, at any rate, I mustn't let Mr. Campbell hear me say that it is. Do you mind waiting a moment while I settle my little business with him? I want to hear all your news."

His little business amounted to no more than an arrangement that he should call in about three days for his "things", whatever they were, and when this had been settled, we left the shop together.

"Which way are you walking?" he asked.

"I really don't know," I answered. "I think I had some dim idea of seeing the town and taking a look at the shops."

"Then," said he, "as you are a country mouse, whereas I am a town sparrow of the deepest dye, perhaps I may be permitted to act as conductor and expositor of the wonders of the Metropolis, while you give me the news from Maidstone."

"There is little to tell you excepting that I have lost my father. He died quite suddenly, about two months ago, from heart failure."

"Ah!" said Mr. Davenant, "I had a presentiment that it was so. Seeing you in mourning, I was afraid to ask after him, and I need not tell you how deeply I sympathise with you. I remember how much you were to one another. What a mercy it is that you were married!"

To this I made no reply, and for a time we walked on slowly without speaking. But though nothing was said, much was thought, at least by me. For I had to make up my mind now, and once for all, on a point that I felt to be of vital importance. Should I tell him how things were with me? Or should I let him think that all was well, and that I was a normal married woman? Something – I did not ask myself what – urged me to tell him everything. But caution, prudence, whispered – and that none too softly – that it were better not. The sudden wave of emotion that had surged over me at the sound of his voice was still a vivid and startling memory, and it counselled reticence.

Thus two opposing forces contended, on the one hand, an emotional impulse, on the other the admonitions of reason, and it is needless to say that reason played losing game. Swiftly I argued out the issues. Sooner or

386

later, the inevitable question must come, and with it the choice of an evasion or a straightforward answer. If it was to be evasion, then I put Jasper Davenant out of my life at once and for ever, for the evasion could never be maintained, must shut out this gleam of sunshine that came to me from the old, happy days as if to light up my sombre, lonely life, and wend on my pilgrimage without a friend save the companions of my working days.

And reason whispered again that it were better so.

Chapter XIV
Jasper Davenant

The silence that had fallen between me and my companion remained unbroken (with one exception, when he briefly drew my attention to the old stone name-tablet, inscribed "*Wardour Streete 1686*") until we came opposite a church, standing back from the road, and distinguished by a sort of *tumour* – containing a clock – on its spire. Here Mr. Davenant halted, and looking up at the tower, remarked, "A quaint-looking church, this, odd and ugly, but yet not without a certain character and picturesqueness. Quite an aristocratic church, too, for it is the burial place of a king."

"Indeed," said I. "Which of the kings is buried there?"

"He was but a shabby little king – Theodore of Corsica – and he has the shabbiest little moralizing monument. But he was a somewhat original monarch in his way, for, being in acute financial difficulties, he conceived the brilliant idea of making over his kingdom to his creditors. Would you care to see the monument?"

I assented, without enthusiasm, and we mounted the steps to the grimy churchyard, where presently, against the wall of the church, we found the monument. And still, as we deciphered the weathered inscription, I debated the question whether I should or should not tell him, and still I reached no conclusion.

"By the way," my companion said, suddenly, "I am acting the showman on the assumption that you are the complete and perfect country bumpkin. But perhaps you are, by now, a fully acclimatized Londoner. How long have you been living in town?"

"About a month."

"Then the hay-seed is still in your hair, so to speak. I still address a country cousin, and have not presumed unduly, though, no doubt, you are beginning to learn the rudiments. I heard Mr. Campbell speak of Wellclose Square, for instance, as a region known to you."

"Yes. That is where I live."

As I caught his look of astonishment my heart began to race, for I knew that the inevitable question was coming.

"I suppose your husband is connected with the docks?"

"No," I replied. "And he doesn't live at Wellclose Square. I am not living with my husband, Mr. Davenant. I never have lived with him, and it is not my intention ever to live with him."

The deed was done. The murder was out. And though I knew that I had taken the wrong course, I drew a deep breath of relief. As to Mr. Davenant, he was, for a few moments, too much taken aback to make any comment. At length he said, somewhat gloomily, "I am sorry to hear this, Mrs. Otway. Very sorry. It sounds as if your domestic affairs were not very comfortable."

"They are not," I answered. "But, as I have told you so much, I should like to tell you what the position really is. Would you mind?"

"Mind!" he exclaimed. "Of course I want to know, if you are willing to tell me. Aren't we old friends? I am most concerned about you."

"Thank you, Mr. Davenant. I should like to tell you how this extraordinary position has come about. Shall we sit down? This place is quieter than the street."

He dusted the wooden bench with his handkerchief, and we sat down just below the shabby monument of the poor, little, bankrupt king. And there I told once again that tragic story of cross-purposes and well-meant blundering. I had intended to give him but a bare outline of the catastrophe, but it could not be. For the bald fact was that I had sold myself to Mr. Otway for money, and my womanly pride and self-respect would not be satisfied with anything short of a complete justification such as might be accepted by a scrupulous, high-minded man. And as I poured out my miserable history, glancing at him from time to time, I was surprised and almost alarmed at the change that came over him. He was a sunny-natured man, buoyant, high-spirited, playful and humorous, though all in a quiet way. But now, as he listened to my story, the genial face grew rigid, the humorous mouth set hard and stern, and the short, sharp questions that he put from time to time, came in a voice that was strange to me.

"So now," said I, when I had come to the end of my recital, "you will understand why I refuse to recognize this marriage, and why I elect to live the life of a spinster, though without a spinster's privileges."

In a moment his face softened, and his clear, hazel eyes looked into mine with grave tenderness.

"Yes," he said, "I understand. I wish I could say more. I wish I could tell you adequately how I grieve for you – for all the sorrow that you have had to endure and for the maimed life that lies before you. But words are poor instruments." He laid his hand on mine for an instant, and added, "Yet I hope you will feel what I want to express in these threadbare phrases."

I thanked him for the sympathy, which he had indeed made very clearly evident, and for a time neither of us spoke. Nevertheless, I could see that he was cogitating something. Once or twice he seemed about to speak, for he looked at me, but then again bent his gaze reflectively on the ground. At length, with some hesitation, he said, "I hope you won't think me inquisitive or impertinent, but I feel rather anxious as to – as to how you are placed. I gather that this man Otway does not – er – contribute – "

"He is quite willing to. But I can't allow him to maintain me if I repudiate the marriage."

"No. At least I think you are quite wise not to. But – you don't mind my asking, do you? Are you properly provided for? I'm really not – "

"Of course, you're not," I interrupted, smiling at his diffidence. "As to my means – well, I don't quite know what they will be eventually, but at present I am living in a reasonable state of comfort. I am not anxious about the future."

My answer did not seem to satisfy him completely, for he continued to cogitate rather uneasily. But, now that I had the key, I could read pretty clearly, without the aid of any magic crystal, what was passing in his mind. He knew that I lived in a squalid east-end neighbourhood. He had seen me at the dealers, and evidently surmised that I was not there as a buyer, that I was in straitened circumstances – perhaps in a state of actual poverty – and that I was disposing of my jewellery and valuables to enable me to live. That, I had no doubt, was what he suspected, and the question that he was debating so earnestly was whether he could, without impertinence, extract any further information and whether our friendship was intimate enough to allow of his making any kind of offer of help.

I should have liked to set his mind at rest, but, in truth, I was none too confident about my future. That depended largely on the nature of Mr. Campbell's offer, on my ability to earn a reasonable livelihood.

"Well," Mr. Davenant said, at length, "I hope your confidence is justified. But in any case, I suppose you have friends?"

"There's no need for you to worry about me," I replied, evasively – for I had no near relatives from whom I could claim assistance. "I am in quite comfortable circumstances at present. And now let us put away my bothersome affairs and talk of something more pleasant."

"Very well," said he. "Let us choose an agreeable topic and discuss it in all its bearings as we used to do." He drew his watch from his pocket, and, glancing at it, continued, "It is now nearly one o'clock. What do you say to the question of lunch as an agreeable topic for our debate?"

I admitted that the subject was not without its attractions.

"Then," said he, "I will suggest that a club is an appropriate place in which to consume it, and that a mixed club satisfies the most extreme proprieties."

"I should hardly have suspected you of a mixed dub."

"In strict confidence," he replied, "between you and me and our friend Theodore of insolvent memory, I have another – unmixed – for normal club purposes. This one is my lunch club. It is quite near to my chambers, and is quieter and more pleasant than a restaurant. And it has a special character of its own, as is indicated by its name. It is called 'The Magpies' Club'."

"That sounds rather ominous."

"Doesn't it? But it isn't a burglars' club. Its members are collectors and connoisseurs – furniture and china maniacs and so forth, and the main function of the club is to enable them to show their specimens to one another and to exchange or sell duplicate pieces. May I take it that you consent to honour the 'Magpies'?"

I accepted the invitation gladly, for a month's residence in the East End had made me decidedly appreciative of the amenities of the more civilized regions. We decided to walk to Essex Street, in which the club had its premises, and to go by way of the side streets for greater quiet and ease of conversation.

"You spoke just now of your chambers," said I. "Does that mean that you are in practice now?"

"Yes. But not in the law. I finished my legal studies and got called, but then I decided to give up the Bench and the Woolsack, though they shouted for me never so loudly, and return to an old love. I am now an architect."

"Is a barrister allowed to practice as an architect?"

"On that I am not quite clear, but it really doesn't matter to me. It is a question for the benchers or other authorities."

"Have you been in practice long?"

"Exactly three weeks to-day. And when I tell you that I have already received a commission to design and erect a greenhouse no less than twelve-feet-by-eight in plan, you will realize that I am mounting the ladder of professional success, with the speed of an eagle with a balloon attachment. My client, by the way, is a member of the club."

Thus gossiping, we made our way by devious routes through the less frequented streets, by Garrick Street, Covent Garden, and Drury Lane until, by the Law Courts, we emerged into the Strand, crossed to Essex Street, and presently arrived at the roomy old-fashioned house in which the Magpies had their meeting-place.

It was a pleasant, homely club, and certainly there could be no question as to its eminent respectability, for the aspect of the members – mostly middle-aged and many of them elderly – bordered on the frumpish. The room in which we selected our table was a large, oblong apartment, quietly furnished and decorated and provided with a glazed museum case, which occupied the centre, while a sort of dais at one end was devoted to the display of pieces of furniture exhibited by the members. I noticed, too, that the walls were occupied by pictures, each of which bore a written descriptive label.

"Are you interested in ancient ivories?" Mr. Davenant asked, as we looked into the glass case, in which a collection of very brown and cracked specimens were exhibited by a Mr. Udimore-Jones. "For my part, I find it difficult to develop great enthusiasm over the dental arrangements of superannuated elephants, carved into funny shapes by piously-facetious middle-agers. Look out! Here comes my client. Let us sneak off to our table. A-ha! Too late! She's seen us."

"Which is your client?" I asked, looking round furtively.

"The elderly damsel with the smile – a Miss Tallboy Smith. There! She has caught my eye now. Did you ever see such a set of teeth? She had better be careful or Udimore-Jones will have her."

We were edging away towards our table, with a feeble hope of escape, when she caught us.

"Now, I don't believe you've seen my cup," she exclaimed, with an engaging smile. "You must see it. It is not only genuine Nantgarw, but the roses on it are unquestionable Billingsleys."

"Observe," said Mr. Davenant, "the pride of the inveterate collector. You'd think she had painted those roses herself."

"Indeed, you wouldn't," retorted Miss Tallboy-Smith, "not if you had seen them and knew anything about ceramic painting. And as to pride, isn't it something to be proud of? Nantgarw porcelain is rare, and roses painted by Billingsley are rare, and when you have them both in a single piece, why then, you see, you – "

"Then," said Mr. Davenant, "you multiply the rarity of the one by the rarity of the other, and the product of the multiplication is the rarity of the piece as a whole."

"Isn't he absurd?" she simpered, "treating me to a complete private view of the 'ancient ivories'."

"Perfectly incorrigible. Don't you agree with me, Miss – Mrs. – "

"Otway," said I.

"Oh, really! Now I wonder – my brother knew a Mr. Otway – Oh, but he was a money-lender. That wouldn't be – But won't you come and look at my cup?"

392

We returned to the glass case, of which Miss Tallboy Smith opened a door and lifted from its shelf a dainty porcelain teacup.

"Just feel how thin and light it is," she said, holding it out to me.

"I wouldn't if I were you," said Mr. Davenant. "This Nantgarw stuff crumbles like a baked egg-shell, and it's hideously valuable."

"Don't take any notice of him," said Miss Tallboy Smith. "Just feel it – it's positively delicious to touch, and look at the lovely roses – no one but William Billingsley could have painted those roses. And, if there could be any doubt, you have only to turn the piece up and look at the bottom. There is Billingsley's personal mark – the number seven. That's infallible."

I took from her hand the delicate, translucent cup, and was admiring the freedom and softness of the flower painting when she drew nearer and said in a warning whisper, "Here comes Major Dewham-Brown. If he tries to sell you anything, don't buy it. He only brings his bad bargains here."

She had barely uttered her warning when a brassy voice behind me exclaimed, "How d'you do, Miss Tallboy Smith? And how are you, Davenant?" And a tall, smart, rather stupid-looking man with a large nose – which seemed to have been produced at the expense of his eyes and chin – sailed into my field of vision.

"Ha!" said he. "Pretty cup, that. Worth a pot of money, too, I expect, though I don't know much about 'em. And that reminds me that I've got rather an interesting thing that I picked up the other day, bit of old church plate, seventeenth century, if not earlier. Like to see it?"

Without waiting for a reply, he fished out of a "poacher's" pocket a flat object wrapped in a silk handkerchief.

"Curious piece, this, interested me very much. The *repoussé*-work on it is remarkably fine." He unfolded the handkerchief as he spoke, and at length extracted, with a sort of conjuror's flourish, a small, circular, silver platter – apparently a *paten*, to judge by its size. This he handed to Miss Tallboy-Smith, who grinned at it indulgently and passed it to Mr. Davenant, who, having looked it over without enthusiasm, handed it to me.

A very brief inspection, with the piece in my hand, was enough to make Miss Tallboy-Smith's warning unnecessary, for, apart from the unsuitability of the ornament – if it was really meant for a paten – it was an obvious electrotype, which had, however, been pickled, polished, and sulphured with intent to deceive. Having noted this fact, I returned the piece to its owner with a few words of polite and colourless commendation of the design, and the Major, chilled by the lack of enthusiasm, invested his treasure once more in its silken wrapping and went off in search of a more appreciative audience. Under cover of his parting courtesies to Miss Tallboy-Smith, Mr. Davenant and I retreated to our table.

"That antique of the Major's looked to me rather like fake," said my companion, when we had ordered our lunch. "It was so very venerable."

"It is an electrotype, sulphured to give an appearance of age," said I.

"Is it, by Jove? Now, how did you spot it as an electrotype?"

"It was the disagreement between the back and the face that first attracted my attention. The face was *repoussé* – pretty coarse too – but there was not a vestige of a toolmark on the back, where, of course, most of the punch-marks would be – nothing but the smooth surface of the deposited metal."

Mr. Davenant chuckled. "I seem to have imported an expert Magpie. Oh! But I remember now that you and your father used to do all sorts of wonderful works in metal. Ha, ha! Poor old Dewham-Brown! He little suspected that he was dealing with a practical artificer."

Here the advent of food put a temporary stop to conversation, for we were both pretty sharp-set, but during the progress of the meal I looked about me and was vastly entertained by the proceedings of the Magpies. The glass case was the centre of interest, around which a small crowd of enthusiasts gathered, eagerly discussing the exhibits, which the proud owners expounded, with their noses flattened against the glass, or tenderly lifted out for closer inspection. And now and again a new exhibitor would arrive with a bag or attaché case, from which fresh treasures were disgorged into the glazed sanctuary.

"I suppose," said I, "your members will have nothing to do with any but antique works?"

"Not as a rule," Mr. Davenant replied. "The collector is usually a lover of old things. But there are exceptions. A good many of the pictures shown here are modern – some, I suspect, are shown by the artists themselves. Then we have one member who collects modern pottery exclusively – not commercial stuff, of course, but the work of modern artist-potters, like De Morgan, the Martin Brothers, and other individual workers. Fine stuff it is, too. I have a few pieces myself. And, talk of the old gentleman – there he is. I'll fetch him over and make him show us what he has got in that bag."

He rose from the table, and crossed the room, and I saw him accost a very tall, pleasant-looking young man who was bearing down on the glass case with a good-sized hand-bag, but readily allowed himself to be led over our table.

"Now, Hawkesley," said Mr. Davenant, "my guest wants to see what really high-class modern pottery is like. What have you got?"

"I have only three pieces with me," replied Mr. Hawkesley, "and they are all of the same type, what I call 'mystery-ware'."

"What is the mystery about it? Mr. Davenant asked.

"The mystery is, who makes it? As far as I know, there is only one dealer who has it, and he absolutely refuses to say where he gets it. I have never seen any of it exhibited – excepting here – and nobody can tell me the name of the potter or anything about it beyond the fact that it seems to be the exclusive monopoly of this one dealer, and that he has very little of it, and charges accordingly. But it is wonderful stuff." He lifted out of his bag a couple of jars and a bowl – handling them with that curious delicacy that one often notices in persons with large, strong, supple hands – and placed them carefully on the table.

"You see," he continued, "there are two methods of treatment, which are sometimes combined, as on this jar, and these two styles are based on two very different types of old work – the old English slip-ware, such as the Wrotham and Staffordshire and Toftware, and the old French Henri Deux, or Oiron ware. In the one, the ornament is produced by laying on pipes or threads of coloured slip – that is, clay in the semi-liquid state, in the other by inlaying coloured paste or enamel in cavities in the body, which seems to be made with tools like those used by book-binders. This covered jar – which looks almost like a piece of fine Japanese *cloisonné* – and this bowl show the inlay method, and this other jar is an example of the slip decoration, but with one or two spots of enamel inlay."

"I think I prefer the pure inlay," said Mr. Davenant.

"So do I," said Mr. Hawkesley, "and so, I think, does the artist. All his finest work is done by the inlay method, though he uses the slip decoration with such skill and taste that it is virtually a new method. The old Wrotham and Toftware looks very primitive by the side of this scholarly, refined work."

I turned the three pieces of pottery over in my hands and warmly commended the judgment of the collector. No modern work that I had ever seen approached it for perfection of finish or grace of design, while the colour-scheme combined richness, delicacy, and restraint in a truly marvellous manner. It seemed to unite the brilliancy of enamel to the sober beauty of old tapestry. And even the little blue bird, inlaid on the bottom of each piece to form the potter's mark, was finished with care and taste.

"May one inquire as to the local habitation and name of the dealer?" Mr. Davenant asked.

"You may," was the reply. "His name is Maurice Goldstein, and he is to be found at Number 56 Hand Court, Holborn. And I should like to wring his neck."

We both laughed at the vindictive tone in which this benevolent wish was uttered, and at the sudden ferocity of aspect that swept over the usually good-humoured, kindly face.

"Why this homicidal craving?" Mr. Davenant asked.

"Don't you see," the other demanded, indignantly, "that this infernal Goldswine – I beg your pardon – "

"You needn't," said I.

"That this miserable huckster is grinding the face of some poor artist, that he is not only devouring the earnings of this industrious, painstaking worker, but – for his own paltry profit – he is robbing that artist of the credit – of the fame – to which his genius and his enthusiasm entitle him. Look at this lovely jar! I gave that mean worm ten guineas for it. How much do you suppose he gave the potter?"

"Ten shillings, perhaps," suggested Mr. Davenant.

"Probably not much more, though there is getting on for a week's work in it."

"Still," I said, with a mischievous desire to stir up his indignation afresh, "the potter probably enjoys making these beautiful things. The work is its own reward."

"I can't agree to that," Mr. Hawkesley rejoined, warmly. "He doesn't enjoy being hard-up and having to work for a pittance. Besides, it isn't just. This man makes a jar that is going to give me a life-long pleasure. I want to pay him for that pleasure. I want to know who he is, to shake his hand and thank him and tell him that he is the salt of the earth. And this dealer hides him away and just feeds on him like the beastly parasite that he is."

He gathered up the treasured masterpieces, and having wished us *adieu*, with a sudden return to his customary geniality, crossed to the glass case to find a vacant niche for his samples of "mystery ware".

"I like Jack Hawkesley," said my companion, as we watched him.

"So do I," I agreed warmly. "He takes a human interest in the artist. I wish more collectors were like him."

"Yes," said Mr. Davenant. "He is a good type of rich man. Would that there were more Hawkesleys." He poured out the coffee which the waitress had just brought and then asked, "What do you think of this club – as a feeding and resting place, I mean?"

"It seems a comfortable, homely place, and the members and their exhibits are quite interesting."

"I find it so. You wouldn't care to join, I suppose? It is cheap, as clubs go – five guineas a year and no entrance fee. I should think you would find it a great convenience, living so far from the centre of town."

"It would be a great convenience. But should I be eligible? I am not a collector, you know."

"No, but you are something of an expert. At any rate, Hawkesley and I would manage the formalities. Think it over, and if you decide to honour us, drop me a line. This is my address – 56 Clifford's Inn."

He handed me his card, and when he had made a note of my address, I prepared to depart.

"I have wasted a fearful amount of your time, Mr. Davenant," said I, "but it has been a very pleasant interlude for me."

"Has it really? I hope it has. For my part, I have enjoyed myself just as I did in the old days when you used to let me wag a philosophic chin at you, and I am reluctant to let you go so soon. Mayn't I see you to the station, or wherever you are going?

"I thought of walking back to get myself acquainted with London."

"Then let me put you on the right road and show you some of the short cuts."

"But what about your work?"

He regarded me with that quaint, humorous smile that I had always found so attractive. "My work is, at present, of a somewhat intermittent type. This is one of the intermissions. Let us fare forth and study the architectural beauties of the Metropolis."

And we fared forth accordingly.

The short cuts discovered by my companion did not in the least conform to Euclid's definition of a straight line, and their brevity was relieved by sundry excursions into alleys and by-streets and incursions into churches and other ancient buildings. They led us by way of the Temple and its old round church, Mitre Court, Fetter Lane, Nevill's Court, Gough Square, and so to St. Paul's Churchyard and into the Cathedral, thence by Paul's Alley, Paternoster Row, Cheapside and Lombard Street, dropping into one or two churches on our way, until we came out on Great Tower Hill, and drifted slowly down Royal Mint Street. And all the while we gossiped pleasantly of this wonderful city and its wonderful, inexhaustible past, and my guide expounded, with all his old gaiety and brightness – and with astonishing knowledge of his subject – until I had almost forgotten Wellclose Square and the sinister shadow that hung over my life, and seemed to be back in the untroubled days of my girlhood.

But not quite. For, even as I talked – or more often listened – with the liveliest interest and pleasure, a project was maturing in my mind. I had, in fact, conceived a brilliant idea. Mr. Davenant's suggestion that I should join the club had started a train of thought that ran as an undercurrent – in the subconscious mind, perhaps, as Lilith would have said. It had begun vaguely when I saw the modern pictures on the walls, and the modern works in the glass case and the Major hawking round his little platter. Here was a place in which the work of the unknown artist could be shown and perhaps sold – my own work, Lilith's work, the Titmouse's, Philibar's, even Miss Polton's. For five guineas a year I could open this emporium, not only to myself, but to my fellow-workers, could slip past the dealer and secure his profits for us all. I say it was a brilliant idea – at least, it appeared so to me, and throughout that long peregrination, made delightful by the sympathetic companionship of my newly-recovered friend, it germinated and grew until, as we halted to say good-bye at the corner of Cable Street, it had grown to full maturity.

"I have been thinking," said I, "of your suggestion – about joining the club, you know. It would be nice to have a place to go to for a rest or a meal, in the centre of town. And I shall often want such a place."

His face brightened perceptibly – perhaps at the implied assurance that I could afford to spend five guineas.

"Then, may I put your name up for election?"

"Will you be so kind?"

"Won't I? It will be jolly, and we shan't lose sight of one another again, though that was my fault for not writing. I was often on the point of sending you a letter, and then I felt a silly diffidence – thought that you might consider I was presuming on a mere acquaintanceship. However, I will propose *you* for membership at once, and in about a week's time you will be a full-blown Magpie. Then I will send you a line – though, of course, you will get the official notification."

He handed me my bag, and with a hearty hand-shake, we said "Good-bye," and went our respective ways.

It was but a few minutes' walk to Wellclose Square, and I took it slowly, for now that my companion was gone and I was bereft of his buoyancy and vitality, I was suddenly aware of intense bodily fatigue. Moreover, I felt a certain reluctance to bring to a definite close what had been an interval of quiet but perfect happiness. And so, in spite of my fatigue, I sauntered on, loitering awhile in St. George's churchyard and stopping to look up at the quaint stone name-tablet at the corner of Chigwell Lane, until weariness and growing hunger drove me homewards. And even then, it was not without regret that I pulled the brass bell-knob and, as it were, wrote "*Finis*" to this pleasant and eventful chapter.

Chapter XV
The Magic Pendulum

The weighty question whether my handicraft would yield me a livelihood was answered on the following morning by the arrival of a letter from Mr. Campbell, and it was answered, though not very emphatically, in the affirmative. The prices that he offered, provisionally – and advised me not to accept – were appallingly low, very little above those of mere commercial goods. But even so, it would be possible, by hard work and spare living, to eke out a bare subsistence. And it was fair to assume that Mr. Campbell's offer was, as indeed he explicitly stated, a minimum, on which an advance might be expected. Accordingly, I declined the offer and decided to await the results of actual sales to his customers.

I was turning these matters over at the breakfast table when Lilith came and took a vacant chair by my side.

"Well, Sibyl," she said, in a low voice, "how did you fare yesterday? Did you have any success?

"Yes. I came back with an empty bag."

"And a full purse?"

"Ah! That is another matter. The tide of handicraft doesn't seem exactly to lead on to fortune."

"I want to hear all about it," said Lilith. "But we can't discuss it here. Let us have a quiet talk up in my room after breakfast. If you will run up when you've finished, I will join you in a few minutes."

I assented gladly, for Lilith, apart from what the irreverent Titmouse characterised as her "crystal-gazing tosh", was a sound adviser on business affairs, and a few minutes later I betook myself upstairs to her studio. I had scarcely seen this room before, for there was an unwritten law, sternly enforced by Miss Polton, forbidding the boarders to enter one another's workrooms except by invitation and on specific business, and I now looked about me with a good deal of curiosity.

It was a queer room. The two sides of Lilith's personality, like two separate persons, seemed to have parcelled it out into two distinct territories. There was the working territory – neat, precise, business-like, strangely free from the usual muddle and disorder of a woman-artist's studio, the big water-colour easel, the orderly painting cabinet, the *papier-mache* lay figure, quaintly arrayed in a walking costume such as might have been seen in a Regent Street shop window (miraculously

399

built up, as I observed, of draperies, pinned, tied or lightly stitched together), the charcoal studies from the figure, pinned up on the wall for reference, with careful pencil drawings of heads, hands, and feet, and one or two casts of faces and hands. The working department was a model of matter-of-fact efficiency.

In curious contrast to this was the domain of Lilith, the mystic. In a well-lighted corner stood a small table supporting a black velvet cushion on which reposed a crystal globe of the size of a cricket ball. Above the table a couple of book-shelves exhibited a collection of volumes treating of Spiritualism, Telepathy, Apparitions, Psychical Research, and other occult subjects. On the upper shelf stood a box filled with the letters of a dissected alphabet, while, hanging on the wall, was a small heart-shaped object with tiny castors, which I assumed to be Planchette, and by its side a single Egyptian bead suspended at the end of a silken thread.

Yet these two aspects of this strange girl's character were not without a connecting link. On the walls were several framed paintings signed *"Winifred Blake"*, mystical figure subjects, recalling, but not imitating, the works of Burne Jones and Rosetti, exquisitely drawn and delicately painted in water-colour. The work on the easel was a similar drawing of a frieze-like character, the figures nude but with lightly indicated draperies, and one of the nude figures had been traced on to a fashion-plate board and was already partly clothed in the walking costume.

My survey of the room and its contents was interrupted by the arrival of its occupant, who having seated me in the easy chair, perched herself on her painting-stool and opened the examination.

"Now," said she, "I don't want to be inquisitive, but I do want to know just how you got on. Did you carry out the methods that I proposed?

"I did – at least as far as the silent willing was concerned – though not very thoroughly. I don't think I did much in the way of suggestion."

"And did you sell your work?"

"Yes, I think I may say I did," and here I gave her an account of Mr. Campbell's two alternative offers.

"You have done admirably, Sibyl," she said enthusiastically. "Your first essay has been a perfect success. And now, tell me, are you convinced?"

As I could not truthfully say that I was, I took refuge in polite evasion, which, however, Lilith brushed aside with some impatience.

"I can never understand this kind of scepticism," said she. "You have the cause and effect before your eyes, but yet you refuse to recognise the connection. You take your work to this man. Outside the

400

shop you will that he shall buy it. You go in and he does buy it. What more could you want?"

"But he might have bought the things if I hadn't willed, you know."

"Yes," she agreed, "he might. But that is not the way we reason about material things. I strike a match and apply it to a laid fire, and the fire burns. It might have burned if I had not applied the lighted match, but no one doubts the connection between the lighted match and the lighted fire. Physical causes and effects are accepted with unquestioning faith, but as soon as we come to spiritual or psychical phenomena, this extraordinary scepticism springs up – this curious refusal to admit and accept the obvious."

"I am not asserting that there was no connection between the silent willing and the purchase of my work," said I. "All I say is that I don't regard the connection as proved. I can't decide for or against because there doesn't seem to be enough evidence either way."

"Yes, I suppose you are right," she admitted, reluctantly. "But I should like to convince you, because I am sure you have very unusual powers."

She was silent for a short space, and then, suddenly, she asked, "Have you ever been to a séance, Sibyl?"

"Never," I replied.

"Well," said she, "you ought to go to one – not to any of those silly public shows conducted by mere mountebanks, but to a private séance, carried out by really earnest people who are seeking to extend our knowledge. Would you care to come to one with me?"

"It would be rather interesting," I replied, without much enthusiasm.

"It would," said she. "You were speaking of evidence just now. Well, at a genuine séance you would obtain evidence that I think would convince you of the reality of psychical phenomena. I have a friend – a Mr. Quecks – who has given me some most remarkable demonstrations, and I have no doubt that he would be very pleased for you to accompany me to one of them."

"Is Mr. Quecks a medium?" I asked.

"No, I shouldn't describe him as a medium, though he is very sensitive and has most extraordinary powers. But he is a profound student of super-normal phenomena and deeply interested in psychical research. May I ask him to show you some of his experiments?"

"Thank you, Lilith, and I hope you will find me less disappointing than you have to-day. I am really quite curious about these things, although I admit a rather sceptical frame of mind. I was wondering, before you came up, what you do with that bead on the string."

"That," replied Lilith, all agog at the question, "is the *pendule explorateur* – the magic pendulum. It is an instrument of the kind known in psychical science as an *autoscope* – an appliance for, as it were, bringing the subconscious into view."

"But how does it work?"

"It works by the influence of the subconscious mind upon the muscles. Let me show you – but you shall try it yourself because you are an unbeliever."

She removed the crystal ball and its cushion from the table, and taking the bowl of loose letters, turned out its contents and rapidly arranged the letters in a circle, forming a clock-wise alphabet. Then she took the pendulum down from its hook.

"Now," said she, "what you have to do is this, you rest your elbow on the table to steady your hand, and you hold the string with the thumb and finger, letting the bead hang just clear of the table in the centre of the circle, and you must keep your hand perfectly still and steady."

"But if I do, the bead will remain still, too."

"No, it won't, excepting just at first. Presently it will begin to swing, apparently of its own accord, but really in accordance with your mental state. For instance, if you let it hang inside a glass and you will that it shall strike the hour, it will strike the hour. If you will – or I hold your other hand and will – that it shall swing round in a circle to the right or left, it will swing round in the direction willed. But that is an exercise of the conscious will. In the experiment that we are making now, we tap the subconscious. If there is any thing or person occupying your subconscious mind, the pendulum will spell out the name of that thing or person by swinging towards the letters. Let me put the chair comfortably for you, so that you can keep quite still."

As I listened to Lilith's explanation I began to wish heartily that I had never embarked on this experiment. Of course, I did not believe for a moment that this absurd pendulum would develop the occult powers that Lilith claimed for it, but yet her confidence shook mine. And I had a very strong feeling that, on this day of all days, I should prefer to keep my subconscious mind to myself. However, there was no escape, so I seated myself and proceeded to carry out Lilith's directions.

For nearly half-a-minute the bead hung quite motionless from my steady hand. Then it began almost imperceptibly to oscillate. My eye had already taken in the positions of the letters which might be incriminating, and now I observed with uneasy surprise that the faint oscillations of the pendulum were taking a direction towards the letter *J*. I could detect no movement in my hand, but, nevertheless, the oscillations grew wider and wider until the bead, as if possessed by a private demon, swung briskly half-way across the circle.

"That is pretty definite," said Lilith. "It is swinging towards U – or is it J? The circle ought to have been bigger, so that the letters need not have been opposite to one another. But I'll write down both, U or J."

The swing of the pendulum now began to shorten, and then, almost abruptly, it changed its direction to one at right angles, and I observed with astonishment that it was pointing direct to A.

"It's either A or P," said Lilith. "I'll put them both down."

Once again the pendulum changed the direction of its swing, and Lilith noted down E or S, and so, to my growing consternation, it continued to take up quite distinct changes of direction until six variations had occurred, when the pendulum became stationary and then began to swing round in a circle.

"It has finished," said Lilith – whereupon I instantly dropped the pendulum. "It is a word of six letters, U or J, A or P, E or S, A or P, E or S, F or R. Let us see if we can make out what the word is. It is a pity the letters were opposite, it muddles it up so. They ought to be in a half-circle, but then they would be too close. But let us try a few combinations. $U\ P\ E\ A\ S\ F$, it can't be that. $U\ P\ S\ A\ S\ F$, it can't be that. We'll try it with $J - J\ A\ E\ P\ E\ F$, that isn't it. $J\ A\ S\ B\ S\ F$, that can't be the word. Do the letters suggest anything to you, Sibyl? Is there any name that might be lurking in your subconscious mind, beginning with U or J? Try to think. What did you do in town yesterday?"

"Oh, various things. I went to the dealer, of course, and then I went to a private show of pottery and antiques."

"Pottery," mused Lilith, scanning the letters that she had written down. "Let me see, Upchurch? No, that won't do." She looked the letters through again and then asked eagerly, "There wasn't any Wedgwood there, I suppose?"

Now it happened that while Mr. Hawkesley was talking to us I had noticed an old gentleman tenderly placing a very fine green Wedgwood cup and saucer in the show case. So I could, and did, answer truthfully.

"Yes, there was, a beautiful green Jasper-ware cup and saucer."

"There!" Lilith exclaimed triumphantly. "Jasper! That is the word! And yet I don't suppose you have given that cup and saucer a thought since you saw it."

"I had forgotten its existence until you spoke of Wedgwood."

"Exactly," said Lilith. "And that is the mysterious peculiarity of the subconscious. You see a thing or a person perhaps only for a moment, and straightway forget it. It seems to be gone for ever. But it is not. It has sunk into the subconscious, to remain there unnoticed possibly for years until some chance association, or perhaps a dream, brings it to the surface. But all the time it has been there. And at any moment it can be brought into view by the use of some kind of autoscope such as the pendulum or the crystal."

"The crystal is an autoscope, too, is it?" I asked.

"Yes, but of quite a different kind. The pendulum acts by the effects of the subconscious mind upon the muscles, the crystal by the effects of the subconscious mind on the centres of visual perception."

"That sounds very learned, but tell me exactly what you do with the crystal."

"As to me, personally," replied Lilith, "I do very little with it. Crystal vision – or '*scrying*', to use the technical term – is a rather rare faculty. I am a very poor scryer. But in the case of a really gifted observer, the most astonishing results are obtained. The method of using the instrument is this: The scryer sits in a restful position with the crystal before her (all the best scryers, I think, are women) and gazes steadily at the bright lights in it, keeping the conscious mind in a passive state – thinking of nothing, in fact. After a time the lights in the crystal grow dim, a kind of cloud or mist seems to float before it, and in this cloud, and gradually taking its place, the picture or vision appears, sometimes dim and vague, but often quite clear and bright, like the little pictures that you see in a convex mirror or a silver ball."

"And what is this picture? I mean what is its subject?

"That varies. It may be a scene from the past that had been forgotten by the conscious memory, or something that never happened at all – just a jumble of bits of memory like a dream. Or it may be the picture of some event that is going to take place in the near future."

"But," I objected, "how can an event which has not yet occurred be in your subconscious mind?"

"I know," said Lilith. "The whole subject of pre-recognition is a very difficult one. But there seems to be no doubt that prophetic visions do really occur. And then there is clairvoyance – seeing across space and through obstacles. A really gifted scryer, by concentrating her thought on a particular person or place as she looks into the crystal, can see that person or place, no matter how great the distance may be – can see exactly what the person is doing or what is happening at the place."

"Really!" I exclaimed. "That sounds like rather an undesirable faculty. Doesn't it strike you, Lilith, as a very great intrusion on the privacy and liberty of the subject to scry a person without his or her consent? Supposing the scryer should happen to discover the scryed one in the act of taking her – or his – morning tub. Wouldn't it be rather a liberty?"

Lilith laughed (but I could see that the idea was new to her.) "You are dreadfully matter-of-fact, Sibyl. But, of course, you are quite right. We shouldn't misuse our powers. As for me, I have very little power of the kind to misuse, for I have never seen anything more than a sort of vague picture of unrecognisable figures in undistinguishable surroundings. But I think you might do better, for I am still convinced that you have special gifts. Would you like to try the crystal, Sibyl?

"Not now, thank you, Lilith. We ought to get to work after all this gossip. And that reminds me that, before you came up, I was looking at your exquisite paintings and wondering if you are not, to some extent, wasting your great talents."

"In what way?" she asked.

"Of course," I said, "these designs would make magnificent tapestries or wall decorations. But if you can't get a wall, you might condescend to a smaller surface. Have you ever tried designing and painting a fan?"

"No," she replied.

"I wish you would," said I. "You would do it splendidly with your power of design and your delicate technique. And Phillibar could make the sticks and carve the guards, or I could do you a pair in silver *repoussé*, and a jewelled pin and loop. Will you think over the proposal?"

Lilith picked up the crystal on its cushion and, smiling at me, said,

"I will make a bargain with you. If you will take the crystal to your room and give it a thorough trial whenever you have time, I will get out a design for a fan. Do you agree?"

I held out my hand for the crystal. Primarily, my desire was to introduce Lilith to Fame and Fortune through the medium of the Magpies Club, but the startling success of the magic pendulum had aroused my curiosity in regard to the other "autoscope", though I have to confess that, when I had borne it to my room, I concealed it guiltily in a locked drawer, where it should be secure from the prying eyes of the servant-maid, and above all from the observation of the sarcastic and sceptical Titmouse.

But there were other matters than crystals and magic pendulums to be thought of. There was, for instance, the set of twelve spoons which Mr. Campbell had asked me to make and to which he had again referred in his letter. I knew now that I should be paid for them at a reasonably remunerative rate, and this, and the congenial nature of the task, encouraged me to get to work. But before I could begin there was the motive of the design to be considered, and since the apostles were ruled out as obsolete, I had to find some other group of twelve related objects.

After a whole day's anxious thought, I fixed upon the Signs of the Zodiac as furnishing a picturesque and manageable motive, and with this scheme in my mind, I fell to work in earnest, first with the pencil and then with the wax and metal.

But busy as I was, and happy in the interest of my work, I was yet aware of a change, of a something new that had come into my life. From the little workshop which had been my world, I found my thoughts straying out into the larger world, and particularly that part of it which is adjacent to Temple Bar, and if at times I viewed this change with some misgivings, I was more often conscious of a sense of exhilaration such as one feels when embarking on some new adventure.

In due course I received notice of my election as a member of the Magpies Club, and by the same post a letter from Mr. Davenant asking me to celebrate the event by lunching with him there, and, as I had occasion to go into town to replenish my silver and some other materials, I accepted his invitation, intending to return to Wellclose Square in the afternoon. But it appeared that a loan collection of antique silver was being exhibited at the South Kensington Museum, and that he had hoped to have the pleasure of inspecting it under my expert guidance. Now, to a craftsman (or crafts-woman) of small experience, there is no technical education to compare with the study of admitted masterpieces. I felt that strongly, and I felt that I needed that technical education, furthermore, I felt that the attempt to explain the merits of the old work to an attentive and sympathetic listener would help me to concentrate my own attention. And perhaps it did. At any rate, I spent a long and pleasant afternoon at the museum, and we subsequently discussed the exhibits (and various other matters) very companionably over the dinner table at the club.

"It has been a jolly day for me, Mrs. Otway," said Mr. Davenant, as he wished me "Good-bye" at the Underground Station. "I've learned no end about silver – you are a perfect encyclopaedia of knowledge in regard to goldsmith's work. And the delightful thing to think of is that we've only scratched the surface of the museum. The place is inexhaustible. Do you think I may hope for the pleasure of another visit there with you before long?"

I gave what I intended to be an ambiguous answer. But it was not ambiguous to me, and I suspect that Mr. Davenant went on his way with a feeling that a precedent had been created.

When I arrived home, I found a letter awaiting me from Mr. Otway. It was not entirely unexpected, for I had felt pretty certain that he would presently hear further from his mysterious correspondent. It now appeared that he had received one or two short letters, ostensibly of the nature of warnings, but actually threatening, though in vague, indefinite terms, and one more recently of a more explicitly menacing character. These he wished me to see and discuss with him, and he asked me to make an appointment, at my convenience, to meet him for that purpose. I replied, suggesting, as before, the Tower Wharf, and there, a couple of evenings later, I met him.

In appearance he had by no means improved. His pale face had a strained, wild expression, his eye-lids were puffy and covered with curious, minute wrinkles. His hands were markedly tremulous, and his fingers bore the deep stains that mark the inveterate cigarette smoker. His dress was noticeably less neat than it had used to be, indeed, he presented a distinctly shabby and neglected appearance. Oddly enough, too, he seemed to have grown somewhat stouter.

I should have been less than human if these plain indications of sustained misery had awakened in me no feeling of pity. That his sufferings were the indirect result of his indifference to the happiness or misery of others, could not entirely stifle compassion, and I found myself speaking to him in a tone almost sympathetic.

"I am afraid, Mr. Otway," said I, "you are letting these nonsensical letters worry you quite unnecessarily. You are not looking at all well."

"I am not at all well, Helen," he replied, dejectedly.

"And I think you are smoking too much."

"I am. And I am drinking too much – I, who have been a temperate man all my life. And I have to take drugs to get a decent night's rest. This worry is breaking me up."

"Oh, come, Mr. Otway," I protested, "you mustn't give way in this manner. What is it all about, after all? Just a wretched blackmailer whom you know to be an impostor, whose threats you know to be mere empty vapourings."

"That is not quite true, Helen. The man is an impostor, no doubt. He doesn't really know anything. There is nothing for him to know. But he could create a great deal of trouble. He could, in fact, cause the – ah – the inquiry to be re-opened and – ah – "

"Exactly. And if it were re-opened? There would be unpleasant comment on the fact that a detail of the evidence had been withheld at the inquest. But that is the worst that could happen."

Mr. Otway looked at me with a sort of dumb gratitude that was quite pathetic, but his gloom was in nowise dispelled by my optimism.

"It is very good of you, Helen," said he, "to speak in this cheerful, confident tone. But I assure you, you minimize the danger. There is no saying what construction might be put upon the suppression of that detail, what considerations of motive might be read into it – especially as

407

there was what they would call collusion between us to suppress it. But let me show you the last letter – the others are of no consequence."

He produced his wallet and, after some awkward fumbling, drew out the letter, which he held out to me with a hand that shook so that the paper rattled. Like the last, it was typewritten unskilfully, and characterized

by the same semi-illiterate confusion in the wording, which ran thus:

Mr. Lewis Otway,

The writer of this warns you once more to look out for trouble. The person that I spoke of knows that some thing was held back at the inquest at least they say so and that they know why your wife won't live with you and that she knows all about it too and that someone knows more than you think anybody knows. This is a friendly warning.

From a Well Wisher

I returned the letter to Mr. Otway after reading it through twice, and I must confess that my confidence was somewhat shaken. If the writer was merely guessing, he seemed to have an uncanny aptitude for guessing right. As to his claim to possess some further knowledge, I did not see how that could be possible. When the fatal interview took place between my father and Mr. Otway, there were – to the best of my belief – only three persons in the house. Of those actually present at the interview there was only a single survivor – Mr. Otway himself – and he alone knew with certainty what occurred. The claim was therefore almost certainly false. And yet, even as I dismissed it, there crept into my mind once again a vague discomfort, a doubt whether there might not be something that I was unaware of, and that Mr. Otway knew, some dreadful secret that I, of all persons in the world, had been instrumental in guarding from discovery. And as I glanced at Mr. Otway – haggard, wild, trembling, and terrified out of all proportion to the danger, so far as it was known to me – the horrid doubts seemed to deepen into something like suspicion.

"Of course," said he, when he had returned the letter to the wallet, "I realize that you are right, that there is nothing to be done but to wait for this person to show his hand more plainly. It would be madness to apply to the police. They would immediately ask if there had been any evidence withheld and why you were not living with me. And if they succeeded in getting hold of the writer of this letter, we should have more to fear from them than from the writer himself. He may be, as you believe, a mere blackmailer who is preparing to extort money, but if he were brought to bay he would try to justify his threats."

With this I could not but agree. The implied allegations in this letter were, in point of fact, true, and any attempt to obtain help from the police would probably result in their truth being made manifest.

"Have you no idea whatever," I asked, "who might be the writer of this letter? He can hardly be a complete stranger. Have you no suspicion? Can you think of no one who might have written it?"

He looked at me furtively and cleared his throat once or twice before replying, and when he did answer, his manner was hesitating and even evasive.

"Suspicions," he said, "are – er – not very – ah – helpful. I have no facts. The mere – ah – conjecture that this person or that might possibly be concerned – if a motive could be supplied – and – ah – if one can think of no motive – "

He left the sentence uncompleted, giving me the vague impression that he was reserving something that he did not wish to discuss.

We were silent for some time, and I was beginning to consider bringing the interview to an end when he suddenly turned to me with a gesture of appeal.

"Helen," he said earnestly, "is it not possible for me to prevail on you to – ah – to reconsider your decision and – ah – to – to – to terminate this – er – this unhappy separation. Consider my loneliness, Helen, my broken health and this trouble – which is our joint trouble – and – ah – "

"Mr. Otway," I answered, "it is not possible. I assure you it is not. I am deeply distressed to think of your unhappiness and to see you looking so ill, but I could not entertain what you suggest. You must remember that we are strangers. We have never been otherwise than separated. As we are, so we must continue."

"You don't mean that we must always remain apart?" he exclaimed. "It was only meant to be a temporary separation."

"At any rate," I rejoined, "the time has not come to consider a change. But I shall be glad to hear how things go with you and to give you any help that I can."

I rose and held out my hand, which he took reluctantly (though it was the first time that I had ever offered to shake hands with him).

"I am driving you away, Helen," he said.

"No, indeed," I replied. "I had to go. You will write to me if anything fresh happens?"

409

He promised readily, and we turned and walked away in opposite directions. When I had gone a little way, I paused to look back at him, and as I noted his dejected droop and his air of something approaching physical decrepitude, I felt a pang – not of remorse, but of regret that I could not in some way lighten the burden of his evident misery. It is true that his unhappiness was of his own making, and that in wrecking his own life he had wrecked mine and my father's. But vindictiveness is a character alien to the civilized and developed mind. For what he had done I still loathed him, but it pained me to think of the haunting dread, the abiding fear that was his companion night and day.

Chapter XVI
The Sweated Artist

I had told Mr. Otway that I had to go, but I did not tell him why. If I had, he would probably have been considerably startled. For the fact is that while we were talking I had formed a resolution which had rapidly matured – the resolution to go to Dr. Thorndyke and make a clean breast of the whole affair. He had invited me to call on him and report from time to time, especially if I should be in need of advice or help, and I had been intending to write and propose a visit. Now, however, I decided to call on the chance of his being disengaged, and if he should be unable to see me, to make an appointment.

From the Tower Wharf I made my way quickly to Mark Lane, noting as I entered the station that it was a quarter-to-six, and as the train rumbled westward I turned over the situation and decided on what I should say. That some trouble was brewing I had little doubt, and though I did not share Mr. Otway's alarm, I was more than a little uneasy. For, at the best, the re-opening of the inquiry into my father's death must entail a scandal and exhibit my conduct in a decidedly questionable light, and such a scandal would be a disaster. As a discredited witness, how could I face my comrades at Wellclose Square? And how should I stand with Jasper Davenant? These were unpleasant questions to reflect on. And underneath these reflections was the uneasy feeling that perhaps there was something more in Mr. Otway's fear than was known to me, something of which I had hardly dared to think.

From the Temple Station I found my way without difficulty to Dr. Thorndyke's chambers at Number 5A, King's Bench Walk, and was relieved to find the outer oak door open and a small brass knocker on the inner one tacitly accepting the possibility of visitors. I plied it modestly, and was immediately confronted by Mr. Polton, whose countenance, at the sight of me, became covered with a net work of benevolent and amicable wrinkles.

"The doctor is up in the laboratory looking over his apparatus, but I expect he has nearly finished. I'll go and tell him you are here. Have you had tea?"

I had not and admitted the fact, whereupon Mr. Polton nodded meaningly, and having offered me an arm-chair, took his departure. In a minute or two Dr. Thorndyke entered the room and greeted me with a cordiality that put me at my ease instantly.

411

"I have been wondering when you were coming to see me. In fact, I have seriously considered calling at Wellclose Square to see how you were getting on. Polton will bring you some tea in a moment, and then you must tell me all your news. I hope you are comfortable in your new home."

"I am very happy, indeed, Dr. Thorndyke, and very grateful to you for finding me such a congenial home. And I have made quite a promising start in my new profession, too. But I have really come to ask your advice – and to make a confession."

"A confession," said Dr. Thorndyke, looking at me gravely. "Is it necessary? And have you given it due consideration?"

"Yes, I think so. There is only one point. I should have told you this secret before, but as another person is involved in it, I felt that it would be a breach of confidence. But I now feel that my legal adviser should be told everything."

"That is so. Advice can only be based on known facts. And I may say that anything that you may tell me in my professional capacity is a privileged communication. A lawyer cannot be compelled to reveal anything that his client has told him, and is, in fact, forbidden to do so. You are, therefore, committing no breach of confidence in giving me any necessary information."

"I am glad to know that, because, when I last spoke to you about my affairs, I held back something that you may consider important."

"Something relating to the inquest?" he asked.

"Yes. Did you suspect that I had?"

"I suspected that Mr. Otway was holding something back when he gave his evidence – but here is your tea, with all the little lady-like extras, just to show you what an old bachelor can do in the way of domestic miracles. I am ashamed of you, Polton. I call that embroidered tea-cloth sheer ostentation."

Mr. Polton laid out the dainty service, beaming with satisfaction at the doctor's recognition of his efforts to maintain the credit of the establishment, and as he went out I heard him close the outer door.

"Polton evidently smells a conference," commented Dr. Thorndyke. "The infallible way in which he always does the right thing without a word of instruction almost makes me believe in telepathy – which might be awkward if he were not as secret as an oyster. Now don't hurry, but tell me quietly what you want me to know."

Thus encouraged, I gave him the suppressed facts relating to the loaded stick that I had seen in Mr. Otway's hand, and then told him about the mysterious letters. He listened very attentively, and seemed deeply interested, for he questioned me at some length about Mr. Otway's establishment at Maidstone, his mode of life, and such of his antecedents as were known to me.

"Is the stick in your possession or has Mr. Otway got it?" he asked.

"I suppose he has it. At any rate, I have never seen it since that day."

"And you know nothing of any of his associates, other than the housekeeper?"

"Nothing whatever."

"Is Mrs. Gregg still with him?"

"I believe so, but I am not sure."

"And you know nothing of his present mode of life excepting that he lives in Lyon's Inn Chambers?"

"No. I really know nothing about him."

"It is very satisfactory for you," Dr. Thorndyke observed. "You are quite in the dark. These letters suggest an intention to extort money, but they may come from a personal enemy or from someone who has some design other than direct blackmail. And the question is, what cards does that person hold? Is he acting on a mere guess or has he any actual knowledge? The problem involves two questions: Was there anyone in the house that morning besides you, your father, and Mr. Otway? And did anything occur on that occasion beyond what Mr. Otway told you? The answer seems to be in the negative in both cases, but we cannot be certain on either point. Meanwhile, your position is very unpleasant, and Mr. Otway's still more so, for his apprehensions, though perhaps exaggerated, are not entirely groundless. He has behaved with consummate folly. Whether his account of the tragedy be true or false, if he had had the courage to give it in full at the inquest, it must have been accepted in the absence of contrary evidence. But that is by no means the case now. If the inquiry were re-opened, a jury would tend to regard his suppression of certain facts as evidence of the importance of those facts.

"As to advice, there is nothing that you can do but try to forget these menacing letters. I will make a few cautious enquiries – though we have very little to go on – and you must let me know at once if there are any fresh developments."

This ended the conference, but not the conversation, for Dr. Thorndyke insisted on a full account of my progress as a craftswoman, and even called down Mr. Polton to give an expert opinion on Mr. Campbell's prices, which opinion was to the effect that they were as good as could be expected.

"So," said Dr. Thorndyke, as I rose to depart, "you have justified your rather bold choice of a profession. You have already made it an economic success, and with more experience on the commercial side, you will probably earn a very satisfactory livelihood."

This was encouraging enough, backed as it was by Mr. Polton's practical experience. But with the other results of this conference I was much less satisfied. Indeed, my talk with Dr. Thorndyke, though it had relieved me of the burden of concealment, so far from setting my apprehensions at rest, had rather increased them. Not only was it evident that he regarded these mysterious letters as indications of a real danger, but he clearly entertained the possibility that Mr. Otway might have something more than I knew to conceal. In fact, I was by no means sure that he did not suspect Mr. Otway of having killed my father.

Here, then, was abundant matter for reflection, and that none of the most pleasant, and during the next few days my mind was very full of these new complications, of this dark cloud which had arisen over my brightening horizon. Again and again I recalled in detail the incidents of that terrible morning when my dear father was snatched from me, but no new light, either on the tragedy itself or on these sinister echoes of it, came to me. I even tried Lilith's crystal – having first locked my door – but either my faith was weak or I lacked those special psychical gifts with which its owner credited me. I did, indeed, get as far as the cloud, or mist, of which Lilith had spoken, which gathered before my eyes and blotted out the crystal. But that was all. When the mist cleared away, no picture emerged from it, but only the crystal ball with the diminutive image of my own head reflected on its bright surface.

But anxieties sit lightly on the young and healthy. As the days passed, the gloomy impressions faded and I became once more absorbed in my work. The Zodiac spoons were progressing apace, and were going to do me credit, and daily I became conscious of growing facility, of increasing skill, which not only lessened my labour but was itself a source of pleasure. To do a thing with ease is to do it with enjoyment, and, incidentally, added skill means added speed and greater earning power. Already I began to speculate on what Mr. Campbell's idea of "a good price" would turn out to be.

Moreover, there were other distractions. Once or twice a week I looked in at the club, and these visits had a pleasant way of developing into impromptu jaunts – to picture galleries, exhibitions, museums, and even on one or two occasions a concert or a matinée. Of the relations which were growing up between Jasper Davenant and me I did not care to think much. Perhaps the ostrich is a wiser bird than we are apt to imagine, for it does, at least, avoid the pains of anticipation. Sooner or later, no doubt, some understanding would have to be arrived at, but meanwhile Mr. Davenant was a delightful companion – gay, cheerful, buoyant, humorous, but withal a man of earnest purpose and a serious outlook on life. In all our junketings was little, real frivolity, the fun and

414

gaiety were but the condiments to season the more solid and serious interests. In so far as a friendship between a young man and a young woman, which must necessarily stop at friendship, can be, our friendship was unexceptionable. But, of course, there was the qualification. However, as I have said, I let the future take care of itself and drifted pleasantly with the stream.

About this time, I made quite a startling discovery. It happened that in one of my journeys to town I had seen in a bookseller's window a book on studio pottery, and, thinking that it might be useful to Miss Finch, I had bought it, but had forgotten to give it to her. In the middle of my morning's work I suddenly remembered the book, which I had put in a cupboard in the workshop, and got up from my bench to take it to her. Her "works" were at the bottom of the garden, in an outhouse which had once been a ship-smith's shop, but, close neighbours as we were, and close friends, too, I had only once been in her workshop, when, on an off day, she had shown me her wheel, her lathe, and her small glass kiln. About her work she was extraordinarily secretive – but then, she was a reticent girl in general, so far as her own affairs were concerned, though she showed a warm interest in her friends, and was, indeed, very affectionate and lovable.

As I came round the clump of bushes that hid her premises from the house, the silence and repose of the place gave me some qualms, and for a moment I hesitated to interrupt her work. However, I pocketed my scruples and rapped boldly on the door, whereupon the familiar voice at its highest pitch – several ledger lines above the stave – demanded who was there.

"It is I, Peggy – Helen Otway," I replied apologetically. There was a pause of nearly half-a-minute, and then she unlocked and opened the door, looking rather embarrassed and very pink.

"I always lock myself in when I am at work," she explained.

"Well, Peggy, don't let me disturb you. I've only brought you a book that I got for you in town."

"Oh, come in, Sibyl," said she. "Of course I don't mind you."

She took the volume from me, and quickly turning over the pages and glancing at the illustrations, exclaimed, "What a ripping book! I shall enjoy reading it. And how sweet of you to think of getting it for me!" She linked her arm affectionately in mine and conducted me into her domain, passing through the outer room, which was devoted to plaster work – the making of moulds and "bats" – to the clay room, where the little gas engine and the mysterious wheel stood idle and a general tidying-up appeared to have taken place. Here we stood chatting rather disjointedly, she still turning over the pages of the book with approving comments, and I looking about me with a craftsman's curiosity respecting the materials and appliances of an unfamiliar craft. And here I got my first surprise, for, on a side bench I noticed a collection of what were evidently bookbinder's tools. Was it possible that the secretive Titmouse was a bookbinder as well as a potter? I determined to inquire into this, but meanwhile my attention was attracted by the bench at which she had evidently been working, as suggested by the displaced stool. On this bench stood an object of some size – about twelve inches high – enveloped in a damp cloth. By its side were a spray-diffuser, a number of little spatulas and tiny modelling tools, and several little covered pots of a creamy, white earthenware delicately ornamented with floral decoration in a warm blue. Venturing to lift the cover of one, I found it to be filled with little rolls of brightly-tinted clay that looked like coloured crayons.

"You are mighty fastidious about your apparatus," I remarked, picking up the dainty little pot and wiping some smears of clay from its surface.

"And why not?" demanded Peggy. "Why shouldn't one have pretty things to work with? The old craftsmen did. I've seen some old planes and chisel-handles beautifully carved, and I am sure they did better work for having beautiful tools to work with. I would have pretty tools myself if I could make them."

"You shall, Peggy," said I. "You shall show me what you want and I will make them for you."

As I was speaking, I absently turned the little pot upside down and glanced at the bottom. And then I really did get a shock. There was only a single spot of ornament on the base, but that spot was a revelation, for it was a little blue bird.

I smothered the exclamation that rose to my lips and put the pot down on the bench. What could be the meaning of this? Had Peggy, like Mr. Hawkesley, been attracted by Mr. Goldstein's wares? Or was it possible – "Won't you show me what you were doing, Peggy?" I asked.

She turned scarlet at the question, and looked so distressed that I felt it a cruelty to press her. But cruel or not, I meant to get to the bottom of the mystery.

"I'd rather not, Sibyl, if you don't mind," she said, shyly.

"But why? What an extraordinary little person you are."

"Well," she said, doggedly, "if you must know, I am not allowed to show my work to anyone."

"Not allowed by whom?"

"By the dealer who takes all my work. For some reason, best known to himself, he makes a secret of it – won't allow anyone to know who makes it."

"But apart from the dealer, Peggy, you wouldn't mind my seeing your work?

"Of course I shouldn't. I should like you to see it. But a promise is a promise, you know."

"Of course," I agreed, and then I stepped quickly up to the bench and very carefully picking up the damp cloth, lifted it clear of the object which it covered, which turned out to be a jar standing on a small turntable. Peggy sprang forward with a gasp of consternation, but she was too late. The deed was done – moreover, the murder was out, for in the moment when my first glance fell on the jar, Mr. Hawkesley's "mystery ware" had ceased to be a mystery so far as I was concerned.

The appearance of the jar was rather curious, but perfectly unmistakable. The clay, in its "green" state – unbaked and still somewhat plastic – was of a cool, grey colour, and the surface of the squat, octagonal body and the short neck and rim was covered with rich and intricate floral ornament, very minute, sharp and delicate. In the completed part this ornament was of dull blue and finished flush with the surface, in the unfinished part it was simply indented and had the appearance of what bookbinders call "blind tooling," but was somewhat deeper.

From the work, my eyes turned with a sort of respectful wonder to the creator, who stood by my side with an air partly embarrassed, partly defiant. To me there was something very impressive in the thought that this unassuming little lady was actually a master craftsman (I am compelled to use the masculine form, there being no feminine equivalent), the creator of masterpieces which would live in the great collections of the future for the admiration of generations yet unborn. And in the first shock of surprised admiration and pride in my friend's achievement I had nearly blurted out all that I knew. But reflection suggested a better plan.

"My dear Peggy!" I exclaimed. "I never dreamed that you did work of this quality."

"There's nothing very wonderful about it," she replied, regarding the jar with a kind of affectionate disparagement. "It is only a poor imitation of the beautiful Oiron ware. That pottery has always interested me, partly because it is so lovely, and partly because, according to tradition, it was made by a woman – Helene de Hangest-Gerilis. But my work isn't a patch of hers, and it isn't even as good as I could do."

"How is that?"

"Well, you see, it ought to have more modelled ornament than I put on. It ought to be more important. Her pieces were most elaborately modelled – many of them had figures in the full round. But I can't afford to carry my work as far as that. It would take too long. Besides, I have to work to order, to some extent, and my orders are to keep to moderately, simple pieces."

"Your orders! From the dealer, I suppose? Tell me about him, Peggy, and how it is that you are such a slave."

"I'm not a slave," she retorted doggedly. "But I have a contract with a dealer. He takes the whole of my work, and he makes it a condition that I shan't sell anything to any one else or let anybody know what kind of work I do. I oughtn't to have let you in, but I know that I can trust you not to breathe a word to anyone of what you have seen here."

Mr. Hawkesley was right, then, and I recalled with sympathetic vindictiveness his desire to wring the dealer's neck.

"Concerning this contract, Peggy," said I. "You say the dealer has the right to the whole of your work. Did he pay you anything for this privilege?"

"Yes. He paid five pounds when the agreement was signed, but he deducted it from the payment for the first lot of pieces."

"Then it was only payment on account, not payment for the exclusive right to all your work. And with regard to the prices, how are they fixed?

"Oh, the dealer fixes the prices, of course. He knows more about it than I do."

"Evidently. But what sort of prices does he fix?"

"Oh, ordinary prices, I suppose. He will probably give me fifteen shillings for this jar."

"And how long will it take you to make it?"

"Let me see," she said, reflectively. "There is the throwing and turning, that doesn't take very long. Then this one had to be shaped after it was turned. Then there comes the decorating, of course that is what takes the time. Including the cover, I should say there is nearly a week's work in that jar. And then it has to be fired and glazed, but the firing and glazing are done in batches."

"And all this for fifteen shillings a week!" I exclaimed.

"Say a pound," said she. "That is about what I earn. It isn't much, is it? But I have a little money of my own, though I spent most of it on fitting up the workshop."

"And what period does this precious contract cover? When does it expire?

"Expire?" she repeated, a little sheepishly. "I don't know that it expires at all. No period is mentioned in it."

"Peggy," I said, solemnly, "you should alter your potter's mark. Take out the little blue finch and put in a little green goose. But, seriously, we must see into this. I am a lawyer's daughter – not that I profess to have inherited a knowledge of law. But I am certain that this agreement is not binding. Will you let me show it to a friend of mine who is a lawyer? In strict confidence, of course."

"Yes, if you like, Sibyl. But I don't see that it matters. I like doing the work and I do make a living by it. What more would you have?"

"I thought you said you would like to do something more ambitious – the very best work of which you are capable. Wouldn't you?"

She was silent for a while, and a far-away, wistful look stole into her face. Suddenly she said, "Sibyl, I'm going to show you something, but you mustn't tell anyone." She led me to a large cupboard, the door of which she unlocked and threw open. On the single shelf was a model in red wax of a tall candlestick or lamp-holder of the most elaborate design, the shaft and capital-like socket enriched – though sparingly – with fine relief decoration, and the base occupied by a spirited and graceful group of figures, beautifully modelled and full of life and expression.

"That," she said, "is to be my *chef d'art* – though it doesn't look much in the wax. You must think of it in ivory-white, with a rich coloured inlay and perhaps some under-glaze painting. It has taken me months, doing a bit whenever I have had time, or when I couldn't resist the temptation to go on with it. Now it is finished, as far as the modelling goes, and the next thing will be to mould it. But I shan't actually make the piece at present, because I don't mean him to have it – the dealer, you know. If I finished it now, it would be his, of course."

"Yes, by the contract it would. And it mustn't. This piece ought to give you a position in the front rank of artist potters. But I mustn't waste any more of your time. You will let me have that agreement, won't you?"

She promised that I should have it at lunch-time, and with this I went back to my workshop to consider a plan that had come into my mind for her enlightenment and emancipation. But it turned out that there was no need for scheming on my part, for chance or Providence offered me the opportunity ready-made. That very evening I received a short note from Mr. Davenant informing me that Miss Tallboy-Smith had acquired a collection of English and French soft porcelain, and that she proposed to exhibit the whole of her new acquisition for a week at the club.

"She rather wants," he said, "to make the opening day something of a function, and has asked Hawkesley and me to be there to lunch. Can you come, too? It would please her if you could – and you know how delighted Hawkesley and I would be. Besides, I think it will really be a very interesting show."

Here was the very chance that I wanted. Forthwith, I swooped down on the unsuspecting Titmouse and secured her agreement to bear me company to a "pottery show" without giving too many particulars. Then I wrote to Mr. Davenant telling him that I was bringing a guest who was deeply interested in pottery and porcelain, and suggesting that we might form a party of four at a small table.

By the same post I sent off Peggy's agreement to Dr. Thorndyke, with the request that he would tell me whether it was or was not legally binding. And, having thus laid the train, as I hoped, for the discomfiture of Mr. Goldstein, I felt at liberty to return to my own affairs.

Chapter XVII
The Apotheosis
of the Titmouse

The respective merits of hard and soft porcelain have been, from time to time, warmly debated by collectors and experts, but never, perhaps, have they been more earnestly discussed than on the occasion of the opening of Miss Tallboy-Smith's exhibition. During the half-hour which preceded lunch, the central glass case and the additional show-cases which had been set up for the occasion were surrounded by groups of eager connoisseurs, and the contrasting virtues of the *pate tendre* and the more durable, if less beautiful, true porcelain were once more considered and expounded.

The attendance of the members and their friends must have been highly gratifying to Miss Tallboy-Smith, though it was no greater than was warranted by the importance of the exhibition, for the collection included representative pieces, not only of Chelsea, Bow, Nantgarw, Pinxton, and other English ware, but also of the old, French soft paste porcelain, including several early examples of Sevres. The preliminary glance at the collection had furnished material for conversation, as I could see by observing the occupants of the long central table, at the head of which sat the beaming hostess, supported by Major Dewham-Brown (who talked little, but consumed his food with intense concentration of purpose), and even our own small table, tucked away inconspicuously in a corner, was not immune from the influence of soft porcelain, for Mr. Hawkesley and my guest discussed the topic with a wealth of knowledge that reduced Mr. Davenant and me to respectful and attentive silence.

Our two friends were evidently very pleased with one another, and not without reason. For Mr. Hawkesley was much more than a mere collector – he was an enthusiastic and learned student of all kinds of ceramic work, while as to my friend Peggy, her conversation revealed a familiarity with all kinds of materials and processes that made me feel quite shy as I thought of the artless handbook with which I had presented her.

But, indeed, Miss Peggy was quite transfigured. She had met with a kindred spirit. And under the influence of contagious enthusiasm, the usually silent and secretive Titmouse blossomed out in a manner that surprised me. As I listened to the animated duet of her chirping treble with Mr. Hawkesley's robust baritone, I found it difficult to identify her with the quiet little potter who was wont to work behind locked doors in the old shipsmith's shop at Wellclose Square.

After lunch, the siege of the showcases began again on a more portentous scale. Glass cases were opened for more complete inspection of their contents, and pieces were even handed out to be handled, stroked, and smelled at by the more infatuated devotees. As neither Mr. Davenant nor I could be included among the latter, we were satisfied by a comparatively brief inspection of the treasures, after which we retired to a sheltered seat to look on and talk.

"Just look at those two china maniacs!" exclaimed Mr. Davenant. "They are as thick as thieves already. And what is Miss Finch going to do with that *bleu de roi* vase? Is she going to kiss it? No, she has given it back to the Tallboy-Smith. Well, well, enthusiasm is a fine thing. By the way, she is a nice little lady, this friend of yours, pretty and picturesque, too, and uncommonly well turned out. I'm beginning to have a new respect for Wellclose Square."

I looked at the Titmouse with a sort of motherly pride (though she was about my own age). The word picturesque described her admirably with her warm colour, her graceful hair, and the trim, petite figure that was so well set off by the simple, artistic dress – in which I seemed to trace the hand of Lilith. She was my importation to the Magpies, and I felt that she was doing me credit.

"I have often wondered," Mr. Davenant said, after a reflective pause, "what made you choose such an unlikely locality as Wellclose Square for a residence, and, indeed, how you came to know of its existence. Very few middle-class people do. I hope Miss Vardon will not consider me unduly inquisitive."

"Mrs. Otway will not," said I.

"Mrs. Otway is a myth – a legal fiction. I refuse to recognise her existence. She is a mere creature of documents, of church registers. The real person is Miss Helen Vardon."

"That sounds rather like nonsense," said I, "but, of course, it can't be, because the speaker is Mr. Davenant. Perhaps there is some hidden meaning in these cryptic observations."

"There isn't," he rejoined, "or, at any rate, it shan't remain hidden. I mean that I refuse to recognise your connection with this man, Otway, or to associate you with his beastly name."

"But it is my beastly name, too, according to law and custom."

"I don't care for law and custom," said he. "The name Otway is abhorrent to me, and it doesn't properly belong to you. I shall call you

Miss Vardon, unless you let me call you Helen, and I don't see why you shouldn't, considering that we are old and intimate friends."

"It would undoubtedly have the support of a well-established precedent. There was a certain bishop who was called Peter because that was his name. That precedent would apply to Helen, but it certainly would not to Miss Vardon."

"Then," he rejoined, "let us follow this excellent precedent. Let it be Helen. Is that agreed?

"I don't seem to have much choice, for if 'Mrs. Otway' is a legal fiction, 'Miss Vardon' is an illegal one."

"Well, don't let us have any fictions at all. Let us adhere to the actual baptismal facts."

"Very well, Mr. Davenant."

"But why 'Mr. Davenant'? My baptismal designation is Jasper.'

"And a very pretty name, too," said I. "But the precedent does not apply in your case. You have not married Mr. Otway."

"No, thank Heaven! If I had, there would be a case of petty treason. But neither have you, for that matter. You have only gone through a ridiculous ceremony which means nothing and signed a document which sets forth what is not true."

"It seems to me," I said, "that we are not adhering to our agreement to avoid fictions. My marriage, unfortunately, is perfectly real and valid in the eyes of the law."

"The law!" he exclaimed, contemptuously. "Who cares for the law? Have we not the pronouncement of that illustrious legal luminary, Bumble C.J., that the law is a ass and a idiot? And, mark you, he was specially referring to matrimonial law. Now, who would base his actions and beliefs on the opinions of an ass and a idiot?

"And to think," said I, "that you have abandoned the law for mere architecture! With your gift for casuistry, you ought to have been a Chancery lawyer, or else a Jesuit. But here is Miss Tallboy-Smith. She thinks we are neglecting her treasures."

But our hostess had not come to utter reproaches. On the contrary, she was brimming over with pleasure and gratitude.

"My dear Mrs. Otway," she exclaimed, beaming on me and grasping my hands affectionately, "I can't thank you enough for bringing that dear young lady, Miss Finch, to see my porcelain. She is a sweet girl, and she simply knows everything about china. It is perfectly wonderful. She might be a potter herself. And her love of the beautiful things and her enjoyment in looking at them has given me, I can't tell you how much, pleasure. You must really bring her to see my whole collection. Will you? I shall love showing it to her."

I agreed joyfully, for this would mean another nail in the coffin of Mr. Goldstein, and as Peggy and Mr. Hawkesley joined us at this moment, I was able to complete the arrangement and fix a date.

As Miss Tallboy-Smith bustled away, Mr. Hawkesley put in his claim.

"I don't see," said he, "why I should be left out in the cold. I've got a collection, too, and I think it would really interest Miss Finch, for she tells me she has seen very little modern pottery. Won't you bring her to see it, Mrs. Otway?"

Again I accepted gladly, with Peggy's consent. My scheme was working rapidly towards a successful conclusion, and I felt that I could push it forward energetically, for that very morning I had received a letter from Dr. Thorndyke returning the agreement and denouncing it as legally worthless and utterly opposed to public policy.

"As to fixing a date," said Mr. Hawkesley, "I suggest that we all adjourn to my rooms now. Come and have a cup of tea with me and then we can look over the crockery. How will that do?"

It suited Peggy and me quite well, and we said so.

"And you, Davenant?" asked Mr. Hawkesley.

"Well, I had one or two cathedrals to finish," was the reply, "but they must wait. Art is long – deuced long, in my case. Yes, let us adjourn and combine crockery and tea – which, as Pepys reminds us is a 'China drink', and therefore appropriate to the occasion."

On this, we sallied forth and made our way to the Strand, where we chartered a couple of hansoms to convey us to Dover Street, Piccadilly, where Mr. Hawkesley had his abode in one of those fine, spacious, dignified houses that one finds in the hinterland of the West End of London. His rooms were on the first floor, and when we arrived there by way of a staircase which would have allowed us to walk up four abreast, we were received by a sedate and impassive gentleman, whose appearance and manner suggested a Foreign Office official of superior rank.

"Would you let us have some tea, please, Taplow?" said Mr. Hawkesley, addressing the official deferentially. Mr. Taplow opened a door for us, and having signified a disposition to accede to the request, departed stealthily.

As we entered the large, lofty room, well lighted by its range of tall windows, I looked about me curiously, for I was instantly struck by the absence of pottery among its ornaments. The available wall-spaces were occupied by important pictures – all modern, the mantelpiece and other suitable surfaces supported statuettes of marble or bronze – again all modern. But of ceramic ware there was not a trace, with the single exception of a small framed cameo relief. Rather did the apartment suggest the abode of a furniture collector, for one side of the room, opposite the windows, was occupied by a range of armoires, or standing cupboards, mostly old French or Flemish.

"You don't favour the glass case, I notice, Hawkesley," said Mr. Davenant.

"No," was the reply. "They are well enough for public museums, but they are unlovely things. And one doesn't want to look at one's whole collection at once. I like to take the pieces out singly and enjoy them one at a time. You see, each piece is an individual work. It was the product of a separate creative effort, and ought to be enjoyed by a separate act of appreciation."

"You seem, Mr. Hawkesley," said I, "to have a preference for modern work. Do you think it is as good as the old?"

"I think," he replied, "that the best modern work is as good as any that was ever done. Of course, I am not speaking of commercial stuff. That is negligible in an artistic sense. I mean individual work, done under the same conditions and by the same class of men as the old craft work. That is quite good. The pity is that there is so little of it. But I am afraid the supply is equal to the demand."

"Don't you think," said Mr. Davenant, "that that is partly the fault of the modern craftsman? Of his tendency to confine himself to fine and elaborate, and therefore costly, productions? Of course, the old work was not cheap in the modern factory sense of cheapness. The pottery and china that was made at the Etruria works or those of Bow or Chelsea was by no means given away. But the prices were practicable for every day purposes, whereas modern studio pottery is impossible for domestic use. And the same is true of other craftwork, such as book-binding, fine printing, textiles, metal work, and so on. If the modern craftsman caters only for the collector and ignores the utilitarian consumer, he can't complain at being ousted by commercial production."

Here the arrival of Mr. Taplow with the tea arrested what threatened to prove a too-interesting discussion. I should have liked to continue it – on another occasion. At present, my desire was rather to "cut the cackle and get to the hosses". Accordingly, while the tea was being consumed, I rather studiously obstructed any revival of the debate by keeping up a conversation of a general and somewhat discursive character, and as soon as we appeared to have finished I introduced the subject of Ceramics.

"Is that plaque on the wall a Wedgwood cameo?" I asked.

"Oh, no," Mr. Hawkesley replied. "That is an example of Solon's wonderful *pate-sur-pate* work. It is done with white porcelain slip on a dark, coloured ground. Come and look at it."

We all rose and gathered round the plaque while Mr. Hawkesley descanted on its beauties, which were, indeed, evident enough.

"It is lovely work," said he, "so free and spontaneous. The Wedgwood reliefs look quite stiff and hard compared with these of Solon's. I have some of his vases with the same kind of decoration, and we may as well look at those first."

He wheeled a travelling turn-table towards a fine Flemish armoire of carved oak, and opening the latter, displayed a range of pieces of this beautiful work, at the sight of which Peggy's eyes glistened. One after another they were carefully placed on the turn-table, viewed from all points, admired, discussed and replaced. The other contents of the armoire were less important works – mostly French – but all received respectful attention. The next receptacle, a French armoire of carved walnut, was devoted to modern stone-ware by the Martin Brothers, Wells, and other individual workers, concerning which our host was specially enthusiastic.

"There," said he, placing on the turn-table a wonderful Toby jug of brown Martin ware, "Show me any old salt-glaze ware that is equal to that! Look at the modelling! Look at the beautiful surface and the quality of the actual potting! And then go and look at the stuff in the shop windows. Just good enough for the slavey to smash."

"Well," Mr. Davenant remarked, "you can't say that she doesn't appreciate its qualities and do justice to them. If former generations had been as energetic smashers as the present, collectors of old stuff would have had to seek their treasures in ancient rubbish-heaps."

"Yes, that is a fact," agreed Mr. Hawkesley, as we moved on to the next cupboard. "When domestic pottery was more valuable it got more respectful treatment. Now this cupboard is only partly filled. I keep it for the work of one artist whose name I don't know. I've shown you some of the ware, Mrs. Otway, but it may be new to Miss Finch."

As he unlocked the door my heart began to thump, and I cast an anxious eye on Peggy. For I knew what was coming, but I didn't know how she would take it. At the moment she was looking at the closed door with pleased expectancy. Then the door swung open, and in a moment she turned pale as death. For one instant I thought she was going to faint, and so, apparently, did Mr. Davenant, for he made a quick movement towards her. But the deadly pallor passed, and was succeeded as rapidly by a crimson flush, but her quick breathing and the trembling of her hand showed how great the shock had been.

Meanwhile, Mr. Hawkesley, all unconscious, was glancing over the row of vases, jars, and bowls, and expatiating on the peculiar beauties of the "mystery ware". The pieces were separated into two groups, the works in pure inlay and those combining the inlay with slip decoration and embossed ornament, and one of the latter he presently lifted from its shelf and placed on the turn-table.

"Now, isn't that a lovely jar, Miss Finch?" said he. "And doesn't it remind you of the beautiful St. Porchaire, or Oiron ware?"

Peggy gazed at the jar with an inscrutable expression as she slowly rotated the turn-table. "It is somewhat like," she agreed, "at least, the method of work is similar."

"Oh, don't give my favourites the cold shoulder, Miss Finch," said Mr. Hawkesley. "I think I prize my pieces of this ware more than anything that I have. It is so very charming and so interesting. For, you see, it is *real* pottery, I mean that, beautiful and precious as it is, it is quite serviceable for domestic purposes, whereas much of the studio pottery is made for the gallery or the cabinet."

"You haven't discovered yet where it is made, I suppose?" I asked.

"No," he replied. "Its origin is still a mystery and something of a romance – which may be one reason why I am so devoted to it. I often speculate about the potter, and invent all sorts of queer theories about him."

"As for instance?"

"Well, sometimes I fancy that he may be in debt to this dealer – that he may have had advances or loans and be unable to pay them off and get free. It is quite possible, you know. Then, sometimes I have thought that he may be one of those poor creatures who drink or take drugs, and that the dealer may keep him slaving in some cellar for his bare maintenance and his miserable luxuries. But I've given that idea up. This work is too sane and reasonable and painstaking for a drunkard or drug-taker. But, whoever and whatever he is, I wish I could find him out, and thank him for all the pleasure that he has given me, and help him to get a proper reward for his labour, which I am sure he does not."

"I don't know why you are so sure," said Mr. Davenant. "This ware is pretty expensive, isn't it?"

"Not if you consider that each piece is an individual work on which a great deal of time and labour has been expended. The price that I paid Goldstein for this particular piece was seven guineas, which wouldn't represent very high remuneration if the artist had the whole of it."

"Seven guineas, Mr. Hawkesley!" exclaimed Peggy, incredulously.

"Yes, Miss Finch, and I should say very cheap at the price."

I glanced at Peggy with malicious satisfaction, for her cheeks were aflame with anger and the light of battle was in her eyes.

"What a shame!" she protested. "How perfectly scandalous! The grasping, avaricious wretch! To charge seven guineas for a piece that he bought for fifteen shillings!"

For a few seconds there was an awesome silence. Peggy's exclamation had fallen like a thunderbolt, and the two men gazed at her in speechless astonishment, while she, poor Titmouse, stood, covered with blushes and confusion, looking as if she had been convicted of pocketing the spoons.

"You actually know," Mr. Hawkesley said, at length, "that Goldstein gave only fifteen shillings for that jar?"

"Yes," she stammered faintly, "I – I happen to have – to be aware – that – that was the amount paid – "

She broke off with an appealing glance at me, and I proceeded to "put in my oar".

"It's no use, Peggy. The cat is out of the bag – at least her head is, and we may as well let out the rest of her. The fact is, Mr. Hawkesley, that this ware is Miss Finch's own work."

I now thought that Mr. Hawkesley was going to faint. Never have I seen a man look so astonished. He was thunderstruck.

"Do you mean, Mrs. Otway," he exclaimed, "that Miss Finch actually makes this ware herself?"

"I do. It is her work from beginning to end. She does the potting, the decorating, the firing, and the glazing. And she does it without any assistance whatever."

Mr. Hawkesley gazed at Peggy with such undissembled admiration and reverence that I was disposed to smile – though I liked him for his generous enthusiasm – and the unfortunate Titmouse was reduced to an agony of shyness.

"This is a red letter day for me, Miss Finch," said he. "It has been my dearest wish to meet the creator of that pottery that I admire so intensely, and now that wish is gratified, it is an extra pleasure to find the artist so much beyond – "

He paused to avoid the inevitable compliment, and Mr. Davenant held up a warning finger.

"Now, Hawkesley," said he, "be careful."

"I know," said Mr. Hawkesley. "It is difficult to steer clear of banal compliments and yet to say what one would like to say, but really the personality of the mysterious artist has furnished a very pleasant surprise."

"I can believe that," said Mr. Davenant. "I can imagine, for instance, that you find Miss Finch a very agreeable substitute for the intoxicated gentleman in the cellar."

At this we all laughed, which cleared the air and put us at our ease.

"But," said Mr. Davenant, "proud as we are to have made the acquaintance of a distinguished potter, we are haunted by the spectre of that fifteen shillings. We get the impression that Miss Finch's business arrangements want looking into."

"Yes," agreed Mr. Hawkesley, "they do indeed. Why do you let this fellow have your work, at such ridiculous prices, too?"

"It isn't so ridiculous as it looks," replied Peggy. "When I began, I couldn't sell any of my work at all. It was frightfully discouraging. No one would have any thing to do with it. My first work was simple earthenware, and even the cheap china shops wouldn't have it. Then I chanced upon Mr. Goldstein, and he bought one or two simple, red earthenware jars and bowls for a few pence each. It didn't pay me, but still it was a start. Then I experimented on this pipe-clay body with slip decoration and coloured inlay and showed the pieces to Mr. Goldstein, and he advised me to go on and offered to take the whole of my work, if I signed an agreement. So I signed the agreement, and he has had all my work ever since."

"At his own prices?"

"Yes. I didn't know what the things were worth."

"Well," said Mr. Davenant, "my law is a trifle rusty, but I should say that that agreement would not hold water."

"It won't," said I. "We have just had counsel's opinion on it, and our adviser assures us that it is worthless, and that we can disregard it."

"Then," said Mr. Davenant, "you had better formally denounce it at once."

"Why trouble to denounce it?" demanded Mr. Hawkesley. "Much better let me call on Goldstein and make him tear up the duplicate. He has got a fine, handy warming-pan hanging up in his shop. I saw it only this morning."

"The connection is not very clear to me," said I.

"It would be clear enough to him," was the grim reply.

Mr. Davenant chuckled. "Your methods, Hawkesley, appeal to me strongly, I must admit, but they are not politic. Legal process is better than a warming-pan, even if it were filled with hot coals. Let us hand the agreement to a reputable solicitor, and let him write to Goldstein stating the position. Miss Finch won't hear any more of her benefactor after that."

After some discussion, in which I supported Mr. Hawkesley's proposal, the less picturesque method of procedure was adopted, and Mr. Davenant was commissioned to carry it out.

"And we will have a one woman show of Blue Bird Ware at the club," said Mr. Hawkesley. "I will take my whole collection there and exhibit it with a big label giving the artist's name in block capitals. The pottery collectors will just tumble over one another to get specimens of the work when the artist is known."

The rest of Mr. Hawkesley's collection received but a perfunctory consideration. Even the gorgeous De Morgan earthenware, glowing with the hues of the rainbow, came as something of an anti-climax, and we closed the last of the cabinets with almost an air of relief.

"And now," said Mr. Hawkesley, as he pocketed his keys, "I suggest that we mark this joyful occasion by a modest festival – say, a homely little dinner at the club and an evening at the play. Who seconds my proposal?"

"We shall have to go as we are then," said I, "as we can't change."

"I think we can enjoy ourselves in morning dress," he rejoined, "and as we shall all be in the same shocking condition, we can keep one another in countenance."

The proposal was accordingly adopted with acclamation and carried into effect with triumphant success, and some slight disturbance of the orderly routine of the establishment in Wellclose Square, for it was on the stroke of midnight when Miss Polton, blinking owlishly, opened the green door to admit the two roisterers who had just emerged from a hansom-cab.

"It has been a jolly day!" Peggy exclaimed fervently as we said "Good-night" on our landing. "And it will be a jolly to-morrow, too."

"Yes, you will be able to get on with your masterpiece now, and when it is finished we can show it at the club and you will be able to sell it for a small fortune."

"I shan't want to sell it," she said. "If it is good enough, and if it wouldn't seem too forward or improper, I should like to give it to Mr. Hawkesley – as a sort of thank-offering, you know."

"Thank-offering for what?"

"For his appreciation of my work. I really feel very grateful to him, as well as to you, Sibyl, dear. You see, he not only liked the things, but he thought of the worker who made them. All the time that I was working alone, with the door locked, from morning to night to fill that cormorant's pockets, Mr. Hawkesley was thinking of me, the unknown worker, looking for me and wanting to help me. I don't forget that it is you who have got me out of Mr. Goldstein's clutches. But I do feel very,

430

very grateful to Mr. Hawkesley. Don't you think it is quite natural that I should, Sibyl?"

"I think you are a little green goose," said I, and kissed her, and so ended the day that saw the end of her servitude and the dawn of prosperity and success.

Chapter XVIII
Among the Breakers

My preoccupation with Peggy Finch's affairs had to some extent submerged my own, but now that my little friend had triumphantly emerged from the house of Bondage, I returned to my labours with a new zest. In spite of the various interruptions, the Zodiac spoons had made steady progress, and it was but a few days after our momentous visit to Mr. Hawkesley's rooms that, almost regretfully, I put the finishing touches to the Fishes spoon – the last of the set.

It had been a pleasant labour, and as I laid out the completed set, I was not dissatisfied. True, there had been difficulties, but difficulties are the salt of craftsmanship. Some of the signs, such as Aries, Taurus, Leo, Virgo, and Capricornus, had been quite simple, the head of the Ram, the Bull, or other symbolic creature furnishing an obvious and appropriate knop for the spoon. But others, such as Gemini, Pisces, and especially Libra, had been less easy to manage. Indeed, the last had involved a slight evasion, for, since it seemed quite impossible to work a pair of scales into a presentable knop, I had relegated them to the shoulder of the bowl and formed the knop of a more or less appropriate head of Justice blindfolded. So all the difficulties had been met by a pleasant and interesting exercise of thought and ingenuity, and the work – my magnum opus, for the present – was finished. And it was rounded off by a very agreeable little addition, for Phyllis Barton, who had seen and greatly admired the set, had made a delightful little case to contain it – just a pair of walnut slabs hinged together, the lower slab having twelve shaped recesses to hold the spoons and the lid ornamented with shallow carvings of a winged hour-glass and the phases of the moon.

I made up the spoons into a parcel and the case into another, so that they should not be treated together in a single transaction, and having advised Mr. Campbell by a letter on the previous day, set forth one morning for Wardour Street. The silent willing which should have preceded my entry to the shop was inadvertently omitted, for as I crossed the street I observed Mr. Campbell exchanging blandishments with a large Persian cat of the "smoky" persuasion, and, as he saw me at the same moment, I had no choice but to enter straightway.

He received me with the most encouraging affability – indeed, he even condescended to shake hands – and was evidently pleased to see me. And his reception of my work was still more encouraging. There was none of the buyer's proverbial disparagement. He was frankly enthusiastic. He held up each spoon separately at arm's length, wagging his head from side to side, he inspected it through a watchmaker's lens, he stroked it with a peculiarly flexible thumb, and finally laid it down with a grunt of satisfaction.

Then came the question of terms, and when he offered twenty-four guineas for the set, I was quite glad that the silent willing had been omitted. For I should probably have willed eighteen.

Having settled the price of my own work, I produced the wooden case. Phyllis had priced it at half-a-guinea, which was ridiculous. I boldly demanded a guinea for it.

"That's a long price," said Mr. Campbell, pulling a face, of proportionate length. But I watched his thumb travel ling over the clean-cut carving, I saw him delicately fitting the spoons, one by one, into their little niches, and I knew that that guinea was as good as in Phillibar's pocket.

"It is a long price, Mrs. Otway," he repeated, cocking his head on one side at the case. "But it's a pretty bit of work, and it's the right thing – that's what I like about it. So suitable, it would be a sin to put those spoons into a velvet-lined case, as if they were common, stamped, trade-goods. Very well, Mrs. Otway, I'll spring a guinea for the case, and I should like to see some more work from the same hand."

This was highly satisfactory (though it was not without a pang of bereavement that I saw the little case closed and hidden from my sight for ever in a locked drawer), and when I had received the two cheques – I asked for a separate one for Phyllis – I tripped away down Wardour Street as buoyantly as if I had not a care in the world.

The association of ideas is a phenomenon that has received a good deal of attention. It was brought to my notice on this occasion when I found myself opposite St Anne's Church, for no sooner had my eye lighted on its quaint warty spire than my thoughts turned to Mr. Davenant – or rather, I should say, to Jasper. Perhaps he was in my mind already, possibly in the subconscious, as Lilith would have said, and the church spire may have acted as an autoscope – it would not have had to be an exceptionally powerful one. At any rate, my thoughts turned to him and to the Magpies Club, and it was not unnatural that my steps should take a similar direction.

As I followed the well-remembered route, I reflected on the changes that a few short months had brought. In that brief space a new life had opened. The solitary, friendless orphan who had sought sanctuary in Miss Polton's house – how changed was her condition! Happy in her work, in her home, in her friends, for had she not her Lilith, her Phyllis, her Peggy – and Jasper? And here a still, small voice asked softly but insistently a question that had of late intruded itself from time to time. Whither was I drifting? My friendship with Jasper was ripening apace. But ripening to what? There could be but one answer, and that answer only raised a further question. In normal circumstances the love of a man and a woman finds a permanent satisfaction in marriage. But where marriage is impossible love, is a mere disaster, a voyage with nothing but rocks and breakers at the end.

So whispered the still, small voice into ears but half-attentive, and as I neared the bottom of Essex Street it became inaudible, for approaching the club-house from the opposite direction was Jasper himself.

"Well!" he exclaimed, "this is a piece of luck! And yet I had hoped that you might be coming into town to-day. Is it business or pleasure?"

"It has been business, and now I hope it is going to be pleasure. I am taking the rest of the day off."

"Now, what a very singular coincidence! I am actually taking the rest of the day off myself."

"Your coincidences," I remarked, "somehow remind me of the misadventures of the bread-and-butter fly: They always happen."

"Quite so," he agreed. "But then, you see, if they didn't happen they wouldn't be coincidences. Do we begin by fortifying ourselves with nourishment?

"I don't know what you mean by 'begin', but I came here to get some lunch."

"So did I – another coincidence, by the way. Shall we take our usual little table in the corner?"

We seated ourselves at the table and, as we waited for our lunch to be brought, I ventured on a few inquiries into Jasper's professional affairs.

"You seem to take a good many days off," I remarked.

"I do. There is, so to speak, a distinctly marked 'off side' to my practice."

"And when you are away, what happens? Do you keep a clerk?"

Jasper grinned. "You over-estimate the magnitude of my practice. No, I have a simpler and more economical arrangement. I let my little front office to a law writer, at a peppercorn rent, subject to the condition that he shall interview my clients in my absence, furnish evasive answers to their questions, and supply ambiguous and confusing information."

"But don't the clients get rather dissatisfied?"

Again Jasper smiled. "That question," said he, "involves an important philosophic principle. A famous philosopher has proved his

434

own existence by the formula '*cogito, ergo sum*' – I think, therefore I am – implying that if he didn't exist he couldn't think. Now, that principle applies to my clients. Before they can be dissatisfied, they must exist. But they don't exist. Therefore they are not dissatisfied. *Q.E.D.*"

"I don't believe you care whether they exist or not – but that is the worst of having an independent income."

"It is a misfortune, isn't it? But I bear up under it surprisingly. Will you have some of this stuff? It is called a pelion. I heard the waitress describing it as a pea-lion, apparently misled by the analogy of the peacock and the pea-hen. Evidently she is no zoologist."

At this moment Miss Tallboy-Smith entered the room and halted at our table to exchange greetings and remind me of my engagement.

"Tell Miss Finch not to forget," said she. "It's next Wednesday. I shall have my things back from here by then, and I understand that Mr. Hawkesley has secured the cases for a special exhibition of studio pottery. You must bring Miss Finch to that, too."

Like Jasper's proxy, I gave an evasive answer to this, for I knew that wild horses would not drag Peggy to an exhibition of her own work. But evidently Mr. Hawkesley had made no confidences so far.

"Have you ever seen the Diploma Gallery at the R.A.?" Jasper asked when Miss Tallboy-Smith had flitted away. "If you haven't, we might look in there for an hour this afternoon."

As I had never seen the diploma works, I fell in readily with the suggestion, and accordingly, when we had finished lunch, we strolled thither and spent a very pleasant hour examining and comparing the works of the different academicians, old and new. From Burlington House we drifted into the Green Park, and presently took possession of a couple of isolated and lonely-looking chairs. For some time we gossiped about the pictures at which we had been looking in the gallery, then our talk turned on to the affairs of my friend Peggy.

"Hawkesley seems to have appointed himself Miss Finch's advertising agent," Jasper remarked. "And he'll do the job well. He is an energetic man, and he knows all the pottery connoisseurs. I met him yesterday, and had to listen to Blue Bird ware by the yard."

"I like him for his enthusiasm," said I.

"So do I," agreed Jasper. "And it is quite a little romance. His admiration of the pottery is perfectly genuine, as we know, but there is something in what he calls 'the personality of the artist'. I think he is distinctly 'taken' with your pretty little friend. How does she like him?"

"I think she is decidedly prepossessed. At any rate, she is profoundly grateful to him for discovering her work, and especially for the interest that he took in the unknown worker."

"There you are, then," said Jasper. "There are the ingredients of a life-size romance. Fervid admiration on the one side, gratitude on the other, and good looks and good nature on both. We shall see what we shall see, Helen, and I, for one, shall look on with the green eyes of envy."

"Why will you? Do you want Peggy Finch for yourself?"

"I want Hawkesley's good fortune. If he loves this little maid and thinks she cares for him, he can ask her to marry him. That is what makes me envious."

I made no reply – indeed, there was nothing to say, and already the sound of the breakers was in my ears.

"I suppose, Helen," he said, after a long pause, "you realize that I love you very dearly?"

"I know that we are the best of friends, and very deeply attached to one another."

"We are much more than friends, Helen," said he, "at least, there is much more than friendship on my side. You are my all – all that matters to me in the world. You live in my thoughts every moment of my life. When we are apart I yearn for the sight of you – I reckon the hours that must pass before I shall see you again, and when we are together the happy minutes slip away like grains of golden sand. But I need not tell you this. You must have seen that I love you."

"I have feared it, Jasper – and that I might presently lose the dearest friend that I have in the world."

"That you will never do, Helen, dearest, if I have the happiness to be that friend. Why should you?"

"It seems that it has to be. Our friendship has been a sweet friendship to me – too sweet to last, as I feared, and if some might cavil at it, it was innocent and wronged no one. But if it has grown into – into what I had feared it might, then it has become impossible. More than friends we can never be, and yet we cannot remain friends."

We were both silent for more than a minute, and both were very grave. Then Jasper asked, with a trace of hesitation, "Helen, if we were as those other two are – if you were free – would you be willing to marry me?"

It was a difficult question to answer in the circumstances, and yet I felt it would be an unpardonable meanness to dissemble.

"Yes," I answered, "of course I should."

"Then," said he, "I don't see why we can never be more than friends."

"But, Jasper, how can we? I am a married woman."

436

"I don't admit that," said he. "Your marriage is a fiction. You are really a spinster with a technical impediment to the conventional form of marriage. Your so-called husband is a stranger to whom you have no ties. You don't like, or even respect him, and certainly you have no obligations of duty to him, seeing that he induced you by a mere fraudulent pretence to go through this form of marriage with him."

"I am not thinking of Mr. Otway," said I. "He is nothing to me. I owe him no duty or consideration, and I would not sacrifice a single hair of my head for him. But the fact remains that I am, legally, his wife, and while he lives I can contract no other marriage."

"But is that quite true, Helen?" he objected.

"Certainly it is, unless you consider a bigamous marriage as an exception, which it is not."

"Of course I do not. Bigamy is a futile and fraudulent attempt to secure the appearance of a legal sanction. No one but a fool entertains bigamy."

"Then I don't see the meaning of your objection."

"What I mean," said he, "is that a fictitious marriage does not exclude the possibility of a real marriage."

"Still I do not quite follow you. What do you mean by a real marriage?"

"A real marriage is a permanent, life-long partnership between a man and a woman. Ordinarily, such a partnership receives the formal endorsement of the State for certain reasons of public policy. But it is the partnership which is the marriage. The legal endorsement is an extrinsic and inessential addition. Now, in your case the State has accepted and endorsed a marriage which does not exist – which is a pure fiction. The result is that if you contract a real marriage, the State will withhold its endorsement. That is all. It cannot hinder the marriage."

"This is all very ingenious, Jasper," said I, "and it does credit to your legal training. But it is mere sophistry. The position, as it would appear to a plain person of ordinary common sense, is that a woman who is legally married to one man and is living as the wife of another, is a married woman who is living with a man who is not her husband."

"That is the conventional view, I admit," said he. "But it is a mistaken view. It confuses the legal sanction – which is not essential – with the covenant of life-long union, which is the essence of marriage – which, in fact, is the marriage."

"But what is the bearing of this, Jasper?" I asked. "We seem to be discussing a rather abstract question of public morals. Has it any application to our own affairs?

"Yes, it has. At least, I think so, though I feel a little nervous about saying just what I mean."

"I don't think you need be. At any rate, there had better be a clear understanding between us. Tell me exactly what you do mean."

He considered awhile, apparently somewhat at a loss how to begin. At length, with evident embarrassment, he put his proposal before me.

"The position, Helen, is this, You and I have become deeply attached to one another, I may say – since you admit that you would be willing to marry me – that we love one another. It is no passing fancy, based on mere superficial attractions. We are both persons of character, and our love is founded on deep-seated sympathy. We have been friends for some years. We liked one another from the first, and as time has gone on we have liked one another better. Our friendship has grown. It has become more and more precious to both of us, and at last it has grow into love – on my side, into intense and passionate love.

"We are not likely to change. People of our type are not given to change. We love one another and we shall go on loving one another until the end.

"If our circumstances were normal, we should marry in the normal manner. That is to say, we should enter into contract publicly with certain formalities which would confer a definite legal status and render our contract enforceable in a court of law. But our circumstances are not normal. We are willing to comply with the formalities but we are not allowed to. We are not in the position of persons who, for their own purposes, lightly disregard the immemorial usages of society – who dispense with the formalities because they would avoid the responsibilities of formal marriage. We wish to enter into a lifelong partnership, we desire to undertake all responsibilities, we would welcome the formalities and the secure status. But the law refuses. There is a technical disability.

"We have, therefore, two alternatives. We may give up the marriage which we both desire, or we may marry and dispense with the formalities and the legal status. Supposing we give up the marriage. Just consider, Helen what it is that we give up. It is the happiness of a whole life-time. The abiding joy of the sweetest, the most sympathetic, companionship that is possible to a man and a woman. For though we are lovers, we are still friends, and friends we shall remain until death parts us. Our tastes, our interests, our sympathies make us prefer one another as companions to all other human beings. Of how many married couples can this be said? To us has been given that perfect comradeship that makes married life an enduring delight, a state of happiness without a cloud or a blemish. And this is what we give up if we let this disability, this technical impediment, hinder us from marrying.

"On the other hand, supposing we marry and dispense with the formalities, what do we give up? Virtually nothing. The legal security is of no value to us, for each of us is secure in the constancy of the other. If we enter into a covenant, we shall abide by it, not by compulsion, but because we shall never wish to break it. As to the legal status and the social recognition, is it conceivable that two sane persons should give up a life's happiness for such trumpery? Surely it is not. No, Helen, let us boldly take our destiny into our own hands. Let us publicly denounce this sham marriage and cancel it for ever. I ask you, dearest, to give me the woman of my heart for my mate, my friend, my wife, forever – to take me, unworthy as I am, for your husband, who will try, as long as he draws the breath of life, to make up to you by love and worship for what you have sacrificed to make him happy."

As I listened to Jasper's appeal – delivered with quiet but impressive earnest – I think I was half-disposed to yield. It was not only that I admired the skill with which he put his case and the virile, masterful way in which he trampled down the obstructing conventions, but deep down in my heart I felt that he was right – that his separation of the things that really mattered from those that were trivial and inessential was true and just. But there was this vital difference between us – that he was a man and I was a woman. Our estimates of the value of the conventions were not the same. Without the legal sanction, I might be his wife in all that was real, but the world would call me his mistress.

"Jasper, dear," I said, "it is impossible. I admit the truth of all that you have said, and I wish – Oh! Jasper, how I wish, that I could accept the happiness that you offer me! You need not tell me that our companionship would be a delight for ever. I know it. But it cannot be. Even if I could accept it for myself, I could not accept it for you. I could not bear to think that, through me, you had been put outside the pale of decent society. For that is what it would mean. You – a gentleman of honour and reputation – would become a social outcast, a man who was living with another man's wife, who, if he were admitted at all to the society of his own class, would have to be introduced with explanations and excuses."

"I think you exaggerate the social consequences, Helen," said he. "I propose that we should write to Otway and formally repudiate the marriage. Then, if we were boldly and openly to state our position and the exceptional circumstances that had driven us to it, I believe that we should receive sympathy rather than condemnation. I don't believe we should lose a friend – certainly not one whose loss would afflict us. And Otway could take his remedy, if he cared to."

"You mean he could divorce me," I said, with something like a shudder.

"Yes. But I am afraid he wouldn't."

"I don't think he would. But if he did, it would be an undefended suit, and the stigma of the Divorce Court would be on us for ever."

"It would be unpleasant, I admit," he replied. "But think of the compensations. Think of the joy of being together always, of having our own home, of going abroad and seeing the world together."

"Don't, Jasper!" I entreated. "It is too tantalizing. And even all this would not compensate me for the knowledge that I had dragged you from your honourable estate to a condition of social infamy."

"You need not consider me," he rejoined. "I have thought the matter out and am satisfied that I should gain infinitely more than I should lose, for I should have you, who are much more to me than all the rest of the world."

"You haven't thought of everything, Jasper," said I. "You know of the folly I committed at the time of my father's death – in withholding facts at the inquest, I mean – and you have excused it and treated it lightly. But others would view it differently. And now there is this blackmailer of whom I have told you. At any moment, a serious scandal may arise, and in that scandal you would be implicated."

"It wouldn't matter to me," said he. "Nothing would matter to me if only I had you."

"So you think now. But, Jasper, think of the years to come. Think how it might be in those years when the social ostracism, the loss of position and reputation, had grown more and more irksome. If we should regret what we had done, if we should blame ourselves – even, perhaps, secretly blame one another – "

"We should never do that, Helen. We should always be loyal. And there wouldn't be any social ostracism. At any rate, I am quite clear as to my own position. I want you for my wife. To get you I would make any sacrifices and count them as nothing. But that is only my position. It isn't necessarily yours – or rather, I should say your sacrifices would be greater than mine. A woman's point of view is different from a man's."

"It is, Jasper. I realise fully how essentially reasonable your proposal is, and I am proud of, and grateful for, the love that has impelled you to make it. But to me the thing is impossible. That is the only answer I can give. What it costs me to give that answer – to refuse the happiness that you offer me, and that I crave for – I cannot tell you. But even if it breaks my heart to say 'no', still, that must be my answer."

For a long time neither of us spoke. As I glanced furtively at Jasper, the dejection, the profound sadness that was written on his face wrung my heart and filled me with self-accusation. Why had I not foreseen this? Why had I, who had nothing to give in return, allowed his friendship to grow up into love under my eyes? Had I not acted towards this my dearest friend with the basest selfishness?

Presently he turned to me, and, speaking in quiet, even tones, said, "It would not be fair for me to make an appeal on my own behalf. I may not urge you to accept a relation which your feeling and judgment reject. But one thing I will ask. I have told you what I want, and you are to remember that I shall always want you. I will ask you to reflect upon what we have said to-day, and if perchance you should come to think differently, remember that I am still wanting you, that I am still asking you, and tell me if you can give me a different answer. Will you promise me this, Helen?"

"Yes," I replied, "I promise you, Jasper."

"Thank you, Helen. And meanwhile we remain friends as we have been?"

"We can never be again as we have been," said I. "Friendship may turn to love, but love does not go back to friendship. That is as impossible as for the fruit to change back into blossom. No, dearest Jasper, this is the end of our friendship. When we part to-day it must be farewell."

"Must it be, Helen? Must we part for ever? Could we not go back to the old ways and try to forget to-day?

"I shall never forget to-day, nor will you. For our own peace of mind, we must remain apart and try to avoid meeting one another. It is the only way, Jasper, hard as it will be."

I think he agreed with me, for he made no further protest. "If you say it must be, Helen, then I suppose it must," he said, dejectedly. "But it is a hard saying. I don't dare to think of what life will be without you."

"Nor I, Jasper. I know that when I say 'Good-bye' to you, the sun will go out of my life and that I can look for no other dawn."

Again we fell silent for a while, and again I reproached myself for having let it come to this.

"Don't you think, Helen," he said at length, "that we might meet sometimes, say at fixed intervals – even long, intervals, if it must be so – just that we might feel that we had not really lost one another completely?"

"But that is what I should wish to avoid. For we have lost one another. As to me, it has no significance. I have nothing to give and nothing to lose. I am shackled for life to Mr. Otway. But you have your life before you, and it would only be fair that I should leave you free."

"Free!" he exclaimed. "I am not free and never shall be. Nor do I wish to be free. I am yours now and forever. And so I would wish it to be. We may not be married in any outward form, but we are married in the most real sense. Our hearts are married. We belong to one another for ever while we live, and neither of us will ever wish to change. You know it is so, dearest, don't you?"

What could I say? He had spoken my own thoughts, had expressed the wish that I had not dared to acknowledge. Weak and unjust it may have been, but the thought that in the dark days of our coming separation we should still be linked, if only by an invisible thread, came as something like a reprieve. It left just a faint spark of light to relieve the gloom of the all too sombre future. In the end, we agreed to a monthly letter and a meeting once a year. And so, having fixed the terms of our sentence, we tried to put our troubles away and make the best of the few hours that remained before the dreaded farewell.

But despite our efforts to get back to our wonted cheerful companionship, the swiftly-passing hours were filled with sadness and heart-ache. Instinctively we went and looked at things and places that recalled the pleasant jaunts that were to be no more, but ever Black Care rode behind. It was like the journey of two lovers in a tumbril that rolled its relentless way towards the guillotine, for at the end of the day was the parting that would leave us desolate.

And at last the parting was upon us. At the corner of Cable Street we halted and faced one another. For a few moments we stood in the gathering gloom, hand clasped in hand. I dared not speak, for my heart was bursting. Hardly did I dare to look at the man whom I loved so passionately. And Jasper could but press my hand and murmur huskily a few broken words of love. And so we parted. With a last pressure of the hand I turned away and hurried along Cable Street. I did not dare to look back, though I knew that he was gazing after me, for the street swam before my eyes and I could barely hold back my sobs.

I did not go straight home. The tumult of emotion sent me hurrying forward – whither I have no recollection save that somewhere in Shadwell a pair of friendly policemen turned me back with the remark that it "was no place for the likes of me." At length, when the first storm of grief had passed, and I felt myself under control, I made my way to Wellclose Square, and pleading the conventional headache, retired at once to my room.

And there, in quiet and seclusion, with tears that no longer need be restrained, with solemn rites of grief, I buried my newborn happiness – the happiness that had died almost in the moment of its birth.

Chapter XIX
Illusions and Disillusion

It is a generally accepted belief that of all the remedies for an aching heart, the most effective is distraction of the mind from the subject of its affliction. And probably the belief is well founded. But it usually happens that the sufferer is the last to recognize the virtues of the remedy, preferring to nurse in solitude a secret grief and to savour again and yet again the bitterness of the Dead Sea fruit of sorrow.

So it was with me in these unhappy days. The seclusion of the workshop gave me the opportunity for long hours of meditation, in which I would trace and retrace the growth of my love for Jasper, would think with passionate regret of what might have been, and speculate vaguely upon the future. So far from seeking distraction in these first days of my trouble, I kept aloof from my comrades, so far as I could – shut myself in the workshop, or in my room, or wandered abroad alone, following the great eastern thoroughfares where I was secure from the chance of meeting a friend.

But the distractions which I would have avoided came unsought. First, there was the visit with Peggy to Miss Tallboy. It was due but a day or two after my parting with Jasper, and I loathed the thought of it, but it had to be, for who could say how much it might mean to Peggy? And as it turned out, I should never have forgiven myself if I had failed her. I had looked for a rather dull, social call flavoured with porcelain. But it was quite otherwise. Miss Tallboy-Smith had at length heard of Peggy's genius and had invited a few specially choice connoisseurs to meet her, including Mr. Hawkesley – unless he had invited himself. At any rate, there he was, reverential and admiring, but yet with a certain air of proprietorship which I noted with interest and not without approval. It was quite a triumph for Peggy, and she took it very modestly, though with very natural satisfaction. To me, however, there was a fly in the ointment, though quite a small one, for Mr. Hawkesley proposed an exploration of the Wallace Collection, which Peggy had never seen, and which I felt bound, for her sake, to agree to. But I looked forward with prospective relief to the time – not far distant, I suspected – when these two pottery enthusiasts would be intimate enough to dispense with a chaperon.

Then there came a distraction of another kind. One evening after tea, Lilith took me apart, and looking at me with some concern, said,

"Our Sibyl has not been herself of late. I hope she is not being worried about anything."

"We all have our little troubles, Lilith," I replied, "and sometimes we don't take them so resignedly as we should."

"No," she rejoined. "Resignation is easier when the troubles are someone else's. But we are very concerned to see you looking so sad – not only Margaret and I, but all of us. We are all very fond of you, Sibyl, dear, and any of us would think it a privilege to be of help to you in any way. You know that, don't you?"'

"I have good reason to. No woman could have found kinder or more helpful friends than I have in this house."

"Well," she said, "friends are for use as well as for companionship. Don't forget that, if there is any little service that any of us can render you."

I thanked her very warmly, and she then opened a fresh topic.

"Some time ago, Sibyl, we were speaking of psychical experiments, and I suggested that you might like to see some carried out by my friend, Mr. Quecks, who is an authority on these subjects. Mr. Quecks was away from home at the time, on a lecturing tour in Kent, but he is home again now. I wrote to him about you and have had one or two talks with him, and he has asked me to invite you to a little demonstration that he is giving to some friends next Friday evening. Would you care to come with me?"

I would much rather not have gone, but I knew that a refusal would disappoint Lilith, who had set her heart on converting me. Accordingly, I accepted the invitation, and we were arranging details of the expedition when Peggy joined us. As soon as she heard what was afoot she was all agog.

"Oh, what fun!" she exclaimed. "You'll let me come, too, won't you, Lilith? I did so enjoy it last time."

Lilith, however, was by no means eager for her company, for the Titmouse was a rank unbeliever, and made no secret of it.

"What is the use of your coming, Peggy?" said she. "You don't believe in the super-normal. You would only come to scoff."

"Perhaps I should remain to pray," rejoined Peggy. "It is no use preaching to people who are already convinced. And I should just love it. That Quecks man is so frightfully amusing. He is the funniest little guffin you ever saw, Sibyl. Won't you let me come, Lilith?"

"Of course you can come if you really want to," Lilith replied with evident reluctance. "But you shouldn't speak of Mr. Quecks as if he were a mountebank or a buffoon. He may not be handsome, but he is a very learned man and very sincere."

"I beg your pardon, Lilith," said Peggy. "I won't call him a guffin any more. And thank you ever so much for letting me come."

The arrangements being thus settled, it is only fair to Peggy to say that she endeavoured, as far as possible, to treat the demonstration quite seriously. Even in our private conversations she made no further disparaging references to Mr. Quecks, though I did gather that her anxiety to be present at the séance was not unconnected with a desire to keep an eye on him to see that he did not impose on me.

Mr. Quecks' house was situated in a quiet street off Cromwell Road, Kensington, and the "demonstration" took place in a large room intermediate in character between a library and a drawing-room, lighted by three electric bulbs, all of which were encased in silk bags, so that the illumination was of a twilight dimness. The visitors were about a dozen in all, and while we were waiting for the late arrivals Mr. Quecks made a few observations on super normal phenomena in general.

To me he required no disparagement from Peggy or anyone else, his own appearance doing all that was necessary in that respect. The first glance at him impressed me disagreeably, but then he was a manifestly uncomely man, with a large, bald face and long, greasy black hair, which was brushed straight back and accumulated in an untidy bush at the nape of his neck. He spoke unctuously, and his manner was confident, persuasive, didactic, and authoritative, and he gave me the impression of a man who was accustomed to dealing chiefly with women – his present audience was composed of them exclusively.

"In interpreting the results of the experiments which we are about to perform," he observed, "we have to bear in mind that psychical and super-normal phenomena, inasmuch as they are not concerned with material things, are not directly appreciable by the senses. We cannot see or touch the subliminal self, either our own or that of others. But neither can we see the electric current or the Hertzian waves. We know of their existence and properties indirectly, through their effects. Electricity can be transformed into heat, light or sound, and these can be perceived by means of the radiator, the electric lamp, or the telephone, which act directly on our senses. So it is with the hidden subconscious self. Invisible itself, it can be made to produce effects which are perceptible to the conscious mind through the senses, and through those effects its own existence is revealed."

This sounds reasonable enough, but the experiments themselves were rather disappointing on the whole. Perhaps I expected too much, or perhaps the preoccupied state of my mind did not allow me to bring to them sufficient interest or attention. Moreover, Mr. Quecks had an assistant (I had almost said "confederate") whose appearance pleased me no more than his own – a wall-eyed, taciturn woman of about thirty-five, of the name of Morgan, who acted as the "percipient" – the word "medium", I noticed, was not used – and helped to prejudice me against the experiments.

We began with a demonstration of thought-transference, which I found dull, tiresome, and unconvincing. Probably I was unreasonable, but the apparent triviality of the proceedings, which resembled a solemn and unspeakably dull drawing-room game, influenced my judgment. The percipient, Miss Morgan, being seated, blindfolded, in the middle of the room, a pack of playing cards and another pack of cards, each of which bore a single capital letter, were produced. A card was drawn out at random and held up behind the percipient and in view of everyone else, including Mr. Quecks, who held the percipient's hand. Miss Morgan then guessed the card or the letter. Sometimes she guessed correctly, sometimes nearly correctly, some times quite incorrectly. The proportion of correct guesses, Mr. Quecks informed us, was vastly greater than could be accounted for on the law of probabilities. And I dare say it was. But the exhibition left me cold, as did those of table-tilting and planchette writing which followed. Even the "pendule explorateur", which had so impressed me on a previous occasion, fell flat on this. For, since that rather startling experience, I had given some thought to the magic pendulum, and believed that I had found at least a partial explanation of its powers. Accordingly, when my turn came to try the "autoscope", I took the string in my fingers and shut my eyes, and when Mr. Quecks objected to this, I gazed fixedly at the opposite wall, seeing neither the pendulum nor the clockwise alphabet. Under these conditions the pendulum was a complete failure, it would spell nothing. But when I looked steadily at the pendulum and the letters, the swinging ball spelled out clearly the word that I chose – Lilith.

I was thus in a decidedly sceptical frame of mind when the next set of experiments began, and even these produced, at first, no effect on me other than a slight tendency to yawn. Their object was to demonstrate the existence of a "psychometric" power or faculty – that is to say, a power to detect in certain material objects a permanent impression left by contact with some particular person. Such a faculty, Mr. Quecks explained to us, was possessed by certain exceptionally sensitive persons. He had it to some extent himself, but in Miss Morgan it was developed in a really remarkable degree, as the experiments which were to follow would convince us.

Hereupon Miss Morgan was once more blindfolded, all the lights but one were switched off, so that the room was almost in darkness, and the demonstration began. One of the visitors, at Mr. Quecks' whispered request, slipped a ring from her finger and passed it to him. By him it was handed to Miss Morgan, who solemnly applied it to her forehead. Then followed an interval of expectant silence, in which I thought I heard a faint giggle from Peggy Finch, who sat in the row in front of me.

At length Miss Morgan opened her mouth and spake. It seemed that she was seeing visions, and these she described in detail. Naturally I was unable to check them, nor could I judge whether they had any relation to the ring. The owner of that article stated, at the close of the experiment, that the visions, as described, corresponded closely to certain places and events which were known to her and to no one else. Which seemed conclusive enough, but yet it left me only with a feeling that the whole proceeding was ridiculous and trivial.

The next experiment was performed with a glove from the hand of another visitor, and when this was concluded, Mr. Quecks whispered to a lady in the front row, who whispered to Peggy, who turned to me.

"He wants your handkerchief, Sibyl," she said in a low whisper.

I took my handkerchief from my pocket and gave it to Peggy, who squeezed it up into a ball and passed it to the lady in front, who passed it to Mr. Quecks, who handed it to Miss Morgan, who, in her turn, applied it to her forehead as if it had been an ice-bag, and assumed an attitude of intense mental concentration. And again the sound of a suppressed giggle came from the neighbourhood of the Titmouse.

Then Miss Morgan began to speak.

"I seem to be passing through the country – swiftly – very swiftly, past great, wide fields and woods. They are strange-looking woods. The trees are all in lines – in straight lines . . . But wait! Are they trees? No, they can't be, they are too small. No – they are plants growing up poles – they must be vines. It is a vineyard – and yet they don't look quite like vines. No, no! Of course, I see now, they are hops. It is a hop-garden. And now I am passing another. Now I have come out on to a road on the top of a hill. There are hills all round, and in the hollow there seems to be a town . . . and I seem to see water in the town . . . yes, it is water. It is a river . . . But I don't see any ships . . . only some red things . . . Oh, yes! I see, the red things are sails – red sails. I thought sails were always white."

She paused, and in the intense silence I leaned forward, listening eagerly. All my indifference and boredom had vanished. This was quite a different affair from the card-guessing and planchette-reading. She had described Maidstone vividly, accurately – or at least so it seemed to me, Maidstone as it would appear to one approaching the bridge from the west. Of course it might be mere guessing, but –

448

"I seem," Miss Morgan resumed, "to be descending a hill by a broad street . . . What is that in front of me? Is it – yes I see it is a bridge. Yes I see it plainly now. I am coming towards it. But what on earth is this thing on my left hand? It seems to be a mass of gold and yet . . . and yet it looks like an elephant. That's ridiculous, of course. It can't be . . . But it certainly looks like gold . . . and yet it . . . it really does look like an elephant! Well, I can make nothing of it. And now it is gone and I am on the bridge." Again she paused, and I sat gazing at her in blank astonishment. There could now be no question as to the reality of the visions, unless the whole exhibition was a fraud. The idea of skilful guessing could not be entertained for a moment. The description did not merely fit Maidstone, the detail of the golden elephant on the brewery by the bridge fixed the identity of the place I beyond the possibility of doubt. It was either a genuine – and most amazing – psychical phenomenon or an outrageous imposture. But an imposture, to which Lilith must have been a party, was more incredible than the super-normal itself.

As these thoughts passed swiftly through my mind, Miss Morgan resumed her description.

"I am standing on the bridge, but it is beginning to grow indistinct. By the riverside I can just see a great house, an old, old house, which seems to stand by the water's edge, and beyond it trees and a church tower. Now it is gone and I can see nothing. Is this all? . . . No, I see, very, very faintly, a small crowd of people. They seem to be in a field. And I make out a number of white objects in the field. They look rather like sheep, but they are very still. Oh! they are not sheep at all, they are tombstones. And I see now that the people are all in black and that they are standing round an open grave. It must be a funeral . . . Yes, there is the clergyman in his surplice . . . But it is beginning to fade.

"Now I can only just see the dark shapes of the people and now they are gone too. This must be all, I think." She paused for a few moments and then exclaimed,

"No it isn't! Something else is coming. It is very dim, but it looks like a man sitting at a table. Yes! But I can't see what he is doing. He is not writing. He has something in his right hand, and keeps moving it up and down. Oh, I see now, it is a hammer. He seems to be hammering some bright object – a piece of metal, I think . . . Yes, it is quite clear now. But it isn't a man at all, it is a woman. I saw her distinctly for a moment, but she has grown dim again . . . Now she has gone and I can see nothing . . . I think that is all . . . Yes, that is all. Nothing else seems to come."

She removed the handkerchief from her forehead and held it out towards Mr. Quecks, who took it from her and tiptoed round to where I was sitting.

"Thank you, Mrs. Otway," he whispered. "It seemed a very successful experiment, but you can judge better than I can."

"It was, indeed, most successful," I replied, as he gave me back my handkerchief. "I am positively amazed at the detailed accuracy of the description."

"You think the correspondence is closer than could be accounted for by coincidence or chance guessing?" he asked.

"There can be no question of chance," I replied. "The descriptions were much too detailed and circumstantial."

"That is most interesting," said he. "For there can be no other explanation but that of genuine psychometric faculty. Miss Morgan is a stranger to you, and, moreover, she did not know whose handkerchief it was. The remarkable success of this experiment seems to support Miss Blake's estimate of your unusual psychic gifts. You evidently have the power of imprinting your personality on inanimate objects in an exceptional degree. I should almost think it likely that you would be a successful scryer. Have you made any experiments with the crystal?"

"Yes. But they are all complete failures. I could see nothing."

"That is not unusual in early experiments," said he. "There is a difficulty in concentrating. I wonder if you would care to make a trial now under my guidance. I think I could help you to visualize some simple scene. Will you try?"

The astonishing success of Miss Morgan's experiment had revived all my former curiosity, and I assented readily, much to Mr. Quecks' satisfaction. The nature of the new experiment was explained to the company, and the necessary preparations made. An easy chair was placed for me in the middle of the room, and the chairs for the others arranged behind it, so that I should not have my attention distracted by seeing them. As I passed Lilith on my way to the chair, I greeted her with a smile, and was a little surprised at the lack of response on her part. I thought she would be gratified to see me taking so active a part in the proceedings, but apparently she was not – indeed, I had never seen her look so ungenial.

When I had taken my seat, Mr. Quecks directed me to lean back and adopt a position of complete physical rest. A black, velvet cushion was then placed in my lap and on the cushion was laid the crystal globe, itself almost black in the dim twilight save for a single spark where it reflected the light of the one electric lamp.

450

"You will look fixedly at the bright spot of light," said Mr. Quecks, who had seated himself beside me. "Concentrate your attention on it and think of nothing else. Don't let your mind wander, and don't move your eyes. Think of the bright spot and look at it. Soon a mist will come before your eyes, then you will feel a sort of drowsiness. You will grow more and more drowsy, but your eyes will keep open and you will still see the mist. You are seeing it now – " (This was quite correct.) " – it grows denser, now you are beginning to feel drowsy – just a little drowsy – but your eyes are wide open, still you are getting drowsy – rather more drowsy – "

He seemed to repeat these words over and over and over again like a sort of chant, and his voice, which had been at first soft and confidential, took on a peculiar sing-song quality, and at the same time began to grow more and more distant until it came to me thin and small like the voices that are borne from far-away ships on a calm day across the water of a quiet anchorage. And, meanwhile, a strange somnolence fell upon me. I felt as if I were in a dream. Yet my eyes were wide open, and before them floated the mist, out of which shone the single spark of light. And the little, thin voice went on chanting far away, but I could no longer make out what it said. Nor was I attending to it. I was gazing into the mist at the tiny spark – gazing fixedly, unwinkingly, without effort.

Presently the mist seemed to clear a little, and the spot of light began to grow larger. Now it looked like a hole in the shutter of a dark room, and now it was as though I were looking through an opera glass or a telescope, but I could make out nothing save a confused blur of light, in the middle of which was a vague, dark shape. But still the area of light grew larger, and now I could see that there were other shapes, all dim, vague and shadowy. Then in an instant it cleared up, as a magic-lantern picture sharpens when the lens is focussed. The dark shape was Mr. Otway.

He stood, stooping forward, gazing at something on the floor – something that lay by the fireplace, motionless, with upturned waxen face. It was horribly distinct. I could see my father's face settling into the rigidity of death, I could see the crimson streak on his temple, I could even see the sparkle of the silver knob on the stick that Mr. Otway grasped.

The vision lasted, as it seemed, but for a few seconds. Then it grew dim and confused and quickly faded away into blank darkness, and I found myself sitting up in the chair, wide awake, but bewildered and a little frightened. The lights were full on, and the visitors were all gathered around my chair gazing at me with a very odd intentness.

"Did you see anything in the crystal?" Mr. Quecks asked, suavely.

"Yes," I answered, not quite so suavely. "How long have I been asleep?"

Mr. Quecks looked at his watch. "Just five and twenty minutes," he replied.

I got up from the chair, and, addressing Peggy, who was looking at me a little anxiously, asked, "What has been happening, Peggy? Have I been talking nonsense?"

"No," she answered. "You've been asleep, and you've been guessing cards and doing most extraordinary sums – multiplying and dividing fractions and all sorts of things. That's all. But," she added in a lower tone, "he'd no business to hypnotize you without your permission. You didn't give him permission, did you?"

"No, I didn't," I replied.

At this moment Lilith came up to us and put the same question.

"No," I answered. "I didn't understand that I was to be hypnotised."

"I thought not," said she in a tone of evident vexation. "It doesn't happen to matter as things have turned out, but it was quite improper. I shall speak to Mr. Quecks about it when you are gone."

"Aren't you coming with us, then?" asked Peggy.

"No," replied Lilith. "I have some matters to talk over with him, so I must stay a little while, but I shall follow you in about half-an-hour."

Shortly after this the meeting broke up, and Peggy and I took our departure. As we sat in the train, I tried to extract from my companion some details of what had happened, but I found her curiously unwilling to pursue the topic. I gathered, however, that, as soon as the hypnotic trance was completely established, Mr. Quecks suggested to me that I should have a distinct vision of some scene that I had witnessed "in the old town that Miss Morgan had seen and shortly before the funeral that she had described." Then, after an interval, he had put a number of problems in multiplication and division of large numbers and fractions, which I had solved with extraordinary ease and rapidity. As to the nature of my vision, Peggy displayed no interest, but turned the conversation on to subjects quite unconnected with Mr. Quecks or psychical science.

When we arrived home, she followed me to my room and suggested that we should wait there for Lilith, which was what I had intended to do. And here again she showed a marked tendency to avoid the subject of Mr. Quecks and his experiments. But as she sat in my chair gossiping, I caught her eye, from time to time, travelling almost furtively towards the clock on the mantelpiece, and I wondered if she was feeling anxious about Lilith, who had to make her way alone through the rather unsavoury neighbourhood of Ratcliff. Whatever she was feeling, however, she kept up a flow of conversation – which was, itself, a rather

452

unusual phenomenon – and presently grew quite confidential about herself – which was more unusual still. It was clear that her friendship with Mr. Hawkesley was now quite firmly established, and they evidently saw a good deal of one another – but this I knew already. And it was clear that their sympathy in tastes was running parallel to a very strong liking of a more personal kind.

After a pause in this confidential gossip, Peggy suddenly looked down a little shyly, and, turning very pink, asked hesitatingly,

"Sibyl, dear, you haven't quarrelled with Mr. Davenant, have you?"

"Quarrelled, Peggy!" I exclaimed. "Of course I haven't. Have we ever struck you as quarrelsome people?"

"No, indeed," she replied. "But you don't seem to have seen much of one another lately."

"No, I haven't seen Mr. Davenant for quite a long time," I said.

She was silent for a while, and I noticed that her cheeks were growing more and more pink.

"What is my little chameleon turning that colour for?" I asked.

She looked up at me with a shy smile. "Sibyl," she said, "don't think me inquisitive or impertinent. I am your friend, you know, and we are fond of one another, aren't we?"

"We are the very best of friends, Peggy, dear, so you needn't mind asking me anything that you want to know."

"Well, then, Sibyl, why don't you and Mr. Davenant marry? Anyone can see how fond he is of you, and I'm sure you care for him an awful lot, don't you, now?"

"My Titmouse is becoming an expert authority on these matters," said I, thereby converting poor Peggy to the semblance of a corn-poppy.

"Perhaps I am," she admitted, defiantly. "But why don't you marry him, Sibyl?"

"My dear Peggy," said I, "there is a very substantial reason. Its name is Mr. Otway."

"Sibyl!" gasped Peggy. "I thought you were a widow!"

I shook my head. "No, Peggy. I am a widow in effect, but a married woman by law. I have a husband who is no husband, whom I married in error, whom I have never lived with and could never think of living with, but whom I can never get rid of. That is the position."

She flung her arms around my neck, and laid her cheek to mine.

"My poor, dear Sibyl," she exclaimed. "How dreadful for you! I am so frightfully sorry, dear. And is there no end to this?"

"There is death," said I. "That is all. And that is why I am not seeing much of Mr. Davenant nowadays."

"It is an awful thing, Sibyl," said she. "You and Mr. Davenant could make one another so perfectly happy.' And I don't see why you shouldn't, for that matter."

"Why, how could we, Peggy?"

Again she blushed scarlet, and with a defiant glance at me, replied, "I wouldn't have my whole life wrecked. I should just go off with him, husband or no husband."

"You dreadful little reprobate. And what do you suppose the world would say about you?"

"It could say what it liked so long as I'd got the man I wanted. But it wouldn't really say anything. No one with any sense would think a penny the worse of me. Nor would they of you. Everyone would say that you had done the right thing, seeing that you had no choice. You couldn't be expected to be bound for life to a dummy husband."

At this moment I rose from my chair, and going over to the dressing table, lit a candle. Then I put my hand in my pocket and drew out an unaddressed envelope and a piece of pencil. With the latter I wrote on the envelope my signature and the words "ten minutes to eleven". The whole proceeding seemed quite automatic. I did not know why I was doing it. I had not known that either the envelope or the pencil was in my pocket, for I had not put them there. But I carried out the train of action almost unconsciously and quite without surprise.

When I had written on the envelope, I opened it and drew out a piece of paper. On the paper was some writing in an unfamiliar hand. I held the paper near the candle and read as follows,

"At ten-minutes-to-eleven you will light a candle, take this envelope and a pencil from your pocket, you will write on the envelope your signature and the time. Then you will open the envelope and read this message."

I stood for some seconds gazing at the paper in utter amazement. Then I looked round quickly at the clock. It was ten minutes to eleven. From the clock my glance turned to Peggy, who was sitting watching me with a very uncomfortable expression.

"Do you know anything about this, Peggy?" I asked.

"Yes," she replied. "That Quecks man told you to do it. He wrote the message and put the envelope and pencil in your pocket when you were in a deep sleep. He spoke the message into your ear, and, after about a minute, told you to wake up, and you woke up immediately. It was like his impudence to perform his beastly experiments without getting your permission first."

"It was. But the thing is rather uncanny. I don't like it at all."

"There's nothing in it," said Peggy, though she, too, was evidently not pleasantly impressed. "It's what they call post-hypnotic suggestion. It isn't in any way super-natural. The doctors know all about it."

"Still," said I, "it is a very strange affair. There is something extremely eerie in finding oneself turned into an unthinking automaton worked by somebody else's will. And some of the other experiments were rather startling, Miss Morgan's visions for instance."

"Mightn't they have been just clever guesses?"

"No, Peggy. That is quite impossible. Her descriptions applied to my case in detail and were correct every time. You heard her describe the view from Maidstone Bridge?"

"Yes. And I recognised it from that water-colour over your mantelpiece."

"Well, don't you think it very wonderful and incomprehensible?"

"No, I don't," said Peggy. "How do you suppose she did it?"

"I can only imagine that some influence that I don't understand passed to her from my handkerchief."

"Then you imagine wrong," said the Titmouse. "Your handkerchief was in my pocket all the time. It was my handkerchief that she was smelling at. And her descriptions didn't fit me the least little bit. I don't hammer my pottery, you know."

"But I don't understand. You passed her my handkerchief, didn't you?"

"No, I passed her mine. You see, I'd seen this handkerchief trick before and I had mine ready, rolled up into a ball in my hand. So it was quite easy to make the exchange. But we may as well change back now."

She took a handkerchief from her pocket and handed it to me, and when I had identified it as my own, I produced hers and restored it to her.

"You are a wicked little baggage, Peggy," said I, "though I must admit that the ruse was quite a fair one. But still, I don't quite see how it was done? It was evidently an imposture. But how was it worked? How did she get the information?"

"Why, she got it from Mr. Quecks, and he got it from Lilith."

"You surely don't suggest that Lilith was a party to this fraud?"

"Of course I don't," she replied, indignantly. "Lilith is a lady to the tips of her fingers. That's just where it is. She would never suspect. But we know that she wrote to Quecks about you, and she has talked to him about you, and no doubt he has pumped out all that she knows about you. Then you will remember that he has just come back from a tour in Kent – he is almost certain to have been to Maidstone – and there are such things as picture postcards. There is no mystery as to how it was done, but I do wonder that he was such a fool as to do it before Lilith. I suspect she stayed behind to tell him what she thought of him."

As we were speaking, Lilith came up the stairs, and I ran out to intercept her and bring her in.

"You needn't have waited up for me," said she, "though I am glad you have, for I want to apologise for Mr. Quecks' very improper behaviour."

"Don't think any more about it, Lilith," said I. "It didn't do any harm, and it has enabled Peggy and me to have a little private séance to ourselves."

"Did the post-hypnotic experiment work correctly?"

"Perfectly – and most uncannily."

"Then," said Lilith, "you have gained by that amount of experience. As to the rest of Mr. Quecks' experiments – well, Sibyl, I am afraid we must consider them on the plane of public entertainment rather than on that of genuine research. But it is getting late. We had better go to bed now and talk things over to-morrow."

This advice was forthwith acted on, as to its first half, and if I owed Mr. Quecks a grudge for trying to impose on me, I should have been grateful to him for giving me something to think about other than my own griefs and entanglements.

Chapter XX
Cloud and Sunshine

Reviwing on the morrow my experiences at Mr. Quecks' house, I was conscious of a rather definite change of outlook. Those experiences had made a very deep impression. The vision that I had seen was something outside ordinary, normal experience, and it still haunted me. And then, even more uncanny, there was that strange automatic action which I had carried out with such perfect unconsciousness and yet so exactly and punctually. It was all very well for Peggy to put it aside with the easy explanation that it was merely post-hypnotic suggestion, and that the doctors knew all about it. That explanation explained nothing. The fact remained that I had suddenly become aware that things which I had been accustomed to dismiss as delusions – as the mere superstitions of credulous people – were actual realities. And this discovery created for me a new standard of possibility and truth. Even Miss Morgan's visions, though I knew them to be a rank imposture, had left an impression that was not to be completely effaced. The shock of amazement that they had produced at the time left a vague after-effect, due, no doubt, to the more real and equally mysterious experiences

Concerning these latter I was somewhat puzzled. It was not quite clear to me how I had come to be hypnotized at all, and I took an early opportunity of questioning Lilith on the subject.

"There is no mystery about that," she replied. "The orthodox method of producing the hypnotic trance is to cause the 'subject' to gaze steadily at some bright object – a metal button, a crystal, or even a small piece of white paper. He is told to gaze fixedly at this object, to concentrate his attention on it, and to think of nothing else. The purpose of this is to get rid, as far as possible, of the conscious self and to allow the subconscious self to act without disturbance. When this state of mental abstraction has been established, the 'subject' is ready to receive suggestions. If the operator suggests to him that he is drowsy, he becomes somnolent, and at the same time he becomes much more susceptible to suggestion. Now, if the operator suggests to him that he feels certain sensations, he feels those sensations. If it is suggested that he performs certain actions, he performs them. This is what happened to you. Mr. Quecks induced you to gaze steadily at the crystal, and when you were in the proper state of mental abstraction, he suggested the hypnotic trance. Then he suggested that you would see a vision of some

457

scene that you had looked on shortly before the funeral, and I understand that you did see such a vision."

"Yes, I did, and most astonishingly vivid it was. But, Lilith, when I lit that candle in my room I was not in the hypnotic trance."

"No, that was a post-hypnotic phenomenon, and really a most interesting one. To understand it you must think of the two personalities, the conscious self and the subconscious, or subliminal self. Now the suggestions are made to the subconscious self, while the conscious is dormant or in abeyance. But when the conscious self returns or awakens, the subconscious mind continues to work, although unperceived by the conscious mind. If the suggestion refers, as in your case, to some action to be performed at an appointed time, the subconscious keeps account of the passing time and at the appointed moment sets the machinery in motion. The action itself is perceived by the conscious mind, but the train of subconscious thought has been unperceived, though it has really been quite continuous. It is very curious, though not particularly mysterious."

"And it is only in the hypnotic trance that these suggestions take effect?"

"That," replied Lilith, "is not quite clear. It seems that in ordinary sleep suggestions of the kind may sometimes take effect. And for the same reason. In sleep, the conscious self is in abeyance – is out of action – but the subconscious is active, as we see in the case of dreams and still more strikingly in the case of somnambulism. But the postponed effects of suggestions made during normal sleep need more investigation. I believe that sleep produced by drugs is much more like the hypnotic trance than natural sleep."

"Well," I said, "it is all rather weird and uncanny." And so the subject dropped. But, as I have said, the influence of these strange experiences remained. My former scepticism of the occult and mystical gave place to a state of mind in which I was prepared to admit the possibility of things that I had once regarded as wildly incredible.

Nevertheless, I was but faintly interested in the wonders of psychical research. Indeed, I was not much interested in anything connected with my daily life. I had endeavoured to revive my enthusiasm for my work by setting myself an ambitious task – a silver candlestick of a semi-ecclesiastical design, worked in *repoussé* with enrichments in enamel. But all the pleasure in the work was gone. The various processes– skilfully enough executed, as I noticed with tepid satisfaction – which should have been a joy, were but the routine of industry, and through them all the never-ending heartache, the sense of loss, of bereavement, the feeling that the light had gone out of my life for ever.

458

The passing time seemed to bring no mitigation. Rather did it seem to me that every day I missed my dear companion more.

Perhaps if my loss had been more final – if, for instance, Jasper had been taken from me by Death – I might have striven more determinedly to shape my life anew. But there was a certain inconclusiveness in our separation. Not that I ever, for a moment, considered the possibility of re-opening the question. But still I think there lurked in my mind the feeling that the door was not finally closed. Jasper's words, "Remember that I am still wanting you, that I am still asking you," would come to me unbidden, again and yet again, reminding me that the way was still open, that I could end the separation if and when I chose. And then Peggy's outspoken declaration was not without its effect. For the Titmouse was a very paragon of modesty and maidenly propriety, and when I recalled her robust contempt of conventional points of view, I could not help asking myself sometimes if I had not been too prudish.

All of which was very disturbing. It left me with my resolution unchanged, and yet without that sense of finality that would have set me reconstructing my scheme of life.

So the weeks dragged by till the time for the first monthly letter drew nigh, and the passionate yearning with which I looked forward to it told me that that letter was a mistake. It ought never to have been. The chapter should have been ended and the volume shut irrevocably.

As the time for the letter approached, my unrest took me abroad more than usual, and one day, forsaking the sordid east, I took the train to South Kensington and made my way to the Museum, though with no special object in my mind. I had ascended the steps to the main entrance, and was approaching the doorway, when I came face to face with Miss Tallboy-Smith, who was just emerging. At the sight of me she halted with a dramatic gesture of astonishment.

"Well!" she exclaimed, "so you are really alive! I thought I was never going to see you again. Where have you been? It's ages – centuries – since I have seen you. And dear Miss Finch, too – whatever has become of her? Were you going into the Museum? I have just been wallowing in the Salting Collection. Delightful, isn't it? The very kernel of the Museum. Don't you think so?

"I don't think I have ever seen the Salting Collection," said I.

"Never seen the Salting Collection!" she gasped. "My dear Mrs. Otway! How dreadful! And you a connoisseur, too. Why, it's a Paradise, the collectors' Heaven. Do you believe that people come back after death and frequent their old haunts? I hope it's true. If it is, I shall come to the Salting Collection. I shall divide my ghosthood between that and the Wallace. It will really be very jolly. Unlimited leisure, with all eternity at one's disposal. And no stuffy restrictions, no closing hours or students' days. So convenient, too! You just pass in through the closed door or the wall and float up the stairs. Why, you could even get inside the glass cases! I'm afraid you'll think me an awful old heathen, but I'm not really. And how are you? And how is Miss Finch? And why haven't you been to the club for such an age. And isn't it dreadful about poor Mr. Davenant?"

My heart seemed to stand still, and I think I must have turned pale, for Miss Tallboy-Smith said hastily, "I'm afraid I have startled you, Mrs. Otway, but surely – surely – do you mean to tell me that you haven't even heard about it?"

"I have heard nothing," I said, faintly. "Is he – tell me what has happened."

"I haven't had very full particulars," said she, "but it seems that a cart – or was it a wagon? No, I think it was a cart – and yet I'm not quite sure that it wasn't – but there! I'm not very dear as to the difference between a cart and aagon. What is the difference?"

"It doesn't matter," I said impatiently. "Tell me what happened."

"No," she agreed, "I suppose it doesn't matter. Well, it seems that this wagon – but I think it was really a cart – yes, I'm sure it was – at least, I think so – but at any rate it appears that the wagon had run away – that is, of course, it was the horse that had run away, but as he was tied to the cart, it comes to the same thing. And he got on to the pavement – it was in the Strand, somewhere near that shop where they sell those absurd – now what do they call those things? I am getting so silly about names, and it's quite a common name, too – "

"Never mind what they are called," I entreated. "Do tell me what happened to Mr. Davenant."

"Well, what happened was this: When the wagon got on the pavement, all the people scattered to get out of the way – all except a messenger boy, and he fell down right in front of the cart. Then Mr. Davenant ran out and tried to drag the boy clear of the wagon, and, in fact, he did drag him out of the way, but he wasn't quick enough to save himself, for the horse swerved and knocked him down violently on to some stone steps. He fell with his side on the stone steps, and I understand that his ribs were simply smashed to matchwood."

"And where is he now? Is he in a hospital?

"He was. They took him to Charing Cross Hospital, but he wouldn't stay there. He insisted on going home directly they put on the splints or whatever the things were. And, will you believe me, Mrs. Otway, when I tell you that he has been living alone in those wretched chambers ever since! He wouldn't even have a nurse. Isn't that just like a man?"

"But who looks after him?

"Nobody. Of course there is the charwoman, or laundress as they call them – though why they should be called laundresses I can't imagine. They look more like dustwomen – and the man from the office downstairs looks in sometimes. It's a perfectly scandalous state of affairs. I wish, Mrs. Otway, you would go and see him and make him have a nurse."

"I will certainly go and see him," said I. "I will go now," and I held out my hand to bring the interview to an end.

"How sweet of you, dear Mrs. Otway!" she explained, keeping a firm hold of my hand, which I endeavoured unobtrusively to withdraw. "I felt sure you would go to the rescue. And you will insist on his having a nurse, won't you? He will listen to you, but you will have to be firm. Promise me you will, now."

"I will see that he is properly looked after," I replied.

"Yes, but he must have a nurse, you know – a properly trained and certificated nurse. You can get excellent nurses at that place – now, what is its name? Cavendish – Cavendish something. I am getting so silly about names. Let me see, I did have a card in my purse, perhaps it is there still – " Here she released my hand to open her wrist-bag, and I took the opportunity to retreat down the steps.

"Don't trouble, please," I urged. "I shall manage quite well. Good-bye!" and with this I hurried away, somewhat unceremoniously, across the wide road, and, as soon as I had turned the corner, broke into a run. A couple of minutes later I arrived at the station, breathless, just in time to see a Circle train move out. I could have wept with vexation. It was but a few minutes before the next one would be due, but those minutes dragged like hours. With swift strides I paced up and down the platform in an agony of impatience, turning over and over again Miss Tallboy Smith's confused account of the accident and trying to construct by its aid some intelligible picture of Jasper's condition.

Even when I was in the train its progress seemed intolerably slow and the succession of stations interminable. It was an agony to sit still and passively await the leisurely arrival at my destination, and an unspeakable relief when, at last, I reached the Temple Station, to spring from the train, dash up the stairs and hurry along the embankment. My progress on foot might be slower, but I had the physical sensation of speed.

At the top of Middle Temple Lane I emerged into Fleet Street and, crossing the road, entered Clifford's Inn Passage. I had never been there before and, though I knew the number of Jasper's house, I thought it best to enquire as to its whereabouts. As I passed through the archway, I saw

461

a somewhat clerical-looking man standing at the door of the porter's lodge, and from him learned that No. 54 was in the inner court on the east side of the garden, with which direction I hurried on again. Clearly there came back to me the impressions that seemed so dim at the time, a sense of quiet and repose, of aloofness from the bustle of the city, an old-world, dignified shabbiness that was yet homely and pleasant withal. I crossed a little court, passed through a second archway, and came out into a second, larger court, where the gay foliage of plane trees found a foil in the dingy, red brick of the venerable houses. A glance showed me the narrow alley by the garden, and a dozen paces along its roughly-flagged pavement brought me to the entry of No. 54, on the side of which was painted "*Mr. J. Davenant, Architect*". and below, in smaller lettering, "*Jonathan Weeble, Law Writer*".

I stepped into the entry and, tapping on a door which, by its painted description, appeared to appertain to Mr. Weeble's premises, was bidden to "Come in". Accordingly, I entered and was confronted by a somewhat unkempt young man who was apparently engaged in engrossing a large document which was secured to a sort of evergrown lectern by means of a band of tape.

"I have called," I said, "to enquire about Mr. Davenant. Is he in a very serious condition?"

"He wasn't when I saw him about an hour ago," was the reply.

"Do you think he would be well enough to see me?" The young man, whom I assumed to be Mr. Weeble, inspected me critically, and then replied,

"I should say most emphatically that he would. But we needn't leave it at that. I can soon find out. Won't you sit down?"

He rose briskly and hurried out of the office, and it was only when I heard him ascending the uncovered stairs, two or three at a time, that I remembered that I had given no name.

Mr. Weeble's confident manner had lifted a load of anxiety from my mind, but my agitation was little abated. My fears were relieved, indeed, for evidently Jasper's condition was not such as to occasion alarm, but, as my anxiety subsided, other emotions made themselves felt. I was actually going to see him. Within a couple of minutes we should be together. The intolerable separation would be at an end. And the ecstasy of this thought – the almost painful joy of anticipation – brought home to me the intensity of my yearning to look on him again

The sound of Mr. Weeble's footsteps descending the stairs set my heart throbbing, and as he bustled into the office I stood up, trembling with excitement.

"It's all right," said he. "Mr. Davenant will see you, if you'll go up. First floor, right hand side of the landing. I've left the door open, and you'll see his name above it."

I did not go up the stairs at Mr. Weeble's pace, but I went as rapidly as the trembling of my knees would let me. On the first floor I saw a forbidding, iron-bound door standing ajar, and above it the well-beloved name, painted in white letters. I drew back the heavy door, disclosing a lighter one, also ajar, which I pushed open as I closed the massive "oak" after me. For a moment, I stood on the threshold looking into the quaint, old-world room, with its panelled walls and the soft green light from the plane trees shimmering through the windows. He was reclining by the fire on a low, wooden settee, and held a book in his hand, and even in that instantaneous glance I could see how changed he was – how pale and thin and weary-looking. But as I stepped out from the shadow, the worn face lighted up, the book fell to the floor, and he flung his arms out towards me.

"Helen!"

"Jasper!"

In a moment I was on my knees by his side. His arms were around me and my cheek lay against his. And so for a while we rested with never a word spoken and no sound in the room but the ticking of the clock and the soft rustle of a swaying branch on the window panes. And so I could have rested forever, for at last my heart was at peace.

"Jasper, dear," I said, at length, "how is it with you? Are you badly hurt?"

"Not a bit," he replied. "It is just a matter of a cracked rib and a few bruises, and I've nearly recovered from those."

"But why did you never send me a word? That wasn't friendly of you, Jasper."

"How could I, dearest?" he protested. "A bargain is a bargain. The month wasn't up."

"Jasper!" I exclaimed, "how could you be so silly? Of course you ought to have sent me a message, and I would have come to you instantly."

"I am sure you would, Helen," said he, "which was an additional reason for my keeping to our covenant. It would have seemed a shabby thing to do for, badly as I wanted you, I was never really in any danger. By the way, how did you hear of my little mishap?"

I told him of my meeting with Miss Tallboy-Smith, and he chuckled softly. "She was an old goose to frighten you with those lurid stories, but I'm very grateful to her, all the same. I have wanted you, Helen."

He drew me closer to him and stroked my hair fondly, and again we were silent for a while. The clock ticked on impassively, the plane tree rustled gently on the window, and I was filled with a quiet, restful happiness that I was unwilling to interrupt even by speaking.

Presently Jasper bent down to my ear and whispered, "Helen, darling, you haven't anything to tell me, have you?"

I knew what he meant, of course, and the strange thing is that, though the question came unexpectedly, and though I had not consciously given the subject a moment's, thought, I found my mind completely and finally made up.

"Yes," I replied, "I have. Jasper, dear, I am your own. I can't live without you. The world must say what it will. I can do without the world, but I can't exist without you."

He drew me yet closer to him and kissed me reverently. "Dear heart," he said softly. "Sweet wife. I would try to thank you if words could tell you what your precious gift means to me. But life is before us, and mine shall be one long thanksgiving. You have given me my heart's desire, if love and worship and faithful service can in any degree repay you, they shall be yours as long as our lives endure."

Thus in a few moments were the long weeks of misery and despair blotted out. We were reinstated, and, indeed, much more than reinstated, we were admitted and accepted lovers. And, just as my mind had, so to speak, made itself up without conscious thought on my part, so now that I had entered into this new covenant it seemed quite inevitable and satisfying. Its nonconformity with social conventions left me completely undisturbed.

Presently Jasper made me draw up a low, rush-bottomed chair that I might sit comfortably by his side while we talked. But, in fact, we talked little, for there is a sort of telepathy born of perfect sympathy that makes speech superfluous. We were both very happy and very deeply moved, and it seemed more companionable to sit, hand clasped in hand, and let our thoughts run on undisturbed by speech, knowing that the thoughts of each were but a reflection of the other's.

Anon came Mr. Weeble, stamping slowly up the stairs like an infirm coal-porter and making such a prolonged to-do about inserting the latch-key into the outer door that we both laughed. A very discreet man was Mr. Weeble.

"I've just come to see if I can do anything," said he, when Jasper had introduced me. "I generally make his tea and straighten out his bandages. Shall I make the tea now or are you taking charge, Mrs. Otway?"

"I will make the tea," said I, "but while you are tidying up the bandages, I will run out and get some fresh cakes."

"Yes," said Mr. Weeble, "that would be a good idea. Our stock is rather low and a trifle old and fruity. And talking of cakes, that reminds me that an old rooster called a day or two ago and left one. I put it in a spare deed-box and forgot all about it. I'll go and fetch it up."

"A rooster, you say, Weeble," said Jasper. "May we assume that you are speaking figuratively?"

"Yes," replied Mr. Weeble. "Elderly party with an automatic smile and the rummiest name I ever heard. Now what was her name? Something double-barrelled – Bigboy-Jones, was it?"

"Tallboy-Smith, I expect," said Jasper.

"That was it. I sent her a letter of thanks the same day in your handwriting and signed it with your name. Are you starting now, Mrs. Otway? You'll find a very good cake-shop in Fetter Lane near the top on the left-hand side."

I took a brief bag of Jasper's and his latchkey and sallied forth into Fetter Lane by the postern gate, and as I walked up the quaint, old street I found myself looking into the homely shops and inspecting the ancient timber houses with a queer sort of proprietary air, as if I belonged to the neighbourhood. I found the cake-shop – it was really an old-fashioned baker's shop, such as one might find in a country town – and as I made a selection of the wares, based on experience of Jasper's tastes, I found myself almost unconsciously considering the merits of the establishment as a source of supply for a family of two. If the change in my mental state was sudden, it was certainly complete, as I sauntered back down Fetter Lane with my bag of provisions, care-free and filled with a delightful sense of emancipation, loitering to look into shop windows or to peer up strange courts and alleys that I might not return prematurely, I could not but contrast my condition with that in which I had set forth in the morning – hopeless, heart weary, despondent. When I arrived at Jasper's chambers, Mr. Weeble had already gone, but he had filled the kettle and set it to boil on the gas-stove in the kitchen, where I found it murmuring placidly and breathing out little clouds of steam. The kitchen was a delightful absurdity. About the magnitude of a good-sized china cupboard, it suggested, with its range of shelves and little chemical sink, a doctor's dispensary or a chemist's laboratory. Yet it was very orderly and quite convenient, and it had the advantage that, while I was engaged in the preparations for the meal, my heart singing in unison with the kettle's song, I could look out of a tiny window on the moss-grown garden, or through the open door see Jasper watching me with a smile of ecstasy, and receive his instructions as to where the various articles were

465

to be found. It was all very pleasant and intimate, and every little, homely detail helped to bring home to me the reality of my happiness.

During the very leisurely tea we gradually approached the subject of our future arrangements, which had evidently been very carefully thought out by Jasper.

"I'm not quite such a graven image as I look," said he. "I don't believe it's necessary for me to keep so immovable. But that is the doctor's business. I just do as I'm told. However, my bandages are coming off in a few days, and I understand that I shall be practically well in a fortnight. Until I am well, we had better let things remain as they are, and I think it would be better for you not to come and see me again in the interval."

"Do you mean that I am to leave you, a helpless invalid all alone and no one to look after you?"

"Yes," he replied. "Of course, I shall want you dreadfully, but as to my being alone and helpless, that is merely a sentimental view of the case. You can see for yourself that I am quite comfortable and well cared-for – Weeble never forgets me for an instant. And I think it most necessary that, until we are definitely married, we should have the most scrupulous regard for the conventions. We can't get the sanction either of the Law or the Church to our marriage – therefore, it is the more necessary for us to treat it ourselves with the utmost respect and seriousness. We are not going to enter into a casual and irresponsible relationship. We are going to contract a marriage, and I propose that we do so publicly and with proper formalities suited to the dignity and importance of the transaction."

"But," I asked, "what formalities are possible?

"My proposal," he replied, "is this: We shall appoint a day and a time to meet here, and have two witnesses in attendance. Weeble could be one and the Inn porter, Mr. Duskin, the other. In the presence of those witnesses we shall formally agree to take one another as husband and wife. Each of us shall make a written declaration to the same effect, reciting the circumstances which render the unusual procedure necessary, and, in your case, denouncing and repudiating your marriage with Otway. These declarations we shall respectively read to the witnesses – who will also read them – and we shall each sign our declaration in the presence of the witnesses. I am not quite clear whether it would be legal for them to counter-sign as witnesses. If not, we shall add a note stating that the signatures were made in their presence. Then we shall exchange declarations and we shall notify Mr. Otway and whosoever else may be concerned, or whom we wish to inform, of what has taken place. Does that meet with your approval, Helen?"

"Entirely," I replied, "excepting the sentence of banishment. Don't you think I might just look in on you now and again to see if you want anything?"

"It is only a fortnight, dearest," said he, "and we can write as often as we please. Until we are married, we can't be too careful to avoid provoking criticism."

I made no further objections, for I felt that he was right, and, moreover, I could not but perceive that this rather excessive primness, like the formalities which he had proposed, was simply an unconscious expression of chivalrous respect, a protest in advance against any unfavourable criticisms of me. And in accordance with what I felt he would consider prudent, I took leave of him comparatively early, so as to avoid a second meeting with Mr. Weeble, who, I learned, came in every night between eight and nine to help him to get to bed.

"I shall write to you every day," I said, as I drew on my gloves, "and you must promise that, if there is anything that I can do for you, you will let me know and never mind about Mrs. Grundy. Is that agreed?"

He gave the required promise, and when I had handed him back his latch-key, I stooped and kissed him, and as I looked back at him before closing the iron-bound door, I could not but contrast this parting with the miserable farewell of less than a month ago.

Chapter XXI
A Dreadful Inheritance

It has always been, and still is, somewhat of a puzzle to me to account for the sudden and complete change in my point of view in regard to my union with Jasper. Lilith would doubtless have explained it as a case of subconscious reflection, and probably she would have been right. My impression is that Peggy's matter-of-fact attitude toward marriage unsanctioned by law had a more profound effect, than I was aware of, and that her words – which I had certainly recalled from time to time – had remained in my mind subconsciously exercising a continuous influence. Or it may be that I had found a life of separation impossible, and had realised it consciously only when I found myself once more in Jasper's presence.

But, however it may have happened, the fact remains that I accepted the new order without a qualm. The conditions that I had scouted as unthinkable now seemed entirely reasonable and acceptable. The only twinge of misgiving that I ever had was produced by the draft of the declaration that Jasper sent for my approval and criticism. For that well-meant document, with its half-defiant, half-protesting phrases, did certainly bring home to me with uncomfortable vividness the fact that this marriage was not like any other marriage, and that I was not as other married women were. But I sent it back approved and tried to forget it, and quietly went on with my preparations for the new life.

Outwardly, however, I made no change in my habits, and even tried to suppress the gaiety and buoyancy of spirit that I felt, lest the sudden change from my recent depressed condition should attract notice. I still lived my life apart, only too happy in my solitude, and spent most of my time in the workshop conning over Jasper's letters, or meditating on the happy days that were drawing so near. For a time the candlestick was sadly neglected, until I had the sudden inspiration of finishing it as a wedding-gift to Jasper. And then all the joy of work revived and blossomed into unsuspected skill. Tracer and punch seemed to travel along their appointed paths unguided, the spindle-shanked chasing hammer became a familiar demon and appeared to develop a volition of its own, and the little enamel furnace roared with glee.

So the days sped by, each bringing me nearer to the golden gate of my enchanted garden, and each so filled with quiet happiness that I could not wish it shorter. About the end of the first week came a letter from

Jasper saying that the bandages had been discarded, and that he had taken a walk and had appeared quite well and strong. A day or two later came another fixing the date and time of our meeting. It was to be on the following Thursday – only five days ahead – at six o'clock in the evening. The formalities were to be carried out immediately on my arrival, we should then dine quietly at the club, spend the evening at a concert or the theatre, and take the boat-train either to Flushing or Calais, which ever I preferred.

The arrival of this letter, though I had been daily expecting it, came as quite a shock, and turned my tranquil happiness into feverish excitement which I had some difficulty in concealing. The fixing of an actual date and the selection of a definite region in which to spend the honeymoon (I chose the north of France) gave a reality to this Great Adventure and brought it out of the undefined future into the present. For now I had to carry out the final preparations. Lightly as I might travel, I must take some luggage, and this would entail a conveyance, and this in its turn involved something in the nature of a public departure, so that, if I had desired to disappear secretly – which I did not – the thing would have been impossible. Yet I was, naturally, loath to say much about my immediate intentions, preparing to make my explanations by letter after the event, and this the prevailing good manners of the little community made quite easy. I notified Miss Polton and my more intimate friends that I was going away on a visit of uncertain duration, and, whatever curiosity they may have felt, no further particulars were asked for as I went about my immediate preparations – the packing of those few things that I must needs take away with me – unnoticed, or at least uncommented on, and then began unobtrusively to arrange the rest of my possessions for the final removal.

On Wednesday – the day before that of my departure – a letter arrived from Mr. Otway. It reached me just after lunch, and I glanced at it before rising from the table. The subject was the same as that of previous ones, but it was evident that something in the nature of a crisis was approaching. The extreme agitation of the writer was shown not only in the matter and the impassioned, rather incoherent manner, but even in the handwriting, which was ill-formed and slovenly, in great contrast to Mr. Otway's usual business-like neatness.

My dear Helen, (it began)

I have not troubled you for quite a long time with my miserable affairs – which are, to some extent, your affairs too. But they are going from bad to worse, and now I feel that I am coming to the limits of endurance. I cannot bear this much longer. My health is shattered, my peace of mind is wrecked, and my brain threatens to give way. Death would be a boon, a relief, and I feel that it is not far off. I cannot go on like this. Those wretches leave me no peace. Hardly a week passes but I get some new menace, and now – but I can't tell you in a letter. It is too horrible. Come to me, Helen, for the love of God! I am in torment. Have pity on me, even though you have never forgiven me. I cannot come to you, for I am now unable to leave my bed. I am a wreck, a ruin. Come to me just this once, and if you cannot help me, at least give me the comfort of your sympathy. You will not be troubled by me much longer.

Your distracted husband,

Lewis Otway

The emotions that this letter aroused were mixed and rather conflicting. Never had I felt a deeper loathing of Mr. Otway than now that I was being forced to accept what I knew in my heart to be but a counterfeit of marriage. I had been robbed of my birthright, and he had robbed me. Never was I less in a mood to offer him sympathy in the troubles that he had created for himself and me by his callous selfishness. And yet I decided to go to him. Whether the decision was due to some sort of compunction for the blow that I was going to strike on the morrow, or whether to curiosity, or to a desire to verify his foreboding of approaching death, I cannot say. Certainly the last consideration entered into the mixture of motives, and probably was the determining factor. At any rate, I decided to go. Dimly, I perceived that I ought to have consulted Jasper, though I was unaware of the possible legal significance that my visit might acquire. I formed my decision at once, and early in the afternoon set forth westward with the letter in my pocket.

I did not go direct to Mr. Otway's chambers. Promptly as I had made up my mind, I felt the necessity of thinking over the circumstances and forecasting the possibilities. On my way westward I made a halt at a tea-shop, and while I awaited the leisurely service I drew out the letter and read it through again. Clearly the blackmailers were becoming more urgent and possibly more definite. It seemed as though they had adopted some new tactics. But it was not the blackmailers who interested me. I found my eye travelling again and again to those two sentences that hinted at the possibility of Mr. Otway's death.

470

"I feel that it is not far off." And again, "You will not be troubled by me much longer." Had he any solid grounds for these forebodings? Or were they merely the offspring of abiding terror, or perchance simply rhetorical flourishes designed to arouse my sympathy? These were questions of no small moment to me, for Mr. Otway's death would set me free and in an instant unravel the tangled skein of my relations with Jasper.

As I drank my tea with reflective deliberation, I turned these questions over in my mind, not disguising from myself the cool, impassive, egoism of my attitude. My feeling in respect of Mr. Otway was devoid of any trace of sentimentalism. I viewed him as the insurance director views the generalised "proposer", – but inversely, for I was interested in his decease, not in his survival. I loathed him, but I did not hate him. I did not wish him ill. If I could have saved him from suffering I would have done so, even at the cost of some considerable effort. But if he had stood in the face of instant death, and I could have averted that peril by moving a finger, I would not have moved a finger.

That was my position. As I rose from the table and returned the letter to my pocket, what was in my mind was that Mr. Otway seemed to think that he was going to die, and I hoped that he was right.

When I reached Lyon's Inn Chambers the sun was already low and the gloom of the evening was beginning to settle on the closed-in block of buildings. I ascended the ill-lit stone stairs to the second floor, where the light on the landing was so dim that I had difficulty in deciphering Mr. Otway's name above the door of his "set", and as I did so, I noted with surprise that the inscription was faded and obscure, and had the appearance of having been in existence for many years, whereas Mr. Otway had, as I believed, but recently entered on his tenancy.

The door was opened by Mrs. Gregg, who stood in the gloom of the entry confronting me without a word.

"Good evening, Mrs. Gregg," I said. "Mr. Otway has asked me to call on him – "

"Ye need make no excuses," she interrupted, "for coming to see your lawful husband."

"Thank you, Mrs. Gregg," I replied. "Is Mr. Otway disengaged?"

"No," she answered, "he is expecting a visitor."

"How very unfortunate," said I. "He wanted particularly to see me, I know."

"Perhaps you could look in some time to-morrow?" she suggested.

"No, I am afraid I can't. If Mr. Otway is unable to see me this evening I must write to him. I shall not have another opportunity to call for some considerable time."

471

She reflected for a few moments, and I gathered that she was unwilling to take the responsibility of cancelling the interview.

"Could you call again a little later?" she asked, at length. "He will have finished with his visitor by about half-past seven, or say a quarter-to-eight. Could you look in again at eight?"

I had not wanted to be out as late as this would make me, but if I was to see Mr. Otway at all, it would have to be to-night. Eventually I accepted the arrangement – somewhat, I think, to Mrs. Gregg's relief.

As I descended the stairs I heard the footsteps of two persons – apparently a man and a woman – ascending. On the first-floor landing I met the man, who turned out to be the lamplighter. Just as I had passed him he lit the landing lamp, and its light, which came from behind me, fell full on the woman who was coming up. It was only a momentary glimpse that I caught as she passed me on the stairs, but I recognised her instantly. She was Mrs. Campbell, the wife of the Ward Street dealer.

It was an odd meeting, and it gave me the material for a good deal of thought and speculation. Mr. Otway's chambers were the only ones on the second floor, from which it seemed probable that Mrs. Campbell was the visitor whom he was expecting. This was a rather queer coincidence, but it was not the only one. That sudden recognition of the face, thrown into strong relief against the dark background by the bright lamplight, had set my memory working. I remembered how, when I had seen Mrs. Campbell in the shop and had heard her speak, her face had seemed to suggest something familiar, and her accent and the intonation of her voice had called up some accent and tone that I had heard before. It had been but a vague impression at the time, but now, in the new setting and aided by association, the impression became quite definite. The face that hers had suggested was Mr. Otway's face, but the really odd thing was that her voice and accent suggested not Mr. Otway's but *Mrs. Gregg's*. And this very queer resemblance was made yet more queer by a singular discrepancy. Mrs. Gregg spoke with a distinct Scottish accent. It was a peculiar one, different from that of any other Scots person whom I had ever heard speak, but it was quite pronounced. Mrs. Campbell, on the other hand, had no trace whatever of a Scottish accent, of that I was quite sure. But I was equally sure of the resemblance between the two, subtle and elusive as it was.

Here, then, was a problem the consideration of which gave me quite a considerable amount of occupation, and, helped me to while away the hour-and-a-half that I had to wait. The almost fantastic oddity of the coincidence might have made me reject my impressions as mere delusions, but, on the one hand, there was Mrs. Campbell evidently making for Mr. Otway's chambers, and, on the other, was the fact that it was Mr. Otway who had introduced me to the shop in Wardour Street. However, I could get no farther than speculation, and, as speculation tends rapidly to exhaust its limited material, I presently dismissed the problem and returned to the consideration of Mr. Otway's health and its bearing on my own future.

The hour-and-a-half I spent in a leisurely survey of Lincoln's Inn and the Temple. My perambulations with Jasper had brought home to me that London is an entertainment in itself, that no observant person need be dull who has access to its historic streets and picturesque backwaters. And now it was very pleasant to revisit the scenes of former rambles – to be repeated often in the future – and meanwhile to reflect on the happenings of the present and let my thoughts stray to the new life that was about to open, and the time slipped away so agreeably that when the three-quarter chime was struck in a polite undertone by the genteel clock in the Inner Temple, it came to me as quite a surprise.

On the stroke of eight I rang the bell of Mr. Otway's chambers, and was forthwith admitted by the taciturn Mrs. Gregg. In silence she conducted me along a narrow corridor that led from the entrance lobby, across a largish room furnished partly as a library, partly as a dining-room and by a communicating door into the bedroom, when – still without uttering a word departed, shutting the door after her.

Mr. Otway half-rose in bed as I entered, and made a vague gesture of welcome, finally extending his hand, which I shook formally.

"This is really good of you, Helen," said he, "to come and see me, and to come so promptly. I am sorry Mrs. Gregg sent you away. There was no need. My other visitor could have been put off."

"It is of no consequence," said I. "My time was my own to-night. What is the new trouble – for I infer from your letter that there is some new development. Is there any definite threat?"

Again he half-rose in bed, and looking at me with anxious intensity said, in a low, suppressed tone. "Helen, just see that the door is properly shut."

I did so, and he then begged me to draw the chair, which had been placed for me, closer to him. This I also did, and, having seated myself, looked at him expectantly.

Still half-raised in bed, he bent his head as near to me as he could, and in a whisper said, "Helen, I want to ask you a question. What became of your father's stick?"

The question, whispered with such strange secrecy, and accompanied by a singular look compounded of eagerness, fear, and suspicion, somewhat startled me, for I remembered, even as he spoke, that the same question had been asked by Dr. Thorndyke.

473

"I haven't the least idea," I replied. "Haven't you got it?

"No. I never had it. I have never seen it since the – ah – the occasion when – ah – you remember – "

"Of course I remember. I have good reason to."

"Ah – no doubt. Yes. But are you quite sure – I thought you might have taken it away with you."

"But, Mr. Otway, you let me out of the house yourself. You saw me go, and you must have seen that I was not taking it. And you know that I never came to the house again."

He sank back on his pillow with a gesture of despair.

"Yes," he murmured, "that seems to be so. It must be so, I suppose."

"It is so," I said. There is no question about it. When I went away that morning, the stick was in your house. But why are you asking me about it? Is it of any importance?

He turned towards a table that stood by the opposite side of the bed and, taking up a bunch of keys, unlocked a deed-box that was on the table, and took from it a sheet of paper.

"Read that," said he, handing me the paper.

The document was a type-written letter of a similar character to the previous ones, and of about the same length. It ran thus,

Mr. Lewis Otway,

Some funny questions are being asked. What about Mr. Vardon's stick – the loaded stick with the silver, knob to hide the lead loading? Where is it? Somebody says they know where it is and who's got it. And they say there is a bruise on the silver top, and they say something about a smear of blood and a grey hair sticking to it. Do you know anything about it? If you don't, you'd better find out. Because I think you'll hear from that somebody before you are many weeks older or else from the police.

A Well Wisher

As I came to the end of this document I raised my eyes and met Mr. Otway's fixed on me with a very singular expression. But he quickly averted his gaze, possibly embarrassed by the steady intensity of my own. For this letter, together with Mr. Otway's agitated questionings, had revived the old doubts in my mind. Could there be any truth in this veiled accusation? Was it possible that I had really made a hideous mistake in shielding this man? As these doubts flashed through my mind, some

474

reflection of them may have appeared in my expression as I steadily, looked Mr. Otway in the face. At any rate, he looked away as I have said, and when I handed him back the letter, he took it in a hand that shook like a dipsomaniac's, and replaced it in the deed-box without a word.

For a space we were both silent, and I sat looking at him and his surroundings with profound distaste. The close, stuffy air of the room aroused a faint disgust, the objects on the bedside table – the cigarette box, the large spirit decanter and siphon and a bottle of veronal tablets – conveyed a disagreeable impression of drinking and drug-taking. And the man himself, with his pasty face, his baggy eyelids, creased with multitudinous wrinkles, his drooping, tremulous underlip, was distinctly repellent. The whole atmosphere of the place and its occupant was unwholesome, sordid, and abnormal.

Yet, unwholesome and unhealthy as he looked, there was no striking change in Mr. Otway's appearance, nothing new to justify, so far as I could judge, his alarming account of himself. His aspect supported the suggestions of the spirit-bottle, the cigarettes, and the veronal. He looked distracted, terrified, nerve-shaken, but he did not, to my eye, look like a dying man. I inspected him critically during that interval of silence, and arrived, almost regretfully, I fear, at the conclusion that his forebodings were merely the result of a chronic state of fear – if they were real and not deliberately assumed to excite my sympathy.

I think he must have had a feeling that I was regarding him with disfavour, for presently he turned towards me with a deprecating air and sighed wearily.

"I am afraid, Helen," said he, "that you are very tired of me and my troubles. But you must try to be patient. It may not be for long."

"Why do you say that?" I asked. "Is your health really bad, apart from the worry of these letters?"

"My health gets worse from week to week," he replied. "Not that I am suffering from any definite disease. But the constant alarm and anxiety, the shocks which keep coming one on top of another, are breaking me up. I get no interval of peace in which to recover. I am in a constant state of worry and depression by day, which leads to that," and he pointed to the spirit-decanter, "and it is even worse at night unless I secure a little rest by those things," pointing to the veronal bottle, "and cigarettes, whisky, and veronal don't make for a long life or robust health."

"Still," I said, "you mustn't exaggerate or alarm yourself unnecessarily. You are not in very good condition, I can see, but there is no reason to suppose that you are in a dangerous state. Couldn't you cut off these drugs and the whisky and go away for a change?"

He shook his head.

"I couldn't go away," he said. "They would find me out and follow me. And as to cutting off the stimulants and the sedatives, that is impossible. Bad as they are, they are the last bulwark against something worse."

"What do you mean?" I asked.

He did not answer immediately, but seemed to be considering my question and debating whether he should make any further confidences. At length he turned to me somewhat abruptly with an expression which I had never seen on his face before, a wild expression strangely unlike his usual, heavy stolidity, suggesting excitement and terror, with yet a curious dash of exultation.

"Helen," he said with a singular intensity of voice and manner, "there are men who are born into this world under sentence of death. The black cap hangs over their cradles. Throughout their lives they have continually to watch – to evade the execution of the sentence if they can. But the time comes when they can escape no longer. They are tired of evasion, of the struggle to escape, and then they give themselves up, and that is the end.

"I am one of those men, Helen. My mother put an end to her own life. My only brother put an end to his life. My mother's father made away with himself. It is in the blood. My mother was found hanging from a tree in an orchard. My brother disappeared and was found a month later hanging from a peg in a disused wardrobe. My grandfather hanged himself from a beam in the loft. Perhaps there were others. At any rate, there it is. The fathers have eaten sour grapes and the children's teeth are set on edge."

He paused, and I sat looking with uneasy surprise at the unwonted animation in his face, the faint flush, the awakening light in his eyes, the suppressed eagerness of his manner. There was something weirdly unpleasant about this new phase.

"You mustn't allow these fancies to disturb you," I said feebly.

"They are not fancies," he retorted. "They are weighty realities. I thought for a long time that the inheritance had passed me by. But when the first of those letters came, I knew that the legacy had fallen in. And every new menace sets the impulse working. Whenever one of those letters comes I feel it. I find myself thinking of my mother and my brother, and wondering if they felt the same. Then I take a stiff whisky, and the feeling goes off. But I don't care, nowadays, to go to bed until I have taken a dose of veronal."

"Why not?" I asked.

He drew himself to the edge of the bed, and, thrusting his head out, peered into a shadowy corner of the room with a sort of half-terrified, half-exultant leer that seemed to stir the very marrow of my bones.

"What is it, Mr. Otway?" I asked, staring into the corner but seeing nothing.

"Do you see it, Helen?" he said, rolling his eyes at me and then looking back into the corner, which was in a line with the bed-head. "That great hook, or bent peg. I can't imagine what it was put there for, but there it is, like a great metal finger – beckoning, beckoning."

I looked at the object that he indicated – a massive curved peg or hook fixed to the wall about seven feet from the floor – and shivered slightly. Its appearance was horribly suggestive.

"When I used to lie awake," Mr. Otway continued, still gazing into the corner, "after the first letters came, I could lie on my left side, because then it was behind me and I seemed to feel it drawing me. I had to turn so that I could see it, and whenever I looked at it, it seemed to beckon. And so it does now."

"I should have it unscrewed and taken away," said I.

"Yes," he replied, reflectively, "perhaps it might be – and yet I don't know. Perhaps I might be more restless if it were *not* there. It is, in a way, a satisfaction to know that – ah – that I hold a trump card that I can play if – ah – if all the other cards are against me."

As he spoke, he looked at me with that same curious half-frightened, half-exultant expression that made me wonder whether perhaps his inheritance included a dash of insanity. Then he rolled back to the middle of the bed and lay staring at the ceiling, and by degrees the excitement faded out of his face and he recovered his usual stolid gravity of expression.

Presently he glanced at the little carriage clock that stood on the table and, turning to me, said, "I usually take my veronal about this time. Would you mind giving me a glass of water and the tablets?"

I rose from my chair, and as I did so my little wrist-bag, which had been reposing, forgotten, on my lap, slipped to the floor. I picked it up and hung it on the knob of the chair-back, and then fetched the water-bottle and tumbler from the wash-stand. Having filled the tumbler and handed it to Mr. Otway, I picked up the veronal bottle, and seeing that it was a new one, broke the seal, withdrew the cork and pulled out the cotton-wool packing.

"Three tablets, please," said Mr. Otway.

I handed him the bottle, and as he took it and shook out the three tablets he smiled grimly.

477

"You are the most cautious woman I have ever met," he remarked. "But you are quite right to make me responsible for my own poison."

He took the tablets one at a time, crunching each between his teeth very thoroughly before washing it down, with water. Then he mixed what looked to me a very stiff allowance of whisky, with a very little soda water, and swallowed it at a draught.

"I find that the stimulant makes the veronal act more rapidly," he explained. "I shall be asleep in about half-an-hour. Do you mind staying with me until I drop off?"

I agreed to this, although it was getting late, but, conscious that it was probably the last service I should ever render him, I did not feel that I could refuse. So I sat down again in the chair and watched him, noting that already – probably as a result of the stimulant – he was quieter in manner and more peaceful in appearance. Even when he reverted to the subject that had occasioned my visit, his manner was quite calm.

"There is something very mysterious about that stick," he remarked. "Recalling the circumstances, I remember putting it down in the corner by the writing-table. I never saw it again, and never gave its whereabouts a thought. I assumed that you had taken it, but I now realise that I was mistaken. Apparently it has got into undesirable hands and we haven't heard the last of it, I fear."

"You had better not think any more about it, Mr. Otway," I said. "There is nothing to be done, and the less you worry the less harm these people will be able to do you."

"Yes," he agreed, "that is good advice, and I can follow it now. But if I should wake up in the small hours of the morning it will be very different. That is the worst time, Helen. Then this persecution seems beyond bearing. The horror of it makes me sweat with fear. I seem to hear the police on the stairs. I find myself listening for the sound of the bell. It is horrible – horrible! And then I think of that wardrobe, unnoticed all those weeks, and the figure inside in the dark. And then – "

He made a motion of his eyes towards the shadowy corner and involuntarily I glanced at the great peg high up on the wall.

He did not speak again for some time, and I sat silently watching him and thinking – thinking of his dreadful heritage and all that it might mean. Was it a reality, this legacy of death that he saw coming to him? Was it true that even now the black cap hung over his bed? Supposing it were? Supposing that this very night, in the chilly middle watch, he should wake with all his terrors clutching at his heart! Should creep out of his bed and – Here my glance stole into the shadowy corner and, as I looked, my mind seemed to picture a dim shape filling the wall space below the big, massive peg. There were no details and hardly any form –

478

it was just a shape, vague and rather horrible. I shivered slightly, but I did not try to blot out the mental picture. It was a gruesome thing, that dim, elongated shape, but it did not disturb me much, for it set going other associated trains of thought. There was the ceremony to-morrow evening, the witnesses with their doubtful rights of attestation, protesting that all was in order – and protesting in vain. There were two Ishmaelites going forth hand-in-hand into the wilderness, ready to meet scorn with defiance – but still Ishmaelites. And at the thought, the shape upon the wall space below the peg seemed to grow less dim, to loom out more distinctly. That shape was Mr. Otway – dead. The late Mr. Otway. No longer a legal impediment, but just a fiction that had ceased to exist.

From the dark corner I turned my eyes on to the living man as he lay motionless, breathing softly with an occasional faint snore, and now and again puffing out his cheeks. He was not asleep, for I could see his eyes open and close at intervals, but he was evidently growing somnolent. I watched him with deep interest, almost with fascination, as one might look on a condemned man making his last journey in the hangman's cart. This was a condemned man, too, a potential suicide. At any moment he might set forth on his last journey, and his arrival at his destination would set the Ishmaelites free. He was ready to go, but he awaited the determining influence that would start him on his journey. What form would that final cause take? Would it be some sudden shock of alarm? Or the cumulative effect of prolonged, abiding fear?

I leaned forward and spoke softly to him.

"Do you know, Mr. Otway, what caused your brother – "

He opened his eyes and looked at me, dully. "What did you say, Helen?" he asked.

"I was wondering if you knew – if there was anything in particular that caused your brother to take his life."

He cogitated sleepily for a while before replying. At length he answered, in a drowsy voice, "I am not very clear about it. He had had a good deal of worry of one kind and another, financial and domestic. I don't know that anything unusual had occurred, but he had been in a nervous, depressed state for some time."

Having made this reply, Mr. Otway closed his eyes and took a deep breath, and I reflected on the significance of his answer. There had apparently been no specific cause of his brother's suicide, but just the accumulating effects of nervousness and depression, which exploded when they reached a certain degree of intensity. His condition, in fact, seemed to have been almost identical with Mr. Otway's present condition.

Once more my eyes wandered away to the shadowy corner, and again the wall space below the great hook-like peg became occupied by that elongated shape. Now I seemed to visualise it more completely. It was no longer a mere shape. It had parts – recognisable members. There were the limp-dangling arms, the downward-pointing toes, the shadowy head lolling sideways. It was very horrible, yet I found myself viewing it without horror, but rather with a certain detached interest. I was getting used to it, and was disposed to consider it in terms of its significance.

It was not a person. It was a thing which had replaced a person who had ceased to exist. That person had had a wife. But the wife had ceased to exist, too. In her place was a widow – a free, unattached woman in whom were vested all the rights and liberties of spinsterhood, including the power to contract a valid and regular marriage. The shape was an ugly and forbidding thing, but it held precious and desirable gifts.

From the shape projected by my own imagination my eyes turned to the actual man – the man who was convertible into such a shape. He was fast asleep now, lying on his back, breathing a little stertorously and blowing out his cheeks at each breath. He was an unpleasant spectacle, and the sound of his breathing was disagreeable. He ought not to be lying on his back, for sleepers who lie on their backs are apt to dream, and dreams are not good for men with a tendency to suicide. And sleepers who breathe stertorously are apt to dream ugly dreams.

This consideration set my thoughts working afresh. Supposing this man should have a dream presenting his waking terrors with all the added intensity and vividness of a nightmare, the heavy footfalls of the police upon the stairs, the hands groping in the darkness of the landing for the bell-pull! Or if his dream should show him that wardrobe with its dreadful occupant! What would happen? And even as I put the question to myself my imagination supplied with startling vividness the answering picture. I saw the affrighted sleeper suddenly awaken in uncontrollable panic, scramble from his bed and shuffle hurriedly towards the corner under the peg.

The mental construction of the scene was singularly complete and orderly. I even found myself filling in the details of the means. There, indeed, was the peg. But a man cannot hang himself without some means of suspension. And these must be immediately available or the impulse might die away before they were found. I glanced around the room to see what means were to hand, and at once my eye lighted on an old-fashioned bell-rope that hung beside the head of the bed. Its perfect suitability was evident at a glance – provided that it could be detached without ringing the bell. But the necessity for cutting it rather than pulling it down would be obvious, even to a suicide.

480

The means, then, were all ready to hand. And there was the man, charged with this self-destructive tendency, sleeping in the very posture calculated to start it into action.

I sat still, watching him with absorbing interest, and as these thoughts shaped themselves with more and more distinctness, an impulse of which I was barely conscious formed itself and steadily grew in intensity. At length I leaned forward and spoke in a low voice.

"Mr. Otway, you should not lie in that position."

There was no answer, and he made no sign. The heavy breathing went on with uninterrupted regularity, the eyes remained closed. Again I spoke, this time more loudly, clearly and distinctly.

"Mr. Otway, can you hear me? If you lie as you are lying, you will probably dream. You may have bad, dangerous dreams. You may dream of your mother and your brother. You may dream that the peg on the wall is beckoning to you. And then you may wake in a panic and think that the peg is still beckoning. And then – "

I stopped suddenly. What was this that I was doing? Was it a warning to avert disaster? So the words were framed. But I knew it was nothing of the kind. It was suggestion, pure and almost undisguised. The dreadful truth struck me like a blow and seemed to turn me into stone. I sat rigid as a statue, still leaning forward with my lips parted as if to complete that awful sentence, every moment more appalled by this frightful thing that I had done. There came to me in a flash a vision of my own automatism after the séance. I heard Lilith telling me how the sleep of the drugged resembles the hypnotic trance, and again it came to me how I had been sitting looking at that terrible peg on the wall and – without conscious intention – creating by my will the awful shape beneath it.

How long I should have sat, bent forward as if frozen into rigid immobility by the horror of this hideous thing, it is impossible to say. The realization of what I had done, that had fallen on me like a thunderbolt, had petrified me in a posture of arrested action. It seemed to have deprived me of the power of movement.

The place was intensely silent. The monotonous breathing of the sleeping man – the snoring intake alternating with the soft, blowing expiration – made no impression on the profound quiet, and the rapid ticking of the little carriage clock on the table seemed only to make it more intense.

Suddenly something stirred in the outer room. I sprang to my feet with a gasp that had almost been a shriek. Probably it was only Mrs. Gregg, but in my overwrought state the sound was vaguely alarming. I stood for a few moments, my heart thumping and my breath coming short and fast, then I stole on tip-toe across the room and softly opening the door, peered into the outer room. It was in darkness except that a bright beam of moonlight poured in at the window, but this gave enough light to show that there was nobody in the room.

Still fearful of I knew not what, I stepped softly through the doorway and looked about me suspiciously. The moonlight struck on a large cupboard or wardrobe, which instantly suggested the lurking-place of some eavesdropper and at the same time aroused horrible associations connected with Mr. Otway's brother, so that, in spite of my alarm, I was impelled to pluck at the handle to satisfy myself that no figure was hidden within. But the cupboard was locked, or, at any rate, would not open.

Then I looked under the table and peered into the darker corners of the room, growing – naturally – more and more nervous every moment, and pausing from time to time to listen, or to look back through the doorway into the bedroom, where I could see Mr. Otway lying motionless like a sepulchral effigy.

Suddenly something stirred softly quite near to me – the sound seemed to come from the cupboard. I could have screamed with terror. The last vestige of my self-possession was gone, and in sheer panic I fled across the room and down the corridor to the entrance lobby. This place was in utter darkness, and as I frantically groped for the latch, I felt my skin creep and break out into a chilly sweat. At last I found the latch, dragged the door open, and darted out, and as the clang of the closing door filled the building with hollow echoes, I ran swiftly down the stairs.

Once out in the inhabited streets, my alarm subsided somewhat, but still the image of that motionless figure in the bedroom, the sinister-looking peg on the wall, and the recollection of those dreadful words that I had spoken into the sleeper's ears pursued me with an abiding horror. I walked quickly out into the Strand, and I was in the act of hailing a cab when I remembered that I had left my wrist-bag hanging on the chair-back by Mr. Otway's bedside. My purse was in that bag. But if it had contained my entire worldly possessions I could not have summoned up courage enough to go back for it.

The cab drew up by the kerb. I hesitated a moment, but reflecting that it was yet hardly ten o'clock, and that someone would be waiting up from whom I could borrow the fare, I gave the cabman the address, with the necessary explanations, entered the cab, and shut the door. But as the crazy vehicle – it was an ancient four-wheeler – rattled over the uneven roadways of the side streets, the scene in that warm and stuffy bedroom was re-enacted again and again. And yet again I looked on that ill omened cupboard in the ghostly moonlight, speculated on the mysterious sounds in the living room, wondered uncomfortably if there had been a watcher or a listener, and if so, whether that eavesdropper knew the meaning of silent willing and suggestion.

Chapter XXII
The Catastrophe

Viewed by the cheerful light of the morning sun as it streamed in through my bedroom window, the phantoms of the previous night dwindled to mere scarecrows. On the panic-stricken state in which I had fled from Mr. Otway's chambers I was now disposed to look back with faint amusement. Even the words which I had spoken into Mr. Otway's ears as he slept had no longer any terrifying significance, though I had to admit that they were not susceptible of any satisfactory interpretation. They had been spoken under the influence of an impulse which I could not account for, and did not care to examine too closely, but which I vaguely connected with my excursions into psychical research – a subject which I decided to avoid as far as possible in the future.

As to Mr. Otway, if his account of his family was correct, it seemed quite probable that, sooner or later, he would make away with himself, though seeing that he was now well past middle life, the propensity could hardly be as strong as he had represented it. On the other hand, he was now being subjected to a very excessive nervous strain, and was undoubtedly letting his mind run on the subject of suicide. If the blackmailers continued to keep up an increasing pressure, as they seemed inclined to do, the breaking-point might be reached quite soon. And I could not disguise from myself that the catastrophe, if and when it occurred, would not present itself to me as a personal misfortune.

With this I dismissed Mr. Otway and his affairs, and let my thoughts roam into more attractive regions. For this was the day of days. In a matter of a few hours my separation from Jasper would be at an end. We should be united, never again to part.

As I rose and dressed, this was the burden of my thoughts. The weeks of separation and loneliness were gone, and the hours that lay between the present and that final meeting were running out apace like the grains of sand in an hourglass that is nearly spent. I hurried over breakfast that I might the sooner escape to be alone with my happiness, and most of the morning I spent in the workshop, arranging my apparatus so that it might easily be packed, in case I should not come back to superintend the removal myself. The candlestick, which was finished and successful beyond my expectations, I took upstairs to place in my trunk that I might give it to Jasper this very day. And then I paid a visit to my friend Peggy, whom I found in her workshop chirruping gaily and very busy making a complicated set of plaster moulds from the dissected wax model of her masterpiece. But I did not stay long with her, for the making of piece-moulds is an engrossing occupation and one better followed in solitude.

As I entered the house from the garden I encountered our little housemaid with a telegram in her hand.

"This has just come for you, ma'am," said she, holding it out towards me. "The boy is waiting to see if there is any answer."

I suppose that to most persons unaccustomed to receiving telegrams, the appearance of the peremptory, orange-tinted envelope is a little portentous. Especially so was it to me at that moment, with the crisis of my life so near at hand, and my heart beat tumultuously as I tore open the envelope and unfolded the flimsy paper. It bore but a brief message, but when I had read that message, the joy of life, the half-timorous happiness that had come to me with the morning sunlight, went out in a moment, like a wind-blown taper, and left me desolate.

Cancel appointment for to-day and do not come to the club.
Letter follows.

Jasper

That was all. There was really nothing very alarming in it. But to me it came as a dreadful anti-climax, strung up, as I was, to the highest pitch of nervous tension. With a trembling hand I refolded the paper, and, having told the maid that there was no answer, ran up to my room and bolted myself in.

It was a terrible blow. Only now, by the bitterness of the disappointment, did I realise the heart-hunger that I had endured, the intense yearning for the moment in which my beloved companion would be restored to me. And then, beyond this sudden collapse of my happiness, almost in the moment of its realisation, was the mystery, the suspense, the uncertainty. What could it be that had happened? Had Jasper's condition suddenly grown worse? That could hardly be, for he was practically well – at least, he had so regarded himself – and moreover there was that cryptic reference to the club. Why must I not go to the club?

There was something very mysterious in that prohibition! The more I reflected on the matter, the more puzzling did it appear. On the other hand, the very mystery in which the affair was shrouded was itself a relief. For, of course, I never for one moment had the faintest doubt of Jasper's loyalty, nor could I entertain the possibility of his having changed his views on the subject of our marriage. Something had occurred to hinder it, but Jasper was my own and I was his, and that being so, the hindrance, whatever it might be, could be but temporary.

So I comforted myself and made believe that all was well, though when by chance my eye lighted on the trunk, packed and even provided with a blank label, I could hardly keep back the tears. At lunch, I let Miss Polton know that my visit was postponed, and immediately after the meal I prepared to go out and seek relief in a long, sharp walk. By the time I returned, the letter from Jasper would probably have arrived and I should know how matters stood.

I had put on my outdoor clothes and was just about to start, when, opening the drawer in which I kept my wrist-bag, I suddenly remembered my loss of the night before. The bag contained, not only my purse, but my card-case and one or two other things I could not conveniently do without. The prohibition to go to the club could hardly, I reflected, extend to Lyon's Inn Chambers, though they were in the same neighbourhood. At any rate, I wanted the bag, and in my restless state a journey with a defined purpose offered more relief than an aimless walk through the streets.

During the short journey from Mark Lane to the Temple I turned over and over again the words of the telegram without obtaining any glimmer of enlightenment. If I had been less sure of Jasper, I should have been intensely wretched, but now, as the shock subsided, my optimism revived and I found myself looking forward to Jasper's letter with a confident expectation of reassuring news.

Emerging from the Temple Station, I walked up Arundel Street, and, crossing the Strand, presently passed through Half-Moon Alley and cast a glance of friendly recognition at the old gilded sign, so pleasantly associated with the scarlet parasol that hung outside the umbrella-maker's shop in Bookseller's Row. The two signs recalled the old delightful explorations with Jasper, and put me in quite a cheerful frame of mind, which lasted until I found myself once more ascending the bare and rather sordid stone stairs of Lyon's Inn Chambers. Then there came a marked change. As I walked up the cold, gloomy staircase a feeling of depression settled on me. I passed the grimy lantern that had looked on my head-long, terror-stricken flight, and some of the forgotten qualms came back. I breathed again the close air of that unpleasant bedroom, I saw again the unwieldy figure in the bed, with its pasty face and puffy eyelids, and even the sinister-looking peg on the wall came forth with uncomfortable vividness from the recesses of memory. By the time I reached the landing, my distaste for the place had grown so strong that I was half-inclined to turn back and complete the transaction by means of a letter.

This weakness, however, I overcame by an effort of will and resolutely rang the bell. There was a short interval and then the door opened, revealing the figure of Mrs. Gregg, who, according to her custom, stood and stared stonily at me without uttering a word.

"Good afternoon, Mrs. Gregg," said I. "When I went away last night I left my wrist-bag behind."

"Ye did," she answered, "and ye left the bedroom door open and the gas full on. I found it so this morning."

"I am very sorry," I said.

"'Tis no matter," she rejoined, impassively, and continued to stare at me in a most singular and embarrassing fashion.

"Could I have my bag, please, Mrs. Gregg?" I asked.

"Ye could," she replied, but still she made no move nor any suggestion that I should enter, and still continued to look at me with the strangest, most enigmatic expression.

"I hope," said I, by way of relieving the extraordinarily uncomfortable situation, "that Mr. Otway is better today."

"Do ye?" said she, and then, after a pause, "Maybe ye'd wish to see him?"

"I don't think I will disturb him, thank you," I replied.

"Ye need have no fear," said she. "Ye'll no wake him."

"Well, I don't think I have time to see him to-day. I just called to get my bag."

"And is that all ye've come for?" she demanded, glowering at me in the most astonishing manner.

"What else should I have come for?" I asked.

She thrust her head forward and replied in a mysterious tone, "I thought maybe ye'd come to ask where your husband is."

"I don't understand you, Mrs. Gregg. Is Mr. Otway not at home?"

"He is not," she replied, and as I made no answer she asked, "Shall I tell you where he is?"

"It really isn't any business of mine, Mrs. Gregg," said I.

"Is it not?" she demanded. "Will it no interest ye if I tell ye that your husband is in St. Clement's Mortuary?"

"In the mortuary!" I gasped.

"Aye, in the mortuary." She glared at me in silence for a few moments, and then, suddenly grasping my arm, exclaimed, "Woman! Do ye ken yon peg on the bedroom wall? Aye, ye may well turn pale. Ye'd ha' turned paler if ye'd seen what I saw by the gaslight this morn hangin' from yon peg."

I gazed at her for a few moments in speechless horror, until she seemed to sway and shimmer before my eyes. Then, for the first and only time in my life, I must have fainted, for I remember no more until I found myself lying on the floor of the lobby, with Mrs. Gregg kneeling beside me slapping my face with a wet towel.

I rose with difficulty, feeling very weak and shaken. Mrs. Gregg silently handed me my bag and preceded me towards I he door, where, with her hand on the latch, she turned and faced me.

"Weel, mistress," said she, "'tis a fit ending, seeing how it began. Ye've been a poor wife, but ye'll make a bonny widow, though I doubt it will stay long at that."

To this insolent and brutal speech I made no reply. I was completely broken, physically and mentally. I tottered out on to the landing and slowly descended the stairs, holding on to the iron hand-rail, my horror of the place urging me to hasten away, my trembling limbs and lingering faintness bidding me go warily. As I walked unsteadily up Holywell Street, a newspaper boy, running down the narrow thoroughfare, halted and held out a paper.

"Here y'are, Miss. Sooicide in Lyon's Inn. The housekeeper's story."

I hurried past him with averted face, but out in the Strand there were others, shouting aloud the dreadful tidings or displaying posters on which the hideous fact was set forth in enormous type. And it seemed as if each and all of them were specially addressing themselves to me. I returned down Arundel Street, instinctively making for the station, but as I approached it a fresh group of newsboys made me swerve to the left and pursue my way along the Embankment on foot.

As I walked on, and the air and exercise helped me to recover physically from the shock, I began to collect my faculties. At first I had been utterly bewildered and overborne by a sense of horror and guilt. I had sent this wretched man to his death. I had ordained the means, the manner, and the time of his death, and it had duly befallen according to my directions. Morally – and perhaps even legally – it amounted to murder. I had willed, I had suggested, and that which I had willed and suggested had come to pass. That was what had flashed into my mind in the very moment in which Mrs. Gregg had made her dreadful communication.

But now, as I walked on, I began to argue the case in my own favour. In the first place, I told myself, it was not certain that the act of the dead man had any connection with the willing or the suggestion. It might have been a mere coincidence. I tried to dwell on this view, but it would not do. The coincidence was too complete to be explained away by any such casuistry. I could not in this way escape the responsibility for Mr. Otway's death.

Then I considered the question of intention. I told myself – truthfully enough – that I had not consciously willed that Mr. Otway should kill himself. I had not even been conscious of any intention to suggest to him that he should kill himself. But though I did make some sort of point in my own defence, it was extremely unconvincing I had allowed my mind to dwell with hardly-disguised satisfaction on the possibility of his suicide (in a particular manner at a particular time), and between that and actual willing the distinction was not very obvious. And then there were those words, spoken to him in his sleep. It was not conscious, deliberate suggestion – but what was it? The impulse to speak those words was apparently evolved from the subconscious. But does no moral responsibility attach to subconscious intentions?

So I argued, back and forth, round and about, but always came back to the same conclusion. Mr. Otway was dead, and it was my act that sent him to his death. Locked up in my own breast this dreadful secret might remain, but it was my companion for life. There was no escape from it. But *would* it remain locked up in my own breast? That was another question that began to loom up with a very real menace. How much did Mrs. Gregg know? She might easily have overheard our conversation and even those final, fatal words. And if she had, would she understand their significance? Now that I came to consider the circumstances, there was something rather alarming in the manner of this inscrutable woman, something threatening and accusatory which I had vaguely felt at the time. And as I reflected on this and the possibilities that it suggested, a fear of something more substantial than my own accusing conscience began to creep around my heart.

When I arrived home, Jasper's letter was awaiting me. But it contained nothing new. He had seen the posters, had bought an early paper, and had immediately sent off the telegram. His tone was that of matter-of-fact satisfaction. The legal impediment to our marriage had now been removed. No declarations were necessary now. We could marry like other people. We were free.

That was the burden of the letter. All our troubles were at an end. Until everything was settled, we had better avoid meeting. But when the chapter was closed with all due formalities we could sing "*Nunc Dimittis*" and thenceforth live only for one another.

I laid the letter down. All that it said was true. The picture that my imagination had drawn under the guidance of desire as I had sat looking into the shadowy corner of the bedroom in Lyon's Inn had become a reality. The fetters that I had forged and put on that fatal morning in the little church at Maidstone, had fallen off and given me back my freedom.

And even as I told myself this, some voice from within seemed to whisper a *caveat*, and my heart was sensible of a chill of fear.

BOOK III – CRIME

Chapter XXIII
The Dead Hand

The entry of Mr. Otway into my life inaugurated a long succession of disasters. The very first words that I heard him speak shattered the peace of a lifetime. Thence-forward, like the Ancient Mariner, I was haunted by a malign influence which seemed to exhale continuously from his ill-omened personality. And even now that he was dead that malignant spirit was not at rest. His very corpse, lying in the mortuary, was a centre whence radiated sinister influences that crept into my secret soul and enveloped me from without. During his life Mr. Otway had been my evil genius, and death had but transformed him into a malicious poltergeist.

His first, tentative appearance in this character was made on the very evening of my second visit to Lyon's Inn Chambers, when the coroner's officer called at Wellclose Square to serve the subpoena for the inquest. The announcement of his arrival caused me some qualms of vague alarm, which I knew in my heart to be nothing but the stirring of my own conscience. For the purpose of this inquest was to find an answer to the question, "How did Lewis Otway come by his death?" And that question I could have answered in four words – *Silent Willing and Suggestion*. But I had no intention of answering that question, and hence, as I entered the room into which the officer had been shown, I was consciously on the defensive.

I had, however, no occasion to be. The officer was a civil, fatherly man in a constable's uniform, sympathetic, deferential and not at all inquisitive.

"I have called, ma'am," he began, "on a very sad errand. I don't know whether you have heard the dreadful news – "

"Of Mr. Otway's death?" said I.

"Ah! Then you have heard. That is a relief. Well, I have called to let you know that the inquest is arranged for the day after to-morrow, at three p.m. in the room adjoining the mortuary." He gave me a few explicit directions as to how to find the latter and then added, "If there is any information that you could give us that would guide us in starting the inquiry, we should be glad. Or the names of any witnesses that we ought to subpoena."

491

I reflected. The threatening letters must necessarily be referred to at the inquest. I should have to mention them myself, even if Mrs. Gregg knew nothing of them.

"I happen to know," I replied, "that Mr. Otway had received a number of anonymous letters and that he was greatly worried about them."

"Blackmailing letters?" he asked.

"I don't think any demands for money were made," I replied.

"Do you know what was their nature? Were they threatening letters?"

"Yes, indirectly. The two or three that I saw had reference to the death of my father, who died very suddenly and who was alone with Mr. Otway at the time. They suggested a suspicion that Mr. Otway was responsible for my father's death."

The officer looked at me quickly and then became deeply reflective.

"Will it be possible to produce those letters at the inquest?" he asked, after a cogitative pause.

"They are not in my possession," I answered, "but if the coroner will make an order for their production I will endeavour to have it carried out."

"Thank you, ma'am," said he, and then, as an after-thought, added, "If you could make it convenient to call at the coroner's office to-morrow, say at about two o'clock, I could give you the order and perhaps help you to carry it out."

The latter suggestion appealed to me strongly and I fell in with it at once. Thereupon the officer picked up his helmet with an air of satisfaction, and, having handed me the subpoena, moved towards the door. I accompanied him along the hall and let him out, and as I wished him good evening and launched him down the steps, another figure emerged from the darkness and passed him on the way up.

"Does Mrs. Otway live here?" the newcomer enquired. I glanced at him with faint suspicion, for the exact incidence in time of his arrival with the officer's departure suggested a connection between the two events.

"I am Mrs. Otway," said I.

"Oh, indeed! Could I have a few words with you on a matter of some importance? I will not detain you more than a few minutes."

I hesitated, eyeing my new visitor dubiously. But there were no reasonable grounds for a refusal, and I eventually ushered him into the little parlour that the officer had just left, and indicated the vacant chair.

"The matter concerning which I have taken the liberty of calling on you, Mrs. Otway," said he, "is connected with – er – with the painful

492

occurrence – er – at Lyon's Inn Chambers. A most deplorable affair. Most distressing for you – most distressing! Pray accept my sincere sympathy."

"Thank you, Mr. – "

"Hyams is my name – you may have heard your late husband speak of me. We have been acquainted a good many years."

"He has never spoken of you to me, Mr. Hyams. But what can I do for you?

"Well, I can put my business in a nut-shell. Your husband, at the time of his death, had certain valuable property of mine in his possession. I should like to get that property back without delay."

He had certainly wasted no time. Unsentimental as was my own attitude, I felt this haste to be almost indecent.

"I should think you will have no difficulty," said I, "if you apply in the proper quarter."

"That is what I am doing," he retorted. "You are is widow. His property is in your hands."

"Not at all," I replied. "Pending probate of the will, the property is vested in his executors."

He looked at me in not unnatural astonishment. I suppose the phraseology that I had acquired from my father was unusual for a woman.

"Who are the executors?" he asked.

"I don't know," I replied.

"But," said he, "I suppose you have seen the will."

"No, I don't know that there is a will. I am only assuming the existence of one from my knowledge of Mr. Otway's business-like habits."

"But this is very unsatisfactory," said Mr. Hyams. "There is portable property of mine worth several thousand pounds lying in his chambers for anyone to pick up, and those chambers in charge of a woman who probably has access to his keys. It really isn't business, you know."

"What is the nature of the property?" I asked.

"It is a collection of very valuable stones, the who lot contained in a little box that anyone could carry away in his pocket."

"Then," said I, "the probability is that he has deposited the box with his bankers."

"Who are his bankers?" he asked.

"I really don't know."

"You don't know!" he exclaimed. "But you must have seen his cheques. I presume he made you an allowance?"

"I accepted no allowance from him and I have never seen one of his cheques."

Mr. Hyams looked at me with undisguised incredulity, "A most extraordinary state of affairs," he commented. "Can you give me the address of his lawyers?"

"I am sorry, Mr. Hyams, that I cannot. I don't even know if he has a lawyer. I know nothing whatever about Mr. Otway's affairs."

Mr. Hyams' countenance took on an expression that was very much the reverse of pleasant. "I suppose, Mrs. Otway," said he, "you realise that you are talking to a man of business and that you are telling a rather unlikely story.

"I realise it very clearly, Mr. Hyams," I replied, "and I realise also the difficulty of your position. What I recommend you to do is to go to Lyon's Inn and see the housekeeper, Mrs. Gregg. She has been with Mr. Otway many years and can probably tell you all that you want to know."

Mr. Hyams shut his mouth tightly, rose deliberately and picked up his hat.

"Then," said he, "the position, as I understand it, is this: You don't know whether there is or is not a will, you don't know the name of your husband's bankers, you don't know who his lawyer is, you don't know anything about his affairs, and you disclaim any responsibility in regard to property that was in his custody when he died."

"Yes," I agreed, "that is the position – a very unsatisfactory one for you, I must admit. Perhaps I may be able to help you later, when I know more about Mr. Otway's affairs. Will you leave me your address?"

He was on the point of refusing, but prudence triumphed over anger and he laid on the table a card on which I read the name, "*David Hyams, Dealer in Precious Stones*," and the address, "*501 Hatton Garden*."

"If I learn anything fresh I will write to you," I said, whereupon he thanked me curtly and gruffly and walked towards the door with pursed-up lips and a lowering, truculent expression and took his departure without another word.

When he was gone, I reflected at some length on the significance of his visit. The interview had brought home to me very vividly my anomalous position. Mr. Otway had been a total stranger to me. Of his past, of his recent habits and mode of life, his friends, his occupation – if he had any – his family and social status, I knew nothing. My father had referred to him as a retired solicitor and as a collector of, or dealer in, precious stones. Vaguely, I had conceived him as a man of some means – perhaps a rich man. But I knew nothing of him and had given him and his affairs barely a thought. He was a stranger who had come into my life

494

for but a moment, and had straightway gone out again, leaving a trail of desolation to show where he had been.

That was the real position. But to strangers to the world at large, it would seem incredible. I was Mr. Otway's widow. I had been his wife in law if not in fact. And the world would hold me to the legal relationship. The dead man, lying in the mortuary, seemed about to make good the claims that the living man had been forced to abandon. My status as a wife had been a mere fiction, my status as a widow was an undeniable reality.

The clear perception of the extent to which I was involved in the dead man's affairs gave my visit to the coroner's office a new importance. For now, while seeking information for official use at the inquest, I must gather what knowledge I could for my own guidance under cover of the coroner's order. The address of the office – in Blackmoor Street, Drury Lane – was printed on the subpoena, and there, after a few enquiries, I made my appearance punctually on the following day.

My friend of the previous evening – whose name I discovered to be Smallwood – was in the office, looking over some documents with the aid of a pair of spectacles, which gave him a curiously unconstabulary aspect. He rose when I entered, and, opening a drawer, took out a sheet of paper.

"This is what you asked for, Mrs. Otway," said he (upon which a young man at a desk looked up quickly), "the coroner's request for the production of the letters that you told me about. Can I give you any other assistance?"

"If you could accompany me to the chambers and be present during the search for the letters, I should be glad," I replied. "You see," I added, seeing that he looked somewhat surprised, "I am almost a stranger to the housekeeper, I know nothing about the household or Mr. Otway's arrangements, and I shall be accountable to the executors if there are any, for any interference with the papers or their removal. I should very much prefer to have a reliable witness."

He saw the position at once, and, greatly to my relief, agreed to come with me, or rather to follow me in a few minutes. Thereupon I left the office and walking at a leisurely pace into Drury Lane presently made my way into the Strand by way of Maypole Alley and turned eastward towards Lyon's Inn Chambers.

At the entrance, I waited for a minute or two and then slowly ascended the stairs to Mr. Otway's landing, growing more and more uncomfortable with every step. For the bare stone staircase set my memory working very unpleasantly, recalling again my headlong flight and the terrible episode that had preceded it – that episode that would so gladly have sponged out of my recollection for ever.

I stood at the door with my hand on the bell, listening for Mr. Smallwood's steps on the stair, and so might have remained until he arrived, but suddenly the door opened and Mrs. Gregg confronted me. Apparently she had some means of observing a visitor from within.

"What are ye standing there for?" she demanded. "Why did ye not ring?"

"I was just about to ring when you opened the door," I replied.

She smiled sourly and looked at me in that strange, inscrutable fashion of hers that I found so disconcerting.

"And what might your business be?" she demanded.

"I have come about some letters of Mr. Otway's – some anonymous letters that he has received from time to time. Perhaps you know about them?

"You mean, perhaps I have been in the habit of reading his letters. Weel, mistress, I have not. I know nothing about his letters."

"Perhaps you can show me where his letters were kept."

"Indeed, I'll do no such thing. What! Do you think I'll have you scratching up in his chambers and pawing over his letters and papers and him not under-ground yet?"

At this moment I caught the welcome sound of footsteps on the stairs. Mrs. Gregg listened suspiciously, and as Mr. Smallwood came into sight there was a visible change in her demeanour.

"What does he want, I wonder?" she said.

"He has come to receive the letters and to be present at the search for them," I replied, producing the coroner's order. She glanced at the paper, and, as Mr. Smallwood stepped up to the door, she motioned us to enter.

"Come in," she said, gruffly. "'Tis no affair of mine, but I'll no hinder ye."

We were just about to enter when footsteps were again audible on the stairs, and we waited to see who this other visitor might be. Somewhat to my surprise it turned out to be Mr. Hyams, who certainly seemed to have a genius for coincidences.

"Now this is quite a lucky chance," said he, doing himself, as I suspected, less than justice. "I didn't expect to find you here, Mrs. Otway. I presume you are just having a look round."

"I have come to search for some documents that have to be put in evidence," said I. "The coroner has asked for them."

"Well," said Mr. Hyams, "you might, at the same time, see if you can find any trace of my property."

496

"What property is that?" demanded Mrs. Gregg.

"A parcel of stones – a very valuable collection – that Mr. Otway had from me on approval."

Mrs. Gregg snorted. "Man," said she, "ye're talkin' like a fool. Do you suppose Lewis Otway would have left a valuable parcel of stones lying about in his rooms like a packet of snuff? Ye'll find no stones here."

"That may or may not be," said Mr. Hyams. "At any rate, I'll stay and see if anything turns up."

During this dialogue we had gradually moved from the lobby down the corridor and now entered the living room. As we crossed it I looked curiously at the large cupboard and wondered idly what I could have found so alarming in its appearance on the night of my visit. But if the living room had, by the light of day, lost its disturbing qualities, it was otherwise with the bedroom. I opened the door with trepidation, and as I did so and was confronted by the disordered bed, the horror of the place began to come back to me. Nevertheless, I entered the room with a firm step and with my eyes on the bedside table, which appeared to be in the same condition as when I had last seen it. I had just noted this when I felt my arm grasped, and turning quickly found Mrs. Gregg at my side. Her eyes were fixed on me and with her disengaged hand she was pointing towards the corner by the bed-head. Involuntarily my gaze followed the direction in which she was pointing and lighted on the fatal peg, which now bore a loop of the red bell-rope with two free ends. Of course I had known it was there, but yet the sight of it made me turn sick and faint, and I must have shown this in the sudden pallor of my face, for when, controlling myself by an intense effort, I turned to speak to her she was looking at me with a leer of triumph.

"Can we have Mr. Otway's keys?" I asked.

"Ye'll find them in the right dressing table drawer," she answered. "I'm no party to this, but I'll no hinder ye."

Mr. Smallwood opened the drawer and produced a bunch of keys which he handed to me. I looked them over and selecting the most likely-looking ones, tried them, one after the other, on the deed-box. The fourth key fitted the lock, and when I had turned it and raised the lid of the box, the letter which Mr. Otway had shown me lay in full view. I took it out and laid it on the table and then proceeded to lift out the remaining contents of the box. There was not much to remove: A cheque-book, a pass-book, a small journal, a memorandum book, a bundle of share-certificates, a canvas bag containing money, and at the bottom of the box a foolscap envelope endorsed, "*Anonymous Letters*".

I opened the unsealed envelope and drew out the letters which I glanced through one by one. There were seven in all, of which I had already seen three. When I had looked at them, I returned them to the envelope, adding the last letter, and then began to replace the other things in the box.

"I see a cheque-book there, Mrs. Otway," said Mr. Hyams, who had followed my proceedings with intense interest. "May I make a note of the banker's address?"

I handed him the cheque-book and continued to replace the contents of the box. When I had finished I paused with the box open, waiting for him to return the cheque-book, and at this moment I became aware, with a start of surprise, that an addition had been made to our party.

The newcomer was a short, stout, middle-aged man, with rather prominent dark eyes. He stood in the open doorway of the bedroom watching us with a slightly unpleasant smile. As he noted my surprised look his smile became broader and more unpleasant.

"Make yourselves at home, ladies and gentlemen," said he. "These are public premises – at least I assume they are, as I found the door open."

Mr. Hyams looked round with a start – as, indeed, did the others.

"May I ask who you are, sir?" he enquired.

"You may," was the suave reply. "My name is Isaacs – of the firm of Isaacs and Cohen, solicitors. I am one of the executors of Mr. Lewis Otway's will. And having regard to my responsibilities in that capacity, I may, perhaps, venture to enquire as to the nature of these proceedings. You, sir, appear to be in possession of the testator's cheque-book. Did you happen to require the loan of a fountain pen?"

Mr. Hyams turned very red and hastily laid down the cheque-book.

"That," he exclaimed angrily, "is perfectly unwarranted. I was simply making a note of the banker's address."

"With what object?"

"With the object of enquiring whether certain property of mine, which was in Mr. Otway's custody, had been deposited in the bank."

"What is the nature and value of this property?" asked Mr. Isaacs.

"It is a collection of precious stones of the approximate value of four-thousand pounds."

"Then," said Mr. Isaacs, "I can give you the information you want. No property, other than documents, has been deposited at the bank."

"In that case," said Mr. Hyams, "the stones must be in these rooms."

"It is quite probable," Mr. Isaacs agreed.

"Is there any objection to ascertaining, now, whether they are here?"

"Yes, there is," replied Mr. Isaacs. "The will has not been proved and no letters of administration have been issued. Pending probate of the will, I propose to take possession of these premises and seal all receptacles that may contain valuable property. I shall interfere with nothing until I have letters of administration."

"And how soon will that be?" asked Mr. Hyams.

"Seven days must elapse before the will can be proved. Under the circumstances, there may be some further delay. And now I should like to know what has been taking place. You, for instance, madam – "

"I am Mrs. Lewis Otway," said I, "and I have come here, by the coroner's direction, to look for some letters that are to be put in evidence."

"Have you found them?"

"Yes," I answered, "they are here and, as you are an executor, I had better hand them to you, and you can deliver them to the coroner's officer if you think fit."

I handed him the envelope and the coroner's letter, which he read, and then asked, "Did you have to make a very extensive search?"

"No, she didn't," said Mrs. Gregg. "She kenned fine where to look for them and she found them at the first cast."

On this I noticed that Mr. Hyams cast a quick, suspicious glance at me and I thought it wise to explain.

"I looked first in this box because I had seen Mr. Otway put one of these letters into it."

"Quite so," said Mr. Isaacs. "Very natural." But obvious as the explanation was, I could see that it had left Mr. Hyams unconvinced.

I now returned the cheque-book to the deed-box, locked the latter, and handed the keys to Mr. Isaacs, who delivered the anonymous letters to the coroner's officer and took his receipt for them on a slip of paper. My business being now at an end, I offered my card to Mr. Isaacs, took his in return, and departed in company with Mr. Smallwood.

"A queer business, this, ma'am," the officer remarked as we descended the stairs. "Regular mix-up. Seem to be a lot of Jews in it."

I reflected on Mr. Smallwood's remark, which seemed hardly justified by the facts – two Jews only having appeared in the case, so far as I knew. And yet I seemed to be aware of a sort-of Semitic atmosphere surrounding Mr. Otway. There were, for instance, the Campbells, and then Mrs. Gregg, although a Scotswoman, might easily, but for her strong Scottish accent, have passed for a Jewess, while Mr. Otway, himself, had been distinctly Semitic in appearance.

At the entry, where we separated, Mr. Smallwood halted to give me a final injunction.

499

"You had better be in good time to-morrow, ma'am," said he, "because it will be necessary for you to view the body so that you can give evidence as to the identity of the deceased."

I thanked him for the reminder, but would much rather have been without it. For the prospect filled me with a vague alarm, and now the mental picture of the sleeping man, which had haunted me by night and by day, began to be replaced by one more dreadful, and one which I felt that my visit to the mortuary would attach to me for ever.

Chapter XXIV
The Gathering Clouds

The distaste which I felt for my errand did not prevent me from following Mr. Smallwood's advice on the subject of punctuality. It was some minutes short of half-past two when I turned into the mean little street off Drury Lane in which the mortuary was situated. I had found the place without much difficulty and had still less in finding the mortuary itself for, as I entered the street, I observed a procession of about a dozen men passing in through a narrow gateway, watched attentively by a small crowd of loiterers. Assuming the former to be the jury, I walked slowly past on the opposite side and continued for the length of the short street. I had just turned to retrace my steps when the men filed out of the gateway and proceeded to enter a building a few yards up the street, and immediately afterwards Mr. Smallwood appeared at the gate. He saw me at once and waited for me to approach.

"I am glad you have come in good time, ma'am," said he. "The jury have just been in to view the body and the coroner will like to open the inquest punctually. This is the way."

He preceded me down a narrow passage, at the end of which he pushed open a door. Following him, I entered the mortuary, a bare, stone-floored hall containing two large slate-topped tables, one of which was occupied by a recumbent figure covered by a sheet. Mr. Smallwood removed his helmet and together we advanced slowly towards the awesome, shrouded form, lying so still and lonely in its grim surroundings. Very quietly, the officer picked up the two upper corners of the sheet and drew it back, retiring then a couple of paces as if to avoid intruding on my meeting with the dead.

Strung up as I was, the first impression was less dreadful than I had anticipated. The face was pale and waxen, but it was placid in expression and more peaceful than I had ever seen it in life. The hunted, terrified look was gone and had given place to an air of repose, almost of dignity. For a few moments I was sensible of a feeling of relief, but then my glance fell upon a contorted length of crimson rope that lay on the slate table, and instinctively my eye turned to the uncovered throat. And as I noted the shallow groove under the chin, faintly marked with an impression of the strands of the rope, the shocking reality came home to me with overwhelming horror. Before my eyes arose that awful shape

501

upon the bedroom wall and the hardly less dreadful image of the sleeping man unconsciously receiving the message of his doom.

With a new horror – an incredulous horror of myself – I looked on the pale, placid face and seemed to read in it a gentle reproach. He had gone to his death at my bidding. He had stood unsteadily on the brink of the abyss, and I had pushed him over.

It seemed incredible. There had been no conscious intention, no guilty premeditation. I would have told myself that there was no connection other than mere coincidence. But there the plain, undeniable facts were. Unconsciously – or subconsciously – my will had created that premonitory shape upon the wall, the terrible words had formed themselves and issued from my lips. And straightway the thing that my thoughts and words had foreshadowed had come to pass. This waxen-faced effigy that lay on the stone table, as its living counterpart had lain that night in the bed, was its fulfilment, its realisation.

"Better not stay too long, ma'am," said Mr. Smallwood. And as he spoke I became suddenly aware that I had reached the limits of endurance. My knees began to tremble and I breathed the tainted air with difficulty.

"Better come away now," continued Mr. Smallwood. "It's been rather too much for you. Good afternoon, Mrs. Gregg."

I looked up quickly and perceived Mrs. Gregg, who must have come in without making a sound, standing at the foot of the table watching me intently. That penetrating stare and the singular, enigmatical expression would have been disturbing at any time. But now I was conscious of actual fear. As I tottered unsteadily along the passage to the street, the menace of that watchful, inscrutable gaze followed me. How much did this woman know? What had she heard? And if she had overheard those last words of mine, how much had she understood of their import? These were weighty questions, the answers to which I should doubtless hear within an hour or two.

When I was ushered by Mr. Smallwood into the room in which the inquest was to be held, the court was already assembled and ready to begin. The jurymen sat along one side of a long table and one or two reporters occupied a part of the other, while a row of chairs accommodated the witnesses and persons interested in the case, including Mr. Isaacs, Mr. Hyams, Mr. and Mrs. Campbell, and a youngish man whom I did not recognise. I took my seat at the end of the row, and Mrs. Gregg, who had followed us in, seated herself near the middle.

As I took my seat the coroner addressed one of the reporters, "Let me see, what paper do you represent?"

502

"I am not a pressman, sir," was the reply. "I am commissioned to make a report for Dr. Thorndyke."

"Dr. Thorndyke! But what is his connection with the case? I know nothing about him."

"I only know that he has asked me to make a verbatim report of the evidence."

"Hmm," grunted the coroner. "I'm not sure that it is quite in order for private individuals to send their reporters to an inquest."

"It is an open court, sir," the reporter observed.

"I know. But still – However, I suppose it doesn't matter. Well, gentlemen, I think we are ready to begin. The witnesses are all present and it is on the stroke of three. I need not occupy your time with any preliminary statement. It seems quite a straightforward case and you will get the facts from the evidence of the witnesses. We are here, as you know, to inquire into the circumstances of the death of Lewis Otway, whose body you have just viewed, which occurred either on the night of the 18th instant or the morning of the 19th. The body was found hanging from a peg in his bedroom by his housekeeper, Mrs. Gregg, and it will be best to take her evidence first."

Mrs. Gregg was accordingly called, and having taken a position near the head of the table, was sworn and proceeded to give her evidence.

"My name is Rachel Gregg, age fifty-one. I was housekeeper to the deceased, Lewis Otway."

"How long," asked the coroner, "had you known the deceased?"

"Thirty-three years."

"What was the deceased's occupation?"

"He was a retired solicitor, but he was a connoisseur in precious stones, and, I think, dealt in them to some extent."

"Was he in financial difficulties of any kind, so far as you know?"

"No. I believe he was quite a well-to-do man."

"Had you any reason to suspect him of an intention to take his life?

"Yes. He used to say that he expected, if ever he had any trouble, that he would hang himself. The tendency to suicide was in the family. His only brother hanged himself, his mother hanged herself, and his mother's father hanged himself."

"But that was only a tendency that might not have affected him. Had you any reason to expect that he actually might commit suicide? Was there anything in his manner, in the state of his mind or in his circumstances that led you to believe that he might take his life?

"Not until recently. He always used to be quite cheerful in a quiet way until he got married. After that he was never the same. His marriage seemed to bring all sorts of trouble into his life."

"Tell us exactly how this change came about."

"His marriage took place about eight months ago – on the 25th of last April when he was living at Maidstone. It was quite sudden. I knew nothing of it until the day before, when he told me he was going to marry a Miss Helen Vardon, and that the marriage was to take place secretly because the lady's father had refused his consent. On the morning of the marriage I saw Mr. Otway go out, and soon afterwards I went out myself to do some shopping. When I came back, I found the new Mrs. Otway in the study and her father, Mr. Vardon, lying dead on the floor. Mr. Otway had gone to fetch a doctor. It appeared that Mr. Vardon had called directly after the newly-married couple had arrived home from the church and that there had been a quarrel and Mr. Vardon had fallen down dead. I understand that Mr. Vardon was alone with Mr. Otway at the time.

"Soon after I arrived, Mrs. Otway left the house and went back to her own home, and Mr. Otway told me that she refused to live with him. At any rate, she never did live with him, and she never came near him until the night of his death."

"Do you know if the deceased agreed to this separation?"

"Apparently she made him agree. But it was a great trouble to him, and I know that he tried more than once to get her to live with him."

"Do you know what was the cause of the separation?"

"No. Mr. Otway never mentioned it to me."

"You say that the separation was a great trouble to the deceased. Did it obviously affect his spirits?

"Yes. He was very depressed after his wife went away, and he never recovered. He seemed to get more and more low-spirited."

"Do you know of any other reasons than the separation from his wife why he should have been depressed in spirits?"

"Yes. Mr. Vardon's sudden death was a great shock to him. He felt that he had been partly the cause of it, by quarrelling with Mr. Vardon. Then there was a great deal of talk in Maidstone about the affair and people blamed Mr. Otway for what had happened, and later rumours began to get about that there had been foul play – that Mr. Otway had actually killed Mr. Vardon. These rumours got on his nerves so badly that he gave up his house at Maidstone and moved to London."

"You have spoken of a quarrel between the deceased and Mr. Vardon. Do you know what the quarrel was about?"

"I believe it was about the secret marriage, but I was not in the house at the time."

"Were there any other causes for the mental depression which you say the deceased suffered from?"

"I think so, but I can't say for certain. There were some letters that came about once a month which seemed to worry him a good deal. I used to see him reading them and looking very anxious and depressed, and after a time he began to get very nervous and fidgety and couldn't sleep at nights unless he took a dose of veronal. And I noticed that he was smoking much more than he used to, and taking much more whisky."

"Did you ever see any of the letters that you have spoken of?"

"I never read one, but I saw the outsides and I noticed that they all bore the post-mark of East London."

Here the coroner drew from the large envelope six of the letters which I had found in the deed-box, and handed them, in their envelopes, to Mrs. Gregg.

"Do you recognise any of these letters?"

Mrs. Gregg turned the envelopes over in her hand, looked closely at the post-marks and replied, as she returned them, "Yes, these look like the letters that I spoke of."

The coroner laid the letters on the table, and after a few moments reflection said, "Now, Mrs. Gregg, we want you to tell us what you know of the circumstances of Mr. Otway's death. You spoke of a visit from Mrs. Otway."

"Yes. She came to Lyon's Inn Chambers on Wednesday night, about half-past-six and told me that Mr. Otway had written to her asking her to come. As Mr. Otway was then expecting another visitor, I asked her to call again about eight, which she agreed to do. Mr. Otway had been rather poorly for the last few days – very nervous and despondent, and had been sleeping badly – and for three days had kept to his bed. I told him that Mrs. Otway was coming at eight o'clock and he then said that he had some private business to talk over with her and that I need not sit up. I gave him his supper at half-past-seven and just after I had cleared it away Mrs. Otway came. I showed her into the bedroom and went to the kitchen to finish up my work. At half-past-nine I went to bed – a little earlier than usual because I thought they would like the place quiet for their talk. At a quarter-to-seven on Thursday morning I got up, and as soon as I was dressed, went into the living room to tidy it up. Then, to my great surprise, I saw that the door of the bedroom, which opens out of the living room, was wide open and that the gas in the bedroom was full on.

"Thinking that Mr. Otway might be worse, I called out to him to ask if he wanted anything, but there was no answer. I could see the bed from where I was and could see that he was not in it, so I called to him again, and as there was still no answer, I went into the bedroom. At first I thought he was not there, but suddenly I saw him in a corner of the room that was in deep shadow. He seemed to be standing against the wall, with his arms hanging down straight and his head on one side, but when I went nearer I saw that he was hanging from a large peg and that his feet were three or four inches off the floor. He had hanged himself with a length of bell-rope that he had cut off with his razor – at least that was what it looked like, for the razor was lying open on the bed. I picked up the razor and ran to him and cut the loop of rope, and as he fell, I let him down on the floor as gently as I could. He seemed to be quite dead and his skin felt cold, so I ran out to fetch a doctor. Just outside the buildings I met a policeman and told him what had happened, and he told me to go back to the chambers and wait, which I did. A few minutes later he arrived at the chambers with a doctor, who examined the body and said that Mr. Otway had been dead some hours."

"Did you see any means by which the deceased could have raised himself to the peg from which he was hanging?"

"Yes. There was an overturned chair lying on the floor nearly underneath him. It looked as if he had stood on it to fix the loop of rope and then kicked it away. Mrs. Otway's bag was lying on the floor by the side of the chair."

"Mrs. Otway's bag! What bag was that?"

"A little wrist-bag such as ladies use to carry their purses and handkerchiefs. She called for it the same day and I gave it to her. She had not heard what had happened, and when I told her she fell down in a dead faint."

The coroner reflected for a while with wrinkled brows, and I caught the eyes of one or two of the jurymen regarding me furtively. After a somewhat lengthy pause, the coroner asked, "Do you know what time Mrs. Otway left the chambers?"

"I heard the outer door slam about half-an-hour after I had gone to bed. That would be about ten o'clock."

"Did you see Mrs. Otway or the deceased after you let her in?"

"No. I did not go into the bedroom again. I went into the living room twice and could hear them talking."

"Could you hear what they were talking about?"

"I could hear a few words now and then. When I went into the living room the first time they seemed to be talking about suicide. I heard Mr. Otway say something about a peg on the wall."

"And when you went in the second time?"

"They seemed still to be talking about suicide. I heard Mrs. Otway ask the deceased what drove his brother to hang himself."

"You heard nothing suggesting a quarrel or disagreement?"

"No. They seemed to be talking in quite a friendly way."

"Do you know what kind of terms they were on?"

"No. I never saw them together before except for a few minutes on the wedding day."

"You spoke of a visitor who came to the deceased earlier in the evening. Who was that visitor?

"A Mrs. Campbell. Her husband is a jeweller and curio-dealer whom the deceased had known for a good many years, and used to have business dealings with. I understand she came on business and she only stayed about ten minutes."

"Is that all you know about the case?"

"Yes, I think I have told you all I know about it."

The coroner glanced at the jury. "Do any of you gentlemen, wish to ask the witness any questions?" he inquired.

Apparently none of them did, and when the coroner had complimented Mrs. Gregg on the clear manner in which she had given her evidence, she was dismissed.

There was a short interval in which the coroner read over his notes and the jury conferred together in low under tones. Then the coroner observed, "We had better dispose of the police and medical evidence as they are merely formal and will not take much time. We will begin with the constable."

The policeman was then called and briefly corroborated Mrs. Gregg's evidence. When he had finished, the doctor, whom he had brought to the chambers, took his place, and having been duly sworn deposed as follows:

"My name is John Shelburn. I am a member of the Royal College of Surgeons and a Licentiate of the Royal College of Physicians, and am acting as *locum tenens* for the police surgeon of Saint Clement Danes. At seven-twenty-eight a.m., on Thursday, the 18th of October, I was summoned by the last witness to accompany him to Lyon's Inn Chambers, where a man was reported to have hanged himself. I went with the constable to a set of chambers, over the door of which was painted the name of Mr. Lewis Otway. I went into the bedroom where the gas was alight, the blinds down, and the curtains drawn. There, lying on the floor near the wall, I found the dead body of a tall, heavily built man, about fifty or fifty-five years of age, dressed in a suit of pyjamas. The surface of the body was cold and *rigor mortis* was well established. I should say the man had been dead about eight hours. Around the neck was a double loop of red bell-rope, and a portion of the same was hanging from a large peg on the wall about seven feet from the floor. The rope had apparently been cut down for the purpose as a portion was still attached to the bell-wire and the severed tassel lay on the bed, on which were impressions of feet, as if someone had stood on the bed to cut it off. The length of rope had been joined at the ends with the kind of knot known as a 'granny' and formed into what is known as a weaver's loop, which had been passed over the head and the standing part of the rope hitched over the peg. This would form a running loop, like this – "

Here the witness produced a piece of thick string and demonstrated the arrangement on his thumb and the knob of a chair-back.

"I released the double loop from the neck and found a shallow groove on the throat corresponding to the rope. The countenance of the deceased was calm – as it usually is in cases of hanging – and there were no signs of violence or anything remarkable about the body. A chair, on which the deceased had apparently stood to adjust the rope on the peg, was lying close by and near to it on the floor was a lady's hand-bag. The rope had been cut with some sharp instrument – probably a razor, as I was informed by the housekeeper. I looked round the room but saw nothing of any significance excepting a half-empty whisky decanter and a nearly-full bottle of veronal tablets on a table by the bed."

"Can you tell us at what time death took place?"

"Only approximately. I have said that the man appeared to have been dead about eight hours. That would give us eleven o'clock on the night of the 18th as the time at which death occurred. But I will not bind myself to that time exactly. It might have been an hour earlier or later."

"After hearing your evidence and that of the other witnesses which you have also heard, it is a mere formality to ask your opinion as to the cause of death."

"Yes. The cause of death was obviously suicidal hanging."

This concluded the surgeon's evidence, and when he had been dismissed, the coroner turned to the jury.

"We have now, gentlemen," said he, "established the fact of death and its immediate cause. Our next move is to seek to establish the contributory circumstances – the more remote causes. We have ascertained that this unfortunate man committed suicide. The question that we now have to consider is: *Why* did he commit suicide? Possibly the evidence of his widow may help us to answer that question. Helen Otway."

As I rose to take my place at the table I was dimly aware of a certain ill-defined movement on the part of the jury and the spectators such as one may notice in a church at the conclusion of a sermon. But in the present case the cause was evidently a concentration rather than a relaxation of attention. Clearly, my evidence was anticipated with considerable interest.

"Your name is – ?

"Helen Otway. My age is twenty-four and I live at 69 Wellclose Square."

"Have you viewed and do you identify the body now lying in St. Clement's mortuary?"

"Yes. It is the body of Lewis Otway, my late husband."

"When did you last see the deceased alive?"

"On the night of Wednesday, the 18th of October."

"Tell us, please, what took place on that occasion."

"I went to see the deceased in consequence of a letter that I had received from him asking me to do so. I arrived at about half-past-six and was informed by Mrs. Gregg that the deceased was expecting another visitor."

"Did you know who that other visitor was?"

"No, but as I went down the stairs I met Mrs. Campbell coming up and assumed that she was the visitor."

"You know Mrs. Campbell, then?"

"Only by sight. I have seen her in her husband's shop. Mrs. Gregg asked me to call again at eight, and I agreed to do so, and did so. I was then admitted by Mrs. Gregg, who conducted me to the bedroom and left me there, shutting the door as she went out. I did not see her again that night. The deceased was in bed and had by his side a table on which were a spirit decanter, a siphon of soda water, a box of cigarettes, a bottle of veronal tablets, and a deed-box."

"Did you notice anything peculiar in his appearance?"

"No. He was not looking well, but he seemed less ill than I had expected from his letter, which conveyed the impression that he was in a dangerous condition."

"Have you got that letter?"

"Yes," I replied, "I have it here." As I spoke, I drew the letter from my pocket and handed it to the coroner who glanced through it and then laid it down with some other papers.

"We will consider this letter," said he, "with the others that you have handed to me later. Will you now tell us what passed between you and the deceased?"

"At first we talked about an anonymous letter that he had received a day or two previously. He showed me the letter, and when I had read it, he locked it in the deed-box."

"We will deal with the anonymous letters presently. What else did you talk about?"

"The deceased repeated the statement that he had made in the letter, that he did not expect to live much longer. I asked him if he had any reason for saying this and he then told me that there was a strong family predisposition suicide, that his brother, his mother, and his mother's father had all hanged themselves, and that since he had received the anonymous letters, he had been conscious of an impulse to make away with himself in the same manner."

"Had you not known previously of this family tendency?"

"No. He had never mentioned it before, and I knew nothing of his family."

"Did the deceased speak as if he actually intended to make away with himself?"

"No, but he spoke of an impulse which he found it difficult to resist, and he mentioned that a large peg on the bedroom wall seemed to fascinate him and to make the impulse stronger. I advised him to have it taken away."

"Previous to this conversation, had you ever thought it possible that the deceased might commit suicide?

"No, the possibility never entered my mind."

The coroner considered these replies and made a few further notes, then he proceeded to open a fresh subject.

"Now, Mrs. Otway, with regard to your relations with the deceased: Were you on friendly terms with him?"

"Not particularly. We were practically strangers."

"A witness has stated that you refused to live with the deceased and that you never had lived with him. Is that true?"

"Yes, it is quite true."

"Had you quarrelled with the deceased?"

"No, there was no quarrel. Our marriage was a business transaction, and immediately after the ceremony I discovered that my consent had been obtained, as I considered, by misrepresentation."

"We don't want to be inquisitive, Mrs. Otway, but we wish to understand the position. Could you give us a few more particulars?"

"Do you wish me to describe the circumstances of my marriage and the separation from my husband?"

"If you please."

"My marriage with Mr. Lewis Otway took place under the following circumstances: I accidentally overheard a portion of a conversation between Mr. Otway and my father, from which I gathered that Mr. Otway claimed the immediate payment of five-thousand pounds held by my father – who was a solicitor – in trust. It appeared from the conversation that my father was unable immediately to produce the money, and Mr. Otway threatened to take criminal proceedings for misappropriation of trust funds. To this my father made no very definite reply. Then Mr. Otway offered to abstain from any proceedings and to allow the claim to remain in abeyance on the condition that a marriage should take place between him and me. This my father refused very emphatically and angrily, and Mr. Otway left our house.

"Being greatly alarmed on my father's account, I communicated with Mr. Otway and informed him that I was prepared to accept his offer on the terms stated – namely, that he should release my father from the immediate claim and secure him from any proceedings in connection with it. Mr. Otway accepted the conditions, and as it was certain that my father would strongly object, we agreed not to inform him until after the marriage had take place.

"In accordance with this arrangement we were married privately on the 25th April of the present year and we went together from the church to Mr. Otway's house. I had left a letter for my father informing him of what had been done, and very shortly after our return from the church he came to the house. From an upper window I saw him enter the garden and I was very much alarmed at his appearance. I had heard that he suffered from complaint of the heart and had been warned against undue excitement and exertion, and I could see that he was extremely excited and was looking very ill. Mr. Otway let him in and, in answer to a question, admitted that the marriage had taken place. Then I heard my father ask Mr. Otway if he had told me about a letter that he – my father – had sent, and when Mr. Otway gave an evasive reply my father called him a scoundrel and accused him of having tricked and swindled me.

"I heard no more of what was said, as the two men went into the study and shut the door, but a minute or two later I heard a heavy fall, and, running down to the study found my father lying on the floor and already dead. There was a small wound on his temple and Mr. Otway, who was stooping over the body, held my father's walking-stick – a thick Malacca cane with a loaded silver knob – in his hand. He stated that my father had threatened him with the stick and that he had taken it away from him and that during the struggle my father had fallen insensible, striking his head on the corner of the mantelpiece as he fell."

"Did you believe him?"

"I think, at the moment, I did not. But on reflection, remembering how ill my father had looked, I had no doubt he was speaking the truth."

"Was there an inquest on your father's death?"

"Yes. The jury found, in accordance with the medical evidence, that death was due to heart failure caused by excitement and anger."

"And after this you refused to live with the deceased?

"Yes. I asked him about my father's letter and he said he had not seen it. I went with him to the letter-box and there we found it. The postmark showed that it had come by the first post and my father's address was on the outside of the envelope. There were no other letters in the box. I had no doubt that Mr. Otway had seen the letter and put it back in the box."

"Was that why you refused to live with him?"

"Partly. The letter stated that my father was able to meet his liabilities and gave a date on which payment would he made. Consequently the threatened proceedings against my father were impossible and Mr. Otway had obtained my consent by false pretences. But further, Mr. Otway's action had been the cause of my father's death, and this alone would have made it impossible for me to live with him as his wife."

"Did the deceased agree to the separation?"

"Yes. He saw that the position was impossible, but he hoped that the separation might be only temporary – that we might become reconciled at some future time."

"Did you consider this possible?"

"No. I held him accountable for my father's death and could never have overcome my repugnance to him."

The coroner noted down this answer and having glanced over his notes reflectively, looked up at the jury.

"Do any of you, gentlemen, wish to put any questions on this subject?" he asked.

The jurymen looked at one another and looked at me, and one of them remarked that, "This young lady seems to have rather easy-going ideas about the responsibilities of marriage."

"That," said the Coroner, "is hardly our concern. The next matter that we have to consider is that of certain letters received by the deceased from some unknown person or persons. There are seven of them and they seem by the postmarks to have been sent at intervals of about three weeks and to have been posted somewhere in the East end of London. We will begin with the first." He handed a letter to me and asked, "Have you seen that letter before?"

"Yes," I replied. "The deceased showed it to me one day last June when I met him by appointment at his request. He seemed to be extremely worried about it."

The coroner took the letter from me and read it aloud.

512

Mr. Lewis Otway,

The undersigned is writing to put you on your guard because Somebody knows something about how Mr. Vardon came by his death and that somebody is not a friend, so you had better keep a sharp look-out for your enemy and see what they mean to do. I can't tell you any more at present.

A Well Wisher

"Do you know," the coroner asked, "who wrote that letter?"

"No, I do not."

"Have you no idea at all? Is there no one whom you suspect?"

"I have not the least idea who sent that letter."

"You say that the deceased was extremely worried about it. Do you know why he was worried?"

"I understand that there had been rumours in Maidstone that Mr. Otway had killed my father. Those rumour seemed to have preyed upon his mind and made him unreasonably nervous."

The coroner nodded gravely and opened another letter and as he read aloud the well-remembered phrases I realised that I should need all the courage and self-possession at my command.

The writer of this warns you once more (the letter ran,) *to look for trouble. The person that I spoke of knows that something was held back at the inquest – at least they say so, and that they know why your wife won't live with you and that she knows all about it too and that someone knows more than you think anybody knows. This is a friendly warning.*

From a Well Wisher

The coroner looked keenly at me as he finished reading.

"Can you explain the meaning of this letter?" asked. "It refers to something that was held back at the inquest. Was anything held back, so far as you know?"

"I remember that there was one omission in the evidence. Mr. Otway made no mention of my father's stick."

"Was it not mentioned at the inquest at all?"

"No."

"Did you not give evidence?"

"Yes, but I was merely asked if I confirmed Mr. Otway's evidence, which I did."

"You confirmed Mr. Otway's evidence! But that evidence was not correct. The duty of a witness is to state the whole truth, whereas Mr. Otway had withheld a highly material fact. How was it that you did not supply this very important fact?"

"It did not appear to me to be of any importance. The medical evidence showed that death was due to heart failure."

"Medical evidence!" the coroner exclaimed, testily. "There is too much of this 'medical evidence' superstition in these courts. People speak as if doctors were infallible. It was your duty as a witness to state all that you knew, not to decide what was or was not of importance. And I cannot understand how you came to hold such an opinion. You found your father lying dead with a wound on his head and a man standing over him with a loaded stick, and you considered this fact of no consequence?"

"I see now that I ought to have mentioned it."

"What was the verdict?

"The verdict was in accordance with the medical evidence – Death from Natural Causes."

"Did the medical witness or witnesses know that Mr. Otway had had a loaded stick in his hand?"

"No."

"Did anybody besides yourself and Mr. Otway know about the loaded stick?"

"Mrs. Gregg came into the room when Mr. Otway had gone for a doctor. She saw the stick in a corner and picked it up to examine it. She asked whose it was and remarked on its weight."

"Did she know it had been in Mr. Otway's hand at the time of your father's death?"

"I have no reason to suppose that she knew."

"Well," said the coroner, "it is a most extraordinary affair. You heard Mr. Otway give his evidence, you knew that that evidence was incomplete, and yet, though the dead man was your own father and you have declared an unconquerable repugnance to Mr. Otway, you allowed this garbled evidence to pass unchallenged. It is an amazing affair. However," he continued turning to the jury, "that is not our concern. But what *is* our concern, for the purposes of this inquiry, is that we now begin to see daylight. We can now understand the extraordinary effect these letters seem to have had on the man whose death we are investigating. Lewis Otway, when he gave his evidence at the inquest, suppressed a most important and damaging fact which he believed to be

514

known only to himself and his wife. Thereby he obtained a verdict of Death from Natural Causes, which exonerated him from all blame. Had all the facts been known, the verdict might have been very different.

"Now the receipt of these letters must have destroyed his sense of security. Apparently someone else – and that someone evidently an enemy – knew of this damaging fact and knew of the further damaging fact that it had been suppressed at the inquest. In effect, these letters held out a threat of a charge of murder, or at least manslaughter. It is no wonder that they alarmed him. But we had better take the rest of the evidence. There is this letter the deceased wrote to his wife, which I will read. It is dated the 17th of October, and this is what it says,

My dear Helen,

I have not troubled you for quite a long time with my miserable affairs – which are, to some extent, your affairs too. But they are going from bad to worse, and now I feel that I am coming to the limits of endurance. I cannot bear this much longer. My health is shattered, my peace of mind is wrecked, and my brain threatens to give way. Death would be a boon, a relief, and I feel that it is not far off. I cannot go on like this. Those wretches will not leave me in peace. Hardly a week passes but I get some new menace and now – but I can't tell you in a letter. It is too horrible, Come to me, Helen, for the love of God! I am in torment! Have pity on me, even though you have never forgiven me. I cannot come to you, for I am now unable to leave my bed. I am a wreck, a ruin. Come to me just this once, and if you cannot help me, at least give me the comfort of your sympathy. You will not be troubled by me much longer.

Your distracted husband,

Lewis Otway

When the coroner finished reading the letter (which evidently made a deep impression on the jury) he looked at me gravely.

"Before passing to the next letter, I must ask one or two questions about this one. What did you understand from the phrases '*I feel that it (death) is not far off. I cannot go on like this. You will not be troubled by me much longer.*' Did they not suggest to you an intention to commit suicide?"

"No. I understood them as referring to his state of health."

"If you had known of the family tendency to suicide, how would you have understood these passages?"

"I should have suspected that he contemplated suicide."

"But you say you were not aware of this tendency?"

"No, I was not."

"He refers to his '*miserable affairs – which are to some extent your affairs too.*' What did you understand him to mean by that?"

"I understood him to refer to the fact that I was partly responsible for the omission of certain details in the evidence at the inquest."

"When you received this pitiful letter, what did you do?"

"I went to him the same day to find out what the trouble was. He then showed me an anonymous letter that he had received."

"Is this the one?" the coroner asked, handing it to me, and when I had glanced at it and identified it, he proceeded to read it to the jury.

Mr. Lewis Otway,

Some funny questions are being asked. What about Mr. Vardon's stick – the loaded stick with the silver knob to hide the lead loading? Where is it? Somebody says they know where it is and who's got it. And they say there is a bruise on the silver-top, and they say something about a smear of blood and a grey hair sticking to it, Do you know anything about that? If you don't you'd better find out. Because I think you will hear from that somebody before you are many weeks older or else from the police.

A Well Wisher

As he laid down the letter, the coroner looked at me curiously.

"There are one or two important questions, Mrs. Otway," said he, "that arise out of this letter. The first is, What has become of this stick?"

"I don't know what has become of it. I saw Mrs. Gregg replace it in the corner by the writing table and never saw it again. The deceased asked me the same question when he showed me the letter, but I reminded him that I did not take the stick with me when I left his house and that I never went to the house again."

"It never occurred to you to ask what had become of your father's stick?"

"No. I always assumed that it was in Mr. Otway's possession."

516

"You have told us that Mrs. Gregg had seen the stick in Mr. Otway's house. Had anyone else seen it there?"

"I don't know of anyone else having seen it, but, of course, it may have been seen there by other persons. I know nothing of what went on in that house. I never entered it after my father's death."

"With the exception of Mr. Otway and yourself, did anyone know that you had seen that stick in Mr. Otway's hand on the occasion of your father's death?"

"So far as I am aware, no one else knew."

"There is a statement in that letter referring to a bruise on the silver knob and a smear of blood with a grey hair sticking to it. Is it possible, so far as you know, that that statement might be true?

"I cannot say that it is impossible."

"After your father's death, did you examine the stick?"

"No. I saw it in Mrs. Gregg's hands, but I did not look at it closely."

At this point a police superintendent who had been sitting near to the coroner's table, rose and, approaching the table, stooped over it and spoke to the coroner in a low voice. The latter listened attentively and nodded once or twice, and when the superintendent had returned to his seat he addressed me.

"I think that will do, Mrs. Otway – for the present, at any rate. We may have to ask you one or two questions later. Do any of the jury wish to ask anything before the witness sits down?"

As none of the jury responded, I returned to my seat, and the coroner then recalled Mrs. Gregg.

"You have heard the last witness state that she saw you take up Mr. Vardon's stick. What made you examine that stick?"

"I did not examine it. I noticed it standing in the corner and saw that it was a strange stick – that it was not Mr. Otway's. I took it out of the corner to look at it and then noticed that it was heavily loaded at the top."

"Can you say whether there was or was not a bruise or a blood smear on the knob?"

"I cannot. I did not look closely at the knob. I just picked the stick up, felt its weight, and put it back in the corner."

"Did you know that Mr. Otway had had that stick in his hand when Mr. Vardon fell dead?"

"No. I never heard of that until to-day."

"Could anyone other than Mrs. Otway have known, so far as you are able to say?

"I can't say. I should think not. I did not get back to the house until it was all over. But I thought, and believe, that there was no one in the house but those three – Mrs. Otway and her husband and her father."

"Do you know what became of that stick?"

"I do not. I put it back in the corner and never saw it again. It was not in the corner when I tidied up the room the next day."

"Thank you, Mrs. Gregg. That will do."

Having dismissed the witness, the coroner turned to the jury.

"I had hoped, gentlemen," said he, "to finish the case to-day, but, as you have seen, its apparent simplicity was rather illusory. Some rather curious issues have arisen which will have to be considered in detail. Moreover, there appears to be a suspicion that property of very great value has been removed from the premises – at least, it seems to be missing. Under these circumstances, the police authorities ask for an adjournment to enable them to make some enquiries, and I am sure you will agree with me that this, and certain other matters, should be cleared up before a verdict is returned. I therefore propose to adjourn the enquiry for fourteen days."

The court rose, and I rose with it. As I stood up and turned towards the door, I saw Jasper standing at the back of the hall. He made no sign, nor did I, and as soon as our eyes had met, he turned and walked out. I did not attempt to follow, for I understood at once that he did not consider it desirable that we should recognise one another in this place. Moreover, I was detained for a minute or two by the coroner, who informed me, with a curious dry civility, that he wished me to attend at the adjourned meeting of the court, as further evidence from me might be required and after him, by Mr. Isaacs, who, as executor, was responsible for the funeral arrangements and who promise to inform me when the date had been fixed.

As I emerged from the gateway I glanced up the street with a wistfulness which I would hardly acknowledge to myself. But, of course, Jasper was already out of sight. Feeling very lonely, weary, and exhausted, I walked slowly down Drury Lane, considering what I should do next. And suddenly there came on me a longing for the quiet and comfort of the club. It was quite near, and once there I could wash, refresh, and rest in peace, alone, or at least among civilised people. And it was even possible that Jasper might be there.

At this thought I must have unconsciously quickened my pace, for a few minutes later found me passing through the entrance hall, telling myself that, of course, Jasper would not have come there. Nevertheless as I opened the door to the large room my eye instantly sought the familiar table in the corner, and when I saw Jasper sitting by it with a wishful gaze fixed on the door, my weariness and loneliness seemed to drop from me like a garment.

Chapter XXV
Suspense – and a Discovery

"I had hoped," said Jasper, as we met by the table, "that you would come on here. I had to take the chance. You understood why I made myself scarce as soon as you had seen me?"

"I assumed that you thought it better that we should not be seen together just at present."

"It is more than unadvisable," said he. "It is vitally important. We will talk about that letter – but not here. There is a lot that I have to say to you, but we had better have our talk where we cannot be seen, or possibly overheard. I propose that I run off now – nobody has seen us here yet – and wait for you at my chambers. You just have a wash to freshen you up and come along at once. Don't stop for tea, I will have some ready for you. And you had better come by the least frequented way. Go down the Embankment, up Middle Temple Lane, along Crown Office Row, cross King's Bench Walk to Mitre Court, come out into Fleet Street by Mitre Court Passage, cross to Fetter Lane, and into Clifford's Inn by the postern gate."

"All this sounds very secret and mysterious," said I.

"It is necessary," he replied. "We mustn't be seen together if we can help it. Remember, the jury and other interested parties are local men, and might easily run against us in the public thoroughfares. So I will run off now and you will come along as soon as you can."

To this arrangement I agreed, although the precautions seemed to me somewhat excessive, and he hurried away while I went in quest of hot water and the other means of ablution.

The process of purification did not take long, for the temptation to linger luxuriously over the ceremonial of the toilet was combated by curiosity and anxiety to rejoin Jasper. In a few minutes I emerged, greatly refreshed and sensible of a very healthy appetite, and set forth by the prescribed route towards Clifford's Inn, reflecting earnestly as I went on Jasper's rather mysterious attitude. I did not have to ply the knocker, for as I reached the landing I found Jasper standing at his open door.

"Now," said he, when I had entered and he had softly closed both the massive "oak" and the inner door, "we are secure from observers and eavesdroppers, and we can pow-wow at any length we please."

"You are very secret and portentous," I remarked. "What is it all about?"

"The secrecy and portentosity," he replied, "are possibly by-products of a legal training. We will discuss that presently. Meanwhile, the need of the moment is to provide nourishment for a starving angel."

He placed an easy chair for me by the fire, and then retired to the little kitchen, from which issued a gentle din of crockery very grateful to my ear. Presently he emerged with a tray on which were a teapot and two covers, and having deposited it on a small table, placed the latter by my chair and removed the covers with a flourish.

"There is only one cup and one plate," said I, noting that the "nourishment" had been provided on a scale of opulence appropriate to masculine conceptions of appetite.

"Dear me!" exclaimed Jasper. "How many cups and plates do you generally use?"

"Go and get another plate and cup and saucer," I commanded, severely.

When he had made the necessary addition to the table appointments, he drew up a second armchair, and, as he poured out the tea, he said, gravely, "We have had a long probation, Helen, dearest – at least, it seems so to me, and it is not over yet. But this little interlude should hearten us for what remains. To me it is a glimpse into a future of perfect happiness and comradeship. Do you realise, Helen, that we are now a normal, engaged couple, free to marry when we choose?"

Of course I had realised that we were free, but as I thought of the shrouded figure that even now reposed under its sheet in the mortuary, I doubted whether the word "normal" was fully applicable.

"It is perfect peace and happiness to be here with you, Jasper," I replied, "but I think I shall feel more normal when we can meet without all this secrecy. And even now I don't quite understand it. Why is it so important that we should not be seen together?"

"That is fairly obvious, I think," he replied. "I am going to be very frank with you, Helen, because I have complete confidence in your courage and strength of character. There is no use in blinking the fact that you are in a difficult situation. That coroner man thinks *you* wrote those anonymous letters, and he suspects that you knew about Otway's suicidal tendencies."

"But I distinctly said I did not."

"Yes, but, you see, the person who wrote those letters is not a person whose statements would carry any weight, and he thinks you are that person. He thinks you have tried to drive Otway to suicide, and he will be looking for a motive. There is a fairly obvious motive already, as you were encumbered with a husband whom you didn't want, but if you add another husband whom you *did* and *do* want, the motive for getting rid of the unwanted one becomes much more definite. That is the kind of motive he will be on the look-out for. Hence the necessity for the utmost caution on our part. If a witness could be produced who could depose to having seen us together, it might be possible for him to put some inconvenient questions."

"Could he not question me on the subject apart from any such witness?"

"I don't think it would be admissible for the coroner to suggest the existence of a lover if he had no facts. And that brings us to the point that I was going to raise. You ought to be represented either by counsel or by a solicitor – preferably by counsel, as a barrister is more agile – more accustomed to deal with the sudden exigencies that arise in court."

"You seem to suggest that I am charged with having brought about Mr. Otway's death."

"I wouldn't use the word 'charged', as I don't know that there is any such offence recognised by law. Morally, to cause a man to commit suicide would be much the same as to murder him, but I can't say off-hand what the legal position would be. My impression is that it would not be an offence that could be dealt with by law unless the act of murder could be proven. Nonetheless, I would be happier to see you with some reliable counsel we could trust."

It was then I thought of Dr. Thorndyke. He had shown a kind interest in my affairs, even to the extent of having a shorthand reporter at the inquest. Surely he would be ideal, if I could persuade him to take up the role of my advocate. I broached the possibility to Jasper, explaining Dr. Thorndyke's interest in the case.

"The very man!" Jasper said enthusiastically. "You must see him, Helen, and soon. He is a local resident, luckily, and lives only a few moments' walk from here."

So fast did things seem to be moving that I was reluctant to take on another visit after my already busy day, but Jasper was insistent that I should seek out Dr. Thorndyke's help. "I wish I could accompany you," he said, "but it is best if we are not seen out together. Will you see him?"

"Perhaps." I temporised, still feeling that to take on the services – and the cost! – of such a distinguished advocate was an extreme reaction to my current situation.

We talked a little longer, and then I took my leave, getting directions to Dr. Thorndyke's rooms from Jasper.

"I suppose," said he, as he bade me farewell, "we had better not meet again until this affair is over. It is only a fortnight, and after that we shall be free. Meanwhile, we can write as often as we please."

I agreed to this the more readily as I saw that another meeting with Jasper would make it difficult for me to escape from his demand that I should invoke Dr. Thorndyke's help. Nevertheless, as I took my way through Clifford's Inn Passage into Fleet Street, I found myself looking forward somewhat gloomily to the lonely and anxious fortnight lay ahead.

For several days nothing out of the ordinary occurred. My friends at Wellclose Square, who knew approximately what my position was, were quietly sympathetic, but never referred to the matter, excepting the incorrigible Peggy, who frankly congratulated me on my newly-acquired freedom.

"It's horrid for you, Sibyl," said she, "but still it is for the best, though he might have managed it a little more decently – a level crossing, you know, or 'found drowned', or something of that sort."

"You are a callous little wretch, Peggy," said I.

"I don't care," she replied, defiantly. "You know it is true. I am awfully sorry for you now. It must be perfectly beastly to have to answer all those impertinent questions, and have your answers printed in the newspapers. But it will soon be over, and then you can forget it and have a good time. I shall dance at your wedding before I am six months older."

I had to pretend to be shocked, but the Titmouse's optimism did me good. For there was a bright side to the picture, and it was just as well to gather encouragement from an occasional glance at it.

About ten days after the first sitting of the inquest I received a letter from Mr. Isaacs. He had already written to me briefly to inform me that the funeral had been postponed by the coroner's direction until after the adjourned inquest, but had then said nothing about the will. The present letter supplied the omission, and its contents surprised me very much. It appeared that the will been proved and that I was the principal beneficiary. "The testator," said Mr. Isaacs, "has bequeathed to you the bulk of his personalty – upwards of eight-thousand pounds – and the lease of the premises in Lyon's Inn Chambers, together with the furniture and effects contained therein. You are also constituted the residuary legatee. The chambers have now been evacuated by Mrs. Gregg, and are at your disposal. They are at present locked up, and the keys are in my possession pending your instructions and advice as to whether you intend to occupy the premises, to let them or to dispose of the lease. A copy of the will can be seen at my office, and, of course, the original can be examined at Somerset House."

The provisions of this will caused me, as I have said, considerable surprise. I had regarded myself as having no pecuniary claim on Mr.

Otway, and had not considered myself as concerned in his will at all. Now it was evident that, selfish as he had been during his life, he had been anxious at least to make some atonement after his death for the injury he had done me, and the fact did not tend to make my sense of guilt less acute.

Before I had replied to Mr. Isaacs' letter, I received two other communications. One was from Jasper, and though it was written in a tone of quiet cheerfulness, its contents filled me with alarm. It appeared that Jasper, becoming uneasy at my continued neglect to take any measures to secure a counsel to represent me, had called on Dr. Thorndyke with the object of retaining him. "We have had rather bad luck," he continued, "though I don't suppose it will matter. Dr. Thorndyke would have been pleased to represent you, but unfortunately he has been commissioned at the last moment by the Home Office to make an independent investigation of the case. He gave me the name of a suitable counsel – a rising junior named Cawley – with whom I have made the necessary arrangements. So your interests will be looked after, and we can trust Thorndyke to clear up the obscurities of the case."

The other letter was from Dr. Thorndyke himself, and confirmed Jasper's account.

> *Your friend, Mr. Davenant,* (it said) *called on me to-day to ask me to watch the proceedings of the inquest on your behalf, which I would have done with great pleasure if I had been at liberty. But I had just received instructions from the Home Office to look into the case and give evidence at the adjourned inquest, so I referred your friend to Mr. Cawley, who is an excellent counsel and will be able to do all that is necessary."*

> *Mr. Davenant expressed great disappointment that I should be, as he expressed it, "retained by the other side". But I pointed out to him that there is no "other side". I am not a "witness advocate". My evidence would be the same whichever side employed me. I never undertake to represent a particular interest, but merely to obtain what facts I can and give those facts impartially in my evidence and I always make it clear to clients that they employ me at their own risk – at the risk that the facts elicited may be unfavourable to them. So, although I am not retained by you, I shall act precisely as if I were. I shall find out all I can, and tell the*

court all I know. This will, presumably, be entirely in your interest.

And now I am going to ask a favour of you. I wish to examine and make a plan of the premises at Lyon's Inn Chambers, and I understand that the tenancy of the Chambers is now vested in you. Will you be so kind as to lend me the keys and authorise me to make this survey? If you will, I shall be able to make my evidence more complete.

If Jasper's letter had alarmed me, Dr. Thorndyke's positively terrified me. The cool, relentless impartiality, the unhuman indifference to everything but the actual truth that the letter conveyed appalled me, and I even seemed to read a direct menace in its tone. If I had employed him, I should have done so at my own risk, so he seemed to hint. His intention was to *"find out all he could and tell the court all he knew"*. How much would he find out? How much did he know already? He had a verbatim report of the evidence so far. He had Mrs. Gregg's statement that "they seemed to be talking about suicide." He would know all about suggestion and silent willing. Was it possible that he already knew that I had sent that wretched man on his last journey? When I recalled all that my father had said of his amazing powers of inference, when I remembered how unerringly he had detected the reservations in Mr. Otway's evidence and mine, I could not but feel that my chance of keeping my guilty secret was infinitesimal. The probability was that it was discovered already.

As to his request, obviously I had no choice but to grant it, and I was on the point of writing to Mr. Isaacs to instruct him to hand the keys to Dr. Thorndyke when it occurred to me that it might be well to avoid unnecessarily taking the former gentleman into my confidence. I knew nothing about Mr. Isaacs, and was not particularly prepossessed by him, not did I know the object of the proposed survey of the premises, concerning which indeed I was somewhat mystified and rather uncomfortable. Eventually I decided to call at Mr. Isaacs' office for the keys and deliver them myself to Dr. Thorndyke.

Accordingly I wrote a short a note to the latter informing him of my intentions, and on the following morning betook myself to Mr. Isaacs' office, which was situated in New Inn. I could see that my visit was somewhat unexpected, and evidently aroused the solicitor's curiosity.

"You will see," said be, "that the keys are all labelled, and I have made a rough inventory of the furniture and effects. Perhaps you would like me to come with you and check it."

"Thank you," said I, "but I don't think I will check the inventory to-day. We will postpone that until I take formal possession. At present I am merely going to take a look at the premises."

When I said this, I had, of course, no intention of going to the chambers at all, but as I walked down Wych Street with the keys in my bag, I reflected that, as I had said I was going, I had better go. Moreover, it was possible that the arrangement of the place had been disturbed and that some things might need to be replaced, for I assumed that Dr. Thorndyke would wish to see the premises as they were on the night of the tragedy. And then I was not without some curiosity concerning this place which had been the scene of events so momentous to me.

At the bottom of Wych Street I turned round by the "Rising Sun" and walked along Holywell Street to the entrance of Lyon's Inn Chambers, and as I, once again, ascended the gloomy stone stairs, the sinister atmosphere of the place enveloped me as it had done on previous occasions, and induced a vague sensation of fear. When I reached the landing and stood at the ill portal, the feeling had grown so pronounced that I hesitated for a while to enter the chambers. At length I summoned up courage to insert the key, and as the massive door swung open I stepped into the lobby.

But my nervousness by no means wore off. Leaving the outer door ajar, I walked quickly down the corridor, peered into the kitchen and the little, empty room that had presumably been occupied by Mrs. Gregg – apparently the furniture had belonged to her – crossed the living room and entered the bedroom. Here nothing seemed to have been changed. Even the great peg – on which, of course, my eye lit instantly – still bore the end of crimson rope, the bed had been stripped, but the bedside table stood intact even to the bottle of veronal tablets. I looked about me quickly and nervously, noting the arrangement of the furniture and comparing it with my recollections of that unforgettable night, and when I had decided that it was unaltered, I turned to go.

As I crossed the living room, the large, wardrobe-like cupboard attracted my attention, and I recalled the mysterious sounds that had seemed to issue from it. Was it possible, I wondered, that Mrs. Gregg could have been concealed in it that night and have overheard those last incriminating words of mine. She had not referred to them in her evidence, but the inquiry was not finished yet. I resolved to settle the question whether it was physically possible for her to have been concealed in the cupboard, and having tried the door and found it locked, I turned the keys over one by one until I found one labelled "*Cupboard in Living Room*". It was a rather unusual type of key, with a solid stem instead of the more usual barrel, and when I had inserted it and opened the door, I noticed that the key-hole passed right through the lock, so that the door could be locked from the inside as well as the outside. The cupboard itself was fitted like a wardrobe with a single shelf just above my eye level, beneath which a short woman like Mrs. Gregg could have easily stood upright. Thus the construction of the cupboard and the peculiar form of the lock made it at least possible that an eavesdropper might have been concealed that night, and that was all that I could say.

Before shutting the door I stood on tip-toe to see if there was anything on the shelf. In the semi-darkness of the interior I could see some kind of metallic object, and reaching in, took hold of it. As I drew it into the light of day I gave a gasp of astonishment. It was my father's stick. I took it down and turned it over curiously in my hands, marvelling how it should have got into this receptacle, and a turned it over, there came into view a flattened dent on the silver knob covered by a thick smear of blood to which two hairs had stuck. I looked at the hairs closely, but could come to no opinion as to whether or not they were my father's. One of these was white and the other a brownish grey. My father's hair had been iron grey as a whole, but I could not judge what the appearance of individual hairs might have been. If these were really his, then the man who had gone to his account was my father's murderer. It was a dreadful thought, but yet not without a certain compensation. As I looked at this relic of that day of wrath I felt my heart hardening. If the message that it bore was a true message, then I need have no more compunction for what I had done. If I had known with certainty that Mr. Otway had killed my father, those words which had slipped from me subconsciously would have been consciously uttered with full and deliberate intent and without a qualm.

I stood for a while with the stick in my hand considering what I should do with it. That its mysterious reappearance would create a complication I plainly foresaw, but to take it away and conceal it would be not only dishonest but very unsafe, for it was almost certain that someone knew of its existence. It must have been seen when the inventory was taken. Eventually I replaced it on the shelf and locked the cupboard, and having put the keys back in my bag made my way to the door, which had been standing ajar all this time.

As I walked slowly to the Temple, I turned over in my mind the significance of this strange discovery. Someone must have known of the presence of this stick in the chambers, and that someone was either Mr. Otway or Mrs. Gregg. But both had declared positively that they had never seen it, and it was difficult to imagine why either of them should have kept it hidden away and disclaimed all knowledge of it. I could make nothing of the problem. Only one thing was clear to me. I must let

Dr. Thorndyke know of my discovery, for it did not incriminate me in any way and might give him a clue to some of the elements of the mystery, the unravelment of which would be to my advantage. The door of Dr. Thorndyke's chambers was opened by Mr. Polton, who greeted me with a friendly smile, all creases and wrinkles.

"I'm sorry to say that The Doctor is not at home, ma'am," said he, "and he will be sorry, too. He would have liked to see you, I am sure."

"It doesn't matter, Mr. Polton," said I. "I have only called to leave these keys. But I should like to leave a message. Will you ask him not to disturb things more than he can help, as the inventory has not been checked yet, and will you tell him that the stick is in the large cupboard in the living room? You won't forget, will you?"

"I shan't forget," he replied, with a slight emphasis on the last word, "but I never trust my memory in important matters. Would you mind writing The Doctor a little note?"

He produced writing materials and placed a chair by the table, and I sat down and briefly put my message into writing. When I had given him the note – which he set in a conspicuous place on the mantelpiece – he looked at me as if he had something to say, and I waited to hear what it was.

"I have got an old verge watch to pieces upstairs," he said at length. "I don't know whether you would care to have a look at the movement. It's worth looking at. If you want to know what workmanship is, you should look at the inside of a good, old watch."

I was not, at the moment, much interested in watches or workmanship, but I could not resist his companionable enthusiasm – to say nothing of the implied compliment. So we went up together to the workshop, where he exhibited with a craftsman's delight the delicate wheels, the engraved plates, and the little chased pillars, and even brought out a microscope that I might appreciate the finish bestowed on the links of a fusee-chain that was hardly thicker than a horse-hair.

As the day of the adjourned inquest drew near, my anxiety – intensified by the consciousness of my guilty secret – grew more acute. My position was, as Jasper had said, a difficult one in any case. But the really alarming element in it was the introduction of Dr. Thorndyke into the case. The suggestion factor in the suicide would probably remain unsuspected by the coroner and the jury. But would it escape Dr. Thorndyke's almost superhuman penetration? I could not believe that it would, for the hint of it was plain in Mrs. Gregg's evidence. And if it were detected, it would be revealed. Of that I had not the shadow of a doubt. Dr. Thorndyke was a kindly, even a genial man, but he was Justice personified. He would investigate the case with relentless accuracy and completeness, and he would tell the truth to the last word. Of that I felt certain. If he held my fate in his hands I was lost.

Of the view of the case taken by outsiders I had an unpleasant illustration the day before the adjourned sitting. It was furnished by an article in an evening paper that I had taken up to my room to read. Glancing over its pages, my eyes was caught by the words "*Lyon's Inn*", and I read as follows:

> *The new Lyon's Inn seems to be emulating the reputation of the old. Within that ancient precinct occurred the famous Weare murder, forgotten of the present generation, but immortalised in those rather brutal verses of Tom Hood's . . . .*

> "*They cut his throat from ear to ear,*
> *His brains they battered in.*
> *His name was Mr. William Weare,*
> *He lived in Lyon's Inn.*"

> *The drama of Lyon's Inn Chambers, however, is not a murder – at least we hope not. It is at present regarded as a suicide. But there are some queer features in the case. There is, for instance, a handsome young wife, who, it seems, flatly refused to live with her elderly husband from the very wedding day. There is a series of unaccountable anonymous letters, and there is a rumour of a hoard of precious gems spirited away from the chambers, apparently on the very night when Mr. Lewis Otway hanged himself from a peg on his bedroom wall. So the adjourned inquest, which opens at 11 a.m. to-morrow, may elicit some curious revelations.*

As I laid the paper down, a cold hand seemed to settle on my heart. The writer had exaggerated nothing. He had not even stated all the accusing facts. But even so, put quite impartially, the article exhibited me as the central figure of the tragedy, as the visible agent of the sinister events that had befallen in those ill-omened chambers. And could I say that it misstated the case? Of the anonymous letters, indeed, and the stolen gems – if stolen they were – I knew nothing. But the central fact of the case was Mr. Otway's death. For that the coroner held me accountable. And, though he misjudged the evidence as to the means, I could not but admit that the coroner was right. The coming inquiry was, in effect, the trial of Helen Otway.

528

Chapter XXVI
The Adjourned Inquiry

The second sitting of the inquest was a much more portentous affair than the first. The large room, or hall, in which it was held was nearly full when I entered, and it was evident that a considerable proportion of the occupants were spectators, attracted hither, no doubt, by the picturesque comments of the newspapers. But besides these were a number of persons connected with the inquiry. Behind the coroner's chair sat a group of police officers. Mr. Isaacs and Mr. Hyams were again present. The witnesses now included Mr. and Mrs. Campbell and a youngish man who sat next to them. The side of the long table allotted to the press was filled by reporters – among whom I noticed the gentleman employed by Dr. Thorndyke, and there was one or two

men whom I judged to be lawyers representing the various parties interested. My own counsel, Mr. Cawley, a shrewd-looking man of about thirty-five, introduced himself to me as I took the seat reserved for me, and gave me a few words of advice.

"I think," said he, "I have had all the necessary instructions from Mr. Davenant, who, I see, is here." (I had had an instantaneous glimpse of him as I entered the room.) "His impression is that the coroner is disposed to put a certain amount of blame on you for your husband's death. If that is so, you will have to be rather careful about answering questions, especially any questions that the jury may put. Don't be in a hurry to answer any doubtful questions. Give me time to object if they seem inclined to go beyond the evidence."

I promised to bear his advice in mind, and then asked, "Do you know if Dr. Thorndyke is giving evidence to-day?"

"I presume he is," was the reply, "but I notice that he is not present and that his reporter is."

At this point the coroner laid down the papers which he had been looking over and opened the proceedings with a short address to the jury.

"The adjournment of this inquiry, gentlemen," said he, "which was decided upon a fortnight ago, is amply justified by the mass of new facts which are now available. These new facts bear chiefly on the property which, as you heard at the last sitting, was believed to be missing, but in other directions they throw a very curious light on the case. The first witness will be Superintendent Miller, of the Criminal Investigation Department."

529

As his name was spoken, the officer rose and took his place by the table. He took the oath and disposed of the preliminaries with professional facility, and then waited gravely for the coroner's next question.

"You had some knowledge of the deceased, Lewis Otway, and his affairs, I understand?" said the coroner.

"Yes. I have known of his existence for more than twenty years."

"Will you tell us what you know of him?"

"I first made his acquaintance about twenty-three years ago. He was then practising as a solicitor – chiefly as a police-court advocate – and was known by his real name, Lewis Levy, which he subsequently changed to Otway. After a time, he began to engage in business as a money lender, and it was at this time that he took the name of Otway. Presently he began to combine with money-lending a certain amount of trafficking in precious stones, and it was then that the police began to keep a somewhat close watch on him, with the idea that he might be also acting as a receiver. We never really had anything against him, but we always had the impression that he did some business as a middleman, or disposer of stolen jewels.

"When I first knew him, he had living with him a young woman named Rachel Goldstein. She was nominally his housekeeper, but there were two children – a boy named Morris, and a girl named Judith – whom he admitted to be his. When he changed his name to Otway, Rachel Goldstein took the name of Gregg and used to pass as a Scotch woman. The children lived with their parents until they grew up, when Otway (or Levy) provided for them in a way that made the police watch still more closely. Judith married a David Samuels, who traded under the name of Campbell as a dealer in works of art, especially goldsmith's work and jewellery, and Morris Goldstein started as a dealer in antiques, with a shop in Hand Court, and some workshops in Mansell Street, Whitechapel, where most of the antiques were made.

"Now both these men were practical working jewellers. It was believed that Otway financed them both, and it was known that he was the lessee of the premises that they occupied. Moreover, as soon as they were established in business, Otway gradually abandoned the money-lending, and occupied himself almost exclusively in dealing in gem stones. He was an exceedingly good judge of stones, and was quite successful as a legitimate dealer, but the police had an impression that he did a considerable amount of business that was not legitimate. I want it to be quite clear that I am not making any accusations, I am referring merely to an impression that the police had. It may have been quite a

530

mistaken impression, but I mention it because the matter bears directly on this enquiry.

"The idea of the police, then, was that Otway dealt to a considerable extent in stolen property. We supposed that he obtained this property – precious stones, without the mounts – not from the thieves, but from the receivers, and that he disposed of them with the aid of his son and son-in-law. Both those men did a fairly large trade in high-class jewellery. They did not touch commercial goods, but dealt exclusively in work produced individually by skilled goldsmiths and jewellers, some of whom they kept regularly employed. They also did a good deal of repairing and re-setting, and their transactions were always with private customers, not with the trade.

"Our idea of the way it was worked was this: We thought that when Otway had got a collection of stolen stones, he would pass on some of them to these two men. They would then commission their craftsmen to make some articles of jewellery, and would provide them with stones which had been bought from the regular dealers, and the purchase of which could be proved if necessary. Then, when the jewels were delivered – or even after they had been sold to a private buyer – Campbell or Goldstein would take the purchased stones out of their settings and replace them by stolen stones. And a similar method could have been employed when jewels were brought for alteration, repair, or re-setting. This kind of substitution would be very difficult to trace, for it is not easy to identify particular stones and prove that they are not the ones referred to in the dealers' receipts. As a matter of fact, we never did trace any stolen gems excepting on a single occasion, and then the evidence was not good enough for us to risk a prosecution.

"And now we come to the case that concerns this enquiry. About a year ago, there was a burglary at the premises of Messrs. Middleburg, of New Bond Street, the well-known jewellers, and, among other things, a collection of valuable stones, worth about five-thousand pounds, was carried off. It was a small collection, but all the stones were individually of considerable value, and several of them were remarkable, either in respect of size or other peculiarities. The collection has never been traced, and none of the stones has reappeared either here or abroad, and the police have reason to believe that the whole collection is still in this country.

"When these stones disappeared so completely, the police formed the opinion that they had passed into the possession of Otway, and that he was holding them up until an opportunity occurred to issue them one by one. At this time he was living at Maidstone – he had been there a year or two, but he had kept his old chambers at Lyon's Inn, and often stayed in them for a week or more at a time. Last May or June he left Maidstone and came back to his old chambers, and we then began to keep a closer watch on him.

"About a couple of months ago he bought – or rather took on approval – from Mr. Hyams, of Hatton Garden, a collection of stones of which I have seen the list. These stones were carefully selected by Otway, and the remarkable thing about them is that, taken as a whole, they are singularly like the stolen collection. Among the stolen stones, for instance, there were two large tourmalines, one green and one deep blue, both table stones with step-cut backs, four emeralds, two step-cut and two cut – *en cabochon* – two large chrysoberyls, one brilliant-cut, green and one *en cabochon*, yellow, one pale-blue diamond, and one pale-pink. Now, the collection taken from Mr. Hyams includes tourmalines, emeralds, chrysoberyls, and diamonds, of almost exactly the same size, colour, and cutting, and there are many other passable duplicates of the stolen stones.

"When I became aware of this, I inferred that Otway was making arrangements to release the stolen stones, and I caused a still closer watch to be kept on him, but up to the present not one of the missing stones has been discovered. Now I understand that the Hyams collection has disappeared, and if that is so, it seems probable that the person who has taken it is also in possession of the stolen collection. But that, of course, is only a guess."

"Quite so!" said the coroner, "and it is a matter that is more in your province than in ours. Is there anything more that you have to tell us that is relevant to the enquiry?'

"No, I think that is all."

"You will be remaining here, in case we want to refer to you again?"

"Yes, I want to hear Dr. Thorndyke's evidence, and, of course, I want to hear the verdict."

"I am afraid you may have a long time to wait, for I have had a telegram from Dr. Thorndyke saying that he has been detained at Maidstone, and has missed his train. It is a great nuisance for us all. However, we will go on with the evidence. The next witness will be Mr. Samuel Isaacs."

As the superintendent retired to his seat and Mr. Isaacs approached the table, I reflected rapidly on what I had just heard. Dr. Thorndyke had apparently been down to Maidstone. Was his visit connected with the present enquiry? And if so, what was it that he had been investigating? The locality suggested some kind of research in which I was concerned, but at the nature of that research I could make no guess whatever.

However, there was no time to speculate on the subject, for Mr. Isaacs had been sworn, and was ready to begin his evidence.

"You were solicitor to the deceased, I understand, Mr. Isaacs?"

"Yes, I am one of the executors of his will."

"In that capacity have you heard of any property said to be missing from the chambers which he occupied?

"I have. Mr. Hyams has made a claim to have restored to him a parcel of precious stones, valued at about four-thousand pounds, which he states was his property, and which he asserts the deceased had in his possession."

"Have you examined the premises with a view to discovering that property?"

"Yes, I have examined the premises very thoroughly, and have made a complete inventory of all the effects of the deceased. I have gone through the contents of the safe and all other receptacles, and have checked the property which he had deposited at his bank. I have made a most exhaustive search, but have failed to find any trace of the parcel referred to, or of any precious stones whatever."

"Is it possible that you may have overlooked the parcel?"

"I should say it is impossible. My opinion is that the parcel is not on the premises, and it certainly is not at the bank."

The coroner and a legal-looking gentleman at the table both noted down this reply. Then the former said, "You are, no doubt, in a position to tell us what was the state of the deceased man's affairs. Was there any kind of financial embarrassment?"

"I should say, certainly not. The gross value of the estate – which is entirely personal – is a little over seventeen-thousand pounds, and the liabilities, so far as they are known to me, are quite trivial."

"Can you tell us roughly, what are the main provisions of the will, that is, if it has been proved?

"It has been proved. The principal beneficiary is the widow, who receives eight-thousand pounds, and the lease of the chambers in Lyon's Inn, with the furniture and effects, and is made residuary legatee. Rachel Gregg – or Goldstein – receives one-thousand, and Morris and Judith, each two-thousand pounds, and the lease of the premises in which they respectively carry on their business. There are a few small legacies – less than a thousand pounds in the aggregate – so that there will probably be a residue of about three-thousand pounds, which will go to the widow."

"What is the date of this will?"

"It is dated the 10th June last.

"Do you know whether the provisions of the will were known to the widow, or the other beneficiaries?"

"I do not know. They were not disclosed by me until probate had been granted."

"Thank you," said the coroner. "I think we need not trouble you any further, unless the jury wish to ask any questions."

The jury did not, but the legal-looking gentleman at the table did, and springing up like a Jack-in-the-box, he addressed the coroner.

"As representing Mr. Hyams, sir," said he, "I should like to ask the witness whether, in the event of the missing gems not coming to light, their loss would be chargeable to the estate?"

The countenance of Mr. Isaacs hereupon assumed that peculiar expression known to students of sculpture as "the archaic smile".

"You are asking me to admit liability," he replied, "I can't do that, you know. There is a recognised procedure in these cases, with which I have no doubt you are acquainted."

The questioner sat down with a jerk, and Mr. Cawley stood up.

"May I ask the witness, sir, whether, in the event of this loss being adjudged to be chargeable to the estate, that loss would affect equally all the beneficiaries?"

"No," replied Mr. Isaacs, "it would not. It would fall, in the first place, on the residuary legatee. It would only affect the estate as a whole in so far as the amount of the charge exceeded that of the residue."

"Thank you," said Mr. Cawley. "There is one other question that I should like to ask. The present will is dated the 10th of last June. Did the execution of that will involve the revocation of a previously-existing will?"

"Yes, it did. After his marriage, the deceased re-acknowledged the existing will by a fresh signature and attestation, but he revoked this will when he made the new one."

"Could you tell us who were the beneficiaries under that will?"

Mr. Isaacs fixed a thoughtful (and somewhat beady) eye on the coroner's pewter ink-pot, and cogitated for a few moments.

"Is it necessary, sir, for me to answer that question?" he asked at length, looking up at the coroner.

"Is the point material?" the latter asked, looking at Mr. Cawley.

"I submit, sir, that it may become highly important," was the reply.

The coroner reflected with his eyes fixed on Mr. Cawley. Then he nodded. "Yes," he said, "I think you are right. We must ask you to answer the question, Mr. Isaacs."

Mr. Isaacs bowed. "The beneficiaries under that will were Rachel Goldstein, Morris Goldstein, and Judith Samuels."

"In what proportions was the property devised?"

534

"The bulk of the personalty was divided between Morris and Judith. Rachel Goldstein – or Gregg – received two-thousand pounds, but she was also the residuary legatee."

"And the value of the estate?

"I can't tell you that. I only know what it is now."

Mr. Cawley sat down, and Mr. Isaacs retired to his seat. Then the coroner pronounced the name of Mr. Hyams, and its owner took his place by the table.

"We have heard, Mr. Hyams," said the coroner, "of certain property of yours which was in the deceased man's custody. Will you give us a few particulars of the transaction. When, for instance, did it come into the possession of the deceased?"

"Two months ago – on the tenth of August, when the deceased called at my office and asked me to let him have a selection of stones for a special purpose. He said that he had an opportunity of disposing of a number of pieces of jewellery to a wealthy American gentleman, and that he had discovered an extremely clever artist whom he proposed to commission to make them. They were to be important pieces – chiefly pendants, brooches, and bracelets. The stones were to be exceptional in size and quality, and he wanted an assortment for Mr. Campbell – who was conducting the transaction – to show the intending purchaser. He had a list in his pocket-book, which he referred to as he made his selection from my stock. The stones which he selected were rather unusual – the sort of stones that appeal to collectors and connoisseurs, rather than ordinary wearers of jewels. And some of them were very valuable – one ruby alone that he took was worth fifteen-hundred pounds. The total value of the parcel that he carried away with him was four-thousand-two-hundred pounds."

"I understand that he did not pay you for them?"

"No, he was not proposing to keep them all. They were a selection to show to the customer. I made out a full list, and he signed a receipt at the foot of it. I had known the deceased for many years, and had often had similar dealings with him."

"And did he never return these stones, or any part of the collection?"

"No. From the time that he left my office with the stones in his pocket, I never saw him or heard from him again."

This was the sum of Mr. Hyams' evidence, and when he had retired the name of Judith Samuels was called. The new witness took her place at the table, and, after the usual preliminaries, proceeded to give her evidence.

"I am the wife of David Samuels who trades under the name of Donald Campbell. He is a dealer in works of art, principally goldsmith's work and jewellery. He is a practical jeweller himself, but most of the alterations and repairs are put out. The new work that he sells, or which is commissioned by customers, is executed for him by independent goldsmiths, not by workmen employed by him."

"You visited the deceased on the night preceding his death, I understand. Is that so?"

"Yes. I came to his chambers about half-past-six, and left about seven o'clock."

"Did you notice anything unusual in his manner or appearance?"

"He was not looking very well, and he seemed rather depressed, but he brightened up as we talked. He was very much interested in the business which I had come to discuss."

"What was the nature of that business?"

"It was connected with a collection of stones that he had got on approval from Mr. Hyams to carry out a commission that he expected to get from a very wealthy American gentleman, to whom he had an introduction. He did not disclose the name of the gentleman, but it was understood that if he secured the commission, my husband should conduct the negotiations and get the work executed."

"Did you gather that he had the stones in his possession?"

"Yes, he showed them to me. They were in a small wooden box, the different kinds of stones wrapped up separately in little paper packets. He took the box from a deed-box on the table by his bed-side, and put it back there when he had shown me the stones."

"Did you make any arrangements as to the disposal of these stones?"

"No final arrangements. He advised that we should get some of our artist goldsmiths to submit designs for the customer to see, and he suggested that my husband should ask Mrs. Otway to design and execute a pendant to take some of the finest stones."

"Mrs. Otway!" exclaimed the coroner. "What Mrs. Otway do you refer to?"

"I mean Helen Otway, the wife of the deceased."

"Are we to understand that Mrs. Otway is a designer of jewellery?"

"She is not only a designer, she is a practical goldsmith, and a very clever one too. My husband admires her work exceedingly and has paid her some very high prices. He paid her, for instance, twenty-five guineas for a set of silver tea-spoons."

The looks of astonishment that the coroner, the jury, and the press-men bestowed on me might, in other circumstances, have flattered my

536

vanity. Now, I could see that Mrs. Campbell, without (so far as I knew) departing one single jot from the truth, was enveloping me in the most hideous entanglements.

After a pause – filled in with strenuous note-taking – the coroner again addressed the witness. "It has been given in evidence that the deceased had received a number of anonymous letters. Do you know anything about these letters?"

"I know nothing beyond what I heard when the evidence was given."

"Have you any means of judging who wrote these letters?"

"I have heard the evidence, and I can make a pretty good guess who wrote them."

"That is not quite what I mean. Have you any information about them other than what you gathered from the evidence?"

"No, I never heard of them until then."

This concluded Mrs. Campbell's evidence. When she had retired Mrs. Gregg was recalled and questioned concerning the missing stones.

"Did you know that the deceased had these stones in his possession?"

"Yes. He showed them to me on one occasion, and I often saw him looking at them. He was very fond of precious stones. He used to set them out on a small square of black velvet, and try them in different lights, and look at them through a magnifying glass."

"When did you last see these stones?"

"After Mrs. Campbell – that is the last witness – had left and just before Mrs. Otway arrived. The deceased was then sitting up in bed looking at a large green stone. I reminded him that Mrs. Otway was due at eight, and he then put the stones back in their box, and put the box away in the deed-box that was on the table."

"When did you first learn that the stones were missing?"

"The day after the discovery that the deceased had committed suicide, when Mrs. Otway came to the chambers with Mr. Hyams and the coroner's officer. She came to search for the anonymous letters, and she went straight to the deed-box, and there they were. But the stones were not there. I saw her take all the things out of the deed box for Mr. Hyams to see and there were no stones there."

"Thank you." said the coroner "That will do. We must now, gentlemen, see if Mrs. Otway can give us any further information."

I once more took my place at the table and was again sensible of a generally heightened curiosity on the past of the jury and the spectators.

"We may as well dispose of the question of the missing stones," said the coroner, "for though it does not affect our enquiry directly but is rather the business of the police, it seems to have an important, indirect bearing. You have heard, Mrs. Otway, the evidence of Judith Samuels, and Rachel Goldstein – or Gregg. Can you throw any light on the disappearance of these stones?"

"No, I cannot."

"Did you know that the deceased had these valuable stones in his possession?"

"No, I never heard of the stones until Mr. Hyams called on me on the evening of the day on which Mr. Otway's death was discovered."

"Do you know, or have you any idea, where those stones are now?"

"I do not know, and I have no idea where they are."

"Did you know that the deceased was a dealer in precious stones?"

"No. My father told me that the deceased collected gem-stones, and that he sometimes had dealings in them. But I supposed that he was merely a collector, not a professional dealer."

"How long had you known the deceased when you married him?"

"I had known of his existence about a year, but I had hardly ever spoken to him. He was virtually a stranger to me."

"Had you never heard of the suicidal tendency in his family?"

"Never until the night preceding his death, when he told me."

"It has been stated that you are a practical goldsmith, and that you have executed work for Mr. Samuels, or Campbell. Is that true?"

"I work as a goldsmith and I have sold some of my productions to Mr. Campbell, but I have never been employed by him. I work as an independent artist."

"Has he ever supplied you with precious stones?"

"No. I purchase my own materials."

"Have you ever done any alterations or resettings for him?"

"No. I have done no work of any kind for him, or anyone else. I work on my own account, and sell what I make."

The coroner nodded, and glanced over his notes. After a pause he asked, "At what time on the night of your visit to the deceased did you leave his chambers?"

"A little before ten o'clock."

"What was the condition of the deceased when you left? Did he seem particularly depressed or worried?"

"He was asleep when I left."

"Asleep!" exclaimed the coroner, "How long had he been asleep?"

"Not very long, perhaps a quarter-of-an-hour. When he took his usual dose of veronal, he asked me to stay with him until he went to sleep, and I did so."

"I see that the housekeeper states that when she entered the living room in the morning, the bedroom door was wide open, and the gas full on. What was the condition of affairs when you left?"

"The gas was full on, and I did not shut the bedroom door. I was not aware that the housekeeper had gone to bed and assumed that she would look in on the deceased and make what arrangements were usual for the night."

"But if you had turned down the gas, and shut the bedroom door, that would have prevented the housekeeper from going to the deceased."

"No. It did not appear to matter either way."

"When you went away, did you leave your hand-bag behind?"

"Yes, I had hung it on the back of my chair, and when I got up to go, I forgot about it."

"When did you discover that you had left it behind?"

"I first remembered it when I hailed a cab at the corner of Holywell Street to take me home."

"Why did you not then go back for it?"

"I did not like to disturb Mrs. Gregg and the deceased, as it was so late."

"Was your purse in the bag?"

"Yes, but that was of no consequence. I knew there would be someone sitting up who could pay the cabman."

"The housekeeper has told us that you came to fetch the bag on the following day."

"Yes, in the afternoon, about three. It was then that I first heard of Mr. Otway's death."

"The housekeeper states that, when she told you what had happened, you fell down in a dead faint. Is that so?"

"Yes. It gave me a great shock, especially as Mrs. Gregg told me the bad news so very abruptly."

"Were you expecting to hear that the deceased had committed suicide?"

"No, the subject was not in my mind."

"Is that not rather remarkable, having regard to your conversation with the deceased on the previous night?"

"I don't think so. That conversation had certainly given me the impression that there was a danger that the deceased might be driven to suicide if this persecution were continued. But I had not supposed that the danger was immediate."

"And that pitiful letter that you received from the deceased? Did that convey no note of warning?"

"At the time when I received it, I was not aware of any predisposition to suicide on the part of the deceased. What he told me caused me some alarm, but he became so much calmer after our talk that I thought the danger was past, so far as the immediate future was concerned."

"And when you went to his chambers on the following day, you felt no uneasiness as to what might have happened?"

"No. The possibility that anything unusual might have happened was not in my mind at all."

"Well," said the coroner, "it seems to me rather remarkable that the possibility did not even occur to you. However, we are dealing with the facts, and if those are the facts, there is no more to be said. We will now pass on to the consideration of the will. When did you first learn that the deceased had made a fresh will?"

"Four days ago, when I received a letter from Mr. Isaacs informing me of the fact that I was one of the beneficiaries."

"Had the deceased never mentioned to you that he had made a will in your favour? Was there no stipulation on your part at the time of the marriage that he should make such a will?

"No. Nothing ever passed between us on the subject."

"And had you no knowledge or belief that a will affecting you had been executed?"

"I had no knowledge or belief that such a will had been executed nor any expectation that it would be. I did not consider myself as having any pecuniary claim on the deceased."

"Did you not receive an allowance from the deceased?"

"No. He wished to make me an allowance, but I declined to accept it."

"But you were entitled to an allowance for maintenance. Why did you refuse to accept it?

"I did not consider that I had any claim on the deceased so long as I insisted on living apart."

"Then do we understand that you subsist entirely on your own means or earnings?"

"Yes, entirely."

"Would you kindly tell us what those means and earnings respectively amount to? And what are their sources?"

"I have a small private income – about sixty pounds a year – derived from the realisation of my father's estate. I cannot estimate my earnings very exactly, as I have been working only a few months. Probably I shall be able to earn from a hundred-and-fifty to two-hundred pounds a year, when I am established. Up to the present, I have sold all my work to Mr. Campbell."

"How did you first become acquainted with Mr. Campbell – or Samuels, to give him his correct name?"

"The deceased recommended him to me when I first came to London. He stated that he had known him for many years."

"Did you know that Mr. Campbell was related to the deceased?"

"Not until I heard it here to-day."

The coroner considered a while, turning over his notes reflectively. At length he said, "Before you sit down, Mrs. Otway, I should like to ask you again about those anonymous letters. You have stated that you have no idea who wrote them."

"That is so," I replied.

"When you discussed them with the deceased, did neither of you arrive at any conclusion as to who might have written them?"

"The deceased assured me that he could make no guess as to who had sent them. Naturally I could not, since all his acquaintances, whether friends or enemies, were unknown to me."

"And you adhere to your statement that you know nothing about these letters?"

"I know nothing about them whatever, excepting that the deceased received them, and that I have only known by his telling me."

"And with regard to your father's stick? You have stated that you have no knowledge as to what became of it, or where it is now. Do you adhere to that statement too?

"That statement was correct when I made it, but the stick has since come to light."

"Indeed!" exclaimed the coroner. "When and how did that happen?"

"It occurred three days ago, when I went to look over the chambers in Lyon's Inn. I chanced to open a large cupboard in the living room, and there, on the single shelf at the top, I saw the stick lying at the back, and hardly visible in the deep shadow."

"In-*deed*!" said the coroner, with a strong emphasis on the second syllable. It was perfectly evident that he did not believe me, and he made no secret of it. Nor were the jury any better impressed. In the silence that followed my statement they whispered together eagerly, and disbelief was writ large on the faces of them all.

"Had you any particular occasion to look over the chambers?" the coroner asked after an interval.

"Yes, I had received a letter from Dr. Thorndyke saying that be wished to make a survey of the premises and asking me to give him permission and the necessary facilities to do so. I accordingly went, on

541

the following day, and fetched the keys from Mr. Isaacs to leave them at Dr. Thorndyke's chambers. On the way, I called in at Lyon's Inn to see what condition the chambers were in."

"And to plant the stick for Dr. Thorndyke to find, eh?" said one of the jurors, with a truculent leer.

Mr. Cawley rose instantly to protest, but he was anticipated by the coroner, who said severely, "That, sir, is quite out of order. Members of the jury must not suggest motives or actions on the part of witnesses which are not given in evidence. They may have their opinion, but those opinions must not be expressed until all the evidence has been heard and the verdict has to be considered." Having administered this reproof, he again turned to me.

"When you looked over the chambers, did you examine the other furniture and receptacles. Did you, for instance look in the other cupboards and drawers?"

"No."

"Only this one cupboard? Now what made you look into this cupboard in particular?"

I saw the awkwardness of the question, but I also saw that a complete explanation of my motives would land me on much more dangerous ground. My immediate motive had been to ascertain what the inside of the cupboard was like, and this was as much as I dared tell.

"I wished to see what kind of a cupboard it was – whether it had shelves, drawers, or simply an open space."

"Did you take the stick out of the cupboard?"

"Yes, I took it out to examine it and see if the statement in the letter as to the bruise, the blood-smear and the hairs was correct."

"And was the statement correct?"

"Yes, there was a bruise on the silver knob, and a thick smear of what looked like dried blood, to which two hairs had stuck."

"Did those hairs look to you like hairs from your father's head?"

"I could not say. They might have been. They were short and looked as if they had come from the head of a grey-haired man. My father's hair was grey."

"What did you do with the stick?"

"I put it back in the cupboard."

"Why did you not bring it here?"

"I thought it best to leave it where I found it."

"Are the keys of the chambers in your possession now?"

"No, I left them at Dr. Thorndyke's chambers, and he has not yet returned them. I left a note informing him that the stick was in the cupboard."

"May I ask why you did that?"

"Dr. Thorndyke mentioned in his letter that he was investigating the case on instructions from the Home Office, and I wished to give him any assistance that I could."

"But," the coroner exclaimed irritably, "don't you understand that this *court* is investigating the case? That a coroner's court is the proper authority to carry out such investigations? I don't know why this medical specialist has been brought into the case at all. I have not asked for his assistance. It is quite irregular and most unnecessary. And how did this gentleman come to write to you?"

"He wanted to survey the premises, and someone – I don't know who – had told him that I was the present lessee."

The coroner grunted in evident displeasure. The importation of Dr. Thorndyke into the case was clearly a sore point, for he rejoined, "The whole affair is highly unsatisfactory. I am not clear that you had any right to give permission to any unofficial person to survey these premises without obtaining my consent, or that he had any right to ask you. The jury have surveyed the premises, and that ought to be enough. However, we shall see what comes of these mysterious investigations. Meanwhile, I think that is all we have to ask you, Mrs. Otway, unless the jury have any questions to put."

The jury, warned, perhaps, by the result of the last question put by a juryman, had no question to ask, and I returned to my seat by Mr. Cawley, in time to hear Mr. Isaacs recalled.

"You have heard," said the coroner, "the very remarkable evidence given by the last witness concerning the finding of a stick in a large cupboard in the living room of the chambers in Lyon's Inn?"

"I have."

"In your previous evidence you stated that you had made a minute search of those chambers, and drawn up an inventory of their contents. Do you remember whether, when you made that search, you examined that particular cupboard?"

"Yes, I remember quite clearly that I examined it, and found it empty. I have marked it 'empty' in the inventory."

"Are you sure that it was really empty? Is it not possible that this stick lying in the shade on the shelf might have been overlooked?"

"It is quite impossible. I made a most exhaustive search, and I used an electric torch for examining cupboard interiors. Moreover, the object that I was looking for a little parcel of precious stones – was much smaller, and less conspicuous than a walking stick. I could not have missed a large object like that. And I have quite a clear recollection of looking on that shelf – it was the only shelf in the cupboard – and throwing the light of the torch along it. I had to stand on tip-toe to see in distinctly, and so I suppose, had Mrs. Otway."

"Do you swear that the cupboard was empty when you examined it?"

"I swear that it was absolutely empty."

The coroner entered the reply in his notes, and then asked, "Did you receive any communication from Dr. Thorndyke respecting his proposed survey of the chambers at Lyon's Inn?"

"He called to enquire in whom the tenancy of the chambers was vested, but did not state why he wanted know. I told him that the widow was the lessee. I don't know how he got her address. I didn't give it to him. I may say that when I had finished the inventory I locked up the chambers, and kept the keys until I delivered them up to Mrs. Otway."

"Thank you," said the coroner. "That is all I wanted you to tell us. And that, gentlemen," he continued, turning to the jury, "appears to be the whole of the evidence, with the exception of Dr. Thorndyke's, and the question now arises, what are we to do? Let me explain the position, and then you can decide on our procedure.

"This enquiry was adjourned to enable the police to make some investigations in connection with it. On their application, Dr. John Thorndyke, who, I may inform you is an eminent medico-legal expert, was instructed by the Home Office to proceed to Maidstone to conduct an exhumation of the body of the late John Vardon, the father of Mrs. Otway. He was to make an examination of the body, and ascertain if possible, whether the cause of the said John Vardon's death was as stated at the inquest, or whether, as is hinted in these anonymous letters, he died from the effects of violence. The question is an important one, but it is more important to the police than to us. Then, it seems that the Home Office further instructed this gentleman to carry out an independent investigation into the facts of this case which we, in our humble and inefficient way, are trying to investigate. It is an extraordinary proceeding, and one that I do not in the least understand, but then I am not a medico-legal specialist. I am only a mere coroner, and you are only a mere coroner's jury. It is just as well that we should know our place.

"Well, I understand that Dr. Thorndyke has made an examination of the body of Lewis Otway, and, as you have heard, he has made a survey of the deceased man's chambers. We, also, have surveyed these chambers, but apparently our survey doesn't count, and Dr. Shelburn, whose evidence you have heard, examined the body within a few hours of death. It would seem as if medical evidence were the last thing we want. Meanwhile I have had a telegram from Dr. Thorndyke saying that he has been detained at Maidstone, and has missed his train. I don't

544

know when he will arrive here. He may be here in a few minutes, or he may arrive in an hour or two. It is for you to decide what is to be done. We have a great deal of evidence to consider. We do not seem to need any more medical evidence, and the question of Mr. Vardon's death is not of vital importance to this enquiry.

"The question is shall we wait to hear Dr. Thorndyke's evidence or shall we proceed to consider the great mass of evidence that we already have? It is for you to decide, gentlemen."

The jury conferred for a couple of minutes, and then the foreman announced their decision. "The jury say, sir, that we are enquiring into the death of Lewis Otway, not John Vardon. They would like to proceed with the consideration of the evidence without waiting for Dr. Thorndyke."

"I am entirely with you, gentlemen," said the coroner. "I think that the evidence that we have heard will prove amply sufficient to guide us to our verdict, and we can still revise our opinions if the expert witness should have something fresh to tell us."

Chapter XXVII
The Indictment

During the short interval, in which the coroner took a final glance over his notes, there was a general stirring among the occupants and a suggestion of preparation for the next act. Jurymen re-settled themselves in their seats, reporters straightened their backs and looked about them, the police officers and the spectators conversed in low undertones. At length the coroner laid on the table before him a single sheet of paper – probably an abstract of the evidence – sat back in his chair, and looked towards they jury, whereupon a deep silence fell upon the court, and he began his address.

"It is hardly necessary to remind you, gentlemen, that we are assembled for the purpose of ascertaining how, when, and by what means Lewis Otway came by his death, but it may be necessary to remark that our enquiry is not entirely concerned with the immediate causes of that death but is also – and in fact, principally – concerned with the more remote contributory circumstances. For in this case, the 'How, when, and by what means' are simple enough. We have the testimony of an eye-witness who saw the deceased hanging dead from a peg on the wall, under conditions strongly suggestive – in fact characteristic – of suicide, and we have the testimony of the deputy-police surgeon that all the appearances were those of suicide, and we have his expert opinion that the cause of death was undoubtedly suicidal hanging. Indeed, we may say that the immediate cause of death is self-evident, and that the whole of our enquiry is concerned with the remote cause. We are not asking '*Did* this man commit suicide?' for the evidence of the first two witnesses settled that question. We are asking ourselves, '*Why* did he commit suicide?' The questions that we have to answer are, Was that suicide the spontaneous act of the deceased, for which he alone is responsible? Or was the deceased driven to suicide by the deliberate, purposive, and malicious acts of some other person, or persons? And if the latter appears to be the case, 'Who is, or are, that person or persons, and what degree of criminal responsibility attaches to such acts?'

"Now we have at our disposal a considerable mass of rather miscellaneous evidence, and, I think the best way to deal with it will be to sketch out lightly the general course of events, and fill in the details later. The deceased, Lewis Otway, is the central figure of our picture, and the history that we have to trace is *his* history. As to what we may call *his* past, that does not much concern us. Among the Ancient Egyptians the deceased was conceived as being brought before the tribunal of Osiris to answer for his conduct during his earthly life. We are not a tribunal of that kind. We are not trying Lewis Otway. If, as the police suspect, he had feathered his nest with a certain amount of illicit plumage, that is not our concern. Our interest in him is mainly confined to his connection with a particular series of events which began with his marriage and ended with his death. Let us now trace that succession of events, at first in outline, and then in more detail.

"Lewis Otway first comes into our view on the occasion of his marriage. As presented in the evidence of his widow, Helen Otway, that marriage offers us the spectacle of an act of the most amazing folly. We see an elderly man – and an unattractive one at that, as you must have observed – marrying by compulsion, under threats, and greatly against her wishes, a young woman of very unusual physical attractions, of great talent, and of exceptional mental gifts, and strength of character. You have seen this lady, and have heard her give her evidence, and you can confirm my description of her.

"It was, I repeat, an act of amazing folly. For she must, in any case, have detested him. His conduct towards her was cruel and unscrupulous to the last degree, and in marrying her he could not fail to introduce a bitter enemy into his household. But there were added causes for that repugnance to him which she has freely admitted. In the first place, she believed that her consent had been secured by actual fraud. And in the second place, Otway's action was the undoubted cause – whether directly or indirectly, we need not enquire at this stage – of John Vardon's death. So that our history opens with the tableau of an elderly man who has married a young, beautiful, and clever wife who loathes him, and has abundant reason for loathing him.

"And now we pass on to the second scene – a scene almost more amazing than the first. Within an hour or two of the marriage ceremony, the young wife has repudiated the marriage, and demanded a separation for an indefinite period – practically a permanent separation. But it is not the demand that is so astonishing. The really astounding thing is that the husband seems to have agreed to this demand without demur. Consider the extraordinary inconsistency of his conduct. On the one hand we see this man, in his eagerness to possess this beautiful girl, trampling without scruple on her happiness, and her father's, oblivious of everything but his own desires. On the other, we see him meekly submitting to a demand which – natural as it may have been – the law would not have supported.

"Whence this sudden compliance? Why did he consent? He need not have consented. The marriage was quite regular. No suit for nullity

547

could have been sustained, whereas he could have sued at once for restitution. Why did he agree in this incomprehensible manner to surrender his unquestionable rights?

"But this is not the only inconsistency. The conduct of the wife is even more inexplicable. When Otway gave evidence at the inquest on Mr. Vardon, he omitted all reference to the loaded stick, which is not unnatural, seeing that it was a highly incriminating circumstance. But that suppression of a material fact made his evidence in effect, false evidence. For the truth is, according to the terms of the witnesses oath, the whole truth. Yet Helen Otway, when she gave evidence, confirmed this virtually false testimony, and she also suppressed – or, at least, omitted – the facts relating to the loaded stick. Her explanation is that, feeling convinced that her father died from a heart attack, she did not consider the stick incident of any importance. In estimating the credibility of that explanation, you will bear in mind that the verdict was 'Death from Natural Causes', but that the jury were not in possession of the facts. You will also bear in mind that this woman had seen her father lying dead, with a wound on his head, and this man, whom she loathed, and detested, standing over the body, grasping a formidable weapon. But whatever view you take of the explanation, the fact remains that at the inquest she not only refrained from accusing him, but she withheld a material fact which, if it had been disclosed, might have put Otway in the dock on a charge of murder.

"Here, then, are two cases of incomprehensible inconsistency of conduct. But they are only incomprehensible so long as they are considered separately. Consider them together and a perfectly intelligible suggestion emerges. The husband had the power to compel his wife to live with him – and he did not exercise it. The wife had the power to expose the husband to a suspicion of having committed a capital crime – and she did not exercise it. The appearance is that of a surrender by each of the power to injure the other – in short, of a bargain or agreement, involving collusion to suppress evidence.

"But this suggestion of collusion raises another question, which we shall consider later, but which we may note in passing. What was really the cause of Mr. Vardon's death? Did he die from natural causes as the coroner's jury believed and affirmed? Or was his death due to violence inflicted by Otway? It is by no means clear that Otway did not kill him, either inadvertently or with malice. And supposing Otway to have killed Mr. Vardon, was the fact known to Helen Otway? If it was, Otway's easy compliance is the more readily understood, for he would be absolutely in his wife's power. But we shall consider these points at more length presently, and perhaps we may get further light on them from the

548

evidence of Dr. Thorndyke – if he should arrive before the verdict is agreed on.

"The next phase of this drama opens about two months after the marriage. On the 21st of June, the deceased received an anonymous letter, the first of a series of seven, which were sent thereafter at fairly regular intervals of about a fortnight. Now, let us consider those letters from various points of view in relation to their probable authorship. You have heard them read, and know their general purport. They all contain veiled threats to make certain exposures. Some are vague and some are more explicit, but there is a general crescendo note, culminating in the last letter, which pretty openly makes an accusation of murder and threatens criminal proceedings.

"First, what is the purpose of these letters? It is clearly not to levy blackmail. They hold out menaces, but there is no suggestion of an attempt to extort money. Those menaces are incomprehensible until we supply an explanatory fact. The man to whom these letters were sent suffered from a strong inherited predisposition to suicide. The very obvious inference to which we are forced, in the absence of any other explanation, is that the purpose of these letters was to convert that latent tendency into action – to produce a state of mind in which the deceased would be likely to take his own life.

"But that purpose implies knowledge on the part of the writer that this inherited tendency existed, and consequently limits the possible authorship to persons possessing such knowledge. The only persons known by us to possess such knowledge are the deceased's own family. His widow has sworn that she had no knowledge of this tendency, and if you believe her statement to be true, you will tend to exclude her from the possible authorship of these letters.

"Next we have to consider the characters of the letters themselves. They all bear the East-London postmark, but there is not much in that. Anonymous letter-writers commonly post their letters in districts remote from their own residences. Still, we must take it into consideration. The two persons known to us who occupy premises in East London are Morris Goldstein and Helen Otway.

"Then as to the style of the letters. They are rather markedly uneducated in manner. The composition is ungrammatical and the phraseology vulgar. But that does not help us much, for, on the one hand, none of the persons known to us is grossly uneducated, and on the other it is usual for anonymous letter-writers to disguise their personality. Obviously, it is easy enough for an educated person to write an apparently illiterate letter.

"The next point is a much more important one. We have decided that the purpose of these letters was to produce in the deceased a state of mind which would render his suicide probable. Now, what was the motive behind that purpose? Who could have wished the deceased to commit suicide, and why should that person have wished it?

"The possible motives in this case are, in effect, the usual motives of murder, with full premeditation – viz revenge, or hatred, direct profit, and indirect profit by the elimination of an undesired person. Let us consider each of these motives in relation to the known facts of this case.

"First as to hatred or revenge. The only persons known to us are the family of the deceased and his wife. His family certainly had a grievance against him, for the children were illegitimate, and the mother was unmarried. But it was an old grievance, and the family appeared to be on quite amicable terms. The children were quite well provided for, and their mother continued to live with the deceased. There was, indeed, a new factor of possible discord. The deceased had married, and that marriage was manifestly to the disadvantage of his family, a fact of which it is necessary to take due account.

"When, however, we turn to the consideration of the wife, the facts are much more striking. She had suffered grievous injuries from the deceased. He had ruined her life. He had virtually condemned her to perpetual spinsterhood, since she would not live with him and she could not marry anyone else. He had caused the death of her father, and she has admitted that she had an unconquerable repugnance to him. That is actually known to us, and there is a further possibility that he was actually her father's murderer, though we must leave that out of consideration in the absence of positive evidence. But on the evidence which is before us, you will see that the motive of personal animosity is much more evident in the case of the wife than in that of the family.

"We now come to the motive of direct profit, and the question that we ask ourselves is: 'Who stood to benefit by the death of Lewis Otway?' And as soon as we ask that question, a very striking fact comes into view. The first letter is dated by the postmark, the 21st of June. But on the 10th of that month – only eleven days previously – the deceased had made a new will. By the provisions of that will Helen Otway, stood to gain from eight- to twelve-thousand pounds by the death of her husband.

"But did anyone else stand to gain by Lewis Otway's death? Observe that we are still dealing with the same group of persons – the only persons known to us in connection with the case. Well, the family of the deceased stood to gain by his death, though to a much smaller extent, but the fact that must instantly impress us is the opposite effects of the new will on the family and the wife respectively. The execution of the new will involved the revocation of a previous will, which had left the bulk of the estate to the family. The position of affairs is consequently this: Up to the 10th of June, the family, jointly, stood to benefit by Lewis Otway's death to the extent of the bulk of his estate and the wife did not stand to benefit at all. After the 10th of June, the wife stood to benefit by Otway's death to the extent of the bulk of his estate, and the family to a relatively small extent.

"But the first of the anonymous letters was sent almost immediately after the 10th of June. That is to say, it was sent almost immediately after the family had ceased to be and the wife had become the principal beneficiary.

"From the motive of direct profit, we turn to that of indirect profit, by the elimination of a person whose existence was a hindrance, a danger, or an inconvenience, Is there anyone known to us who could have regarded the deceased in that light? We cannot attribute any such view to his family, for, as I have said, they appear to have been on quite amicable terms, and the deceased seems to have maintained an interest in his children's welfare to the last. But what are we to say with regard to the wife? She was married against her wishes to a man unsuitable in age, uncomely in appearance, a man whom she loathed – and had good reason to loathe – who, while she repudiated him as a husband yet held her chained to him for life, who stood inexorably between her and any marriage which she might wish to contract, whose existence condemned her for life to the dubious position of a married woman who is not living with her husband. Think, gentlemen, of this woman – young, handsome, clever, accomplished, capable – think of what life might have been to her, and what it was with this millstone hung round her neck! And then ask yourselves whether – apart from all pecuniary considerations – she did not stand to gain incalculably by his death, whether his elimination from her life would not have opened to her the gates of a world of happiness and freedom.

"And it is here that the importance of that further evidence, which we unfortunately have not yet heard, appears. For if it should now transpire that Otway did actually kill John Vardon and that Helen Otway was privy to the homicide, then there would be yet another powerful reason why she should desire to be rid of him. But this evidence is not in our possession and we must, therefore, leave this aspect of the case out of our consideration. Nor is it essential. The facts within our knowledge are amply sufficient to enable us to answer the question whether Helen Otway's position would or would not have been improved by the death of her husband.

"And now we come to something much more definite. Hitherto we have been dealing with the question, 'Who *might* have written these letters?' We shall now consider the more specific question, 'Who *could* have written them?'

"There seems to be only one possible answer. The writer of those letters had knowledge that was possessed by only two persons – the deceased and his wife. One letter refers to something that was held back at the inquest. But who knew that anything had been held back at the inquest? No one, according to the evidence, but those two persons. Of course, it is possible that there may have been some watcher secreted in that house at Maidstone who knew that Lewis Otway had stood over the body of John Vardon with a loaded stick in his hand. But the evidence before us is to the effect that there was no one in the house but John Vardon, Lewis Otway, and Helen Otway. Consequently, unless Lewis Otway wrote these letters to himself, there is nobody, so far as we know, who could have written them but Helen Otway.

"The last letter refers explicitly to the loaded stick, and even describes its condition minutely and, as it appears, correctly. The writer had, therefore, presumably seen the stick and very probably had possession of it. But where was that stick? The deceased certainly did not know where it was, the housekeeper states that she had never seen it since that fatal morning, and Helen Otway has denied all knowledge of its whereabouts. No one knew what had become of it.

"But if its disappearance was a mystery, its reappearance is a greater mystery still. The account given by Helen Otway is obviously unsatisfactory. She went to the chambers, for no very apparent reason. When there she did not examine the various cupboards, drawers, and other receptacles, but she went direct to this particular cupboard, unlocked it, stood on tiptoe, and looked on the shelf. And behold! There was the missing stick. She took it out, examined it, and put it back. And she not only put it back, but she went out of her way to inform a person who is to give evidence on this enquiry that the stick was to be found in that cupboard.

"Now, how did that stick get into that cupboard, and when was it put there? You have heard Mr. Isaacs swear that it was not there when he made out the inventory, and you will probably agree that he could hardly be mistaken. A stick is a fairly large and conspicuous object, whereas he was searching for a small and inconspicuous one. Clearly the stick was put into the cupboard after his search was made. But when he had finished, the chambers were locked up, and the keys remained in his possession until he delivered them up to Helen Otway. Bearing these facts in mind, you have to consider whether you can accept Mrs. Otway's

552

statement, or whether it is more probable that she took the stick to the chambers, and put it into the cupboard herself.

"We now come to the incidents of that terrible night. What really happened in those chambers on that occasion will probably never be known. But the accounts that we have are full of sinister suggestions. We cannot, for instance, but note the fact that after this, the first and only visit from his wife, Lewis Otway made away with himself. Why he did the dreadful deed on this particular occasion, and at this particular time, is not clear. According to his wife's account he was much calmer, and more cheerful after their talk, and she left him peacefully asleep. That is what she has told us. But what are the facts? Within an hour or two hours after she had left, his dead body was hanging from that peg. Nay! There is even a more dreadful possibility. The medical witness has told us that death took place about eleven, 'But it might have been an hour later or earlier'. So that it is physically possible – since Mrs. Otway left the chambers about ten – that the suicide may have actually taken place before she left. It is a horrible suggestion, and I should not have made it but for the fact that there are certain appearances which seem to support it.

"You must have been struck by the singular circumstance that when Mrs. Otway took her departure she left the gas full on, and the bedroom door open. You have heard her explanation, but we are not concerned with that for the moment. The remarkable thing is that in the morning, the gas was still full on, and the bedroom door still open. Now how could that have been? If the deceased was asleep when his wife left, then he must have arisen, made his preparations, and finally hanged himself, not only with the gas full on – which might easily have been the case – but with the door open, which is improbable in the extreme. Men do not usually commit suicide *coram publico*. Commonly suicides lock themselves in their rooms or otherwise seek security from interruption. Yet this man, whose bedroom opened directly into the living room and whose housekeeper might still have been about, cuts down the bell-rope, arranges the chair, and hangs himself, all in a brightly-lighted room with the door open. It is certainly against common probabilities.

"But there are other suggestions of a similar tendency. If the fully-lighted gas and the open door suggest a hurried and agitated departure, so does the forgotten hand-bag containing the purse. And you will have noted that Mrs. Otway remembered that she had left her purse behind when she hailed a cab at the corner of Holywell Street. Now why did she not go back for it? She was quite near Lyon's Inn. She could have left the cab waiting, or brought it to the gate. She says she did not like to disturb Mrs. Gregg. But she has also said that she thought that Mrs. Gregg was still up and about. The explanation is not convincing, but on the other hand there is a strong suggestion of dislike to the idea of going back – a dislike which we can understand well enough if we believe that the tragedy had already been enacted, and that the body was even then hanging on the wall.

"Then, too, the disappearance of the precious stones points in the same direction. They might have been taken when the deceased was asleep, but the theft would have been far easier if he was dead. But, of course, we cannot say with certainty that Helen Otway took the stones. We can only consider the evidence. That evidence, however, is almost overwhelmingly strong. It goes to show that the stones were in the deed-box within half-an-hour of Helen Otway's arrival. There is no reason to suppose they were then removed. It is practically certain that they were there when she arrived, and they were never seen there or anywhere else after she left. And there is a further corroborative circumstance. To ordinary persons, unmounted precious stones illicitly obtained are difficult to dispose of. But this woman is not an ordinary person. She is a working goldsmith and jeweller who buys her own materials and sells the finished works to individual buyers. She could easily dispose of stolen gems in a manner that would render them untraceable.

"The theft of these stones is not directly our business. It is that of the police. But indirectly it is of great importance. For it furnishes strong support to the suggestion that the deceased was already dead when Helen Otway took her hurried departure. But what is the importance of that suggestion? The answer to that question will be found in the consideration of certain further facts and certain points of criminal law.

"First, we must notice that if the deceased committed suicide while Helen Otway was in the chambers, he must have done so with her consent and connivance. But was it only a matter of consent? Is there not a suggestion that some direct means may have been employed to induce or compel him to commit suicide? On this point we have very little information. But we have the evidence of Rachel Goldstein or Gregg that she overheard the conversation between Helen Otway and the deceased on two separate occasions, and that on both occasions they seemed to be talking about suicide. There seems to be a strong suggestion that some active, direct, means were employed – persuasion, threats, or perhaps the mysterious agency of suggestion. We cannot say that it was so, but it would be in close agreement with the known circumstances and quite consistent with the course of action exhibited by the anonymous letters.

"Supposing such active, direct means to have been employed, what degree of criminal responsibility would their employment entail? With regard to the letters, though the moral responsibility for their effect is beyond question, I should hesitate to give an opinion as to the exact legal position. But in the case of direct means there is no doubt at all. The law on the subject is quite clear. Let us consider it for a moment.

"First as to the legal nature of suicide. In law, suicide is murder. It has been expressly laid down that a person cannot commit manslaughter on himself. But since suicide is necessarily murder, it follows that any person who is accessory to suicide is accessory to murder. If such person aids or abets any other person in so killing himself, that person is an accessory before the fact, or a principal in the second degree in the murder so committed, an accessory before the fact being defined as one who directly or indirectly counsels, procures, or commands any person to commit any felony or piracy which is committed in consequence of such counselling, procuring, or commandment.

"Here, then, is the importance of the matter. The criminal responsibility attaching to the anonymous letters may be involved in some obscurity, but if it can be proved that any person counselled, procured, or commanded the deceased to kill himself, that person can be dealt with as a principal in the second degree in the murder of the deceased. It is for you to say whether, in your judgment, such action can be proved in the case of any person, and if so, who that person is.

"There is only one more item of evidence that I shall refer to, and that I shall touch upon only lightly. You have heard the witness Rachel Goldstein state that when she informed Helen Otway that the deceased had hanged himself, Mrs. Otway fell down in a dead faint. You have heard the explanation that Mrs. Otway gave, and you must decide what weight you attach to it, whether you can regard this fainting as due to the shock of an unexpected tragedy, or as the culminating effect of prolonged and extreme nervous tension. In any case, its evidential value is but small.

"And now, as our expert witness has still not arrived, let us take a last look over the evidence to see what material we have for our verdict." Here the coroner paused, a laying a number of sheets of paper in a row before him glanced rapidly through them.

I watched him with a dreadful fascination, even as a bird might watch the stealthy approach of a snake – terrified, but despairing of any hope of escape. So I had listened to this terrible summing-up – all false and erroneous in detail, but so horribly true in regard to the central fact. Through that dense fog of error and false appearances the coroner had seen the essential truth, that Lewis Otway had gone to his death at my bidding. Like some great spider he had wound around me a network of horrid entanglements, and now he was about to wind up the final turns.

555

At length he looked up and laid his hand on one of the papers. Then he turned once more towards the jury and began his summary of the evidence. And at that moment, unnoticed, apparently, by anyone save myself, Dr. Thorndyke entered silently by a side door, and seated himself on a vacant chair.

Chapter XXVIII
The Verdict

The arrival of Dr. Thorndyke seemed to me to close the last avenue of escape. The coroner had guessed at my guilty secret, but he only offered his guess as a speculative possibility on which no decisive opinion could be founded. But Dr. Thorndyke was not a guesser. If he had penetrated to that secret he would offer no speculative probabilities, but definite evidence, which would reduce the matter to certainty.

It was a terrible thought. Self-accusation – the denunciations of a guilty conscience – had been dreadful enough. But there is a world of difference between self-accusation in secret and a public criminal indictment, between calling oneself a murderess, and standing in the dock to answer the charge.

During the coroner's address I furtively watched Dr. Thorndyke. But I could gather nothing from his face. As he sat motionless, with his eyes steadily bent on the coroner, his expression denoted nothing but a grave and concentrated attention. After the first quick glance round the court, he never looked at me. What was in his mind I could not guess, though I felt that he held my fate in the hollow of his hand.

"There is no need, gentlemen," the coroner began, "for us to go through the mass of evidence again. We have looked over it as a whole, and we have seen that certain striking suggestions emerge from it. In our last glance we have to bring those suggestions to a definite focus. Our inquiry deals with a man who committed suicide, but the appearances suggest that that suicide was not a voluntary, spontaneous act, but was the effect of a compelling force exerted by some other person.

"Who was that other person? The compelling force seems to have been exerted by means of certain menacing letters. The person who procured the suicide of the deceased was therefore the writer of those letters. Now who was the writer of those letters? The question is best answered by asking certain other questions.

"First: Had the deceased any enemies? Well, we know of one, and one only. His wife, Helen Otway, has confessed to a deep repugnance to him. She had suffered grievous injuries at his hands, and she resented those injuries profoundly.

"Second: Who gained most by his death? Again, the answer is his wife, Helen Otway.

"Third: Did anyone stand to gain in any other way by his death? The answer again is yes, and the person who stood to gain – by liberation from an intolerable bondage – was Helen Otway.

"Fourth: Who could have written those letters? Who possessed the secret knowledge that those letters exhibit? Only one such person is known to us besides the deceased himself. That person is Helen Otway.

"Fifth: Who was the last person who was with him before his death? Again the answer is Helen Otway.

"Sixth: Is there any evidence of the use of more direct means to procure or compel this act of suicide? And if so, by whom do those means appear to have been employed? The answer is that there *is* such evidence, and that the person who appears to have used those means is Helen Otway. There is evidence suggesting that she was actually present when the suicide took place. There is evidence of a hurried flight and unwillingness to return for the purse that she had left behind. There is the open door, the lighted gas, and the missing jewels, which were in the chambers when she arrived, and which were never seen after she left. And then there is the mysterious stick which had vanished, and which reappeared so strangely after her unexplained visit to the chambers.

"That, gentlemen, is in brief the whole of the evidence, with the exception of that relating to John Vardon's death. That evidence is important to this enquiry, for if it should be proved that John Vardon was killed by Lewis Otway, and that Helen Otway was privy to the homicide, that would furnish a further motive for procuring the suicide of the deceased – the motive of the removal of the sole accomplice in a serious crime. But that evidence is not vitally important, and it is for you to decide whether you will still await the arrival of Dr. Thorndyke, or whether you will proceed to consider your verdict on the evidence that you have heard."

As the coroner concluded, Dr. Thorndyke rose and advanced to the table, placing on an empty chair a small green-covered suit-case. The coroner looked up at him sharply and with somewhat definitely unfriendly recognition.

"How long have you been here, sir?" the former demanded.

"About seven minutes," Dr. Thorndyke replied glancing at his watch. "You were just beginning your summary when I entered."

"You should have announced your arrival immediately," said the coroner. "However, as you are here, you had better take the oath, and give your evidence without further delay."

The coroner's brusque, and even rude manner, did not appear to disturb Dr. Thorndyke in the smallest degree. With the same impassive expression and quiet, composed demeanour, he took the oath and disposed of the usual preliminaries.

"We understand," said the coroner, "that you have made an examination of the body of the late John Vardon."

"Yes. I proceeded to Maidstone on instructions from the Home Office and conducted an exhumation of the body of John Vardon, of which I then made an examination. The object of the proceeding was to ascertain whether the cause of death had been correctly stated at the inquest."

"And what was the result of your examination – I don't think we want minute details."

"I found that the cause of death was, as stated at the inquest by the medical witnesses, failure of an extremely dilated heart. There was a small wound on the right side of the forehead adjoining the temple, which I examined very thoroughly. It was a glancing wound caused by a very oblique impact, and was such a wound as might have been produced in the manner described – by striking the corner of the mantelpiece in falling. There was no injury to the bone nor to the brain or its membranes. It was quite a trivial wound, and was not either wholly or partially the cause of death."

"Could that wound have been caused by a blow with a loaded stick?"

"I should say not. It was an oblique tear in the scalp and was apparently produced by some object more angular than the knob of a stick."

"Well," said the coroner, "that seems to dispose of the question of Mr. Vardon's death. It is a thousand pities that it was not cleared up more completely at the time. However, it is cleared up now, and that, really, is all, I think, that we want you to tell us, unless you have some other information. I understand that you had a sort of roving commission to investigate the matter of this enquiry?"

"I received instructions to make certain investigations with a view to my giving evidence at this inquest, and I have made such investigations as seemed to me to be necessary."

"Yes. You have, in fact, held a sort of one-man inquest on your own account. Well, the question is, do you suppose that you are in a position to tell us anything that we do not know already?"

"I am quite sure that I am. If you will allow me to present a summary of the facts in my possession – "

"I shall allow nothing of the kind. You will be good enough to answer questions like any other witness."

Dr. Thorndyke bowed with the same immovable serenity, and the coroner proceeded with his examination.

"Have you had much experience of cases of suicide?"

"I have."

"Have you had personal experience of any cases in which the suicidal act was procured, or brought about, by acts of persons other than the suicide, performed by them with deliberate intent?"

"Yes, I have had experience of several such cases."

"In those cases, what methods were used to procure the other person to commit suicide?"

"The majority were cases in which two persons agreed mutually to commit suicide together. In the less common cases in which the procurer did not propose to commit suicide – the method employed was usually some form of suggestion."

"Can you give us an instance of the employment of suggestion?"

"A very typical case occurred in my practice some years ago. A young man, who had a strong inherited predisposition to suicide, was caused by certain persons, who stood to benefit very considerably by his death, to make away with himself. The method adopted was this, The victim was made to believe that a certain Chinese jewel in his possession carried a curse, that all previous owners of it had hanged themselves, and that the appointed time for the suicide was made known by the apparition of a dead mandarin. When by frequent repetitions of this story the suitable state of mind had been produced, one of theses persons dressed himself in a mandarin's costume and presented himself to the victim, with the result that, within an hour or two, the latter hanged himself."

"In that case," observed the coroner, "the suggestion seems to have been in two stages. Is that usual?"

"One could hardly call it usual, as the cases are so rare. But it is the most obvious and effective method – to produce a suicidal state of mind by preparatory suggestion, and then, as it were, to explode the mine by a definite determining suggestion."

"Are you acquainted with the evidence which has been given in this inquiry?"

"I have read a verbatim report of the first proceedings, and I have heard your summary of the whole case."

"You have, then, read the evidence relating to the anonymous letters. What opinion did you form as to the purpose of those letters?"

"I formed the opinion that their purpose was to impel the deceased to commit suicide."

"Do you consider that, in the case of a person predisposed to suicide, they would be likely to produce that effect?"

"I should say that they would have a tendency to induce a suicidal state of mind."

"And suppose such a person, having received a series of such letters, and being greatly depressed by them, should be engaged – in his bedroom, the last thing at night – in a conversation on suicide, his own suicide, and that of relatives who had killed themselves, what would you expect to be the effect of such conversation?"

"It would not be possible to predict the effect, but the tendency would be to reinforce the influence of the letters."

"And what would be the condition of such a person in regard to his susceptibility to further suggestion?

"His susceptibility to further suggestion would probably be increased."

"Looking at this case as a whole, by the light of your experience of suicide, do you regard the death of the deceased as the result of his own spontaneous act or as due in part to the acts of some other person or persons?

"I regard his death as due entirely to the acts of some other person or persons."

At these terrible words my heart seemed to stand still. There was a fearful certainty and confidence in Dr. Thorndyke's tone that chilled my very blood. He did not guess. He knew. In the short pause that followed, I set my teeth and waited for my condemnation.

"You consider that the suggestion conveyed in the letters and in that conversation and by other possible means operated so as to convert the deceased into an automaton? Is that what you mean?"

"No. I do not consider that the letters or the conversation had any effect in causing his death."

The coroner frowned, perplexedly. "I don't think I quite understand," said he. "There seems to be – if you will pardon me – some self-contradiction. You state that the letters and the conversation would tend to produce a suicidal state of mind, but yet, though the letters were actually received and the conversation occurred, neither had any effect in causing the death which followed them. Do I state the case correctly?"

"Yes, quite correctly."

"Then I do not understand you in the least. You appear to be flatly contradicting yourself. I think you will agree that we are not making much progress."

"We are not making any progress at all. The examination has not elicited a single, relevant fact."

"Indeed, sir!" exclaimed the coroner. "And, pray, whose fault is that?

"I suggest," Dr. Thorndyke replied, suavely, "that it is due to the method of examination."

The coroner turned purple. "This is insufferable!" he exclaimed, "that a witness should presume to instruct an experienced officer of justice in the duties of his office! But I suppose we must be humble in the presence of an expert. May I ask, sir, what you object to in my methods of examination?"

"The lack of result," Dr. Thorndyke replied, "is due to the fact that your examination has been conducted to support a particular theory, and that theory happens to be the wrong theory."

"Again, I don't understand you," the coroner said, angrily. "No theory has been advanced by me. Will you be good enough to explain what theory you are alluding to?"

"I allude to the theory, which you seem to have adopted, that the deceased Lewis Otway committed suicide by hanging himself from a peg on the bedroom wall. That theory is erroneous. It is practically certain that Lewis Otway did not commit suicide, and it is quite certain that he never hung from that peg on the bedroom wall."

"But," exclaimed the coroner, "we have the evidence of a witness who saw the deceased hanging from that peg, and not only saw him, but cut him down and found him to be dead."

"As a witness," said Dr. Thorndyke, "I am not concerned with the testimony of other witnesses, but only with the facts as ascertained by me."

"No doubt," retorted the coroner. "But we are concerned with the testimony of all the witnesses, and the statement of this witness that she saw the body hanging from the peg, and that she cut it down from the peg, is a clear statement on a question of fact. If that statement is true, the deceased hung from that peg. If he did not hang from that peg the statement is false. You say that he never hung from that peg. On what facts do you base that statement?

"On the strength of the peg and the weight of the body of the deceased. The strength of the peg – that is, the maximum weight it was capable of supporting – was under one-hundred-seventy-five pounds. But the body of the deceased weighed two-hundred-thirty-one pounds – that is half-a-hundredweight in excess of the greatest weight that the peg was capable of supporting."

"What method did you employ to measure the strength of the peg?"

"I used simple weights, which I thought preferable to a dynamometer for purposes of evidence. These weights I had conveyed to the chambers, and I carried out the experiment in the presence of Mr. Anstey, K.C., and my assistant, Francis Polton. I hung from the peg a wooden tray, slung by a chain, the total weight of which was ten pounds. On this tray I placed – with great care to avoid shocks – two half-hundredweights. I then added weights, five pounds at a time, until the total weight, including that of the tray and chain, reached one-hundred-seventy pounds. This was evidently very near the limit of what the peg would bear, for it was bending noticeably under the weight, and when I added another five pounds the peg doubled under, breaking half-way through. I have brought it with me for your inspection." He opened the green suit-case and produced the peg, which he handed to the coroner.

"You see," he said, "that, in spite of its massive appearance, it had very little strength. It is merely a piece of thinnish, brass tube."

The coroner was impressed, but puzzled. "You consider," said he, as he handed the peg to the foreman of the jury, "that the test is conclusive?"

"Quite," replied Dr. Thorndyke. "Clearly, a peg which breaks under a weight of one-hundred-seventy-five pounds could not have supported a body weighing two-hundred-thirty-one pounds."

"Yes," agreed the coroner, "that appears to be undeniable." He again reflected for a few moments, and then said, "I notice that you went to the chambers provided with this apparatus. The suggestion is that you had already a definite suspicion in your mind. Is that the case?

"Yes, I had already come to the conclusion that the deceased had never hung from that peg."

"Will you tell us what led you to that conclusion?"

"When I received instructions to investigate the case, I proceeded to make an inspection of the body, and it struck me, at once, that the appearances were not quite in agreement with the alleged facts, which I had learned from a verbatim report of the evidence. The amount of injury to the structures of the neck was much less than I should have expected in the case of so heavy a man, and the characteristic signs of death by hanging were absent. It is my invariable rule, in all cases of suspicious death, no matter what the apparent cause of the death may be, to examine the contents of the stomach and the secretions. In this case the procedure appeared to be necessary, and I made a careful examination of the contents of the stomach. The examination disclosed the presence of small quantities of veronal and alcohol, but when I tested for alkaloids, I obtained from the stomach and its contents no less than twenty-three minims of nicotine, the alkaloid of tobacco.

"Now nicotine – which differs from all other alkaloids but conein, the alkaloid of hemlock, in being a liquid – is an intensely poisonous substance. The fatal dose has not been exactly ascertained, but it may be stated at not more, than five minims – that is, roughly, five drops. So that the quantity of this virulent poison actually obtained from the stomach of the deceased was about four times the fatal dose. But this was only a part of the quantity that had been swallowed, for the examination was made ten days after death, by which time an appreciable amount of the poison would have been lost by *post mortem* diffusion. I also examined the liver and other organs and the secretions, and in these I detected minute quantities of nicotine. The evidence afforded by these minute quantities is very important. Nicotine is a poison that acts with great rapidity – in fact, with the exception of hydrocyanic acid (prussic acid), it is probably the most rapidly-acting poison known. The importance, therefore, of these minute traces of the poison in remote organs is this: Their existence proves that the poison entered the stomach during life – while the blood was still circulating, and the minuteness of the quantity absorbed proves that death occurred very rapidly – practically instantaneously.

"But the very large quantity of the poison and the evidence of its almost instantaneous effect created this dilemma: A witness had stated that she saw the deceased hanging from the peg, but since death was practically instantaneous, he could not have hanged himself after taking the poison, and obviously he could not have taken the poison after he had hanged himself. This discrepancy, coupled with the absence of appreciable injury to the neck, raised a doubt as to whether the deceased had ever hung from the peg at all. That doubt was increased by certain other circumstances. There were, for instance, *post mortem* lacerations of the hamstring muscles and other muscles of the thighs, which could not be accounted for in the case of a body which had hung vertically, fully extended. There were faint impressions below the knees of some coarse-textured fabric, not part of his clothing, and there was the condition of a length of red, worsted rope by which the deceased was said to have been suspended. Both ends of this rope – which had formed part of a loop – had been cut through with a very sharp instrument, and both ends were cut cleanly right through. But this could not possibly have happened in the alleged circumstances. If a body of this great weight had been suspended by two thicknesses of a flimsy, woollen rope, and an attempt had been made to cut that rope, the cutting instrument would not have passed right through, but would have divided the rope until the remaining portion was too weak to sustain the weight, and then that portion would have broken, leaving a ragged end. Having regard to the great evidential importance of the question, I decided to clear up the doubt, if possible, by examining the peg itself. There are not many pegs which could carry this great weight without either bending, breaking, or pulling out of the woodwork, and I thought it probable that an actual test with weights would settle the question. I accordingly obtained the keys from Mrs. Otway, went to the chambers, and applied the tests as I have stated."

"If the deceased was not suspended at all," the coroner objected, "how do you account for the marks of the rope on his neck?"

"He was suspended – or rather partially suspended. I looked about the chambers for the probable means of suspension, and decided that this was the knob of the bedpost at the right-hand side of the head of the bed. On this side of the bed was a hard jute matting, the texture of which corresponded exactly with the impressions on the knees, the faintness of which is accounted for by the partial protection furnished by the pyjamas. The procedure seems to have been this: The rope was secured to the neck of the deceased immediately after death, while he was lying on the bed. It was then hitched over the knob of the bedpost and the body drawn off the bed so that it was supported against the bedpost in a kneeling position. This would account for the shallowness of the marks on the neck, the impressions of the matting on the knees, and the *post mortem* lacerations of the muscles. With regard to these latter, it is evident that the body was left suspended in an approximately kneeling position for a good many hours – probably for the purpose of producing as deep an indentation as possible on the neck – and that during that time cadaveric rigidity became well established, so that when the rope was cut and the body allowed to fall to the floor, the legs were found to have stiffened and to be firmly set in the kneeling posture. As the deceased was to be represented as having hanged himself from the peg, it would be necessary to straighten out the legs by force, but as the muscles were already rigid, the forcible extension would tend to produce such lacerations as were found. These lacerations were, of course, under the skin and would not be noticeable excepting on close examination."

"Is that the whole of your evidence?" the coroner asked, as Dr. Thorndyke paused.

"It is the whole of my evidence concerning the immediate circumstances of the death of Lewis Otway. I have certain other information, but you will probably not consider it of much importance to the enquiry. I have examined the two hairs that were found adhering to Mr. Vardon's stick. They were not his hairs. As a matter of fact, the wound on his head was on a part in which there was no hair, but in any case, these were not his hairs. One of these was apparently a hair of Lewis Otway's – probably taken from his hair brush. His hair was white, but was dyed with a stain containing sulphide of lead. This hair was of a similar character and stained with the same material. The other was white and appeared to be a woman's hair. It was cut at both ends, and was evidently part of a much longer hair. I have also made some enquiries concerning the anonymous letters. Mrs. Otway consulted me about them a month or two back, and I promised her to look into the matter, and did so. I collected very few facts, but if I may look at the letters, I can tell you at once whether those facts throw any light on the authorship of these letters."

"It really is not of much importance to us," said the coroner, "though it may be important evidence in another place. Still, you may as well look at the letters."

He handed the bundle of letters to Dr. Thorndyke, who examined each of them closely, holding them up to the light to inspect the watermark and comparing them with some other letters which he produced from his pocket.

"I think," said he, as he returned the letters to the coroner, "there is no doubt that all these letters were written by Morris Goldstein. I have several letters which were received from and signed by him, which are identically similar in character. All are typed on the same foreign paper – made in Sweden – with an old Calligraph machine which had three type-bars slightly bent – the lower-case 'g' and 's' and the capital 'O'. I have further evidence on the subject, if you care to hear it."

The foreman of the jury interposed at this point. "We don't want to hear any more about those letters. If the deceased did not commit suicide, the letters don't matter."

"They will matter a good deal in another court," said, the coroner, "but I agree with you that they do not affect our probable verdict, but there is one question to which we may as well have a definite answer, and then we need not detain Dr. Thorndyke any longer. You have told us, sir, that the immediate cause of Lewis Otway's death was nicotine poisoning. Can you say whether the poison was taken by the deceased himself, or whether it was administered by some other person?"

"The medical evidence proper furnishes no answer to that question, but from the attendant circumstances I infer that the poison was administered by some other person – probably while the deceased was asleep. But that is only an opinion, based on the circumstantial evidence."

"Exactly. It is really a question for the jury. And now I don't think we need trouble you any further." The coroner bowed, a little stiffly, and as Dr. Thorndyke walked back to his chair, he once more faced the jury.

"Well, gentlemen," said he, "you have heard Dr. Thorndyke's very remarkable evidence, and you will see that it compels us completely to revise our views of the case. The suicide by hanging, which we have been considering at such length, is seen to be an illusion – carefully, elaborately and ingeniously prepared. The question now is, was there a suicide at all? The cause of death was poisoning by nicotine, and death was almost instantaneous. Is this, then, a case of suicidal poisoning or of homicide?

"It is unnecessary for me to dwell on the suggested probabilities. You have heard a witness swear, in the most circumstantial manner, that she saw the deceased hanging from a peg, and that she cut the body down. You now know that the deceased could never have hung from that peg. That statement was false. But what was the object of that false statement? Its object must be considered in conjunction with the illusory appearances produced by an elaborate set of preparations – the cord-marks on the neck, the overturned chair, the end of the rope fastened to the peg – a set of preparations, the only intelligible object of which seems to be the concealment of the real cause of death. And then there is a further series of preparations revealed by the anonymous letters. These we now have reason to believe were written and sent by Morris Goldstein. Our reason for connecting Mrs. Otway with those letters was based on Rachel Goldstein's statement that no one was in the house at Maidstone but Mrs. Otway, and her husband and father. But we can no longer accept that statement. The suggested probability is that she was in the house, and that she either saw, or heard, enough to gather what had taken place. In that case, we seem to detect a carefully-laid plan to procure the suicide of the deceased, and throw suspicion on his wife, and when the suicide failed to occur, the alternative of poison would seem to have been adopted.

"I must draw your attention to the circumstances existing at the time of the tragedy. In the deceased's chambers were precious stones to the value of over four-thousand pounds. Possibly there were stolen gems of a somewhat greater aggregate value. It is highly probable that Rachel Goldstein knew of the deceased's letter to his wife, for as he was bed-ridden at the time, the letter would have been posted by her, and could easily have been opened and read. The time of the interview was arranged by her so that Mrs. Otway should be the last visitor.

"Here then is a group of circumstances furnishing a perfect opportunity for the carrying out of the plan. The gems were within reach, and a visitor was expected on whom could be thrown the suspicion of the theft, and the responsibility of the apparent suicide.

"As to the motive, apart from the theft of the gems, we must remember that here was an illegitimate family into which had been introduced a legitimate wife. Her arrival had affected the interests of the family injuriously, and if a reconciliation between husband and wife should have occurred, those interests would have been still more unfavourably affected.

"But we are not called on to go deeply into the question of motive. This is a coroner's inquest, and our business is to decide how and by what means the deceased met with his death. That decision is with you, gentlemen. You have heard the evidence, and I shall now leave you to consider your verdict."

As the coroner ceased speaking, and silence fell upon the court I allowed myself, for the first time, to think of my own position. Previously I had not dared, for when Dr. Thorndyke had made his dramatic statement, the revulsion of feeling had been so great that I had much ado to restrain myself from bursting into hysterical tears or laughter. But now I was more calm, and could think upon the change that a few magic words had wrought in my condition. I was free – free in body and soul. My imagined guilt had been a delusion, the silent willing and suggestion, a myth. I had never had any conscious intention to procure Lewis Otway's suicide, and no suicide had been procured. The death of that wretched man – my evil genius – had been brought about by no act of mine, conscious or unconscious. I was guiltless. I was free.

The jury took but a short time to consider their verdict. In a few minutes, the foreman intimated that they had come to a unanimous decision. The coroner then formally put the question.

"Have you considered the evidence, gentlemen, and are you agreed upon your verdict?"

"We are," replied the foreman. "Our verdict is that the deceased, Lewis Otway, met his death as the result of a poisonous dose of nicotine administered to him by Rachel Goldstein."

"Do you say that the poison was administered inadvertently or with malice?"

The foreman consulted his colleagues, and then replied, "With malice."

"That," said the coroner, "amounts to a verdict of wilful murder against Rachel Goldstein, and I may say, that I am entirely in agreement with you."

As the coroner concluded, I looked at Mrs. Gregg. Her face was set, and had turned a horrible, livid grey. Presently she rose slowly from her chair, and looked furtively over her shoulder, and as she did so she looked into the face of Superintendent Miller.

Epilogue

The history that I have set forth in the foregoing pages is the history of an episode. That episode opened with instantaneous abruptness, and in an instant it came to an abrupt end. The fatal words that I had overheard in my father's house had been as an incantation that had cast over me a malign spell. In the moment in which they were spoken the sinister shadow of Lewis Otway had fallen upon my life, and in the long months that followed it had never lifted. Even the death of the unhappy wizard had left the spell still working, the shadow deepening from hour to hour, until Dr. Thorndyke, like a benevolent magician, had spoken the counter-charm. Then, in an instant, the spell was broken, the shadow lifted and lifted for ever.

And with the breaking of the spell and the lifting of the shadow, the episode is at an end, and my tale is told. Yet I am loth to lay down my pen until the reader who has followed my pilgrimage through the valley of the shadow has been given at least one glimpse of me straying in the sunshine, "along the meads of asphodel." I would crave his attendance at the sombre, old church of St. Clement Danes, where, on a bright May morning, was spoken another incantation that opened to four faithful hearts the gates of a Paradise of life-long happiness and love. I would bid him admire sweet Peggy, tripping forth, all smiles and blushes, beside her stalwart husband to foregather with Jasper and me and our friends from Wellclose Square and the Temple in the ancient rooms in Clifford's Inn.

But my tale is told. The curtain is rung down, and I may not linger before it, babbling over the extinguished footlights on an empty stage – perchance to an empty house.

The End

A New Dr. Thorndyke episode.

1923 Hodder & Stoughton Cover

Preface

By *one of those coincidences which are quite inadmissible in fiction, but of frequent occurrence in real life, an incident in the story of* The Cat's Eye *has found an almost exact duplicate in an actual case which has been reported in The Press.*

The real case was concerned with a most alarming misadventure which befell a distinguished police official of high rank. The fictitious incident occurs in Chapter Ten of this book, and the reading of that chapter will inevitably convey the impression that I have appropriated the real case and incorporated it in my story, a proceeding that the reader might properly consider to be in questionable taste.

It seems, therefore, desirable to explain that Chapter Ten was written some months before the real tragedy occurred. Indeed, by that time, the book was so nearly completed that it was impracticable to eliminate the incident, which was an integral part of the plot.

The coincidence is to be regretted, but worse things might easily have happened. But for the circumstance that I had to lay this book aside to complete some other work, The Cat's Eye *would have been in print when the crime was committed, and it might then have been difficult for anyone – even for the author – to believe that the fictitious crime had not furnished the suggestion for the real one.*

RAF
Gravesend,
19th June, 1923

Chapter I
In the Midst of Life

I am not a superstitious man. Indeed superstition, which is inseparably bound up with ignorance or disregard of evidence, would ill accord with the silken gown of a King's Counsel. And still less am I tainted with that particular form of superstition in which the fetishism of barbarous and primitive man is incongruously revived in a population of, at least nominally, educated persons, by the use of charms, amulets, mascots, and the like.

Had it been otherwise, had I been the subject of this curious atavistic tendency, I should surely have been led to believe that from the simple gem whose name I have used to give a title to this chronicle, some subtle influence exhaled whereby the whole course of my life was directed into new channels. But I do not believe anything of the kind, and therefore, though it did actually happen that the appearance of the Cat's Eye was coincident with a radical change in the course and manner of my life, and even, as it seemed, with my very personality, and though with the Cat's Eye the unfolding of the new life seemed constantly associated, still I would have it understood that I use the name merely as a label to docket together a succession of events that form a consistent and natural group.

The particular train of events with which this history deals began on a certain evening near the end of the long vacation. It was a cloudy evening, I remember, and very dark, for it was past eight o'clock and the days were drawing in rapidly. I was returning across Hampstead Heath towards my lodgings in the village, and was crossing the broken, gorse-covered and wooded hollow to the west of the Spaniards Road, when I heard the footsteps of someone running, and running swiftly, as I could judge by the rapid rhythm of the footfalls and the sound of scattering gravel. I halted to listen, noting that the rhythm of the footsteps was slightly irregular, like the ticking of an ill-adjusted clock, and even as I halted, I saw the runner. But only for a moment, and then but dimly. The vague shape of a man came out of the gloom, passed swiftly across my field of vision, and was gone. I could not see what he was like. The dim shape appeared and vanished into the darkness, leaving me standing motionless, listening with vague suspicion to the now faint footfalls and wondering what I ought to do.

Suddenly the silence was rent by a piercing cry, the cry of a woman calling for help. And, strangely enough, it came from the opposite direction to that towards which the fugitive was running. In an instant I turned and raced across the rugged hollow towards the spot from whence the sound seemed to come, and as I scrambled up a gravelly hillock I saw, faintly silhouetted on the murky skyline of some rising ground ahead, the figures of a man and a woman struggling together, and I had just noted that the man seemed to be trying to escape when I saw him deal the woman a blow, on which she uttered a shriek and fell, while the man, having wrenched himself free, darted down the farther slope and vanished into the encompassing darkness.

When I reached the woman, she was sitting up with her right hand pressed to her side, and as I approached she called out sharply, "Follow him! Follow that man! Never mind me!"

I stood for a moment irresolute, for on the hand that was pressed to her side I had noticed a smear of blood. But as I hesitated, she repeated, "Follow him! Don't let him escape! He has just committed a dreadful murder!"

On this I ran down the slope in the direction that the man had taken and stumbled on over the rugged, gravelly hillocks and hollows, among the furze bushes and the birches and other small trees. But it was a hopeless pursuit. The man had vanished utterly, and from the dark heath not a sound came to give a hint as to the direction in which he had gone. There was no definite path, nor was it likely that he would have followed one, and as I ran forward, tripping over roots and sandy hummocks, the futility of the pursuit became every moment more obvious, while I felt a growing uneasiness as to the condition of the woman I had left sitting on the ground and apparently bleeding from a wound. At length I gave up the chase and began to retrace my steps, now full of anxiety lest I should be unable to find the spot where I had left her, and speculating on the possibility that the victim of the murder of which she had spoken might yet be alive and in urgent need of help.

I returned as quickly as I could, watching the direction anxiously and trying vainly to pick up landmarks. But the uneven, gorse-covered ground was a mere formless expanse intersected in all directions by indistinct tracks, confused by the numbers of birch-trees and stunted oaks, and shut in on all sides by a wall of darkness. Presently I halted with a despairing conviction that I had lost my way hopelessly, and at that moment I discerned dimly through the gloom the shape of a piece of rising ground lying away to the right. Instantly I hurried towards it, and as I climbed the slope, I thought I recognised it as the place from which I had started. A moment later, the identity of the place was confirmed beyond all doubt, for I perceived lying on the ground a shawl or scarf which I now remembered to have seen lying near the woman as she sat with her hand pressed to her side, urging me to follow her assailant.

But the woman herself had disappeared. I picked up the shawl, and throwing it over my arm, stood for a few moments, peering about me and listening intently. Not a sound could I distinguish, however, nor could I perceive any trace of the vanished woman. Then I noticed, a few yards away, a defined path leading towards a patch of deeper darkness that looked like a copse or plantation, and following this, I presently came upon her, standing by a fence and clinging to it for support.

"The man has got away," said I. "There is no sign of him. But what about you? Are you hurt much?"

"I don't think so," she answered faintly. "The wretch tried to stab me, but I don't think – " Here her voice faded away, as she fell forward against the fence and seemed about to collapse. I caught her, and lifting her bodily, carried her along the path, which appeared to lead to a house. Presently I came to an open gate, and entering the enclosed grounds, saw before me an old-fashioned house, the door of which stood ajar, showing a faint light from within. As I approached the door, a telephone bell rang and a woman's voice, harsh and terrified, smote my ear.

"Are you there? This is Rowan Lodge. Send to the police immediately! Mr. Drayton has been robbed and murdered! Yes, Mr. Drayton. He is lying dead in his room. I am his housekeeper. Send the police and a doctor!"

At this moment I pushed open the door and entered, and at my appearance, with the insensible woman in my arms, the housekeeper shrieked aloud, and dropping the receiver, started back with a gesture of wild terror.

"My God!" she exclaimed, "What is this? Not another!"

"I hope not," I replied, not, however, without misgivings. "This lady tried to hold the man as he was escaping and the villain stabbed her. Where can I lay her down?"

The whimpering housekeeper flung open a door, and snatching a match-box from the hall table, struck a match and preceded me into a room where, by the light of the match that flickered in her shaking hand, I made out a sofa and laid my burden on it, rolling up the shawl and placing it under her head. Then the housekeeper lit the gas and came and stood by the sofa, wringing her hands and gazing down with horrified pity at the corpse-like figure.

"Poor dear!" she sobbed. "Such a pretty creature, too, and quite a lady! God help us! What can we do for her? She may be bleeding to death!"

577

The same thought was in my mind, and the same question, but as I answered that we could do nothing until the doctor arrived, the woman – or rather girl, for she was not more than twenty-six – opened her eyes and asked in a faint voice, "Is Mr. Drayton dead?"

The housekeeper sobbed an indistinct affirmative and then added, "But try not to think about it, my dear. Just keep yourself quite quiet until the doctor comes."

"Are you sure he is dead?" I asked in a low voice.

"I wish I were not," she sobbed. Then, with an earnest look at the young lady – who seemed now to be reviving somewhat – she added, "Come with me and see, and do you lie quite still until I come back, my dear."

With this she led me out of the room, and turning from the hall into a short corridor, passed quickly along it and stopped at a door. "He is in there," she said in a shaky voice that was half a sob. She opened the door softly, peered in, and then, with a shuddering cry, turned and ran back to the room that we had just left.

When she had gone I entered the room half-reluctantly, for the atmosphere of tragedy and horror was affecting me most profoundly. It was a smallish room, almost unfurnished save for a range of cabinets such as insect collectors use, and opposite one of these a man lay motionless on the floor, looking, with his set, marble-white face and fixed, staring eyes, like some horrible waxwork figure. I stooped over him to see if there were any sign of life. But even to a layman's eye the fixity, the utter immobility was unmistakable. The man was dead beyond all doubt. I listened with my ear at his mouth and laid my finger on the chilly wrist. But the first glance had told me all. The man was dead.

As I stood up, still with my eyes riveted on the face, set in that ghastly stare, I became conscious of a certain dim sense of recognition. It was a strong, resolute face, and even in death, the fixed expression spoke rather of anger than of fear. Where had I seen that face? And then in a flash I recalled the name that the housekeeper had called through the telephone – Mr. Drayton. Of course. This was the brother of my neighbour in The Temple, Sir Lawrence Drayton, the famous Chancery lawyer. He had spoken to me of a brother who lived at Hampstead, and there could be no doubt that this was he. The likeness was unmistakable.

But, as I realised this, I realised also the certainty that this crime would become my professional concern. Sir Lawrence would undoubtedly put the case in the hands of my friend John Thorndyke – the highest medico-legal authority and the greatest criminal lawyer of our time – and my association with Thorndyke would make me a party to the investigation. And that being so, it behoved me to gather what data I could before the police arrived and took possession.

The mechanism of the crime was obvious enough, though there were one or two mysterious features. Of the cabinet opposite which the body lay, one drawer was pulled out, and its loose glass cover had been removed and lay shattered on the floor beside the corpse. The contents of this drawer explained the motive of the crime, for they consisted of specimens of jewellery, all more or less antique, and many of them quite simple and rustic in character, but still jewels. A number had evidently been taken, to judge by the empty trays, but the greater part of the contents of the drawer remained intact.

The rifled drawer was the second from the top. Having turned up the gas and lit a second burner, I drew out the top drawer. The contents of this were untouched, though the drawer appeared to have been opened, for the cover-glass was marked by a number of rather conspicuous fingerprints. Of course these were not necessarily the prints of the robber's fingers, but they probably were, for their extreme distinctness suggested a dirty and sweaty hand such as would naturally appertain to a professional thief in a state of some bodily fear. Moreover, the reason why this drawer should have been passed over was quite obvious. Its contents were of no intrinsic value, consisting chiefly of Buckinghamshire lace bobbins with carved inscriptions and similar simple objects.

I next drew out the third drawer, which I found quite untouched, and the absence of any fingerprints on the cover-glass confirmed the probable identity of those on the glass of the top drawer. By way of further settling this question, I picked up the fragments of the broken glass and looked them over carefully, and when I found several of them marked with similar distinct fingerprints, the probability that they were those of the murderer became so great as nearly to amount to certainty.

I did not suppose that these fingerprints would be of much interest to Thorndyke. They were rather the concern of the police and the Habitual Criminals Registry. But still I knew that if he had been in my place he would have secured specimens, on the chance of their being of use hereafter, and I could do no less than take the opportunity that offered. Looking over the broken fragments again, I selected two pieces, each about four inches square, both of which bore several fingerprints. I placed them carefully face-to-face in a large envelope from my pocket, having first wrapped their corners in paper to prevent the surfaces from touching.

I had just bestowed the envelope in my letter-case and slipped the latter into my pocket when I heard a man's voice in the hall. I opened the

579

door and, walking along the corridor, found a police inspector and a sergeant in earnest conversation with the housekeeper, while an elderly man, whom I judged to be the doctor, stood behind, listening attentively.

"Well," said the inspector "we'd better see to the lady. Will you have a look at her, Doctor, and when you've attended to her, perhaps you will let us know whether she is in a fit state to answer questions. But you might just take a look at the body first." Here he observed me and inquired, "Let me see. Who is this gentleman?"

I explained briefly my connection with the case as we walked down the corridor, and the inspector made no comment at the moment. We all entered the room, and the doctor stooped over the body and made a rapid inspection.

"Yes," he said, rising and shaking his head, "there's no doubt that he is dead, poor fellow. A shocking affair. But I had better go and see to this poor lady before I make any detailed examination."

With this he bustled away, and the inspector and the sergeant knelt down beside the corpse but refrained from touching it.

"Knife wound, apparently," said the inspector, nodding gloomily at a small pool of blood that appeared between the outstretched right arm and the side. "Seems to have been a left-handed man, too, unless he struck from behind, which he pretty evidently did not." He stood up, and once more looking at me, somewhat inquisitively, said, "I had better have your name and address, sir."

"My name is Anstey – Robert Anstey, KC, and my address is 8A Kings Bench Walk, Inner Temple."

"Oh, I know you, sir," said the inspector with a sudden change of manner. "You are Dr. Thorndyke's leading counsel. Well, well. What an odd thing that you should happen to come upon this affair by mere chance. It's quite in your own line."

"I don't know about that," said I. "It looks to me rather more in yours. If they have got these fingerprints in the files at Scotland Yard, you won't have much trouble in finding your man or getting a conviction."

As I spoke, I drew his attention to the fingerprints on the broken glass, saying nothing, however, about those on the upper drawer.

The two officers examined the incriminating marks with deep interest, and the inspector proceeded carefully and skilfully to pack several of the fragments for subsequent examination, remarking, as he laid them tenderly on the top of a cabinet, "This looks like a regular windfall, but it's almost too good to be true. The professional crook, nowadays, knows too much to go dabbing his trade-marks about in this fashion. These prints and the knife rather suggest a casual or amateur of some kind. The fellow not only didn't wear gloves, he didn't even trouble to wipe his hands. And they wanted wiping pretty badly. Are all these cabinets full of jewellery?"

"I really don't know what they contain, but they are pretty insecure if their contents are valuable."

"Yes," he agreed. "A single locked batten to each cabinet. One wrench of a jemmy and the whole cabinet is open. Well, we'd better have a few words with the housekeeper before we go over the room in detail. And she won't want to talk to us in here."

With this he led the way back to the hall, and I could not but admire the diplomatic way in which he managed to get me away from the scene of his intended investigation.

As we entered the hall, we met the doctor, who was repacking his emergency bag at the door of the room.

"I think," said he, "my patient is well enough to give you a few necessary particulars. But don't tire her with needless questions."

"She is not seriously hurt, then?" said I, with considerable relief.

"No. But she has had a mighty narrow escape. The brute must have aimed badly, for he struck viciously enough, but the point of the knife glanced off a rib and came out farther back, just transfixing a fold of skin and muscle. It is a nasty wound, but quite superficial and not at all dangerous."

"Well, I'm glad it's no worse than that," said the inspector, and with this he pushed open the door of the room and we all entered, though I noticed that the sergeant regarded me with a somewhat dubious eye. And now, for the first time, I observed the injured lady with some attention, which I was able to do at my leisure while the examination was proceeding. And a very remarkable-looking girl she was. Whether she would have been considered beautiful by the majority of persons I cannot say, she certainly appeared so to me. But I have always felt a great admiration of the pictures of Burne-Jones and of the peculiar type of womanhood that he loved to paint, and this girl, with her soft aureole of reddish-gold hair, her earnest grey eyes, her clear, blonde skin – now pale as marble – the characteristic mouth and cast of features, might have been the model whose presentment gave those pictures, to me, their peculiar charm. She seemed not of the common, everyday world, but like some visitor from the regions of legend and romance. And the distinction of her appearance was supported by her speech – by a singularly sweet voice, an accent of notable refinement, and a manner at once gentle, grave, and dignified.

"Do you feel able to tell us what you know of this terrible affair, Madam?" the inspector asked.

"Oh yes," she replied. "I am quite recovered now."

"Was Mr. Drayton a friend of yours?"

"No. I never met him until this evening. But perhaps I had better tell you how I came to be here and exactly what happened."

"Yes," the inspector agreed, "that will be the shortest way."

"Mr. Drayton," she began, "was, as you probably know, the owner of a collection of what he called 'inscribed objects' – jewels, ornaments, and small personal effects bearing inscriptions connecting them with some person or event or period. I saw a description of the collection in the *Connoisseur* a short time ago, and as I am greatly interested in inscribed jewels, I wrote to Mr. Drayton asking if I could be allowed to see the collection, and I asked, since I am occupied all day, if he could make it convenient to show me the collection one evening. I also asked him some questions about the specimens of jewellery. In reply he wrote me a most kind letter – I have it in my pocket if you would like to see it – answering my questions and not only inviting me most cordially to come and look at his treasures, but offering to meet me at the station and show me the way to the house. Of course I accepted his very kind offer and gave him a few particulars of my appearance so that he should be able to identify me, and this evening he met me at the station and we walked up here together. There was no one in the house when we arrived – at least he thought there was not, for he mentioned to me that his housekeeper had gone out for an hour or so. He let himself in with a key and showed me into this room. Then he went away, leaving the door ajar. I heard him walk down the corridor and I heard a door open. Almost at the same moment, he called out loudly and angrily. Then I heard the report of a pistol, followed immediately by a heavy fall."

"A pistol!" exclaimed the inspector "I thought it was a knife wound. But I mustn't interrupt you."

"When I heard the report, I ran out into the hall and down the corridor. As I went, I heard a sound as of a scuffle, and when I reached the door of the museum, which was wide open, I saw Mr. Drayton lying on the floor, quite still, and a man climbing out of the window. I ran to the window to try to stop him, but before I could get there he was gone. I waited an instant to look at Mr. Drayton, and noticed that he seemed to be already dead and that the room was full of the reek from the pistol. Then I ran back to the hall and out through the garden and along the fence to where I supposed the window to be. But for a few moments I could not see anyone. Then, suddenly, a man sprang over the fence and dropped quite near me, and before he could recover his balance, I had run to him and seized him by both wrists. He struggled violently, though

582

he did not seem very strong, but he dragged me quite a long way before he got free."

"Did he say anything to you?" the inspector asked.

"Yes. He used most horrible language, and more than once he said, 'Let go, you fool! The man who did it has got away!'"

"That might possibly be true," I interposed, "for, just before I heard this lady call for help, a man passed me at a little distance, running so hard that I was half-inclined to follow him."

"Did you see what he was like?" the inspector demanded eagerly.

"No. I hardly saw him at all. He passed me at a distance of about thirty yards and was gone in an instant. Then I heard this lady call out and, of course, ran towards her."

"Yes," said the inspector. "Naturally. But it's a pity you didn't see what the man was like." Then, once more addressing the lady, he asked, "Did this man stab you without warning, Miss – "

"Blake is my name," she replied. "No. He threatened several times to 'knife' me if I didn't let go. At last he managed to get his left hand free. I think he was holding something in it, but he must have dropped it, whatever it was, for the next moment I saw him draw a knife from under his coat. Then I got hold of his arm again, and that is probably the reason that he wounded me so slightly. But when he stabbed me I suddenly went quite faint and fell down, and then he escaped."

"He held the knife in his left hand, then?" the inspector asked. "You are sure of that?"

"Quite sure. Of course, it happened to be the free hand, but – "

"But if he had been a right-handed man he would probably have got his right hand free. Did you see which side he carried his knife?"

"Yes. He drew it from under his coat on the left side."

"Can you give us any description of the man?"

"I am afraid I can't. I am sure I should recognise him if I were to see him again, but I can't describe him. It was all very confused, and, of course, it was very dark. I should say that he was a smallish man, rather slightly built. He wore a cloth cap and his hair seemed rather short but bushy. He had a thin face, with a very peculiar expression – but, of course, he was extremely excited and furious – and large, staring eyes, and a rather pronounced, curved nose."

"Oh, come," said the inspector approvingly, "that isn't such a bad description. Can you say whether he was dark or fair, clean shaved or bearded?"

"He was clean shaved, and I should say decidedly dark."

"And how was he dressed?"

583

"He wore a cloth cap, and, I think, a tweed suit. Oh, and he wore gloves – thin, smooth gloves – very thin kid, I should say – "

"Gloves!" exclaimed the inspector. "Then the fingerprints must be the other man's. Are you sure he had gloves on both hands?"

"Yes, perfectly sure. I saw them and felt them."

"Well," said the inspector, "this is a facer. It looks as if the other man had really done the job while this fellow kept watch outside. It's a mysterious affair altogether. There's the extraordinary time they chose to break into the house. Eight o'clock in the evening. It would almost seem as if they had known about Mr. Drayton's movements."

"They must have done," said the housekeeper. "Mr. Drayton went out regularly every evening a little after seven. He went down to the village to play chess at the club, and he usually came back between half-past-nine and ten. And I generally sat and worked in the kitchen on the other side of the house from the museum."

"And did he take no sort of precautions against robbery?"

"He used to lock the museum when he went out. That was all. He was not at all a nervous man, and he used to say that there was no danger of robbery because the things in the museum were not the kind of things that burglars go for. They wouldn't be of any value to melt or sell."

"We must just look over the museum presently and see what the collection consists of," said the inspector. "And we must see how they got in and what they have taken. I suppose there is a catalogue?"

"No, there isn't," replied the housekeeper. "I did suggest to Mr. Drayton that he ought to draw up a list of the things, but he said it was not a public collection, and as he knew all the specimens himself, there was no need to number them or keep a catalogue."

"That is unfortunate," said the inspector. "We shan't be able to find out what is missing or circulate any descriptions unless you can remember what was in the cabinets. By the way, did Mr. Drayton ever show his collection to visitors other than his personal friends?"

"Occasionally. After the *Connoisseur* article that Miss Blake was speaking of, two or three strangers wrote to Mr. Drayton asking to be allowed to see the jewellery, and he invited them to come and showed them everything."

"Did Mr. Drayton keep a visitors' book, or record of any kind?"

"No. I don't remember any of the visitors, excepting a Mr. Halliburton, who wrote from the Baltic Hotel in the Marylebone Road. I remember him because Mr. Drayton was so annoyed about him. He put himself to great inconvenience to meet Mr. Halliburton and show him the jewellery that he had asked to see, and then, he told me, when he came, it was quite obvious that he didn't know anything at all about jewellery, either ancient or modern. He must have come just from idle curiosity."

"I'm not so sure of that," said the inspector. "Looks a bit suspicious. We shall have to make some inquiries at the Baltic. And now we had better go and have a look at the museum, and perhaps, Doctor, you would like to make a preliminary examination of the body before it is moved."

On this we all rose, and the inspector was just moving towards the hall when there came a sharp sound of knocking at the outer door, followed by a loud peal of the bell.

Chapter II
Sir Lawrence Declares
a Vendetta

At the first stroke of the knocker we all stood stock still, and so remained until the harsh jangling of the bell gradually died away. There was nothing abnormal in either sound, but I suppose we were all somewhat overstrung, for there seemed in the clamorous summons, which shattered the silence so abruptly, something ominous and threatening. Especially did this appear in the case of the housekeeper, who threw up her hands and whimpered audibly.

"Dear Lord!" she ejaculated. "It is Sir Lawrence – his brother! I know his knock. Who is to tell him?"

As no one answered, she crept reluctantly across the room, murmuring and shaking her head, and went out into the hall. I heard the door open and caught the sound of voices, though not very distinctly. Then the housekeeper re-entered the room quickly, and a man who was following her said in a brisk, somewhat bantering tone, "You are very mysterious, Mrs. Benham." The next moment the speaker came into view, and instantly he stopped dead and stood staring into the room with a frown of stern surprise.

"What the devil is this?" he demanded, glaring first at the two officers and then at me. "What is going on, Anstey?"

For a few moments I was tongue-tied. But an appealing glance from the housekeeper seemed to put the duty on me.

"A dreadful thing has happened, Drayton," I replied. "The house has been broken into and your brother has been killed."

Sir Lawrence turned deathly pale and his face set hard and rigid, until it seemed the very counterpart of that white, set face that I had looked on but a few minutes age. For a while he stared at me frowningly, neither moving nor uttering a word. Then he asked gruffly, "Where is he?"

"He is lying where he fell, in the museum," I replied.

On this he turned abruptly and walked out of the room. I heard him pass quickly down the corridor and then I heard the museum door shut. We all looked at one another uncomfortably, but no one spoke. The housekeeper sobbed almost inaudibly and now and again uttered a low moan. Miss Blake wept silently, and the two officers and the doctor stood looking gloomily at the floor.

Presently Sir Lawrence came back. He was still very pale. But though his eyes were red, and indeed were still humid, there was no softness of grief in his face. With its clenched jaw and frowning brows, it was grim and stern and inexorable as Fate.

"Tell me," he said, in a quiet voice, looking from me to the inspector, "exactly how this happened."

"I don't think anyone knows yet," I replied. "This lady, Miss Blake, is the only person who saw the murderer. She tried to detain him and held on to him until he stabbed her."

"Stabbed her!" he exclaimed, casting a glance of intense apprehension at the recumbent figure on the sofa and stepping softly across the room.

"I am not really hurt," Miss Blake hastened to assure him. "It is only quite a trifling wound."

He bent over her with a strange softening of the grim face, touching her hand with his and tenderly adjusting the rug that the housekeeper had spread over her.

"I pray to God that it is as you say," he replied. Then, turning to me, he asked, "Has this brave young lady been properly attended to?"

"Yes," I answered. "The doctor here – Dr. – "

"Nichols," said the medicus. "I have examined the wound thoroughly and dressed it, and I think I can assure you that no danger is to be apprehended from it. But, having regard to the shock she has sustained, I think she ought to be got home as soon as possible."

"Yes," Sir Lawrence agreed, "and if she is fit to be moved, I will convey her to her home. My car is waiting in the road. And I will ask you, Anstey, to come with me, if you can."

Of course I assented, and he continued, addressing the inspector, "When I have taken this lady home I shall go straight to Dr. Thorndyke and ask him to assist the police in investigating this crime. Probably he will return here with me at once, and I will ask you to see that nothing – not even the body – is disturbed until he has made his inspection."

At this the officer looked a little dubious, but he answered courteously enough. "So far as I am concerned, Sir Lawrence, your wishes shall certainly be attended to. But I notified Scotland Yard before I came on here, and this case will probably be dealt with by the Criminal Investigation Department, and, of course, I can enter into no undertakings on their behalf."

"No," Sir Lawrence rejoined, "of course you can't. I will deal with the Scotland Yard people myself. And now we had better start. Is Miss Blake able to walk to the car, Doctor? It is only a few yards to the road."

"I am quite able to walk," said Miss Blake, and as Dr. Nichols assented, we assisted her to rise, and Sir Lawrence carefully wrapped her in the rug that Mrs. Benham had thrown over her. Then I picked up the shawl, and tucking it under my arm, followed her as she walked slowly out supported by Sir Lawrence.

At the garden gate we turned to the left, and passing along the path, came very shortly to a road on which two cars were standing, a large closed car, which I recognised as Sir Lawrence's, and a smaller one, presumably Dr. Nichols'. Into the former Miss Blake was assisted, and when the carriage rug had been wrapped around her, I entered and took the opposite seat.

"What address shall I tell the driver, Miss Blake?" Sir Lawrence asked.

"Sixty-three Jacob Street, Hampstead Road," she replied, and then, as neither the driver nor either of us could locate the street, she added, "It is two or three turnings past Mornington Crescent on the same side of the road."

Having given this direction to the driver, Sir Lawrence entered and took the vacant seat and the car moved off smoothly, silently, and with unperceived swiftness.

During the journey hardly a word was spoken. The darkness of the heath gave place to the passing lights of the streets, the rural quiet to the clamour of traffic. In a few minutes, as it seemed, we were at the wide crossing by the Mother Red-Cap, and in a few more were turning into a narrow, dingy, and rather sordid by-street. Up this the car travelled slowly as the driver threw the light of a powerful lamp on the shabby doors, and at length drew up opposite a wide, wooden gate on which the number "*63*" was exhibited in large brass figures. I got out of the car and approached the gate in no little surprise, for its appearance and the paved truckway that led through it suggested the entrance to a factory or builders yard. However, there was no doubt that it was the right house, for the evidence of the number was confirmed by a small brass plate at the side, legibly inscribed "*Miss Blake*" and surmounted by a bell-pull. At the latter I gave a vigorous tug and was immediately aware of the far-away jangling of a large bell, which sounded as if it were ringing in an open yard.

In a few moments I detected quick footsteps which seemed to be approaching along a paved passage. Then a wicket in the gate opened and a boy of about twelve looked out.

"Whom did you want, please?" he asked in a pleasant, refined voice and with a courteous, self-possessed manner which "placed" him instantly in a social sense. Before I had time to reply, he had looked past me and observed Miss Blake, who, having been helped out of the car, was now approaching the gate, on which he sprang through the wicket and ran to meet her.

"You needn't be alarmed, Percy," she said in a cheerful voice. "I have had a little accident and these gentlemen have very kindly brought me home. But it is nothing to worry about."

"You look awfully white and tired, Winnie," he replied, and then, addressing me, he asked, "Is my sister hurt much, sir?"

"No," I answered. "The doctor who attended to her thought that she would soon be quite well again, and I hope she will. Is there anything that we can do for you, Miss Blake?"

"Thank you, no," she replied. "My brother and a friend will look after me now, but I can't thank you enough for all your kindness."

"It is I," said Sir Lawrence, "who am in your debt – deeply in your debt. And I do pray that you may suffer no ill consequences from your heroism. But we mustn't keep you standing here. Goodbye, dear Miss Blake, and God bless you."

He shook her hand warmly and her brother's with old-fashioned courtesy. I handed the boy the folded shawl, and having shaken hands with both, followed my friend to the car.

"Do you think Thorndyke will be at home?" he asked as the car turned round and returned to the Hampstead Road.

"I expect so," I replied. "But I don't suppose there will be very much for him to do. There were plenty of fingerprints in evidence. I should think the police will be able to trace the man without difficulty."

"Police be damned!" he retorted gruffly. "I want Thorndyke. And as to fingerprints, weren't you the leading counsel in that Hornby case?"

"Yes, but that was exceptional. You can't assume – "

"That case," he interrupted, "knocked the bottom out of fingerprint evidence. And these fingerprints may not be on the files at the registry, and if they are not, the police have no clue to this man's identity, and are not likely to get any."

It seemed to me that he was hardly doing the police justice, but there was no use in discussing the matter, as we were, in fact, going to put the case in Thorndyke's hands. I accordingly gave a colourless assent, and for the rest of the short journey we sat in silence, each busy with his own reflections.

At length the car drew up at the Inner Temple gate. Drayton sprang out, and signing to the driver to wait, passed through the wicket and strode swiftly down the narrow lane. As we came out at the end of Crown Office Row, he looked eagerly across at King's Bench Walk.

"There's a light in Thorndyke's chambers," he said, and quickening his pace almost to a run, he crossed the wide space, and plunging into the entry of number 5A, ascended the stairs two at a time. I followed, not without effort, and as I reached the landing the door opened in response to his peremptory knock and Thorndyke appeared in the opening.

"My dear Drayton!" he exclaimed, "you really ought not, at your age – " he stopped short, and looking anxiously at our friend, asked, "Is anything amiss?"

"Yes," Drayton replied quietly, though breathlessly. "My brother Andrew – you remember him, I expect – has been murdered by some accursed housebreaker. He is lying on the floor of his room now. I told them to leave him there until you had seen him. Can you come?"

"I will come with you immediately," was the reply, and as with grave face and quick but unhurried movements, he made the necessary preparations, I noticed that – characteristically – he asked no questions, but concentrated his attention on providing for all contingencies. He had laid a small, green, canvas-covered case upon the table, and opening it, was making a rapid inspection of the apparatus that it contained, when suddenly I bethought me of the pieces of glass in my pocket.

"Before we start," said I, "I had better give you these. The fingerprints on them are almost certainly those of the murderer." As I spoke, I carefully unwrapped the two pieces of glass and handed them to Thorndyke, who took them from me, holding them daintily by their edges, and scrutinising them closely.

"I am glad you brought these, Anstey," he said. "They make us to some extent independent of the police. Do they know you have them?"

"No," I replied. "I took possession of them before the police arrived."

"Then, in that case," said he "it will be as well to say nothing about them." He held the pieces of glass up against the light, examining them closely and comparing them, first with the naked eye and then with the aid of a lens. Finally he lifted the microscope from its shelf, and placing it on the table, laid one of the pieces of glass on the stage and examined it through the instrument. His inspection occupied only a few seconds. Then he rose, and turning to Drayton, who had been watching him eagerly, said, "It may be highly important for us to have these fingerprints with us. But we can't produce the originals before the police, and besides, they are too valuable to carry about at the risk of spoiling them. But I could make rough, temporary photographs of them in five minutes if you will consent to the delay."

"I am in your hands, Thorndyke," replied Drayton. "Do whatever you think is necessary."

"Then let us go to the laboratory at once," said Thorndyke, and taking the two pieces of glass, he led the way across the landing and up the stairs to the upper floor on which the laboratory and workshop were situated. And as we went, I could not but appreciate Thorndyke's tact and sympathy in taking Drayton up with him, so that the tedium of delay might be relieved by the sense of purposeful action.

The laboratory and its methods were characteristic of Thorndyke. Everything was ready and all procedure was prearranged. As we entered, the assistant, Polton, put down the work on which he was engaged, and at a word, took up the present task without either hesitation or hurry. While Thorndyke fixed the pieces of glass in the copying frame of the great standing camera, Polton arranged the light and the condensers and produced a dark-slide loaded with bromide paper. In less than a minute the exposure was made, in another three minutes the print had been developed, roughly fixed, rinsed, squeegeed, soaked in spirit, cut in two, and trimmed with scissors, and the damp but rapidly drying halves attached with drawing pins to a small hinged board specially designed for carrying wet prints in the pocket.

"Now," said Thorndyke, slipping the folded board into his pocket and taking from a shelf a powerful electric inspection lamp, "I think we are ready to start. These few minutes have not been wasted."

We returned to the lower room, where Thorndyke, having bestowed the lamp in the canvas-covered "research-case", put on his hat and overcoat and took up the case, and we all set forth, walking quickly and in silence up Inner Temple Lane to the gate, and taking our seats in the waiting car when Drayton had given a few laconic instructions to the driver.

Up to this point Thorndyke had asked not a single question about the crime. Now, as the car started, he said to Drayton, "We had better be ready to begin the investigation as soon as we arrive. Could you give me a short account of what has happened?"

"Anstey knows more about it than I do," was the reply. "He was there within a few minutes of the murder."

The question being thus referred to me, I gave an account of all that I had seen and heard, to which Thorndyke listened with deep attention, interrupting me only once or twice to elucidate some point that was not quite clear.

"I understand," said he when I had finished, "that there is no catalogue or record of the collection and no written description of the specimens?"

"No," replied Drayton. "But I have looked over the cabinets a good many times, and taken the pieces out to examine them, so I think I shall be able to tell roughly what is missing, and give a working description of the pieces. And I could certainly identify most of them if they should be produced."

"They are not very likely to be traced," said Thorndyke. "It is highly improbable that the murderer will attempt to dispose of things stolen in such circumstances. Still, the possibility of identifying them may be of the greatest importance, for the folly of criminals is often beyond belief."

Chapter III
Thorndyke Takes Up
The Inquiry

The outer door of the house was shut, although the lower rooms were all lighted up, but at the first sound of the bell it was opened by a uniformed constable who regarded us stolidly and inquired as to our business. Before there was time to answer, however, a man whom I at once recognised as Inspector Badger of the Criminal Investigation Department came out into the hall and asked sharply, "Who is that, Martin?"

"It is Sir Lawrence Drayton, Dr. Thorndyke, and Mr. Anstey," I replied, and as the constable backed out of the way we all entered.

"This is a terrible catastrophe, Sir Lawrence," said Badger. "Dreadful, dreadful. If sincere sympathy would be any consolation – "

"It wouldn't," interrupted Drayton, "though I thank you all the same. The only thing that would console me – and that little enough – would be the sight of the ruffian who did it dangling at the end of a rope. The local officer told you, I suppose, that I was asking Dr. Thorndyke to lend his valuable aid in investigating the crime?"

"Yes, Sir Lawrence," replied Badger, "but I don't know that I am in a position to authorise any unofficial – "

"Tut, tut, man!" Drayton broke in impatiently, "I am not asking you to authorise anything. I am the murdered man's sole executor and his only brother. In the one capacity his entire estate is vested in me until it has been disposed of in accordance with the will, in the other capacity, the duty devolves on me of seeing that his murderer is brought to account. I give you every liberty and facility to examine these premises, but I am not going to surrender possession of them. Has any discovery been made?"

"No, sir." Badger replied a little sulkily. "We have only been here a few minutes. I was taking some particulars from the housekeeper."

"Possibly I can give you some information while Dr. Thorndyke is making his inspection of my poor brother's body," said Drayton. "When he has finished and the body has been laid decently in his bedroom, I will come with you to the museum and we will see if anything is missing."

Badger assented, with evident unwillingness, to this arrangement. He and Drayton entered the drawing-room, from which the inspector had just come, while I conducted Thorndyke to the museum.

The room was just as I had seen it last, excepting that the open drawer had been closed. The stark, rigid figure still lay on the floor, the set, white face still stared with stern fixity at the ceiling. As I looked, the events of the interval faded from my mind and all the horror of the sudden tragedy came back.

Just inside the door Thorndyke halted and slowly ran his eye round the room, taking in its arrangement, and no doubt fixing it in his memory. Presently he stepped over to where the body lay, and stood a while looking down on the dead man. Then he stopped and closely examined a spot on the right breast.

"Isn't there more bleeding than is usual in the case of a bullet-wound?" I asked.

"Yes," he replied, "but that blood hasn't come from the wound in front. There must be another at the back, possibly a wound of exit. "As he spoke, he stood up and again looked searchingly round the room, more especially at the side in which the door opened. Suddenly his glance became fixed and he strode quickly across to a cabinet that stood beside the door, and as I followed him, I perceived a ragged hole in the front of one of the drawers.

"Do you mean, Thorndyke," I exclaimed, "that the bullet passed right through him?"

"That is what it looks like," he replied. "But we shall be able to judge better when we get the drawer open – which we can't do until Badger comes. But there is one thing that we had better do at once." Stepping over to the table on which he had placed the research-case, he opened the latter and, taking from it a stick of blackboard chalk, went back to the body. "We must assume," said he, "that he fell where he was standing when he was struck, and if that is so he would have been standing here." He marked on the carpet two-rough outlines to indicate the position of the feet when the murdered man fell, and having put the chalk back in the case, continued, "The next thing is to verify the existence of the wound at the back. Will you help me to turn him over?"

We turned the body gently on to its right side, and immediately there came into view a large, blood-stained patch under the left shoulder, and at the centre of it a ragged burst in the fabric of the coat.

"That will do," said Thorndyke. "It is an unmistakable exit wound. The bullet probably missed the ribs both in entering and emerging, and passed through the heart or the great vessels. The appearances suggest almost instantaneous death. The face is set, the eyes wide open, and both the hands tightly clenched in a cadaveric spasm. And the right hand seems to be grasping something, but we had better leave that until Badger has seen it."

594

At this moment footsteps became audible coming along the corridor, and Badger entered the room accompanied by the local inspector. The two officers looked inquiringly at Thorndyke, who proceeded at once to give them a brief statement of the facts that he had observed.

"There can't be much doubt," said Badger when he had examined the hole in the drawer front, "that this was made by a spent bullet. But we may as well settle the question now. We shall want the keys in any case."

He passed his hand over the dead man's clothes and, having located the pocket which contained the keys, drew out a good-sized bunch, with which he went over to the cabinet. A few trials with likely-looking keys resulted in the discovery of the right one, and when this had been turned and the hinged batten swung back, all the drawers of the cabinet were released. The inspector pulled out the one with the damaged front and looked in inquisitively. Its contents consisted principally of latten and pewter spoons, now evidently disarranged and mingled with a litter of splinters of wood, and in the bowl of a spoon near the back of the drawer lay a distorted bullet, which Badger picked up and examined critically.

"Browning automatic, I should say," was his comment, "and if so we ought to find the cartridge case somewhere on the floor. We must look for it presently, but we'd better get the body moved first, if you have finished your inspection, Doctor."

"There is something grasped in the right hand," said Thorndyke. "It looks like a wisp of hair. Perhaps we had better look at that before the body is moved, in case it should fall out."

We returned to the body, and the two officers stooped and watched eagerly as Thorndyke, with some difficulty, opened the rigid hand sufficiently to draw from it a small tuft of hair.

"The spasm is very marked," he observed as he scrutinised the hair and felt in his pocket for a lens, and when, with the aid of the latter, he had made a further examination, he continued, "The state of the root-bulbs shows that the hair was actually plucked out – which, of course, is what we should expect."

"Can you form any opinion as to what sort of man he was?" Badger asked.

"No," replied Thorndyke, "excepting that he was not a recently released convict. But the appearance of the hair agrees with Miss Blake's description of the man who stabbed her. I understand that she described him as a having rather short but bushy hair. This hair is rather short, though we can't say whether it was bushy or not. Perhaps more complete examination of it may tell us something further."

"Possibly," Badger agreed. "I will have it thoroughly examined, and get a report on it. Shall I take charge of it?" he added, holding out his hand.

"Yes, you had better," replied Thorndyke, "but I will take a small sample for further examination, if you don't mind."

"There is no need for that," protested Badger. "You can always have access to what we've got if you want to refer to it."

"I know," said Thorndyke, "and it is very good of you to offer. Still this will save time and trouble." And without more ado he separated a third of the tuft and handed the remainder to the inspector, who wrapped it in a sheet of note-paper that he had taken from his pocket and sourly watched Thorndyke bestow his portion in a seed-envelope from his pocket-book, and after writing on it a brief description, return it to the latter receptacle.

"You were saying," said Badger, "that this hair agrees with Miss Blake's description. But it was suggested that it was the other man who really committed the murder. Isn't that rather a contradiction?"

"I don't think so," replied Thorndyke. "The probabilities seem to me to point to the other man as the murderer."

"But how can that be?" objected Badger. "You say that this hair agrees with Miss Blake's description of the man. But this hair is obviously the hair of the murderer. And that man was left-handed and the wound is on the right breast, suggesting that the murderer held his pistol in his left hand."

"Not at all," said Thorndyke. "I submit that this hair is obviously not the hair of the murderer. Look at those chalk marks that I have made on the floor. They mark the spot on which the deceased was standing when the bullet struck him. Now go back to the cabinet and look at the chalk marks and see what is in a direct line with them."

The inspector did so. "I see," said he. "You mean the window."

"Yes. It was open, since the robber evidently came in by it, and the sill is barely five feet from the ground. I suggest – but merely as a probability, since the bullet may have been deflected – that the other man was keeping guard outside, and that when he heard a noise from this room he looked in through the window and saw his confederate on the point of being captured by the deceased, that he then fired, and when he saw deceased fall, he made his escape. That would account for the man who was seen by Miss Blake making his appearance after the other man had gone. He may have had to extricate himself from the dead man's grasp, and then he had to climb out of the window. But the position of the empty cartridge-case – if we find it – will settle the question. If the

596

pistol was fired into the room through the window, the cartridge-case will be on the ground outside."

He opened his research-case and, taking from it the electric lamp, walked slowly to the window, throwing the bright light on the floor as he went. The two officers followed, and all scrutinised the floor closely, but in vain. Then Thorndyke leaned out of the window and threw the light of his lamp on the ground outside, moving the bright beam slowly to-and-fro while the inspector craned forward eagerly. Suddenly Badger uttered an exclamation.

"There it is, Doctor! Don't move the light. Keep it there while I go out and pick the case up."

"One moment, Badger," said Thorndyke. "We mustn't be impetuous. There are some other things out there more important than the cartridge-case. I can see two distinct sets of footprints, and it is above all things necessary that they should not be confused by being trodden into. Let us get the body moved first. Then we can take some mats out and examine the footprints systematically and recover the cartridge-case at the same time. If we are careful, we can leave the ground in such a condition that it will be possible to go over it again by daylight."

The wisdom of this suggestion was obvious, and the inspector proceeded at once to act on it. The sergeant and the constable were sent for, and by them the body of the murdered man was carried, under the inspector's supervision, to the bedroom above. Then a couple of large mats were procured from Mrs. Benham and we all issued from the front door into the garden. Here, however, a halt was called, and at Thorndyke's suggestion, the party was separated into two, he and Badger to explore the grounds inside the fence, while the local inspector and the others endeavoured to follow the tracks outside.

I did not join either party, nor did Sir Lawrence. We both realised the futility of any attempt to trace the fugitives, and recognised that the suggestion was made by Thorndyke merely to get rid of the unwanted supernumeraries. Accordingly we took up a position outside the fence, which we could just look over, and watched the proceedings of Thorndyke and Inspector Badger, as they passed slowly along the side of the house, each with the light of his lantern thrown full on the ground.

They had gone but a few paces when they picked up on the soft, loamy path the fairly clear impressions of two pairs of feet going towards the back of the house. Both the investigators paused and stooped to examine them, and Badger remarked, "So they came in at the front gate-naturally, as it was the easiest way. But they must have been pretty sure that there was no one in the house to see them. And that suggests that they knew the ways of the household and that they had lurked about to watch Mr. Drayton and Mrs. Benham off the premises."

"Is it possible to distinguish one man from the other?" Drayton asked.

"Yes, quite easily," Badger replied. "One of them is a biggish man – close on six feet, I should say – while the other is quite a small man. That will be the one that Miss Blake saw."

They followed the tracks to the back of the house, and as we followed on our side of the fence Thorndyke called out, "Be careful, Anstey, not to tread in the tracks where they came over the fence. We ought to get specially clear prints of their feet where they jumped down. Could you get a light?"

"I'll go and get one of the acetylene lamps from the car," said Drayton. "You stay where you are until I come back."

He was but a short time absent, and when he returned he was provided with a powerful lamp and a couple of small mats. "I have brought these," he explained "to lay on any particularly clear footprints to protect them from chance injury. We mustn't lose the faintest shadow of a clue."

With the aid of the brilliant light Drayton and I explored the ground at the foot of the fence. Suddenly Sir Lawrence exclaimed, "Why, these look like a woman's footprints!" and he pointed to a set of rather indistinct impressions running parallel to the fence.

"They will be Miss Blake's," said I. "She ran round this way. Yes, here is the place where the man came over. What extraordinarily clear impressions this ground takes. It shows the very brads in the heels."

"Yes," he agreed, "this is the Hampstead sand, you know, one of the finest foundry-sands in the country."

He laid one of the mats carefully on the pair of footprints, and we continued our explorations towards the back of the house. Here we saw Thorndyke and the inspector, each kneeling on a mat, examining a confused mass of footprints on the ground between the museum window and the fence.

"Have you found the cartridge-case?" I asked.

"Yes," replied Thorndyke. "Badger has it. It is a 'Baby Browning'. And I think we have seen all there is to see here by this light. Can you see where the big man came down from the fence? He went over where I am throwing the light."

We approached the spot cautiously, and at the place indicated perceived the very clear and deep impression of a large right foot with a much less distinct print of a left foot, both having the heels towards the fence, and a short distance in front of them the soft, loamy earth bore a clear impression of a left hand with the fingers spread out, and a fainter print of a right hand.

I reported these facts to Thorndyke, who at once decided to come over and examine the prints. Handing his lamp over a few paces farther along the fence, he climbed up and dropped lightly by my side, followed almost immediately by Inspector Badger.

"This," said the inspector, gazing down at the foot and hand-prints, "bears out what we saw from the inside. He wasn't any too active, this chappie. Probably fat – a big, heavy, awkward man. Had to pull the garden seat up to the fence to enable him to get over, though it was an easy fence to climb with those big cross-rails, and here, you see, he comes down all of a heap on his hands and knees. However, that doesn't help us a great deal. He isn't the only fat man in the world. We had better go indoors now and have a look at the room and see if we can find out what has been taken."

We turned to retrace our steps towards the gate, pausing on our way to lift the mats and inspect the footprints of the smaller man, and as we went Drayton asked if anything of interest had been discovered.

"No," replied Badger. "They got in without any difficulty by forcing back the catch of the window – unless the window was open already. It isn't quite clear whether they both got in. The big man walked part of the way round the house and along the fence in both directions, and he pulled a garden seat up to the fence to help himself up. The small man came out of the window last, if they were both inside, and I expect it was he who dropped this – must have had it in his hand when he climbed out – " And here the inspector produced from his pocket a ring, set with a single round stone, which he handed to Sir Lawrence.

"Ah," said the latter, "a posy-ring, one of the cat's eye series. There were several of these and a set of moonstone rings in the same drawer."

"You know the collection pretty well, then. Sir Lawrence?"

"Fairly well. I often used to look over the things with my poor brother. But, of course, I can't remember all the specimens, though I think I can show you the drawer that this came from."

By this time we had entered the house and were making our way to the museum. On entering the room, Drayton walked straight to the cabinet which I remembered to have seen open, and pulled out the second drawer from the top.

"This is the one," said he. "They have taken out the glass top – I suppose those are the pieces of it on the floor."

"Yes," said Badger. "We found it open, and it seems to be the only drawer that has been tampered with."

Drayton pulled out the top drawer and, having looked closely at the glass cover, remarked, "They have had this one open, too. There are distinct fingerprints on the glass, and they have had the cover off for there are finger-marks on the inside of the glass. I wonder why they did that."

"I can't imagine." said Badger. "They don't seem to have taken anything – there wasn't anything worth taking, for that matter. But they could see that without lifting off the glass. However, it is all for the best. We'll hand this glass cover to the Fingerprint Department and hope they will be able to spot the man that the fingers belong to."

As he spoke, he made as if he would lift off the cover, but he was anticipated by Thorndyke, who carefully raised the glass by its leather tab, and taking it up by the edges, held it against the light and examined the fingerprints minutely both on the upper and under surfaces.

"The thumbs are on the upper surface," he remarked, "and the fingers underneath, so the glass was lifted right out and held with both hands."

He handed the glass to the inspector, who had been watching him uneasily, and now took the cover from him with evident relief, and as Badger proceeded to deposit it in a safe place, he pushed in the top drawer and returned to the consideration of the second.

"There are evidently several pieces missing from this drawer," said he, "and it may be important to know what they are, though it is rather unlikely that the thieves will try to dispose of them. Can you tell us what they are, Drayton?"

"I can tell you roughly," was the reply. "This drawer contained the collection of posy-rings, and most of them are there still, as you can see. The front row were rings set with moonstone and cat's eye, and most of those are gone. Then there was a group of moonstone and cat's eye ornaments, mostly brooches and earrings, and one pendant. Those have all disappeared. And there is another thing that was in this drawer that has apparently been taken, a locket. It was shaped like a book and had a Greek inscription on the front."

"So far as you can see, Sir Lawrence," said Badger, "has anything of value been taken – of real value, I mean?"

"Of negotiable value, you mean," Drayton corrected. "No. Most of the things were of gold, though not all, but the stones were probably worth no more than a few shillings each. The value was principally in the associations and individual character of the pieces. All of them had inscriptions, and several of them had recorded histories. But that would be of no use to a thief."

"Exactly," said Badger. "That was what was in my mind. There is something rather amateurish about this robbery. It isn't quite like the work of a regular hand. The time was foolish, and then all this shooting and stabbing is more like the work of some stray foreign crooks than of a regular tradesman. And, as you say, the stuff wasn't worth the risk – unless there's something else of more value. Perhaps we had better go through the other cabinets."

He produced the bunch of keys from his pocket and had just inserted one into the lock of the next cabinet when Drayton interposed.

"There is no need for that, Inspector. If the cabinets are locked and have not been broken open, their contents are intact, and I can tell you that those contents are of no considerable intrinsic value."

With this he drew the key from the lock and dropped the bunch in his pocket, a proceeding whereat the inspector smiled sourly and remarked, "Then in that case, I think I have finished for the present. I'll just pack up this glass cover and see if those others were able to follow the tracks of either of these men. And I'll wish you gentlemen goodnight."

Sir Lawrence accompanied him to the drawing-room, and as I learned later, provided the official party with refreshment, and when we were alone I turned to Thorndyke.

"I suppose we have finished, too?"

"Not quite," he replied. "There are one or two little matters to be attended to, but we will wait until the police are clear of the premises. They will keep their own counsel and I propose to keep mine, unless I can give them a straight lead." He opened his research-case and was thoughtfully looking over its contents when Drayton returned and announced that the police had departed.

"Is there anything more that you want to do, Thorndyke?" he asked.

"Yes," was the reply. "For one thing, I should like to see if there are any more fingerprints." As he spoke, he pulled out the drawers of the cabinet one after the other, and examined the glass covers. But apparently they had not been touched. At any rate, there were no marks on any of the glasses.

"They must have been disturbed soon after they got to work," said Drayton "as they opened only two drawers."

"Probably," Thorndyke agreed, taking from his case a little glass-jar filled with a yellowish powder and fitted with two glass tubes and a rubber bulb. With this apparatus he blew a cloud of the fine powder over the woodwork of the rifled cabinet, and when a thin coating had settled on the polished surface, he tapped the wood gently with the handle of his pocket-knife. At each tap a portion of the coating of powder was jarred on the surface, and then there appeared several oval spots to which it still adhered. Then he gently blew away the rest of the powder, when the oval spots were revealed as fingerprints, standing out white and distinct against the dark wood. Thorndyke now produced from his pocket the hinged board, and opening it, compared the photographs with these new fingerprints, while Drayton and I looked over his shoulder.

"They are undoubtedly the same," said I, a little surprised at the ease with which I identified these curious markings. "Absolutely the same – which is rather odd, seeing that there are the marks of only two digits of the left hand and four of the right. It almost looks as if those particular fingers had got soiled with some greasy material and that the other fingers were clean and had left no mark."

"An admirable suggestion, Anstey," said Thorndyke. "The same idea had occurred to me, for the prints of these particular fingers are certainly abnormally distinct. Let us see if we can get any confirmation." He blew upon each of the fingerprints in turn until most of the powder was dislodged and the markings had become almost invisible. Then, taking my handkerchief, which was of soft silk, and rolling it into a ball, he began to wipe the woodwork with a circular motion, at first very lightly but gradually increasing the pressure until he was rubbing quite vigorously. The result seemed to justify my suggestion, for as the rubbing proceeded, I could see, by the light of Drayton's lamp, thrown on at various angles, that the fingerprints seemed to have spread out into oval, glistening patches, having a lustre somewhat different from that of the polished wood.

Sir Lawrence looked on with keen interest, and as Thorndyke paused to examine the woodwork, he asked, "What is the exact purpose of this experiment?"

"The point is," replied Thorndyke, "that whereas the fingerprint of the mathematical theorists is a mere abstraction of form devoid of any other properties, the actual or real fingerprint is a material thing which has physical and chemical properties, and these properties may have considerable evidential significance. These fingerprints, for instance, contain some substance other than the natural secretions of the skin. The questions then arise: What is that substance? How came it here? And is it usually associated with any particular kind of person or activity? The specimens that Anstey so judiciously captured may help us to answer the first question, and our native wits may enable us to answer the others. So we have some data for consideration. And that reminds me that there are some other data that we must secure."

"What are they?" Drayton asked eagerly.

"There are those impressions in the sand outside the fence. I must have permanent records of them. Shall we go and do them now? I shall want a jug of water and a light."

While Drayton went to fetch the water, Thorndyke and I took our way out through the garden to the outside of the fence, he carrying his research-case, and I bearing Drayton's lamp. At the spot where we had laid down the mat we halted, and Thorndyke, having set down his case, once more lifted the mat.

"They are small feet," he remarked, glancing at the footprints before stooping to open the case. "A striking contrast to the other man's."

He took from his case a tin of plaster of Paris, and dipping up a small quantity in a spoon, proceeded very carefully to dust the footprints with the fine, white powder until they were covered with a thin, even coating. Then he produced a bottle of water fitted with a rubber ball-spray diffuser, and with this blew a copious spray of water over the footprints. As a result, the white powder gradually shrank until the footprints looked as if they had received a thin coat of whitewash.

"Why not fill the footprints up with liquid plaster?" asked Drayton, who came up at this moment carrying a large jug.

"It would probably disturb the sand," was the reply, "and moreover, the water would soak in at once and leave the plaster a crumbling mass. But when this thin layer has set it will be possible to fill up and get a solid cast."

He repeated the application of the spray once or twice, and then we went on to the place where the other man had come over. Here the same process was carried out, not only with the footprints but also with those of the hands. Then we went back to the first place, and when Thorndyke had gently touched the edge of the footprints and ascertained that the thin coating of plaster had set into a solid shell, he produced a small rubber basin, and having half filled it with water, added a quantity of plaster and stirred it until it assumed the consistency of cream, when he carefully poured it into the white-coated footprints until they were full and slightly overflowing.

"You see the advantage of this?" said Thorndyke as he cleaned out the basin and started to walk slowly back to the site of the second set of prints.

"I do, indeed," replied Drayton, "and I am astonished that Badger did not take a permanent record. These casts will enable you to put the actual feet of the accused in evidence if need be."

"Precisely – besides giving us the opportunity to study them at our leisure, and refer to them if any fresh evidence should become available."

The second set of footprints and the impressions of the hands received similar treatment, and when they had been filled, Thorndyke proceeded to pack up his appliances.

"We ought to give the casts a good twenty minutes to set hard," he said, "though it is the best plaster and quite fresh and has a little powdered alum mixed with it to accelerate setting and make the cast harder. But we mustn't be impatient."

"I am in no hurry," said Drayton. "I shall stay here tonight – one couldn't leave Mrs. Benham in the house all alone. The car can take you back to your chambers and drop Anstey at his lodgings.

"Tomorrow we must make some arrangements of a more permanent kind. But the great thing is to get on the track of these two villains. Nothing else seems to matter. There is my poor brother's corpse, crying aloud to Heaven for justice, and I shall never rest until his murderers have paid their debt."

"I sympathise with you most cordially, Drayton," said Thorndyke, "and it is no mere verbal sympathy. I promise you that every resource at my disposal shall be called in to aid, that no stone shall be left unturned. It is not only the office of friendship – it is a public duty to ensure that an inexcusable crime of this kind shall be visited with the most complete retribution."

"Thank you. Thorndyke," Sir Lawrence said with gruff earnestness. And then after a short pause, he continued, "I suppose it is premature to ask you, but do you see any glimmer of hope? Is there anything to lay hold of? I can see for myself that it is a very difficult and obscure case."

"It is," Thorndyke agreed. "Of course, the fingerprints may dispose of the whole difficulty, if they happen to be on the files at the Habitual Criminals Registry. Otherwise, there is very little evidence. Still, there is some, and we may build up more by inference. I have seen more unpromising cases come to a successful issue."

By this time the stipulated twenty minutes had expired, and we proceeded to the first set of footprints. The plaster, on being tested, was found to be quite firm and hard, and Thorndyke was able, with great care, to lift the two chalky-looking plates from their bed in the ground. And even in the rather unfavourable light of the lamp their appearance was somewhat startling, for, as Thorndyke turned them over, each cast presented the semblance of a white foot, surprisingly complete in detail so far as the sole was concerned.

But if the appearance of these casts was striking, much more so was that of the second set, for the latter included casts of the handprints, the aspect of which was positively uncanny, especially in the case of the deeper impression, the effect of which was that of a snowy hand with

604

outspread, crooked, clutching fingers. And here again the fine loam had yielded an unexpected amount of detail. The creases and markings of the palm were all perfectly clear and distinct, and I even thought that I could perceive a trace of the ridges of the fingertips.

Before leaving the spot, we carefully removed all traces of plaster, for it was certain that the footprints would be examined by daylight, and Thorndyke considered it better that the existence of these casts should be known only to ourselves. The footprints were left practically intact, and it was open to the police to make casts if they saw fit.

"I think," said Thorndyke when we had re-entered the house and were inspecting the casts afresh as they lay on the table, "it would be a wise precaution to attach our signatures to each of them, in case it should be necessary at any time to put them in evidence. Their genuineness would then be attested beyond any possibility of dispute."

To this Drayton and I agreed most emphatically, and accordingly each of us wrote his name, with the date, on the smooth back of each cast. Then the "records" were carefully packed and bestowed in the research-case, and Thorndyke and I shook our host's hand and went forth to the car.

Chapter IV
The Lady of Shalott

The modern London suburb seems to have an inherent incapacity for attaining a decent old age. City streets and those of country towns contrive to gather from the passing years some quality of mellowness that does but add to their charm. But with suburbs it is otherwise. Whatever charm they have appertains to their garish youth and shares its ephemeral character. Cities and towns grow venerable with age, the suburb merely grows shabby.

The above profound reflections were occasioned by my approach to the vicinity of Jacob Street, Hampstead Road, and by a growing sense of the drab – not to say sordid – atmosphere that enveloped it, and its incongruity with the appearance and manner of the lady whose residence I was approaching. However, I consoled myself with the consideration that if "Honesty lives in a poor house, like your fair pearl in your foul oyster," perhaps Beauty might make shift with no better lodging, and these cogitations having brought me to the factory-like gateway, I gave a brisk tug at the bell above the brass plate.

After a short interval the wicket was opened by my young acquaintance of the previous night, who greeted me with a sedate smile of recognition.

"Good afternoon," I said, holding out my hand. "I have just called to learn how your sister is. I hope she is not much the worse for her rather terrifying experiences last night."

"Thank you," he replied with quaint politeness, "she seems to be all right today. But the doctor won't let her do any work. He's fixed her arm in a sling. But won't you come in and see her, sir?"

I hesitated, dubious as to whether she would care to receive a stranger of her own class in these rather mean surroundings, but when he added, "She would like to see you, I am sure, sir," my scruples gave way to my very definite inclination and I stepped through the wicket.

My young friend – who wore a blue linen smock – conducted me down a paved passage, the walls of which bore each a long shelf on which was a row of plaster busts and statuettes, into an open yard in which a small, elderly man was working with chisel and mallet on a somewhat ornate marble tombstone, amidst a sort of miniature Avebury of blocks and slabs of stone and marble. Across the yard rose a great barn-like building with one enormous window high up the wall, a great double door, and a small side door. Into the latter my conductor entered and held it open for me, and as I passed in, I found myself in total darkness. Only for a moment, however, for my young host, having shut the door, drew aside a heavy curtain and gave me a view of huge, bare hall with lofty, whitewashed walls, an open timber roof, and a plank floor relieved from absolute nakedness by one or two rugs. A couple of studio easels stood opposite the window, and in a corner I observed a spectral lay-figure shrouded in what looked like a sheet. At the farther end, by a large, open fireplace, Miss Blake sat in an easy-chair with a book in her hand. She looked up as I entered, and then rose and advanced to meet me, holding out her left hand.

"How kind of you, Mr. Anstey, to come and see me!" she exclaimed. "And how good it was of you to take such care of me last night!"

"Not at all," I replied. "But I hope you are not very much the worse for your adventures. Are you suffering much pain?"

"I have no pain at all," she replied with a smile, "and I don't believe this sling is in the least necessary. But one must obey the doctor's orders."

"Yes," interposed her brother, "and that is what the sling is for. To prevent you from getting into mischief, Winnie."

"It prevents me from doing any work, if that is what you mean, Percy," said she, "and I suppose the doctor is right in that."

"I am sure he is," said I. "Rest is most essential to enable the wound to heal quickly. What sort of night did you have?"

"I didn't sleep much," she replied. "It kept coming back to me, you know – that awful moment when I went into the museum and saw that poor man lying on the floor. It was a dreadful experience. So horribly sudden, too. One moment I saw him go away, full of life and energy, and the next I was looking on his corpse. Do you think those wretches will really escape?"

"It is difficult to say. The police have the fingerprints of one of them, and if that person is a regular criminal, they will be able to identify him."

"Will they really?" she exclaimed. "It sounds very wonderful. How are they able to do it?"

"It is really quite simple. When a man is convicted of a crime, a complete set of his fingerprints is taken at the prison by pressing his fingers on an inked slab and putting them down on a sheet of paper – there is a special form for the purpose with a space for each finger. This form is deposited, with photographs of the prisoner, in one of the files of the Habitual Criminals Registry at Scotland Yard. Then, when a strange fingerprint turns up, it is compared with those in the files, and if one is found that is an exact facsimile, the name attached to it is the name of the man who is wanted."

"But how are they ever able to find the facsimile in such a huge collection, for the numbers in the files must be enormous?"

"That also is more simple than it looks. The lines on fingertips form very definite patterns-spirals, or whorls, closed loops like the end grain of wood, open curves, or arches, and so on. Now each fingerprint is filed under its particular heading – whorl, loop, arch, etc. – and also in accordance with the particular finger that bears the pattern, so the inquiry is narrowed down to a comparatively small number from the start. Let us take an instance. Suppose we have found some fingerprints of which the left little finger has a spiral pattern and the ring finger adjoining has a closed loop. Then we look in the file which contains the spiral left little fingers and in the file of looped left ring fingers, and we glance through the lists of names. There will be certain names that will appear in both lists, and one of those will be the name of the man that we want. All that remains is to compare our prints with each of them in turn until we come to the one that is an exact facsimile. The name attached to that one is the name of our man. Of course, in practice, the process is more elaborate, but that is the principle."

"It is wonderfully ingenious," said Miss Blake, "and really simple, as you say, and it sounds as if it were perfectly infallible."

"That is the claim that the police make. But, as you see, the utility of the system for the detection of crime is limited to the cases of those criminals whose fingerprints have been registered. That is what our chance depends on now. The man who murdered Mr. Drayton left prints of his fingers on the glass of the cabinet, and the police have taken the glass away to examine. If they find facsimiles of those fingerprints in the register, then they will know who murdered Mr. Drayton. But if those fingerprints are not in the register, they won't help us at all. And as far as I know, there is no other clue to the identity of the murderer."

Miss Blake appeared to reflect earnestly on what I had said, and in the ensuing silence I continued my somewhat furtive observation of the great studio and its occupants. Particularly did I notice a number of paintings, apparently executed in tempera on huge sheets of brown paper, pinned on the walls somewhat above the level of the eye, figure subjects of an allegorical character, strongly recalling the manner of Burne-Jones, and painted with something considerably beyond ordinary competence. And from the paintings my eye strayed to the painter – as I assumed and hoped her to be – and a very striking and picturesque figure she appeared, with her waxen complexion, delicately tinged with pink, her earnest grey eyes, a short, slightly *retrousse* nose, the soft mass of red-gold hair and the lissom form, actually full and plump though with the deceptive appearance of slimness that one notes in the figures of the artist whose style she followed. I noted with pleasure – not wholly aesthetic, I suspect – the graceful pose into which she seemed naturally to fall, and when my roving eye took in a "planchette" hanging on the wall and a crystal ball reposing on a black velvet cushion on a little altar-like table in a corner, I forbore to scoff inwardly as I should have done in other circumstances, for somehow the hint of occultism, even of superstition, seemed not out of character. She reminded me of the Lady of Shalott, and the whispered suggestion of Merlinesque magic gave a note of harmony that sounded pleasantly.

While we had been talking, her brother had been pursuing his own affairs with silent concentration, though I had noticed that he had paused to listen to my exposition on the subject of fingerprints. In the middle of the studio floor was a massive stone slab – a relic of some former sculptor tenant – and on this the boy was erecting, very methodically, a model of some sort of building with toy bricks of a kind that I had not seen before. I was watching him and noting the marked difference between him and his sister – for he was a somewhat dark lad with a strong, aquiline face – when Miss Blake spoke again.

"Did you find out what had been stolen?"

"Yes," I answered, "approximately. There was nothing missing of any considerable value. Only a few pieces had been taken, and those were mostly simple jewels set with moonstones or cat's eyes."

"Cat's eyes!" she exclaimed.

"Yes, a few posy-rings, some earrings and, I think, one pendant."

"Was the pendant stolen?"

"Yes, apparently. Sir Lawrence mentioned a cat's-eye pendant as one of the things that he missed from the drawer. Does the pendant interest you specially?"

"Yes." she answered thoughtfully. "It was this pendant that I went there to see. It was illustrated in the *Connoisseur* article, and I wrote to poor Mr. Drayton because I wanted to examine it. And so," she added in a lower tone and with an expression of deep sadness, "the pendant became, through me, the cause of his death. But for it and me, he would not have gone to the house at that time."

"It is impossible to say whether he would or not," said I, and then, to change the subject, as this seemed to distress her, I continued. "There was another thing missing that was figured in the *Connoisseur* – a locket – "

"Of course!" she exclaimed. "How silly of me to forget it." She rose hastily, and stepping over to an old walnut bureau that stood under the window, pulled out one of the little drawers and picked some small object out of it.

"There," she said, holding out her hand, in which lay a small gold locket, "this is the one. I recognised it instantly. And now see if you can guess how it came into my possession."

I was completely mystified, and said so, though I hazarded a guess that it had in some way caught in her clothing.

"Yes," said she, "it was in my shawl. You remember I said that the man whom I was trying to hold had something in his hand and that he must have dropped it when he drew his knife. Now it happened that my shawl had just then slipped off in the struggle and that he was standing on it. The locket must have dropped on the shawl, and this little brass hook, which someone has fastened to the ring of the locket, must have hooked itself into the meshes of the shawl – which is of crocheted silk, you will remember. Then you picked the shawl up and rolled it into a bundle, and it was never unrolled until this morning. When I shook it out to hang it up, the locket fell out, and most unfortunately, as it fell it opened and the glass inside got broken. I am most vexed about it, for it is such an extremely charming little thing. Don't you think so?"

I took the little bauble in my hand, and, to speak the literal truth, was not deeply smitten with its appearance. But policy, and the desire to make myself agreeable, bade me dissemble. "It is a quaint and curious little object," I admitted.

"It is a perfectly fascinating little thing," she exclaimed enthusiastically. "And so secret and mysterious, too. I am sure there is some hidden meaning in those references inside, and then there is something delightfully cabalistic and magical about that weird-looking inscription on the front."

"Yes," I agreed, "Greek capitals make picturesque inscriptions, especially this uncial form of lettering, but there is nothing very recondite in the matter, in fact it is rather hackneyed. '*Life is short but Art is long*'."

"So that is what it means. Percy couldn't quite make it out, and I don't know any Greek at all. But it is a beautiful motto, though I am not sure that I don't prefer the more usual form, '*Art is long but Life is short*'."

"That is the Latin version, '*Ars longa, Vita brevis*'. Yes, I think I agree with you. The Latin form is rather more epigrammatic. But what other inscription were you referring to?"

610

"There are some references to passages of Scripture inside. I have looked them out, all but one. Shall I get my notes and let you see what the references are?" She looked at me so expectantly and with such charming animation that I assented eagerly. Not that I cared particularly what the references were, but the occupation of looking them out promised to put us on a delightfully companionable footing. And if I was not profoundly interested in the locket, I found myself very deeply interested in the Lady of Shalott.

While she was searching for her notes, I examined the little bauble more closely. It was a simple trinket, well made and neatly finished. The workmanship was plain, though very solid, and I judged it to be of some considerable age, though not what one would call antique. It was fashioned in the form of a tiny book with a hinge at the back and a strong loop of gold on each half, the two loops forming a double suspension ring. To one of the loops a small brass hook had been attached, probably to hang it in a show-case. On the front was engraved in bold Greek uncials "*O BIOC BPAXYO H AE TEXNH MAKPH*" without any other ornament, and on turning the locket over I found the back – or under-side as a bookbinder would say – quite plain save for the hallmark near the top. Then I opened the little volume. In the back half was a circular cell, framed with a border of small pearls and containing a tiny plait of black hair coiled into a close spiral. It had been enclosed by a glass cover, but this was broken and only a few fragments remained. The interior of the front half was covered with extremely minute engraved lettering which, on close inspection, appeared to be references to certain passages of Holy Scripture, the titles of the books being given in Latin.

I had just concluded these observations when Miss Blake returned with a manuscript book, a Bible, and a small reading-glass.

"This," she said, handing me the latter, "will help you to make out the tiny lettering. If you will read out the references one at a time, I will read out the passages that they refer to. And if any of them suggest to you any meaning beyond what is apparent, do, please, tell me, for I can make nothing of them."

I promised to do so, and focusing the glass on the microscopic writing, read out the first reference, "*Leviticus 25:41*".

"That verse," she said, "reads: '*And then shall he depart from thee, both he and his children with him, and shall return unto his own family, and unto the possession of his fathers shall he return.*'"

"The next reference," said I, "is "*Psalms 121:1*.""

"The reading is: '*I will lift up mine eyes unto the hills, from whence cometh my help.*' What do you make of that?"

"Nothing," I replied, "unless one can regard it as a pious exhortation, and it is extraordinarily indefinite at that."

"Yes, it does seem vague, but I feel convinced that it means more than it seems to, if we could only fathom its significance."

"It might easily do that," said I, and as I spoke I caught the eye of her brother, who had paused in his work and was watching us with an indulgent smile, and I wondered egotistically if he was writing me down a consummate ass.

"The next," said I, "is *Acts 10:5*."

"The reading is: '*And now send men to Joppa, and call for one Simon, whose surname is Peter.*'"

"I begin to think you must be right," said I, "for that passage is sheer nonsense unless it covers something in the nature of a code. Taken by itself, it has not the faintest bearing on either doctrine or morals. Let us try the next one, *Nehemiah 8:4*."

"That one is just as cryptic as the others," said she. "It reads, '*And Ezra the scribe stood upon a pulpit of wood, which they had made for the purpose, and beside him stood Mattithiah, and Shema, and Anaiah, and Urijali, and Hilkiah, and Maaseiah, on his right hand, and on his left hand, Pedaiah, and Mishad, and Malchiah, and Hashum, and Hashbadana, Zechariah, and Meshullam.*'"

At this point an audible snigger proceeding from the direction of the builder revived my misgivings. There is something slightly alarming about a schoolboy with an acute perception of the ridiculous.

"What is the joke, Percy?" his sister asked.

"Those fellows' names, Winnie. Do you suppose there really was a chap called Hashed Banana?"

"Hashbadana, Percy," she corrected.

"Very well. Hashed Badada then. But that only makes it worse. Sounds as if you'd got a cold."

"What an absurd boy you are, Percy," exclaimed Miss Blake, regarding her brother with a fond smile. Then, reverting to her notes, she said, "The next reference appears to be a mistake, at least I don't understand it. It says '*3 Kings 7:41*'. Isn't that so?"

"Yes. '*3 Lib. Regum 7:41*'. But what is wrong with it?"

"Why, there are only two Books of Kings."

"Oh, I see. But it isn't a mistake. In the Authorised Version the two books of Samuel have the alternative title of the *First* and *Second Books of Kings*, and the *First Book of Kings* has the subtitle '*Commonly called the Third Book of the Kings*'. But at the present day the books are invariably referred to as the *First* and *Second Books of Samuel* and the *First* and *Second Books of Kings*. Shall we look it up?"

She opened the Bible and turned over the leaves to the *First Book of Kings*.

"Yes," she said, "it is as you say. How odd that I should never have noticed it, or at any rate, not have remembered it. Then this reference is really '*1 Kings 7. 41*'. And yet it can't be. What sense can you possibly make of this: '*The two pillars, and the two bowls of the chapters that were on the top of the two pillars, and the two networks, to cover the two bowls of the chapters which were upon the top of the pillars.*' It seems quite meaningless, separated from its context."

"It certainly is rather enigmatical," I agreed. "This is an excerpt from what was virtually an inventory of Solomon's Temple. If the purpose of this collection of Scripture texts was to inculcate some religious or moral truths, I don't see the bearing of this quotation at all. But we may take it that these passages had some meaning to the original owner of the locket."

"They must have had," she replied earnestly. "Perhaps we may be able to find the key to the riddle if we consider the whole series together."

"Possibly," I agreed, not very enthusiastically. "The next reference is *Psalms 31:7*."

"The verse is, '*I will be glad and rejoice in thy mercy, for thou hast considered my trouble, thou hast known my soul in adversities.*'"

"That doesn't throw much light on the subject," said I. "The last reference is *2 Timothy 4:13*."

"It reads: '*The cloak that I left at Troas with Carpus, when thou comest, bring with thee, and the books, but especially the parchments.*'" She laid down her notes and, looking at me with the most intense gravity, exclaimed, "Isn't that extraordinary? It is the most astonishing of them all. You see, it is perfectly trivial, just a message from St. Paul to Timothy on a purely personal matter of no importance to anybody but himself. But the whole collection of texts is very odd. They seem utterly unconnected with one another and, as you say, without any significance in respect of either faith or morals. What is your opinion of them?"

"I don't know what to think," I replied. "They may have had some significance to the original owner of the locket only, something personal and reminiscent. Or they may have been addressed to some other person in terms previously agreed on. That is to say, they may have formed something in the nature of a code."

"Exactly," she agreed eagerly. "That is what I think. And I am just devoured by curiosity as to what the message was that they were meant to convey. I shan't rest until I have solved the mystery."

I smiled, and again my glance wandered to the planchette on the wall and the crystal ball on the table. Evidently my new and charming friend was an inveterate mystic, an enthusiastic explorer of the dubious regions of the occult and the supernormal. And though my own matter-of-fact temperament engendered little sympathy with such matters, I found in this very mysticism an additional charm. It seemed entirely congruous with her eminently picturesque personality.

But at this moment I became suddenly aware that I had made a most outrageously long visit and rose with profuse apologies for my disregard of time.

"There is no need to apologise," she assured me cordially. "It is most kind of you to have given so much time to a mere counterfeit invalid. But won't you stay and have tea with us? Can't you really? Well, I hope you will come and see us again when you can spare an hour. Oh, and hadn't I better give you this locket to hand to Sir Lawrence Drayton?"

"Certainly not," I replied. "You had better keep it until you see him, and perhaps in the interval you may be able to extract its secret. But I will tell him that it is in safe hands." I shook her hand warmly, and when I had made a brief inspection of Master Percy's building, that promising architect piloted me across the yard and finally launched me, with a hearty farewell and a cordial invitation to "come again soon", into the desert expanse of Jacob Street.

Chapter V
Mr. Halliburton's Mascot

Emerging into the grey and cheerless street, I sauntered towards the Hampstead Road and, having reached that thoroughfare, halted at the corner and looked at my watch. It was barely four o'clock, and as I had arranged to meet Thorndyke at the Euston Road corner at half-past-four, I had half-an-hour in which to cover something less than half-a-mile. I began to be regretful that I had refused the proffered tea, and when my leisurely progress brought me to the door of an establishment in which that beverage was dispensed, I entered and called for refreshment.

And as I sat by the shabby little marble-topped table, my thoughts strayed back to the great bare studio in Jacob Street and the strange, enigmatical, but decidedly alluring personality of its tenant. To say that I had been favourably impressed by her would be to understate the case. I found myself considering her with a degree of interest and admiration that no other woman had ever aroused in me. She was – or, at least, she appeared to me – a strikingly beautiful girl, but that was not the whole, or even the main, attraction. Her courage and strength of character, as shown in the tragic circumstances of the previous night, her refinement of manner and easy, well-bred courtesy, her intelligence and evident amiability, and her frank friendliness, without any sacrifice of dignity, had all combined to make her personality gracious and pleasant. Then there were the paintings. If they were her work, she was an artist of some talent. I had meant cautiously to inquire into that, but the investigation of the locket had excluded everything else. And the thought of the locket and the almost childish eagerness that she had shown to extract its (assumed) secret, led naturally to the planchette and the crystal globe. In general I was disposed to scoff at such things, but on her the mysticism and occultism – I would not call it superstition – seemed to settle naturally and to add a certain piquancy to her mediaeval grace. And so reflecting, I suddenly bethought me of the cat's eye pendant. What was the nature of her interest in that? At first I had assumed that she was a connoisseur in jewels, and possibly I was right. But her curious interest in the locket suggested other possibilities, and into these I determined to inquire on my next visit – for I had already decided that the friendly invitations should not find me unresponsive. In short, the Lady of Shalott had awakened in me a very lively curiosity.

My speculations and reflections very effectively filled out the spare half-hour and brought me on the stroke of half-past-four to the corner of the Euston Road, and I had barely arrived when I perceived the tall, upright figure of my colleague swinging easily up Tottenham Court Road. In a few moments he joined me, and we both turned our faces westward.

"We needn't hurry," said he. "I said I would be there at five."

"I don't quite understand what you are going for," said I. "This man, Halliburton, seems to have been no more than a chance stranger. What do you expect to get out of him?"

"I have nothing definite in my mind," he replied. "The whole case is in the air at present. The position is this: A murder has been committed and the murderers have got away almost without leaving a trace. If the fingerprint people cannot identify the one man, we may say that we have no clue to the identity of either. But that murder had certain antecedents. Halliburton's visit was one of them, though there was probably no causal relation."

"You don't suspect Halliburton?"

"My dear fellow, I suspect nobody. We haven't got as far as that. But we have to investigate everything, person, or circumstance that makes the smallest contact with the crime. But here is our destination, and I need not remark, Anstey, that our purpose is to acquire information, not to give it."

The Baltic Hotel was a large private house not far from the Great Central Station, distinguished from other private houses only by an open street door and by the name inconspicuously inscribed on the fanlight. As we ascended the steps and entered the hall, a short, pleasant-faced man emerged from an office and looked inquiringly from one of us to the other. "Dr. Thorndyke?" he asked.

"Yes," replied my colleague, "and I assume that you are the manager, Mr. Simpson. I must thank you for making the appointment, and hope I am not inconveniencing you."

"Not at all," rejoined the other. "I know your name very well, sir, and shall be delighted to give you any assistance that I can. I understand that you want Mr. Halliburton's address."

"If you have no objection, I should like to have it. I want to write to him."

"I can give it to you off-hand," said the manager. "It is Oscar Halliburton, Esquire, Wimbledon."

"That doesn't seem a very sufficient address," remarked Thorndyke.

"It is not," said the manager. "I had occasion to write to him myself and my letter was returned, marked '*Insufficiently addressed*'."

"Then, in effect, you have not got his address?"

"That is what it amounts to. Would you like to see the visitors' book? If you will step into my private office, I will bring it to you."

He showed us into his office, and in a few moments entered with the book, which he laid on the table and opened at the page on which the signature appeared.

"This does not appear to have been written with the hotel pen," Thorndyke remarked when he had glanced at the adjoining signatures.

"No," the manager agreed. "Apparently he used his own fountain pen."

"I see that this entry is dated the 13th of September. How long did he stay?"

"He left on the 16th of September – five days ago."

"And he received at least one letter while he was here?"

"Yes, one only, I believe. It came on the morning of the 16th, I remember, and he left in the evening."

"Do you know if he went out much while he was here?"

"No, he stayed indoors nearly all day, and he spent most of his time in the billiard-room practising fancy strokes."

"What sort of man was he – in appearance, for instance?"

"Well," said Simpson rather hesitatingly, "I didn't see much of him, and I see a good many people. I should say he was a biggish man, medium colour, and rather sunburnt."

"Any beard or moustache?"

"No, clean shaved and a good deal of hair – rather long, wanted a crop."

"Any distinctive accent or peculiarity of voice?"

"I didn't have much talk with him – nor did anybody else, I think. He was a gruffish, taciturn man. Nothing peculiar about his voice, and as to his accent, well, it was just ordinary, very ordinary, with perhaps just a trace of the cockney, but only a trace. It wasn't exactly the accent of an English gentleman."

"And that is all that you remember about him?"

"That is all."

"Would you have any objection to my taking a photograph of this signature?"

The manager looked rather dubious. "It would hardly do for it to be known – " he began, when Thorndyke interrupted.

"I suggest, Mr. Simpson, that whatever passes between us shall be regarded as strictly confidential on both sides. The least said, the soonest mended, you know."

"There's a good deal of truth in that, said the manager with a smile, "especially in the hotel business. Well, if that is understood, I don't know that I have any objection to your taking a photograph. But how are you going to manage it?"

"I have a camera," replied Thorndyke, "and I see that your table lamp is a sixty-watt. It won't take an unreasonably long exposure."

He propped the book up in a suitable position and, having arranged the lamp so as to illuminate the page obliquely, produced from his pocket a small folding camera and a leather case of dark slides, at which Mr. Simpson gazed in astonishment. "You'll never get a useful photograph with a toy like that," said he.

"Not such a toy as you think," replied Thorndyke as he opened the little instrument. "This lens is specially constructed for close-range work, and will give me the signature the full size of the original." He laid a measuring tape on the table, and having adjusted the camera by its engraved scale, inserted the dark slide, looked at his watch, and opened the shutter.

"You were saying just now, Mr. Simpson," he resumed as we sat round the table watching the camera, "that you had occasion to write to Mr. Halliburton. Should I be indiscreet if I were to ask what the occasion was?"

"Not at all," replied the manager. "It was a ridiculous affair. It seems that Mr. Halliburton had a sort of charm or mascot which he wore suspended by a gold ring from a cord under his waistcoat – a silly little bone thing, of no value whatever, though he appears to have set great store by it. Well, after he had left the hotel he missed it. The ring had broken and the thing had dropped off the cord – presumably, he supposed, when he was undressing. So a couple of days later – on the eighteenth – back he came in a rare twitter to know if it had been picked up. I asked the chambermaids if any of them had found the mascot in his room or elsewhere, but none of them had. Then he was frightfully upset and begged me to ask them again and to say that he would give ten pounds to anyone who should have found it and would hand it to him. Ten pounds!" Mr. Simpson repeated with contemptuous emphasis. "Just think of it! The price of a gold watch for a thing that looked like a common rabbit bone! Why, a man like that oughtn't to be at large."

I could see that my colleague was deeply interested, though his impassive face suggested nothing but close attention. He put away his watch, closed the lens-shutter and the dark slide, and finally bestowed the little apparatus in his pocket. Then he asked the manager, "Can you give us anything like a detailed description of this mascot?"

"I can show you the thing itself," replied Simpson. "That is the irony of the affair. Mr. Halliburton hadn't been out of the house half-an-hour when the boy who looks after the billiard-room came bursting into my office in the devil's own excitement. He had heard of the ten pounds reward and had proceeded at once to take up all the rugs and mats in the billiard-room, and there, under the edge of a strip of cocoa-nut matting, he had found the precious thing. No doubt the ring had broken when Halliburton was leaning over the table to make a long shot. So I took it from the boy and put it in the safe, and I wrote forthwith to the address given in the book to say that the mascot had come to light, but, as I told you just now, the letter was returned marked '*Insufficiently addressed*'. So there it is, and unless he calls again, or writes, he won't get his mascot, and the boy won't get his ten pounds. Would you like to see the treasure?"

"I should, very much," replied Thorndyke, whereupon the manager stepped over to a safe in the corner of the room and, having unlocked it, came back to the table holding a small object in the palm of his hand.

"There it is," said he, dropping it on the table before Thorndyke, "and I think you will agree with me that it is a mighty dear ten pounds' worth."

I looked curiously at the little object as my colleague turned it about in his hand. It was evidently a bone of some kind, roughly triangular in shape and perforated by three holes, one large and two smaller. In addition to these, a fourth hole had been drilled through near the apex to take a gold suspension ring, and this was still in position, though it was broken, having chafed quite thin with wear in one part and apparently given way under some sudden strain. The surface of the bone was covered with minute incised carving of a simple and rather barbaric type, and the whole bone had been stained a deep, yellowish brown, which had worn lighter in the parts most exposed to friction, and the entire surface had that unmistakable polish and patina that comes with years of handling and wear.

"What do you make of it, sir?" asked Mr. Simpson.

"It is the neck bone of some small animal," Thorndyke replied. "But not a rabbit. And, of course, the markings on it give it an individual character."

"Would you give ten pounds for it?" the manager asked with a grin.

"I am not sure that I wouldn't," Thorndyke replied "though not for its intrinsic value. But yours is not a 'firm offer'. You are not a vendor. But I should like very much to borrow it for a few hours."

"I don't quite see how I could agree to that," said Simpson. "You see, the thing isn't mine. I'm just a trustee. And Mr. Halliburton might call and ask for it at any moment."

"I would give you a receipt for it and undertake to let you have it back by ten o'clock tomorrow morning," said Thorndyke.

"M'yes," said Simpson reflectively and with evident signs of weakening. "Of course, I could say I had deposited it at my bank. But is it of any importance? Would you mind telling me why you want to borrow the thing?"

"I want to compare it carefully with some similar objects, the existence of which are known to me. I could do that tonight and, if necessary, send the specimen back forthwith. As to the importance of the comparison, who can say? If Halliburton should turn up and give a practicable address, there would be nothing in it. But if he should never reappear and it should become necessary to trace him, the information gathered from an exhaustive examination of this object might be of great value."

"I see," said Simpson. "In a sense it is a matter of public policy. Of course that puts a different complexion on the affair. And having regard to your position and character, I don't see why I shouldn't agree to your having a short loan of the thing. But I should like to have it back by nine o'clock tomorrow morning, if you could manage it."

"I promise you that it shall be delivered into your hand by a responsible person not later than nine o'clock," said Thorndyke. "I will now give you a receipt, which I will ask you to hand to my messenger in exchange for your property, and again, Mr. Simpson, I would suggest that we make no confidences to anyone concerning this transaction."

To this the manager assented with decided emphasis, and our business being now concluded, we thanked Mr. Simpson warmly for his courtesy and his very helpful attitude and took our departure.

"You seem extraordinarily keen about that precious bone, Thorndyke," I remarked as we walked back along the Marylebone Road, "but I'm hanged if I see why. It won't tell you much about Halliburton. And if it would, I don't quite see what you want to know. He is obviously a fool. You don't need much investigation to ascertain that, and like most fools, he seems easily parted from his money. What more do you want to know?"

"My learned friend," replied Thorndyke, "is not profiting sufficiently by his legal experience. One of the most vital principles that years of practice have impressed on me is that in the early stages of an inquiry, no fact – relevant or irrelevant, that is in any way connected with the subject of the inquiry – should be neglected or ignored. Indeed, no such fact can be regarded as irrelevant, since, until all the data are assembled and collated, it is impossible to judge the bearing or value of anyone of them.

"Take the present case. Who is Mr. Halliburton? We don't know. Why did he want to examine Mr. Drayton's collection? We don't know. What passed between him and Mr. Drayton when he made his visit? Again we don't know. Perhaps there is nothing of any significance to know. The probability is that Halliburton has no connection with this case at all. But there is no denying that he is in the picture."

"Yes, as a background figure. His name has been mentioned as one of the visitors who had come to see the collection. There were other visitors, you remember."

"Yes, and if we knew who they were we should want to know something about them, too. But Halliburton is the only one known to us. And your presentation of his position in relation to what has happened does not state the case fairly at all. The position is really this: Halliburton – a complete stranger to Drayton – took considerable trouble to obtain an opportunity to examine the collection. Why did he do this? You have quoted Mrs. Benham as saying that he apparently knew nothing about jewellery, either ancient or modern. He was not a connoisseur. Then, why did he want to see the collection? Again, he wrote for the appointment, not from his own residence but from an hotel, and when we come to that hotel we find that he has left no verifiable address, and the vague locality that he gave may quite possibly be a false address. And further, that this apparent concealment of his place of abode coincides with a very excellent reason for giving a correct address, the fact that he has lost – and lost in the hotel, as he believes – certain property on which he sets a high value. And if you add to this the facts that within four days of his visit to Drayton the collection was robbed, that the robbers clearly knew exactly where it was kept and had some knowledge of the inmates of the house and their habits, you must admit that Halliburton is something more than a background figure in the picture."

I was secretly impressed by the way in which Thorndyke had "placed' Mr. Halliburton in respect of the inquiry, but, of course, it wouldn't do to say so. It was necessary to assert my position.

"That," I replied, "is the case for the prosecution, and very persuasively stated. On the other hand, it might be said for the defence, 'Here is a gentleman who lives in the country and who comes up to spend a few days in town – '"

"For the apparent purpose," Thorndyke interrupted, "of practising the art of billiards, a sport peculiar to London."

"Exactly. And while he is in London, he takes the opportunity of inspecting a collection which has been described in the Press. A few days after his visit, the collection is robbed by some persons who have probably also seen the published description. There is no positive fact of any kind that connects him with those persons, and I assert that the assumption that any such connection exists is entirely gratuitous."

Thorndyke smiled indulgently. "It seems a pity," he remarked, "that my learned friend should waste the sweetness of his jury flourishes on the desert air of Marylebone Road. But we needn't fash ourselves, as I believe they say in the North. There was a lady named Mrs. Glasse whose advice to cooks seems to be applicable to the present case. We had better catch our hare before we proceed to jug him – the word "jug' being used without any malicious intent to perpetrate a pun."

"And do I understand that the capture is to be accomplished by the agency of the rabbit-bone that my learned senior carries in his reverend pocket?"

"If you do," replied Thorndyke, "your understanding is a good deal in advance of mine. I am taking this little object to examine merely on the remote chance that it may yield some information as to this man's antecedents, habits, and perhaps even his identity. The chance is not so remote as it looks. There are very few things which have been habitually carried on a man's person which will not tell you something about the person who has carried them. And this object, as you probably noticed, is in many respects highly characteristic."

"I can't say that I found the thing itself particularly characteristic. The fact that the man should have carried it and have set such a ridiculous value on it is illuminating. That writes him down a superstitious ass. But superstitious asses form a fairly large class. In what respects do you find this thing so highly characteristic, and what kind of information do you expect to extract from it?"

"As to the latter question," he replied, "an investigator doesn't form expectations in advance, and as to the former, you will have an opportunity of examining the object for yourself and of forming your own conclusions."

I determined to make a minute and exhaustive inspection of our treasure trove as soon as we arrived home, for obviously I had missed something. It was clear to me that Thorndyke attached more importance to this object than would have been warranted by anything that I had observed. There was some point that I had overlooked and I meant to find out what it was.

But the opportunity did not offer immediately, for, on our arrival at his chambers, Thorndyke proceeded straight up to the laboratory where we found his assistant, Polton, seated at a jeweller's bench, making some structural alterations in a somewhat elaborate form of pedometer.

"I've got a job for you, Polton," said Thorndyke, laying the mascot on the bench. "Quite a nice, delicate little job, after your own heart. I want a replica of this thing – as perfect as you can make it. And I have to return the original before nine o'clock tomorrow morning. And," he added, taking the camera and dark slides from his pocket, "there is a photograph to be developed, but there is no particular hurry for that."

Polton picked the mascot up daintily, and laying it in the palm of his hand, stuck a watchmaker's glass in his eye and inspected it minutely.

"It's a queer little thing, sir," he remarked. "Seems to have been made out of a small cervical vertebra. I suppose you want the copy of the same colour as this and as hard as possible?"

"I want as faithful a copy as you can make, similar in all respects, excepting that the reproduction can scarcely be as hard as the original. Will there be time to make a gelatine mould?"

"There'll have to be, sir. It couldn't be done any other way, with these undercuttings. But I shan't lose any time on that. If I have to match the colour I shall have to make some experiments, and I can do those while the gelatine is setting."

"Very well, Polton," said Thorndyke. "Then I'll leave the thing in your hands and consider it as good as done. Of course the original must not be damaged in any way."

"Oh, certainly not, sir," and forthwith the little man, having carefully deposited the mascot in a small, glass-topped box on the bench, fell to work on his preparations beaming with happiness. I have never seen a man who enjoyed his work so thoroughly as Polton did.

"I am going round to The College of Surgeons now," said Thorndyke. "No callers are expected, I think, but if anyone should come and want to see me, I shall be back in about an hour. Are you coming with me, Anstey?"

"Why not? I've nothing to do, and if I keep an eye on you I may pick up a crumb or two of information."

Here I caught Polton's eye, and a queer, crinkly smile overspread that artificer's countenance. "A good many people try to do that, sir," he remarked. "I hope you will have better luck than most of them have."

"It occurs to me," Thorndyke observed as we descended the stairs, "that if the scribe who wrote *The Book of Genesis* had happened to look in on Polton, he would have come to the conclusion that he had grossly overestimated the curse of labour."

"He was not much different from most other scribes," said I. "A bookish man – like myself, for instance – constantly fails to appreciate the joy of manual work. I find Polton an invaluable object lesson."

"So do I," said Thorndyke. "He is a shining example of the social virtues – industry, loyalty, integrity, and contentment – and as an artificer he is a positive genius." With this warm appreciation of his faithful follower, he swung round into Fleet Street and crossed towards the Law Courts.

Chapter VI
Introduces an Ant-eater
and a Detective

As we entered the hall of The College of Surgeons, Thorndyke glanced at the board on which the names of the staff were painted and gave a little grunt of satisfaction.

"I see," he said, addressing the porter, "that Mr. Saltwood hasn't gone yet."

"No, sir," was the reply. "He is working up at the top tonight. Shall I take you up to him?"

"If you please," answered Thorndyke, and the porter accordingly took us in charge and led the way to the lift. From the latter we emerged into a region tenanted by great earthenware pans and jars and pervaded by a curious aroma, half-spirituous, half-cadaveric, on which I commented unfavourably.

"Yes," said Thorndyke, sniffing appreciatively, "the good old museum bouquet. You smell it in all curators' rooms, and though, I suppose, it is not physically agreeable, I find it by no means unpleasant. The effects of odours are largely a matter of association."

"The present odour," said I, "seems to suggest the association of a very overripe Duke of Clarence and a butt of shockingly bad malmsey."

Thorndyke smiled tolerantly as we ascended a flight of stairs that led to a yet higher storey, and abandoned the discussion. At the top, we passed through several long galleries, past ranges of tables piled up with incredible numbers of bones, apparently awaiting disposal, until we were finally led by our conductor to a room in which two men were working at a long bench, on which were several partially articulated skeletons of animals. They both looked up as we entered, and one of them, a keen-faced, middle-aged man, exclaimed, "Well, this is an unexpected pleasure. I haven't seen you for donkey's years, Thorndyke. Thought you had deserted the old shop. And I wonder what brings you here now."

"The usual thing, Saltwood. Self-interest. I have come to negotiate a loan. Have you got any loose bones of the Echidna?"

Saltwood stroked his chin and turned interrogatively to his assistant. "Do you know if there are any, Robson?" he asked.

"There is a set waiting to be articulated, sir. Shall I fetch them?"

"If you would, please, Robson," replied Saltwood. Then turning to my colleague, he asked, "What bones do you want, Thorndyke?"

"The middle cervical vertebrae – about the third or fourth," was the reply, at which I pricked up my ears.

In a few minutes Robson returned carrying a cardboard box on which was a label inscribed "*Echidna hystrix*".

Saltwood lifted the lid, disclosing a collection of small bones, including a queer little elongated skull.

"Here you are," said he, picking out a sort of necklace formed of the joints of the backbone, "here is the whole vertebral column, minus the tail, strung together. Will you take it as it is?"

"No," replied Thorndyke, "I will just take the three vertebrae that I want – the third, fourth, and fifth cervical – and if I let you have them back in the course of the week, will that do?"

"Perfectly. I wouldn't bother you to return them at all if it were not for spoiling the set." He separated the three little bones from the string, and having wrapped them in tissue paper and handed them to Thorndyke, asked, "How is Jervis? I haven't seen him very lately, either."

"Jervis," replied Thorndyke, "is at present enjoying a sort of professional holiday in New York. He is retained, in an advisory capacity, in the Rosenbaum case, of which you may have read in the papers. My friend Anstey here is very kindly filling his place during his absence."

"I'm glad to hear that I'm filling it," said I, as Saltwood bowed and shook hands. "I was afraid I was only half-filling it, being but a mere lawyer destitute of medical knowledge."

"Well," said Saltwood, "medical knowledge is important, of course, but you've always got Thorndyke to help you out. Oh – and that reminds me, Thorndyke, that I've got some new preparations that I should like you to see, a series of tumours from wild animals. Will you come and have a look at them? They are in the next room."

Thorndyke assented with enthusiasm, and the two men went out of the room, leaving me to the society of Robson and the box of bones. Into the latter I peered curiously, again noting the odd shape of the skull, then I proceeded to improve the occasion by a discreet question or two.

"What sort of beast is an Echidna?" I asked.

"*Echidna hystrix*," replied Robson in a somewhat pompously didactic tone, "is the zoological name of the porcupine ant-eater."

"Indeed," said I, and then tempted by his owlish solemnity to ask foolish questions, I inquired, "Does that mean that he is an eater of porcupine ants?"

"No, sir," he replied gravely. (He was evidently a little slow in the uptake.) "It is not the ants which are porcupines. It is the ant-eater."

626

"But," I objected, "how can an ant-eater be a porcupine? It is a contradiction in terms."

This seemed to floor him for a moment, but he pulled himself together and explained, "The name signifies a porcupine which resembles an ant-eater, or perhaps one should say, an ant-eater which resembles a porcupine. It is a very peculiar animal."

"It must be," I agreed. "And what is there peculiar about its cervical vertebrae?"

He pondered profoundly, and I judged that he did not know but was not going to give himself away, a suspicion that his rather ambiguous explanation tended to confirm.

"The cervical vertebrae," he expounded, "are very much alike in most animals. There are exceptions, of course, as in the case of the porpoise, which has no neck, and the giraffe, which has a good deal of neck. But in general, cervical vertebrae seem to be turned out pretty much to one pattern, whereas the tail vertebrae present great differences. Now, if you look at this animal's tail – " Here he fished a second necklace out of the box and proceeded to expound the peculiarities of its constituent bones, to which exposition I am afraid I turned an inattentive ear. The Echidna's tail had no bearing on the identity of Mr. Halliburton.

The rather windy discourse had just come to an end when my two friends reappeared and Saltwood conducted us down to the hall. As we stepped out of the lift he shook our hands heartily, and with a cheery *adieu*, pressed the button and soared aloft like a stage fairy.

From the great portico of the College we turned eastward and walked homewards across Lincoln's Inn, each of us wrapped in his own reflections. Presently I asked, "Supposing this mascot of Halliburton's to be the neck bone of an echidna, what is the significance of the fact?"

"Ah!" he replied. "There you have me, Anstey. At present I am concerning myself only with the fact, hoping that its significance may appear later. To us it may have no significance at all. Of course there is some reason why this particular bone should have been used rather than some other kind of bone, but that set of circumstances may have – probably has – no connection with our inquiry. It is quite probable that Halliburton himself has no such connection. On the other hand, the circumstances which determined the use of an echidna's vertebra as a mascot may have an important bearing on the case. So we can only secure the fact and wait for time and further knowledge to show whether it is or is not a relevant fact."

"And do you mean to say that you are taking all this trouble on the mere chance that this apparently trivial and meaningless circumstance may possibly have some bearing?"

"That is so. But your question, Anstey, exhibits the difference between the legal and the scientific outlook. The lawyer's investigations tend to proceed along the line of information wanted. The scientists tend to proceed along the line of information available. The business of the man of science is impartially to acquire all the knowledge that is obtainable. The lawyer tends to concern himself only with that which is material to the issue."

"Then the scientist must accumulate a vast number of irrelevant facts."

"Every fact," replied Thorndyke, "is relevant to something, and if you accumulate a great mass of facts, inspection of the mass shows that the facts can be sorted out into related groups from which certain general truths can be inferred. The difference between the lawyer and the scientist is that one is seeking to establish some particular truth while the other seeks to establish any truth that emerges from the available facts."

"But," I objected "surely even a scientist must select his facts to some extent. Every science has its own province. The chemist, for instance, is not concerned with the metamorphoses of insects."

"That is true," he admitted. "But then, are we not keeping within our own province? We are not collecting facts indiscriminately, but are selecting those facts which make some sort of contact with the circumstances of this crime and which may therefore conceivably be relevant to our inquiry. But methinks I perceive another collector. Isn't that our friend Superintendent Miller crossing to King's Bench Walk and apparently bearing down on our chambers?"

I looked at the tall figure, indistinctly seen by the light of a lamp, and even as I looked, it ascended the steps and vanished into our entry, and when, a couple of minutes later, we arrived on our landing, we found Polton in the act of admitting the Superintendent.

"Well, gentlemen," the officer said genially, as he subsided into an armchair and selected a cigar from the box which Thorndyke handed to him "I've just dropped in to give you the news – about this Drayton case, you know. I thought you'd be interested to hear what our people are doing. Well, I don't think you need trouble yourselves about it anymore. We've got one of the men, at any rate."

"In custody?" asked Thorndyke.

"No, we haven't actually made the arrest, but there will be no difficulty about that. We know who he is. I just passed those fingerprints in to Mr. Singleton and he gave me the name straight away. And who do you think it is? It is our old friend, Moakey – Joe Hedges, you know."

"Is it really!" said Thorndyke.

628

"Yes, Moakey it is. You're surprised. So was I. I really did think he had learned a little sense at last, especially as he seemed to be taking some reasonable precautions last time. But he always was a fool. Do you remember the asinine thing that he did on that last job?"

"No," replied Thorndyke, "I don't remember that case."

"It was a small country house job, and Moakey did it all on his own. And it did look as if he had learned his lesson, for he undoubtedly wore gloves. We found them in his bag and there was not a trace at the house. But would you believe it, when he'd finished up, all neat and ship-shape, he must stop somewhere in the grounds to repack the swag – after he had taken his gloves off. Just then the alarm was raised and a dog let loose, and away went Moakey, like a hare, for the place in the fence where he had hidden his bicycle. He nipped over the fence, mounted his bike, and got clear away, and all trace of him seemed to be lost. But in the morning, when the local police came to search the grounds, they found a silver tray that Moakey had evidently had to drop when he heard the dog, with a most beautiful set of fingerprints on it. The police got a pair of photographs at once – there happened to be a dark room and a set of apparatus in the house – and sent a special messenger with them to Scotland Yard. And then the murder was out. They were Moakey's prints, and Moakey was arrested the same day with all the stuff in his possession. He hadn't had time to go to a fence with it. So the fingerprints didn't have to be put in evidence."

"Did Moakey ever hear about the fingerprints?" Thorndyke asked.

"Yes. Some fool of a warder told him. And that's what makes this case so odd, to think that after coming a cropper twice he should have gone dabbing his trademarks over the furniture as he has, is perfectly incredible. And that isn't the only queer feature in the case. There's the stuff. I got Sir Lawrence to show it to me this morning, and I assure you that when I saw what it was, you could have knocked me down with a feather. To say nothing of the crockery and wineglasses and rubbish of that sort, and the pewter spoons and brass spoons and bone bobbins, the jewellery was a fair knockout. There was only one cabinet of it, and you'll hardly believe me, Doctor, when I tell you that the greater part of it was silver, and even pinchbeck and brass – or latten, as Sir Lawrence calls it – set with the sort of stones that you can buy in Poland Street for ten-bob-a-dozen. You never saw such trash!"

"Oh come. Miller," Thorndyke protested, "don't call it trash. It is one of the most interesting and reasonable collections that I have ever seen."

"So it may be," said the Superintendent, "but I am looking at it from the trade point of view. Why, there isn't a fence outside Bedlam who'd give a fiver for the whole boiling. It's perfectly astonishing to me that an experienced tradesman like Moakey should have wasted his time on it. He might just as well have cracked an ironmonger's."

"I expect," said I, "he embarked on the job under a mistake. Probably he saw, or heard of, that article in the *Connoisseur* and thought that this was a great collection of jewels."

"That seems likely," Miller agreed. "And that may account for his having worked with a chum this time instead of doing the job single-handed as he usually does. But it doesn't account for his having used a pistol. That wasn't his way at all. There has never been a charge of violence against him before. I always took him for the good old-fashioned, sporting crook who played the game with us and expected us to play the game with him."

"Is it clear that it was Moakey who fired the shot?" asked Thorndyke.

"Well, no, I don't know that it is. But he'll have to stand the racket unless he can prove that somebody else did it. And that won't be so very easy, for even if he gives us the name of the other man – the small man – and Miss Blake can identify him, still it will be difficult for Moakey to prove that the other man fired the shot, and the other chap isn't likely to be boastful about it."

"No," said Thorndyke, "he will pretty certainly put it on to Moakey, But between the two we may get at the truth as to what happened."

"We will hope so," said Miller, rising and picking up his hat. "At any rate, that is how the matter stands. I understand that Sir Lawrence wants you to keep an eye on the case, but there's really no need. It isn't in your line at all. We shall arrest Moakey and he will be committed for trial. If he likes to make a statement we may get the other man, but in any case there is nothing for you to do."

For some minutes after the Superintendent's departure, Thorndyke sat looking into the fire with an air of deep reflection. Presently he looked up as if he had disposed of some question that he had been propounding to himself and remarked, "It's a curious affair, isn't it?"

"Very," I agreed. "It seems as if this man, Moakey, had thrown all precaution to the winds. By the way, do you suppose those fingerprint people ever make mistakes? They seem pretty cocksure."

"They would be more than human if they never made a mistake," Thorndyke replied. "But, on the other hand, the identification of a whole set of fingerprints doesn't leave much room for error. You might get two prints that were similar enough to admit of a mistake, but you would hardly get two sets that could be mistaken for one another."

"No, I suppose not. So the mystery remains unexplained."

"It remains unexplained in any case," said Thorndyke.

"How do you mean?" I asked. "If they had made a mistake and these were really the fingerprints of some unknown person, that person might be a novice and there would be no mystery about his having taken no precautions."

"Yes, but that is not the mystery. The real mystery is the presence of a third man who has left no other traces."

"A third man!" I exclaimed. "What evidence is there of the presence of a third man?"

"It is very obvious," replied Thorndyke. "These fingerprints are not those of the small man, because he wore gloves. And they are not the fingerprints of the tall man."

"How do you know that?" I asked.

Thorndyke rose, and opening a cabinet, took out the plaster cast of the tall man's left hand, which he had made on the previous night, and the pair of photographs.

"Now," said he, "look at the print of the left forefinger in the photograph. You see that the pattern is quite clear and unbroken. Now look at the cast of the forefinger. Do you see what I mean?"

"You mean that pit or dent in the bulb of the finger. But isn't that due to an irregularity of the ground on which the finger was pressed?"

"No, it is the puckered scar of an old whitlow or deep wound of some kind. It is quite characteristic. And the print of this finger would show a blank white space in the middle of the pattern. So it is certain that those fingerprints did not belong to either of these two men."

"Then, really," said I, "the fact that these are Moakey's fingerprints serves to explain this other mystery."

"To some extent. But you see, Anstey, that it introduces a further mystery. If there were *three* men in that room, or on the premises, how comes it that there were only *two* sets of footprints?"

"Yes, that is rather extraordinary. Can you suggest any explanation?"

"The only explanation that occurs to me is that one of these men may have let Moakey into the house by the front door, that he may have been in the room when Miss Blake entered – he might, for instance, have been behind the door – and have slipped out when she ran to the window. He could then have to run into the drawing-room and waited until she rushed out of the house, when it would be easy for him to slip out at the front door and escape."

"Yes," I said dubiously, "I suppose that is possible, but it doesn't sound very probable."

"It doesn't," he agreed. "But it is the only solution that I can think of at the moment. Of course there must be some explanation, for there are the facts. Inside the house are traces of three men. Outside are traces of only two. Have you any suggestion to offer?"

I shook my head. "It is beyond me, Thorndyke. Why didn't you ask Miller?"

"Because I am not proposing to take the police into my confidence until I have evidence that they are prepared to do the same by me. They will probably assume that the tall man was Moakey – he is about the same height. The information that we obtain from the cast of that man's hand is not, you must remember, in their possession."

"No, I had forgotten that. And now I begin to appreciate my learned senior's foresight in taking a permanent record of that handprint."

"Yes," said Thorndyke. "A permanent record is invaluable. It allows of reference at one's leisure and in connection with fresh evidence, as in the present case. And, moreover, it allows of study under the most favourable conditions. That scar on the finger was not noticeable in the impression in the sand, especially by the imperfect light of the lamp. But on the cast, which we can examine at our ease, by daylight if necessary, it is plainly visible. And we have it here to compare with the finger, if ever that finger should be forthcoming. I now make a rule of securing a plaster cast of any object that I cannot retain in my possession."

Here, as if in illustration of this last statement, Polton entered the room bearing a small tray lined with blotting paper, on which lay three objects – a diminutive glass negative and two mascots. He laid the tray on the table and invited us to inspect his works, tendering a watchmakers eyeglass to assist the inspection.

Thorndyke picked up the two mascots and examined them separately through the glass, then with a faint smile, but without remark, he passed the tray to me. I stuck the glass in my eye and scrutinised first one and then the other of the mascots, and finally looked up at Polton, who was watching me with a smile that covered his face with wrinkles of satisfaction.

"I suppose, Polton," I said, "You have some means of telling which is which, but I'm hanged if I can see a particle of difference."

"I can tell 'em by the feel, sir," he replied "but I took the precaution to weigh the original in the chemical balance before I made the copy. I think the colour matches pretty well."

"It is a perfect reproduction, Polton," said Thorndyke. "If we were to show it to Superintendent Miller he would want to take your fingerprints right away. He would say that you were not a safe person to be at large."

At this commendation, Polton's countenance crinkled until he looked like a species of human walnut, and when the photograph of the signature had been examined and pronounced fit for the making of an enlargement, he departed, chuckling audibly.

When he had gone, I picked up one of the mascots and again examined it closely while Thorndyke made a similar inspection of its twin.

"Had you any definite purpose in your mind," I asked "when you instructed Polton to make this indistinguishable copy?"

"No," he replied. "I thought it wise to preserve a record of the thing, but, for my own information, a plain plaster cast would have answered quite well. Still, as it would not take much more trouble to imitate the colour and texture, I decided that there might be some advantage in having a perfect replica. There are certain imaginable circumstances in which it might be useful. I shall get Polton to make a cast of the Echidna's vertebra, so that we may have the means of demonstrating the nature of the object to others, if necessary, and by the way, we may as well make the comparison now and confirm my opinion that the animal really was an Echidna."

He produced the little packet that Saltwood had given him and, laying the little bones on the table, compared them carefully with the mascot.

"Yes," he said at length, "I was right. Mr. Halliburton's treasure is the third cervical vertebra of a young but full-grown Echidna."

"How did you recognise this as an Echidna's vertebra?" I asked, recalling Mr. Robson's rather obscure exposition on the subject. "Aren't neck vertebrae a good deal alike in most animals?"

"In animals of the same class they are usually very much alike. But the Echidna is a transitional form. Although it is a mammal, it has many well-marked reptilian characters. This vertebra shows one of them. If you look at those corner-pieces – the transverse processes – you will see that they are separate from the rest of the bone, that they are joined to it by a seam or suture. But in all other mammals, with a single exception, the transverse processes are fused with the rest of the bone. There is no separating line. That suture was the distinguishing feature which attracted my attention."

"And does the fact of its being an Echidna's bone suggest any particular significance to your mind?"

"Well," he replied, "the Echidna is far from a common animal. And this particular bone seems to have been worked on by some barbarian artist, which suggests that it may have been originally a barbaric ornament or charm or fetish, which again suggests personal connections and a traceable history. You will notice that the two letters seem to have been impressed on the ornament and have no connection with it, which suggests that the bone was already covered with these decorations when it came into the late owner's possession."

I took up the glass and once more examined the mascot. The whole surface of the little bone, on both sides, was covered with an intricate mass of ornament consisting principally of scrolls or spirals, crude and barbaric in design but very minutely and delicately executed. In the centre of the solid part of the bone an extremely small "U" had been indented on one side and on the same spot on the reverse side an equally minute "H". And through the glass I could see that the letters cut into the pattern, whereas the hole for the suspension ring was part of the original work and was incorporated into the design.

"I wonder why he used small letters for his initials instead of capitals," said I.

"For the reason, I imagine, that they were small letters. He wanted them merely for identification, and no doubt wished them to be as inconspicuous as possible. Any letters are a disfigurement when they are not part of the design, and capitals would have been much worse than small letters."

"These seem to have been punched, on with printer's types." I remarked.

"They have been punched, not cut – but not, I should say, with printer's types. Type metal – even the hard variety which would be used for casting these little 'Pearl' or 'Diamond' types – is comparatively soft, and the harder varieties are brittle. It would scarcely be strong enough to bear hammering into bone. I should say these letters were indented with steel punches."

"Well," I said "we have got a vast amount of entertainment out of Mr. Halliburton and his mascot. But it looks rather as if that were going to be the end of it, for if Moakey is one of the robbers, we may take it that the others are just professional crooks. And thereupon Mr. Halliburton recedes once more into the background. Isn't that the position?"

"Apparently it is," replied Thorndyke. "But we shall see what happens at the inquest. Possibly some further evidence may be forthcoming when the witnesses give their accounts in detail. And possibly Moakey himself may be able to throw some further light on the matter. They will probably have him in custody within a day or two."

"By the way," I said, "have you examined the hair that poor Drayton had grasped in his hand?"

"Yes. There is nothing very characteristic about it. It is dark in colour and the hairs are rather small in diameter. But there was one slightly odd circumstance. Among the tuft of dark hairs there was one light one – not white – a blonde hair. It had no root and no tip. It was just a broken fragment. What do you make of that?"

"I don't know that I make anything of it. I understand that a man may sometimes find a woman's hair sticking to his coat in the neighbourhood of the shoulder or chest, though I have no personal experience of such things. But if on the coat, why not on the head? My learned senior's powerful constructive imagination might conceive circumstances in which such a transfer of hair might occur. Or has he some more recondite explanation?"

"There are other possible explanations," Thorndyke replied. "And as the hour seems to preclude a return to Hampstead tonight, and seems to suggest a temporary tenancy of Jervis's bedroom, I would recommend the problem for my learned friend's consideration while awaiting the approach of Morpheus or Hypnos, whichever deity he elects to patronize."

This gentle hint, enforced by a glance at my watch, brought our discussion to an end, and very shortly afterwards we betook ourselves to our respective sleeping apartments.

Chapter VII
The Vanished Heirloom

The tragic events at The Rowans had excited a considerable amount of public interest, and naturally that interest was manifested in a specially intense form by the residents in the locality. I realised this when, in obedience to the summons which had been left at my lodgings, I made my way to the premises adjoining the High Street in which the inquest was to be held. As I approached the building, I observed that quite a considerable crowd had gathered 'round the doors awaiting their opening, and noticed with some surprise the proportion of well-dressed women composing it.

Observing that the crowd contained no one whom I knew, I began to suspect that there was some other entrance reserved for authorised visitors, and was just looking round in search of it when the doors were opened and the crowd began to surge in, and at that moment I saw Miss Blake approaching. I waited for her to arrive, and when we had exchanged greetings, I proceeded to pilot her through the crowd, which passed in with increasing slowness, suggesting that the accommodation was already being somewhat taxed.

I was not the only person who observed the symptoms of a "full house". A woman whom I had already noticed making her way through the throng, with more skill and energy than politeness, came abreast of me just as I had struggled to the door and made a determined effort to squeeze past. Perhaps if she had been a different type of woman I might have accepted the customary masculine defeat, but her bad manners, combined with her unprepossessing appearance, banished any scruples of chivalry. She was a kind of woman that I dislike most cordially: Loudly dressed, flashy, scented like a civet cat, with glaring golden hair – manifestly peroxided, as was evident by her dark eyebrows – pencilled eyelids, and a coat of powder that stared even through her spotted veil. My gorge rose at her, and as she stuck her elbow in my ribs and made a final burst to get in before me, I maintained a stolid resistance.

"You must excuse me," I said, "but I am a witness, and so is this lady."

She cast a quick glance at me, and from me to Miss Blake, then – with a bad enough grace and without replying – she withdrew to let us pass, and ostentatiously turned her back on us.

The room was already crowded, but that was no concern of ours. We were present, and when our names should be called, the coroner's officer would do all that was necessary.

"I suppose," said Miss Blake, "we ought to have come in by another door. I see Sir Lawrence and Mrs. Benham are sitting by the table, and isn't that Dr. Thorndyke next to Sir Lawrence?"

"Yes," I replied. "I don't think he has been summoned, but, of course, he would be here to watch the case. I see Inspector Badger, too. I wonder if he is going to give evidence. Ah! You were right. There is another door. Here come the coroner and the jury. They will probably call you first as you are the principal witness, unless they begin with the medical evidence or Sir Lawrence. I see Dr. Nichols has just come in."

As the coroner and the jury took their seats at the table, the loud hum of conversation died away and an air of silent expectancy settled on the closely-packed audience. The coroner looked over a sheaf of type-written papers, and then opened the proceedings with a short address to the jury in which he recited the general facts of the case.

"And now, gentlemen," he said in conclusion, "we will proceed to take the evidence, and we had better begin with that of the medical witness."

Hereupon Dr. Nichols was called and, having been sworn, described the circumstances under which he was summoned to The Rowans on the night of the 20th of September, and the result of his subsequent examination of the body of the deceased. "The cause of death," he stated, "was a bullet-wound of the chest. The bullet entered on the right side between the third and fourth ribs, and passed completely through the chest, emerging on the left side of the back between the fourth and fifth ribs. In its passage it perforated the aorta – the greater central artery – and this injury might have produced almost instantaneous death."

"Could the wound have been self-inflicted?" the coroner asked.

"Under the circumstances, it could not, for although death was practically instantaneous, no weapon was discovered. If the injury had been self-inflicted, the weapon would have been found either grasped in the hand or lying by the body."

"Was the weapon fired at close quarters?"

"Apparently not. At any rate there was no singeing of the clothes or any other sign indicating a very close range."

That was the sum of Dr. Nichols' evidence, and on its conclusion the local inspector was called. His evidence, however, was of merely formal character, setting forth the time at which he received the alarm call from Mrs. Benham and the conditions existing when he arrived. When it was finished there was a short pause. Then the next witness was

637

called. This was Sir Lawrence Drayton, who, after giving evidence as to the identity of the deceased, answered a few questions respecting the collection and his brother's manner of life, and the articles which had been stolen.

"The report, then," said the coroner, "that this was a collection of valuable jewellery was erroneous?"

"Quite erroneous. The deceased never desired, nor could he afford, to accumulate things of great intrinsic value."

"Do you know if many strangers came to see the collection?"

"Very few. In fact I never heard of any excepting those who came after an article on the collection had appeared in the *Connoisseur*."

"Do you know how many came then?"

"There was a small party of Americans who came by appointment and were introduced by one of the staff of the South Kensington Museum. And there was a Mr. Halliburton, who wrote from some hotel for an appointment. All I know about him is that he was apparently not specially interested in anything in the collection excepting the pieces that were illustrated in the magazine. I believe he wanted to buy one of those, but I don't remember which it was."

That was the substance of Drayton's evidence, and when he had returned to his seat, the next witness was called.

"Winifred Blake."

Miss Blake rose and, having made her way to the table, took the oath and proceeded to give her evidence. After one or two preliminary questions, the coroner allowed her to make her statement without interruption, while the jury and the audience listened with absorbed interest to her clear and vivid account of the events connected with the crime. When she had finished her narration – which was substantially the same as that which I had heard from her on the night of the tragedy – the coroner thanked her for the very lucid manner in which she had given her evidence and then proceeded to enlarge upon one or two points relating to the possible antecedents of the tragedy.

"You have mentioned, Miss Blake, that you were led to communicate with the deceased by a certain article which appeared in the *Connoisseur*. Did that article give you the impression that the collection described was an important collection of valuable jewellery?"

"No. The article explicitly stated that the chief value of the pieces was in their history and associations."

"Are you an expert or connoisseur in jewellery?"

"No. As an artist I am, of course, interested in goldsmith's and jewellers work, but I have no special knowledge of it. My interest in this collection was purely personal. I wished to examine one of the pieces that was illustrated."

"Would you tell us exactly what you mean by a personal interest?"

"The *Connoisseur* article was illustrated with two photographs, one of a locket and the other of a pendant. The pendant appeared to me to resemble one which was an heirloom in my own family and which disappeared about a hundred-and-fifty years ago and has never been seen since. I wanted to examine that pendant and see if it really was the missing jewel."

"Was the missing pendant of any considerable value?"

"No. It was a small, plain gold pendant set with a single cat's eye, and the pendant shown in the photograph appeared to answer the description exactly so far as I could judge. Its actual value would be quite small."

"You say that the actual, or intrinsic, value of this jewel would be trifling. Had it, so far as you know, any special value?"

"Yes. It appears to have been greatly prized in the family, and I believe a good many efforts have been made to trace it. There was a tradition, or superstition, connected with it which gave it its value to members of the family."

"Can you tell us what was the nature of that tradition?"

"It connected the possession of the jewel with the succession to the estates. The custom had been for the head of the family to wear the jewel, usually under the clothing, and the belief was that so long as he wore the jewel, or at any rate had it in his possession, the estates would remain in the possession of the branch of the family to which he belonged, but if the jewel passed into the possession of a member of some other branch of the family, then the estates would also pass into the possession of that branch."

The coroner smiled. "Your ancestors," he remarked, "appear to have taken small account of property law. But you say that efforts have been made to trace this jewel and that a good deal of value was set on it. Now, do you suppose that this tradition was taken at all seriously by any of the members of your family?"

"I cannot say very positively, but I should suppose that anyone who might have a claim in the event of the failure of the existing line would be glad to have the jewel in his possession."

"Is there, so far as you know, any probability of a change in the succession to this property?"

"I believe that the present tenant is unmarried and that if he should die there would be several claimants from other branches of the family."

"And then," said the coroner with a smile, "the one who possessed the cat's eye pendant would be the successful claimant. Is that the position?"

"It is possible that some of them entertain that belief."

"Have you any expectations yourself?"

"Personally I have not. But my brother Percival is, properly speaking, the direct heir to this estate."

"Then why is he not in possession? And what do you mean exactly by the 'direct heir'?"

"I mean that he is the direct descendant of the head of the senior branch of the family. Our ancestor disappeared at the same time as the jewel – he took it with him, in fact. The reason that my brother is not in possession is that we cannot prove the legality of our ancestor's marriage. But it is always possible that the documents may be discovered – they are known to exist – and then, if a change in the succession should occur, my brother's claim would certainly take precedence of the others."

"This is very interesting," said the coroner, "and not without importance to this inquiry. Now tell us, Miss Blake, would you yourself attach any significance to the possession of this jewel?"

Miss Blake coloured slightly as she replied, "I don't suppose it would affect the succession to the property, but I should like to know that the jewel was in my brother's possession."

"In case there might be some truth in the belief, hmm? Well, it's not unnatural. And now, to return for a moment to the man whom you tried so pluckily to detain. You have given us a very clear description of him. Do you think you would be able to recognise him?"

"I feel no doubt that I could. As an artist with some experience as a portrait painter, I have been accustomed to study faces closely and quickly and to remember them. I can form quite a clear mental picture of this man's face."

"Do you think you could make a drawing of it from memory?"

"I don't think my drawing would be reliable for identification. It is principally the man's expression that I remember so clearly. I might be wrong as to the details of the features, but if I were to see the man again I am sure I should know him."

"I hope you will have an opportunity," said the coroner. Then, turning to the jury, he asked, "Do you wish to ask this witness any questions, gentlemen?" And on receiving a negative reply, he thanked Miss Blake and dismissed her with a bow.

My own evidence was taken next, but I need not repeat it since it was concerned only with those experiences which I have already related in detail. I was followed by Mrs. Benham, who, like the preceding witnesses, was allowed to begin with a statement describing her experiences.

"How did it happen," the coroner asked when she had finished her statement, "that there was no one in the house when the thieves broke in?"

"I had to take a message for Mr. Drayton to a gentleman who lives at North End. It is quite a short distance, but I was detained there more than a quarter-of-an-hour."

"Was the house often left?"

"No, very seldom. During the day I had a maid to help me. She went home at six, and after that I hardly ever went out."

"Were you alone in the house in the evenings when Mr. Drayton was at the club?"

"Yes. From about seven to between half-past-nine and ten. Mr. Drayton used to lock the museum and take the key with him."

"Did many persons know that deceased was away from the house every evening?"

"A good many must have known, as he was a regular chess-player. And anybody who cared to know could have seen him go out and come back."

"On the night of the murder did he go out at his usual time?"

"Yes, a little after seven. But, unfortunately, he came back nearly two hours earlier than usual. That was the cause of the disaster."

"Exactly. And now, Mrs. Benham, I want you to tell us all you know about the visitors who came to see the collection after the article had appeared in the *Connoisseur*. There were some Americans, I believe?"

"Yes. A small party – four or five – who came together in a large car. They sent a letter of introduction, and I think Mr. Drayton knew pretty well who they were. Then about a week later, Mr. Halliburton wrote from The Baltic Hotel to ask if he might look over the collection, and naming a particular day – the sixteenth of this month – and Mr. Drayton made the appointment, although it was very inconvenient."

"Was Mr. Halliburton known to the deceased?"

"No, he was a complete stranger."

"And did he come and inspect the collection?"

"Yes, he came, and Mr. Drayton spent a long time with him showing him all the things and telling him all about them. I remember it very well because Mr. Drayton was so very vexed that he should have put himself to so much inconvenience for nothing."

"Why 'nor nothing'?" asked the coroner.

641

"He said that Mr. Halliburton didn't seem to know anything about jewellery nor to care about any of the things but the two that had been shown in the photographs. He seemed to have come from mere idle curiosity. And then he rather offended Mr. Drayton by offering to buy one of the pieces. He said that he wanted to give it for a wedding present."

"Do you know which piece it was that he wanted to buy?"

"The pendant. The other piece – the locket – didn't seem to interest him at all."

"Did you see Mr. Halliburton?"

"I only saw his back as he went out. Mr. Drayton let him in and took him to the museum. I could see that he was rather a big man, but I couldn't see what he was like."

"And are these the only strangers that have been to the house lately?"

"Yes, the only ones for quite a long time."

The coroner reflected for a few moments, then, as the jury had no questions to ask, he thanked the witness and dismissed her.

The next witness was Inspector Badger, and a very cautious witness he was, and like his namesake, very unwilling to be drawn. To me, who knew pretty well what information he held, his evasive manoeuvres and his portentous secrecy were decidedly amusing, and the foxy glances that he occasionally cast in Thorndyke's direction made me suspect that he was unaware of Superintendent Miller's visit to our chambers. He began by setting forth that, in consequence of a telephone message from the local police, he proceeded on the evening of the twentieth instant to "The Rowans' to examine the premises and obtain particulars of the crime. He had obtained a rough list of the stolen property from Sir Lawrence Drayton. It included the pendant and the locket which had been illustrated in the article referred to.

"Should you say there was any evidence of selection as to the articles stolen?" the coroner asked.

"No. Only two drawers had been opened, and they were the two upper ones. The top drawer contained nothing of any value, and I infer that the thieves had only just got the second drawer open when they were disturbed."

"Did you ascertain how many men were on the premises?"

"There were two men. We found their footprints in the grounds, and moreover, both of them were seen. And certain other traces were found."

"Dr. Nichols has mentioned that some hair was found grasped in the hand of deceased. Has that been examined?"

"I believe it has, but hair isn't much use until you have got the man to compare it with."

"I suppose not. And with regard to the other traces. What were they?"

The inspector pursed up his lips and assumed a portentous expression.

"I hope, sir," said he, "that you will not press that question. It is not desirable in the interests of justice that the information that is in our possession should become public property."

"I quite agree with you," said the coroner. "But may we take it that you have some clue to the identity of these two men?"

"We have several very promising clues," the inspector replied with some disregard, I suspected, for the exact wording of the oath that he had just taken.

"Well," said the coroner, "that is all that really concerns us," and I could not but reflect that it was all that really concerned Mr. Joseph Hedges, alias Moakey, and that the inspector's secrecy was somewhat pointless when the cat had been let out of the bag to this extent. "I suppose," he continued, "it would be indiscreet to ask if any information is available about the Mr. Halliburton whose name has been mentioned."

"I should rather not make any detailed statement on the subject," replied Badger, "but I may say that our information is of a very definite kind and points very clearly in a particular direction."

"That is very satisfactory," said the coroner. "This is a peculiarly atrocious crime, and I am sure that all law-abiding persons will be glad to hear that there is a good prospect of the wrongdoers being brought to justice. And I think if you have nothing more to tell us, Inspector, that we need not trouble you any further." He paused, and as Badger resumed his seat, he took a final glance over his notes, then, turning to the jury, he said, "You have now, gentlemen, heard all the evidence, excepting those details which the police have very properly reserved and which really do not concern us. For I may remind you that this is not a criminal court. It is not our object to fix the guilt on any particular persons but to ascertain how this poor gentlemen met with his most deplorable death, and I am sure that the evidence which you have heard will be sufficient to enable you, without difficulty, to arrive at a verdict."

On the conclusion of the coroner's address, the jury rapidly conferred for a few moments, then the foreman rose and announced that they had agreed unanimously on a verdict of wilful murder committed by some person or persons unknown, and they desired to express their deep sympathy with the brother of the deceased, Sir Lawrence Drayton, and when the latter had briefly thanked the jury, through the coroner, the proceedings terminated and the court rose.

As the audience were slowly filing out, Sir Lawrence approached Miss Blake and, having shaken hands cordially and inquired as to her convalescence, said, "That was a very remarkable story that you told in your evidence – I mean the simultaneous disappearance of your ancestor and this curious heirloom. As a Chancery barrister, unusual circumstances affecting the devolution of landed property naturally interest me. In the court in which I practise one sees, from time to time, some very odd turns of the wheel of Fortune. May I ask if any claim has ever been advanced by your branch of the family?"

"Yes. My father began some proceedings soon after my brother was born, but his counsel advised him not to go on with the case. He considered that without documentary evidence of my ancestor's marriage, it was useless to take the case into court."

"Probably he was right," said Drayton. "Still, as a matter of professional interest – to say nothing of the interest that one naturally feels in the welfare of one's friends – I should like to know more about this quaint piece of family history. What do you think, Anstey?"

"I think it would be interesting to know just at what point the evidence of the relationship breaks off, and how large the gap is."

"Precisely," said Drayton. "And one would like to know how the other parties are placed. What, for instance, would be the position if the present tenant were to die without issue, who are the heirs, and so on."

"If it would interest you," said Miss Blake, "I could give you fairly full particulars of all that is known. My grandfather, who was a lawyer, wrote out an abstract for the guidance of his descendants, quite a full and very clear narrative. I could let you have that or a copy of it, if I didn't feel ashamed to take up your time with it."

"Let me have the copy," said Drayton. "I don't suppose anything will come of it from your point of view, but it strikes me as an interesting case which is at least worth elucidating. Do you know Dr. Thorndyke?"

"We know one another by repute," said Thorndyke. "Miss Blake used to board with Polton's sister. You were speaking of the curious circumstances that Miss Blake mentioned in reference to the cat's eye pendant."

"Yes," said Drayton. "I was saying that it would be worthwhile to get the facts of the case sorted out."

"I quite agree with you," said Thorndyke. "The same idea had occurred to me when Miss Blake was giving her evidence. Do I understand that there are documents available?"

"I have a full resume of the facts relating to the change in the succession," said Miss Blake, "and a copy which I am going to hand to Sir Lawrence."

"Then," said Thorndyke, "I shall crave your kind permission to look through that copy. I am not much of an authority on property law, but – "

"*Nihil quod tetigit non ornavit*," I murmured, quoting Johnson's famous epitaph on the versatile "*Goldie*".

"Quite right, Anstey," Drayton agreed warmly. "All knowledge is Thorndyke's province. Then you will let me have that copy at your convenience, Miss Blake?"

"Thank you, yes, Sir Lawrence," she replied. "You shall have it by tomorrow. Oh, and there is something else that I have to give you, and I may as well give it to you now. Did Mr. Anstey tell you that I had found the missing locket? I have brought it tied round my neck for safety. Has anyone got a knife?" As she spoke she unfastened the top button of her dress and drew out the little gold volume which was attached to a silken cord.

"Don't cut the cord," said Drayton. "I want you to keep the locket as a souvenir of my poor brother. Now don't raise objections. Anstey has told me that the little bauble has found favour in your eyes, and I very much wish you to have it. It was a great favourite of my brother's. He used to call it 'The Little Sphinx' because it always seemed to be propounding a riddle, and it will be a great satisfaction to me to feel that it has passed into friendly and sympathetic hands instead of going to a museum with the other things."

"It is exceedingly kind of you, Sir Lawrence," she began, but he interrupted, "It is nothing of the kind. I am doing myself a kindness in finding a good home for poor Andrew's little favourite. Are you going by train or tram?"

"I shall wait for the tram," she replied.

"Then we part here. Dr. Thorndyke and I are taking the train to Broad Street. Goodbye! Don't forget to send me that copy of the documents."

The two men swung off down the road to the station, and as a tram appeared in the offing, a resolution which had been forming in my mind took definite shape.

"I don't see," said I, "why I should be left out in the cold in regard to this family romance of yours. Why shouldn't I come and collect the copy to deliver to Sir Lawrence and have a surreptitious read at it myself?"

"It would be very nice of you if you could spare the time," she replied. "I will even offer special inducements. I will give you some tea,

645

which you must be wanting by this time, I should think, and I will show you not only the copy but the original documents. One of them is quite curious."

"That settles it then," said I. "Tea and documents, combined with your society and that of your ingenious brother, form what the theatrical people would call a galaxy of attractions. Here is our tram. Do we go inside or outside?"

"Oh, outside, please. There is quite a crowd waiting."

I was relieved at this decision, for I was hankering for a smoke, and as soon as we had taken our places in a front seat on the roof, I began secretly to feel in the pocket where the friendly pipe reposed and to debate within myself whether I might crave permission to bring it forth. At length the tobacco-hunger conquered my scruples and I ventured to make the request.

"Oh, of course," she replied. "Do smoke. I love the smell of tobacco, especially from a pipe."

Thus encouraged, I joyfully produced the calumet and felt in my pocket for my pouch. And then came a dreadful disappointment. The pouch was there, sure enough, but its lean sides announced the hideous fact that it was empty. There were not even a few grains wherewith to stave off imminent starvation.

"How provoking!" my companion exclaimed tragically. "I am sorry. But you shan't be deprived for long. You must get down at a tobacconist's and restock your pouch, and then after tea you shall smoke your pipe while I show you the documents, as you call them."

"Then I am comforted," said I. "The galaxy of attractions has received a further addition." Resignedly I put away the pipe and pouch, and reverting to a question that had occurred to me while she was giving her evidence, I said, "There was one statement of yours that I did not quite follow. It was with regard to the man whom you were trying to hold. You said that you were quite confident that you would recognise him and that you could call up quite a clear and vivid mental picture of his face, but yet you thought that, if you were to draw a memory portrait of him, that portrait might be misleading. How could that be? You would know whether your portrait was like your recollection of the man, and if it was, surely it would be like the man himself?"

"I suppose it would," she replied thoughtfully. "But there might be some false details which wouldn't matter to me but which might mislead others who might take those details for the essential characters."

"But if the details were wrong, wouldn't that destroy the likeness?"

"Not necessarily, I think. Of course, a likeness is ultimately dependent on the features, particularly on their proportion and the spaces between them. But you must have noticed that when children and beginners draw portraits, although they produce the most frightful caricatures – all wrong and all out of drawing – yet those portraits are often unmistakable likenesses."

"Yes, I have noticed that. But don't you think the likeness is probably due to the caricature? To the exaggeration of someone or two characteristic peculiarities?"

"Very likely. But that rather bears out what I said. For those caricatures, though easily recognisable, are mostly false, and if one of them got into the hands of a stranger who had never seen the subject of the portrait, for purposes of identification, he would as probably as not look for someone having those characteristics which had been quite falsely represented."

"Yes, and then he would be looking for the wrong kind of person altogether."

"Exactly. And then my drawing would probably be far from a correct representation of my recollection of the face. It isn't as if one could take a photograph of a mental image. So I am afraid that the idea of a memory drawing for the purpose of identification must be abandoned. Besides, it would be of no use unless we could get hold of the man."

"No. But that is not impossible. The police have apparently identified one of the men and expect to have him in custody at any moment. He may give information as to the other, but even if he does not, the police may be able to find out who his associates were, and in that case a memory drawing which was far from accurate might help them to pick out the particular man."

"That is possible," she agreed. "But then if the police could get hold of this man's associates and let me see them, I could pick out the particular man with certainty and without any drawing at all. Isn't that a tobacconist's shop that we are approaching?"

"It is. I think I will get off and make my purchase and then come along to the studio."

"Do," she said, "and I will run on ahead and see that the preparations for tea are started."

I ran down the steps and dropped off the tram without stopping it, but by this time we had passed the shop by some little distance and I had to walk back. I secured the new supply and, having stuffed it into my pouch, came out of the shop just in time to see the tram stop nearly a quarter of a mile ahead and Miss Blake get off, followed by a couple of other passengers, and walk quickly into Jacob Street. I strode forward at a brisk pace in the same direction, but when I reached the corner of the street she had already disappeared. I was just about to cross to the side on which the studio was situated when my attention was attracted by a woman who was walking slowly up the street on my side. At the first glance I was struck by something familiar in her appearance and a second glance confirmed the impression. She was smartly – and something more than smartly – dressed, and in particular I noted a rather large, elaborate, and gaudy hat. In short, she was very singularly like the woman who had jostled me in the doorway of the hall in which the inquest was held.

I slowed down to avoid overtaking her, and as I did so she crossed the road and walked straight up to the gate of the studio. For an instant I thought she was going to ring the bell, for after a glance at the number on the gate she turned to the side and read the little nameplate, leaning forward and putting her face close to it as if she were near-sighted. At that moment the wicket opened and Master Percy stepped out on to the threshold, whereupon the woman, after one swift, intense glance at the boy, turned away and walked quickly up the street. I was half-disposed to follow her and confirm my suspicion as to her identity, but Master Percy had already observed me, and it seemed, perhaps, more expedient to get out of sight myself than to reveal my presence in attempting to verify a suspicion of which I had practically no doubt, and which, even if confirmed, had no obvious significance. Accordingly I crossed the road, and having greeted my host, was by him conducted down the passage to the studio.

Chapter VIII
A Jacobite Romance

In the minds of many of us, including myself, there appears to be a natural association between the ideas of tea and tobacco. Whether it is that both substances are exotic products, adopted from alien races, or that each is connected with a confirmed and accepted drug habit, I am not quite clear. But there seems to be no doubt that the association exists and that the realisation of the one idea begets an imperative impulse to realise the other. In conformity with which natural law, when the tea-things had been, by the joint efforts of Miss Blake and her brother, removed to the curtained repository – where also dwelt a gas ring and a kettle – I proceeded complacently to bring forth my pipe and the bulging tobacco-pouch and to transfer some of the contents of the latter to the former.

"I am glad to see you smoking," said Miss Blake as the first cloud of incense ascended. "It gives me the feeling that you are provided with an antidote to the documents. I shall have less compunction about the reading."

"You think that the 'tuneless pipe' is similar to the tuneful one in its effects on the 'savage breast'. But I don't want any antidote. I am all agog to hear your romance of a cat's eye – that is, if you are going to read out the documents."

"I thought I would read the copy aloud and get you to check it by the originals. Then you can assure Sir Lawrence that it is a true copy."

"Yes. I think that is quite a good plan. It is always well to have a copy checked and certified correct."

"Then I will get the books and we will begin at once. Do you want to hear the reading, Percy, or are you going on with your building?"

"I should like to come and listen, if you don't mind, Winnie," he replied and, as his sister unlocked the cabinet under the window, he seated himself on a chair by the now-vacant table. Miss Blake took from the cabinet three books, one of which – an ordinary school exercise-book – she placed on the table by her chair.

"That," she said, "is the copy of both originals. This – " handing to me a little leather-covered book, the pages of which were filled with small, clearly-written, though faded, handwriting " – is the abstract of which I spoke. This other little book is the fragmentary original which is referred to in the abstract. If you are ready I will begin. We will take the abstract first."

I provided myself with a pencil with which to mark any errors and, having opened the little book announced that I was ready.

"The abstract," said she, "was written in 1821, and reads as follows . . . ."

A Short History of the Blakes of Beauchamp Blake near Wendover in the County of Buckinghamshire, From the Year of Our Lord 1708

This history has been written by me for the purpose of preserving a record of certain events for the information of my descendants, to whom a knowledge of those events may prove of great importance, and its writing has become necessary by the circumstance that, whereas the only existing written record has been reduced by Time and ill-usage to a collection of disconnected fragments, the traditions passed on orally from generation to generation become year by year more indistinct and unreliable.

I shall begin with the year 1708, at which time the estate of Beauchamp Blake was held by Harold Blake. In this year was born Percival Blake, the only son of Harold aforesaid. Seven years later occurred a rising in favour of the Royal House of the Stuarts, in which act of rebellion the said Harold Blake was suspected (but never accused) of having taken part. In the year 1743, Harold Blake died and his only son, Percival, succeeded to the property.

In or about the year 1742, Percival Blake married a lady named Judith Weston (or Western). For some unknown reason this marriage took place secretly, and was, for a time at least, kept secret. Possibly the marriage would not have been acceptable to Percival's father, or the lady may have been a Papist. This latter seems the more probable, inasmuch as the marriage was solemnised, not at the church of St. Margaret at Beauchamp Blake, but at a little church in London near to Aldgate, called St. Peter by the Shambles, the rector of which, the Reverend Stephen Rumbold, an intimate friend of Percival's, became subsequently not only a Papist but a Jesuit. In the next year, 1743, a son was born and was christened James. No entry of this birth appears in the registers of St. Margaret's, so it is probable that it was registered at the London church. Unfortunately, this register is incomplete. Several pages have been torn out, and as these missing pages belong to the years 1742 and 1743, it is to be presumed that they contained the records of the marriage and the birth.

About the year 1725, Percival came to London to study medicine, and about 1729 or 1730 he completed his studies and took his degree at Cambridge, of which University he was already a Bachelor of Arts. From this time onwards he appears to have practised in London as a physician, and it was probably at this period that he made the acquaintance of Judith Western and Stephen Rumbold. Even after the death of his father and his own succession to the property, he continued to practise his profession, making only occasional visits to his estate in Buckinghamshire.

Like his father, Percival Blake was an ardent supporter of the Stuarts, and it is believed that he took an active part in the various Jacobite plots that were heard of about this time, and when, in 1745, the great rising took place, Percival was one of those who hastened to join the forces of the young Pretender – a disastrous act, to which all the subsequent misfortunes of the family are due.

On the collapse of the Jacobite cause, Percival took immediate measures to avert the consequences of his ill-judged action from his own family, and in these he displayed a degree of foresight that might well have been exhibited earlier. From Scotland he made his way to Beauchamp Blake and there, in one of the numerous hiding-places of the old mansion, concealed certain important documents connected with the property. It is not quite clear what these documents were. Among them appear to have been some of the title-deeds, and there is no doubt that they included documents proving the validity of his marriage with Judith and the legitimacy of his son James. Meanwhile, he had sent his wife and child, with a servant named Jenifer Gray, to Hamburg, where they were to wait until he joined them. He himself made his way to a port on the East Coast, believed to have been King's Lynn, where he embarked, under a false name, on a small vessel bound for Hamburg, but while he was waiting for the vessel to sail, he circulated a very circumstantial account of his own death by drowning while attempting to escape in an open boat.

This was at once a fortunate and unfortunate act, fortunate inasmuch as it completely achieved his purpose of

651

preventing the confiscation of the property, unfortunate inasmuch as it effectually shut out his own descendants from the succession. On the report of his death (unmarried, as was believed, and so without issue) a distant cousin, of unquestionable loyalty to the reigning house, took possession of the estate without opposition and without any suggestion of confiscation.

One thing only, appertaining to the inheritance, Percival took with him. Among the family heirlooms was a jewel consisting of a small pendant set with a single cymophane (vulgarly known as a "cat's eye") and bearing an inscription, of which the actual words are unknown, but of which the purport was that whosoever should possess the jewel should also possess the Blake estate – a foolish statement that seems to have been generally believed in the family and to which Percival evidently attached incredible weight. For not only did he take the jewel with him but, as will presently appear, he made careful provision for its disposal.

From this time onward the history becomes more and more vague. It seems that Percival joined his wife and child at Hamburg, and thereafter travelled about Germany, plying his profession as a physician. But soon he was overtaken by a terrible misfortune. It appears that a robbery had been committed by a woman who was said to be a foreigner, and suspicion fell upon Judith. She was arrested and, on false evidence, convicted and sent, as a punishment, to labour in the mines somewhere in the Harz Mountains. Percival made unceasing efforts to obtain her release, but it was three years before his efforts were crowned with success. But then, alas, it was too late. The poor lady came back to him aged by privation and broken by long-standing sickness, only to linger on a few months and then to die in his arms. On her release he carried her away to France, and there, at Paris, about the year 1751, she passed away and is believed to have been buried in the cemetery of Pere Lachaise.

The death of his wife, to whom he seems to have been devotedly attached, left Percival a broken man, and about eighteen months later, he himself died, and is believed to have been buried beside Judith. But in these sad months he occupied himself in making provision for the recovery of the family inheritance by his posterity when circumstances should have become more favourable. To this end he wrote a summary of the events connected with and following the Jacobite rising and had it sewn into a little illustrated Book of Hours, *which, together with the cymophane jewel, he gave into the keeping of Jenifer Gray, to be by her given to the child James when he should be old enough to be trusted with them. The exact contents of the little book we can only surmise from the fragments that remain, but they seem to have been a short account of his own actions and vicissitudes, and no doubt gave at least a clue to the place in which the documents were hidden. Nor can we tell what the exact form of the jewel was or the nature of the inscription, for Percival's references to the latter as "a guide" to his descendants are not clearly understandable. At any rate, the jewel has disappeared and the written record is reduced to a few fragments. Jenifer Gray (who seems to have been an illiterate and foolish woman) apparently gave the little book to the child to play with, for the few leaves that remain are covered with childish scrawls, and she may have sold the jewel to buy the necessaries of life, for she and the boy were evidently but poorly provided for.*

On reaching the age of fourteen, James was apprenticed to a cabinetmaker in Paris and apparently became very skilful workman. When he was out of his time (Jenifer Gray having died in the meantime) he came to England and settled in London, where, in time, he established an excellent business.

Into this his son William (my father), was taken, first as an apprentice, then as partner, and finally as principal. By my father the prosperity of the house was so well maintained that he was able to article me to an attorney, to whom I am chief clerk at this time of writing.

This record, together with what remains of Percival Blake's manuscript, will, I trust, be preserved by my descendants in the hope that it may be the instrument by which Providence may hereafter reinstate them in the inheritance of their forefathers.

John Blake
16 Symond's Inn, London
20th June, 1821

As she finished reading, Miss Blake let the book fall into her lap and looked at me as if inviting criticism. I closed the little original, and laying it on the table, remarked, "A very singular and romantic history, and a very valuable record. The detailed narrative presents a much more convincing case than one would have expected from the bare statement that you gave in your evidence. Your great-grandfather was a wise man to commit the facts to writing while the memory of the events was comparatively recent. How much is there left of Percival's manuscript?"

"Very little, I am sorry to say," she replied, picking up the remaining volume and handing it to me, "but I have made a copy of these fragments, too. It follows the copy of John Blake's abstract, and I will read it out to you if you will check it by the original."

I turned the little book over in my hand and examined it curiously. It was a tiny volume, bound in gold-tooled calf, now rusty and worn and badly broken at the joints. The title-page showed it to be a *Book of Hours – Horae Beatae Mariae Virginis –* printed at Antwerp by Bakhasar Moretus and dated 1634, and on turning over the leaves I perceived that it was illustrated with a number of quaint but decorative woodcuts. The inside of the cover seemed to have been used as a sort of unofficial birth register. At the top, in very faded writing, was inscribed "*Judith Weston*", and underneath a succession of names beginning with "*James, son of Percival and Judith Blake, born 3 April 1743*", and ending with Winifred and Percival, the daughter and son of Peter and Agnes Blake. Between the cover and the title-page a number of fly-leaves of very thin paper had been stitched in, and those that remained were covered with minute writing of a pale, ghostly brown, largely defaced by spots, smears, scribblings and childish drawings. But most of them had disappeared, and the few that were left hung insecurely to the loosened stitches.

When I had completed my inspection, I opened the book at the first fly-leaf, and adjusting the reading-glass which Miss Blake had placed on the table, announced that I was ready, whereupon she resumed her reading.

"The first page reads:

> . . . *to my cousin Leonard, who, as the heir-at-law, would, I knew, be watching the course of events. Indeed, I doubt not that if he had known of my marriage, he would have used his influence at the Court to oust me. But the news of my death I felt sure would bring him forward at once, and his loyalty to the German King would make him secure to the succession. So he and his brood should keep the nest warm*

until the clouds had passed and the present troubles should be forgotten. Only to my own posterity, the true heirs, must be provided a key wherewith to re-enter on their inheritance, and to this end I searched the muniment chest and took therefrom all the –

This was the end of the page, and as she broke off. Miss Blake looked up.

"Isn't it exasperating?" said she. "There seems to be only one page missing in this place, but it is the one that contains the vital information."

"It is not very difficult to guess what he took," said I. "Evidently he abstracted the title-deeds. But the question is, what did he do with them?"

"Yes," said Miss Blake, "that is the important question, and unfortunately we cannot answer it. That he hid them in a secure hiding-place is evident from the next two pages. The first reads:

Will Bateman, the plumber, made me a tall leaden jar like a black-jack to hold the documents, with a close-fitting lid, which we luted on with wax when we had put the documents into it. And this jar I set in the hiding-place, and on top of it the great two-handled posset-pot that old Martin, the potter, made for my mother when I was born, which I prize dearly and would not have it fall into the hands of strangers. When all was ready, we sent for the carpenter, who is a safe man and loyal to the Prince, and bade him close the chamber, which he did so that no eye could detect the opening. So the writings shall be safe until such time –

"The next page reads:

. . . and the other documents which I obtained from Mr. Halford, the attorney. I had feared that their absence might be a bar to the succession, but he assured me it was not so, but only that it would hinder the sale of the property. So I am satisfied, and I am confident that Leonard will never guess the hiding-place in which they are bestowed, nor will he ever dream what that hiding-place conceals.

When I had done this I began forthwith to spread the report of my death among strangers, both in the coffee-houses and at the inn whereat I lodged while I was waiting for the ship to sail from –

"There the page ends, and there seems to be quite a lot missing, for the next one speaks of the disaster as having already occurred."

> *Nor, indeed, would they listen to her protestations (spoken, as they were, in a strange tongue), and still less to my entreaties. And so she was borne away from my sight, brave, cheerful, and dignified to the last, as befitted an English gentlewoman, though it seemed then as if we should never look on one another again. So I left with the child and Jenifer and must needs continue to live at Eisenach (that I might be near my darling, though I could never see her) and must minister for my daily bread to the wretches who people that accursed land –*

"There seems to be only one or two pages missing here, for the next page runs:

> *. . . this joyful day (as I had hoped it would be) and set forth from Eisenach with the child and Jenifer to meet my poor darling on the road. A few miles out we saw the cart approaching, filled with the prisoners released from the mines. I looked among them, but at first saw her not. Then a haggard old woman held out her arms to me and I looked again. The old woman was Judith, my wife! But, O God, what a wreck! She was wasted to a very skeleton, her skin was like old parchment, her hair, that had been like spun gold, was turned to a strange black and her whole aspect –*

Miss Blake paused and said in a low voice, "It is a dreadful picture. Poor Judith! And poor Percival! And the rest of the story is just as sad. The next page takes up the thread just after Judith's death."

> *And when it was over and I saw them shovel in the earth, I felt moved to beg them not to fill the grave but to leave room for me. I went away through the snow with Jenifer and the boy. But I was alone. Judith had been all to me, and my heart was under the new-turned sods. Yet I bethought me, if it should please God to take me, I must not go without leaving some chart to guide my son back to our home, should such return be possible in his lifetime, or to guide his children or his children's children. Therefore, that*

same sad day I began to write this history on the fly-leaves
that my dear wife had had sewn into her little book of –

"There seems to be only one page missing before the next, but it was an important one, so far as we can judge. Indeed, it almost appears as if all the most significant pages were lost. The next page reads:

. . . gave me a string from his bass viol, which he says
will be the best of all. So that matter is as secure as care and
judgement can make it. This book and the precious bauble I
purpose to hold until I feel the hand of death upon me, and
then I shall give both into the keeping of Jenifer, bidding her
guard them jealously as treasures beyond price, until my son
attains the age of fourteen. Then she shall give them to him,
adjuring him to preserve the book in a safe place and never
to lend or show it to any person whatsoever, and to wear the
trinket hung around his neck under his clothing so that none
shall know –

"That is the last complete page. There remains a half-page, which seems to have been the concluding one. It reads:

. . . and that is all that I can do, since one cannot look
into the future. When the time is ripe, my son, or his
descendants, can go forward with open eyes. This history
and the trinket shall guide them. Wherefore I pray that both
may be treasured by them to whom I thus pass on the
inheritance.

As Miss Blake finished her reading she closed the book and sat looking thoughtfully at her brother, who had listened with rapt attention to the pathetic story. Half-reluctantly, I shut the little *Book of Hours* and laid it on the table.

"It is a tragic little history," I said, "and these soiled and tattered leaves and the faded writing and the old-fashioned phraseology make it somehow very real and vivid. I wonder what became of the cat's eye pendant. Is nothing at all known of the way in which it was lost?"

"Nothing," she replied. "The boy James was only seven years old when his father died, so he would hardly have remembered, even if he knew of the existence of the jewel. It may have been lost or stolen or, more probably, Jenifer sold it to buy the necessaries of life. She must have been pretty hard pressed at times."

"She must have been a duffer," said Percy, "if she sold it after what she had been told. Couldn't she have popped it and kept up the interest?"

"You seem to know a good deal about these matters, Percy," his sister remarked with a smile.

"Well," said he, "I should think everybody knows how to raise the wind if they are hard up. There's no need to sell things when you've got an uncle."

"We don't know that she did sell it," said Miss Blake. "She may even have 'popped' it, to use your elegant expression. All that we know is that it disappeared. And now it has disappeared again, if this pendant that was stolen was really the Blake pendant."

"Is there any reason to suppose that it was?" I asked.

"Only that it agreed with what little we know of the missing jewel, and cat's eye pendants must be very rare. Unfortunately, the *Connoisseur* article doesn't help us much. It gives a photograph, from which we could identify the pendant if we knew exactly what it was like, but the description fails just at the vital point. It doesn't say anything about the inscription on the back. It was in order to find out what that inscription was that I asked poor Mr. Drayton to let me see the jewel. Would you like to see the photograph?"

"I should, very much, if you have a copy."

She fetched from the cabinet a copy of the *Connoisseur* and, having found the article, handed the open magazine to me. There were two photographs on the page, one of the little book-locket and the other of a simple, lozenge-shaped pendant of somewhat plain design, set with a single, rather large stone, smooth-cut and nearly circular. The letterpress gave no particulars and did not even mention the inscription.

"I suppose," said I, "there is no doubt that this pendant did bear an inscription of some kind. There is no reference to it here."

"No particular reference, unfortunately. But this was a collection of inscribed objects. Every specimen bore an inscription, if it was only a name and a date. The article, you will see, says so, and Mr. Drayton told me so himself."

"You didn't ask him what was written on this pendant?"

"No, I didn't want to tell him about our family tradition unless I found that it really was the Blake pendant. Perhaps I might not have told him even then, for the inscription might have told us all we wanted to know, though I must confess to a certain superstitious hankering to possess the jewel, or, at least, to see it in Percy's possession."

"You were telling Sir Lawrence that proceedings to establish a claim were actually begun by your father."

"Yes, but our solicitor was not at all hopeful, and the counsel whom he retained very strongly advised my father not to go on. He thought that, with the apparently well-founded belief in Percival's death and the absence of any real evidence of his marriage and survival, we had no case. So the action was settled out of court and the tenant at the time agreed to pay most of the costs."

"Do you remember who was the solicitor for the tenant?"

"Yes. His name was Brodribb, and my father thought he treated us very fairly."

"He probably did. I know Mr. Brodribb very well, and I have the highest opinion of him as a lawyer and as a man. I have often been retained by him, and I have usually been very well satisfied to be associated with him. Do you know what the position was when your father began his action? I mean as to the possible heirs. Was the present tenant then in possession?"

"No, he was a Mr. Arnold Blake, a widower with no surviving children. But he knew the present tenant, Arthur Blake, although they were not very near relatives, and was prepared to contest the claim on his behalf. Arthur Blake was then, I think, in Australia."

"And I gather that you don't know much about him?"

"No, excepting that I understand that he is unmarried, which is all that really matters to us."

"And did Brodribb know about this little book and John Blake's abstract?"

"I think my father must have told him that we had some authentic details of the family history, but I don't know whether he actually showed him the originals."

"And with regard to the pedigree since Percival – have the marriages and births all been proved?"

"Yes. My father had them investigated and obtained certificates of all of them, and I have those certificates, though I am afraid they are never likely to be called for."

"Well," I said, "as a lawyer, I shouldn't like to hold out any hopes even if the death of the present tenant without issue should seem to create a favourable situation. But, of course, if it should ever become possible to prove the marriage of Percival and Judith and the birth of James, that would alter the position very materially. And now I must tear myself away. I have been most keenly interested in hearing your romance, and I have no doubt that Sir Lawrence will be equally so. If you will give me the copy, I will leave it at his chambers tonight or tomorrow morning."

She gave me the manuscript book, which I slipped into my pocket, and then she and Percy escorted me across the yard and let me out at the wicket.

Chapter IX
Exit Moakey

From Jacob Street I made my way to The Temple with the intention of letting Thorndyke look through Miss Blake's manuscript – since he had expressed a wish to see it – before delivering it to Drayton. And as I sat on the omnibus roof I reflected on the events of the afternoon. In spite of my legal training and experience, the romance of the lost inheritance had taken a strong hold on me. The two narratives, and especially the older one, diffused an atmosphere of reality that was very convincing. It was practically certain that the two manuscripts were genuine, and if they were, there could be no doubt that my young friend Percy was the direct descendant of the Jacobite fugitive, Percival Blake. Nor could there be much reasonable doubt that the descent was legitimate. Percival plainly referred to Judith as his wife and there seemed to be no reason for supposing that the marriage had not taken place at the time stated in John Blake's abstract. In short, I found myself wondering whether Mr. Peter Blake's counsel had not been a little over-cautious, or whether he might not have been influenced by a possible financial straitness on the part of the said Peter unfavourable to a warmly-contested action at law.

If he had been over-cautious, it was unfortunate, for he had missed an opportunity. The death of Arnold Blake without a direct successor would have made things comparatively easy for a new claimant with a good case, whereas now, with Arthur Blake in possession, the difficulties would be much greater. It is one thing to maintain a claim against other claimants, but quite another to oust a tenant who has established a title by actual possession. And, to judge by their surroundings and mode of life, my friends were but poorly equipped for any action at all.

From the manuscripts and their story, my thoughts strayed to the woman whom I had seen examining Miss Blake's nameplate. I did not like that incident at all. It might mean nothing. The woman might happen to live in the neighbourhood and have made her inspection from mere idle curiosity. But that was not what the appearances suggested. The woman had been at the inquest, and from Hampstead she must have travelled in the same tramcar that had conveyed Miss Blake and me. Then she had seemed to have followed Miss Blake, at some distance, on the opposite side of the road. There was a suggestion of purpose in the whole proceeding that I found disquieting and rather sinister, and it was not made less so by the very unprepossessing appearance of the woman herself.

When I let myself into our chambers with my key – or rather Jervis' – I found the sitting-room vacant, but as an inspection of the hat-rack in the lobby suggested that Thorndyke was somewhere on the premises, I went up to the laboratory, and there I found him in company with Polton and an uncanny-looking apparatus consisting of a microscope with an attachment of miniature hot-water pipes.

"This is a new form of magic," said I, "at least it is new to me. What is going on?"

"This is just a microscope with a warm stage," Thorndyke explained. "We are making it a hot stage for the purposes of the present experiment."

"And what is the experiment?" I asked with sudden curiosity, for I had just observed that the object on the microscope stage was an irregular-shaped piece of glass on which I could distinguish a very clear fingerprint.

"The experiment is connected with the fingerprints on the piece of glass that you so very fortunately secured at The Rowans. This is a portion of it which I have cut off with a glazier's diamond and which bears a duplicate print. You remember my pointing out to you that a real fingerprint – as distinguished from a statistical or mathematical fingerprint – has chemical and physical properties. Well, we are endeavouring to determine the chemical nature of the substance of which this fingerprint is composed by inference from its physical properties. We are now ascertaining its melting-point, in fact I may say that we have ascertained it. It is fifty-three degrees centigrade. And this fact, in conjunction with its other observed physical properties, tells us that it is Japanese wax."

"Indeed," said I. "Then that goes to show that the man who made these fingerprints had been handling Japanese wax."

"That is the obvious inference."

"Does that throw any light on the man's personality or occupation? What is Japanese wax used for?"

"For a variety of purposes. Very largely for the manufacture of wax polishes for boots and furniture, for the preparation of foundry wax and the various waxes used by jewellers, engravers, and lapidaries. It is also used in pharmacy in the making of certain plasters and cerates."

"Do you think," I asked, "that this man could have got it on his fingers by touching the furniture?"

"No," replied Thorndyke. "The cabinets were French-polished, and I saw no trace of wax polish on them. Besides, there is more wax than would have been taken up in that way."

"Does the presence of this wax suggest anything to you?"

"Well," replied Thorndyke, "of course there are possibilities. But one mustn't expect to apply a fact as soon as it is discovered. We have ascertained what this substance is. Let us put this item of knowledge in its proper mental pigeon-hole and hope that we shall find a use for it presently."

"I have a strong suspicion, Thorndyke," said I, "that you have found a use for it already. However, I won't press you. I know my place. The mantle of Jervis is on me – and trailing a few yards along the ground. I am not permitted to cross-examine my reverend senior."

"There really isn't any need for you to do so," said he. "I have no exclusive information. You are in possession of all the facts that are known to me."

"That is not strictly true, you know, Thorndyke," I objected. "We share the mere observed facts of this case, I admit, but you have a body of general knowledge which I have not, and which gives many of these observed facts a significance that is hidden from me. However, we will let that pass. You are the investigating wizard, I am only a sort of familiar demon. Which reminds me that I have been devilling for you this afternoon. I think you said that you would like to look over the documents relating to Miss Blake's claim."

"Yes, I should be interested to see them."

"Well, I've got a copy, which I have compared with the originals, and which I am to hand over Drayton. Would you like to have it now?"

"Yes, I have finished up here. Let us go downstairs and look over the documents together."

"You had better take the copy down with you and run through it while I am having a wash. Then I will come down and hear your reverend pronouncements on the case." I produced the manuscript book from my pocket and, having handed it to him, retired to the bedroom of which I was tenant *ex officio*, while he descended to the sitting-room with the manuscript in his hand.

When I came down after a leisurely wash and brush up, I found Thorndyke sitting with the open book before him and a slip of paper and a pencil in his hand. Apparently he had finished the reading and was jotting down a few dates and other particulars.

"This is a singularly interesting story, Anstey," said he, "and extraordinarily picturesque in its setting. It enables us to understand Miss Blake's view as to her brother's claim, which sounded a little extravagant

663

when baldly stated in her evidence. And, in fact, it looks as if that claim were a perfectly sound one. If it were only possible to produce satisfactory evidence of the marriage of Percival and Judith Blake and of the legitimacy of James, I should take the case into Court with perfect confidence – under suitable conditions, of course."

"You mean, if there were any question as to the succession."

"Yes. And such a question may arise at any moment if the present tenant is unmarried. It seems to me a matter of vital importance to find out as much as possible about this present tenant, Arthur Blake, I mean as to his heir, his relatives, and connections generally, and the chances of his marrying. Miss Blake's brother is but a child, and many things may happen before he is a middle-aged man."

"Yes," I agreed. "It would be a good deal more to the point than fussing about this ridiculous cat's eye. Miss Blake's keenness about that is a mystery to me."

"Don't forget," said Thorndyke, "that the pendant is believed to bear an inscription that might be helpful to the possessor, though it is difficult to imagine in what way it could be."

"Very difficult," said I. "But it isn't the inscription that she is so keen on, it is the thing itself. She has a sort of half-belief in some occult quality inherent in this jewel, in fact she is infected by the family superstition. It is incomprehensible to me."

"It is always difficult for one temperament to understand another," said he. "But this state of mind is quite a common one. That absurd little bone of Halliburton's is a case in point, and quite a representative instance. It was obviously a mascot – that is to say, an object credited with occult properties and the power to influence events, and how many people are there who, openly or secretly, cherish similar charms or fetishes. The Stock Exchange, the Stage, and the Sporting Clubs are full of them."

"Yes, that is true," I agreed, and then, suddenly remembering the mysterious woman, I said, "By the way, a rather queer thing happened this afternoon. I accompanied Miss Blake home from Hampstead, but I got off the tram to get some tobacco and let her go on ahead. She had gone indoors before I arrived at the studio, and as I was approaching her house, I saw a woman cross the road and go deliberately up to the door and read the name on the plate."

"Yes," said Thorndyke, looking at me interrogatively.

"Well, the point is that that woman had followed us from Hampstead."

"Indeed!" he exclaimed with sudden gravity. "You are sure of that?"

"Yes. I recognised her before she crossed. You may have noticed her at the inquest, a brassy-haired baggage with a spotted veil and a face powdered like a clown's."

"Yes, I noticed her. She was sitting near to you, by the door. I took particular note of her because she stood up while Miss Blake was giving her evidence, and seemed deeply interested in her and in you."

"Well, that is the woman."

"But this is very serious, Anstey. What a pity you didn't follow her and find out where she went to!"

"I had half-a-mind to, but Master Percy – Miss Blake's brother – came to the door at that moment and saw me, so it was hardly possible."

"It is very unfortunate," said Thorndyke. "You see the importance of the matter? Miss Blake stood up in open Court and swore that she was confident she could identify the man who stabbed her. Now that man is not only a robber. He is, at least, an accessory to the murder of Andrew Drayton, and his apprehension would probably reveal the identity of the actual murderer – if he is not the murderer himself – to say nothing of the charge against him of wounding with intent. Of course, if the police are right about those fingerprints, there is not so much in it. They will arrest Moakey and probably get the other man as well. But if the police clue should fail – and I should not be surprised if it does – Miss Blake represents the whole of the evidence against these two men. Apart from her, a conviction would be impossible unless the men were taken with the stolen property in their possession, which they are not likely to be. Even if the men were arrested they could not be identified, excepting by her, and would have to be released. I consider that her position is one of extreme danger. Did you tell her of this incident?"

"No, I thought there was no use in making her uneasy."

"She ought to be warned, Anstey. And she ought to be most cautious about exposing herself to the possibility of an attack of any kind. I am expecting a visit from Superintendent Miller – he sent me a note asking for an interview at seven o'clock, so he will be here in a few minutes. When we have seen him, we shall know how the case stands, but the fact of his wanting an interview suggests that the police bark has got into shoal water."

Punctually at seven o'clock the Superintendent's characteristic official rat-tat announced his arrival, and as I let him in, a subtle something in his manner seemed to confirm Thorndyke's surmises.

"I suppose," said he as he took the armchair and lighted the customary cigar, "you've guessed what I wanted to talk to you about? It's this Drayton case, you know."

Thorndyke nodded. "Any new developments?" he asked.

"Well, yes, there are. We've got a bit of a setback. It seems that the fingerprint people made a mistake. Never known them to do such a thing before, but I suppose nobody is infallible. It turns out that those fingerprints are not Moakey's after all."

As the Superintendent made this statement, he fixed a stony gaze on the opposite wall. Glancing at Thorndyke, I noted that my colleague's countenance had taken on that peculiar woodenness that I had learned to associate with intense attention not unmingled with suspicion.

"I can't think how they came to make such a stupid mistake," the Superintendent continued, still staring fixedly at the wall. "Might have got us into a horrid mess."

"I should have thought," said Thorndyke, "that mistakes might easily be made with such multitudes of records. Whose fingerprints are they?"

"Ah!" said Miller, "there you are. We don't know. They don't seem to have 'em at the registry. So our only clue is gone."

"Haven't you opened up in any other direction?" Thorndyke asked.

"We've notified all the likely fences, of course, but that's no good. These coveys are not likely to try to plant the stuff with a murder charge hanging over them. Then we made some inquiries about that man Halliburton. But they turned out a frost. The chap has disappeared and left no address. We've got his signature, and we've got a damn silly rabbit bone that some fool has taken the trouble to cut a pattern on, that he left behind at the hotel, and as he seemed to value the thing, we put an advertisement in the papers saying that it had been found. But there are no answers up to the present, and not likely to be. And then Halliburton probably had nothing to do with the affair. So we're rather up a tree. And it's annoying, after thinking it was all plain sailing, and letting the papers give out that we were in full cry. Of course, they are all agog for the next act – and, by the way, one of them has got a portrait of you – I think I've got it. Yes, here it is."

He produced from his pocket a copy of *The Evening Courier* and opened it out. On the front page was an excellent portrait of my colleague, with the descriptive title, "*Dr. John Thorndyke, the Famous Criminal Expert, Whose Services are Being Retained in the Case*".

"That ought to help you, sir," said the Superintendent with a grin. "You won't be a stranger to our friends if you should happen to meet them. It is a pity their photographs can't be given, too."

"Yes, it would be more to the point. But now, Miller, what is it that you want me to do? I assume that you have come to suggest some sort of co-operation?"

"Well," said Miller, "you are retained in the case, and I rather suspect that Sir Lawrence would like you to carry on independently. But there is no sense in our getting at cross-purposes."

"Not the least," Thorndyke agreed. "It is a criminal case, and our objects are identical – to secure the offenders and recover the property. Do I understand that you are prepared to offer me facilities?"

"What facilities do you want?"

"At this moment I am not wanting any, excepting that I should like to look at the fingerprints. There would be no objection to that. I suppose?"

The Superintendent looked uncomfortable. "I don't know why there should be," said he, "but you know what Singleton and his crowd are. They don't like unofficial investigators in their department. And," Miller added with a grin, "they aren't very fond of you – and no wonder, they haven't forgotten that Hornby case. But it wouldn't help you a bit if you did look at the prints. You can take it from me that Moakey is not the man. There's no mistake this time. They have checked the fingerprints quite carefully, and you can rely on what they say. So it would be no use your examining them – unless," he added with a shrewd look at Thorndyke, "you've got a fingerprint registry of your own."

As a matter of fact it was known to me that Thorndyke had a collection in a card-index file, but it was a mere appendix to the reports of cases dealt with, which had no bearing on the present case.

"I daresay you are right," Thorndyke agreed "One doesn't learn much from stray fingerprints. And you've nothing more to tell us?"

"Nothing," was the reply. "And you, sir? I suppose you haven't struck anything that would give us a lead?"

"I have not begun to work at the case," said Thorndyke. "I have been waiting for your report, to see if the case was as simple as it appeared."

"Yes," said Miller, "it did look simple. Seemed as if there was nothing to do but make the arrest. And now we have nothing to go on at all. Well," here he rose and began to move towards the door, "if we can help you in anyway I hope you will let us know, and, of course, if you can put us on to anything we shall thank you kindly."

As our visitor's footsteps died away on the stairs, Thorndyke softly closed the door and moved to the window, where he stood meditatively regarding the retreating officer as the latter crossed to Crown Office Row.

"That was a queer interview," said he.

"Yes," I agreed. "I don't see why he made the appointment. He hadn't much to tell us."

"I am not quite sure of that," said Thorndyke. "I have a sort of feeling that he came here to tell us something and *didn't* tell it – at least he *thinks* he didn't."

"It seemed to me that he told us nothing," said I.

"It probably seemed so to him," replied Thorndyke. "Whereas, if I am not mistaken, he has made us a free gift of a really valuable piece of information."

"Well, it may be so," said I, "but for my part, I can't see that he gave us a particle of information excepting that the case against Moakey has fallen through. Perhaps it is a technical point that is outside my range."

"Not at all," he replied. "It is just a matter of observation and comparison. You were present when Miller called last time and you have been present today. You have heard all that passed and have had the privilege of observing the Superintendent's by-no-means unexpressive countenance. Just recall the conversation and consider it by the light of all the known circumstances and see if it does not yield a very interesting suggestion."

I recalled without difficulty the brief conversation and reflected on it in connection with the Superintendent's rather aggressively nonchalant air. But from that reflection, nothing emerged but wonder at my colleague's amazing power of rapid inference. Finally I resolved to write down the conversation and think it over at my leisure.

"I take it," said I, "that you don't believe Miller is in such a fog as he professes to be?"

"On the contrary," Thorndyke replied, "I think that he is not only in a fog but hard aground. The fact that he meant to conceal and in effect disclosed (as I believe) is a leading fact. But I don't think he realises whither it leads. And, of course, it may not be a fact, after all. I may have drawn an erroneous inference. Obviously, the first thing to do is to test my hypothesis rigorously. In twenty-four hours I shall know whether it is true or false, since the means of verification are quite simple."

"I am glad of that," I said sourly, "for the fog in which you assume that Miller is enveloped is clear daylight compared to that which surrounds me."

"I think you will find that the fog will clear up under the influence of a little reflection," said Thorndyke. "But we are forgetting Miss Blake. You see the bearing of Miller's tidings on her position. Moakey is out of the case. The fingerprints are unknown, and therefore practically valueless. The police evidently have no clue at all. Miss Blake represents the only danger that threatens these men, and we may be pretty sure that they know it. If she could be eliminated, their position would be absolutely secure. And, remember, these are desperate men to whom a human life is of no account when set against their own safety. It is an unseemly hour at which to call on a lady, but I think she ought to be warned without delay."

"I entirely agree with you," said I. "We can't stand on ceremony, and after all, it is barely eight o'clock. A taxi will take us there in quarter-of-an-hour."

"Then let us start at once," said he, stepping into the lobby for his hat and stick. Leaving a slip of paper on the table for Polton's information, we set forth together and walked rapidly up Inner Temple Lane to the gate. As we emerged, a taxi-cab drew up to deposit a passenger and we hurried forward to secure the reversion when the present tenant should give up possession. A few moments later we had taken our seats and were bowling up Chancery Lane to the soft hum of the taxi's engine.

Chapter X
A Timely Warning

As the cab rolled swiftly through the quietening streets I turned over once more the two statements that had been made by Superintendent Miller and compared them. Together they had yielded to the amazingly quick intelligence of my friend Thorndyke something that the speaker had not intended to convey. What was the something? The first statement had set forth that the fingerprints were those of Joseph Hedges – or Moakey, as his associates had nicknamed him – the second had set forth that the fingerprints were *not* his, but those of some person who had yet to be identified. The two statements contradicted one another, of course, but the first was admittedly based upon a mistake. What was the fact that emerged from the contradiction?

I revolved the question again and again without seeing any glimmer of light. And then, suddenly, the simple explanation burst upon me. Of course! The prints were those of fingers smeared with Japanese wax. But Japanese wax is used for making furniture polish. There was the solution of this profound mystery. They were Mrs. Benham's fingerprints – or perhaps those of the murdered man – made in the process of applying furniture polish to the cabinet. This, the only clue, evaporated into a myth and left Miss Blake's identification the only link with the vanished murderer.

"I think I have found the solution to the fingerprint problem, Thorndyke," said I.

"Ah!" said he, "I thought you would if you reflected on it. What is it?"

"They are Mrs. Benham's fingerprints, or else Drayton's. They were made in the course of polishing the furniture."

"An excellent suggestion, Anstey," he replied, "which doesn't seem to have occurred to the police. I suspected it as soon as I saw the waxy material of the fingerprints. It doesn't happen to be the correct explanation, I am glad to say, for it would be a singularly unilluminating one. I took the fingerprints both of Mrs. Benham and the deceased this morning before the inquest, but I didn't think it necessary to mention the matter to the police. It is quite clear to me that they are not laying their cards on the table. In point of fact, they have only one card, and my impression is that they are mistaking the back of that for the face. But here we are at our destination."

We sprang out of the cab and, having dismissed it, gave a pull at the studio bell. The wicket was opened by Miss Blake herself, and I hastened to make the necessary apologies.

"I have come back again, you see, Miss Blake, and with reinforcements. It is an unholy time for making a call, but we have come on a matter of business. Dr. Thorndyke thought it advisable that you should be told something and given certain advice without delay."

"Well," she said graciously, "you are both very welcome, business or no business. Won't you come in?"

"Is Percy in the studio?"

"Yes. He has finished his home lessons and is doing a little building before going to bed."

"Then we had better say what we have to say here, or perhaps in the passage."

We stepped through the wicket and closed it, and as we stood in the dark entry, Miss Blake remarked, "This is very secret and portentous. You are filling me with curiosity."

"Then we will proceed to satisfy it. To begin with, do you remember a woman who jostled us rather rudely at the door when we were going in to the inquest?"

"Yes, I remember the incident, but I didn't notice the woman particularly, except that she gave me a rather impertinent stare and that she was a horrid-looking woman."

"Well, she either lives about here or she followed us deliberately from Hampstead. She must have come on the same car as we did, for when I turned into Jacob Street I saw her prowling up the opposite side of the road, and when she came opposite this house, she crossed and looked at the number on the door – and the name on your plate."

"That was very inquisitive of her," said Miss Blake. "But does it matter?"

"It may be of no significance at all," said Thorndyke. "But under the special circumstances it would be unwise to ignore the warning that it may convey."

"What are the special circumstances?" she asked.

"They are these," he replied. "You heard Inspector Badger say in his evidence this morning that the police have a very promising clue? Well, that clue has broken off short. I believe the police have now no clue at all, and the murderers pretty certainly know it. But you stated publicly that you are confident that you could identify the man whom you saw. That statement is certain to be known, or to become known, to these men, and they will consequently know that you are a serious menace to their safety, and the only one, that your ability to recognise one of them

671

is the only circumstance that stands between them and absolute, perfect security. But for this one fact they could walk abroad, safe from any possible recognition. They could stand outside Scotland Yard and snap their fingers at the police. Now, I don't want to be an alarmist. But it is necessary to recognise a danger and take the necessary means to guard against it. You see what I mean?"

"I think so. You mean that if I were out of the way these men would be safe from any possibility of discovery, and that it is consequently to their interest to put me out of the way."

"Yes, stated bluntly, that is the position. And you know what the characters of these men are."

"They are certainly not persons who would stick at trifles. Yes, I must admit that your view of the position seems a reasonable one, though I hope things are not as bad as you fear. But what precautions could I take?"

"I suggest that, for the present, you don't go out after dark – at any rate, not alone. That you avoid going about alone as far as is possible, that you especially shun all unfrequented places where you might be suddenly attacked, and that, on all occasions, you bear this danger in mind in considering any unusual circumstances."

"All this sounds rather alarming," she said uneasily.

"It *is* alarming," Thorndyke agreed, "and I am extremely sorry to have to impress it on you. But I would further impress on you that you have friends – two of them are now present – who are deeply concerned as to your safety and who would consider it a privilege to be called upon at any time for help or advice. I am always at your service, and I am sure Mr. Anstey is too, as well as Sir Lawrence Drayton."

"Then," said Miss Blake, "the compensations are greater than the evil for which they compensate. I welcome the danger if it brings me such kind friends. And now you really must come in for a little while, or Percy will accuse me of gossiping with "followers' at the gate."

She led the way down the paved passage and I steered Thorndyke with an expert hand past the scattered monoliths and the unfinished tombstone until we reached the door, where Miss Blake stopped to hold aside the curtain. As we entered Percy looked up from his work and then, in his quaint, self-possessed way came forward to welcome us.

"How do you like my tower now it's finished, Mr. Anstey?" he asked, regarding his work complacently, with his head on one side.

We stood by him looking at the building – a model of a church tower some three feet in height – and I observed with a sort of proprietary pride that Thorndyke was deeply impressed.

"This is really a remarkable piece of work," said he. "Where do you get your bricks?"

"I make them of clay," replied Percy, "and let them dry hard. I make one as a model and make a plaster mould of it. Then all the rest are just squeezes from the mould. So I can get any shaped bricks that I like, and as many of them as I want. It's much cheaper than buying them, and besides, the bought bricks are no use for serious work."

"No," Thorndyke agreed, "you couldn't build a tower like that with ready-made bricks, at least with none that I have ever seen. Are you going to be an architect?"

"Yes," the boy replied gravely, "if we can afford it. If not I shall be a mason. Mr. Wingrave – out in the yard, you know – lets me do a bit of stone-cutting sometimes. I shouldn't mind being a mason, but I should like to work on buildings, not on tombstones. I love buildings."

Thorndyke looked at the boy with keen and sympathetic interest. "It is a good thing," said he, "to know what you want and to have a definite bent and purpose in life. I should think you ought to be a happy man and a useful one if you keep up your enthusiasm. Don't you think so, Miss Blake?"

"I do indeed," she replied. "Percy has a real passion for buildings and he knows quite a lot about them. His copy of Parker is nearly worn out. And I don't see why he shouldn't be an architect and make his hobby his living."

As she was speaking, I looked at her and noticed that she was wearing the locket suspended from a bead necklace.

"I see you have taken your new acquisition into wear," I remarked.

"Yes," she replied. "I have just hooked it to this necklace, but I must get some more secure attachment. Have you seen this locket, Dr. Thorndyke?"

"No," he answered, and as she unhooked it and gave it to him to inspect, he continued, "This is what poor Mr. Drayton used to call his 'Little Sphinx', isn't it?"

"Yes, because it seemed always to be propounding riddles. But the riddles are inside."

"One of them is outside," said Thorndyke, "though it is not a very difficult one. I mean the peculiar construction and workmanship."

"What is there unusual about that?" she asked eagerly.

"Well," he replied, "it is not ordinary jeweller's construction. The normal way to make a locket is to build it up of sheet metal. The sides would be made first by bending a stout strip into a hoop of the proper shape – nearly square, in this case – and joining the ends with solder. Then the back and front would be soldered on to the hoop and the latter

673

cut through vertically with a fine saw, dividing the locket into two exactly similar halves. Then the hinge and the suspension ring would be soldered on, and the flange fastened in with solder. But in this case the method has been quite different. Each half of the locket was a single casting, which included half a hinge and one suspension ring. Probably both halves were cast from a single half-model and the superfluous part of the hinge filed off. Then each half was worked on the stake and pitch-block to harden the metal and the final finishing and fitting done with the file and stone. The engraving must have been done after everything but the hinge was finished."

"It must have been very awkward to engrave that small writing inside, with the edges projecting," said Miss Blake.

Thorndyke opened the locket, and taking his Coddington lens from his pocket, examined the writing closely. "If you look at it through the lens," said he, "you will see that it is not engraved. It is etched, which would have disposed of the difficulty to a great extent."

Miss Blake and I examined the minute writing, and through the lens it was easy to see that the delicate lines were bitten, not engraved.

"You were saying," said Miss Blake, as the locket and lens were passed to Percy (who, having examined the inscription, extended his investigations to his fingertips and various other objects before reluctantly surrendering the lens) "that the riddle of the construction is not a difficult one. What is the answer to it?"

"I think," he replied, "the inscription inside supplies the answer. That inscription was clearly put there for some purpose to which the original owner attached some importance. It apparently conveyed some kind of admonition or instruction which was hardly likely to be addressed to himself. But if the message was of importance, it was worthwhile to take measures to ensure its permanence. And that is what has been done. There are no loose or separable parts, no soldered joints to break away. Each half of the locket is a single piece of solid metal, including the hinge and suspension ring. And you notice that the hinge is unusually massive, and that each half of the locket has its own suspension ring, so that if the hinge should break, both halves would still be securely suspended. And there was no loose ring to chafe through and break."

"Don't you think," she asked, "that there was originally a loose ring passing through both of the eyes?"

"No," he answered. "If you look carefully at the two eyes you will see that the holes through them have been most carefully smoothed and rounded. Evidently the locket was meant to be suspended by a cord or thong, and the position of the eyes with a hole through from back to front shows that the cord was intended to be tied in a single knot where it passed through – a much more secure arrangement than a chain, anyone link of which may, unnoticed, wear thin and break at any unusual strain."

"And you think that the message or whatever it was that the inscription conveyed was really something of importance?" As she asked the question, Miss Blake looked at Thorndyke with a suppressed eagerness at which I inwardly smiled. The Lady of Shallot evidently had hopes of Merlin.

"That is what the precautions suggest," was his reply. "It appeared important to the person who took the precautions."

"And do you suppose that it would be possible to guess what the nature of the message was?"

"One could judge better," he replied "if one knew what passages the reader is referred to."

"I can show you the passages," she said. "I have looked them up, and Mr. Anstey and I went over them together and could make nothing of them."

"That doesn't sound very encouraging," said Thorndyke as she ran to the cabinet and brought out her book of notes. "However, we shall see if a further opinion is of any help." He took the note-book from her and read through the entries slowly and with close attention. Then he handed the book back to her.

"One thing is fairly evident," said he. "The purpose of the writer was not pious instruction. Whatever was intended to be conveyed did not lie on the surface, for the individual passages are singularly barren of meaning, while the collection as a whole is a mere jumble of quotations without any apparent sequence or connection. The passages must have had some meaning previously agreed on or, more probably, they formed the key of a code or cipher used for secret correspondence."

"If they form the key of a cipher," said Miss Blake, "do you think it would be possible to work out the cipher by studying them?"

"I suppose it would be possible," he replied, "since a cipher must work by some sort of rule. But people who make ciphers do not take great pains to make them easily decipherable to the uninitiated. And then we are only guessing that they are the key to a cipher. They may be something quite different, some form of cryptogram that would be utterly unintelligible without some key or counterpart that we haven't got. Do you think of trying to decipher them or extract the hidden meaning?"

"I am rather curious about them," she admitted, "and rather interested in ciphers and cryptograms."

"Well," said Thorndyke, "you may succeed. More probably you will draw a blank – but in any case I think you will get a run for your money."

Once more with his lens he examined the locket inside and out, not omitting the hallmark on the back, on which he dwelt for some time. Then, still holding the locket in his hand, he said, "You ought to have this cover-glass replaced. The hair is part of the relic and ought not to be exposed to loss or injury."

"Yes," said she, "I ought to get it done, but I don't much like trusting it to an unknown jeweller."

"Would you like Polton to do it for you?" Thorndyke asked. "He is not a stranger, and you know he is a first-class workman."

"Oh, if Mr. Polton would do it I should be delighted and most grateful. Do you think he would?"

"I think he would be highly flattered at being asked," said Thorndyke. "I will take it back with me if you like, and get him to put in the fresh glass at once."

Miss Blake accepted this offer joyfully, and taking the locket from Thorndyke, she proceeded, with great care and a quantity of tissue paper, to make it into a little packet. While she was thus engaged, the bell in the yard rang loudly and Percy ran out to open the gate. In less than a minute he re-entered the studio carrying a brown-paper parcel.

"Miss Winifred Blake," he announced. "Shall I see what's in it, Winnie?"

"I suppose you won't be happy till you do," she replied, whereupon he gleefully cut the string and removed the paper, exposing a cardboard box, of which he lifted the lid.

"My eye, Winnie!" he exclaimed. "It's tuck. I wonder who it's from. And it's for us both. *To Winifred and Percival Blake, With Love*". Whose love, I wonder. Can you spot the handwriting?" He passed a slip of paper to his sister and exhibited a shallow box filled with large chocolate sweets on which he gazed gloatingly.

Thorndyke, who had just received the little packet from Miss Blake and was putting it into his pocket, watched the boy attentively, interested, as I supposed, by the sudden descent from the heights of architectural design to frank, boyish gluttony.

"I don't recognise the writing at all," said Miss Blake, "and I can't imagine who can have sent this."

"Well, it doesn't matter," said Percy. "Let's sample them." He passed the box to his sister – still closely watched by Thorndyke, I noticed – and as she put out her hand to pick up one of the sweets, my colleague asked in a significant tone, "Are you sure that you don't know the handwriting?"

The tone in which the question was asked was so emphatic that she looked at him in surprise. "No," she answered, "the writing is quite strange to me."

"Then," said he, "the writer is possibly a stranger."

She looked at him with a puzzled expression, and I noticed that he was gazing at her with a strange fixity. After a pause he continued. "We were speaking just now of unusual circumstances. Would not a gift of food from a stranger be an unusual circumstance?"

In an instant his meaning flashed upon me, and upon her too, for she took the box quickly from her brother and her face became deathly pale.

"I think, Percy dear," she said, "if you don't mind very much, we won't touch these tonight. Do you mind?"

"Of course I don't," he replied, "if you would rather keep 'em till tomorrow."

Nevertheless the boy looked curiously at his sister, and it was clear to me that he saw that there was "something in the wind". But he asked no questions and made no comment, sauntering back to his tower and looking it over critically.

"It's really time you went to bed, Percy," Miss Blake said after a pause.

"Is it?" he asked. "What's the time?"

"It is getting on for ten, and you have to be up at half-past-six."

"It's always 'getting on' for ten, you know," said he. "The question is, how far has it got? But there! It's no good arguing. I suppose I shall get chucked out if I don't go peaceably." He offered a friendly hand to me and Thorndyke in succession, and having given his sister a hug and a kiss, took his departure. And again I thought I detected in his manner a perception of something below the surface that accounted for his sudden dismissal.

"I suspect Master Percy smells a fox," said I, "but is too polite to mention it."

"It is very likely," said Miss Blake. "He is wonderfully quick and observant, and he is extraordinarily discreet. In most respects he is quite a normal boy, but in others he is more like a man."

"And a very well-bred man, too," said I.

"Yes, he is nice boy and the best of brothers. But now, Dr. Thorndyke, about these sweets. Do you really think there is anything wrong with them?"

"I don't say that," replied Thorndyke, "but, of course, when you have swallowed one, it is too late to inquire. May I look at that paper?"

Miss Blake took the slip of paper from the box and handed it to him, and once more the lens came into requisition.

"Yes," he said, after somewhat prolonged examination of the writing, "this is not reassuring. It is quite clear that this writing was traced over a previous writing in lead pencil. A hard rubber has been used to take out the pencil marks, but the ink has fixed them in several places. If you look at the writing carefully through the lens you can see the fine, dark pencil line forming a sort of core to the broader ink line. And you can also distinguish several minute crumbs of blackened rubber – little black rolls with pointed ends."

"But why should it have been written first in pencil?" Miss Blake asked.

"For the purpose of disguising the handwriting," replied Thorndyke. "It is a common practice. Of course, in the case of a forger copying a signature, its purpose is obvious. He takes a pencil tracing of the original signature, goes over it in ink and rubs out the pencil – if he can. But it is used in producing feigned handwriting as well. It is difficult to write direct with a pen in a hand which is quite different from one's own. But if a preliminary trial sketch is done in pencil, and touched up if necessary, and then traced over deliberately with the pen, the result may be quite unlike one's own handwriting. But, in any case, this underlying pencil writing is manifestly abnormal and therefore suspicious. Shall we see if there is anything unusual in the appearance of the sweets?"

She passed him the box, which he placed on the table under the gaslight and looked over systematically. Then he turned the sweets, one after the other, on their sides, and when they were all in this position, he again looked them over.

"It seems hardly possible," said I, "that the woman – if it is she whom you suspect – could have prepared a set of poisoned sweets in such a short time. It was past four o'clock when she came and looked at the plate, and it is not ten yet. There doesn't seem to have been time."

"There has been about five hours," said Thorndyke, "and I see by the postmark on the wrapper that the parcel was posted in this neighbourhood barely two hours ago. That leaves three hours, which would have been sufficient. But she might have had the things prepared in advance, and merely waited for the inquest to get the name and particulars. And the sender may not be this woman at all. And again, there may be no poison in the sweets. We are only taking precautions against a possibility. But looking at these things all together, there seems to me to be a suggestion of their having been patched with liquid chocolate round the sides. If that is so, they will have been cut open horizontally and the halves fitted together again, and the purpose of the

678

patching will have been to hide the join. Here is a very well-marked specimen. I think we will take it as a test case."

He picked out the sweet, and with his pocket-knife, began very delicately to scrape away the outer coat of chocolate all round the sides, while we drew up our chairs and watched him anxiously. Presently he paused and silently held the sweet towards us, indicating a spot with the point of his knife, and looking at that spot where the outer coating had been scraped away, I could clearly make out an indented line. He then resumed his scraping, following the line, until he had worked round the whole circumference. And now it was quite obvious that the sweet had been divided into an upper and a lower half and the two parts rejoined.

"I am afraid it is a true bill, Thorndyke," said I.

"I think so," he agreed, "but we shall soon see." He inserted his knife into the encircling crevice, and giving it a gentle turn, raised the top half, which he then lifted off. At once I could see that the exposed surfaces of the white interior of the sweet were coated with a glistening white powder, worked into the soft material of the filling. Thorndyke produced his lens, and through it examined the cut surface for a few moments. Then he passed the half sweet and the lens to me.

"What do you suppose this stuff is, Thorndyke?" I asked, when I had inspected the sweet, and then passed it and the lens to Miss Blake. "It looks like finely powdered china or white enamel."

"It looks like – and I have no doubt is – arsenious acid, or white arsenic, as it is commonly called, and I should say there is rather more than two grains in this sweet. It is a heavy substance."

"Is that a fatal dose?" I asked.

"Yes. And it is extremely unlikely that only one sweet would have been eaten. Two or three would contain a dose that would produce death very rapidly."

We were silent for a few moments. Suddenly Miss Blake burst into tears and buried her face in her hands, sobbing almost hysterically. Thorndyke looked at her with a curious expression, stern and even wrathful, and yet with a certain softness of compassion, but he said nothing. As to me, I was filled with fury against the wretch who had done this unspeakable thing, but, like Thorndyke, I could find no words that were adequate.

Presently Miss Blake recovered her self-possession somewhat, and as she wiped her eyes, she apologised for her outburst.

"Pray forgive me!" she exclaimed. "But it is horrible – horrible! Just think! But for the infinitely unlikely chance of your coming in tonight Percy would have eaten at least two or three of those sweets. By now he would have been dead, or dying in agony, and I unable to help him! It is a frightful thought. Nobody would have known anything until Mrs. Wingrave came in the morning and found our bodies! And the wretch may try again."

"That won't matter much," said Thorndyke. "You are now on your guard. It will be best to think as little of this episode as you can. It has been a narrow escape, but it is past. You must fix your attention on the future."

"But what can we do?" she asked despairingly.

"You must walk warily and never for one moment forget this implacable, ruthless enemy. No opportunity must be given. Do not go out after dark without efficient protection, and avoid going abroad alone at any time. You had better not to go to the gate after nightfall, neither you nor Percy. Can you not arrange for someone to answer the bell for you?"

"I could ask Mrs. Wingrave, the sculptor's wife. Their rooms open on the yard. But what could I tell her?"

"You will have to tell her as much as is necessary. And, of course, Percy must be told. It is very unfortunate, but we can take no risks. You must impress upon him that under no circumstances whatever must he eat or drink anything that is given or sent to him by strangers or of which he does not know the antecedents. Does he go to school?"

"Yes. He goes to the Elizabeth Woodville Grammar School, near Regents Park. He usually gets home about five o'clock. Sometimes I go and meet him, but he has some school-fellows who live near here and who generally walk home with him."

"Then let him come home with them. There is no reason to suppose that he is in any danger apart from you. And let me impress upon you again that Mr. Anstey and I are always at your service. While this danger lasts – I hope it will soon pass – don't scruple to make any use of us that circumstances may require. If you have to go anywhere at night, we can always arrange for you to have an escort. At a pinch, we could secure the help of the police, but we don't want to do that unless we are compelled. And – it seems contradictory advice to give you – but having taken all precautions, try not to think about this incident of tonight, or to dwell on the danger more than is necessary to keep your attention on the alert. And now we must wish you good night, Miss Blake. I will take these sweets with me for more complete examination."

"I can never thank you enough for all your kindness," she said, as he wrapped the box in its original paper, "and I shall have no hesitation in treating you as the good and generous friends that you have proved tonight. I feel that Percy and I are in your hands, and we shouldn't wish to be in better." She walked out with us to the gate, and at the wicket shook our hands warmly, and indeed with no little emotion. And when we had seen the wicket safely closed on her, and taken a look up and down the street, we turned westward and started on our way home.

Chapter XI
The Blue Hair

"What are you going to do, Anstey?" Thorndyke asked as we reached the corner of Jacob Street. "Are you going to Hampstead or are you coming home with me?"

"What are you going to do tonight?" I asked in return.

"I shall make a rough qualitative test of the substance in that sweet," he replied, "just to settle definitely whether it is or is not arsenic."

"Have you any doubt on the subject?" I asked.

"No," he answered. "But still it is not a matter of fact until it has been verified by analysis. My own conviction on the subject is only a state of mind, which is not transferable as evidence. A chemical demonstration is a fact which can be deposed to in sworn testimony."

"Then," said I, "I shall come home with you and hear the result of your analysis, although your certainty would be good enough for me."

We walked down to the bottom of Hampstead Road where we boarded an omnibus bound for Charing Cross. For some time nothing more was said, each of us being immersed in reflection on the events of the evening.

"It is a horrible affair," I said at length, assuming that we were still thinking on the same subject, "and a terrible thing to reflect that the world we live in should contain such wretches."

"It is," he agreed. "But the mitigating circumstance is that these wretches are nearly always fools. That is the reassuring element in the present case."

"In what way reassuring?" I asked.

"I mean," said he, "the palpable folly of the whole proceeding. We have here no subtle, wary criminal who works with considered strategy under secure cover, but just the common arsenic fool who delivers himself into your hands by his own stupidity."

"But what is the evidence of the stupidity?"

"My dear Anstey!" he exclaimed. "Look at the crudity of method. The discharge, broadcast, of a boxful of poisoned food under manifestly suspicious circumstances, with the poison barely concealed, the faked writing, which a common policeman would have detected, the absence of any plausible origin of the gift, and the nature of the poison itself. That alone is diagnostic. Arsenic is typically a fool's poison. No competent poisoner would dream of using such a material."

Why not?" I asked.

"Because its properties are exactly the reverse of those which would make a poison safe to use. The fatal dose is relatively large – not less than two grains and for security, considerably more. The effects are extremely variable and uncertain, making necessary the use of really large doses. The material is rather conspicuous, it is only slightly soluble in water and still less so in tea or coffee, it is easily recognised by simple chemical tests, even in the minutest quantities. It is practically indestructible, and its strong preservative effects on the dead body make it easy to demonstrate its presence years after death. A man who poisons a person with arsenic creates a record of the fact which will last, at least, for the term of his own lifetime."

"That isn't much benefit to the person who has been poisoned," I remarked.

"No," he admitted. "But we are considering the poisoner's point of view. It is not enough for him to succeed in killing his victim. He has to avoid killing himself at the same time. A poisoner sets out to commit a secret murder, and the secrecy is the test of his efficiency. If his methods are easily detectable, and if he leaves a record which stands against him in perpetuity, he is an inefficient poisoner. And that is the case of the arsenic practitioner. He runs a great present risk, since the symptoms of arsenic poisoning are conspicuous and fairly characteristic, and he leaves traces of his crime which nothing but cremation will destroy."

Our discussion had brought us to our chambers, where Thorndyke proceeded straight up to the laboratory, breaking in upon Polton, who was seated at his bench, putting the finishing touches to the large and elaborate pedometer.

"We need not disturb you, Polton," said Thorndyke. "I am just going to make a rough qualitative test for arsenic."

Polton instantly laid down his watchmaker's glass and unlocked a cupboard on the chemical side of the laboratory. "You will want a Marsh's apparatus and the materials for Reinsch's Test, I suppose, sir?" said he.

"Yes. But we will begin with the liquid tests. I shall want a glass mortar and some hydrochloric acid."

Polton put the necessary appliances on the bench and added a large bottle labelled "*Distilled Water*," while I seated myself on a stool and watched the analysis with a slightly vague though highly interested recognition of the processes that I had so often expounded to juries. I saw Thorndyke open the box, take from it the two halves of the divided sweet, and drop them into the little glass mortar and, having poured on them some distilled water and a little acid, rub them with the glass pestle until they were reduced to a muddy-looking liquid. This liquid he carefully filtered into a beaker, when it became clear and practically colourless, like water, and this watery-looking fluid formed the material for the succeeding tests.

Of these the first three were performed in test-tubes into each of which a small quantity of the clear solution was poured, and then to each was added a few drops of certain other clear liquids. The result was very striking. In two of the tubes the clear liquid instantly turned to a dense, opaque yellow, somewhat like yolk of egg, while in the third it changed to a bright, opaque emerald green.

"What are those precipitates?" I asked.

"The two yellow ones," he replied, "are arsenite of silver and arsenic sulphide. The green one is arsenite of copper. As there is sugar and some other organic matter in this solution, I shall not carry these tests any farther, but they are pretty conclusive. How are you getting on, Polton?"

"I think we are ready, sir," was the reply, on which I crossed to the bench on which he had been at work. Here on a tripod over a Bunsen gas-burner, was a beaker containing a number of little pieces of copper foil and a clear, watery liquid which was boiling briskly.

"This is Reinsch's test," Thorndyke explained. "You see that this copper-foil remains bright in the dilute acid, showing that both the metal and the acid are free from arsenic. I shall now introduce a few drops of the suspected liquid, and if it contains arsenic the copper-foil will become grey or black according to the amount of arsenic present." As he spoke, he took the beaker containing the filtered liquid from the mortar and poured about a tablespoonful into that containing the copper-foil. I watched eagerly for the result, and very soon a change began to appear. The ruddy lustre of the copper gradually turned to a steely grey and from that to a glistening black.

"You see," said Thorndyke, "that the reaction is very distinct. The quantity of arsenic present is, in an analytical sense, quite large. And now we will try the most definite and conclusive test of all – Marsh's." He turned to the other apparatus which Polton had made ready, which consisted of a squat bottle with two short necks, through one of which passed a tall glass funnel, and through the other a glass tube fitted with a tap and terminating in a fine jet. The contents of the bottle – lumps of zinc immersed in sulphuric acid – were effervescing briskly, and the tap was turned on to allow the gas to escape through the jet. To the latter Polton now applied a lighted match, and immediately there appeared a little pale violet flame. Picking up a white tile which had been placed in readiness, Thorndyke held it for a moment in the flame and then looked at it.

"You see," said he, "that the tile is quite unsoiled. If there had been the smallest trace of arsenic in the bottle, a dark spot would have appeared on the tile. So we may take it that our chemicals are free from arsenic. Now let us try the solution of the sweet."

He took up the beaker containing the solution of the disintegrated chocolate, and poured very slowly, drop by drop, about a teaspoonful into the funnel of the bottle. Then, after having given it time to mix thoroughly with the other contents, he once more picked up the tile and held it for an instant in the flame. The result was, to me, most striking. In the very moment when the tile touched the flame, there appeared on the white surface a circular spot, black, lustrous, and metallic.

"That," said Thorndyke, "might be either antimony or arsenic. By its appearance it is obviously metallic arsenic, but still we will make the differential test. If it is arsenic it will dissolve in a solution of chlorinated lime. If it is antimony it will not." He removed the stopper from a bottle labelled "*Chlorinated Lime*", and poured a little pool of the solution on the tile. Almost immediately the black spot began to fade at the edges, and to grow smaller and fainter until at length it disappeared altogether.

"That completes our inquiry," said Thorndyke as he laid down the tile. "For the purposes of evidence in a court of law, a more searching and detailed analysis would be necessary. To produce conviction in the minds of a jury, we should have to be able to say exactly how much arsenic was in each of the sweets. That, however, is no concern of ours. The criminal intention is all that matters to us. And now, Anstey, I must leave you for a while to entertain yourself with a book. I have to do some work in the office on another case. But we will take this ill-omened box down and put it in a safe place."

He took the box of sweets, with its original wrapper, and when we descended to the sitting-room. He closed it up, sealed it, and signed and dated it, and having made a note of the particulars of the postmark, deposited it in the safe. Then he retired to the office, where I assumed that he had in hand some work of compilation or reference, for the "office" was in fact rather a miniature law library, in which was stored a singularly complete collection of works bearing upon our special branch of legal practice.

When he had gone, I ran my eye vaguely along the book-shelves in search of a likely volume with which to pass the time. But the box of poisoned sweets haunted me and refused to be ejected from my thoughts. Eventually I brought out Miss Blake's manuscript from the drawer in which I had put it when Miller had arrived, and drawing an easy-chair up to the fire, sat listlessly glancing over the well-remembered pages, but actually thinking of the writer, of the brave, sweet-faced girl and the fine, manly boy to whom she was at once sister and mother. What, I wondered uncomfortably, was to be the end of this? Only by the merest hairbreadth had she and the boy, this very night, escaped a dreadful death. Soon the wretches who had contrived this diabolical crime would discover that their plot had miscarried in some way. What would they do next? It was hardly likely that they would try poison again, but there are plenty of other ways of committing murder. It was all very well to say that they were fools. So they might be. But they were unknown fools. That was the trouble. They could make their preparations unwatched, and approach unsuspected within striking distance. If your enemy is unknown it is almost impossible to be on your guard against him. In one direction only safety lay – in detection. In the moment when the identity of the criminals should become known, the danger would be at an end.

But when would that moment arrive? So far as the position was known to me, it was not even in sight. The police admitted that their clue had broken off short and apparently they had no other – at least that was Thorndyke's opinion. But what of Thorndyke himself? Had he any clue? My feeling was that he had not. It seemed impossible that he could have, for these two men had, as it were, dropped down out of the sky and then vanished into space. No one knew who they were, whence they had come, or whither they had gone. And they seemed to have left not a trace for the imagination to work on.

On the other hand, Thorndyke was Thorndyke: An inscrutable man, silent, self-contained, and even secretive, in spite of his genial exterior. I thought of him, at this very moment, sitting calmly in the office with all his faculties quietly transferred to a fresh case, unmoved by the thrilling events of the evening, though it was he who had instantly seen the danger, he who had immediately suspected the "Greek Gift". And as I thought of him poring over his reports, and marvelled at his detachment, I recalled the many instances of his wonderful power of inference from almost invisible data, and found myself hoping that even now, when to me all seemed dark, some glimmer of light was visible to him.

It had turned half-past-eleven when I heard a light but deliberate step ascending the stair. Instantly I stole on tiptoe to the office, and had just opened the door when a tapping – apparently with the handle of a stick or umbrella – on our "oak" announced the arrival of a visitor.

"Shall I open the door, Thorndyke?" I whispered.

"Yes," he answered. "It is Brodribb. I know his knock. Tell him I shall have finished in a few minutes. And you might run up and tell Polton that he is here. He will know what to do."

I accordingly went out and threw open the "oak", and there, sure enough, was Mr. Brodribb, looking with his fine, rich complexion, his silky white hair, and his sumptuous, old-fashioned raiment, as if he had stepped out of the frame of some Georgian portrait.

"Good evening, Anstey," said he. "Might even say 'Good night'. It's a devil of a time to come stirring you up, but I saw a light in your windows, and I rather particularly wanted to have a word or two with Thorndyke. Is he in?"

"Yes. He is in the office surrounded by a sort of landslide of reports – Assizes, Central Criminal, and various assorted. He will have finished in a few minutes. Meanwhile I will run up and let Polton know you are here."

At the mention of Polton's name, methought his bright blue eye grew brighter, and by the way in which he murmured "Ha!" and smiled as he subsided into an armchair, I judged that – as our American cousins would say – he "had been there before", and this impression was confirmed when I made my announcement in the laboratory, where I found Polton dancing his pedometer up and down and listening ecstatically to its measured tick.

"Mr. Brodribb," said he. "Let me see, it is the sixty-three that he likes. Yes, and Lord, he does like it! It's a pleasure to see him drink it!"

"Well, Polton," said I, "it is an altruistic pleasure, and if it would add to your enjoyment to see me drink some, too, I am prepared to make an effort."

"You couldn't do it as Mr. Brodribb does," said Polton, "and you haven't got the complexion. Still – I'll bring it down in a minute or two, when I've got it filtered into the decanter."

On this I descended and rejoined Mr. Brodribb and, having offered him a cigar, which he declined – no doubt with a view to preserving his gustatory sense unimpaired – sat down and filled my pipe.

"I looked in," said Mr. Brodribb, "on my way home to ask Thorndyke a question. I met Drayton today – only saw him for a few moments – and he said something about wanting some information respecting Arthur Blake of Beauchamp Blake. I understood him to say that the matter arose out of the inquest on his brother – can't see how the devil it could, but that is what I gathered. Now, before I tell him anything, I should like to know what's in the wind. What's he after? Do you happen to know?"

"I think I do, to some extent," said I, and I gave him a brief account of the circumstances and a summary of Miss Blake's evidence.

"I see," said he. "Then this young lady will be Peter Blake's daughter. But what does Drayton want to know? And why does he want to know it? He said something about Thorndyke, too. Now, where does Thorndyke come in?"

As if in answer to the question, my colleague emerged at this moment from the office, slipping a large note-book into his pocket. As he greeted our visitor, I found myself speculating on the contents of that note-book and wondering what kind of information he had been disinterring from those piles of arid-looking reports of Assizes, quarter-sessions, and the Central Criminal Court. The greetings were hardly finished when Polton entered with a tray on which were a decanter, three glasses, and a biscuit jar, and having placed a small table adjacent to Mr. Brodribb's chair, deposited the tray thereon with a crinkly smile of satisfaction and departed after an instantaneous glance of profound significance in my direction.

Thorndyke filled the three glasses and, drawing a chair nearer to the fire, sat down and began to fill his pipe while Brodribb lifted his glass, looked at it reflectively, took an experimental sip, savoured it with grave attention, and again looked at the glass.

"A noble wine, Thorndyke," he pronounced solemnly. "I don't deserve this after coming and routing you out at close upon midnight. But I haven't come for mere gossip. I've just been putting my case to Anstey." And here he repeated what he had told me of his interview with Sir Lawrence. "Now, what I want to know," he concluded, "is, what is Drayton after? He seems disposed to interest himself in Peter Blake's daughter – and his son, too, I suppose."

"Yes," said Thorndyke, "and for that matter, I may say that I feel a benevolent interest in the young people myself – and so, I think, does Anstey."

"Then," said Brodribb, "I'm going to ask you a plain question. Is there any idea of contesting the title of the present tenant of the Blake property – Arthur Blake?"

"I should say certainly not," replied Thorndyke. "Drayton's object is, I think, to ascertain whether there is any prospect of circumstances becoming favourable in the future for the revival of Peter Blake's claim – or rather Percival Blake's, as it would now be. He wants to know who the present heir is, what is his relation to the present tenant, and he would like to know as much as possible about Arthur Blake himself, particularly in regard to the probability of his marrying. And, as I said, Anstey and I are not uninterested in the matter."

"Well, if that is all," said Brodribb, "I can answer you without any breach of confidence to my client. As to the heir, his name is Charles Templeton, but what his relationship to Arthur Blake is, I can't say at the moment. He is a pretty distant relative, I know. With regard to Arthur

Blake, I can tell you all about him, for I have made some inquiries on my own account. And I can tell you something that will interest you more than the probability of his marrying – he is trying to sell the property."

"The deuce he is!" exclaimed Thorndyke. "I suppose I mustn't ask why he wants to sell?"

"I don't know that there is any secret about it. His own explanation is that he doesn't care for England and would like to get back to Australia, where he has lived nearly all his life, and I daresay there is some truth in that, for he is like a fish out of water – doesn't understand the ways of an English landowner at all. But I don't think that's the whole of it. He knows about this claim of Peter Blake's, and he knows that Peter Blake's son is living, and then – you know about the title-deeds, I suppose?"

"Yes," said Thorndyke. "Miss Blake has told us the whole story."

"Well, I suspect that, with this claim in the air and the mystery of the whereabouts of the title-deeds, he feels that his tenure of the property is a little insecure. So he would like to sell it and clear off with the money. And, mind you, he is not entirely wrong. Peter Blake's claim was a *bona fide* claim. It broke down from the lack of documentary evidence. But it is always possible for documents to reappear, and if these documents ever should, the position would be very different. And, to tell the honest truth, I shouldn't be particularly afflicted if they did reappear."

"Why wouldn't you?" I asked.

"Well," Brodribb replied, "you know, one gets a sort of sentimental interest in a historic estate which one has known all one's life. I am Arthur Blake's solicitor, it is true. But I feel that I have responsibilities towards the whole family and the estate itself. I have much more sentiment about the old house and its lands than Blake himself has. I hate the idea of selling an old place like that, which has been in one family since the time of Henry the Eighth, as if it were a mere speculative builder's estate. Besides, it isn't playing the game. An inherited estate belongs to the family, and a man who has received it from his ancestors has no right to dispossess his posterity. I told him so, and he didn't like it a bit."

"What sort of man is he?" I asked.

"He's a colonial, and not a good type of colonial. Gruff and short and none too well-mannered, and, of course, he doesn't know anybody in the county. And I should think he is a confirmed bachelor, for he lives – when he is at home – in the new part of the house, with three servants and his man, as if he were in a bachelor flat."

"How did you manage to dig him up?" Thorndyke asked.

689

"I began to make inquiries as soon as it was certain that he would be Arnold Blake's successor. That was years ago. I ascertained his whereabouts and got into touch with him pretty easily, but I really never knew much about him until a few weeks back, when I came across a man who had just retired from the Australian Police. He knew all about Blake, so I took the opportunity to get a pretty full history of him and make out a little dossier to keep by me. You never know when a trifle of information may come in useful."

"No," Thorndyke agreed as he refilled our visitor's glass. "Knowledge is power."

"Quite so," said Brodribb, "and it is well to know whom you are dealing with. But, in fact, this fellow Blake is quite an interesting character."

"So the police seem to have thought," I remarked.

"Oh, I don't think there was anything against Blake," said he, "excepting that he kept rather queer company at times. My friend first heard of him at a mining camp, where the society was not exactly select, and where he ran a saloon or liquor bar. But he gave that up and took to digging, and he seems to have had quite good luck for a time. Then his claim petered out and he moved off to a new district and started a sawmill with some of his mining pals. There, I think, some of his partners had trouble with the police – I don't know exactly what it was, but he moved off again and rambled about doing all sorts of odd jobs – boat-building, farming, working as deck hand on a coaster, carpentering – he seems to have been able to turn his hand to anything – and finally he came across his last partner, a man named Owen, a fellow of his own type, who seemed to be able to do anything but stick to one kind of job. Owen was a colonial – he was born at Hobart – and by trade he was a photo-engraver, but he had worked a small type-foundry, run a local newspaper, and done some other jobs that weren't quite so respectable. Blake ran across him at a new town in a mining district, and the circumstances were characteristic of the two men. Owen had started a pottery, but he had just met with an accident and broken his knee-cap. Thereupon Blake took him in hand and fixed his knee-cap up in splints, and as it happened to be the left knee, so that Owen would not be able to work the potter's wheel for a long time, Blake took over the job, worked the wheel, and turned out the pots and pans, while a woman who was associated with Owen – I don't know what their relations were – helped with the kiln and sold the stuff in the town."

"Why can't you work a potter's wheel with your right foot?" I asked.

"I don't know," replied Brodribb, "but I understand that you can't."

"In an ordinary 'kick-wheel', said Thorndyke, "the 'kick-bar', or treadle, is on the left side, and has to be if the potter is right-handed, to enable him to steady himself with the right foot."

"I see," said I. "And how long did the pottery last?"

"Not long," replied Brodribb. "When Owen got about again, as he couldn't work the wheel, it seems that he got restless and began to hanker for something fresh. Then Blake got a tip from some prospector about some traces of gold in the hills in an outlying district, so they sold the pottery and the three of them went off prospecting, and I think they were engaged in some tentative digging when Blake got my letter telling him that Arnold Blake was dead and that he had come into the property. A deuce of a time he was, too, in getting that letter, for, of course, there was no post out there and they only rode into the town at long intervals."

"And now," said Thorndyke, "he wants to sell the property and get back to his cronies. I should think they would be very glad to see him."

"I don't know that he wants to join his pals again," said Brodribb. "As a man of property, I should think he would keep clear of people of that sort. But in any case, he couldn't. Owen is dead. He must have died soon after Blake left, must have met with an accident when he was alone, for his body was found only a few months ago at the foot of a cliff – just a heap of more or less damaged bones that must have been lying there for several years. The skeleton was found by the merest chance by another prospector."

"How did he know it was Owen's body?" I asked.

"Well, he knew that Owen had been there and had not been seen for a long time, and he found a signet-ring – a rough affair that Owen had made himself and engraved with a representation of a yew-tree. That was recognised as his."

"Why a yew-tree?" I asked.

"That was his private mark, a sort of rebus or pun on his Christian name, Hugh."

"But how was it," Thorndyke asked, "that the woman hadn't reported his death?"

"Oh, she had left him quite soon after Blake's departure. The police had an idea that she had gone off with Owen to the South Sea Islands on one of the schooners. At any rate, she disappeared, and they weren't sorry to see the last of her. She was a shady character – and so, apparently, was Owen, for that matter."

"What was there against her?" I asked.

"Well, I don't know that there was anything very definite, though there may have been. But she turned up rather mysteriously at Melbourne on a Russian tramp steamer, and the police surmised that she had left her country for her country's good and her own. So they entered her name – Laura Levinsky – on their books and kept an eye on her until she went. But, God bless me, what a damned old chatterbox I am! Here am I babbling away at past midnight, and giving you a lot of gossip that is no more your business than it is mine."

"I think," said Thorndyke, "we have all enjoyed the gossip, and as to its irrelevancy, who can tell? At any rate, we gather that there is no immediate prospect of Blake's marrying, which really does concern us."

"No," said Brodribb, "nor of his selling the property, though he has put it into the hands of Lee and Robey, the estate agents. But he won't sell it. Of course there's no magic in title-deeds, and his title is good enough, but no one would buy an important property like that with the title-deeds missing and liable to turn up in the wrong hands. And now I must really be off. You've squeezed me dry if you were out for information, and I've squeezed you dry," he added with a complacent glance at the decanter, "and a devilish good bottle of port it was. You can pass on what I've told you to Drayton, and I'll see if I can let you know what relation the heir, Charles Templeton, is to Arthur Blake. So goodnight and good luck, and my best respects to your wine merchant."

When Brodribb had gone, I stretched myself and yawned slightly.

"Well," I said, "I don't feel sleepy, but I think I will turn in. One must go to bed some time."

"I don't feel sleepy either," said Thorndyke, "and I shall not turn in. I think I will just jot down a few notes of what Brodribb has told us and then have another look at Miss Blake's manuscript before handing it over to Drayton."

"Old Brodribb enjoyed the wine, didn't he?" I remarked. "And, by Jove, it did set his old chin wagging. But he didn't tell us much, after all. Excepting the proposed sale, it was just mere personal gossip."

"Yes. But the sale question is really important. We shall have to think over that. He mustn't be allowed to sell the property."

"Can we prevent him?" I asked.

"I think," replied Thorndyke, "from what Brodribb said, that a threat to apply for an injunction pending an investigation of the title would make him draw in his horns. But we shall see. Goodnight, if you are off."

By the time I had undressed, washed, and turned into bed, I began to suspect that Thorndyke had taken the wiser course. And as I lay in the dark, at first quietly but then with increasing restlessness, the suspicion deepened. The disturbing – indeed, alarming – events of the evening came crowding back into my mind and grew, minute by minute, more vivid. The scene in the studio arose before me with fearful reality, and worse still, the horrible catastrophe, barely averted by Thorndyke's

692

watchfulness and wonderful prevision, actually seemed to befall before my eyes. The dreadful picture that Miss Blake had drawn in a few words painted itself in my consciousness with the most frightful realism. I saw the sculptor's wife peering into the dim and silent studio in the early morning, and heard her shriek of horror as her glance fell on the brother and sister, lying there stark and dead, and Thorndyke's analysis in the laboratory took on a new and fearful significance. At last, after tossing in bed for over an hour, I could bear it no longer, and rose to go down to the sitting-room for a book.

As I entered the room, Thorndyke looked up from the note-book in which he was writing. "You had better have stayed up a little longer," he remarked. "Now you are going to read yourself to sleep, I suppose."

"Yes, I hope so," I replied, and turned to the book-shelves to search for a work of a calm and cheerful tendency. *The Compleat Angler* appearing to fulfil these requirements most perfectly, I picked it out and was just about to move away when my glance lighted on the rather curious collection of objects on the table. They had made their appearance since I retired, and were presumably connected with some kind of investigation which my colleague had been pursuing while I was wooing Hypnos in vain. I looked at them curiously, and speculated on the nature of the inquiry. There was a microscope, and beside it lay the locket, opened and showing the broken glass, and a little, fat, greasy volume which examination showed to be a *Latin Vulgate Bible*.

I laid down the volume and glanced at Thorndyke, whom I found watching me with a faint smile. Then I peered through the microscope and perceived what looked like a thread of blue glass.

"Is this a thread of silk, Thorndyke?" I asked.

"No," he replied, "it is a hair. Apparently a woman's hair."

"But," I expostulated, "it is blue – bright blue! Where on earth did you get it?"

"Out of the locket," he replied.

I stared at him in amazement. "What an extraordinary thing!" I exclaimed. "A blue hair! I never heard of blue hair before."

"Then," said Thorndyke, "my learned friend has made an addition to his already vast store of knowledge."

"I suppose it was dyed?" said I.

"I think," he replied, "we may assume that the blue colour is adventitious."

"But why, in the name of Fortune, should a woman dye her hair blue?" I demanded.

He shook his head. "A curious question that, Anstey, a very curious question. I suggest that when my learned friend has satisfied himself as to the correct method of '*daping or doping with a grasshopper for the chavender or chub*', he might with advantage bring his colossal intellect to bear on it."

"You are an aggravating old devil, Thorndyke," I said with conviction. "You know perfectly well what this thing means, and yet, when you are asked a civil question, you sit there wagging your exasperating old head like some confounded secretive effigy. I'd like to paint your cranium with Stephen's blue-black ink and then put it under the microscope."

He shook the threatened head conclusively. "It would be futile, Anstey," he replied "As a method of producing blue hair it would be a complete failure. The effect of the tannate of iron – on exposure to oxygen – would entirely mask that of the indigo-carmine. No, my friend. Physical experiment is outside the range of a King's Counsel. Reflection is your proper province. And now take your book and go to bed. Consider the chavender or chub and also the possible connection between a blue hair and a gold locket, shun needless and inky strenuosities, and '*be quiet and go a-angling*'."

With this he returned to his note-book, and there being evidently nothing more to be got out of him, I picked up my book and, having shaken my fist at the impassive figure by the table, once more betook myself to bed, there to meditate fruitlessly upon this new and curious problem.

Chapter XII
From the Jaws of Death

On the following morning it seemed natural that my steps should stray in the direction of Jacob Street, not only that I might relieve my anxiety as to my friend whom I had left overnight in so distressed a state, but also to ascertain whether any services that I could render were at the moment in request. As to the former, my mind was completely set at rest as soon as I entered the studio (to which I was conducted by Mrs. Wingrave, who opened the wicket), for I found Miss Blake hard at work and looking as cheerful and interested as if poisoned sweets and brazen-haired Jezebels were things unheard of.

I explained, half-apologetically, the purpose of my visit, and was preparing a strategic retreat when she interrupted me.

"Now, Mr. Anstey, I will not have these formalities. We aren't strangers. You have been, and are, the best and kindest of friends to me and Percy, and we are not only grateful but we value your friendship very much indeed. As to Percy, he loves you."

"Does he?" said I, with an inward glow of satisfaction. "I am proud to know that. And Percy's sister – ?"

She coloured very prettily and smilingly avoided the pitfall. "Percy's sister," she replied, "takes an indulgent view of her brother's infatuation. But I am going to treat you as a friend. I am going on with my work, because it has to be done, even if I didn't like doing it, but it would be very nice and companionable if you would sit down and smoke a pipe and talk to me – that is, of course, if you can spare the time."

"If I could spare the time!" Why, the whole Appeal Court, with the House of Lords thrown in, might have sat and twiddled their thumbs for all I cared. But, in fact, I had nothing to do at all.

"You are sure I shan't hinder you?" I said, feeling for my pipe.

"Perfectly," she answered. "I have done all the troublesome part, you see – posing and draping the model." And she pointed with her pencil to a lay figure: It was an elaborate "stuffed" figure with real hair and a wax face and hands), dressed in the very height of fashion, which stood, posed in what Lewis Carroll would have called an "Anglo-Saxon Attitude", simpering at us idiotically.

"That is a very magnificent costume," I remarked. "I suppose it is one of your own? Or do you keep a wardrobe for the models?"

"It isn't costume at all," she replied with a laugh. "It is just dress material draped on and tacked or pinned in position. You will see if you go round to the other side."

I went round to the "off-side" and, having thus discovered the fraud, asked, "Is this a figure for a subject picture?"

She laughed softly. "Bless your innocent heart, Mr. Anstey, I don't paint pictures. I draw fashion-plates. I have to earn a living, you know, and give Percy a start."

"What a horrid waste of talent!" I exclaimed. "But I had no idea that fashion-plate artists took all this trouble." And I pointed to the smooth card on her easel which bore a masterly, though rather attenuated, nude figure – in the Anglo-Saxon Attitude – lightly drawn in pencil, and looking almost like a silver point.

"Most of them don't," she replied, "and perhaps it isn't really necessary. But I like to make a finished pencil drawing, though it has all to be rubbed out when the pen work has been done over it."

"And the preliminary nude figure," said I. "You do that from a model, I suppose?"

"No," she answered. "I can draw a nude figure well enough for this purpose out of my head. You see, I worked from the model for a long time at the Slade School, and I never threw away a drawing. I have them all bound in books, and I have copied them and drawn them from memory over and over again. In practice, one must be able to rough out a figure out of one's head."

As she talked, her pencil travelled easily and lightly over the smooth fashion-plate board, gradually clothing the nude figure in transparent habiliments, and I sat smoking with infinite contentment and watching her. And a very dainty, picturesque figure she made in her long blue pinafore, with her red-gold hair and waxen skin, as she stood gracefully poised before her easel, hand on hip and the drawing arm flung out straight and swinging easily from the shoulder. I contrasted her lithe form, in which every curve was full of life and grace, with the absurd rigidity of the lay-figure, her simple, dignified garments with the fussy exuberance of the fashionable costume (though, to be sure, that costume was her own creation), and was moved to comments on the effigy that might have lacerated its feelings if it had had any.

"How long will this drawing take you?" I asked presently.

"I shall have it done by this evening," she replied, "and tomorrow morning I shall take it to the office and deliver it to the art editor."

"Couldn't I take it for you?" said I.

"I am afraid not," she answered. "I must go myself to see that it is all right and to get instructions for the next drawings. Besides, why should you?"

"Didn't we agree that you were to keep indoors out of harm's way? Or at least not to go abroad without an escort? If you must take the drawing yourself, you had better let me come with you to see you safely there and back. Do you mind?"

"Of course I should like your company, Mr. Anstey," she replied, "but it seems such a tax on you."

"I wish all taxes were as acceptable," said I. "But I understand that you agree so, if you will fix a time, the escort will assemble at the gate and the bugles will sound 'fall in' with military punctuality."

After a few more half-hearted protests she fixed the hour of half-past-ten for the following morning, and I then took my leave, very well satisfied with the progress of this friendship that was becoming so dear to me, and even sensible of a dawning hope that a yet closer intimacy might someday become possible.

Punctually at the appointed time, the Hampstead tram set me down at the end of Jacob Street, when I proceeded to collect the convoy and make sail for Bedford Street, Covent Garden, which was the abiding-place of the art editor to whom the drawing was consigned. But if the outward voyage was characterised by business-like directness, it was quite otherwise with the homeward, which was marked by so many circumnavigations and interrupted by so many ports of call – including the National Gallery – that it was well on in the afternoon when the convoy shortened sail at Sixty-three Jacob Street, and it became necessary for the escort to put into port and take in stores in the form of tea and biscuits. And even then, so satisfactory had the voyage turned out that (to pursue the metaphor to a finish) the charter-party was renewed and further voyages projected.

Expeditions abroad, however, could only be occasional, and even then on a plausible business pretext, for my fair friend was a steady worker and spent long days at her easel and drawing-desk – nor was I entirely without occupation, though Thorndyke made but the smallest demands upon my vacation leisure. In effect, not a day passed without a visit to Jacob Street, and whether my time was spent placidly watching the growth of a new drawing, in executing shopping commissions, or in escort duties, it was all equally pleasant to me, and day-by-day more firmly established my position as the indispensable friend of the little household.

Affairs had been on this footing for about a week when early on a certain afternoon I set forth from The Temple for my daily call, but with a more definite purpose than usual, for I bore with me the locket, in which Polton had fixed a new glass. I rang the studio bell with the customary pleasurable anticipation of the warm and evidently sincere welcome, and listened complacently to Mrs. Wingrave's footsteps as she came along the paved passage, and as the wicket opened I prepared to step jauntily through. But the first words that the worthy lady spoke scattered in an instant all my pleasant thoughts and filled me with alarm.

"Miss Blake has just gone out," she said. "A most sad thing has happened. Poor Master Percy has had an accident. He has broken his leg."

"Where did this happen, and when?" I asked.

"It must have happened about an hour ago," she replied. "I don't know where, but they have taken him into a house near Chalk Farm."

"Who brought the news?" I demanded breathlessly, for, seeing that Percy would be at school at the time mentioned, the story was, on the face of it, highly suspicious.

"It was a lady who brought the message," said Mrs. Wingrave. "She wouldn't come in, but she handed me a note, written in pencil and marked 'urgent'. Miss Blake showed it to me. It didn't give any particulars beyond what I have told you, and the address of the house."

"What was the lady like?" I asked.

"Well," Mrs. Wingrave replied, "I call her a lady, but she was really rather a common-looking woman, painted and powdered and very vulgarly dressed."

"Did you notice her hair?"

"Yes, you couldn't help noticing it. Brassy-looking, golden stuff, frizzed out like a mop – and her eyebrows were as black as mine are."

"Do you know where the note is?" I asked.

"I expect Miss Blake took it with her, but she may have left it in the studio. Shall we go and see?"

We hurried together across the yard and into the studio, where for a minute or so we searched the tables and the unfastened bureau. But there was no sign of the note.

"She must have taken it with her," said Mrs. Wingrave. "But I think I can give you the address, if that is what you want. You don't think there's anything wrong, do you?"

"I am extremely uneasy, Mrs. Wingrave," said I, producing my notebook and a pencil, "and I shall go straight to the house, if I can find it. What is the address? For Heaven's sake don't give me a wrong one!"

"I remember it quite clearly," she replied, "and I think I know the place. It is Number Twenty-nine Scoresby Terrace, a corner house, and the terrace turns out of Sackett's Road on the left side going up from here."

I wrote this down in my note-book and then asked, "How long has Miss Blake been gone?"

"She started less than ten minutes before you came," was the reply. "If you hurry you may possibly over-take her."

We came out of the studio, and as we crossed the yard she gave me very full and clear directions as to how to find the place, some of which I jotted down. Passing a marble tombstone on which her husband had been working, I noticed a number of his tools lying on a sack, and among them a long chisel, almost like a small crowbar. "May I borrow this, Mrs. Wingrave?" I said, picking it up.

"Certainly, if you want to," she replied with a look of surprise.

"Thank you," I said, slipping it up my sleeve. "I may have to force a door, you know." And with this I let myself out at the wicket and strode away swiftly up the street.

I am habitually a rapid walker, and now I covered the ground at a pace that made other pedestrians stare. For Winifred, I felt sure, would have flown to her brother on the wings of terror, and hurry as I might, I should be hard put to it to overtake her. But her terror could have been nothing compared with mine. As I raced along the shabby streets, swinging the chisel openly in my hand – for its presence in my sleeve was a sensible hindrance – the sinister possibilities – nay, probabilities – that, unsought, suggested themselves one after another, kept me in a state of sickening dread. Supposing I failed to find the place after all! It was quite possible, for the neighbourhood was strange and rather intricate. Or suppose I should lose time in searching for the house and arrive at last, only to find – Here I set my teeth and fairly broke into a run, regardless of the inquisitive stares of idlers at doors and street corners. But, for all my terror and horrible forebodings, I kept my wits and held my attention firmly to Mrs. Wingrave's directions, and I derived a faint encouragement from the fact that I had never lost touch of the landmarks and that every hurried step was bringing me nearer to my goal. At length, want of breath compelled me to drop into a walk, but a couple of minutes later, with a gasp of relief, I reached the corner of Sackett's Road and, even as I swung round into the long, straight, dreary street, I caught a glimpse of a woman, at the far end, hurrying forward in the same direction. It was only a momentary glimpse, for in the instant when I saw her she turned swiftly into a by-street to the left. But brief as was the vision, and far away as she was, no doubt was possible to me. It was Winifred.

I drew a deep breath. Surely I should be in time. And perhaps my fears might be groundless after all. The plot might be but the creation of my own uneasy suspicion. At any rate, I was nearly there, and it was hardly possible that in a few short minutes anything could happen – but here all my terrors came crowding on me again, and, breathless as I was, I again broke into a run.

As I reached the corner of Scoresby Terrace and looked at the corner house, my heart seemed to stand still. A single glance showed that it was an empty house, and the horrible desolation of its aspect was made more dreadful by the silence and the total absence of any sign of life. I flew across the road, and barely glancing at the number-twenty-nine-raced up the garden path and tugged furiously at the bell.

Instantly the hollow shell reverberated with a hideous jangling that sounded more ominous and dreadful from the vacancy that the discordant echoes bespoke. But it slowly died away and was succeeded by no answering sound. A deadly silence enveloped the ill-omened place. Not a creak upon the stair, not a sign of life or movement could I detect, though I held my breath to listen. Yet this was the house, and she was in it – and that other! Again I wrenched at the bell, and again the horrible jangling filled the place with echoes, like some infernal peal rung by a company of ghouls. And still there was no answer.

In a frenzy of terror I rushed down the side passage, and bursting open the flimsy gate, ran into the back garden and tried the back door. But it was locked and bolted. Then I darted to the back parlour window, and springing on the sill, shattered, with a stroke of the chisel, the pane above the catch. Passing my hand in through the hole, I drew back the catch and slid up the lower sash. I had noticed that the wooden shutters were not quite closed, but at the moment that I slid up the window-sash, the shutters closed and I heard the cross-bar snap into its socket.

For a moment I had a thought of running round to the front and breaking in the street door. But only for a moment. Rescue, not capture, was my purpose. A glance at the flimsy, decrepit shutters showed me the way in. Thrusting the edge of the long, powerful chisel into the crack close to the lower hinge, I gave a violent wrench, and forthwith the hinge came away from the jamb, the screws drawing easily from the rotten woodwork. Another thrust and another wrench at the upper hinge brought that away too, at a push the whole shutter swung inward and I sprang down into the room. And at that moment I heard the street door shut.

I ran across the room to the door. Of course it was locked and the key was outside. But I was not a criminal lawyer for nothing. In a moment I had the chisel driven in beside the lock, and pressing on the long handle, drove the door back on its hinges, when the lock-bolt and latch disengaged from the striking-plate and the door came open at once.

I ran out into the hall, unlocked the front room, and looked in, but it was empty. Then I flew up the stairs and was about to unlock the door of the first room that I came to, when I became aware of a soft, shuffling sound proceeding apparently from the next room. Instantly I ran to that door, and turning the key, flung it open.

The sight that met my eyes as I darted into the room was but the vision of a moment, but in that moment it imprinted itself upon my memory for ever. Even now, as I write, it rises before me, vivid and horrible, with such dreadful remembrance that my hand falters as it guides the pen. In a corner near the wall she lay – my sweet, gracious Winifred-lay huddled, writhing feebly and fumbling with her hands at her throat. Her face was of the colour of slate, her lips black, her eyes wide and protruding.

It was, I say, but the vision of a moment, a frightful, unforgettable moment. The next, I was on my knees beside her, my open knife was in my hand, its keen edge eating through the knot at the back of her neck that secured the band that was strangling her. A moment of agonised impatience and then the knot was divided and the band hastily unwound – it was a narrow silken scarf – revealing a livid groove in the plump neck.

As I took away the scarf she drew a deep, gasping breath with a hoarse, distressful sound like the breathing of a croup-stricken child. Again and again it was repeated, growing quicker and more irregular, and with each succeeding gasp the horrible purple of face and lips faded away, leaving a pallor as of marble, the dreadfully protruding eyes sank back until they looked almost normal, though wild and frightened.

I watched these changes with a sense of utter helplessness, though not without relief – for they were clearly changes for the better. But I longed to help her, to do something active to advance her recovery. If only I had had Thorndyke's knowledge I might have been of some use. He would have known what to do. But perhaps there was nothing to be done but wait for her natural recovery. At any rate, that was all that I could do. And so I remained kneeling by her side with her head resting on my arm, holding her hand, and looking with infinite pity and affection into the frightened, trustful eyes that sought my own with such pathetic appeal.

Presently, as her breathing grew easier, the gasps began to be mingled with sobs, and then, suddenly, she burst into tears and wept passionately, almost hysterically, with her face buried against my shoulder. I was profoundly moved, indeed I was almost ready to weep myself, so intense was the revulsion now that the danger was past. In the tumult of my emotions I forgot everything but that she was saved, and that I loved her. As I sought to comfort her, to coax away her terrors, to soothe and reassure her, I cannot tell what words of tenderness I murmured into her ear, by what endearing names I addressed her. Stirred as I was to the very depths of my soul, I was aware of nothing but the great realities. In the stress of terror but now barely past and the joy and relief of the hardly hoped for recovery, the world of everyday was forgotten. All I knew was that she was here, safe in my arms, and that she was all in all to me.

By degrees her emotion expended its force and she grew calmer. Presently she sat up, and having wiped her eyes, looked nervously about the empty room.

"Let us go away from this dreadful place," she said in a low, frightened voice, laying her hand entreatingly on my arm.

"We will," said I, "if you are well enough yet to walk. Let us see."

I stood up and lifted her to her feet, but she was very unsteady and weak. I doubt if she could have stood without support, for I could feel her trembling as she leaned on me heavily. Still, with my help, she tottered to the door and crossed the landing, and then, very slowly, we descended the stairs. At the open door of the room which I had entered, we paused to adjust her hat and remove any traces of the struggle before we should emerge into the street. I was still holding the silken scarf, and now put it into my pocket to free my hands that I might assist her in settling her hat and the crumpled collar of her dress. As I looked her over to see that all was in order, I noticed three or four conspicuous golden hairs sticking to her right sleeve. I picked them off and was in the act of dropping them when it occurred to me that Thorndyke might be able to extract some information from them, whereupon I brought out my pocket-book and slipped them between the leaves.

"That is how I got into the house," I said, pointing to the shattered window and the hanging shutter.

She peered fearfully into the empty room and said, "I heard the crash of the glass. It was that which saved me, I think, for that brute heard it too, and rushed away downstairs instantly. How did you break open the shutter?"

"I did it with a chisel of Mr. Wingrave's – and that reminds me that I have left the chisel upstairs. I must take it back to him."

I bounded up the stairs, and running into the room, snatched up the chisel from the floor and ran out again. As I turned the corner of the staircase, I met her beginning to ascend the stair, clinging to the handrail and sobbing hysterically. I cursed myself for having left her, even for a few moments, and putting my arm around her, led her back into the hall.

"Oh, pray forgive me!" she sobbed. "I am all unstrung. I couldn't bear to be alone."

"Of course you couldn't," said I, drawing her head to my shoulder and stroking her pale cheek. "I oughtn't to have left you. But try, Winnie dear, to realise that it is now over and gone. And let us get out of this house."

She wiped her eyes again, and as her sobs died away into an occasional moan, I opened the street door. The sight of the open street and the sunlight seemed to calm her at once. She put away her handkerchief, and clinging to my arm, walked slowly and a little unsteadily by my side down the garden path and out at the gate.

"I wonder where we can get a cab," said I.

"There is a station not very far away, I believe," said she. "Perhaps someone can direct us."

We walked slowly down Sackett's Road, looking about that curiously deserted thoroughfare for some likely person from whom to make inquiries, when I saw a taxi-cab draw up at a house and discharge its passengers. I managed to attract the notice of the driver, and a minute later we were seated in the vehicle travelling swiftly homeward.

During the short journey hardly a word was exchanged. She was quite composed now, but she was still deathly pale and lay back in her seat with an air of intense fatigue and exhaustion. When we reached the studio I helped her out of the cab and, having dismissed it, led her to the gate and rang the bell.

Instantly I heard hurried steps in the passage, the wicket was flung open, and Mrs. Wingrave looked out eagerly. When she saw us, she burst into tears.

"Thank God!" she exclaimed. "I've been in an agony of suspense. Directly Percy came home, I knew that Mr. Anstey must be right – that the message about him was a trap of some sort. What has happened?"

"I'll tell you later, Mrs. Wingrave," Winifred replied. "I don't want to talk about it now. Is Percy at home?"

"No. The two Wallingford boys were with him. He has gone home to tea with them. I thought it best to say nothing, and let him go. They live quite near here."

"I am glad you did," said Winifred, as we crossed the yard, where I replaced the invaluable chisel. "Perhaps we needn't tell him anything about this."

"It might be better not to," said Mrs. Wingrave. "And now go and sit down quietly in the studio and I will bring you some tea. You both look as if you wanted some rest and refreshment." She bustled away towards her own residence and Winifred and I entered the studio.

As I held the curtain aside to let her pass, my companion halted and looked round the great, bare hall with an air of deep reflection – almost of curiosity. "I never thought to look upon this place again," she said gravely, "and I never should but for you. My life is your gift, Mr. Anstey."

"It is a very precious life to me, Winifred," said I. And then I added, "I can't call you Miss Blake."

"I am glad of that," she said, looking at me with a smile. "It would sound very cool and formal now when you have held my life in your hands, and my heart is bursting with gratitude to you." She laid her hand on my arm for a moment, and then, as if afraid of saying too much, returned abruptly to the subject of her brother. "It is fortunate Percy was not at home. I don't think we need tell him, at least not just now. Do you think so?"

"I don't see any necessity," I replied. "He knows the general position and the precautions that have to be taken. Perhaps he can be told later. And now you must just sit on the settee and rest quietly, for you are as pale as a ghost still. I wonder you have not collapsed altogether."

In a few minutes Mrs. Wingrave brought in the tea and placed it on a table by Winifred's settee. I drew up a chair and performed the presidential functions in respect of the teapot and, under the influence of the homely ceremony and the reviving stimulant, my patient began to recover something like her normal appearance and manner. I kept up a flow of more or less commonplace talk, avoiding, for the present, any reference to the terrible events of the afternoon, the details of which I decided to elucidate later when the effect of the shock had passed off.

The postponement, however, was shorter than I had intended, for when we had finished tea and I had carried the tray across the yard and restored it to Mrs. Wingrave, Winifred opened the subject herself.

"You haven't asked me how this thing happened," she said, as I re-entered the studio and sat down beside her in the vacant place on the settee.

"No. I thought you wouldn't want to talk about it just now."

"I don't want to talk about it to Mrs. Wingrave," said she. "But you are my deliverer. I don't mind telling you – besides you ought to know. And I want to know, too, by what extraordinary chance you came to be in that place at that critical moment. When I saw you come into the room, it seemed as if a miracle had happened."

"There was nothing very miraculous about it," said I, "except that I happened to arrive at the studio a little earlier than usual." And here I

704

gave her an account of my arrival and my interview with Mrs. Wingrave and my efforts to overtake her.

"It was very clever of Mrs. Wingrave to remember the address so clearly," said Winifred.

"It is a mercy that she did," said I. "If she had not – but there, we won't think of that. What happened when you got to the house?"

"I rang the bell and a woman opened the door. I hardly saw her until I had entered the hall and she had shut the door, and then – you know how dark the hall was – I couldn't see her very distinctly. But I noticed that she was a good deal powdered and that she had bright, unreal-looking golden hair, though that didn't show much as she had a handkerchief tied over her head and under her chin. And I also noticed that her face seemed in some way familiar to me.

"As soon as she had shut the door the woman said in a rather peculiar voice, 'You must excuse the state of the house, we haven't properly moved in yet. The little man is with the nurse on the first floor, the second room you come to. Will you go up?'

"I ran up the stairs and she followed close behind me. When I came to the second room, I asked, 'Is this the one?' and when she answered 'Yes,' I opened the door and stepped in. Then, of course, I saw it was an empty room, and instantly I suspected that it was a trap. But at that moment the woman threw the scarf over my head and pulled it tight. I turned round quickly, but she dodged behind me and pulled me into the room, and there we struggled and kept turning round and round for hours, as it seemed to me, she trying to get behind me to tie the scarf, and I struggling to keep her in front of me. She still held both ends of the scarf, and though she was not able to pull it quite tight, it was tight enough to make my breathing difficult and to prevent me from calling out. At last I managed to turn quickly and seize her by the hair and the handkerchief that was tied over her head. But the handkerchief came away in my hand and the hair with it. It was a wig. And then, to my horror, I saw that this was not a woman at all. It was a man! The man who stabbed me that night at Hampstead! I recognised him instantly, and the shock was so awful that I nearly fainted. For a moment I felt perfectly helpless, and in that moment he got behind me and tied the scarf and pulled it tight.

"Then there came a tremendous pealing of the bell. The man started violently, and I could feel his hands trembling as he tried to finish tying the knot while I struggled to get hold of his wrists. But, of course, I could not struggle long, for the scarf was so tight that it almost completely stopped my breathing, and the horror of the thing took away all my strength. When the bell rang the second time, he broke into a torrent of curses mixed with a curious sort of whimpering, and flung me violently on the floor. He was just finishing the knot when I heard a crash of glass down below, and at that he sprang to his feet, snatched up the wig and handkerchief, and flew down the stairs.

"After this there seemed a long, long interval. Of course it was only a matter of seconds, I suppose, but it was agonising – that horrible feeling of suffocation. At last I heard a bursting sound down below. Then the street door shut, and then – just as I seemed to be losing consciousness – you came into the room and I knew that I was saved." She paused, and then, laying her hand on mine, she continued, "I haven't thanked you for saving me from that horrible death. I can't. No words are enough. Any talk of gratitude would be mere anticlimax."

"There is no question of gratitude, Winnie," said I. "Your life is more to me than my own, so there is no virtue in my cherishing it. But I needn't tell you that, for I suspect that my secret has slipped out unawares already."

"Your secret?" she repeated.

"That I love you, Winnie dearest. You must know it by now. I suppose I ought not to speak of it just at this time. And yet – well, perhaps I might ask you if you would take time to consider whether we might not, someday, be more to one another than we are now."

She looked down gravely though a little shyly, but she answered without hesitation, "I don't need to take time to consider. I can tell you at once that I am proud to be loved by such a man as you. And it is not a case of gratitude. I should have said the same if you had asked me yesterday – or even longer ago than that."

"Thank you for telling me that, Winnie," said I. "It would have been an unworthy thing if I had seemed to presume on any small service – "

"It would have been an absurd thing to have any such idea, Mr. Anstey."

"Mr. Anstey?" I repeated. "May I humbly mention that I also have a Christian name?"

"I always suspected that you had," she retorted with a smile, "and I must confess to having speculated as to what it might be."

"It takes the prosaic form of Robert, commonly perverted by my own family to Robin."

"And a very pretty name, too," said she. "But you are a foolish Robin to speak in that way about yourself. The mistake you are making," she continued, holding up an admonitory forefinger, "is that you don't realise what an exceedingly nice person you are. But *we* realise it. Mrs. Wingrave is quite fond of you, Percy loves you, and as for Percy's sister,

706

well, she lost her heart longer ago than she is prepared to admit. So let us hear no more ridiculous self-deprecations."

"There shall be no more, sweetheart," said I. "You have taken away the occasion and the excuse. A man who has won the heart of the sweetest and loveliest girl in the whole world would be a fool to undervalue himself. But it is a wonderful thing, Winnie. I can hardly believe in my good fortune. When I saw you that night at Hampstead, I thought you were the most beautiful girl I had ever seen. And now I know I was right. But how little did I dream that that lovely girl would one day be my own!"

"I say again that you are a foolish Robin," said she, resting her cheek against my shoulder. "You think your goose is a swan. But go on thinking it, and she will be as near a swan as she can manage, or failing that, a very faithful, affectionate goose."

She looked up at me with a smile, half-shy but wholly endearing and, noting how her marble-white cheeks had grown pink and rosy, I kissed her, whereupon they grew pinker still.

It was all for our good that Percy lingered with his friends and left us to the undisturbed possession of our new happiness. For me the golden minutes supped away unnumbered – sullenly and relentlessly checked, however, by my unconsulted watch – as we sat, side-by-side and hand clasped in hand. We talked little, not that we were, as Rosalind would say, "Gravelled for lack of matter' (and even if we had been, Rosalind's admirable expedient was always available). But perfect companionship is independent of mere verbal converse. There is no need for speech when two hearts are singing in unison.

At last there came the expected peal of the bell. I might, I suppose, have gone out to open the wicket, but, in fact, I left that office to Mrs. Wingrave.

"I don't think Percy will notice anything unusual," said I. "You look perfectly recovered now."

"I suppose I do," she answered with a smile. "There have been restoratives, you see."

"So there have," I agreed, and *ex abundantia cautelae*, as we lawyers say, I added a sort of restorative codicil even as the quick footsteps pattered across the yard.

Whether Percy observed anything unusual I cannot say with certainty. He was a born diplomatist and a very model of discretion. But I have a strong suspicion that he detected some new note in the harmony of our little society – particularly when I addressed his sister as Winnie did he seem to cock an attentive ear, and when she addressed me as Robin he cocked both ears. But he made no sign. He was a jewel of a boy. No lover could have asked for anything more perfect in the way of a prospective brother-in-law.

But my suspicion of that juvenile diplomat was confirmed – and my admiration of his judgment reached a climax – when the time arrived for me to go, and Winifred rose to accompany me to the gate. This had always been Percy's office. But now he shook hands with me without turning a hair and without even a glance at the studio door. It was a marvellous instance of precocious intelligence.

We had left the studio and were just crossing the yard when suddenly I bethought me of the locket which Thorndyke had entrusted to me for delivery, and which I had, up to this moment, completely forgotten.

"Here is another narrow escape," said I. "The special errand which, to the uninitiated, appeared to be the occasion of my visit here today, has never been discharged. I was to give you your locket, which the ingenious Polton has made as good as new, and had forgotten all about it. However, it is not too late," and here I took the little bauble from my pocket and handed it to her.

"I am glad it came today, of all days," she said as she took it from me. "Now I can wear it as a sort of memento. If we had only known, Robin, we could have got Mr. Polton to engrave the date on the back."

"He can do that later," said I. "It is engraved on my heart already. I can never forget a single moment of this day. And what a wonderful day it has been! What a day of wild extremes! Within a few hours I have suffered the most intense misery and dread that I have ever experienced, and been blessed with the greatest happiness that I have ever known. And as to you, my poor darling – "

"Not a poor darling at all," she interrupted, "but a very rich and proud and happy one. A day of storm and sunshine it has indeed been, but the storm came first, and 'in the evening there was light'. And after all, Robin dear, you can't have a rainbow without rain."

By this tune we had reached the gate, and when I had taken her in my arms and kissed her, I opened the wicket and passed out. As it closed behind me I looked up and down the dreary street, but it was dreary to me no longer. I don't know who Jacob was – I mean this particular Jacob – but as I stopped to look back fondly at the factory-like gate, I felt that I was in some sort under an obligation to him as the (presumptive) creator of the sacred thoroughfare.

Chapter XIII
Thorndyke States His Position

Recalling the events of the evening after leaving the studio, I am sensible of a somewhat hazy interval between the moment when I turned the corner of Jacob Street and my arrival at the familiar precincts of The Temple. After the fashion of the aboriginal Londoner, I had simply set my face in the desired direction and walked, unconscious of particular streets, instinctively or subconsciously heading for my destination by the shortest route. And meanwhile my mind was busy with the stirring incidents of this most eventful day, with its swift alternations of storm and sunshine, its terror, its despair, and its golden reward. So my thoughts now alternated between joy at the attainment of a happiness scarcely hoped for and apprehension of the dangers that lurked unseen, ready to spring forth and wreck the life that was more to me than my own.

Thus meditating, I sped through by-streets innumerable and unnoted, crossing quiet squares and traversing narrow courts and obscure passages, but always shunning the main thoroughfares with their disturbing glare and noise, until I came, as it were, to the surface at the end of Chichester Rents, and turned into Chancery Lane. There the familiar surroundings brought me back to my everyday world, and my thoughts took a new direction. What would Thorndyke have to say to my news? Had he any resources unknown to me for staving off this very imminent danger? And would the terrible episode of the empty house convey any enlightenment to him that I had missed?

Still revolving these questions, I dived down Middle Temple Lane and presently became aware of a tall figure some little distance ahead, walking in the same direction as my own. I had nearly overtaken him when he turned at the entrance to Pump Court and looked back, whereupon a mutual recognition brought us both to a halt.

"I expect we are bound for the same port, Anstey," said he as we shook hands. "I am going to call on Thorndyke. You are still helping him, aren't you?"

"He says I am, and I hope it is true. At any rate, Jervis has not come back yet, if that is what you mean. I suppose, Drayton, you haven't any fresh information for us?"

Sir Lawrence shook his head gloomily. "No," he answered, "I have learned nothing new, nor, I fear, are any of us likely to. Those brutes seem to have got away without leaving a trace that it is possible to make anything of. We can't expect impossibilities even of Thorndyke. But I am not calling on him with reference to the murder case. I want him to come down with me to Aylesbury to help me with an interview. A question of survivorship has arisen, and he knows more about that subject than I do, so I should like him to elicit the facts, if possible."

As we walked through Pump Court and the Cloisters, I debated with myself whether I should tell Drayton of the horror that this day had witnessed. He was an interested party in more than one sense, for he had the warmest regard for Winifred. But I knew that he would be profoundly shocked, and as he continued to talk of the case on which he wanted Thorndyke's advice, I said nothing for the present.

When I let myself and Drayton in with my latch-key, we found Thorndyke seated at the table with a microscope and a tray of reagents and mounting materials, preparing slides of animal hairs to add to his already extensive collection.

"I am ashamed to disturb you at this hour," Drayton began.

But Thorndyke interrupted him. "You are not disturbing me at all. This kind of work can be taken up and put down at any moment."

"It is very good of you to say so," said Drayton, "and I will take you at your word." And thereupon he opened the matter of which he had spoken to me.

"When do you want me to come down to Aylesbury?" Thorndyke asked.

"The day after tomorrow, if you can manage it."

Thorndyke reflected for a few moments as he picked up with his forceps a newly-cleaned cover-glass, and delicately dropped it on the specimen that floated in its little pool of balsam.

"Yes," he said at length, "I think we can arrange that. There isn't very much doing just now."

"Very well," said Sir Lawrence. "Then I will call for you at ten o'clock, and I needn't trouble you with any details now. We can talk the case over on the way down." He rose as if to depart, but as he turned towards the door, he stopped and looked back at Thorndyke.

"I am afraid," said he, "that I have rather neglected our friend Miss Blake. Has either of you seen her lately?"

Thorndyke gave me a quick look, and in the short interval before replying, I could see that he was rapidly debating how much he should tell Sir Lawrence. Apparently he reached the same conclusion as I had, that we could hardly conceal material facts from him, for he replied, "Yes, we have both seen her quite lately – in fact, I think Anstey has just come from her studio. And I am sorry to say, we are both rather anxious about her."

"Indeed," said Drayton, laying down his hat and seating himself. "What is amiss with her?"

"The trouble is," replied Thorndyke, "that she is the sole witness to the identity of the murderers, and they realise it, and they have determined, accordingly, to get rid of her." And here he gave Sir Lawrence an account of the incident of the poisoned chocolates and the circumstances that had led up to it.

Drayton was thunderstruck. As he listened to Thorndyke's vivid and precise narration, he sat motionless, with parted lips and his hands on his knees, the very picture of amazement and horror.

"But, good God!" he exclaimed, when Thorndyke had finished. "This is perfectly frightful! It is a horrible state of things. Something must be done, you know. It is practically certain that they will make some further attempt."

"They have already," said I. And as the two men turned to me with looks of startled inquiry, I recounted – not without discomfort in recalling them – the terrible events of that afternoon.

My two friends listened with rapt attention as I told the hideous story, and on each it produced characteristic effects. Sir Lawrence glared at me with a scowl of suppressed fury, while Thorndyke's face settled into a rigid immobility like that of a stone mask.

When I had concluded, Drayton sprang to his feet and began to pace the room in uncontrollable agitation, muttering and cursing under his breath. Suddenly he halted opposite Thorndyke, and gazing frowningly into his set face, demanded, "Is it not possible to do something? Something radical and effective, I mean? I don't know what cards you hold, Thorndyke, and I am not going to embarrass you by asking for details, but are you in a position to make any kind of move?"

Thorndyke, who had also risen, and now stood with his back to the fire, looked down reflectively for a few moments. At length he replied, "The difficulty is, Drayton, that if we move prematurely, we run a serious risk of failing, and we can't afford to fail."

"Do I understand, then, that you are in a position to take action?"

"Yes. But it would be extremely unsafe, for if we fail once we fail finally. It would be a gamble, and we should quite probably lose. Whereas, if we can wait, we shall have these men to a certainty. We have taken their measure and we know now exactly what kind of persons we are dealing with. You see, Drayton," he continued after a brief pause, "secret crime most commonly comes to light through the efforts of the criminal to cover his tracks. That is so in the present case. All that I know as to the identity of these men I have learned from their struggles to conceal it. But for their multitudinous precautions, I should have known nothing about them. And you see for yourself that they are criminals of the usual kind who will not let well alone. They keep making fresh efforts to secure their safety, and each time they make a move we learn something more about them. If only we can wait, they will surely deliver themselves into our hands."

There was a brief silence. Then Sir Lawrence gave utterance to the thought that was in my own mind.

"That is all very well, Thorndyke, and as a lawyer I fully understand your desire to get a conclusive case before making a move. But can we afford to wait? Are we justified in using this poor young lady as a bait to enable us to catch these villains?"

"If that were the position," replied Thorndyke, "there could be but one answer. But we must remember that the capture of these men is the condition on which her safety depends. If we fail, we fail for her as well as for ourselves."

"Then," asked Drayton, "what do you suggest? You don't propose to stand by passively until they make some fresh attempt to murder her?"

"No. I suggest that more complete precautions be taken to secure Miss Blake's safety, and meanwhile I hope to fill in one or two blanks in my collection of evidential facts and perhaps induce these men to make a move in a new direction. I think I can promise to bring the affair to a climax in one way or another, and that pretty soon."

"Very well," said Drayton, once more taking up his hat. "But who is going to look after Miss Blake?"

"Anstey has taken that duty on himself," replied Thorndyke, "and I don't think anyone could do it better. If he wants assistance or advice, he has only to call upon us."

With this arrangement Drayton appeared to be satisfied, though he still appeared uneasy – as, indeed, we all were. But he made no further suggestion, and very shortly took his leave.

For some time after his departure not a word was spoken. The conversation that had just taken place had given me abundant food for reflection, while Thorndyke, who still stood with his back to the fire, maintained a grim silence. Evidently he was thinking hard, and a glance at his face – stern, rigid, inexorable – assured me that his cogitations boded ill for those who had aroused his righteous anger. At length he looked up and asked, "What measures can you suggest for Miss Blake's protection?"

"I have told her that, for the present, she must not go out of doors on any occasion whatever unless accompanied by me – or, of course, by you or Drayton. She has promised to abide absolutely by that rule and to make no exception to it. She has also promised to keep the studio door locked and to inspect any visitors from the window of the bedroom adjoining before unlocking it."

"If she keeps to those rules she should be quite safe," said Thorndyke. "They are not likely to try to break in. There is a man living on the premises, I think?"

"Yes. Mr. Wingrave is about the place at his work most of the day, and, of course, he is always there at night."

"Then, I think we may feel reasonably secure for the present, and I am glad you have made such complete arrangements, for I was going to suggest that you come down with us to Aylesbury."

"With what object?" I asked. "Drayton won't want me at the conference."

"No. But it just occurred to me that, as we shall be within a mile or two of Beauchamp Blake and can easily take it on our way back, we might go and have a look at the place and see if we can pick up any information on the spot. I believe the question of the sale of the property is more or less in abeyance, but it would be just as well to make a few inquiries locally."

I received the suggestion with some surprise but no enthusiasm.

"Doesn't it seem rather inopportune," I said, "with these imminent dangers impending, to be occupying ourselves in prosecuting this shadowy claim? Surely this is no time for building castles in the air. The chance of young Percival's ever coming into this property is infinitely remote, and we can attend to it when we have done with more urgent matters."

"If we attend to it at all," he replied "we must do so when we have the opportunity. Should the property be sold, Percy's chance will be gone for good. And the conflict between our two purposes is only in your mind. The fact of our keeping an eye on Percy's interests will not hinder our pursuit of the wretches who murdered poor Drayton and would now murder Percy's sister. You can trust me for that."

"No, I suppose it won't," I admitted. "And you seem to take Percy's claim to this estate quite seriously."

"It is impossible to do otherwise," said he. "It may be impossible to prove it, even if an opportunity should arise. But it is a real claim, and what little chance he has ought to be preserved. It mustn't be lost by our negligence."

I was not keen on the expedition, but I knew what Winifred's sentiments would have been, and loyalty to her bade me assent, though in my own mind, I felt it to be a fruitless and somewhat foolish errand.

Accordingly I agreed to form one of the party on the day after the morrow, a decision which Thorndyke received with more satisfaction than the occasion seemed to warrant.

Chapter XIV
Beauchamp Blake

"Can there be any more pleasant place of human habitation than an English country town?" I asked myself the question as I strolled round the market square of the little town of Aylesbury, gazing about me with a Londoner's pleasure in the restful, old-world aspect of the place, I had still more than half-an-hour to wait, but I had no feeling of impatience. I could spend that time agreeably enough, sauntering around, wrapped in pleasurable idleness provocative of reflection, looking at the handsome market-place with its clock-tower and its statues immortalising in bronze the worthies of more stirring times, or at the carriers' carts that rested unhorsed in the square and told of villages and hamlets nestling amidst their trees but a few miles away down the leafy lanes.

Presently my leisurely perambulations brought me opposite a shop of more than common smartness, and here – perhaps because the crowd of market folk was a little more dense – I paused and gazed somewhat absently into the window. I have no idea why I looked into that particular shop window. The wares exposed in it – ladies' hats – have no special attraction to the masculine eye – at least in the state in which they are presented by the milliner, bereft of the principal ornament which should be found underneath them. Nevertheless, I was not the only male observer. Another man had stopped and stood, nearer to the window than I, inspecting the gaily-flowered and feathered headgear with undeniable interest.

The incongruity of this eager scrutiny of things so characteristically feminine struck me with amused curiosity, and I watched the man with a half-suppressed smile. He was a small, slight man, neatly dressed in a suit of tweeds and a tweed hat, and the trouser-clips at his ankles suggested that he had cycled in from the country. I could not see his face, as I was standing nearly behind him, but apparently he became aware, after a time, of my presence – perhaps he saw my reflection in the window – and of the fact that I was observing him somewhat curiously, for he turned away with some suddenness, glancing up at me as he passed and then half-pausing to look at me again before he bustled away and disappeared up an alley.

There was something very odd in that second look. The first had been a mere casual glance, but the second – quick, searching, even startled – suggested recognition, and something more than recognition.

715

What could it have been? And *who* could he be? The face – a clean-shaved, thin, sallow face, not very young, seen only for a moment, left a clear mental image that still remained. And as I visualised it afresh I was conscious of a faint sense of familiarity. I had seen this man before. Where had I seen him, and who was he? And why did he look at me with that singular expression?

I stood where he had left me, cudgelling my brains for an answer to these questions. And even as I stood there, a cyclist passed swiftly across the end of the square and disappeared in the direction of the London Road. He was too far off for his face to be clearly recognizable, but he was a small man, he wore a tweed suit and hat, and trouser-clips, and I had no doubt that he was the same man.

Now who was he? The more I recalled the face, the more convinced I was that I had seen it before. But the identity of its owner eluded me completely. I couldn't place the fellow at all. Probably it didn't matter in the least who he was. But still it was exasperating to be baffled in this way. Unconsciously, I turned and stared into the milliner's window. And then, in a flash it came. The middle of the window was occupied by an enormous hat – a huge, bloated, fungous structure overrun with counterfeit vegetation and bristling with feathers, such a hat as might have adorned the cranium of a foreign queen. A glance at that grisly head-dress supplied the missing link in the chain of association. The face that had looked into mine was the face of the woman who had shadowed Winifred and me from Hampstead, who had lured her to the empty house, and had there revealed herself as a man in disguise. In short, this was the murderer of poor Drayton, and the would-be murderer of Winifred!

And I had held this wretch in the hollow of my hand and I had let him go! It was an infuriating thought. If my quickness of observation had only been equal to his, I should have had him by now safely under lock and key. No wonder he had looked startled. But he must have a remarkably good memory for faces to have recognised me in that instantaneous glance. For he had seen me only once – at the inquest at Hampstead – and then but for a moment. Unless he had got a glimpse of me at the empty house, or – which seemed more probable – had shadowed and watched me when I had been acting as Winifred's escort. At any rate he knew me, better than I knew him, and had managed very adroitly to slip through my fingers.

But what on earth was he doing at Aylesbury? Was it possible that he lived in this neighbourhood? If so, a description given to the police might even yet secure his arrest. I was turning over this possibility when the chiming of a clock recalled my appointment. I glanced up at the dial on the clock-tower and had just noted that the appointed hour had struck when I observed Thorndyke ascending the steps to the platform at the base. This was our rendezvous, and I forthwith hurried across the cobbled square and presented myself, bursting with my news and discharging them in a volley as soon as I arrived.

Thorndyke was deeply interested, but yet I found in his manner something slightly disappointing. He was an impassive man, difficult to surprise or move to any outward manifestation of emotion. Still, knowing this, I was a little chilled by the almost academic view that he took of the incident, and especially by his firm rejection of my plan for invoking the aid of the police.

"It sounds tempting," he admitted, "to swoop down on this man and put an end forthwith to all our dangers and complications, but it would be a bad move. Quite probably the police would decline to take any action. And then what sort of description could you give them? For the purposes of a search it is far too general, and a change of clothing would make it entirely inapplicable. And we must admit the possibility of your being mistaken. And finally, if we gave this information, we should almost certainly lose one man – whom none of us has ever seen, but who is probably the principal. We should have let the cat out of the bag, and all our carefully-laid plans would come to nought."

"I didn't know that we had any carefully-laid plans," said I.

"You know that we are engaged in investigating a murder, that our aim is to secure the two or more murderers, and to elucidate the causes and circumstances of the crime, and that we have accumulated a certain number of data to that end."

"You have," I objected. "I have practically no data at all. May I ask if you know who this sallow-faced little devil is?"

"I have a strong suspicion," he replied. "But suspicion isn't quite what one wants to take into a court of law. I want to verify my suspicions and turn them into conclusive evidence, so that when I play my card it shall be a trump card."

To this I had no reply to make. I knew Thorndyke's methods. For years I had acted as his leading counsel, and always when I had gone into court I had taken with me a case complete to the last detail. Now, for the first time, I was realising the amount of patience and self-restraint that went to the making of a case of unassailable conclusiveness, and I found myself with difficulty overcoming the temptation to make a premature move.

While we had been talking, we had been making our way at an easy pace out of the town on to the London Road, and now Thorndyke, with the one-inch ordnance map in his hand, indicated our route.

717

"Beauchamp Blake," said he, "lies just off the Lower Icknield Way, on the left of the London Road. But there is no need for us to take the shortest way. The by-road through Stoke Mandeville looks more entertaining than the main road, and we can pick up the Lower Icknield Way at the crossroads below the village."

Our route being thus settled, we set forth, turning off presently into the quiet, shady by-road. And as we swung along between the thinning hedgerows, with the majestic elms – now sprinkled with yellow – towering above us and casting athwart the road streaks of cool shadow, we chatted sporadically with long intervals of silence, for we were Londoners on holiday to whom the beauty of this fair countryside was reinforced by a certain pleasant strangeness.

"I have wondered from time to time," I said, after one of the long pauses, "what can be the significance – if it has any – of that blue-dyed hair that you extracted from Winifred's locket." (I had confided to Thorndyke the new relations that had grown up between our fair client and me).

"Ah," he replied. "A very interesting problem, Anstey."

"I have also wondered what made you take the hair out of the locket to examine it under the microscope."

"The answer to that question is perfectly simple," said he. "I took it out to see if it was blue. In the mass the hair looked black."

"But do I understand that you thought it might be blue?"

"I expected to find it blue. The examination was a measure of verification."

"But why, in the name of Fortune, should you expect to find blue hair in a locket? I had no idea that hair ever was dyed blue – except," I added with a sudden flash of recollection, "in the case of ancient Egyptian wigs, and I had an idea that they were not hair at all."

"Some of them, I believe, were not. However, this was not ancient Egyptian hair. It was modern."

"Then, will you tell me what it was that made you expect to find the hair in the locket dyed blue?"

"The expectation," he replied, "arose out of an inspection of the locket itself."

"Do you mean those mysterious and obscure Biblical references engraved inside?"

"No, I mean the external characters, the peculiar construction, the motto engraved on the front, and the hallmark on the back."

"But what," I asked, "was the connection between those external characters and this most extraordinary peculiarity of the hair inside?"

He looked at me with the exasperating smile that I knew so well (and was, in fact, expecting).

"Now, you know, Anstey," said he, "you are trying to pump me, to suck my brains instead of using your own. I am not going to encourage you in any such mental indolence. The proper satisfaction of a discovery is in having made it yourself. You have seen and handled the locket, you have heard my comments on it, and you have access to it for further examination. Try to recall what it is like, and if necessary, examine it afresh. Consider its peculiarities one by one and then in relation to one another. If you do this attentively and thoughtfully, you will find that those peculiarities will yield some most curious and interesting suggestions, including the suggestion that the hair inside is probably blue."

"I shan't find anything of the kind, you old devil," I exclaimed wrathfully, "and you know perfectly well that I shan't. Still, I will take an early opportunity to put the 'Little Sphinx' under cross-examination."

While we had been talking we had passed through the village of Stoke Mandeville, and we now arrived at the crossroads, where we turned to the left into the ancient Icknield Way.

"A mile-and-a-half farther on," said Thorndyke, again consulting the map, "we cross the London Road. Then we turn out of the Icknield Way into this lane, leaving Weston Turville on our left. I note there is an inn opposite the gates of Beauchamp Blake. Does that topographical feature interest you?"

"I think," said I, "that after another couple of miles, we shall be ready for what the British workman calls a 'breaver'. But it is probably only a wayside beerhouse."

Another half-hour's walking brought us to the London Road, crossing which we followed a side road – apparently part of the Icknield Way – which skirted the lake-like reservoir and presently gave off as a branch a pleasant, elm-bordered lane on the right-hand side of which was a tall oak paling.

"This," said Thorndyke, whose stature enabled him easily to look over the fence, "is the little park of Beauchamp Blake. I don't see the house, but I see the roof of a gatekeeper's lodge. And here is the inn."

A turn of the lane had brought into view a gatekeeper's lodge by the main gates of the park, and nearly opposite, the looked-for hostelry. And a very remarkable-looking hostelry it was, considering its secluded position, an antique, half-timbered house with a high, crinkly roof in which was a row of dormer windows, and a larger, overhanging gabled bay supported below by an immense carved corner-post. But the most singular feature of the house was the sign, which swung at the top of a

719

tall post by a horse-trough in the little forecourt, on which was the head of a gentleman wearing a crown and a full-bottomed wig, apparently suspended in mid-air over a brown stone pitcher.

"It seems to me," said I, as we approached the inn, "that the sign needs an explanatory inscription. The association of a king and a brown jug may be natural enough, but it is unusual as an inn-sign."

"Now, Anstey," Thorndyke exclaimed protestingly, "don't tell me that that ancient joke has missed its mark on your superlative intellect. The inscription on the parlour window tells us that the sign is The King's Head, and the pitcher under that portrait explains that the king is James the Second or Third – His Majesty over the water. This is evidently a Jacobite house. Does the sedition shock you? Or shall we enter and refresh? If the landlord's ale is as old as his politics, we ought to find quite exceptional entertainment within, and perhaps pick up a trifle of local gossip that may interest us."

I assented readily, secretly denouncing my slowness in the "uptake". Thorndyke's explanations were always so ridiculously simple – when you had heard them.

The landlord, who looked like a retired butler, received us with old-fashioned deference and inducted us into the parlour, drawing a couple of Wycombe armchairs up to the table.

"What can I do for you, gentlemen?" he inquired.

"Well, what can you do for us?" asked Thorndyke. "Is it to be bread and cheese and beer?"

"I can let you have a cold fowl and a cut of boiled bacon," said the landlord with the air of one who lays down the ace of trumps.

"Can you really!" exclaimed Thorndyke. "That is a repast fit for a king – even for the king over the water."

The landlord smiled slyly. "Ah, you're alluding to my old sign, sir," said he. "T'wouldn't have done to have had him swingin' up there time back. Some others would have been swingin' too. In those days he used to hang in this room over the fireplace, only there was a portrait of King George fixed over him with concealed hinges. When strangers came to the house there was King George – God bless him! – the same as the sign that used to hang outside, but when the villagers or the people from the Hall opposite sat in the room, then George was swung back on his hinges to bring James into view and a pitcher of water was put on the table to drink the toasts over. This was a thriving house in those days. They say that Percival Blake – he was the last of the old family and a rare plotter by all accounts – used to meet some of his political cronies in this very room, and I've no doubt a lot of business was plotted here that never came to anything."

720

"Who has the place now?" asked Thorndyke.

"The present squire is Mr. Arthur Blake, and a queerish sort of squire he is."

"In what way queer?" I asked.

"Well, you see, sir, he's a Colonial – lived in Australia all his life, I understand. And he looks it – a big, roughish-looking man, and very short spoken. But he can ride, I'll say that for him. There isn't a better horseman in the county. Mounts from the off-side, too. I suppose that's their way out there, though it don't suit our rule of the road."

As the landlord gave these particulars, he proceeded, with swift dexterity, to lay the table and furnish it with the materials for the feast, aided and abetted by an unseen female who lurked in the background. When he had put the final touch with a "foam-crowned jug of nut-brown", he showed a tendency to withdraw and leave us to our meal, but Thorndyke was in a conversational mood and induced him, without difficulty, to fetch another tumbler and proceed with his output of local lore.

"Is it true that the place is going to be sold?" Thorndyke inquired.

"So they say," replied the landlord. "And the best thing the squire could do if the lawyers will let him. The place is no good to him."

"Why not?"

"Well, sir, he's a bachelor, and like to remain one it seems. Then he's a stranger to the place and don't appear to take to English ways. He keeps no company and he makes no visits, he don't know any of his neighbours and doesn't seem to want to. He has only kept on one or two of the servants, and he lives with his man – foreign-looking chap named Meyer – in a corner of the house and never uses the rest. He'd be more comfortable in a little farm house."

"And how does he spend his time?" asked Thorndyke.

"I don't know, sir," was the answer. "Mostly loafing about, I should say. He takes photographs, I hear – quite clever at it, too, it seems. And he goes out for a ride every afternoon – you'll see him come out of the gate at three o'clock almost to the minute – and sometimes he goes out in the morning, too."

"And as to visitors? Are strangers allowed to look over the house?"

"No, sir. The squire won't have any strangers about the place at all. I fancy what made him so particular was a burglary that occurred there about a couple of years ago. Not that there was much in it, for they got all the things back and they caught the burglar the very next day."

"That was smart work," I remarked.

"Yes," our friend agreed, "they did the thief very neatly. It was a one-man job and the burglar seems to have been a downy bird, for he worked in gloves so that he shouldn't leave any marks behind. But he took those gloves off a bit too soon, for, when they heard him making off and let the dogs loose, he had to do a bolt, and he dropped one of the things in the park – a silver salver it was, I think – and the police found it the next morning and found some finger-marks on it. They wanted to take the salver up to Scotland Yard to have it examined, but the squire wouldn't have that. He took a photograph of the fingermarks and gave it to the police, and they took it up to Scotland Yard, and the people there were able to tell them at once whose fingermarks they were, and they got the burglar that very evening with all the stolen goods in his possession. Wonderful smart, I call it."

"Do you think," Thorndyke asked, "that we should be able to get a look at the house? Just the outside, I mean?"

"I'll see what can be done, sir," the landlord replied "I'll have a few words with the lodge-keeper. I was butler to the last squire but one, so they know me pretty well. I'll just run across while you are finishing your lunch. But you'd better wait until the squire has gone out, because, if he sees you on the drive, like as not he'll order you out, and that wouldn't be pleasant for gentlemen like you."

"I think we'll take the risk," said Thorndyke. "If he tells us to go, we can go, but I don't like sneaking in behind his back."

"No, sir, perhaps you are right," the landlord agreed, a little dubiously, and departed on his errand, leaving us to finish our lunch – which, in fact, we had practically done already.

In this long conversation I had taken no part. But I had been an interested listener. Not that I cared two straws for the small beer that our host had been retailing. What had interested, and a good deal puzzled me, was Thorndyke's amazing inquisitiveness respecting the private and domestic affairs of a man whom neither of us knew and with whom we really had no concern, for the question of the succession to the property was a purely legal one – and pretty shadowy at that – on which the personal qualities and habits of the present tenant had no bearing whatever. And yet my experience of Thorndyke told me that he certainly had not been asking these trivial and impertinent questions without some reasonable motive. No man was less inquisitive about things that did not concern him.

But the discrepancy between his character and his conduct did not end here. As soon as the landlord had gone and we had filled and lit our pipes, he began to explore his waistcoat pockets and presently produced therefrom Polton's reproduction of Mr. Halliburton's ridiculous mascot, which he laid on the table and regarded fondly.

"Do you usually carry that thing in your pocket, Thorndyke?" I asked.

"Not usually," he replied, "but this is a special occasion. We are on holiday, and moreover, we are seeking our fortune – or at least, hoping that something may turn up."

"Are we?" I said. "I am not conscious of any such hope, and I don't know what you expect."

"Neither do I," he replied. "But I feel in an optimistic mood. Perhaps it is the beer," and with this he picked up the mascot, and opening the split gold ring with a knife-blade, attached it to his watch-chain, closing the ring with a squeeze of his finger and thumb.

It was a singular proceeding. What made it especially so was Thorndyke's openly-expressed contempt of the superstition which finds expression in the use of charms, mascots, and other fetishistic objects and practices. However, we were on holiday, as he had said, and perhaps it was admissible to mark the occasion by playing the fool a little.

In a few minutes the landlord returned and announced that he had secured the consent of the lodge-keeper to our making an inspection of the house, with the proviso that we were not to go more than a couple-of-hundred yards down the drive. "I'll just step across with you," he added, "so that he can see that you are the right parties."

Accordingly, when we had paid the modest reckoning, we picked up our hats and sticks and as our host held open the parlour door, we passed out into the courtyard, glancing up with renewed interest at the historic sign which creaked in the breeze. Crossing the road, we passed through the wicket of the closed gate, under the detached observation of the lodge-keeper, and here our host wished us *adieu* and returned to the inn.

A short walk down the drive brought us to a turn of the road where we came in sight of the house across a stretch of meadows in which a small herd of cows made spots of vivid colour. It was not a large mansion, but what it lacked in size it made up for in character and interest. The two parts were clearly distinct, the newer portion being a Jacobean brick building with stone dressings and quaint corbie-step gables, while the older part – not later than the Sixteenth Century – was a comparatively low structure showing massive timbers with pargetted plaster fillings, a high roof with wide-spreading eaves, and a long row of picturesque dormer windows and large, clustered chimneys.

"It is a grand old house," I said. "What a pity it is that Blake is such a curmudgeon. The inside ought to be even more interesting than the outside."

"Yes," Thorndyke agreed, "it is a splendid specimen of domestic architecture, and absolutely thrown away, if our host was not exaggerating. One could wish for a more appreciative tenant – such as our young friend Percy, for instance."

I glanced at Thorndyke, surprised – not for the first time – at the way in which he tended to harp on this very unresonant string. To me, Percy's claim to this estate was simply a romantic instance of the might-have-been, and none too clear at that. His chance of ever inheriting Beauchamp Blake was a wild dream that I found myself unable to take seriously. But this was apparently not Thorndyke's view, for it was evident that he had considered the matter worth inquiring into, and his last words showed that it still hovered in his mind. I was on the point of reopening the discussion when two men appeared round the corner of the house, each leading a saddled horse. Opposite the main doorway they halted and one of them proceeded to mount – from the off-side, as I noticed. Then they apparently became aware of our presence, for they both looked in our direction, indeed they continued to stare at us with extraordinary attention, and by their movements appeared to be discussing us anxiously.

Thorndyke chuckled softly. "There must be something uncommonly suspicious in your appearance, Anstey," he remarked. "They seem to be in a deuce of a twitter about you."

"Why my appearance?" I demanded. "They are looking at us both. In fact, I think it is you who are the real object of suspicion. I expect they think you have come back for that silver plate."

As we spoke, the discussion came to an end. The one man remained, holding his horse and still looking at us, while the other turned and advanced up the drive at a brisk trot, sitting his mount with that unconscious ease that distinguishes the lifelong, habitual equestrian. As he approached, he looked at us inquisitively and with undissembled disapproval, but seemed as if he were going to pass without further notice. Suddenly, however, his attention became more intense. He slowed down to a walk, and as he drew near to us he pulled up and dismounted. And again I noticed that he dismounted from the off-side.

Chapter XV
The Squire and
the Sleuth-hound

As Mr. Blake approached with the evident intention of addressing us, it was not unnatural that I should look at him with some interest. Not that such interest was in any way justified by his appearance, which was quite commonplace. He was a tall man, strongly built, and apparently active and muscular. His features were somewhat coarse, but his expression was resolute and energetic, though not suggestive of more than average intelligence. But at the moment, as he bore down on us, leading his horse by the bridle-rein, with his eyes fixed on Thorndyke's face, suspicion and a certain dim suggestion of surprise were what I principally gathered from his countenance.

"May I ask what your business is?" he demanded somewhat brusquely, but not rudely, addressing Thorndyke and looking at him with something more than common attention.

"We really haven't any business at all," my colleague replied. "We were walking through the district and thought we should like to have a glance at your very picturesque and interesting house. That is all."

"Is there anything in particular that you want to know about the house?" Mr. Blake asked, still addressing Thorndyke.

"No," the latter replied. "Our interest in the place is merely antiquarian, and not very profound at that."

"I see," said Mr. Blake. He appeared to reflect for a few moments and seemed to be on the point of moving away when he stopped suddenly and a quick change passed over his face. At the same moment I noticed that his eyes were fixed intently on Thorndyke's ridiculous mascot.

"I take it," said he," that you had the lodge-keeper's permission to come inside the gates?"

"Yes," Thorndyke replied. "He gave us permission – through the inn-keeper, who asked him – to come in far enough to see the house. As far as we have come, in fact."

Mr. Blake nodded, and again his eyes wandered to the object attached to Thorndyke's watch-chain.

"You are looking at my mascot," the latter said genially. "It is a curious thing, isn't it?"

"Very," Blake agreed gruffly. "What is it?"

Thorndyke pulled the soft wire ring open, and detaching it from his chain, handed the little object to the other, who examined it curiously and remarked, "It seems to be made out of a bone."

"Yes, the bone of a porcupine ant-eater."

"Ha. You got it somewhere abroad. I suppose?"

"No, replied Thorndyke. "I found it in London, and, of course, it isn't really mine. It belongs to a man named Halliburton. But I don't happen to have his address at the moment, so I can't return it."

Mr. Blake listened to this explanation with a sort of puzzled frown – wondering, perhaps, at my colleague's uncalled-for expansiveness to an utter stranger. But his wonder was nothing to mine, as I heard the usually secretive Thorndyke babbling in this garrulously confidential fashion.

When he had examined the mascot, Mr. Blake handed it back to Thorndyke with an inarticulate grunt, and as my colleague hooked the ring on his watch-chain, he turned away, walked round his horse to the off-side, mounted lightly to the saddle and started the horse forward at a trot. As he disappeared round a bend of the tree-bordered road, I glanced at Thorndyke, who was once more gazing calmly at the house.

"Mine host was right, I observed. "Squire Blake is a pretty considerable boor."

"His manners are certainly not engaging," Thorndyke agreed.

"I didn't notice that he had any manners," said I, "and it seemed to me that you were most unnecessarily civil, not to say confidential."

"Well, you know," he replied, "we are on his premises, and not only uninvited, but contrary to his expressed wishes. We could hardly be otherwise than civil. And after all, he didn't eject us. But I suppose we may as well retire now."

"Yes," I agreed, "he is probably waiting to see us off his confounded land, and possibly speaking his mind to the lodge-keeper."

Both these surmises appeared to be correct, for when we came round the clump of trees at the turn of the road, I saw the squire in earnest conversation with the keeper, who was standing at attention, holding the gate open, and, I thought, looking somewhat abashed. We passed out through the wicket, which was still unfastened, but though the lodge-keeper looked at us attentively, and even a little curiously, Blake gave no sign of being aware of our existence.

"Well," said I, "he is an unmannerly hog. But he has one redeeming feature. He is a man of taste. He did admire you, Thorndyke. While you were talking he couldn't keep his eyes off you."

"Possibly he was trying to memorise my features in case I should turn out to be a swell cracksman."

I laughed at the idea of even such a barbarian as this mistaking my distinguished-looking colleague for a member of the swell mob. But it was not impossible. And certainly the squire had scrutinised my friend's features with an intensity that nothing but suspicion could justify.

"Perhaps," said I, "he suffers from an obsession on the subject of burglars. Our host's remarks seemed to suggest something of the kind. I wonder what he was saying to the lodge-keeper. It looked to me as if the custodian was receiving a slight dressing-down on our account."

"Probably he was," replied Thorndyke. "But I think that, if my learned friend had happened to be furnished with eyes in the back of his head – "

"As my learned senior appears to be," I interjected.

" – he would already have formed a more definite opinion as to what took place. In the absence of the retrocephalic arrangement, I suggest that we slip through this opening in the hedge and sit down under the bank."

Stooping to avoid the thick upper foliage, he dived through the opening and I followed, with no small curiosity as to what it was that my extraordinarily observant colleague had seen. Presumably someone was following us, and if so, as the opening occurred at a sharp bend of the road, our disappearance would have been unobserved.

"It is my belief, Thorndyke," I said, as we sat down under the bank, "that your optical arrangements are like those of the giraffe. I believe you can see all round the horizon at once."

Thorndyke laughed softly. "The human field of vision, Anstey," said he, "as measured by the perimeter, is well over a hundred and eighty degrees. It doesn't take much lateral movement of the head to convert it into three hundred and sixty. The really important factor is not optical but mental. That earnest conversation with the gatekeeper suggested a possibility, though a rather remote one. Ordinary human eyesight, used with the necessary attention, was quite sufficient to show that the improbable had happened, as it often does. Hush! Look through that chink in the hedge."

As he concluded in a whisper, rapid footfalls became audible. Nearer and nearer they approached, and then, through my spy-hole, I saw a man in cord breeches and leggings and a velveteen coat walk swiftly past. The gatekeeper had been dressed thus, and presumably the man was he, though I had not observed him closely enough to be able to recognise him with certainty.

"Now, why is he following us?" I asked, taking the identity for granted.

"We mustn't assume that he is following us at all with a definite intent, though I suspect he is. But he may be merely going the same way. He may have business in Wendover."

"It would be rather amusing to dodge him once or twice and see what his game is," I said with the schoolboy instinct that lingers on, if atavistically, in the adult male.

"It would be highly amusing," Thorndyke agreed, "but it wouldn't serve *our* purpose, which is to ascertain *his* purpose, and keep our knowledge to ourselves. We had better move on now if he is out of sight."

He was out of sight, having reached and turned down the Tring Road. We followed at a sharp walk, and as we came out into the Tring Road, behold him standing in the footway a couple-of-hundred yards towards Wendover, looking about him with a rather foolish air of bewilderment. As soon as he saw us, he lifted his foot to the bank and proceeded to attend to his bootlace.

"We won't notice him," said Thorndyke. "He is evidently an artless soul and probably believes that he has not been recognised. Let us encourage that eminently desirable belief."

We passed him with an almost aggressive appearance of unconsciousness on both sides, and pursued our way along the undulating road.

"I don't think there is much doubt now that he is following us," said I, "and the question is, why is he doing it?"

"Yes," said Thorndyke, "that is the question. He may have had instructions to see us safely out of the district, or he may have had further instructions. We shall see when we get to the station. Meanwhile I am tempted to try a new invention of Polton's. It is slightly fantastic, but he made me promise to carry it in my pocket and try it when I had a chance. Now, here is the chance, and here is the instrument."

He took from his pocket a leather case from which he extracted a rather solidly-made pair of spectacles. "You see," he said, "Polton has long had the idea that I ought to be provided with some means of observing what is going on behind me, and he has devised this apparatus for the purpose. Like all Polton's inventions, it is quite simple and practicable. As you see, it consists of a rigid spectacle-frame fitted with dummy glasses – clear, plain glass – at the outer edge of which is fixed a little disc of speculum-metal worked to an optically true plane surface and set at a minute angle to the glass. As the disc is quite close to the eye, it enables the wearer, by the very slightest turn of the head, to get a clear view directly behind him. Would you like to try it?"

728

I took the spectacles from him and put them on, and was amazed at their efficiency. Although the discs were hardly bigger than split peas, they gave me a perfectly clear view along the road behind us – as if I had been looking through a small, round hole – and this with a scarcely appreciable turn of the head. Viewed from behind, I must have appeared to be looking straight before me.

"But," I exclaimed, "it seems a most practical device, and I shall insist on Polton making me a pair."

"That will please him," said Thorndyke, and he added, reflectively "if only there were a few thousand more Poltons – men who found their satisfaction in being useful and giving pleasure to their fellows – what a delightful place this world would be!"

I continued to wear the magic spectacles all the way to Wendover, finding a childish pleasure in watching the unconscious gatekeeper who was dogging our footsteps and taking ludicrous precautions to keep – as he thought – out of sight. Only as we descended the long hill into the beautiful little town did I take them off, the better to enjoy the charm of the picturesque approach with its row of thatched cottages and the modest clock-turret, standing up against the background of the wooded heights that soared above Ellesborough. At the station we had the good fortune to find a train due and already signalled, but we delayed taking our tickets until our follower arrived, which he did, in evident haste, a couple of minutes later – being, no doubt, acquainted with the times of the trains. As soon as he appeared, Thorndyke sauntered to the booking-office wicket and gave him time to approach before demanding in clear, audible tones, two firsts to Marylebone. The gatekeeper followed, and thrusting his head and shoulders deep into the opening, as if he were about to crawl through, made his demand in a muffled undertone.

"We need not trouble ourselves about him anymore," said Thorndyke, "until we get to London. Then we shall know whether he is or is not trying to shadow us."

When we had settled ourselves in an empty compartment and began to charge our pipes as the train moved off, I returned to the question of our tactics.

"What do you propose to do, Thorndyke, if this fellow tries to follow us home? Shall we let him run us to earth, or shall we lose him?"

"I see no reason why we should make a secret of who we are and where we live. That is apparently what Blake wants to know – that is, if this man is really shadowing us."

"But," I urged, "isn't it generally wiser to withhold information until you know what use is going to be made of it?"

"As a rule, it is," he admitted. "But it may happen that the use made of information by one party may be highly illuminating to the other. We may assume that Blake wants to know who we are simply because he suffers from an obsession of suspicion and thinks that we were in his grounds for some unlawful purpose. But he may have some other object, and if he has, I should like to know what it is, and the best way to find out is to let him have our names and address."

To this I assented, though I was a little mystified. The man Blake was no concern of ours, and it did not seem to matter in the least what suspicions of us had got into his thick head. However Thorndyke probably knew his own business – and meanwhile the presence of this sleuth-hound provided an element of comedy of which I was far from unappreciative, and which my sedate colleague enjoyed without disguise.

When we alighted at Marylebone, we walked quickly to the barrier, but having passed through, we sauntered slowly to the main exit.

"Do you think Polton's spectacles would be very conspicuous?" I asked.

My colleague smiled indulgently. "The new toy has caught on," said he, "and it would be undeniably useful at the present moment. No, put the spectacles on. The discs are hardly noticeable to a casual observer."

Accordingly I slipped the appliance on as we strolled out into the Marylebone Road and was able, almost immediately, to report progress.

"He is watching us from the exit. Which way are we going?"

"I think," replied Thorndyke, "as he is a country cousin, we will make things easy for him and give him a little exercise after the confinement of the train. The Euston Road route is less crowded than Oxford Street."

We turned eastward and started at an easy pace along the Marylebone Road and Euston Road, keeping on the less-frequented side of the street. I was a little self-conscious in regard to the spectacles, but apparently no one noticed them, and by their aid I was able to watch with astonishing ease our artless follower and to amuse myself by noting his conflicting anxieties to keep us in view and himself out of sight. We turned down Woburn Place, crossed Queen Square to Great Ormond Street and, proceeding by Lamb's Conduit Street, Red Lion Street, Great Turnstile, Lincoln's Inn, and Chancery Lane, crossed Fleet Street to Middle Temple Lane. Here we slowed down, lest the sleuth-hound should lose us, and as we were now in our own neighbourhood, I removed the spectacles and restored them to their owner.

At the entrance to Pump Court we separated, Thorndyke proceeding at a leisurely pace towards Crown Office Row while I hurried through the court, and having halted in the Cloisters to make sure that the sleuth was not pursuing me, I darted through Fig-Tree Court and across King's Bench Walk to our chambers, where I found Polton laying a sort of hybrid tea and supper.

To our trusty assistant I rapidly communicated the state of affairs (including the triumphant success of the magic spectacles, at which his face became a positive labyrinth of ecstatic wrinkles) and, having provided ourselves with field-glasses, we stationed ourselves at the laboratory window, from whence we had the gratification of watching Thorndyke emerge majestically from Crown Office Row, followed shortly by the man in the velveteen coat, whose efforts to make himself invisible brought Polton to the verge of apoplexy.

"Hadn't I better follow him and see where he goes to, sir?" the latter suggested.

The suggestion was put to Thorndyke when he entered, but was rejected.

"I don't think we want to know where he goes from here," said he. "But still, seeing that he has come so far, it might be kind of you, Polton, to go down and give him a chance of obtaining any information that he wants."

Polton needed no second bidding. Clapping on his hat, he set forth gleefully down the stairs. But in a minute or two he was back again, somewhat crestfallen.

"It's no go, sir," he reported. "I found him copying the names on the door-post in the entry, and I think he must have got them all down, for when he saw me, he was off like a lamplighter."

Thorndyke chuckled. "And to think," said he, "that our friend, the squire, could have got all the information he wanted by the simple expedient of asking for our cards. Verily, suspicious folk give themselves a deal of unnecessary trouble."

Chapter XVI
Mr. Brodribb's Embassy

There is a certain psychological phenomenon known to those financial navigators who have business on the deep and perilous waters of the Stock Exchange as "jobbing backwards". It is not their monopoly, however. To ordinary mortals – who describe it as "prophesying after the event" – it has been familiar from time immemorial, and has always been associated with a degree of wisdom and certainty strangely lacking in prophecy of a more hasty and premature kind.

Reviewing the curious case of which this narrative is the record, I am tempted to embark on this eminently satisfying form of mental exercise. But when I do so, I am disposed to look with some surprise at the very conspicuous deficiency in the power of "jobbing forward" which I displayed while the events which I am chronicling were in progress. Now, I can see that all the striking and significant facts (only they then appeared neither striking nor significant) which enabled Thorndyke, from the very first, to pursue a steady advance along a visible trail, were in my possession as much as they were in his. But, whereas in his hands they became connected so as to form a continuous clue, in mine they remained separate, and apparently unrelated fragments. At the time, I thought that Thorndyke was hiding from me what material evidence he had. Now it is obvious to me (as also to the acute reader, who has, no doubt, already pieced the evidence together) that he not only concealed nothing, but actually gave me several of the very broadest hints.

So, despite the knowledge that I really possessed, if I had only realised it, I remained utterly in the dark. All that I knew for certain was that Winifred was encompassed by dangers, that human wolves prowled about her habitation and dogged her footsteps when she went abroad.

But even these perils had their compensations, for they gave an appearance of necessity to the constant companionship that my inclinations prompted. It was not a mere pilgrim of love that wended his way daily to Jacob Street, but an appointed guardian with duties to discharge. In the personally-conducted tours through the town, on business connected with the drawings that Winifred continued to produce with unabated industry, I was carrying out an indispensable function, since she was not permitted to go abroad without an efficient escort, and thus duty marched with pleasure.

Intimate, however, as my relations with Winifred had become, and recognised now even by Percy, I abstained from any confidences on the subject of our investigation of the murder. That was Thorndyke's affair, and although he had made no stipulation on the subject, I had the feeling that he expected me to keep my own counsel, as he certainly did himself. Accordingly, in describing our visit to Beauchamp Blake – in which both she and Percy were intensely interested – I said nothing about the man whom I had seen in Aylesbury.

One exception I had nearly made, but thought better of it. The occasion arose one afternoon when we were examining and criticising her latest drawing. As we stood before the easel, a shaft of sunlight, coming in through the great window struck a part of the drawing and totally altered the character of the colouring. I remarked on the change of colour produced by the more intense illumination.

"Yes," said she, "and that reminds me of a very odd discovery that I made the other day and that I meant to tell you about." She unfastened the silken cord by which she wore the mysterious locket suspended from her neck, and opening the little gold volume, held it in the sunbeam so that the light fell upon the coil of hair that it enclosed.

"Do you see?" she asked, looking at me expectantly.

"Yes," I answered. "In the sunlight the hair seems to have quite a distinct blue tint."

"Exactly!" she exclaimed. "Now isn't that very remarkable? I have often heard of blue-black hair, but I thought it was just a phrase expressing intense blackness without any tinge of brown. But this is really blue, quite a clear, rich blue, like the colour of deeply-toned stained glass. Do you suppose it is natural? It can hardly be a dye."

It was then that I had nearly told her of Thorndyke's discovery and his strange and cryptic utterances on the subject. But a principle is a principle. The fact had been communicated to me by him, and I did not feel at liberty to disclose it without his sanction – though, to be sure, there was nothing confidential about it. His examination of the locket had been, apparently, a matter of mere curiosity, for Thorndyke was so constituted that he could not bring himself willingly to leave a problem unsolved, even though its solution promised no useful result. To him the solution was an end in itself, undertaken for the pleasure of the mental exercise. And this locket evidently held a secret. To what extent he had mastered that secret, I could not guess. Nor did I particularly care. It was not my secret, and I had no taste for working out irrelevant puzzles.

"I should hardly think the blue colour can be natural," said I, and then, by way of compromise, I added, "but I expect Thorndyke could tell you. When you come to see us again, you had better show it to him and hear what he says about it."

I took the locket from her hand and looked it over with half-impatient curiosity, remembering Thorndyke's exasperating advice, and recalling his reference to the hallmark on the back, I turned it over and scrutinised the minute device.

"You are looking at the hallmark, or the goldsmith's 'touch', or whatever it is," said Winifred. "It is rather curious. I have never seen one like it before. It certainly is not an ordinary English hallmark. Let me get you a magnifying-glass."

She fetched a strong reading-glass, and through this I examined the mark more minutely. But I could make nothing of it. It consisted of four punch-marks, of which the first was a capital "A" surmounted by a small crown and bearing two palm-leaves, the second a kind of escutcheon bearing the initials "AH" surmounted by a crown, and over that a *fleur-de-lis*, the third bore simply a capital "L", and the fourth the head of some animal which looked like a horse.

"It is a curious and unusual mark," said I, handing back to her the locket and the glass, "but it conveys no information to me, beyond the suggestion that the locket is apparently of foreign workmanship, probably French or Italian, But," I added, with a malicious hope of seeing my reverend senior cornered, "you had better ask Thorndyke about it when you come. He is sure to be able to tell you all about it."

"He seems to be a sort of human encyclopaedia," Winifred remarked as she refastened the locket. "I shall adopt your advice and consult him about that hair, but I shan't be able to come this week. There is quite a big batch of drawings to be done, and that means some long working days. Perhaps you can arrange an afternoon in the latter part of next week for the oracular tea-party."

I promised to ascertain my colleague's arrangements and to fix a day, but the promise was left unredeemed and the "oracular tea-party" was thrust into the background by new and more stirring events, which began to cast their shadows before them that very evening. For, when I entered our chambers, behold Mr. Brodribb and Sir Lawrence Drayton settled in armchairs by the fire, in company with the small table and the inevitable decanter. Evidently some kind of conference was in progress.

"Ha!" said Brodribb. "Here is the fourth conspirator. Now we are complete. I have been devilling for your respected senior, Anstey, and I have called to report progress. Also, as you see, I have captured Sir Lawrence and brought him along as he seemed to be an interested party."

"He is a somewhat mystified party at present," said Drayton, "but probably some explanations are contemplated."

"They are going to begin as soon as Anstey has filled his glass," said Brodribb, bearing in mind, no doubt, the laws of conviviality as expounded by Mrs. Gamp, and as the stipulated condition was complied with, he proceeded, "It was suggested to me by Thorndyke a short time ago that the tenure of the Beauchamp Blake property would be put on a more satisfactory footing if the missing title-deeds could be recovered."

"More satisfactory to the present tenant, you mean," said Drayton.

"More satisfactory to everybody," said Brodribb.

"That would depend on the nature of the documents recovered," Sir Lawrence remarked. "But let us hear the rest of the suggestion."

"The suggestion of our learned and Machiavellian friend was that, since the documents are believed to be hidden somewhere in the house, it would be a good plan to have a systematic survey of the premises carried out by some person who has an expert knowledge of secret chambers and hiding-places."

"Do you know of any such person?" Drayton asked.

Brodribb smiled a fat smile and replenished his glass. "I do," he replied "and so do you. Thorndyke himself is quite an authority on the subject, and, of course, the suggestion was that the survey should be made and the search conducted by him. Naturally. You can guess why, I suppose?"

"I can't," said Drayton, "if you are suggesting any reason other than the one you have given."

"My dear Drayton," chuckled Brodribb, "can you imagine Thorndyke embarking on a search of this kind without some definite leading facts? No, no. Our friend has got something up his sleeve. I've no doubt that he knows exactly where to put his hand on those documents before he begins."

"Do you, Thorndyke?" Sir Lawrence asked, with an inquisitive glance at my colleague.

"Now," the latter replied, "I put it to you, Drayton, whether it is likely that I, who have never been in this house in my life, have never seen a plan of it, and have no knowledge whatever of its internal construction or arrangement, can possibly know where these documents are hidden."

"It certainly doesn't seem very probable," Drayton admitted, and it certainly did not. But still I noted that Thorndyke's answer contained no specific denial, a circumstance that apparently did not escape Brodribb's observation, for that astute practitioner received the reply with an unabashed wink and wagged his head knowingly as he savoured his wine.

"You can think what you like," said he, "and so can I. However, to proceed: The suggestion was that I should put the proposal to the present tenant, Arthur Blake, and expound its advantages, but, of course, say nothing as to the source of the inspiration. Well, I did so. I wrote to him, pointing out the desirability of getting possession of the deeds, and suggesting that he should call at my office and talk the matter over."

"And how did he take it?" asked Drayton.

"Very calmly – at first. He called at my office yesterday and opened the subject. But he didn't seem at all keen on it, thought it sounded rather like a wild-goose chase – until I mentioned Thorndyke. Then his interest woke up at once. The mention of a real, tangible expert put the matter on a different plane, gave it an air of reality. And he had heard of Thorndyke – read about him in the papers, I suppose – and, of course, I cracked him up. So in the end he became as keen as mustard and anxious to get a start made as soon as possible. And not only keen on his own account. To my surprise, he raised the question of the other claimant, Peter Blake's son. Of course he knew about Peter Blake's claim, although it was before his time, and it seems that he read the newspaper report of the curious statement that Miss Blake – Peter's daughter – made at the inquest on Sir Lawrence's brother. Well, in effect, he suggested – very properly, as I thought – that Miss Blake might like to be present when the search was made."

"I certainly think," said Drayton, "she should be, if not actually present, at least represented. There might be some documents affecting her brother directly."

"That was his point, and he authorised me to invite her to be present and to make all necessary arrangements. So the question is, Thorndyke, when can you go down and find the documents?"

"I am prepared to begin the search the day after tomorrow."

"And with regard to Miss Blake? You are acquainted with her, I think?"

"Yes," replied Thorndyke. "We can communicate with her. But my feeling is that it would hardly be desirable for her to be present while the actual survey is being made. It may be a tedious affair, and we shall get on with it better without spectators. Of course I shall know if anything is found and shall probably ascertain its nature, and in that case she can be informed."

Drayton nodded, but he did not seem quite satisfied. "I suppose that will do," said he, "though I would rather that she were directly represented. You see, Thorndyke, you are acting for Blake, and if Anstey goes with you, he is your coadjutor. I wonder if Blake would object to my looking in later in the day. I could, as I have to go down to Aylesbury the day after tomorrow. What do you say, Brodribb?"

"I see no objection," was the reply. "In fact, I will take the responsibility of inviting you to call and see what progress has been made."

"Very well, then," said Drayton, "I will come about four. I shall go down by car, and when I have finished with my client, I can easily take Beauchamp Blake on my way home. And for that matter," he added, "I don't see why Miss Blake shouldn't come with me. My client's wife could entertain her while I am transacting the business, and then she could come on with me to the house. How does that strike you, Thorndyke?"

"It seems quite an admirable arrangement," my colleague replied. "She will be saved the tedium of waiting about, and she will have the advantage of your advice if any delicate inquiries have to be made."

Drayton's suggestion was accordingly adopted, subject to Winifred's consent – which I did not doubt she would give readily, notwithstanding the pressure of her work – and shortly afterwards our two friends took their departure, leaving me a little puzzled as to the origin and purpose of the conference and the projected expedition.

It had been a rather curious transaction. There were several points that I failed to understand. In the first place, what interest had Thorndyke in these title-deeds? Assuming him to take Percy's rather indefinite claim seriously – which he apparently did – was the establishment of the title desirable from his point of view? I should have thought not. It had appeared that Blake was anxious to sell the property and had been restrained only by the insecurity of the title. But if the title were made secure, he would almost certainly sell the estate, which was the last thing that Percy's advisers could wish. Then could it be that our shrewd old friend Brodribb was right? That Thorndyke had actually ascertained or inferred the whereabouts of the missing deeds? In the case of any other person the supposition would have seemed ridiculous. But Thorndyke's power of reasoning from apparently unilluminating facts was so extraordinary that the possibility had to be admitted, and his evasive reply to Drayton's direct question seemed to make it even probable.

"I don't see," said I, with a faint hope of extracting some trifle of information from Thorndyke, "why you are so keen on these title-deeds."

"That," he replied, "is because you persist in thinking in sections. If you would take a larger view of the subject this proposed search would appear to you in a rather different light."

"I wonder if there is really going to be a search," I said craftily, "or whether old Brodribb was right. I am inclined to suspect that he was."

"I commend your respect for Brodribb's opinions," he replied. "Our friend is an uncommonly wide-awake old gentleman. But he was only guessing. Whatever we find at Beauchamp Blake – if we find anything – will be discovered by bonafide research and experiment. And that raises another question. Are you going down with Drayton, or did you propose to come with me?"

"I don't want to be in your way," I replied, a little piqued at the question. "Otherwise I should, of course, have liked to come with you."

"Your help would be very valuable," said he, "if you are willing to sacrifice the other attractions. But if you are going to help me, we had better take a little preliminary practice together. There is a set of empty chambers next door. Tomorrow I will get the keys from the treasurer's office, and we can put in some spare time making careful measured plans. The whole art of discovering secret chambers is in the making of plans so exact as to account for every inch of space, and showing accurately the precise thickness of every wall and floor. And a little practice in the art of opening locked doors without the aid of keys will not be amiss."

This programme was duly carried out. On the morrow we conveyed into the empty chambers a plane table covered with drawing-paper, a surveyor's tape, and a measuring-rod, and with these appliances, I proceeded, under Thorndyke's direction, to make a scaled plan of the set of rooms, showing the exact thickness of all the walls and the spaces occupied by chimneys, cupboards, and all kinds of projections and irregularities. It was a longer business than I had expected, indeed I did not get it completed until the evening was closing in, and when at last I had filled in the final details and took the completed plan to our chambers for Thorndyke's inspection, I found my colleague busily engaged in preparations for the morrow's adventure.

"Well!" I exclaimed, when my plan had been examined and replaced by a fresh sheet of paper, "this is an extraordinary outfit! I hope we shan't have to carry this case home after dark."

It was certainly a most sinister collection of appliances that Thorndyke had assembled in the suitcase. There was a brace and bits, and auger, a bunch of skeleton keys, an electric lantern, a pair of telescopic jemmies, and two automatic pistols.

"What on earth are the pistols for?" I demanded.

"Those," he replied, "are just an extra precaution. Many of these hiding-holes are fitted with snap locks, and it is quite possible to find oneself caught in a trap. Then, if there should be no room to use a jemmy, it might be necessary to blow the lock to pieces."

"Well," I remarked, "it is as well to take all necessary precautions, but if Blake sees those pistols they will need a good deal of explaining, especially as he will certainly recognise us as the two suspicious visitors."

"We need not exhibit them ostentatiously," said Thorndyke. "We can carry them in our pockets, and the jemmies as well. Then if the necessity to use them arises, they will explain themselves."

The rest of the evening we spent in a course of instruction in the arrangement and design of the various kinds of secret chambers, hiding-holes, aumbries, and receptacles for documents, sacred vessels, and other objects that, in times of political upheaval, might need to be concealed. On this subject Thorndyke was a mine of information, and he produced a note-book filled with descriptions, plans, sections, and photographs of most of the examples that had been examined, which we went over together and studied in the minutest detail. By the end of the evening, I had not only acquired an immense amount of knowledge on an obscure out-of-the-way subject, but I had become in so far infected with Thorndyke's enthusiasm that I found myself looking forward almost eagerly to the romantic quest on which the following day was to see us launched.

Chapter XVII
The Secret Chamber

It was close on half-past-eleven when we drew up in Wendover Station. We had just finished our rather premature lunch and had packed up the luncheon baskets and placed them on the seats, and now, lifting down the suitcase and the plane table with its folding tripod, stepped out on to the platform.

"I wonder," said I, "if Blake has sent any kind of conveyance for us. I don't suppose he has."

My surmise turned out to be correct. When we went out into the station approach, the only vehicle in sight was a closed fly, which we decided to charter and, having stowed our impedimenta on the front seat and given the driver the necessary directions, we entered and took possession of the back seat. The coachman climbed to the box and started the horse at a quiet jog-trot, turning into the Aylesbury, or London Road to avoid the steep hill down which we had come to the station on the last occasion. As we passed the fine, brick-towered windmill and came out on the country road, Thorndyke leaned forward and opened the suitcase.

"We had better put the more suspicious-looking objects in our pockets," said he. "We may not want them at all, and then they won't have been seen, whereas if they are wanted, the necessity will explain our having provided ourselves with them."

He took out the bunch of skeleton keys and slipped them into his coat pocket, and then picked out the two telescopic jemmies, one of which he handed to me while he bestowed the other in some kind of interior pocket – into which, I noticed, it disappeared with singular completeness, suggesting a suspicious suitability of the receptacle. Finally he took out the two automatic pistols, and having pocketed one, handed me the other after a careful and detailed explanation of its mechanism and the proper way to hold and fire it. I took the weapon from him and stowed it in my hip-pocket, very gingerly and with some reluctance, for I detest firearms, and as I placed it carefully with the muzzle pointed as far as possible away from my own person, I reflected once more with dim surprise on the circumstance that Thorndyke, whose dislike of these weapons was as great as my own, should have adopted this clumsy and dangerous means of dealing with a somewhat remote contingency. It seemed an excessive precaution, and I found creeping into my mind a faint suspicion that my colleague might possibly have had something more in his mind than he had disclosed, though that was even more incomprehensible, considering the very peaceful nature of our quest.

I was still turning these matters over in my mind when the fly reached the crossroads and entered the lane. Here the appearance of the inn just ahead recalled me to our immediate business, and old Brodribb's observation recurred to me.

"How are you going to start, Thorndyke?" I asked. "I presume you have got some definite programme?"

"I shall be guided by what Blake has to tell us," he replied. "He may have a good plan of the house, and it is possible that he has made some explorations of his own which will give us a start. There is our old friend, the lodge-keeper, mightily surprised to see us."

I caught a passing glimpse of the sleuth, staring at us in undisguised astonishment. Then we swung round into the drive, and the old house came into view. We were evidently expected, for as we approached the house a man came out of the main entrance and stood on the wide threshold awaiting our arrival. Just as the fly was about to draw up opposite the portico, Thorndyke said in a low voice, "If we are offered any refreshments, Anstey, we had better decline them. We have had lunch, you know."

I glanced at him in amazement. It was a most astonishing remark. But there was no time to ask for any explanation, for at that moment the fly drew up, the driver jumped down from his seat and the squire came forward to receive us.

"We have met before, I think," said the latter as we shook hands. "If I had known who you were I should have invited you to look at the house then. However, it isn't too late. I see you have brought your traps with you," he added, with a glance at the plane table and its tripod.

"Yes," said Thorndyke, "we are prepared to make a regular survey, if necessary. But perhaps you have a plan of the house?"

"There is a plan," replied Blake, "though I fancy it is not very exact. I will show it to you. Probably it will give you a hint where to begin."

As I had now settled with the fly-man, we entered the house and Blake conducted us into a large room, furnished as a library and containing a considerable collection of books. On a table by one of the windows was a plan spread out and held open by paperweights.

"You see," said Blake, "this is an architect's plan, made, I think, when some repairs were contemplated. It is little more than a sketch, and doesn't give much detail. But it will help you to take a preliminary look round before lunch."

"We have had lunch," said Thorndyke. "We got that over in the train so that we should have a clear day before us. Time is precious, and we ought to get to work at once. I suppose you have not made any sort of investigation on your own account?"

As Thorndyke mentioned our premature meal, the squire gave him a quick glance and seemed to look a little resentful. But he made no comment beyond answering the question.

"I have not made any regular examination of the house, but I have poked about a little in the old part and I have found one secret chamber, which I have utilised as a photographic dark-room. Perhaps you would like to see that first. There may be some other hiding-places connected with it which I have overlooked. There is a tall cupboard in it which I have used to store my chemicals."

"We may have to empty that cupboard to see if there is anything behind it," said Thorndyke. "At any rate, we had better begin by overhauling it."

He opened the suitcase and took from it the surveyor's tape, which he put in his pocket.

"Hadn't we better take the lamp?" said I.

"You won't want that," said Blake. "There is a portable lamp in the room."

I was half-inclined to take it, nevertheless, but as Thorndyke shut the suitcase and prepared to follow our host, I let the matter rest.

From the library we passed out into a long gallery, one side of which was hung with portraits, presumably of members of the family, and some of them of considerable antiquity, to judge by the style of the painting and the ancient costumes. Then we crossed several rooms – fine, stately apartments with florid, moulded ceilings and walls of oaken panelling, on which I noticed a very respectable display of pictures. The rooms were fully furnished – very largely, I noticed, with the oak and walnut furniture that must have been put in when the new wing was built. But they were all pervaded by a sense of desolation and neglect. They were dusty and looked faded, unused, and forgotten. Nowhere was there a sign of human occupation, nor, I noticed, did we meet, in the whole course of our journey across this part of the house, a single servant or retainer, or, indeed, any living creature whatever.

A door at the end of a short passage, on being unlocked and opened, revealed a short flight of wooden stairs, and when we had descended these we found ourselves in a totally different atmosphere. This was the old timber house, and as we crossed its deserted rooms and trod its uncarpeted oaken floors, our footsteps resounded with dismal echoes among the empty chambers and corridors, conveying a singular sense of remoteness and desolation. The gloomy old rooms with their dirt-encrusted casements, the massive beams in their ceilings, the blackened wainscoting, rich with carved ornament but shrouded with the dust and grime of years of neglect, the gouty-legged Elizabethan tables and ponderous oaken chairs and settles, all these dusty and forgotten appurtenances of a vanished generation of men seemed to have died with their long-departed human associates and to be silently awaiting their final decay and dissolution. It was an eerie place, dead and desolate as an Egyptian tomb.

And yet, strangely enough, it was here that I saw the one solitary sign of human life. We were passing along a narrow gallery or corridor when I noticed, high up in the panelled wall, one of those small interior windows which one sees in old houses, placed opposite an exterior window to light an inner chamber. Looking up at this little window, I saw the face of some person looking down on us. It was the merest glimpse that I caught, for the window was coated with dust and the room behind it in darkness. But there was the face of some human creature, man, woman, or child, and its appearance in this remote, sepulchral place, so far from the domain of the living household, smote upon me strangely and seemed to make even more intense the uncanny solitude of the empty mansion.

I was still speculating curiously on who this watcher might be when our host halted by the wall of a smallish room.

"This is the place," said he, pointing to the wall. "I wonder if you can find the door."

The wainscoting in this room was nearly plain, the only ornament being a range of very flat pilasters and a dado moulding, enriched by a row of hemispherical bosses. Thorndyke ran his eye over the wainscoting, noting more particularly the way in which the pilasters were joined to the intervening panels.

"I suppose," said he, "we had better try the most obvious probabilities first. The natural thing would be to use one of these bosses to cover the release of the lock."

Blake assented (or dissented) with an inarticulate grunt, and Thorndyke then proceeded to pass along the row of bosses, pressing each one firmly in turn. After about a dozen trials, he came to one in the middle of a pilaster which yielded to the pressure of his thumb, sinking in some two inches, in the fashion of a large electric-bell push. Holding the "push" in with his thumb, he pressed vigorously against the adjoining panel, first on one side of the pilaster and then on the other, but in neither case was there any sign of the panel moving, though I added my weight to his.

"You haven't quite hit it off yet," Blake informed us.

Thorndyke reflected for a few seconds. Then, keeping the boss pressed in, he put his other thumb on the next one of the series, which was at the edge of the panel, and gave a sharp push, whereupon this boss also sank in with an audible click and then the whole panel swung inward, disclosing a narrow and wonderfully well-concealed doorway.

"Good," said Blake. "You've solved the problem more quickly than I did. Just hold the door open a moment. It has rather a strong spring, and I generally prop it open with this block." As he spoke he fetched a small block of wood from under an adjacent table and set it against the foot of the door.

"I had better go first," said he, "as I know where to find the lamp." With this he entered before us, striking a wax match and shading it with his hand. The dim illumination showed a narrow, passage-like room, apparently a good deal more lofty than the low-ceiled room from which we had entered it, and dimly revealed a very high cupboard near the farther end. We had groped our way after him a few paces when he turned suddenly. "How stupid of me!" he exclaimed. "I had forgotten that I had left the lamp in the next room. Excuse me one moment."

He slipped past us, and kicking the block away, ran out, pulling the door sharply after him, when it slammed to with a loud click of the latch.

"What the deuce did he kick that block away for," I exclaimed, "and leave us all in the dark?"

"We shall probably find out presently," replied Thorndyke. "Meanwhile, stand perfectly still. Don't move hand or foot."

"Why do you say that?" I demanded with something like a thrill of alarm, for there was something rather disturbing in the tone of Thorndyke's sharply-spoken command. And standing there in the pitchy darkness, locked in a secret chamber in the very heart of this great, empty mansion, there came to me a flash of sudden suspicion. I recalled Thorndyke's mysterious warning to take no food in this house, I remembered the loaded pistol that he had put into my hand, and I saw again that unaccountable face at the window, watching us as Blake led us – whither? "You don't think Blake is up to any mischief, do you?" I asked.

"I can't say," he replied. "Perhaps he will come with the lamp presently. But we may as well see where we are while we are waiting."

I heard a rustling as if he were searching his pockets. Then, suddenly, there broke out a bright light that flooded the little room and rendered all the objects in it plainly visible.

It was a queer-looking room, almost more like a rather irregularly-shaped passage, for none of the walls were straight, and the ceiling sloped up from a height of about eight feet at one end to nearly twelve at the other. Near the farther end was a very high wall-cupboard, and at the extreme end, facing us, was a small door, about three feet above the floor level and approached by a flight of five wooden stairs.

The appearance of the light was reassuring, and still more so was the evidence that it afforded of Thorndyke's foresight in having provided himself with this supplementary lamp. But much less reassuring was his next observation after having flashed his light all over the room.

"I suspect we have seen the last of our host – for the present, at any rate. Look at the top of the cupboard, Anstey."

I looked at the cupboard. It was between eight and nine feet high, and was fitted with folding doors, of which the leaf nearest to us was half-open, and on the top of the half-open door, near the free corner, a little board had been placed with one end resting on the door and the other insecurely supported by the moulding at the top of the cupboard, and on the board, delicately balanced over the door, was a large chemical flask, filled with what looked like water and fitted with a cork.

"What do you make of it?" Thorndyke asked, keeping his powerful inspection-lamp focused on the flask as I gazed at it.

"It looks like some sort of booby-trap," said I. "It is a wonder that flask wasn't shaken down when Blake slammed the door."

"He probably expected that it would be, and it very nearly was, for you can see that it has jarred to the extreme edge. But failing the slam of the door, he no doubt assumes that we, being as he imagines in total darkness, shall grope our way along the wall until we come to the cupboard. Then, the instant we touch the door, down will come the flask. It is quite an ingenious plan."

"But what is the purpose of it?" I demanded. "It can't be a practical joke."

"It isn't," said he. "Far from it. I should say it is very deadly earnest. Unless I am mistaken, that flask is filled with some volatile poison. The instant that it falls and breaks, this room will become a lethal chamber."

At these words, uttered by Thorndyke in tones as calm and emotionless as if he were giving a demonstration to his students, a chill of horror crept over me. My very hair seemed to stir. It was an appalling situation. I stared in dismay and terror at the flask, poised aloft and ready, as it seemed, at the slightest movement, or even a loudly-spoken word, to come crashing down and stifle us with its deadly fumes.

"Great God!" I gasped. "Then we are in a trap! But is there nothing that we can do? The flask is too high up for us to reach it."

"It would be sheer insanity to go near it, said Thorndyke. "But I don't think we need be very disturbed. There must be some way of getting out of this chamber. Let us go and reconnoitre the door, though I daresay our friend has attended to that."

We tiptoed cautiously back to the door and examined its construction. The mechanism was very simple, but like most old locksmith's work, extremely massive. The two bosses outside evidently were the ends of two sliding bars and bolts of wood. The one which Thorndyke had pressed first apparently had a slot which, when it was brought opposite the massive latch, allowed the latter to rise. That at least was what Thorndyke inferred, for, as the latch was in the thickness of the great oaken doorpost (which had a slot to let it escape, when raised) the actual mechanism could not be seen. The second sliding bar, when pushed in, raised the latch itself by means of an inclined plane. Both the sliding bars had been provided with knobs on their inner ends, so that they could be pulled in from inside as well as pushed in from without, but whereas the knob still remained on the bar which raised the latch, that of the bar which released the latch and allowed it to rise had been removed. The end of the bar could be seen, nearly flush with the surface of the doorpost, and in it a small hole in which the knob had evidently been screwed.

"Would it be possible to hook anything, such as a skeleton key, into that hole?" I asked when we had examined it thoroughly.

"I think we can do better than that," said he, hooking the bulls-eye of his inspection-lamp in a button-hole of his coat and feeling in his pocket. "This is a more workmanlike appliance."

He exhibited an appliance that looked like a kind of clasp-knife, but was actually a pocket set of screw-taps, such as are carried by engineers and plumbers. Drawing out the smallest tap, he tried it in the hole, but the latter was too small to admit it. Then, from the same appliance, he drew out a taper reamer, and on trying this in the hole he found that the point entered easily. He accordingly drove it in lightly, rotating it as he pressed, and continued to turn it until the sharp-cutting tool had broached out the hole to a size that would admit the nose of the tap, when he withdrew the reamer and, inserting the tap, gave it a few vigorous turns. Now, on pulling gently at the handle of the tap, it was seen to be fast in the hole, and the sliding bar began to move forward.

"I wonder if our host is hanging about outside," said he.

"What does it matter whether he is or not?" I asked.

"Because I want to try whether we can open the door, and I don't want him to hear."

"But, confound it," said I, "he will see us when we come out."

"We are not going to come out that way if we can find any other."

"Why not?" I demanded. "We want to get clear of that infernal flask, and the sooner we are out the better."

"Not at all," said Thorndyke. "If we come out and show ourselves, the game is up, and there will probably be trouble. Whereas if we can get out another way, we shall put him in a very pretty dilemma. Hearing no sound from us, he will probably assume that his plan has succeeded. And if Drayton should arrive before he has taken the risk of verifying our decease, his explanations should be rather interesting. At any rate, I should like to see what his next move will be, but we must make our retreat secure in case of accidents. I think we can raise the latch without making any noticeable sound. You observe that the pivot has been oiled – and also that the door-spring is new and has apparently been fixed on quite recently."

In my heart I cursed his inquiring spirit, for I wanted to get out of this horrible trap. But I offered no objection, standing by sullenly while he proceeded with calm interest to complete his experiment. Grasping the tap-handle with one hand and the knob with the other, he pulled steadily at the former until the sliding bar was drawn inwards to its full extent, and then at the knob, which came in with similar ease and silence. But when I saw the latch rise and the door begin to swing inwards, I could hardly restrain myself from dragging it open and making a burst for freedom.

The next moment the opportunity was gone. With the same silent care Thorndyke reclosed the door, let the latch down, and slid back the release bar.

"Now," said he, turning away but leaving the tap jammed in the hole, "we can pursue our investigations at our ease. If there is no other exit, we can come out this way, and we have got a clear retreat in case of accidents. What does the appearance of this place suggest to you? I mean as to an exit."

"Well," I answered, "there is a door at the top of those steps. Presumably its function is the ordinary function of a door."

"I doubt it," said he. "It is too blatantly innocent. More probably its function was to occupy pursuers while the fugitive was gaining a start. Still, we will have a thorough look at it, as I expect our host has already done. We had better go one at time, and for Heaven's sake step lightly, and remember that if that flask should come down, you make a bee-line for the door and get outside instantly."

Lighted by Thorndyke's lamp, I crept cautiously along the room with my eyes riveted on the flask and my heart in my mouth. Then Thorndyke followed, and together we ascended the steps to the door and proceeded to examine it minutely. It was provided with plainly visible hinges but had no ostensible latch or lock. Around it were a number of projecting ends of tree-nails, but pressure on them, one after the other, produced no result, nor did the door itself show any sign of yielding, indeed, the form of the hinges suggested that it opened inwards – towards the room – if it would open at all.

"We are wasting time, Anstey," Thorndyke said at length. "The thing is a dummy, as we might have expected. Let us try something more likely. Now, from what I know of these secret chambers, I should say that the most probable exits are the cupboard and the stairs. Both, you notice, seem to be functionless. There is no reason for that great cupboard having been built in here, and these stairs simply lead to a dummy door. And cupboards with sliding shelves and concealed doors in the back, and stairs with movable treads were very favourite devices. The cupboard is unfortunately not practicable while that flask is balanced overhead, so we had better give our attention to the stairs. I suspect that there are two exits, in different directions, but either will do for us."

We stole softly down the stairs, and stooping on hands and knees, brought the light to bear on the joints of the treads and risers, but the dirt of ages had settled on them and filled up any tell-tale cracks that might have been visible. To my eye, the steps looked all alike, and all seemed to be solid oak planks immovably fixed in their positions.

Suddenly Thorndyke dived into his inner pocket and brought forth the telescopic jemmy, which he pulled out to its full length. Then, laying the chisel end on the tread of the bottom stair, he drove its edge forcibly against the angle where the tread and the riser met. To my surprise, the edge entered fully half an inch into the joint, which the dirt had filled and concealed.

"Get your jemmy, Anstey, and push it in by the side of mine," said he.

I produced the tool from my breast pocket, where it had been reposing to my great discomfort, and opening it out, I inserted its edge close to that of Thorndyke's.

"Now," said he, "both together. Push!"

We both bore heavily on the ends of the jemmies, and the sharp chisel ends entered fully an inch, and simultaneously a visible crack appeared along the foot of the riser. We now withdrew the jemmies and reinserted them at the two ends of the tread. Again we drove in together, and the crack widened perceptibly. On this, Thorndyke rose and closely examined the angle of the step above and then that of the third, and here, as he brought the bulls-eye close to the surface of the step, I could see that a narrow crack had opened between the step and the riser.

"It looks," said I, "as if the two steps had shifted."

"Yes," he agreed, "and apparently the pivot, if there is one, is above. Let us get to work again."

We reinserted the jemmies several times in different places, thrusting together and as forcibly as we dared with that horrible flask insecurely balanced above our heads, and at each thrust there was an appreciable widening of the crack, which had now opened fully a quarter of an inch, making it evident that the stairs were really movable.

"Now," said Thorndyke, "I think we might venture to prise."

He reversed his jemmy and inserted the "crow" end into the crack near one extremity, while I inserted mine near the opposite end. Then, at a word from him, we bore on the ends of the levers, and with a protesting groan, the step rose another inch. Thorndyke now laid aside his jemmy, and standing on the bottom step, thrust his fingers into the gaping crack, I did the same, and when we had got a fair grasp, he gave the word.

"Now, both together. Up she comes!"

We both heaved steadily but not too violently. There was a grinding creak as the long-disused joint moved, then suddenly the two steps swung up and stood nearly upright on their pivot, disclosing a yawning hole in which the light showed a narrow flight of brick steps.

Thorndyke immediately stepped in through the opening, and descending a few steps, turned and held the light for me, when I followed.

The steps fell away steeply down a kind of well with walls of brickwork, which was thickly encrusted with slimy growths of algae and fungi, and the steps themselves were slippery with a similar coating and were almost hidden, in places, by great fungous masses which sprouted from the joints of the brickwork. After descending about eight feet, we reached a level floor and proceeded along a narrow brick tunnel, stooping to clear the slime-covered roof. This extended some fifteen yards and ended in what at first looked like a blank wall. On coming close, however, and throwing on it the light of the lantern, I perceived an oblong space of planking about five feet long by three high and three feet above the floor, forming a rude door, very massive and clumsy and furnished with a simple, roughly-fashioned iron latch.

"I don't see any hinges," observed Thorndyke, "so there is probably an internal pivot. Let us prise up the latch first and then see how the door moves."

He slipped the end of his jemmy under the latch, taking a bearing on the brickwork, and levered the great latch up without much difficulty in spite of the rust that had locked it in position. Then, inserting the chisel end into the crack between the door and the jamb, he gave a tentative wrench. The door moved perceptibly, inwards at one end and outwards at the other.

"It is evidently pivoted in the middle," said he. "If you will prise the other end while I work at this, we shall get it open easily."

We accordingly inserted our jemmies at the respective ends and gave a steady thrust, on which the door, with a deep groan and a loud screech from the rusty pivots, swung round on its centre, letting in a flood of cheerful daylight and fresh air, which I inhaled with profound relief. A vigorous pull on the edge brought the door fully open and disclosed a mass of foliage which blocked the view from within and no doubt concealed the door from outside. But in any case it would have been very inconspicuous, for we could now see that the solid planking was covered externally with counterfeit brickwork, very convincingly executed with slices of brick.

Thorndyke reached out and pulled aside a branch of the tree that obscured the view "This door," said he, "seems to open on the edge of the moat, so it was probably made at a time when the moat was full of water. However, we have found our way out, and it is a better one than the cupboard would have given us, for, if that has an exit in the back, it probably leads up to the garrets or the chimneys. Now all we have to do is to remove our traces from the chamber above and make our way out. But there is no need for you to come up."

"I am coming up all the same," said I, and as he turned to re-enter the tunnel, I followed, though I admit, with infinite reluctance. But I did not actually re-enter the chamber. I stood with my head out of the opening and a terrified eye on the accursed flask, while Thorndyke tiptoed across the room to the door. Here he withdrew the tap from the hole, and folding it, dropped it into his pocket. Then he stooped and blew away the wood-dust that had fallen from the reamer on to the floor, and having thus removed every trace (excepting the broached-out hole in the sliding bar), he stepped lightly back and re-entered the opening.

"The problem now," said he, "is to get these stairs back in their place without shaking down the flask."

"Does it matter," I asked, "now that we have a means of escape?"

"Not very much," he answered, "but I would rather leave it there in evidence."

The movable stairs were furnished with a rough wooden handle on the underside to enable a fugitive to replace them from below. This Thorndyke grasped, and with a steady pull, drew the stairs down into their original position, giving a final tug to bring the joints close together. Then once more we began to descend the slippery steps.

We were about half-way down when Thorndyke stopped.

"Listen, Anstey," said he, switching off the light. And as he spoke, I caught the sound of footsteps somewhere overhead. Then I heard the door of the secret chamber open slowly – I could recognise it by the sound of the door-spring – and after a little interval, Blake's voice called out, "Dr. Thorndyke! Mr. Anstey! Where are you?"

Again there was a short pause. The door slowly opened a little farther, the floor above creaked under a stealthy tread, and then I seemed to catch faintly another voice, apparently more distant.

"They are not here," said Blake. "They seem to have got out somehow. Here, catch hold of the lamp. Mind the door! Mind the – "

The door-spring creaked. There was a heavy thud, and an instant later the sound of shattering glass, followed by a startled shout and a hurried trampling of feet.

"The knob! The knob! Quick!" a high-pitched voice shrieked, and at that the very marrow in my bones seemed to creep. For the knob was useless now. Thorndyke's reamer had destroyed the screw-hole.

With the sweat streaming down my face and my heart thumping with sickening violence, I listened to the torrent of curses, rising to yells of terror and anguish and mingled with strange, whimpering cries. I could see it all with horrible distinctness – the two trapped wretches above, frantically turning the knob in the broached-out hole while the poisonous fumes rose remorselessly and encompassed them.

The cries grew thicker and more muffled, and mingled with dreadful coughs and gasps. Then there was a sound of a heavy body falling on the floor and a horrible husky screech broke out, whereat I felt the hair of my scalp stir like the fur of a frightened cat. Three times that appalling screech came through the floor to our pitch-dark lurking-place, the last time dying away into a hideous, quavering wail. Then, once more, there was the thud of a heavy body falling on the floor, and after that an awful silence.

"God Almighty!" I gasped. "Can't we do anything, Thorndyke?"

"Yes," he replied, "we can get out of this. It is time we did."

Even as he spoke I became aware of a faint odour of bitter almonds which seemed every moment to grow more distinct. It was undoubtedly time for us to be gone, and when, once more, the light of his lamp flashed down the stairway, I responded readily to a gentle push and began to descend the steps as rapidly as my trembling knees would let me.

The faint, sinister odour pursued us even to the tunnel and it was with a sigh of relief that I reached the open doorway and looked again on the sky-lit foliage and breathed the wholesome air. We crept out together through the long, low doorway, and grasping the branches of the trees

751

and bushes outside, scrambled down the sloping bank to the dry floor of the moat.

Chapter XVIII
The Cat's Eye

When we stood up at the bottom of the bank, I turned to Thorndyke and asked, "What are we going to do now? We must make some effort to let those poor devils out."

"That," he replied, "is an impossibility. In the first place they are certainly dead by now, and in the second it would be certain death to attempt to open that door. The chamber is full of the vapour of hydrocyanic acid."

"But," I expostulated, "we ought to do something. Humanity demands that we should, at least, make a show of trying to save them."

"I don't see why," he replied coldly. "They are certainly dead, and if they were not, I would not risk a single hair of my head to save their lives. Still, if you have any feeling on the matter, we can go and reconnoitre. But we must look to our own safety."

He struck out along the floor of the moat at a brisk pace, and I kept up with him as well as my trembling knees would let me, for I was horribly shaken by the shocking experiences of the last few minutes, and still felt sick and faint. Thorndyke, on the other hand, was perfectly unmoved, and as he strode along at my side, I glanced at his calm face and found in his quiet, unconcerned manner something inhuman and repelling. It is true that those two wretches who now lay stark and dead on the floor of that dreadful chamber deserved no sympathy. They had digged a pit for us and fallen into it themselves. But still, they were human beings, and their lives were human lives, but Thorndyke seemed to value them no more than if they had been a couple of rats.

About a hundred yards farther along the moat, we came to a cross path, at each end of which was a flight of rough steps up the bank. We ascended the steps on the house side, and these brought us to a small door with a Tudor arch in the head. A modern night-latch had been added to the ancient lock, but it was a simple affair which Thorndyke's picklock opened in a few moments, and the door then yielded to a push. It opened into a corridor which I recognised as the one which we had passed through and where I had seen the face at the window – a dead face it was now, I suspected. We turned and walked along it in the direction in which Blake had led us, and as we neared the end I began to be sensible of a faint odour in the musty air, an attenuated scent of bitter almonds.

"We must go warily," said Thorndyke. "The next room, I think, is the one out of which the secret chamber opens."

He paused and stood looking dubiously at the door, and as he stood hesitating, I pushed past him, and seizing the handle, flung the door open and looked into the room. But it was only an instantaneous glance, showing me the uninterrupted wall, the wooden block lying where Blake had kicked it, and close by, a dead rat. The sight of that little corpse and the sickening smell of bitter almonds that suddenly grew strong in the air as the door opened, produced an instant revulsion. My concern for our would-be murderers was extinguished by a thrill of alarm for my own safety. I drew the door to hurriedly and followed Thorndyke, who was walking quickly away.

"It is no use, Anstey," he said, a little impatiently. "It is mere sentiment, and a silly one at that. All we can do is to open these windows and clear off until the gas has diffused out. It won't take so very long with all the gaping joints in this old woodwork."

"And what are we going to do meanwhile?"

"We must find the housekeeper, if there is one, and let her know the state of affairs. Then we must send information to the police at Aylesbury, and before they arrive, I think it would be well to prepare a written statement, which we can sign in their presence and which should contain all that we are prepared to say about the matter before the inquest."

"Yes," I agreed "that seems to be the best course," and with this we proceeded to open the rusty casements of the corridor and then made our way back to the new wing of the house.

The inn-keeper had certainly been right. Squire Blake had been very far from lavish in the matter of retainers. One after another of the great, dusty rooms we crossed or peered into without encountering a single serving-man or maid. The house seemed to be utterly deserted. At last we came to the entrance hall, and here, as we stood commenting on this extraordinary solitude, a door opened and a faded and shabby elderly woman, looking like a rather superior charwoman, emerged. She looked at us curiously and then asked, "Can you tell me, sir, if Mr. Blake is ready for lunch?"

"I am sorry to say," replied Thorndyke, "that Mr. Blake has met with a mishap. He has locked himself in his dark room and has poisoned himself accidentally with some chemicals."

"Oh dear!" exclaimed the woman, looking at Thorndyke with a sort of stupefied dismay. "Hadn't someone better go and fetch him out?"

"That is not possible at present," said Thorndyke. "The room is full of poison gas."

"But," the woman protested, "he may die if no one goes to his assistance."

"He is dead already," said Thorndyke, "and there is another person in the room with him, who is also dead."

"That will be Mr. Meyer, his valet," said the woman, staring at Thorndyke with a sort of bewildered horror, puzzled, no doubt, by the incongruity between his tragic tidings and his calm, matter-of-fact demeanour. "And you say they have both killed themselves! Lord! Lord! What a dreadful thing!" She clasped her hands, and gazing helplessly from one of us to the other, asked, "What are we to do? Oh! What are we to do?"

"Is there anyone whom we could send into Aylesbury?" asked Thorndyke, "We ought to let the police know of the accident, and we ought to get a doctor."

"There is only the lodge-keeper," she whimpered shakily. "He could go on Mr. Meyer's bicycle. Dear, dear! what an awful thing it is!"

"If you will have the bicycle brought to the door," said Thorndyke, "I will write a note and take it up to the lodge-keeper myself. There are writing materials in the library, I suppose?"

She supposed there were, and showed us into the room, where we found some notepaper and envelopes. Then she departed, wringing her hands and muttering, to fetch the bicycle.

"I shall not give any details in this note," Thorndyke said as he sat down at the table and uncapped his fountain pen. "I shall just tell them that Mr. Blake and his valet have met their deaths – presumably – by poisoning, that it is a police case, and that the Divisional Surgeon had better accompany the police officer."

With this he wrote the note, addressing it to the Superintendent or Chief Constable, and he had just closed and sealed it when the woman reappeared to announce the arrival of the bicycle, which had been brought to the door by a young woman, apparently a housemaid. Thorndyke mounted the machine and rode away swiftly up the drive, and I turned back into the house, followed by the two women, who, now that the first shock had spent itself, were devoured by curiosity and eager to extract information.

Their efforts in this direction, however, were not very successful, for, although the facts must very soon become public property, it seemed desirable at present to say as little as possible, while, as for any explanation of this extraordinary affair, I was as much in the dark as they were. So I maintained a discreet, though difficult, reticence until Thorndyke reappeared, when the two women retired and left us in possession of the room.

"I sent our friend off with the note," said my colleague "and I told him enough to make sure that he will put on the pace. It is only about four miles, and as the police probably have a car, we may expect them pretty soon. I will just draft out a statement of the actual occurrences, and you had better write, on the same paper, a confirmatory declaration. We can read them to the officer and sign them in his presence."

He proceeded to write out a concise, but fairly full, narrative of what had befallen us in this house, with a brief statement of the nature of our business here, and when I had read it through, I wrote at the foot a paragraph confirming the statement and accepting it as my own. This occupied some considerable time, and we had not long finished when there was a somewhat peremptory ring at the bell, and a minute later, the elderly woman – whom I assumed to be the housekeeper – entered, accompanied by a police officer and a gentleman in civilian clothes. The former introduced himself briefly and got to business without preamble.

"Concerning this note, sir," said he. "You have given no particulars. I suppose there is no doubt that Mr. Blake and his valet are really dead?"

"I should say there is no doubt at all," replied Thorndyke. "But I have written out a statement of the particulars, from which you will be able to judge. Shall I read it to you?"

"I think the doctor had better see the bodies first," was the reply.

"Certainly," agreed the doctor. "We don't want to waste precious time on statements. Where are they?"

"I will take you to them," said Thorndyke, "but I must tell you that they are shut in a room which is filled with the vapour of hydrocyanic acid."

The two men gave a startled look at Thorndyke, and as he led the way out into the hall and across the new wing, they followed, talking together earnestly but in low tones. Presently they overtook us, and the officer remarked, "This is a very extraordinary affair, sir. Has no attempt been made to get these men out of that room?"

"No," replied Thorndyke.

"But why not?"

"I think you will see when you get there."

"But," exclaimed the doctor, "surely some effort ought to have been made to save them! You don't mean to say that you have left them in that poisoned air and made no attempt even to open the doors and windows?"

"We have opened some of the neighbouring windows," said Thorndyke, and he proceeded to give a description of the secret chamber and its surroundings, to which the doctor listened with pursed-up lips.

"Well," he remarked dryly, "you seem to have been very careful. Is it much farther?"

"It opens out of the next room but one," replied Thorndyke, and as he spoke I detected in the air a very faint odour of bitter almonds. I fancy the doctor noticed it, too, but he made no remark, and when we reached the end of the corridor and Thorndyke indicated the door that gave access to the room, both men hurried forward. The doctor turned the handle and flung the door open, and he and the officer stepped briskly across the threshold. And then they both stopped short, and I guessed that they had seen the dead rat. The next moment they both backed out hastily and the doctor slammed the door behind him and followed us to the discreet distance at which we had halted.

"The vapour is as you say," said the latter, visibly crestfallen, "in an extreme state of concentration."

"Yes," agreed Thorndyke, "but it is much less than it was. If you will go a little farther away, I will throw the door open and we can then retire and let the vapour diffuse out."

"Do you think it safe, sir?" queried the officer. "There's a fearful reek in there." Then, as Thorndyke approached the door, he and the doctor (and I) walked away quickly up the corridor and, looking back, I saw my colleague, pinching his nostrils together, fling the door wide open, and hurry after us.

When we had retired to a safe distance, the officer halted and said, "You were saying something about a statement, sir. Shall we have it now? I don't understand this affair in the least."

Thorndyke produced the statement from his pocket and proceeded to read it aloud, and as he read, the two men listened with growing astonishment and not very completely concealed incredulity. When he had finished, I read out my statement, and then we both signed the document, the officer adding his signature as the witness.

"Well." he said, as he put the paper in his pocket-book, "this is a most extraordinary story. Can you give any kind of explanation?"

"At the moment," replied Thorndyke, "I am not proposing to go beyond the actual occurrence – certainly not until I have seen the bodies."

The officer looked dissatisfied, and naturally enough. On the facts presented, he would have been quite justified in arresting us both on a suspicion of murder, and indeed, but for Thorndyke's eminent position and my own status as a King's Counsel, he would probably have done so. As it was, he contented himself with the expression of a hope that we should presently be able to throw some light on the mystery, on which remark my colleague offered no comment.

When about half-an-hour had passed, Thorndyke suggested that the vapour had probably cleared off from the room out of which the secret chamber opened and that it might now be possible to open the door of the chamber itself. Our friends were somewhat dubious, however. The sight of the dead rat had effectually dissipated the doctor's enthusiasm and engendered a very wholesome caution.

"Perhaps," said Thorndyke, "as my friend and I know where to find the concealed fastenings of the door, we could open it more safely. What do you say, Anstey?"

I was not much more eager than the doctor, but as Thorndyke would certainly have gone alone if I had refused, I assented with assumed readiness, and we started down the corridor, followed at a little distance by the other two. On entering the room, in which the odour of the poison had now become quite faint, Thorndyke opened both the casements wide and then slid the block of wood close up to the foot of the door.

"Now," said he, "when I say 'ready', take a deep breath, close your mouth, pinch your nostrils, and then push in the right-hand boss. I will press the other one and open and fix the door. Ready!"

I pushed in the boss, and immediately afterwards Thorndyke pressed in the other one. The door yielded, and as we pushed it wide open, he thrust the block in after it. Glancing in, I had a momentary glimpse of the dark chamber with the two dead men lying huddled on the floor and an extinguished lantern by the side of the nearer one. It was but the vision of an instant, for almost as the door opened, I turned with Thorndyke and ran out of the room, but in that instant it was imprinted on my memory for ever. Even as I write, I can see with horrible vividness that dark, gloomy hold and the two sprawling corpses stretched towards the door that had cut them off in the moment of their crime from the land of the living.

The first breath that I took, as I came out of the room, made me aware that the poisonous vapour was pouring out of the chamber of death. Our two friends had also noticed it and were already in full retreat, and we all made our way out of the old wing back to the library, there to wait until the poison should have become dissipated. The officer made one or two ineffectual efforts to extract from Thorndyke some explanation of the amazing events set forth in his statement, and then we settled down to a somewhat desultory conversation on subjects criminal and medical.

We had been in the library rather more than half-an-hour and were beginning to discuss the possibility of removing the bodies, when the doorbell rang, and a few moments later the housekeeper entered, followed by Sir Lawrence Drayton, Winifred, and Mr. Brodribb, The latter came in with a genial and knowing smile, which faded with remarkable suddenness as his eye lighted on the police officer.

"Why, what the deuce is the matter?" exclaimed Sir Lawrence as he also observed the officer.

"The matter is," replied Thorndyke, "that there has been a tragedy. Mr. Blake is dead."

"Dead!" exclaimed Drayton and Brodribb in unison.

"And what." asked the former, "do you mean by a tragedy?"

"Perhaps," said Thorndyke, "the officer would allow me to read you the written statement that I have given him. I may say," he added, addressing the officer "that this lady and these gentlemen are interested parties and that they will all be called as witnesses at the inquest."

This latter statement, utterly incomprehensible to me, seemed to be equally so to every one else present. Sir Lawrence and Brodribb stared in astonishment at Thorndyke, while the officer, with a frown of perplexity, slowly took the statement from his pocket-book and handed it to my colleague without a word. Thereupon the latter, having waited for the housekeeper to withdraw, read the statement aloud, and I watched the amazement growing on the faces of the listeners as he read.

"But, my dear Thorndyke!" Sir Lawrence exclaimed, when he had finished, "this is a most astounding affair. It looks as if this search had been a mere pretext to get you here and murder you!"

"That, I have no doubt, is the case," said Thorndyke, "and that I suspected to be the object when Brodribb conveyed the invitation to me."

"The devil you did!" said Brodribb. "But why should you suspect that Blake wanted to murder you?"

"I think," replied Thorndyke, "that when we have seen the bodies you will be able to answer that question yourself. And I should say," he added, turning to the doctor, "that it would now be possible to get the bodies out. Most of the fumes will have blown away by this time."

"Yes," the doctor agreed, evidently all agog to see and hear the explanation of this mystery. "We had better get a sheet from the housekeeper and then go and see if we can get those poor wretches out."

He set forth in company with the officer, and as soon as the two strangers had left the room, Brodribb attacked my colleague.

"You are a most inscrutable fellow, Thorndyke. Do you mean to tell me that when you proposed this search, you were just planning to give this man, Blake, an opportunity to murder you?"

"To *try* to murder me," Thorndyke corrected.

"And me," I added. "It begins to dawn on me that the post of junior to Thorndyke is no sinecure."

Brodribb smiled appreciatively, and Sir Lawrence remarked, "We seem to be navigating in deep waters. I must confess that I am completely out of my depth, but I suppose it is useless to make any appeal."

"I should rather say nothing more at present," Thorndyke replied. "In a few minutes I shall be able to make the crucial test which I expect will render explanations unnecessary."

I speculated on the meaning of this statement, but could make nothing of it, and I gathered from the perplexed expressions of the two lawyers that they were in a similar condition. But there was not much time to turn the matter over, for, very shortly, the police officer reappeared to announce that the bodies had been removed from the chamber and were ready for inspection and identification.

"It will not be necessary, I suppose," said Drayton, as we rose to accompany the officer, "for Miss Blake to come with us?"

"I think," answered Thorndyke, "that it is desirable and, in fact, necessary, that Miss Blake should see the bodies. I am sorry," he added, "that she should be subjected to the unpleasantness, but the matter is really important."

"I can't imagine in what respect," said Drayton, "but if you say that it is, that settles the matter."

On this we set forth, Thorndyke and the officer leading the way, and as we crossed the great, desolate rooms I talked to Winifred about the old house and the secret chamber to divert her attention from our rather gruesome errand. At the end of the long corridor, as we entered the large room, we saw the doctor standing by two shrouded figures that lay on the floor near a window, with their feet towards us. We halted beside them in solemn silence, and the doctor stooped, and taking the two corners of the sheet, drew it away, with his eyes fixed on Thorndyke.

For a moment we all stood looking down on the two still and ghastly figures without speaking a word, but suddenly Winifred uttered a cry of horror and started back, clutching my arm.

"What is it?" demanded Drayton.

"The man!" she exclaimed breathlessly, pointing to the body of the valet, which I had already recognised. "The man who tried to murder me in the empty house!"

"And who stabbed you that night at Hampstead?" said Thorndyke.

"Yes, yes," she gasped. "It is he, I am certain of it."

Sir Lawrence turned a look of eager inquiry on my colleague.

"This is an amazing thing!" he exclaimed. "How on earth did this fellow come to be associated with Mr. Blake?"

Thorndyke stooped over the dead squire and, unfastening the collar and neckband, drew the shirt open at the throat. There came into sight a stout, silken cord encircling the neck, which Thorndyke gently pulled up, when I saw that there was suspended from it a small gold pendant with a single large stone. As the little jewel was drawn out from its hiding-place, Winifred stooped forward eagerly.

"It is the Cat's Eye!" she exclaimed.

"Impossible!" Sir Lawrence ejaculated. "Let me look at it."

Thorndyke cut the cord and handed the pendant to Drayton, who turned it over in his hand, gazing at it with an expression of amazement and incredulity.

"It is," he said at length. "This is certainly the pendant that was stolen from my poor brother's house. I recognise it without doubt by the shape and colour of the stone, and there is the inscription on the back, '*Dulce Domum*', which I remember now. It is unquestionably the stolen pendant. But what does it mean, Thorndyke? You seemed to know that this man was wearing it."

"The meaning of it is, Sir Lawrence," replied Thorndyke, "that this man – " He pointed down at the dead squire. " – is the man who murdered your brother. It was he who fired the pistol."

Sir Lawrence looked down at the dead man with a frown of disgust.

"Do you mean to tell me, Thorndyke," said he, "that this man murdered poor Andrew just to get possession of this trumpery toy?"

"I do," replied Thorndyke, "though, of course, the murder was not a part of the original plan. But he carried the pistol with him to use if necessary."

"He has got a pistol in his pocket now," said the officer. "I felt it as I was dragging him out of the secret room."

He plunged his hand into the dead man's coat pocket and drew out a small automatic pistol, which he handed to Thorndyke.

"This seems to be the very weapon," said the latter, "a Baby Browning. You remember that we identified the pattern from the empty cartridge-case."

I had noticed a peculiar expression of perplexity gathering on Mr. Brodribb's face. Now the old solicitor turned to Thorndyke and said, "This is a very unaccountable affair, Thorndyke. We didn't know a great deal about Arthur Blake, but it always appeared that he was quite a decent sort of man, whereas this robbery and murder that he actually did commit, and the murder that he was attempting when he met his death, are cases of sheer ruffianism. I don't understand it."

Thorndyke turned to the doctor. "Would you mind telling us," said he, "if there is anything abnormal in the condition of this man's left knee-cap?"

The doctor stared at Thorndyke in astonishment. "Have you any reason to suppose that there is?" he asked.

"I have an impression," was the reply, "that there is an old fracture with imperfect ligamentous union."

The doctor stooped, and drawing up the trouser on the left side, placed his hand on the knee.

"You are quite right," he said, looking up at Thorndyke with an expression of surprise. "There is a transverse fracture with a gap of fully two inches between the fragments."

Suddenly Mr. Brodribb broke out eagerly with a look of intense curiosity at my colleague, "It can't be! What is it that you are suggesting, Thorndyke?"

"I am suggesting that this man was not Arthur Blake. I suggest that he was an Australian adventurer named Hugh Owen."

"But," objected Brodribb, "Owen was reported to have died some years ago. His body was found and identified."

"A mutilated skeleton was found," retorted Thorndyke, "and was identified as that of Hugh Owen by means of a ring which was known to have belonged to Owen. I suggest that the remains were those of Arthur Blake, that he had been murdered by Owen, and that the ring had been put on the body for the purpose of ensuring a false identification."

"That is perfectly possible," Brodribb admitted. "Then who do you suggest that this other man is?"

"I suggest that this other person is a woman named Laura Levinsky."

"Well," said Brodribb, "that need not be left a matter of guesswork. I don't think I mentioned it to you, but that Australian police official told me that Levinsky had a tattoo-mark on the right forearm – the letters H and L with a heart between. Let us see if this person has such a mark."

The police officer bent down over the dead valet, and unfastening the right wristband, drew the sleeve up above the elbow.

"Ha!" exclaimed Brodribb as there were revealed, standing out on the greenish-white skin as if painted in blue ink, the letters "*H*" and "*L*" with a small, misshapen heart between them. "You are right, Thorndyke, as you always are. And I suppose she was a party to the murder?"

"I take it," said Thorndyke, "that these two wretches murdered Arthur Blake, removed all identifiable objects from the corpse, put Owen's ring on its finger, and tumbled it over the cliff, shooting down a mass of rocks and stones on top of it. Then they took possession of all Blake's papers and money and separated, coming to England on different ships. I assume that no measures were ever taken to verify Blake's identity?"

"No," replied Brodribb. "There was no one who could identify him. He sent a letter, in answer to mine, saying when he would arrive. He arrived about the date mentioned, and presented all the necessary credentials. The question of identity was never raised."

For some moments we all stood looking down on the bodies of the two adventures in silence. Presently Drayton asked, holding out the pendant, "What is to be done with this? It was stolen from my brother, but it seems that, as it is an heirloom, it should be handed to Miss Blake."

"For the present," said Thorndyke "it must remain in the custody of the police, as it will have to be put in evidence at the inquest. We will take a receipt for it. But as to its being the missing heirloom, I doubt that very much. It does not agree with the description, and I should suppose that the original jewel will have been hidden with the title-deeds."

"That could hardly be," said Winifred, "though I agree with you that the inscription '*Dulce domum*' doesn't seem to be the right one. But you will remember that Percival's manuscript distinctly says that the jewel was taken away and given to Jenifer to keep for the child James."

"That is not my reading of the manuscript," said Thorndyke. "But we can discuss that on another occasion. If we give our respective names and addresses to the officer, we shall have concluded our business here."

At this hint, the officer produced a large, official notebook in which he entered the names and addresses of all the witnesses in the case, and when the doctor had once more covered the corpses with the sheet, we turned to retrace our steps to the library. As I walked along the corridor at Winifred's side, I glanced at her a little anxiously, for it had been a rather terrible experience. She met my glance, and resting her hand on my arm for a moment, she said in a low voice, "It was a gruesome sight, Robin, that poor little wretch lying there with that awful, fixed stare of horror on her face. But I couldn't feel sorry for her, nor even for the man, though there was something very dreadful – almost pitiful – in the way in which his dead hand clutched that little brass knob. It must have been a frightful moment when he found that the knob was useless and that he and his companion were caught in their own hideous trap. But I can't be sorry for them. I can only think of the relief to know that you are safe and that I am free."

"Yes," said I, "it is an unspeakable relief to feel that you can now go abroad in safety – that that continual menace is a thing of the past, thanks to Thorndyke's uncanny power of seeing through a stone wall."

"I am not sure," said she, "that I am not disposed to quarrel with Dr. Thorndyke for calmly walking you into this murderer's den."

"I don't think there was ever any real danger," I replied. "They couldn't have murdered us by overt methods, and as to the other methods, I have no doubt that Thorndyke had got them all calculated out in advance and provided for. He seems to foresee everything."

763

When we reached the library, and Thorndyke and I had replaced our pistols and jemmies in the suitcase (a proceeding which the police officer watched with bulging eyes and open mouth), Drayton asked, "Have you two got any sort of conveyance? Because, if you haven't, and you don't mind a pretty tight squeeze, I can give you a lift to the station."

We accepted the offer gladly and, having made our *adieux* to the officer and the doctor, we went out and packed ourselves and our impedimenta into the car as soon as the lawful occupants had taken their seats. As we moved off, I observed the housekeeper and two other women watching us with concentrated interest, and at the gate, as we swept past the lodge, I had an instantaneous glimpse of the keeper's face at the window, with another countenance that seemed reminiscent of The King's Head.

The swiftly-gliding car devoured the mile or two of road to the station in a few minutes. We drew up in the station yard and, while the chauffeur was handing out our luggage, Drayton stood up and, laying his hand on Thorndyke's shoulder, said earnestly, "I have spoken no word of thanks to you, Thorndyke, for what you have done, but I hope you understand that I am your debtor for life. Your management of this case is beyond my wildest expectations, and how you did it, I cannot imagine. Someday you must give me the intellectual satisfaction of hearing how the investigation was carried out. Now I can only congratulate you on your brilliant success."

"I should like to second that," said Brodribb, "and talking of success, I suppose you didn't find those deeds after all?"

"No," replied Thorndyke. "They are not there."

"Oh, aren't they?" Brodribb. "Then, if you are so certain where they are not, you probably know where they are?"

"That seems a sound inference," replied Thorndyke. "But we can't discuss the matter here. If you care to come to my chambers tomorrow, at two o'clock, we might go into it further, and, in fact, conduct an exploration."

"Does that invitation include me?" Winifred asked.

"Most undoubtedly," he replied. "You are the principal party to the transaction. And perhaps you might bring *The Book of Hours* with you."

"I believe he has got the deeds stowed away in his chambers," said Brodribb, and although my colleague shook his head, I felt no certainty that the old lawyer was not right.

When the car had moved off, we carried our cases into the station and were relieved to find that we had but a few minutes to wait for a train. I postponed my attack on my secretive colleague until we were snugly established in a compartment by ourselves. Not that I had any expectations. Thorndyke's reticence had conveyed to me the impression that the time for explanations had not yet come, and so it turned out when I proceeded to put my questions.

"Wait till we have finished the case, Anstey," said he. "Then, if you have not worked out the scheme of the investigation in the interval, we can review and discuss it."

"But surely," said I, "we have finished with the case of the murder of Andrew Drayton?"

"Not entirely," he replied. "What you have never realised, I think, is the connection between the problem of the murder and the problem of the missing documents. This is a very curious and interesting case, and those two problems have a very strange connection. But for Owen's determination to possess the cat's eye pendant at all costs, those documents might have lain in their hiding-place, unsuspected, for centuries."

This statement, while it explained Thorndyke's hitherto unaccountable interest in Percy Blake's claim, only plunged the other problem into deeper obscurity. During the remainder of the journey I tried to reconstitute the train of events to see if I could trace the alleged connection between the two problems. But not a glimmer of light could I see in any direction, and in the end I gave it up, consoling myself with the reflection that the morrow would probably see the last act played out and that then I might hope for a final elucidation.

Chapter XIX
A Relic of the '45

At two o'clock punctually on the following afternoon, our visitors made their appearance, and at the very moment when the last of them – Mr. Brodribb – emerged from Crown Office Row, I observed from the window two taxi-cabs, which had entered successively by the Tudor Street gate, draw up before our door. I hailed their arrival with deep satisfaction, for the strange events of the previous day, together with Thorndyke's rather mysterious observations thereon, had made me impatient to see the end of this intricate case and intensely curious to hear how my inscrutable colleague had managed to fit together the apparently unrelated fragments of this extraordinarily complex puzzle. Throughout the morning – while Thorndyke was absent, and, as I suspected, arranging details of the afternoon's adventure – I had turned over the facts again and again, but always with the same result. There were the pieces of the puzzle, and no doubt a complete set, but separate pieces they remained, and obstinately refused to join up into anything resembling an intelligible whole.

"I see, Thorndyke," said Mr. Brodribb as he entered, smiling, rosy, and looking as if he had just come out of a bandbox, "that I did you an injustice. You have not been sitting on the deeds. The chariots are at the door waiting, I suppose, for the band or the stavebearers. We shall be quite an imposing procession."

"We won't wait for the band." said Thorndyke. "As we are all here, we may as well start. Will you conduct Miss Blake down, Anstey?"

"Do I give any directions to the driver?" I asked.

"Yes. You can tell him to put you down at the north-east corner of the Minories."

Accordingly I led the way with Winifred and, having given the destination to the driver, bestowed my charge and myself in the cab. The driver started the engine, and as the cab made a sweep round to the Tudor Street gate, I heard the door of the other cab slam.

"Have you any idea where we are going, Robin?" Winifred asked as the cab whirled round into New Bridge Street.

"None beyond what I have communicated to the driver," I replied. "Apparently we are going to explore the Minories or Aldgate or Whitechapel. It is an ancient neighbourhood, and in the days of Percival Blake it was somewhat more aristocratic than it is now. There are good many old houses still standing about there. You may have seen that picturesque group of timber houses looking on Whitechapel High Street. They are nearly all butchers' shops, and have been, at least, since the days of Charles the Second. In fact, the group is known as Butcher Row, though I think there is an old tavern among them."

"Perhaps we are going to the tavern," said Winifred. "It is quite likely. Many of the old inns had secret hiding-places and must have been the favourite rendezvous of the conspirators of those times."

She continued to speculate on the possibilities of the ancient tavern, which had evidently captured her romantic fancy, and as I looked at her – pink-cheeked, bright-eyed, and full of pleasurable excitement over our adventurous quest – I once more breathed a sigh of thankfulness that the dark days of ever-impending peril were over.

It seemed but a few minutes before the cab drew up at the corner of the Minories, and we had hardly alighted when the other vehicle arrived and disgorged its occupants at our side. The drivers having been paid (and having thereafter compared notes and settled themselves to watch our further proceedings), Thorndyke turned his face eastward and we started together along Whitechapel High Street. I noticed that, now, no one asked any questions. Probably each of us was busy with his own speculations, and in any case, Thorndyke maintained a sphinx-like reticence.

"Are those delightful old houses the ones you were speaking of?" Winifred asked as the ancient, plaster-fronted buildings came in sight.

"Yes," I answered. "That is Butcher Row."

"Or," said Thorndyke, "to give it what is, I believe, its official title, "The Shambles', though the shambles proper are at the back."

"The Shambles!" exclaimed Winifred, looking at Thorndyke with a startled expression. She appeared to be about to ask him some question, but at this moment he turned sharply into a narrow alley, into which we followed him. I glanced up at the name as we entered and read it aloud – "'*Harrow Alley*'."

"Yes," said Thorndyke, "quite a historic little thoroughfare. Defoe gives a very vivid description of its appearance during the Plague, with the dead-cart waiting at the entrance and the procession of bearers carrying the corpses down the narrow court. Here is the old Star and Still Tavern, and 'round the corner there are the shambles, very little changed since the Seventeenth Century."

He turned the corner towards the shambles, and then, crossing the narrow road, dived through an archway into a narrow paved court, along which we had to go in single file. This court presently opened into a squalid-looking little square, surrounded on three sides by tall, ancient,

767

timber-and-plaster houses, the fourth side being occupied by a rather mean but quaint little church with a low brick tower. Thorndyke made his way directly to the west door of the church and, taking from his pocket a key of portentous size, inserted it into the lock. As he did so I glanced at the board that was fixed beside the doorway, from which I learned that this was the church of St Peter by the Minories.

As the door swung open, Thorndyke motioned to us to enter. We filed in, and then he drew the door to after us and locked it from the inside. We stood for a few moments in the dim porch under the tower, looking in through the half-opened inner door, and as we stood there, Winifred grasped my arm nervously, and I could feel that her hand was trembling. But there was no time for speech, for as Thorndyke locked the door and withdrew the key, the inner door opened wide and two men – one tall and one short – appeared silhouetted against the east window.

These are my friends, of whom I spoke to you," said Thorndyke. "Miss Blake, Sir Lawrence Drayton, Mr. Brodribb, Mr. Anstey – the Reverend James Yersbury. I think you have met this other gentleman."

We came out into the body of the church, and having made my bow to the clergyman, I turned to the smaller man.

"Why, it's Mr. Polton!" exclaimed Winifred, shaking hands heartily with my colleague's familiar, who greeted us with a smile of such ecstatic crinkliness that I instantly suspected him of preparing some necromantic surprise for us.

"This is quite a remarkable building," said Sir Lawrence, looking about him with lively interest, "and it appears the more striking by contrast with the shabby, commonplace exterior."

"Yes," agreed the clergyman, "that is rather characteristic of old London churches. But this is rather an ancient structure, it was only partially destroyed by the Great Fire and was almost immediately rebuilt, at the personal cost, it is said, of the Duke of York, afterwards James the Second. Perhaps that accounts for the strong Jacobite leanings of some of the later clergy, such as this good gentleman, for instance."

He led us to a space between two of the windows where a good-sized tablet of alabaster had been let into the wall.

"That tablet," said he, "encloses a cavity which is filled with bones piously collected from the field of Culloden, and the inscription leaves one in no doubt as to the sentiments of the collector. But I believe it was covered with plaster soon after it was put up, to preserve it from destruction by the authorities, and it was only discovered about fifty years ago."

I read the brief inscription with growing curiosity:

"This tablet was raised to the Memory of the Faithful by Stephen Rumbold, sometime Rector of this Church."

"But," said Winifred, "I thought Stephen Rumbold was rector of St. Peter by the Shambles."

"This *is* St. Peter by the Shambles," replied Mr. Yersbury. "The name has only been changed within the last forty years."

Winifred faced me and looked with eager delight into my eyes, and I knew that the same thought was in both our minds. Here, during all the slowly-passing years, the missing deeds had rested, securely hidden with the bones of those patriots at whose side Percival Blake had fought on the fatal field of Culloden. I looked round at Thorndyke, expecting to see some preparations to open this curious little burial-place. But he had already turned away and was moving towards the east end of the church. We followed him slowly until he halted before the pulpit, where he stood for a few moments looking at it reflectively. It was a very remarkable pulpit. I have never seen another at all resembling it. In shape it was an elongated octagon, the panels and mouldings of deep brown oak enriched with magnificent carving. But the most singular feature was the manner in which it was supported. The oblong super-structure rested on twin pillars of oak, each pillar being furnished with a handsome, floridly-ornamented bronze capital, and a bronze base of somewhat similar character. But fine as the workmanship was, the design was more unusual than pleasing. The oblong body and the twin pillars had, in fact, a rather ungainly appearance.

"Here," said Thorndyke, pointing to the pulpit, "is another relic of the Reverend Stephen Rumbold, and one of more personal interest to us than the other. You notice these twin pillars. Aesthetically, they are not all that might be desired, but they serve a useful purpose besides supporting the upper structure, for each of them forms an aumbry – originally designed, no doubt, to conceal the sacred vessels and other objects used in celebrating Mass or Vespers, or in administering Communion in accordance with the rites of the Church of Rome. One of them is still discharging this function. This pillar – " Here he tapped the northern one of the pair. " – contains a chalice and paten, a thurible, and a small pyx. This other pillar contains – well, Polton will show us what it contains, so I need not go into particulars."

"Do I understand," Drayton asked, "that you have opened the aumbries already and verified the existence and nature of the contents?"

"We have not yet opened the aumbries," Thorndyke replied, "but we have ascertained that the things are there untouched. Polton and I made an examination somedays ago with an X-ray apparatus and a fluorescent screen. It was then that we discovered the plate in the second pillar. I wished Miss Blake to be present at the actual opening."

At these words, like an actor taking up a cue, Polton appeared from somewhere behind the pulpit bearing a good-sized leather handbag. This he deposited on the floor and, as we gathered round, he took from it a small, rounded mallet, apparently of lead, covered with leather, and a tool of hard wood, somewhat in shape like a caulking chisel.

"Which pillar shall I begin on, sir?" he inquired, looking round with a sly smile. "The one with church plate or – "

"Oh, hang the church plate!" interposed Brodribb, adding hastily, "I beg your pardon, Mr. Yersbury, but you know – "

"Exactly," interrupted the clergyman, "I quite agree with you. The church plate will keep for another half-hour."

Thereupon Polton fell to work, and we crowded up close to watch. The capitals of the pillars presented each two parts, a lower member, covered with ornament, and above this a plain, cylindrical space extending up to the abacus. It was to the lower part that Polton directed his attention. Having mounted on a chair, he placed the edge of the hardwood chisel against the lower edge of the ornamented member and struck it gently with the leaden mallet. Then he shifted the chisel half-an-inch to the right and struck another blow, and in this way he continued, moving the chisel half-an-inch after each stroke, until he had travelled a third of the way round the pillar, when Thorndyke placed another chair for him to step on.

"Have you oiled the surface?" my colleague asked.

"Yes, sir," replied Polton, tapping away like Old Mortality, "I flooded it with a mixture of paraffin and clock oil, and it is moving all right."

We were soon able to verify this statement, for when Polton had made a complete circuit of the pillar, the plain space above had grown perceptibly narrower and a ring of lighter-coloured wood began to appear below. Still, the leaden mallet continued to deliver its dull sounding taps, and still Polton continued to creep round the pillar.

By the time the second circuit was completed, the sliding part of the capital had risen half-way to the top of the plain space, as was shown by the width of paler, newly-uncovered wood below. And now the sliding member was evidently moving more freely, for there was a perceptible upward movement at each stroke, so that, by the end of the third circuit, the upper, plain space had disappeared altogether and a narrow ring of metal appeared below, and in this ring I perceived a notch about half-an-inch wide.

"I think she's all clear now, sir," said Polton.

"Very well," said Thorndyke. "We are all ready."

He relieved Polton of the mallet and chisel and handed him a tool which looked somewhat like a rather slender jemmy with a long, narrow beak. This beak Polton inserted carefully into the notch, when it evidently entered a cavity in the top of the woodwork. Then he began cautiously to prise at the end of the lever.

For a moment or two nothing happened. Suddenly there was a grating sound, the end of the lever rose, and at the same instant about a quarter of the pillar began to separate from the rest and come forward, showing a joint which had been cunningly hidden by the deep fluting. Polton grasped the top of the loose panel and, with a sharp pull, drew it right out and lifted it clear – but as he was in front of the opening, none of us could see what was within. Then he stepped down from the chair, and Winifred uttered a little cry and clasped her hands.

It was certainly a dramatic moment, especially to those of us who had read the manuscript in the little *Book of Hours.* The pillar was a great shell enclosing a considerable cavity, and in this cavity, standing on the floor, was a tall leaden jar with a close-fitting, flat lid, and on the lid stood a great, two-handled posset-pot. It was all exactly as Percival Blake had described it, and to us, who had formed a mental picture from that description, there was something very moving in being thus confronted with those strangely familiar objects, which had been waiting in their hiding-place for more than a century-and-a-half – waiting for the visit of Percival's dispossessed posterity.

For some time we stood looking at them in silence. At length Thorndyke said, "You notice, Miss Blake, that there is an inscription on the jar."

I had not observed it, nor had Winifred, but we now advanced, and looking closely at the jar, made out with some difficulty on the whitened surface an inscription which had apparently been punched into the metal letter by letter, and which read:

The Contents hereof are the Property of Percival Blake, MD of Beauchamp Blake in Buckinghamshire, or the Heirs of his Body AD 1746

"That," said Sir Lawrence, as Winifred read the inscription aloud, "settles the ownership of the documents. You can take possession of the jar and its contents with perfect confidence. And now perhaps it would be as well to see what is inside the jar."

Polton, who had apparently been waiting for this cue, now lit a small spirit blow-pipe. The posset-pot was tenderly lifted out by Winifred and deposited on a pew-bench, and Polton, having hoisted out the jar and placed it on a chair, began cautiously to let the flame of the blow-pipe play on the joint of the lid, which had been thickly coated with wax. When the wax began to liquefy, he introduced the edge of the jemmy into the joint, and with a deft turn of the wrist, raised the lid, which he then took off.

Winifred peered into the jar and announced, "It seems to be full of rolled-up parchments," – a statement which we all verified in turn.

"I would suggest," said Mr. Yersbury, "that we carry the jar into the vestry. There is a good-sized table there, which will be a convenience if you are going to examine the documents."

This suggestion was instantly agreed to. Polton took up the rather ponderous jar and made his way to the vestry under the guidance of the clergyman, and the rest of us followed, Winifred carrying the precious posset-pot. Arrived at the vestry, Polton set down the jar on the table, and Sir Lawrence proceeded at once to extract the roll of stiff and yellow parchment and vellum documents. Unrolling them carefully – for they were set into a rigid cylinder – he glanced over them quickly with the air of one looking for some particular thing.

"These are undoubtedly the title-deeds," he said, still turning over the pages quickly with but a cursory glance at their contents. "But – Ha! Yes. These are what we really wanted. I had hoped that we should find them here."

He drew out from between the leaves of the deeds two small squares of parchment which he exhibited triumphantly and then read aloud:

> *I hereby certify and declare that on the thirteenth day of June in the Year of Our Lord seventeen-hundred-and-forty-two, at the church of St. Peter by the Shambles, nearby Aldgate, the following persons were by me joined together in Holy Matrimony to wit PERCIVAL BLAKE of Beauchamp Blake in the County of Buckinghamshire, Bachelor and JUDITH WESTERN of Cricklewood in the County of Middlesex, Spinster.*
>
> *Stephen Rumbold, MA,*
> *Rector of the said Church of St Peter by the Shambles*
> *20th May, 1746*

"That," said Sir Lawrence, "is what principally matters, but this second certificate clenches the proof. I will read it out:

> *I hereby certify and declare that James the Son of Percival and Judith Blake of Beauchamp Blake in the County of Buckinghamshire was baptized by me according to the rites of Holy Church on the thirtieth of May in the Year of Our Lord seventeen-hundred-and-forty-three at the Church of St. Peter by the Shambles nearby Aldgate.*
>
> *Stephen Rumbold, MA,*
> *Rector of the said Church of St. Peter by the Shambles*
> *20th May, 1746*

"That," continued Drayton, "with the other certificates, which I understand you have, establishes a direct descent. And seeing that the estate is at present without an owner, this is a peculiarly opportune moment for putting forward a claim. What do you say, Brodribb?"

"I should like," said Brodribb, "to have fuller particulars before giving a definite opinion."

"Oh, come, Brodribb," Sir Lawrence protested, "you needn't be so infernally cautious. We're all friends, you know. Would you be prepared to act for Miss Blake?"

"I don't see why not," replied Brodribb. "I am not committed to any other claimant. Yes, I should be very happy to act for her."

"Then," said Drayton, "we must arrange a consultation and find out exactly how we stand. I will call at your office for a preliminary talk tomorrow, if that will suit you."

"Very well," agreed Brodribb, "come in at one o'clock, and we can lunch together and talk over the preliminaries."

While this conversation was proceeding, I had observed Thorndyke peering inquisitively into the now empty jar. From this he transferred his attention to the posset-pot which Winifred was guarding jealously. It was a fine specimen of its kind, a comparatively large vessel of many-coloured slip-ware. On the front was a sort of escutcheon, on which was a heart surmounted by a "*B*" with the letters "*H*" and "*M*" on either side and the date *1708* below. Just under the rim was a broad band bearing the following quaint inscription:

> *Here is the Gest of the Barly Korne, Glad Ham I the child is Borne – JM*

"Isn't it a lovely old thing?" murmured Winifred. "So human and personal and so charming too."

"Yes," Thorndyke agreed "it is a fine piece of work. Old Martin was something more than a common village potter. Have you looked inside it?"

"No," replied Winifred. She took the knob in her fingers and delicately lifted off the cover, and then she uttered a cry of surprise.

"Why," she exclaimed, "it is the Cat's Eye – the *real* cat's eye this time. And what a beauty!"

She lifted out of the pot a small pendant, curiously like the other one – so much so, in fact, as to suggest that the latter had been a copy. But, whereas the stone in the counterfeit had been a rather dull grey, this one was of a beautiful deep yellow with a brilliant streak of golden light. Attached to the pendant was a slender gold chain and a clasp, which, like the pendant itself, was smooth and rounded with years of wear. After gazing for a while at the flashing stone, Winifred turned the pendant over and looked at the back. The inscription was half-obliterated by wear, but we read without difficulty:

God's Providence is Mine Inheritance

"It is extremely appropriate," she commented when she had read it aloud, "though it isn't quite what one expected. But what I don't understand is how it comes to be here. Percival distinctly says that he had the jewel and that he intended to give it to Jenifer to keep for the child."

"Not the jewel," Thorndyke corrected. "He speaks of 'the bauble' and 'the trinket', never of 'the jewel'."

"You think he was referring to some other trinket?"

"Obviously," replied Thorndyke. And then, looking at Winifred with a smile, he exclaimed, "O blind generation! Don't you see, Miss Blake, that events have shaped themselves precisely as Percival designed? Here is his descendant, the child of his children's children, coming to the hiding-place wearing the precious bauble around her neck and guided by it to the possessions of her fathers. Could anything be more complete?"

Winifred was thunderstruck. For a while she sat, motionless as a statue, gazing at Thorndyke in speechless amazement. At length she exclaimed, "But this is astounding, Dr. Thorndyke! Do you mean that this little locket is the trinket that was given to Jenifer and which she lost?"

"Undoubtedly," he replied, "and the really strange and romantic circumstance is that it was given into your hand by the very impostor who was seeking to rob you forever of your inheritance."

"Then," exclaimed Sir Lawrence, who was almost as overcome as Winifred herself, "it was actually poor Andrew's 'Little Sphinx' that gave you the clue to this hiding place?"

"Yes," replied Thorndyke, "only the sphinx was really an oracle, just waiting for the question to be asked."

Winifred's eyes filled. Impulsively she grasped my colleague's hand, murmuring shakily, "What can I say to you, Dr. Thorndyke? How can I ever thank you for all that you have done for my brother and me?"

"You need say nothing," he replied "but that which is written on the back of the cat's eye."

Our business being now concluded, Sir Lawrence carefully returned the precious documents to the jar and replaced the cover. From without, a dull tapping that had been audible for some time past had told us that Polton was at work on the second pillar. But that was no concern of ours.

"What are we going to do now?" asked Sir Lawrence. "It seems as if we should mark the occasion in some way."

"I agree with you, Drayton," said Thorndyke, "and I have, in fact, arranged a little festival at my chambers – just a simple tavern dinner, since Polton was otherwise engaged. Will that satisfy the requirements?"

"It will satisfy mine," replied Drayton, "and I think I can answer for Brodribb."

"Then," said Thorndyke, "if Miss Blake will consent to combine the function of hostess with that of principal guest, we will capture Polton and betake ourselves to The Temple."

We strolled out into the church, where Polton and the rector were gloatingly examining the newly-recovered sacred vessels, and having thanked the friendly clergyman and bidden him a warm farewell, we went forth in search of conveyances. Polton heading the procession with the heavy jar under his arm, and Winifred tenderly carrying the posset-pot swathed in her silken shawl.

In Whitechapel High Street we had the unexpected good fortune to encounter an unoccupied taxi-cab, which was by universal consent assigned to Winifred, Polton, and me. In this we bestowed ourselves and were forthwith spirited away, leaving our companions to follow as best they could. But they were not far behind, for we had barely arrived in the chambers and disposed of our treasure trove when a second cab drew up in King's Bench Walk and our three friends made their appearance at the rendezvous.

Chapter XX
QED

To an enthusiastic and truly efficient gourmet it might be difficult to assess the respective merits of the different stages of a really good dinner, to compare the satisfactions yielded, for instance, by the first tentative approaches – the little affairs of outposts – with the voracious joy of the grand onslaught on tangible and manducable solids, or again with the placid diminuendo, the half-hearted rear-guard actions, concerned with the unsubstantial trifles on which defeated appetite delivers its expiring kick. For my own part, I can offer no opinion – at any rate, without refreshing my memory as to the successive sensations, but I recall that as our dinner drew to a close, signs of expectancy began to manifest themselves (in Mr. Brodribb's case they seemed to be associated with the advent of the port decanter), and when Polton had evacuated the casualties to an aid-post established in the adjacent office, Sir Lawrence gave expression to the prevailing state of mind.

"I suppose, Thorndyke, you know what is expected of you?"

Thorndyke turned an impassive face towards his guest. "On these triumphal occasions," said he, "I usually smoke a Trichinopoly cigar. On this occasion, I presume, I am expected to refrain."

"Not at all," replied Drayton. "I think we can endure the Trichy with reasonable fortitude. What we can't endure is the agony of curiosity. We demand enlightenment."

"You want to know how the 'Little Sphinx' answered its own riddle. Is that your demand?"

"I understood you to say," said I, "that the problem of the crime and that of the missing deeds were one and the same."

"I said that they were closely connected. But if you want an exposition of the unravelment, it will be more convenient to take them separately and in the order in which they were presented. In which case we begin with the crime."

He paused, and I saw him glance with an indulgent smile towards the office door which was incompletely closed, and from which issued faint sounds of furtive movement which informed us that Polton had elected to take his dinner within earshot of the exposition.

"We had better begin," he proceeded, "with the facts presented to us on the night of the tragedy. First as to the criminals. There were traces of two men, and only two. One of these was a tall man, as shown by the size of his feet. He appeared to suffer from some weakness of the left leg. The sound of his footsteps, as heard by Anstey, suggested a slightly lame man, but as he ran away rapidly he could not have been very lame. Yet there was some distinct disability, since he had to draw up a garden seat to enable him to get over a fence which we climbed easily, and the faint impression of the left foot under the fence showed that, when he jumped down, the weight was taken principally by the right. Examination of the cast of his left hand showed a depressed scar on the tip of the forefinger. We also gathered that he carried a Baby Browning pistol and appeared to be a skilful pistol shot.

"Of the other man we learned less. He was noticeably small and slight, he was left-handed, he had dark hair, and at the time of the robbery he was wearing gloves, apparently of kid or thin leather. But later, when examining the tuft of his hair that was found grasped by the deceased, we made an important discovery. Among those dark hairs was a single blonde hair – not white, but golden – which could not have come from his own head. Of its presence there seemed to be only two possible explanations: Either it had been rubbed off, or had fallen from the head of some other person, or it had become detached from the inside of a wig. But the first explanation was ruled out – "

"How?" demanded Brodribb.

"By its appearance under the microscope. When you find an alien hair, on your coat-sleeve, for instance – "

"I don't," said Brodribb, "at my time of life."

" – If you examine it under the microscope, or even with a strong lens, you will invariably find it to be a dead hair – a hair which has completed its growth and dropped out of its sheath. You can identify it by the presence of the complete bulb and the absence of the inner root-sheath (which would be adherent to it if it had been pulled out while growing). Well, this blonde hair had no bulb. It had both ends broken, which suggested unusual brittleness, as if it had been treated with some bleach, such as chlorine or hydrogen peroxide. But the hair of wigs shows absence of bulbs and is commonly so treated and is usually somewhat brittle. Thus the probability was that this man had recently worn a wig of artificially bleached hair.

"These were our initial data concerning these two men. There were also some fingerprints, but we will consider those separately. The initial data included the character of the things stolen. These were of insignificant intrinsic value and were very easily identifiable. They were thus quite unacceptable to the ordinary professional thief, yet the evidence (of the suspicious visitor) suggested that they knew what they were stealing. One of the things stolen – the cat's eye pendant – was known to have an extrinsic value and to have been eagerly sought by other persons, and there was thus the bare suggestion that this pendant might have been the object of the robbery.

"We now come to the fingerprints. These presented some very remarkable anomalies. In the first place, they were not the fingerprints of either of the robbers. That was certain. The small man wore gloves, so they could not have been his, and the tall man had a depressed scar on the tip of his left forefinger, whereas there was no trace of any such scar on the corresponding fingerprint. But if they were not the fingerprints of either of the robbers, whose fingerprints were they? There was no trace of any third person, and it was practically certain that no third person was present.

"But there was another striking anomaly. Although there were numerous impressions, only six digits were represented – the forefinger and thumb of the left hand and the thumb and the first three fingers of the right. Every impression of the right hand showed the same four digits, every impression of the left showed the same two.

"Now what could be the explanation of this curious repetition? Anstey's very reasonable suggestion was that the man had soiled these particular digits with some foreign substance and that, consequently, the soiled digits alone had made prints. This suggestion received a certain amount of support from the fact that a foreign substance actually was present – it proved, on examination, to be Japanese wax. But though the presence of the wax accounted for the distinctness of the fingerprints that were there, it did not explain *why* the other fingers had made no mark at all. I examined the glass which bore the fingerprints with the utmost minuteness, but in no case was there the faintest trace of the other fingers. Yet those fingers, if they had existed, must have touched the glass, and if they had touched it they would have made marks. The only explanation seemed to be that *there were no other fingers* – that the prints were not real fingerprints at all, but counterfeits made by means of facsimile stamps of rubber, roller-composition, or – more probably – chrome gelatine.

"It seemed a far-fetched hypothesis. But it fitted all the facts, and there seemed to be no other explanation. Thus the use of a set of stamps would explain the existence of a set of fingerprints which were not those of either of the parties present, it would explain the repetition of the same group of digits (on the assumption that only six stamps were available which might easily be the case if these stamps were copies of a particular group of fingerprints), and lastly, it would explain the presence of the Japanese wax."

"How would it?" I asked.

"Well, some foreign substance would be necessary. In a real fingerprint – on glass, for instance – the mark is produced by the natural grease of the fingers. But a rubber or gelatine stamp has no natural grease. It is quite dry, and would make no mark at all unless it were charged with some sticky or greasy material. Now Japanese wax is an ideal material for the purpose. It is markedly sticky and would consequently develop up splendidly with dusting powder. It has no tendency to spread or run, so that it gives very clear impressions, and it might easily be mistaken for natural skin-grease.

"The counterfeit fingerprints hypothesis was, therefore, the only one that explained the facts, and I adopted it provisionally, assuming that the stamps were probably thin plates of rubber or gelatine cemented on the fingertips of the gloves worn by the short man.

"A few days later I received a visit from Detective-Superintendent Miller who informed me that the fingerprints had been identified at the registry as those of a well-known 'habitual' named Hedges, more commonly known as Moakey. Of course this did not alter the position, since there was no evidence that Moakey had ever been on the premises. However, I decided to wait until he was arrested and hear what he had to say. But he never was arrested. A day or two later, the Superintendent called on me again, and this time he settled the matter finally. My impression was, and is, that he came intending to make a clean breast of the matter, but that at the last moment he shied at the responsibility of giving away official secrets. What he actually said was that there had been a mistake, that the fingerprints were not Moakey's after all.

"Of course this was absurd. A mistake might occur with a single fingerprint, but with a set of six it was incredible. What had happened appeared to me quite obvious. The fingerprints had been submitted to the experts, who had at once identified them as Moakey's. Then the executive had set out to arrest Moakey – and had discovered that he was in prison. If that was really what had happened, it furnished conclusive proof that the fingerprints were forgeries.

"At once I set to work to ascertain if it were so. I searched the lists of convictions at assizes, quarter-sessions, and so forth, and eventually ran Moakey to earth. He had been convicted six months previously and sentenced to two years' imprisonment with hard labour. So, at the date of the murder, he had been in prison about six months.

"We were now on solid ground. We knew that the fingerprints were forgeries. But we knew more than this. The forgery of a fingerprint, unlike that of a signature, is a purely mechanical operation, carried out either by photography or by some other reproductive process. The forged print is necessarily a mechanical copy of an existing real print. Whence it

779

follows that the existence of a forgery is evidence of the existence of an original. And more than that, it is evidence that the forger had access to that original. Now these forgeries were copies of Moakey's fingerprints. It followed that we had to look for somebody who had had access to Moakey's fingerprints.

"Fortunately we had not far to look. At the first interview the Superintendent had referred to a previous exploit of Moakey's, a burglary at a country house, when that artist was apprehended and convicted on the evidence of his fingerprints, which were found on a silver salver. A photograph of these fingerprints was immediately taken by the owner of the house and given to the police, who took them straight to Scotland Yard. I looked up the report of that case and had the good fortune to find that the fingerprints were described. There were six of them, the thumb and first three fingers of the right hand, and the forefinger and thumb of the left hand.

"This was extremely interesting. But still more so was the fact that the house which was broken into was Beauchamp Blake, and the further fact that the owner who photographed the fingerprints was Mr. Arthur Blake.

"I need not point out the importance of the discovery. It told us that Arthur Blake had had, and presumably still had, in his possession, a set of negatives with which it was possible to make the stamps of these very fingerprints. It did not, however, follow that he had made the stamps, for that would demand an amount of technical knowledge and skill far beyond that of an ordinary photographer – knowledge ordinarily possessed only by professional photo-engravers. He might have such knowledge or he might have employed someone else. At any rate, he had the negatives and had made them himself.

"But Blake was not only associated with the fingerprints. He was also associated with the stolen property. Of all the persons known to us, he was the most likely to wish to acquire the cat's eye pendant. So, you see, the investigation, which started with a certain connection with Beauchamp Blake, led us straight to Beauchamp Blake again. And there we will leave it for the moment and approach the problem from one or two different directions.

"First we will consider the mysterious woman who came into view on the day of the inquest and who presumably sent the poisoned chocolates. Who was she? And what was her connection with the case? Now, the first thing that struck me in the description of her was her hair. It was of that brassy, golden tint that one associates with bleaches such as hydrogen peroxide. I recalled the stray hair from the small man's head which had suggested that he had worn a wig of precisely this character.

The obvious suggestion was that this woman and that small man were one and the same person. They appeared to be similar in stature. There were good reasons why they should be the same, and no reasons why they should not. But, assuming them to be the same (it was afterwards proved that they were) the question arose: Is this woman a disguised man, or was that man a disguised woman? The latter view was clearly the more probable, for whereas a woman, if she cuts her hair short, will pass easily for a clean-shaved man, a clean-shaved man does not pass so easily for a woman, especially if he is dark, as this person was. It seemed probable, therefore, that this was really a woman – a dark woman wearing a fair wig. But who she was, and what – if any – was her relation to Blake, remained for the present a mystery.

"We now come to the man Halliburton. Obviously he was an object of deep suspicion. His only known address was an hotel. He visited Andrew Drayton without any reasonable purpose. He tried unsuccessfully to purchase the cat's eye pendant, and within four days of his failure the jewel was stolen. Then he disappeared, leaving no trace.

"Anstey and I called at his hotel to make enquiries about him. There we obtained a photograph of his signature, which we have not used, but which will be produced at the inquest, and we acquired some information which has been invaluable. He had lost, and left behind, a mascot which he valued so highly that he offered ten pounds reward for its recovery. We got the loan of it, and Polton made this indistinguishable facsimile." Here Thorndyke passed round Polton's masterpiece for inspection. "Now," he continued, "in connection with this mascot, two very important facts emerged. One was that, as Anstey expressed it, this man was a superstitious ass, a man who believed in the occult properties of mascots and charms. The importance of that becomes evident when we remember that the cat's eye was, in effect, a mascot – an object credited with occult powers affecting the fortunes of its owner. It enables us to understand his anxiety to possess the cat's eye.

"The other important fact emerges from the nature of the thing itself. It is a neck vertebra of an Echidna, or porcupine ant-eater, decorated with aboriginal ornament. The Echidna is an animal peculiar to Tasmania and Australia, and the ornament is distinctive of the locality. This mascot, therefore, established some connection between Halliburton and Australia. But Blake had lived most of his adult life in Australia. There was, however, a difficulty. Punched on the mascot – apparently with typefounder's steel punches – were the letters o and h. The name signed in the hotel register was Oscar Halliburton, and these letters seemed to be his initials. But if that was so, Oscar Halliburton would appear to be a real person and consequently could not be Arthur Blake.

781

"Thus, at this stage of the inquiry, on the hypothesis that the robbery had been committed by Blake, we had two persons whom we could not account for – the unknown woman (possibly a man) and Mr. Oscar Halliburton.

"But just as we appeared to have reached an impasse, Mr. Brodribb threw a flood of light on the problem. For different reasons, Sir Lawrence and I were anxious to obtain some particulars of Arthur Blake and his affairs, and these particulars Mr. Brodribb was fortunately in a position to supply. The information that he furnished amounted to this:

"Arthur Blake appeared to be a decent, industrious man with nothing against him but the rather queer company that he had kept. He had been associated in Australia with a man named Hugh Owen, who was a person of shady antecedents, and who, on his side, was associated with a woman named Laura Levinsky who appeared to be definitely a bad character, and who, like Owen, was under police observation. These two persons seem to have separated immediately after Blake's departure for England, and both disappeared. Levinsky was lost sight of for good, but Owen's body – or rather unrecognisable remains – came to light some years later and was identified by a ring which was known to have belonged to Owen.

"Certain particulars that Mr. Brodribb gave concerning Owen made a considerable impression on me. For instance, it appeared that Owen was originally a photo-engraver by trade and that he had later owned a small type-foundry. Also that he had fractured his left kneecap and that this injury was certainly never completely repaired. But the first thing that struck me on looking at this party of three was that whereas Blake appears to have been a respectable man and most unlikely to have committed an atrocious crime such as the one we were investigating, the same could not be said of his two companions, and inevitably I found the question creeping into my mind: Is it certain that those remains were really the remains of Owen? Or may it have been that they were those of Arthur Blake? That these two criminals had murdered Blake when Brodribb's letter arrived: That Owen had taken the papers and credentials and come to England personating Blake, and that Levinsky had come by another route?

"It seemed, perhaps, a rather violent supposition, but it was quite possible, and the instant it was adopted as a working hypothesis, all the difficulties of the case vanished as if by magic. We could now account for the mysterious woman. We could also account for Halliburton, for the letters on the mascot could be read either way – 'O H' for *Oscar Halliburton* or 'H O' for *Hugh Owen*, and Owen had possessed and used in his type-foundry steel punches exactly like those with which the letters had been made, and further, Owen was a native of Tasmania and had lived many years in Australia. He fitted the mascot perfectly.

"Then Owen had been a photo-engraver – that is to say, he possessed the very kind of knowledge and skill that was necessary to make the stamps for the fingerprints, and he agreed with the taller of the two criminals in that he had a marked weakness of the left leg. In short, the agreements were so striking as to leave little doubt in my mind that our two criminals were Owen and Levinsky, and that the former was in possession of Beauchamp Blake, personating the murdered owner.

"One point only remained to be verified in order to complete this aspect of the case. We had to ascertain whether the man who was posing as Arthur Blake had, in fact, fractured a knee-cap. I was casting about for some means of getting this information when the third attempt was made on Miss Blake's life, and it became evident that the danger to her was too great to admit of further delay. Just then Sir Lawrence asked me to go down with him to Aylesbury, and that proposal suggested to me the plan of visiting Beauchamp Blake and making an unmistakable demonstration. I had learned from Mr. Brodribb something of the squire's habits, and I got further details from the landlord of The King's Head. With the help of the latter I obtained access to the park at the time when the squire would be coming out, and I planted myself, with Anstey, where we were bound to be noticed.

"My object was twofold. First, I wanted to ascertain, if possible, whether the squire had any abnormal condition of the left leg, and if so, whether that condition was probably due to a fractured knee-cap, and secondly, I proposed to make such a demonstration as would convince him (if he were really Owen) that it was useless to murder Miss Blake until he had settled with me, and that it would be highly unsafe to make any further attempts. To this latter end, I attached Polton's facsimile of the mascot to my watch-guard, where it could hardly fail to be seen, and then, as I have said, I planted myself on the road leading to the gate.

"Both purposes were achieved. I was able to verify with my own eyes the landlord's statement that the squire habitually mounted his horse from the off-side – a most inconvenient method of mounting, but one that would be rendered absolutely necessary by a fractured left knee-cap. Then, as I had expected, he recognised me instantly – no doubt from the portrait published in the newspapers – and dismounted to examine me more closely, and when he came near, he saw the mascot and it was obvious that he recognised it. I detached it and handed it to him, giving him such details as must have made clear to him that I knew its history and knew of his connection with it. His manner left me in no doubt that he fully understood the hint and that he accepted my challenge, and

783

further proof was furnished by the fact that he sent a man to shadow us home and ascertain for certain who we were. So that matters were now on a perfectly definite footing, and I may add that further verification, if it had been needed, was supplied by the circumstance that, on this very day, Anstey caught a glimpse of Levinsky, disguised as a man, in the market square at Aylesbury. The rest of the story I think you all know."

"Yes," said Drayton, "we gathered that from your written statement. But what is not clear to me is why you considered it necessary to thrust your head into the lion's jaws. You seem to have had a complete case against these two wretches. Why couldn't you have lodged an information and had them arrested?"

"I was afraid to take the risk," replied Thorndyke. "To us the case looks complete. But how would it have looked to the police? Or to a possibly unimaginative magistrate? Or especially to a jury of ordinary, and perhaps thick-headed, tradesmen and artisans? Juries like direct evidence, and that was what I was trying to produce. I had no doubt that these two persons would try to murder me and Anstey, and that we should prevent them from succeeding. Then we could charge them with the attempt and prove it by direct evidence, after which we could have proceeded confidently with the second charge of the murder of Andrew Drayton."

"I think Thorndyke was right," said I, seeing that Sir Lawrence still looked doubtful. "From my large experience of juries in criminal cases, I feel that this intricate train of inferential evidence would have been rather unconvincing by itself, but that it would have been quite effective if it had come after a charge supported by the testimony of eye-witnesses, such as we should have been."

"Well," said Drayton, "we will agree that the circumstances justified the risk, and certainly the unravelment of this case by means of such almost invisible data is a most remarkable achievement. This exposition has whetted my appetite for the explanation of the other mystery."

"Yes," said Winifred. "I am on tenterhooks to hear how you made the 'Little Sphinx' answer its own riddle. Shall I hand you the locket?"

"If you please, and *The Book of Hours*. And if we can get Polton to put the microscope on the table with the slide that is on the stage, we shall have all that we want for the demonstration."

At this Polton emerged unblushingly from the office and, having put the microscope on the table, carefully adjusted the mirror and then, with brazen effrontery, took a long and intent look through the instrument, under the pretence of seeing that the specimen was properly lighted.

"There is no need for you to go back to the office, Polton," my colleague said with a smile at his familiar. "We shall want your help with the microscope presently. Draw up a chair for yourself."

Polton seated himself opposite the instrument with a smile of intense gratification, and Thorndyke then resumed.

"This investigation was a much simpler affair than the other. You may remember, Miss Blake, showing me the locket that night when I called with Anstey at your studio, and you will remember that we noted the very unusual construction, the evident purpose of the maker to render it as strong and durable as workmanship could make it. This curious construction – which I pointed out at the time – caused me to examine it rather closely. And then I made a rather strange discovery."

Winifred leaned forward and gazed at him with breathless expectancy.

"It was concerned with the hallmark," he continued. "There are, as you see, four punch-marks. The first is a capital '*A*' with two palm-leaves surmounted by a crown. The second is an escutcheon or shape with the initials '*AH*' surmounted by a crown and over that a *fleur-de-lis*. The third is a capital '*L*', and the fourth is the head of an animal which looks like a horse. This grouping shows that the piece is French. The first mark is the town mark, the second the maker's mark, the third is the date letter, and the fourth is the mark of the Farmer of the Duty. Now, I happened to have had occasion to give some attention to the marks on old French plate, and I happened to have read, only an hour or two previously, the fragmentary narrative of Percival Blake. Accordingly, when I examined the hallmark and learned from it that this locket had been made in Paris in the year 1751, that fact at once arrested my attention."

"How did you learn that from the hallmark?" Winifred asked.

"It is the function of the hallmark to give that information," he replied. "The town-mark of Paris is a capital '*A*' surmounted by a crown, but it varies in style from year to year. This one is a Roman capital with two palm-leaves and a very small crown. That is the form used in the middle of the Eighteenth Century, but the date is definitely fixed by the date-letter – in this case a capital '*L*', which indicates the year *1751*.

"It was, of course, a very remarkable coincidence that this locket should have been made at the place and in the year of Judith Blake's death, and it naturally caused me to look at the little trinket more narrowly. Hitherto I had assumed, as you did, that the object that Percival referred to was the cat's eye pendant. But I now recalled that he had not specifically mentioned the pendant, and that he had spoken of it as 'the bauble' or 'the trinket', never as 'the jewel'. It was thus just barely conceivable that this mysterious little object might be the one to which he was referring, and the instant the question was raised, the evidence supporting it began to run together like drops of water.

"First, there was the inscription, '*O BIOC BPAXYO H AE TEXNH MAKPH*' – '*Life is short but Art is long*'. It was the motto of the practitioner of some art or craft. But artists and craftsmen almost invariably use the Latin form, '*Ars longa, Vita brevis – Art is long. Life is short*'. But there is one body of craftsmen who use the Greek form. It is the motto of the London College of Physicians, and moreover it is written by them in the same uncial characters, with the round, *C*-shaped sigma. Now Percival was a physician and a fellow of this very college, and he was an enthusiast who originally practised his profession for love and not from necessity or for a livelihood. What more natural than that he should use the motto of his own college?

"Then there was the construction of the locket – everything sacrificed to permanence and durability. It fitted the circumstances perfectly. And there were the unusual suspension rings, specially adapted to take a cord or thong. I recalled the enigmatic words '*gave me a string from his bass viol, which he says will be the best of all*'. Remembering that the bass viol would be a *viol da gamba* or *violoncello*, not a double-bass, we see that this was true, the stout gut string would last for a century or more.

"Then again there were the scripture references which you showed me. The first was '*And then shall he depart from thee, both he and his children with him, and shall return unto his own family, and unto the possession of his fathers shall he return*'. That was a most striking passage. It was an exact statement of Percival's aim – incidentally illustrating the way in which the other passages were to be treated, and when I noted that the principal word in the last reference was '*parchments*', I felt that a *prima facie* case had been made out. I had little doubt that this locket was the '*precious bauble*' that was handed to – and presumably lost by – Jenifer.

"But after all this was only guesswork. We had to get down to certainties. And, fortunately, there was available an excellent and conclusive test. If the locket was Percival's, the hair in it was almost certainly Judith's. Now there was something very unusual about Judith's hair. During her imprisonment, it had undergone a most extraordinary change. Percival tells us that when she was released, '*her hair, that had been like spun gold, was turned to a strange black*'. This was very remarkable. Judith was evidently a true blonde, and when she was arrested, she must have been getting on for thirty years of age. But the hair of a blonde adult does not turn black from ill-health and grief. It tends rather to turn white. What could be the explanation of the change?

"It is a very curious one. Judith had been labouring in the mines in the Harz Mountains. These mines yield a number of different metals, and some of them are extremely poisonous. They are ancient mines, and in the Middle Ages, when the properties of metals were less understood, the terrible condition to which persons who worked in them were reduced by chronic poisoning was put down to the influence of a race of malignant gnomes who were believed to inhabit the mines and who were known as *kobolds*. In particular, the influence of the kobolds came to be associated with a particular, uncanny ore from which no metal could be – in those days – extracted, and in the end this ore came to be known by the name of these mine-gnomes or kobolds, and that name it bears this day, in the slightly altered form of *cobalt*.

"Now, the metal, cobalt, has one or two very distinctive properties. One is that of imparting a powerful and beautiful blue colour to substances with which it combines. This was the value of the ore, and for this it has been prized from quite ancient times. We find it in use everywhere. The blue of all the Chinese porcelain is cobalt. The blue of the old Delft pottery is cobalt. The blue in all the old stained-glass windows – and modern ones too – is cobalt.

"Then this metal has another curious property which it shares with arsenic and one or two other metals. It is capable of being absorbed into the body and producing poisonous effects, and when so absorbed, it becomes deposited in the skin, or, more correctly speaking, in the epidermis and its appendages – the fingernails and the hair. But whereas the outer skin and the nails wear away and are cast off, the hair – especially a woman's hair – remains attached for long periods. Consequently, in chronic cobalt poisoning, the hair becomes charged with a cobalt compound – probably an oxide – and is stained blue.

"Bearing these facts in mind, we can now understand what had happened to Judith. She had been sent to labour in a mine which yielded cobalt, and probably nickel. Her hair had not turned black, it had turned blue, though, in the mass, it would appear black – a strange, unnatural black, as Percival tells us. Thus, if the hair in this locket was the hair of Judith Blake, it would appear blue when properly examined. I took an opportunity to get possession of the locket, and that very night I removed the remains of the cover-glass and picked out a single hair, which I mounted in Canada balsam and examined under the microscope. That hair is on the stage of the microscope now. Polton will bring it round and let you see it."

Our assistant tenderly carried the microscope round and set it before Winifred, and having adjusted the light and the focus, stepped back to watch the effect.

"But how extraordinary!" she exclaimed as she looked into the eyepiece. "It looks like a thread of blue glass! And how strange and romantic!"

Brodribb and Drayton rose from their chairs and came round, all agog to see this prodigy. In succession they gazed at it with murmurs of astonishment and then went back to their seats, still muttering.

"The appearance of that hair," Thorndyke resumed, "settled the question conclusively. This was Percival's trinket beyond a doubt, and all that remained was to read the message inside. As we now knew what to look for, this presented no difficulty at all. It was no cipher or cryptogram. It was simply a collection of texts, from each of which, as the first one showed, the instructed reader would have no difficulty in picking out the significant word or phrase. We may as well just run through them and see what they tell us.

"Number one, *Leviticus 25: 41*, we have already considered. It is the preamble which indicates the purport of the remainder. I see you have your notebook. Will you read us out the next?"

"Number two," said Winifred, "is *Psalms 121:1*: '*I will lift up mine eyes unto the hills, from whence cometh my help!*' That is the passage, but it doesn't convey any intelligible meaning to me."

"No," said Thorndyke, "it doesn't, because you have got the wrong Psalm. You looked up your reference in the English Authorised Version, overlooking the fact that Percival was probably a Catholic and certainly a resident in France, and also that the references were given with Latin titles, suggesting that he used the Latin *Vulgate*. This happens to be matter of vital importance in this case, as the *Psalms* are not numbered quite alike in the two Bibles. *Psalm 121* in the *Vulgate* is 122 in the Authorised Version. Here is the Douay Bible, which is the official translation of the Vulgate, and if we refer *to Psalm 121:1* in it, we find '*I rejoiced at the things that were said to me, We shall go into the house of the Lord*'. That is quite illuminating. It tells us that we are concerned with a church, and the next reference tells us what church. It is *Actus Apostolorum 10:5*"

"Yes," said Winifred. "'*And now send men to Joppa, and call for one Simon, whose surname is Peter*'."

"That," said Thorndyke, "gives us the church of St. Peter. The next," he continued, glancing at the notebook which Winifred had handed to him, "is *Nehemias 8:4*. '*And Ezra the scribe stood upon a pulpit of wood*' – we need not complete the passage. The pulpit of wood

788

is obviously the significant part. Then we come to *3 Lib. Regum 7. 41* – by the way, that third book of *Kings* might have given you a hint that you were not dealing with the Authorised Version. It reads: '*The two pillars, and the two bowls of the chapters that were on the top of the two pillars*', etc. The meaning of this passage was not very clear. It had some connection with the pulpit of St Peters Church, but what the connection was, it was not easy to guess. Of course, directly one saw the pulpit, the meaning was obvious.

"The next reference is to *Psalm 31:7*, and again you have taken the Authorised Version and got the wrong Psalm. Psalm 31 in the Vulgate is *Psalm 32* in the Authorised Version. Your reading is '*I will be glad and rejoice in thy mercy, for thou hast considered my trouble, thou hast known my soul in adversities*'. This, as you say, seems quite irrelevant, but if you had turned forward to *Psalm 32:7*, you would have read: '*Thou art my hiding-place*' or '*refuge*', as the Vulgate has it, which is very relevant indeed. The last reference is *2 Epist. ad Tim*: '*The cloak that I left at Troas with Carpus, when thou comest, bring with thee, and the books, but especially the parchments*'.

"Thus, taking the references together, they suggest to us the ideas of parchments, a hiding-place, and the two pillars (and their capitals) of the wooden pulpit of the church of St. Peter. It was perfectly plain and simple to a reader who knew the kind of information that was being given and who knew of the existence of this particular church. To a stranger, on the other hand, it was perfectly meaningless and undecipherable."

"It certainly looks very simple now that we have heard the explanation," said Winifred, "but it didn't seem so when I was trying to work it out myself. There didn't seem to be anything to go on."

"No," agreed Sir Lawrence, "there didn't seem to be anything to go on in either case. The clues were perfectly invisible, and I don't believe anyone but our friend would have discovered a particle of evidence."

Brodribb chuckled and reached out for the decanter. "I agree with you, Drayton," said he. "Thorndyke reminds me of that, probably fabulous, kind of Indian juggler who throws a rope into the air and proceeds to climb up it and pull it up after him. He can work without any visible means of support. However, he has conducted our various affairs to a highly satisfactory conclusion, and I propose that we charge our glasses in his honour and invite him to light the Trichinopoly, which, I believe, is his disgusting habit on occasions of this kind."

Accordingly the glasses were filled, the toast pledged, and the virulent little cheroot duly lighted, with which mystical rite the case of

789

the Cat's Eye was formally closed and dismissed into the domain of memory.

There is little more to tell. I am finishing this narrative in a pleasant, panelled room in the old mansion of Beauchamp Blake, one of a suite assigned by Percy to Winifred and me, in which we commonly spend our weekends – for our normal abiding-place is still The Temple. Percy is growing apace and, like his ancestor and namesake, refuses to abandon his professional ambitions. At present he is engaged, under the direction of a famous architect, in restoring the old house to its former comeliness, and only this morning I saw them together superintending the replacement of a perished fascia with a sturdy oaken plank, enriched with fine carving and bearing in raised letters the legend: *"God's Providence is Mine Inheritance"*.

The End

About the Author

Richard Austin Freeman was born on April 11th, 1862 in the Soho district of London. He was the son of a skilled tailor and the youngest of five children. As he grew, it was expected that he would become a tailor as well, but instead he had an interest in natural history and medicine, and so he obtained employment in a pharmacist's shop. While there, he qualified as an apothecary and could have gone on to manage the shop, but instead he began to study medicine at Middlesex Hospital.

Austin Freeman qualified as a physician in 1887, and in that same year he married. Faced with the twin facts of his new marital responsibilities and his very limited resources as a young doctor, he made the unusual decision to join the Colonial Service, spending the next seven years in Africa as an Assistant Colonial Surgeon. This continued until the early 1890's, when he contracted Blackwater Fever, an illness that eventually forced him to leave the service and return permanently to England.

For several years, he served as a *locum tenens* for various physicians, a bleak time in his life as he moved from job to job, his income low, and his health never quite recovered. However, he supplemented his meager income and exercised his creativity during these years by beginning to write. His early publications included *Travels and Live in Ashanti and Jaman* (1898), recounting some of his African sojourns.

In 1900, Freeman obtained work as an assistant to Dr. John James Pitcairn (1860-1936) at Holloway Prison. Although he wasn't there for very long, the association between the two men was enough to turn Freeman's attention toward writing mysteries. Over the next few years, they co-wrote several under the pseudonym *Clifford Ashdown*, including *The Adventures of Romney Pringle* (1902), *The Further Adventures of Romney Pringle* (1903), *From a Surgeon's Diary* (1904-1905), and *The Queen's Treasure* (written around 1905-1906, and published posthumously in 1975.)

In approximately 1904, Freeman began developing a mystery novella based on a short job that he had held at the Western Ophthalmic Hospital. This effort, "31 New Inn", was published in 1905, and it is the true first Dr. Thorndyke story. In 1907, the first Thorndyke novel, *The Red Thumb Mark*, was published.

From Thorndyke's creation until 1914, Freeman wrote four novels and two volumes of short stories. Then, with the commencement of the

First World War, he entered military service. In February 1915, at the age of fifty-two, he joined the Royal Army Medical Corps. Due to his health, which had never entirely recovered from his time in Africa, he spent the duration of the war involved with various aspects of the ambulance corps, having been promoted very early to the rank of Captain. He wrote nothing about Thorndyke during this period, but he did publish one book concerning the adventures of a scoundrel, *The Exploits of Danby Croker* (1916).

Following the war, he resumed his previous life, writing approximately one Thorndyke novel per year, as well as three more volumes of Thorndyke short stories and a number of other unrelated items, until his death on September 28th, 1943 – likely related to Parkinson's Disease, which had plagued him in later years. He is buried in Gravesend.

If you enjoy Dr. Thorndyke, then you'll love
The MX Book of New Sherlock Holmes Stories
Edited by David Marcum
(MX Publishing, 2015-   )

"This is the finest volume of Sherlockian fiction I have ever read, and I have read, literally, thousands." – Philip K. Jones

"Beyond Impressive . . . This is a splendid venture for a great cause!
– Roger Johnson, Editor, *The Sherlock Holmes Journal,*
The Sherlock Holmes Society of London

. . . and more to come!

793

The MX Book of New Sherlock Holmes Stories
Edited by David Marcum
(MX Publishing, 2015-   )

<u>*Publishers Weekly* says:</u>

Part VI: *The traditional pastiche is alive and well . . . .*

Part VII: *Sherlockians eager for faithful-to-the-canon plots
and characters will be delighted.*

Part VIII: *The imagination of the contributors in coming up with variations on the
volume's theme is matched by their ingenious resolutions.*

Part IX: *The 18 stories . . . will satisfy fans of Conan Doyle's originals. Sherlockians will
rejoice that more volumes are on the way.*

Part X: *. . . new Sherlock Holmes adventures of consistently high quality.*

Part XI: *. . . an essential volume for Sherlock Holmes fans.*

Part XII: *. . . continues to amaze with the number of high-quality pastiches . . .*

Part XIII: *. . . Amazingly, Marcum has found 22 superb pastiches . . . This is more catnip
for fans of stories faithful to Conan Doyle's original*

Part XIV: *. . . this standout anthology of 21 short stories written in the spirit of Conan
Doyle's originals.*

Part XV: *Stories pitting Sherlock Holmes against seemingly supernatural phenomena
highlight Marcum's 15th anthology of superior short pastiches.*

The MX Book of New Sherlock Holmes Stories
Edited by David Marcum
(MX Publishing, 2015-   )

Also From MX Publishing

Sherlock Holmes in Montague Street
by Arthur Morrison
Edited, Holmes-ed, and with Original Material
by David Marcum

Separate Paperback Editions

Combined Hardcover Edition

*"It's been suggested that Hewitt was the young Mycroft Holmes,
but David Marcum has a more plausible and attractive theory
– that he was Sherlock, early in his career as an investigator
... these are remarkably convincing in their new guise."*
– Roger Johnson, Editor, *The Sherlock Holmes Journal*,
The Sherlock Holmes Society of London

MX Publishing

MX Publishing is the world's largest specialist Sherlock Holmes publisher, with several hundred titles and over a hundred authors creating the latest in Sherlock Holmes fiction and non-fiction.

From traditional short stories and novels to travel guides and quiz books, MX Publishing caters to all Holmes fans.

The collection includes leading titles such as *Benedict Cumberbatch In Transition* and *The Norwood Author*, which won the 2011 *Tony Howlett Award* (Sherlock Holmes Book of the Year).

MX Publishing also has one of the largest communities of Holmes fans on *Facebook*, with regular contributions from dozens of authors.

www.mxpublishing.co.uk (UK) and *www.mxpublishing.com* (USA)